A Novel

Imperfectly Perfect
Together

B. Montgomery

ISBN: 978-1-7365667-0-1 (Paperback)
ISBN: 978-1-7365667-1-8 (Hardcover)

Cover design by: Author using Canva App
Chapter 2 Picture of Beautiful Tree in UK: Trisha Gerrard
Other Images: Canva App and Microsoft Word
Drawings: Brianne Maijala
Library of Congress Control Number: TXu002193373
Printed in the United States of America

To my best friend, I'm grateful for her love and support over the years. I can't thank her enough for being the first to read my book, while raising two kids and working in the healthcare industry.

To my two greatest blessings, my daughters, who's excitement for these books to be published sent me on this journey, and their excitement is what keeps me going.

"What's amazing to me is, here I was, living a plain old ordinary life, when something extraordinary happened...you!" ~ BriaLynn

Imperfectly Perfect Together

PREFACE

The Imperfectly Perfect Series

This book started off as a typical romance story with the main character, BriaLynn (Brē-ah-Lynn) and David falling in-love; I even thought about the best friends becoming a couple. I had no intentions of ever publishing this book; I was simply writing a story. I'd get only so far before I was inspired to go back and start from the beginning to add things, change things, even take things in a different direction I never saw coming. *Like a consort?*! It never occurred to me when I started writing, *let alone have a woman with a consort*!

Before I knew it, I had over fifteen hundred pages written and my daughters were telling me, "*Mom! You should sell your book!*" I kept telling them, I was just writing a story and I wasn't expecting anyone to read it. When I got to about two thousand pages, they convinced me to publish the books, even though they have never read them...*yet*. :-)

I sent a copy of this book off to the copyright office. Later, I would send a copy to my longtime best friend to read...then nervously waited to hear if I should even bother publishing it. I decided to channel that nervous energy into working on 'Book Two,' which got to be too long and I ended up splitting 'Book Three' from it.

The 'Imperfectly Perfect Together' book is the first of at least four books I hope to publish in this series.

INTRODUCTION

Imperfectly Perfect Alternate World

This is a world that is very similar to ours, but please keep in mind *this is still a fictional world*. The story of 'Book One' takes place mostly in Washington, D.C. and on The Duchy of Newhaven, a fictional island east of Edinburgh, Scotland. This UK is The United Kingdom of Provinces, consisting of only England, Scotland, Wales, and Ireland.

This UK is ruled by the monarchy, yet they still have a parliament of elected officials representing the people running the government, but 'at the leisure of The King.' That means, technically the ruling monarch can override anything at any time; a power *rarely used*, as the purpose of parliament is for the people to have a voice in how their country is run. This is how they avoided a revolution centuries earlier when France was in the midst of their revolution.

The people have a love for their royals and nobles, but the excitement has dwindled over the years with unlikable rulers. It is a little better with the latest king and queen, but it's obvious they are not 'happily married,' and behind the scenes, The Queen Mother is in charge. Now an American marrying into a ruling noble family will spark new excitement into the nobles and royals of their country, because of a tradition that is usually dominated by the men. She will embrace this tradition, and she will do it better than *any* of her predecessors.

CHAPTER 1

Two Imperfect People Perfectly Matched

BriaLynn Harris was raised in the Midwest with her family, but they are not as close knit as one would think of a Midwestern family. In her case, that is not necessarily a bad thing and she would soon realize it is all part of a Divine plan for her. A plan where pieces were put into place years earlier, some even centuries ago, and it all would come together in a very unique way.

BriaLynn has long, dark-brown hair she curls when she wears it down. She is not the skin and bones type, but with all the walking her job requires, plus what she does for solitude, she is confident in her skin. The clothes she wears are the simple, classy, timeless styles to show she is a woman, but they keep her 'assets' appropriately covered. With the way she carries herself, she is treated as a well-respected lady, even by those who don't really like her.

While considering herself an average person, BriaLynn is smart and quick-witted. She is kind-hearted and quick to feel for others, but she's not a pushover either. She has her own brand of sweet and sassy that makes her good at her job in Washington, D.C. She works with politicians, dignitaries, diplomats, royalty, celebrities, and other upper-class and well-known people on anything from their arrival to specific requirements for dietary needs, even putting together fundraisers and other charity events; and for some, it is all the above and a lot more.

BriaLynn's previous marriage was one of friendship. The love between them was like any two family members would have for each other. It wasn't the true, deep, abiding love, two people *need* in order to have a lasting and fulfilling marriage for both the husband and wife. She'll always be grateful for the marriage, two of the most important reasons being her beautiful daughters Emmie and Natty; they are the best parts of her and so much more. Not many people can say this, but BriaLynn and her ex-husband, Jeff, are good friends; she even has a growing friendship with his wife, Olivia. She is relieved Jeff found that true, abiding love she knew was out there for him. She always felt guilty, like she was holding him back from progressing into the person he could be and the love he could've had, if he weren't married to her. He needed to be with someone that inspires him to be better, to do better; *everyone does*!

She was mad at herself for quite some time for staying in the marriage for as long as she did. She prayed to fall in-love with him; unfortunately, no one can force love. Then one day, the answer to her prayers was heard; it was simply 'no.' Her faith lets her be at peace with that now, knowing she'll one day understand, even if it's not this lifetime.

She has also come to another realization about people and love. If people would be patient and wait for that kind of true, adoring, and abiding love, the world would have more happy people and happy families in it. Unfortunately, people's many fears, like the fear of being alone, have them missing glaring truths about why they *shouldn't be* with someone; BriaLynn was one of them.

As for herself and love? BriaLynn feels she's missed her chance. She has worked at convincing herself that true-love is not in the cards for her, but perhaps on the other side of this life. She once believed and hoped true, adoring love was out there for her, but hope can be paralyzing, and it was for her. She eventually moved through her paralyzing state accepting her life was on a *solo* path. Besides, she has always enjoyed her alone time and still does. She reads a lot, goes for walks, plays piano, listens to music; and other things for her to have a form of 'therapeutic spiritual meditation.' Her family and friends feel she is enjoying her solitude a little *too much*, especially when she gets annoyed that solitude gets interrupted.

BriaLynn and her best friend since college, Katie Barnes, have dreamed of a trip to Europe since those college years, but they always focused on England and Scotland since both could trace their ancestral trees there. Katie just got a job promotion which requires a lot of business travel, so she asked for two weeks off before she jumped into her new marketing position. Katie convinces her best friend to go with her, so they could relax and spend some quality time in various places, mending their friendship in the process.

Katie is a sassy auburn-redhead and is the same average size as BriaLynn, but Katie was a little taller. Katie is determined to have this trip help BriaLynn let go of her foolish thinking that she doesn't deserve love; with Bri's loving heart, she deserves that kind of love just as much as any other person! Katie is hoping her BFF will meet someone on their trip that will open her up to dating again when they get back to DC.

Henry and Maggie Bradshaw immigrated from The United Kingdom of Provinces; they were born in Scotland but went to boarding schools in the UK, then he came to the US to study at Harvard and go to law school. Their accents have faded over the decades being in the US, but every so often you hear a hint of their accent in a lengthy conversation, or heated discussion.

Henry is sixty-eight years old with a tall 6'3" trim build. He keeps his full head of silver hair just long enough to have a part on top, and a little bit of a feathered look on the sides. To say this man ages well is an understatement, which is more noticeable with his tailored suits.

Henry first met BriaLynn fresh out of high school, when she came to the East Coast to stretch her wings and go to college; she worked for his law firm as a clerk. When she met *Henry*, she didn't know he was 'Mr. Bradshaw,' of The Bradshaw Law Firm. They had an instant connection he could only describe to Maggie that evening as, "The daughter we never had."

When Maggie met BriaLynn, she whole-heartedly agreed; even their sons would call her "the sister we never had" and protect her as such. BriaLynn was a Bradshaw in every way, so when Katie went to enlist Henry's help planning their vacation, he was more than happy to help and even insisted on funding it.

Henry set up an account for them to use for everything and he made Katie promise they would use it. Henry loved Katie like any father would love his daughter's best friend, which made Katie part of their family, too. Katie's dad split before she was born, her mother died of a drug overdose when Katie was in high school, and she was sent into foster care until she aged out of the system. Neither BriaLynn, nor Katie, asked the Bradshaw's for anything; both girls were content being a part of the family and spending time with them.

Katie took Henry's guidance and suggestions to heart as she planned the trip. They already had their passports, so she focused on investigating and booking flights, hotels, and travel within the country. All BriaLynn had to do was say, 'yes.' After a little coaxing, which included Katie's guaranteed-to-work 'sad puppy dog look,' she had BriaLynn agreeing to go on their adventure. They only had two days to pack before their flight left, but BriaLynn and Katie felt the rush to get ready beat the agony of waiting for their vacation to start.

It was a long flight even for first-class, but they were soon in London. For the next few days, they would be seeing the various famous sights of London, visiting shops, and enjoying the spa at their hotel. It's not long before BriaLynn is feeling among the living; however, she can't shake the feeling that this is a life changing trip for her.

David Worthington was born in Scotland and since it's customary in higher social classes to send children to boarding schools, that's what happened with him and his younger brother James; it's also where he met his best friend, Jack Carlisle. Their accents were more English than Scottish because of being away at English boarding schools. David and Jack went to the US for college, becoming very familiar with the American-English lingo. David went to Harvard for a bachelor's degree in business and then to Columbia for his master's degree in business finance before going to work in his family's conglomerate business, The Worthington Corporation. Jack would go to Columbia for his bachelor's and master's degrees in business finance and investments. He would go on to work for a prominent global finance company, Watchtower Investments Firm, with its main office in Edinburgh. He quickly moved up the ranks and now manages his own team.

David is heir to The Duchy of Newhaven, an island to the east of Scotland, across from Edinburgh. He comes from a long history of nobility. There's an expectation 'The Heir' marries someone with royal bloodlines to show Newhaven would continue in strength.

Unfortunately, over more recent decades, Newhaven's not as popular with the tourists as it once was, even the excitement of their nobility could use a boost. David's mother, Carlotta, who is 'The Duchess of Newhaven,' has been working to increase tourism in Newhaven. There is a small castle on its own island just off of The Worthington Estate that they have finished renovating into a luxury inn. It has been a slow process to increase tourism, and the effort has increased the trickling of tourists, to more like a drizzle, as word gets around that the prices for rooms at The Worthington Inn are extremely affordable. The locals are happy to keep Newhaven's population where it is, with their capitol, Kingsbury, having a larger percentage of that population number; however, the island needs steady tourism to thrive. The Duchess also knows there will be a surge in tourism when David settles down again and starts a family.

David *had hoped* his marriage to Lady Ava Warwood would be the asset to the duchy everyone hoped for. She had the pedigree, her family owns various properties around the UK, in addition to their own family's estate on the border of England and Scotland. One of the European magazines named him, *Sexiest Bachelor*, which David was angry about; it made him uncomfortable in numerous ways. He would later find out Ava was behind it so she could boost *her* social standing, and it was part of her strategy to get him to marry her.

He learned long ago these so-called newspapers and magazines were rubbish, but he felt he was stuck with moving the relationship forward when 'rumors' printed in gossip columns had them engaged, but once again it was Ava behind those rumors. Her one purpose, her motivation like so many of the women he's dated, was to become the next 'Duchess of Newhaven.' Ava had no intentions of love and fidelity in any marriage, which David would learn too late.

Ava was a self-centered upper-class snob and she knows men; *more importantly*, she knows how to *use* men to get what she wants. Using her sandy-blond hair, blue-eyes, and body to grab a man's attention to go after exactly what she wants; and her sights were laser-focused on becoming a duchess. Ava was skilled at manipulation and played the part of a loving girlfriend and marriage material superbly; David scoffs in disgust at himself as he thinks how he fell for it all. 'Hook. Line. *Sunk*!'

His younger brother, James, looks a lot like David. Both have clean cut brown hair, but while James has brown eyes, David has sharp, dark-blue eyes like his mother, Carlotta. James is an inch or two taller than David, but both have fit, muscular frames. David's muscles were more defined since he increased his exercising routine to blow off his anger towards Ava, and more anger towards himself for being so blind.

James was the one who broke it to David about Ava's infidelity, but only after he investigated all the rumors. He knew it would break David's heart, but he also knew David would be hurt more if James didn't tell him what he found out. After James told David, he withdrew himself from almost everyone. Jack worked to keep David from pushing him and his family away, but seeing David put up such thick walls around himself was hard for his loved ones to watch at times.

David would remember the experience to keep himself from falling for whatever game Ava would play to try to get him back. He remembers being stunned when she not only admitted to everything, but she was *relieved* she didn't have to go through the trouble of hiding her affairs anymore. He wished he could've seen the shocked look on her face when she got the divorce papers. She never expected him to go through a scandal of a divorce and she was angry when she called him about it! He told her on the phone that the true scandal would've been if he had found out and did nothing! She was speechless and he hung up before she could say anything back.

Ava would drag David through a very nasty and bitter divorce that only made him swear off any woman he could see any potential at a future with. His family worries about him and wants to see him happy. They know they can't heal his broken heart; however, his heart would need to be open for it to heal. Sadly, to protect himself, he never has anything last longer than a few dates.

CHAPTER 2

Imperfectly Perfect Coffee Shop

After a few days in London, Katie and BriaLynn are riding a train to Edinburgh, Scotland. They watch the landscape out their window of rolling green hills, forests, and such, talking about how they felt a connection to the land which they attributed to their ancestral roots. When they get around to traveling the Edinburgh area, they visit old ruins and castles and feel a deeper connection to their ancestors. Perhaps an ancestor or two stood on the very spot they are standing, or maybe an ancestor strolled passed a younger version of the beautiful old tree they were gazing at now...It was kind of fun to think about!

They discovered a small café, The Primrose, that is popular with the locals, on a corner that wasn't too far of a walk from The Coriander Hotel where they were staying. It's an old-fashioned building with brick walls inside, oak wood accents, white iron tables with glass tops and matching white iron chairs; each table has a small vase for a single flower. It's hard not to feel warm and cozy when you're in there.

BriaLynn considered herself a 'hot-chocolate snob' and had a difficult time finding a cup she could enjoy, other than the brand she had at home. She loves mango and mango-peach smoothies, so when she saw the mango-peach on the menu on their first visit, she ordered one. Blended to perfection, she savored the first taste to the last drop. On a cooler morning, she decided to order a cup of hot cocoa, preparing to order a smoothie, but it wasn't necessary; their hot cocoa was *amazing*! Even their baked goods were melt-in-your-mouth delicious! She and Katie vowed to never have the same thing twice, so they could try more tasty goodies before they leave next week for Ireland.

Sitting at a small table one mid-afternoon, BriaLynn and Katie would have a conversation with the locals. They find out there is an island that was one of the oldest family-ruled duchies in Scotland; maybe even the UK, but they weren't too sure about that one. It has fishing, hiking, horseback riding, green rolling hills and forests for a beautiful drive, and lots of one-of-a-kind shops. The ferry is very inexpensive, and it makes frequent trips back and forth all day; a later night trip is possible, if it's prearranged and with a small additional fee. Bed and Breakfasts were easy to come by, so a spur-of-the-moment overnight trip would be possible. As Katie asks for more information, BriaLynn smiles to herself as she listens to their conversation because even though she loves British accents, sitting there in the café she realizes she loves the Scottish accents 'just a wee bit more.'

As they walk back to their hotel, Katie suggests, "Why don't we go over and see this island? Maybe spend a couple of days?"

Bri agrees and adds, "And if we need more time, we can stay another night." Katie agrees with a huge smile and claps with excitement.

 When they get to The Coriander Hotel, they wait in the lobby to speak to Nicholas, the concierge, about what the locals suggested. When he's free, they talk about what they'd like to do the next couple of days. Nicholas is laughing here and there during the rehashing of the morning's discussion, then informs them that he grew up on Newhaven Island and now lives there again to raise his family. He calls The Worthington Inn to book the rooms and he makes all the travel arrangements for them as well.

David is in his office at The Worthington Corporation Complex in Edinburgh, Scotland. He glances at the clock as he is about to head to a meeting when his assistant, Mary, puts a call from his brother through to his desk phone.

"James," he says with a more business tone than one would expect between brothers, "what can I do for you?"

"Mother said to tell you that there's more preparation to do for The Black-Tie Party they're hosting Saturday evening." James tells him.

"Fine," he grumbles and hangs up on James to go to his meeting.

The meeting doesn't last an hour, so David wraps up his day and pulls work together to take home to the island, along with his laptop. Mary knocks on his open door to let him know his car is out front.

"Tell Paul I'll be down soon." He replies. She nods and goes back to her desk.

After freshening up a bit, David grabs a bottled water and goes down to the lobby. The receptionist, who has a *huge* crush on him, tells him, "Have a good evening, Sir!"

He barely waves as he passes the reception desk, responding plainly, "Ms. Wilson." He walks out the main doors and greets his driver, Paul, who will drive him out to The Worthington Estate. "Paul, I need to make a quick stop by The Coriander Hotel on the way home."

Paul nods, "Yes, Sir."

About ten minutes later, the car pulls up to the hotel. David gets out of the car and Nicholas, The Concierge, greets him, "Good day, Lord Newhaven!"

"Nicholas. How's the family?" David asks walking by.

Nicholas only has time for a short response, "Doing well, Sir!"

David stops at the front desk asking if the manager, Mr. Daniels, is available for a few minutes. The woman grins all starry-eyed as she slightly curtsies before going to find the manager. He takes in the décor of the lobby and the-see-through-elevator-windows, seeing a happy couple kissing as it comes down. He hears the loveliest of giggles coming from somewhere. He absentmindedly searches for the source and only sees the back of a dark brown-haired woman talking to a cute auburn-redhead. He doesn't stare; he makes it look like he's glancing around. Katie notices this handsome man, but he gives off an unfriendly vibe and she forgets about him.

The manager, Mr. Daniels, comes out and greets David. They talk about The Worthington Corporation's purchase of the hotel. Mr. Daniels runs to grab some papers David needs. While David waits, he hopes to catch a glimpse of this brown-haired woman, but he kicks himself for caring. He keeps telling himself he doesn't want to be seriously involved with anyone, although he's having to work harder to convince himself of that lately.

The manager comes back out and they wrap up their conversation shaking hands. Just as he goes to leave, his mystery woman is no longer there, and he finds himself a little disappointed. When he starts to tell himself it's better this way, he sees she is talking to Nicholas and he briefly pauses in mid stride...she is the most beautiful woman he has ever seen! To add torture to his torment, she has a killer American accent! '*Ah, bloody hell*.' He thinks to himself. He barely says 'bye' to Nicholas, nodding to the ladies who are not really paying attention to him anyway, and quickly escapes to his awaiting car.

Paul has the door open, so David doesn't stop until he slides in the back seat, exhaling in relief. Paul saw through the window how flustered David became seeing the two ladies at The Concierge Desk. He wished his boss would give a real woman the time of day. Then again, he panicked... it dawns on Paul that David is *really* attracted to one of them.

Paul puts a finger up and says, "One second, Sir." David nods, happy to be safe in the car and pulls out his phone.

As Paul ducks inside the lobby, he overhears the ladies are going to The Worthington Inn tomorrow. '*Perfect!*' He thinks to himself. The ladies leave and walk outside, Paul nods to them as they pass by him.

He asks Nicholas how long they were staying, "It's for the boss," he throws his thumb over his shoulder gesturing the car.

Nicholas gives a knowing grin. "They're actually going to The Worthington Inn tomorrow for couple days and staying checked in here until Tuesday, when they head to Ireland."

"Great!" Paul says. He looks in the direction they went and asks about the woman who is David's type. "Would you happen to have the brunette's name and number for Lord Newhaven?" Paul asks.

"I shouldn't, but The Inn already has that information." Nicholas smirks as he jots down her name and number.

"I'm hoping to get this going sooner, rather than later." Paul says.

"Then you should know," Nicholas says with a sly grin, "she's single! Although a few men have tried." He gestures towards the bar.

Paul smiles. "One thing Lord Newhaven can be is persuasive." They both chuckle, then Paul thanks Nicholas before he leaves.

David had seen the ladies come out and walk past the car. The beauty's dressed for walking, the other has a book and they're both headed in the direction of the park. He wanted to run after her and get her name and number, but he just couldn't bring himself to do it. David watched them disappear and saw Paul going up to the driver's door. Before Paul sits, he reaches back and hands the folded paper to David.

"What's this?" David asks as he opens the paper. He reads out loud: "BriaLynn Harris." He thinks for a moment. "Her first name sounds Welsh...*interesting*." A flash of 'BriaLynn Worthington' goes through his thoughts. Surprised, his heart beats faster in excitement and he quickly pushes it down.

"It's the phone number for that cute brunette that has caught your eye and yes, Nicholas pronounced it with an 'ah' sound in the middle, too. Brē-ah-Lynn, just like you said." Paul informs him as he pulls forward for David to see her again. "He said she is very single, even though Nicholas says guys have tried." David watches her...then a strong impulse takes over him.

> He texts Bri: "I wish we had time to meet, but I just wanted to say you're the most beautiful woman I've ever seen!"

"Paul, will you pull away like you normally would so we won't be noticed?" David asks.

He does, but asks with a laugh, "Isn't that the idea?"

"I can't drag her into my life..." he trails off, watching her look around, then sees her look back down at her phone.

> Bri: "You have the wrong number, but for what it's worth, it's a great text to send to whoever she is!"

> David: "Aren't you Ms. Harris?"

Bri's mouth drops open and Katie reads it, then whispers. "*Craaap!*"

BriaLynn looks around. "I know, *right!*"

> Bri: "Okay...trying really hard not to get creeped out and think 'stalker' right now!"

She sends the text, then looks around more, but doesn't see anything.

> David: "I'm on my way out of the city right now. Does that make you feel better?"

Just when she wonders if he's driving and texting, he sends a follow-up text.

David: "And no, I'm not driving." (Adding a winking face)

Bri: "Yes and no. Yes, because then you're not following my every move, so you wouldn't see me fall flat on my face if I tripped. No, because you know my name and what I look like! Anyways, maybe it's for the best. Living an ocean apart doesn't make the best geography for any relationship except a long-distance friendship."

David: "I need to plan a trip to New York City. Tell me if you live there or at least a train ride away? I'll even pay for your own room at The Plaza."

Bri: "I won't answer that without knowing *who* I'm talking to." (She adds a zipped-mouth face) "We've already established you're a stalker." (Adding a winking face)

He doesn't catch that he's chuckling, loving her wittiness. Paul hasn't heard him laugh in a while, but even that is with Jack and it isn't the same thing.

David: "Funny." (Smirking face) "I need to take care of some things and there's a party I have to attend this weekend. I'd be rude to break a date this late, plus it would create fodder for the gossip columns. Can we put this on hold until Monday?"

Bri: "Lucky for you, I despise gossip, gossip columns, and the overall media; I try to never touch the stuff! But yes, we can talk on Monday. After Tuesday, though, I'll delete your number since we'll be checking out and leaving that day."

David: "But now that you know I may be in those columns; you might make an exception to your rule!"

Bri: "Not a chance! I refuse to give those disgusting vultures the time of day, especially if I know or care about the people in them!" (She adds a green nauseous face) "I like forming my own opinions of people, so I'm not a fan of being told what to think of others."

David: "Good to know! We'll talk in a few days, then?"

Bri: "I look forward to hearing from you, 'Mystery Stranger.' Will you at least tell me your name?"

David: "No. It'll help you to stay away from learning anything about me and be unknowingly swayed. I'm looking forward to talking with you again soon, Lady Harris."

If he can't talk himself out of it by then.

Bri: "FYI, you just gave me another piece of your puzzle! That world, your world, may not be the best fit...then add we live an ocean apart...let's just leave things here."

This stuns David and his jaw clenches. He's not used to being turned down, let alone like this!

David: "I thought you liked to form your own opinions and here you are judging what you think is 'my world?'"

He doesn't know the history of BriaLynn's job; that it has her working with politicians, diplomats, and dignitaries, various noble and royal titles, and so on. 'Lady' was a title and while David meant it with respect and to be charming, he also told her he was part of *that* world in some way and being concerned with gossip *should've been* her first 'clue' of sorts.

Bri: "It's not judgement when it's my job to work with various people of importance, including those with royal and noble titles. While I know that you were trying to be sweet using 'Lady,' and it was, only people in that social class, or are around that society, would address me like that. People not in that world and trying to be sweet, would've used my first name with 'Lady.' Again, it was just a clue into who you are and why we shouldn't go any further. My sincerest apologies if I offended you in any way. Please enjoy the party!"

David mulls this over, annoyed and stunned. '*What just happened?! Forget it! The last time I let a woman control the relationship, it ended with a bitter divorce! Never again! Maybe it is better this way...*'

David will soon see that Bri not wanting to be a part of his world, is exactly why she is perfect for it.

CHAPTER 3

Imperfect Cracks on Perfect Walls

David and Paul talk along the way, mostly about Paul and his family; on the ferry they discuss the party on Saturday night. As they drive to The Estate, David watches out the window lost in his thoughts. David finally begins to admit to himself he is getting tired of the women he has been taking on dates. None of them challenge him. They're smart *enough* to take on a date; only to be a duchess requires intelligence to not only navigate parties and finesse important people, but there is also a brilliance that a woman would need to actually run a duchy and take it to the next level for their people...*none* of these ladies have what it takes to be a duchess!

David has no problem securing dates, like the one for the party Saturday evening, because they know he is 'The Heir to Newhaven.' These kinds of ladies were serving a purpose of sorts, but now...*now* he feels himself starting to long for a meaningful relationship that would go somewhere. It's getting harder to ignore what's missing...love. His thoughts kept coming back to this beautiful American. '*Ugh*! *Why couldn't he have ignored her*!' Being turned down is new to him and it's an *awful* feeling...

They turn on the all too familiar road with a forest and right before getting to the top of a hill, the forest ends and a span of black iron fence runs along the edge of the property with large, squared, stone posts evenly spaced out, running along the road where there are two large gates with fancy W's at the top-middle of each gate. The driveway leads to The Worthington Manor that sits back a ways but is still visible from the road. The Manor is four-stories right in front and three-stories everywhere else.

Paul pulls through the gates and they proceed down the drive. A large fountain can be seen and the driveway circles around it. The fountain sprays water up the middle, cascading down into the tiers of pools below. David sees that everything is clean and flawlessly tended to as it always is. '*Why am I even here*?' He asks himself. If he knows his mother, and he does, there isn't a thing for him to do.

Paul pulls around to the front of The Manor and David gathers his things before getting out of the car. When he heads inside, he nods to one of the staff who has stepped outside to greet him and takes David's things up to his room. He tries to push out the thought of how nice it would be to be greeted by the woman he loves, *who actually loves him*. His thoughts go to BriaLynn and he allows himself to have a brief moment to picture her with him before he goes inside.

David doesn't know his mother, Carlotta, called The Coriander Hotel and spoke with the concierge, Nicholas, who made the arrangements for the two American ladies staying at The Inn. Nicholas told her that Ms. BriaLynn Harris and Ms. Katherine Barnes, are college best friends on a 'BFF Relaxation Trip.' They are two of the most enjoyable Americans he has met in some time and they are extremely low maintenance; they genuinely appreciate everyone's efforts for whatever it may be.

> "They're just smashing! These ladies just wanted to get away for a couple of weeks. Seems Ms. Barnes received a job promotion and she wanted to decompress before jumping into her new position. Bri, er, Ms. Harris, works in Washington, D.C. but I'm not sure what she does exactly. From what I understand, it involves making the impossible happen: seeing to it that politicians and dignitaries are kept happy."

They both laugh at what is sometimes a contradiction. He continues to tell her they also want to see the land of their ancestors in the UK.

> Carlotta asks, "Oh? Where?" Nicholas says they had mentioned it but apologizes for not remembering. "Nicholas, you've been more helpful than you realize!" Carlotta says to him, excited about what he had told her and the possibility of setting David up with someone different; someone with potential for a meaningful relationship.

Nicholas thanks her and informs her that since they live in a city, they want simple: walking, hiking, horseback riding, maybe visit a few shops.

> "Should be rather simple," he says, "that's how they are."

Carlotta thanks Nicholas again for the information and insights. She calls back to speak with his manager and gives Nicholas a raving review.

Carlotta greets her son when he comes in the door. "David! So good to see you, Sweetie!" She kisses his cheek and hugs him; he returns her hug. She puts her arm in his and leads him to the patio outside for teatime; his father,

Peter, joins them. '*Great.*' David sarcastically thinks to himself, assuming his parents are going to corner him about his date for the party.

"Looks like we'll have a couple of visitors tomorrow. What do we have planned?" Peter innocently asks his wife.

"The Concierge didn't request anything spectacular." She answered. "They're, how did he say it, on their long awaited 'BFF Relaxation Trip,' or something like that, I guess."

He chuckles and asks, "How long is this BFF trip?"

"I didn't ask how long their whole trip is, but I do know they're coming tomorrow morning, staying a night, then leaving Saturday afternoon."

"Ah, and the party is Saturday evening," he says taking a sip from his cup, "perhaps they may feel like staying for the evening? It's always nice to have new people at these things." That gets Carlotta thinking. Peter looks at David and notices he has a glass of lemonade. "Don't feel like tea, Son?"

"I've been bored with tea lately." He says matter-of-factly, taking a drink of his lemonade.

James comes and joins them. With all four sitting together, it's easy to see the family resemblance to each other. Carlotta's hair is greyish white. She has a little extra weight around her mid-section, but she wears it well. She is always put together and business-like in her designer skirts, shirts, dresses, and shoes, not to mention jewelry. She and David share the same striking navy-blue eyes. Peter's hair is graying, which he keeps a clean cut appearance like his sons, although his sons have scruff and beards at times. He and James have brown eyes. All three men are fit, but the sons are more muscularly toned, particularly David since his marriage ended. One 'son' is missing and that is David's best friend, Jack, who is still working in the city today, but will be out tomorrow. Jack is very much Peter and Carlotta's son in every way that matters.

"How are things at The Inn?" David asks James to make conversation.

"Good! We'll be all set for the ladies' arrival tomorrow morning. The Chef's going to try his hand at some American dishes. He's even going to bake the American apple pie."

"Splendid!" Says Peter. "Boys! There's a business opportunity for The Worthington Corporation. Let's go to my study and discuss it, shall we?" He stands and kisses his wife on the cheek, and the three men walk to the door to go inside to Peter's study, but Carlotta asks David to stay a moment.

After the other two men left, she asks, "I'm assuming you have a date for Saturday evening?"

"I do." David says rather flatly.

"Should I expect she's the same type, beautiful and more interested in her looks and social standing, rather than in a relationship?"

Seeing where this was headed and not wanting to disappoint with his mother, he smirks, "But you're already taken, Mother!" He winks at her and she tsks, but she's smiling. "Look, I have yet to meet a woman, other than you, who's professional and business-minded, but can carry herself like a lady and has a heart of gold. Still, even those with hearts get scared off with this world." His mom raises her eyebrow, curious. He walks to the door and stops. "I know you mean well, Mother, but I purposely have dates versus relationships because it's better than marrying the wrong woman again."

"But don't you see, Sweetie? You'll also miss out on the right one if you don't date women with potential!"

He gives her a soft smile, not commenting directly on that. "Must be the day for Americans to be in Scotland; I saw a *beautiful* American at The Coriander Hotel today, Mother. The fact that I noticed, means that hope isn't lost for me to marry again...*someday.*"

"David, this has to do with you taking the time to find someone who makes you happy! All three of my boys need that in their lives!" She smiles sweetly. "Did you at least talk to her and get her name?"

"Paul saw my interest in her after I bolted, and he snuck inside to ask The Concierge for her name and number, then surprised me with them. I actually texted Ms. Harris and got sidelined before we ever met!" Carlotta keeps an excellent poker face as she recognizes the last name of the woman coming tomorrow. David doesn't want to tell her he was so drawn to this woman, that there was something about her that made him want to spend the rest of his life with her. *That* scares him the most; losing control to this pull he has to her! Things would've been so much worse had Ava had control over him in the way he is drawn to this American woman.

Carlotta's keeping her poker face. "I'm confused, Sweetie. How were you 'sidelined' so quickly if you never met?"

"We texted. I wanted to be charming, so I called her 'Lady Harris.' That's how she figured out I was part of the upper-class society, and now believes it'd never work between us. She turned me away, but maybe it's for the best."

"What do you mean?" She asks.

"Mother, what would I do with an American woman when I need a someone with at least one bloodline to even be able to marry them?"

"David Christopher Worthington! You know as well as I do that there are *lots* of women around the world, including American women, who would have the necessary ancestral line. Even the two women coming tomorrow morning!" She throws out there.

"Well, I'll keep my distance all the same." He answers.

"*You always do*, David! If you're always running away, you'll have a very lonely life." She says. He walks back over to her with a small smile and kisses her on the cheek before going to his father's study. '*All is better this way.*' He thinks to himself.

Carlotta is left alone to finish her tea. She smiles to herself as she remembers what The Concierge from The Coriander Hotel said about the two ladies having ancestral ties here. '*Maybe, just maybe, this might be the one who gets through these almost impenetrable walls of his...*' She can't help but also think about how nice it would be to have a daughter-in-law she would enjoy spending time with. She is sad David was so badly hurt that he doesn't want to risk his heart again. James enjoys dating and has been in-love *many* times; Jack loves women and is having fun but he never seems to want to commit to any one woman. He recently broke up with his girlfriend, whom he had dated for a short time...he is next on her list to settle down.

One of Carlotta's assistants, Gabriel, arrives and they begin going through her tasks for the afternoon.

CHAPTER 4

Imperfectly Perfect Stud

Bri and Katie decided to be on the first ferry that Friday morning to Newhaven. The ferry was white with fire-engine red accents, including the top rail of the railing that went around the boat; the roof was black. They took a seat where they could see where they were headed while they talked.

The closer they got to Newhaven, the bigger it seemed; almost like entering a different world. They dock at a pier below a fishing town that centuries ago had been carved into and up the rock face of a cliff; the fishing town nestled into it. On either side of the pier and village, they are flanked by steep, if not straight up and down, cliffs that seem to go around the island, at least as far as they could see.

There is a car waiting for them when they disembark the ferry. The driver, Paul, introduces himself, and as they shake hands, Katie and Bri introduce themselves back to him. David always had an eye and Bri is beautiful; hers is a natural beauty.

Once they are inside the car, they follow the road as it winds its way through and up the little fishing village. They pass through lovely towns, drive by and through some forests, they even roll up and down green hills. Everything really is picturesque!

They turn off the main road and pass another forest, but on the other side of it is a black iron fence with square stone posts that matched the huge multi-story manor sitting a ways back from the road. They pull through the large black iron gates Paul drove David through yesterday afternoon. The driveway circles around a huge fountain in front, but he takes the road that splits off and goes under an arch that has a room above it with windows. '*An old guard post, maybe?*' Bri wonders.

From entering The Estate and all the way through, the landscaping and gardens are incredibly beautiful. They drive along the road that had branched off from the driveway and drive through the forest they first saw from the road. When it opens up, they see The Inn sitting on its own island. There is a wide, tall bridge stretching between the two islands, the outer edges of the bridge are for walkers, runners, bikes, and such. The island's utilities are hidden under the bridge, between the road itself and the arches beneath it.

As Paul drives across the bridge, there are ivy and flowery vines that cover crumbled old walls on either side of the entrance of the island. The front of the castle has more landscaped gardens. The castle itself is fully restored. It's more of a miniature castle, even smaller than The Worthington Manor. The back half of the island, behind The Inn, there is a patio with more gardens before a small grove of lush trees, which runs to the edge of the island. An ivy-covered reenforced safety wall surrounds the island.

They pull up to the door where a gentleman of The Inn's staff opens the car door. Katie climbs out first and they are both greeted by a few people. James is the first to approach them with his hand out.

"James Worthington," he kisses the back of Katie's hand with a slight bow, then moves to Bri. "My family and I would like to welcome you to our estate and hope you have an enjoyable stay!" He bows slightly kissing the back of Bri's hand. They both give him their names and then he introduces them. "Mother, this is Ms. Harris," he gestures one and then the other, "and this is Ms. Barnes. Ladies, this is The Duchess of Newhaven."

Katie hesitates, so Bri does a curtsy first and Katie mimics. "A pleasure to meet you, Your Grace, but you didn't have to come all the way over here to greet us. I'm sure you have more important things to do!"

"Aren't you sweet, Dear." She happily smiles. "My husband and I like to meet our guests when we can, but he's tied up at the moment. He looks forward to meeting you both this evening for dinner."

"With all due respect, Ma'am, I'm thinking you must have us confused with other guests that have importance." Bri says. "We just came for a quiet, low-key, no-fuss, couple of days. We simply want to enjoy the beauty of nature and The Estate, maybe visit a few shops at a local village or two. We're *definitely* no one to fuss over."

Katie shakes her head. "Really, Ma'am. Other than a few of your staff knowing we're here, you'll forget all about us."

"*Nonsense* and no confusion! You're exactly who we expected you to be," she smiles brightly. She hopes Bri will hold David's attention. "Come, let's get you settled and then you both can ride to the main house with James and me. James has a horseback ride being prepared for you both, that's if you're up for it this early?"

Katie looks a little frightened, "Bri's been on a horse before; I'd like to learn."

"No worries!" James says. "The horses we have for both of you are gentle and calm; great for beginners." James informs her to ease her mind. Katie smiles in appreciation and relaxes a bit.

Once settled, they all slide into a golf cart where James drives, Katie sits up front because The Duchess wants to sit in the back with Bri. She's hoping she's right about her being a match for David and wants to get to know Bri a little better.

Bri starts the conversation, "How long has the duchy been in your family, or your husband's family?"

"Hmmm, if I remember correctly, it goes as far back as the 1400's, but Newhaven's history goes back even further, in some shape or form, to the 1100's." She looks at Bri with a smile, "A very long time." She pats Bri's hand.

"I'm still amazed at how old things are here verses the US! The Declaration of Independence goes back to 1776, but further back are the pilgrims and the Mayflower. Then there are the Native Americans, but that is a different conversation altogether. The history of the actual United States of America versus any other country, really makes the US seem likes it's still in its childhood! We could argue it is still in its 'Terrible Two's!'"

The Duchess happily laughs, clasping her hands together, "Sounds like you love history!"

"I love historical things, Your Grace!"

"Please, call me Carlotta."

"I should clarify that, Carlotta; I love hearing about history and historical things, I'm just not sure how much I actually retain!" They both laugh.

James heard the last part of the conversation between Carlotta and Bri. "My brother, David, knows a lot of our history, I'm sure he'd love to talk to someone who would actually appreciate hearing it!" He pulls up just past the back of the house.

"I'm all ears if he has some time to spare for me!" Bri smiles excitedly about learning the history of this beautiful place.

"Oh! You're absolutely delightful!" Carlotta can feel Bri *is* David's match and she begins to formulate a plan...

> Carlotta texts Jack: "Hey there, Handsome Son! David had an American catch his eye, but he's still planning on taking whatever woman he has coming as his date. I need your help! Since you don't have a date, I really think you could have some platonic fun with her and maybe enjoy toying with David's stubbornness."

> Jack: "Sounds like fun! Let's see if we can get David to drop his stubbornness once and for all...or we'll know it's insanity and we'll have to have him committed!" (adds a smirking face)

Carlotta snaps a picture of Bri when she isn't looking.

> Carlotta: "I knew you were my favorite! (she adds a winking face) Here's a pic of her and as you can see, she's beautiful *and* she's the real deal!"

It takes a solid minute for the picture to deliver to Jack.

> Jack: "She's gorgeous! I think he *has* gone mad, Mother! If he lets her go, I vote we lock him in an asylum and throw away the key!"

Carlotta quietly giggles. She sends him another text with a 'thank you' and 'love you' before she joins the conversation with the three as they walk to the stables. Carlotta, James, and Katie are in a discussion about the flowers, shrubs, and other things botany, stopping outside the stables. While they are in their own little conversation, Bri decides to walk into the stables and takes a look around.

The stables are made of oak, or something similar, and is long with stalls on both sides. She walks in and looks at the horses that are still in their stalls, petting a few as she passes by them. There are four horses being brushed before a saddle blanket and saddle go on them. Of the four horses, the one on the far left is in the shadows. It has a commanding and powerful stance making it obvious *he's* a stallion; but the horse softens when he sees Bri. The closer she gets, it's clear he is a big and tall, very beautiful, shiny black stallion. He is not quite as big as a Clydesdale, but big enough that at 5'5" Bri would need to think about how to mount a horse this size! She wouldn't easily be able to stretch her leg up and put her foot in the stirrup.

She locks eyes with this magnificent creature, and it feels as if the two of them can see into each other's soul. She has never connected with any horse like that and she is intrigued. She reaches up to pet him, but a hand *snatches* her wrist to stop her! Bri gasps in shock! Surprised and annoyed, Bri's head snaps to look at who grabbed her wrist.

David recognizes her, but quickly recovers. His voice is commanding as he tells her, "This isn't some petting zoo where you can just walk up and pet anything you want!"

Her eyebrows scrunched together. "*What*?!"

He is still frustrated she turned him down yesterday and now this? "This horse is dangerous to those who don't know how to handle him! It would be best for a novice to keep their distance."

She angrily yanks her wrist out of his hand. "Don't *presume* to know me!"

David's eyebrows furrow as he gets more annoyed. "I don't *presume* to know *you*; I just know my horse!"

"*Obviously, you don't know him like you* think *you do*!" She snips.

"*Oh*?" He gives her a steely look and smugly says, "*By all means*," he steps back, gesturing towards his horse, "show me what I'm missing!"

The handsome brown haired, navy blue-eyed stranger, knows Artemis doesn't let just anyone near him, let alone ride him, except a couple of people. He will scare her away, just like he does everyone else.

She scoffs. "*Why*? I have nothing to prove, *especially to you*, and I could care *less* what you think!" She takes a little bit of a deep breath and bites her lower lip. "*Although...*" she says as she turns to look at the horse, "I suppose I shouldn't punish you for your owner's arrogance." David's jaw clenches. Bri smiles at the horse and turns her full attention to him.

David starts to say something, but stops himself as he watches her, *astounded* by what takes place before his eyes! Bri looks into the horse's eyes again, but it's the horse that makes the first move; gently stepping towards her with his head down to her level, stopping an inch from her face. Bri puts her forehead to his, gently petting the side of his face.

She whispers, "*You're such a handsome boy.*" The horse softly snorts an exhale, relaxing into her hands, his eyes closing as she lifts her head and works her hand down his neck, her other hand still on his cheek.

David can't believe what he is seeing! He is joined by his mother, brother, and Katie. James and Carlotta are just as stunned as everyone else who works in the stables.

"I've never seen anything like it!" Carlotta manages to say in disbelief.

"Does this handsome boy have a name?" Bri asks. The horse nods his head; a reign drops from his neck and hangs down. She looks over at the horse's owner expectantly.

David humorlessly laughs asking, "*You mean you don't know?!*" He can see the side of her face and when she rolls her eyes, it only irks him more. "You seem to think you know my horse better than me!"

"Spoken like an arrogant, entitled, selfish, ill-mannered, condesc–...." She cuts herself off, biting her lips together inside her mouth.

He studies her, fascinated she controlled herself not to finish that sentence. He gives in and grumbles, "*Artemis.*"

His mother whispers sternly, "*David! Where* are *your manners?!*"

David hears her but keeps focused on Bri. "Didn't you hear, Mother? I'm told I have none."

Carlotta scolds him more, "You're proving her right!" David glances and then looks at his mother's face; she has a little glare of her own.

"Hmmm..." Bri looks at the horse, "Did your rude master give you that name because of your *wild side?*" Artemis nods a little. David stifles his urge to smile at that. Bri giggles and kisses Artemis' nose. "Just not with me?" He shakes his head. "Thank you, Handsome! I appreciate that!" She turns to walk away, but stops and whispers to Artemis, only it's loud enough for David to hear as she tips her head in his direction, "Feel free to continue to give him a hard time!" Artemis nods. She kisses the end of her fingers and then touches his nose. She goes to walk away, but David steps in her way. He is *not* about to back down and pushes back.

"You stubbornly got your chance to pet him, but is that all you got?" David asks. He is about to get another lesson with Bri.

Her eyebrow goes up and she crosses her arms. "Why don't you just *ask me* to ride him?"

> James quickly texts Jack: "You won't believe David has finally come face-to-face with a woman who is perfect for him! Fresh from America!"

Jack video calls James right away to watch this in action. James gives him a front row seat.

"Isn't that what this whole show was for, with my mother's prodding, to show me how good you are with horses, particularly my horse, so I could see a common interest and somehow I would be interested in you?"

His mother gasps in shock and is horrified! She angrily says, "*DAVID CHRISTOPHER WORTHINGTON!*"

"*What are you talking about?!*" Bri can't believe what he is accusing her of! "I came in here all by myself, so how would I know this was *your horse?*" Mocking his accent but with added snobbery. "You act as if I should know who you are, like you're someone special when really you're just being asinine!" Jack spits out his drink of water, sitting straight up; *he is hooked!* She continues. "Seems you're a bit stuck on yourself if you think any woman who steps foot on this estate is somehow *in-love with you.*" Bri rolls her eyes and scoffs in disgust. "Get over yourself already, so you can stop tripping over your gigantic ego!"

"*I don't think everyone's in-love with me!*" He gruffly says. "*Now who's presuming?*"

Bri rolls her eyes scoffing again. "That's just it! I don't have to *presume* what you're already proving! You thought I was here to put on a show *for you!* Any good looks you may have are far overshadowed by your conceited superiority in my book! *I don't want to get to know,*" she gestures, "*whoever this is!*" She turns to Artemis. "Artemis and I were having a moment before *you* rudely interrupted! Didn't we, you handsome boy?!" Artemis neighs at David.

"*Great*, now I'm getting attitude from my horse?!" David says more to himself in annoyance.

"*Oh, please!*" She retorts. "Artemis was giving you attitude long before now, or you wouldn't be so nervous about other people being around him!"

There is chuckling and snickering around them. Carlotta, James, Katie, Jack, and all watching their exchange see what David and Bri don't; attraction *with* chemistry...*lots* of chemistry!

"Besides, there are multiple reasons why I don't have to *presume* anything!" She continues to mock his accent. "I work with enough people like you *to know* your type."

"How is it then," he starts to ask, "you work with all these titled people—."

"Entitled is more like it!" She says to herself but he hears it and has an exasperated look.

"*Fine.* Entitled people, yet you cast me off with the lot of them?! *Surely* you know we're not *all* the same?" He says.

His mother holds her breath as she catches his mistake. James is confused and Katie didn't catch it. David hasn't realized what he said yet, but Bri does only she doesn't call him on it just yet. She is so turned off by this point, she just wants to leave.

She says to David, "You're more curious if Artemis will *let me* ride him, but *you're pride* won't let you ask me to try." His micro expression tells her she's right, so she folds her arms in an assertive stance, "It's a shame your pride won't let you ask, because even though I'd rather be in my room right now instead of standing here talking with you any longer, I *might* humor you."

David is irritated but finds himself drawn to her with such a strong magnetic force, *he wants to run*! He's not about to let down his guard; his walls are there to protect him from being hurt again and she proves to be a challenge to everything, even the very strength of his resolve.

"You're wrong." He states.

She smiles an all-knowing-smile, "I'm not. Which is why you won't ask." She shrugs and before he can say anything to the contrary she adds, "Your micro expression gave you away."

"Micro expression?" He asks dismissively. "Sounds like rubbish."

"And here I thought you were an educated man." She exhales and holds the bridge of her nose with her fingers. "I find that the difficult diplomats, politicians, and dignitaries, I work with are much easier to deal with when I can catch their micro expressions." This makes James, Carlotta, and Jack curious, but Bri continues talking to David as she pets Artemis' neck, "Mr. *David* Worthington, I do believe you're the son and brother they've offhandedly mentioned..." gesturing to his mother and brother.

He glances at them, then looks back to her, "So I am."

"Perhaps the next time we meet, we can have a more pleasant exchange, like our texting yesterday," his mouth falls open, as well as the others' mouths. "That's of course *if* you can get over yourself." She unhooks Artemis from the lead rope and takes the reigns. She gets ready to mount, saying, "Unfortunately for you, I don't get all gushy over titles, *Mister* Worthington; titles are *not* a 'pro' on *any* list of mine. If *you* don't respect the title you hold, then how can you expect anyone else?" She doesn't see his jaw clench in frustration towards her words, her attention is with Artemis. "What do you think, Handsome? Should we try this in spite of his rudeness?" She asks Artemis, petting his neck.

Bri steps back as Artemis shifts and he goes down on his front knee for her to get on. She walks up and throws her leg over and hangs on to the saddle, sliding her feet into the stirrups as Artemis stands back up. She purposely doesn't look at David, and he knows it. He can't help but see how beautiful she is when she's angry.

Bri turns Artemis to leave, towards the back door of the stables. David goes to stop her, "Oh no, *Mister* Worthington, we're not stopping now! Let's get out of here, Artemis!" He begins a trot and when he clears the doors, he goes into a run like a bolt of lightning leaving David and the others behind. Bri feels a rush of adrenaline and is exhilarated!

David and the others watch Bri leave, even Jack who lets out a whistle saying, "She's bloody fantastic, David!"

David has an exasperated look telling Jack, "*No.*"

"No, what? 'No' you're not interested, or 'no' I can't go after her?" He smirks.

"*Both!*"

"You like her! Just admit it dam—." Jack is cut off when David ends the video call.

David is frustrated that *anyone* would talk to him like that! His heart wanted to be with her, and he is struggling to hold onto it. It's a very real battle, because he is not ready to admit that he *wants* to lose his heart to her. He saw what Jack saw, that she *is* a gorgeous force to be reckoned with! And with her American accent, he is hooked!

James pats him on his shoulder, "Wow! Not sure how you'll win that one over, but her feistiness is *definitely* sexy!" He laughs.

"I'm not interested!" David says sternly.

"*Riiight...*and if that were true, she wouldn't bother you so much!" James tells him. David scoffs and grabs the first horse he sees, Buttercup, and rides off to find Bri and Artemis.

CHAPTER 5

Imperfectly Perfect Invite

David rides out a few miles and sees no sign of BriaLynn. He knew Artemis was fast but this was crazy!

"Where could she be?" He asks out loud to himself.

He looks around, thinking, and then he remembers a trail he likes to take. He goes to where it leaves the main trail and sure enough, there are fresh hoof-prints in the side trail. There is an irritation as he takes the path, but it disappears when he sees her just admiring the view.

"You came to a great spot with one of the best views on The Estate, but I would've liked to have seen you stay on the main trail."

She continues to stare at the view and replies, "I guess Artemis believed you'd find us if you needed to." David comes up next to her and she adds, "You must up come here often."

"Why do you say that?" He asks.

She gestures Artemis as she replies, "*He* brought me here." They sit on their horses in silence, both pleasantly surprised at just how comfortable the silence is between them. After a while, Bri asks, "Are you wanting to switch horses now?"

"I think Artemis would protest that." David says without looking away from the landscape. "We should be getting back though."

Disappointed, her shoulders have a hint of a slump that he sees out of the corner of his eye. He has this desire come over him to make her feel better...to make her happy...

"We can sit a little longer." He offers.

"No, no," she replies quickly, "it's fine. I have a sneaking suspicion that you have better things to do than to entertain tourists, Mister Worthington, er, Lord *Newhaven*, is it?" She asks, turning Artemis in the direction they came from.

David follows until he can walk along side of Bri. *"You're angry with me."*

"No, not angry, Mister, er, Lord, ugh, how does a commoner address Scottish nobility?!"

"You were right. Officially, it's Lord Newhaven, but you can call me—."

"Lord Newhaven." She says with a snobbery that causes him to cringe.

David gets the horse he's on, in front of Artemis and tells Artemis, "Whoa..." which he obeys 'his master' without David ever touching him or the reins.

Bri looks down at Artemis with a raised eyebrow and disappointment, "Really? All that flirting was just a show for you?" Artemis exhales a snort.

David shifts to face her some and studies her. "Call me whatever you want, I don't care, *as long as* you *never* say that again!"

"Say what? I was just being distinctive with your title. Isn't that what an entitled man prefers?" She snips.

He smirks. "The way you said that would *prove* you're angry with me!"

"Oh, no. You see, if I were angry with you, *you'd know it!* I've accepted dealing with men like you as a part of my professional life, but whether professional or personal, I refuse to rollover for pretentious snobs no matter how exhausting *you* make it."

"*I'm* exhausting?!" David asks with a humorless laugh.

"*And here we go...*" she says under her breath, but he hears her.

David says irritably, "You *think* you know me, *but you don't.*"

"Ah, but this is the only side you show—."

He cuts her off, "I'm not some heartless, unfeeling, Dobber!"

The way she looks at him bewilders him, because she is looking at him compassionately, as if she agrees he *isn't* one. She has no idea what a 'Dobber' is, but simple reasoning would have it lumped in with 'jerk,' or perhaps a worse meaning in their society?

"You're right, you're not a '*Dobber*,' so why *act like one*?!" She watches his surprised face and he quickly looks away, not wanting to answer. "If I'm good at my job, you're acting this way to protect yourself; it's a hard shell or solid wall you use to keep people out. In fact, all of this 'attitude' I'm dealing with, is to be sure you prevent anyone from getting too close. My theory as to why you have these walls?" She asks and he looks down, but she knows he's listening. "You were hurt *so* badly; you blame yourself for not seeing it beforehand *and* you're punishing yourself! Deep down you have a big heart and care a lot about those you love. I mean, you're here when you *obviously* don't want to be, which means you're here at someone's request, perhaps your mother's?" He looks at her and she can read she's right, giving him an understanding smile before she has Artemis go around him and rides back to the stables at a gallop.

David comes off the trail in time to see Bri slide off Artemis. When Artemis sees David, he vocalizes his feelings loudly, making Bri jump because she wasn't expecting it.

Looking at Artemis, David says, "Fine, I'll apologize to her. *Happy?*" Artemis exhales and snorts very noisily. David looks at Bri as she rolls her eyes. "What's with the eye roll?" He asks with a hint of annoyance.

"Why would you apologize if you're not really sorry? Are you scared I might punch your smug face?" There's snickering behind them. "We wouldn't want to mess up your handsome face for whatever woman you're seeing next from your revolving door of mannequins, it might spoil some of your late night fun, wouldn't it?" She smirks.

"*Revolving* door?" He asks.

Bri folds her arms and defiantly asks, "*Am I wrong?*"

"*No.*" He answers, without thinking twice about it.

Her fingers go up to the bridge of her nose again. "Look, I can only guess the person who hurt you terribly was some narcissistic, self-absorbed heiress you loved, but she was more interested in your title or money, or both. Now you're protecting yourself the only way you know how: by *trying to be* the biggest '*Dobber*' there is." She looks at him compassionately and his breath catches this time. "Doesn't that get tiresome and *extremely* lonely?"

Peter and Carlotta were watching not too far away, they could still hear what was being said. "Oh Darlin,' are you hearing this?" Carlotta is on the verge of tears with her excitement.

Peter smiles and kisses her temple. "I am, Mo Stór." He chuckles. "And I'm *really* liking her!"

"David is going to want to run after this," she says, "but I *pray* he doesn't with her."

"Lotti, don't you see! He would've run already, but there's a battle going on inside him and his heart has him planted right here." He smiles, still watching the two. "Nah, Mo Stór, he isn't going to run, but he's not ready to let her in, *not just yet.*"

Carlotta adds, "Well, hopefully it's *before* they leave."

"When he realizes she's seeing *him*, that she's really pushing him to be the better man underneath his tough exterior; *then* your son will drop his walls." She looks at him with a smirk and he winks.

"Well, I asked Jack to take her to The Black-Tie Party tomorrow night and he agreed." She tells him.

Peter lightly laughs, "Jack won't hold back either! Your plan for tomorrow night just might work!"

"Now all I need to do is ask the ladies to stay longer, to be our guests tomorrow night."

He laughs. "And she'll go because David's sweet mother is asking."

Carlotta breaks the standoff between Bri and David. "Bri! Could I borrow you for a wee bit?" Carlotta hopes and prays her plan works! She has already talked with Jack and he is on board, now for her next step.

Bri looks at David. "It's clear I'm not going to back down, *Mister* Worthington, and you don't like it. I make it a point not to back down with people like you, so I think it'd be best if we just stay out of each other's way."

"Fine." David agrees, but he wasn't paying attention because it was all he could do not to grab her and kiss her!

Bri watches as Carlotta walks over to her, happy to see her friendly face. "Bri, I'd like you and Katie to come as *our* personal guests to our Black-Tie Party tomorrow night. Since there are two of you, I thought James could take Katie and our other son, and David's best friend, Jack, would take you. He just broke up with his short-term girlfriend and, if you're alright with it, the two of you could just have a nice time at a fancy party. Do you think your travel arrangements could be pushed back a day or two?" Her face is so hopeful that just like David, Bri can't say 'no' to Carlotta either.

David hears this and shakes his head at his mother saying, "*Mother*, Jack is not a fan of blind dates!"

"I've already talked to him and he had a good look already watching the two of you on a videocall in the stables; however, I sent him a picture of Bri earlier," Carlotta grins at him. "He was quick to snatch her up as a date, *if* she wants to go with him!" Then, she looks at Bri smiling, "Well, what do you think? I know you would have a *lovely* time."

Bri teases, "My first thought is, 'Hey! Where's my picture of this Jack?'" She giggles. "My other thought is more serious: our travel can be moved; *however*, we never packed anything remotely 'black-tie appropriate.'"

Carlotta looks to David, "I'm sure David has a photo on his phone," she gestures to The Manor, "my phone's inside."

"No." David looks at Bri, seemingly interested in her answer about the party, raising an eyebrow to her as if to dare her.

He loves his best friend as a brother, but he is not wanting to give in on anything with her at the moment, because he is afraid he will lose his heart right there! He doesn't realize yet that he has already lost his heart to her; it will just take a bit more time before his mind is ready to admit it.

The corner of her mouth curls into a smile, and his eyebrow goes up in curiosity. She tells Carlotta, "No need..." Giving David an obvious once over, "If David's *any* indicator as to how good-looking Jack is, and even James for that matter, I don't need a picture." She looks at Carlotta, "I'm up for some fun with a good-looking date!"

"Good girl! He's a blond-haired blue-eyed version." She winks. "All three of my sons are very fit and fetching, *usually* gentlemen." Carlotta gives David a disapproving look, as she puts her arm around Bri's arm. "We have lots of dresses for you and Katie to find one to borrow. Then tomorrow we'll have a makeup artist and hair stylist here." She looks at Bri with a twinkle in her eye and a smirk on her face, "I think you'll have a full dance card tomorrow night!" David knows his mother is right, which irks him, too. He selfishly wants *all* her dances.

Bri rolls her eyes smiling, "I highly doubt that! *Every* woman will look their best!" She smiles telling Carlotta, "As soon as Katie gets here, we'll go try on some dresses!"

"I'm so glad to hear it! I'll see to the arrangements with The Inn and your hotel with one of my assistants." She smiles and squeezes Bri's shoulders. "Ah, here's Katie now!" Carlotta waves Katie over and she takes them into The Manor, explaining things as they walk to a room they have devoted to, and named: 'The Dresses and Accessories Room.'

Hours pass when James knocks on the door where Katie and Bri are looking for dresses. He enters when he hears Bri's, "Come in!" He brought tea sandwiches with tea and lemonade. "Thank you!" Bri says.

James walks over to Bri while Katie is behind some racks helping Bri look for a dress; Katie has already found one for herself. "I hope you're okay being escorted by Jack. He's a son, brother, and best friend in this family. David didn't use to be like this; he changed when…" He trails off not wanting to say too much.

"James, he's still there. He's just hiding behind some very thick walls. Now, I won't put you on the spot with David's private life. He does know I've already figured he's been badly hurt, that these walls and protective stances are to keep *everyone* away to some degree."

"More so with anyone he sees potential with, Bri." He gives her a little smile to let her know that meant her, which she is slightly surprised. He clears his throat. "You'll have a great time with Jack, even with his post breakup. He has never had a bad review by *any* date!"

"Honestly, it's fine. No, it's *more* than fine. We can go together with no expectations of anything more than friends and just have fun!"

"Ah, you have the best expectations then," James says and grins, *"low ones."* They all laugh, even Katie.

"I'm being realistic! It comes with being good at my job." She tells him.

"Which is what, exactly?" He's curious.

"Officially, I'm a 'Liaison Officer,' wherever that title came from." She shrugs. "Perhaps it's a fancy enough title to keep people in a position that works with lots of needy politicians, diplomats, dignitaries, royalty, and any other officials from various countries; making sure things run smoothly for housing, galas, facilities, and so on; a glorified babysitter for the horribly behaved. Thankfully, there are more decent and good ones than awful ones." By this point, James is laughing. "I didn't realize it was so funny."

"No, no, it's just my mother would say it's a lot like what she does on a regular basis as The Duchess of Newhaven." James tells her.

Bri laughs. "I can see that."

Katie is standing between a wall and a clothes rack when a dress flies off it. "This is *perfect*, Bri!"

It's a short-sleeved, full-length, navy-blue dress with a straight neckline. The dress outlines her hourglass curves to the knee, then flows out and to the floor. There are burgundy-red and gold colors mixed in the glittery design on the belt and the edges of the sheer cape.

Bri walks out to show Katie, with James still there, and both smile. Katie says, "That's it! That's the dress, Bri!" Katie jumps up and down clapping. "You look great!"

James exhales saying, "Wow! I'd say, 'save me a dance' but Jack is not about to let you out of his sight!"

"What? This is a friendly date." Bri replies.

"Oh, it is! But Jack will have fun poking and pecking away at David's stubbornness and chipping away at his walls." He winks before he goes to the door. "I'll wait right outside to escort you both to The Inn for dinner after you've changed. Hang the dresses on the back of the door," he points to the hook, "and the staff will see to them being ready before the party tomorrow." They nod and thank him, then hurry to change.

After dinner, Bri retires to her room at The Inn to give James and Katie time alone together. She sits on the balcony enjoying the cool breeze as the sun is setting. She is wrapped in a blanket reading her book, but it got a little too dark to continue to read. She watches a guest running up the driveway, but it is too dark to see if it's even a man or woman...realizing it's that dark out, she decides to go inside and go to bed.

CHAPTER 6

Imperfect Leap, Perfect Surprise Dive

Saturday morning, Katie and Bri decide to do different things. Katie wanted to explore some shops, Bri wanted to hike to the waterfall and to clear her head. James offered to take Katie to the shops, hoping David might somehow run into Bri. He quickly runs through a 'How-To' with Bri on driving the golfcart. After a loop around the driveway, she is driving over to The Manor.

David was trying to avoid the guests from The Inn, particularly Bri. He kept replaying the events of yesterday and how frustratingly gorgeous she was standing up to him. He is staring out a second-floor window when he sees a golfcart pulling up. Assuming it was his brother, he goes over to the balcony doors and waits outside to greet him, only he sees Bri climbing out and heading into the gardens.

He could see she had workout pants on that were fitted but not tight. He could barely tell she was wearing a sports bra because she had a shirt over the top of it. She had her hair pulled up into a high ponytail and of course, running shoes. He was intrigued by this woman who not only wasn't afraid to stand up to him, but when most women would be barely dressed just wearing a sports bra and tight shorts to get his, James,' or Jack's attention, she is dressed like she is really going for a hike.

'*Could she seriously not be interested in him? Couldn't she feel the same magnetic pull? No, she had to feel it, or she wouldn't be this feisty of a firecracker.*' His thoughts are being consumed by this woman. He went for a run last night and it was like his feet took him over to The Inn; *he just couldn't stop thinking about her.* Maybe it's her mystery that intrigued him...maybe it's because she is not like any woman he has ever met? Whatever it is, he should be running away, *but he couldn't.* Instead, since he still had his gym clothes on, he is considering a jog to run right into her. '*Ugh! Daft heart!*' He thinks to himself as he makes his way to the gardens.

When David catches up to her, he sees her about to climb up the side of the waterfall and he runs a little faster to climb right up behind her. It's a challenge to catch up, but not impossible. She reaches the top just as he comes up on her heels, startling her a little, but she recovers quickly.

"*Mister* Worthington...what brings you out here?" She folds her arms as she breathes heavily. She was hoping not to see him at all before the party.

"Call me David." He says.

She raises an eyebrow, not particularly amused. "No."

"Fine," he says, with a bit of annoyance. "Who do you think created this trail you just hiked up?" He points to the trail.

"I'll let you have that, but only because something tells me there are stories about this place." She notes.

"There are." But he refuses to share because of his annoyance.

"*Oh-kaaay*..." She watches him. "Well, *this has been fun*..." she says sarcastically and turns to leave.

He smirks, "Where are you going?"

"I'm looking for the path down, but I suppose you guys use this same one."

Sometimes, but he wasn't going to tell her that. "I'm afraid there is really only one way down..."

She studies him, then she looks down at the waterfall. Before she can over think it, he grabs her and jumps off with her. He doesn't realize that her greatest fear is water where she can't touch the bottom, unless it's in a swimming pool. They hit the water and not even one toe feels a rock, but she does feel his hand pull her up with him. When she surfaces, he sees a look of paralyzing fear on her face and his heart sinks.

He pulls her into a hug. "You're okay!" She does notice how comforting it is to be in his arms, but the panic still chokes her, and she is shaking violently. "I'm so sorry. Can't swim?"

She pushes him away and swims over to get out of the water, letting him see for himself she can swim. David follows her over and out of the water. He goes to hug her again, but she pushes past him to start walking the trail; her shaking never fully subsides.

They go through to the gardens and Carlotta is sitting on the patio. "Bri! David! Come join us! We can introduce Jack…" Bri just walks the road in the direction of The Inn. "David? What's wrong?"

David ignores his mother for the moment, catching up to Bri. "Wait, *please?!*" He grabs her upper arm to stop her and turns her to him.

Jack comes onto the patio with Peter after they heard Carlotta call out to David and Bri. It's that moment, Bri fists her hand, but at the last second slaps him *hard* across the face. Jack runs over to them, but Bri has already started running towards The Inn. She is crying and doesn't want anyone to see that, *especially David*. She felt stupid to feel this scared, which made her angrier and frustrated with herself. David watches her run away, rubbing his cheek where she had slapped him.

"*Damn!*" David whispers, still staring in Bri's direction.

"Bloody hell!" Jack is surprised. "What did you do to deserve that?!" He asks as they walk back towards the patio.

Before he can answer, his mother is *angry*, which is rare for her. "David! Explain yourself *this instant!*" She demands with a facial expression to match her anger.

David explains to everyone, "I caught up to her at the waterfall and said there was only one way down. I didn't want her to over think it, so I grabbed her and we jumped."

"And?" Jack encourages him to continue.

"*And* she came to the surface with a terrified panicked look on her face. When I tried to apologize, she pushed me away. We got out and she was shaking so hard; probably still is." He gestures in Bri's direction. "She never said a word on the way back here. I was trying to get her to talk to me and, well…" he rubs his face again, "you saw what happened."

"*You need to go after her!*" Carlotta says with irritation towards David.

"Maybe you should." David says to Jack. "She's too upset and I don't want to make it worse."

Jack nods and jumps into the golf cart. He catches up to Bri and convinces her to get in so he can drive her over to The Inn. She is silent as she climbs in with someone she doesn't even know, but she will risk it since she just wants to go hide in her room.

Jack turns her chin to him and wipes the tears from her cheeks, telling her, "He feels awful."

She closes her eyes and more tears slip down her cheeks before she looks the other way again. He leaves it there for now and starts driving to The Inn.

David *did* feel horrible, but what could he do? She did slap him, so maybe they're even...*or done before they've really started.* '*Ugh!*' The more he thought about it, the angrier he got at himself. His heart had him seeing Bri like *she belongs with him.* When his thoughts go in the direction of kissing her, he shakes his head to stop that way of thinking; *he has to stop thinking that way about her!*

David tries to think about his date, Serene Abrams. She is beautiful, but not sophisticated, which is funny considering she comes from a titled family. Serene wasn't the kind of beautiful Bri is, nor carries herself the way Bri does. Serene loves revealing clothes and revealing her body. David found himself put off by that realization. Bri *could* dress just as revealing as other women, only she doesn't because she chooses elegance over showing a lot of skin, giving her that classy, polished look that revealing clothes could *never* do. He takes a deep breath and exhales, thinking to himself, '*I need to take a shower...a very cold shower.*'

Saturday afternoon, Bri had showered before heading to The Manor with Katie. When the two of them walk into the dressing room, there are two ladies already there and excited to see Bri and Katie.

They speak with a French accent. "Please let us 'elp you!" One of them says to both of them.

The other one grabs Bri and introduces herself as Antionette, her friend is Nicole. They look at the dresses Bri and Katie will be wearing and immediately dive into hair and make-up, then dresses, shoes, the whole deal. Just before the party starts, James comes for Katie.

"You're both beautiful!" He tells them. Katie and Bri carefully hug each other and James kisses Bri on the cheek. He holds his arm out for Katie and they head to the party.

She hears a knock and opens the door to find The Duchess there with, "Wait. *You're Jack?* How did I miss that?" She thinks back to sitting with him in the golf cart.

"It's okay. Your mind was a wee bit preoccupied." He gives her a sweet, handsome smile.

She nods and steps aside as Carlotta and Jack come inside the room. "You look incredibly *dashing!*" She teases with his accent.

"Ha-ha! I better if I'm to escort such a gorgeous woman to this party!" He smiles a wonderful smile as he looks her over.

 Carlotta tells her, "You do look wonderful, Dear!" Holding Bri's arms out to get a better look.

She walks over and takes something out of a safe and brings it over. Carlotta opens a box behind Bri, then she puts the necklace on her while Antionette and Nicole help with the earrings. All three stand in front of her to have a look.

"Perfect!" Carlotta exclaims and they show Bri in a mirror.

The Newhaven Necklace is a V-shaped necklace with a small oval sapphire at the center, then a mixture of small, diamonds, sapphires, emeralds, and rubies, tightly packed together going all the way around the necklace. The earrings match with a small oval sapphire and a cluster of the same gems.

"Your Grace, these are exquisite, but I can't wear these. This is too much!"

"You're wearing the colors of the family tartan and The Newhaven Necklace Set pulls it all together, plus, Jack has a tartan square in the front pocket. You both look *wonderful* together!" Carlotta tells her with a huge smile, but she doesn't mention that David has a tartan square, too. Hopefully, by the end of the evening, her plan has worked and she will be looking stunning *with David.*

Jack has sandy-blond hair and blue-eyes. He is *very* charismatic and incredibly handsome with his build resembling David's, as well as height. They've grown up as brothers and, although Carlotta gave birth to two sons, when she is asked, she tells people she has three sons. Jack's mom died when he was only six and his dad favored his older brother, his heir; Jack was the spare and treated worse than that. Jack was, and is, wanted by the whole Worthington Family and that is where he has always wanted to be.

When Jack looks at Bri, an excited smile spreads across his face and after slowly blowing out his breath, he tells her, "You.are.*breathtaking*!" Then he bows a little and kisses her hand, "The pleasure of escorting you tonight is *all* mine, Gorgeous! Which is what I'm going to call you." He winks.

A little earlier that evening, David was standing outside the entrance to their Grand Ballroom, as his date, Serene, arrived. Serene is a bleach-blond with highlights in her hair, blue-eyed beauty, who oozes high maintenance with her straightened hair, long manicured nails with glittering gold polish, and nude colored lipstick with her over done makeup. She is wearing a fitted glittering gold dress with thick straps at the top, a plunging neckline, and the dress barely goes down a third of her thighs. She has matching gold stilettos with a bunch of crisscrossing straps on them; the shoes cost more than the dress, which her entire look was *far* into the five-digit price range.

There are no kilts tonight and like Jack, David is wearing a square of the family tartan in the front pocket of his tux jacket, as are all the men with a family tartan. Serene's dress being gold had David sarcastically thinking, '*At least she managed to where one color.*' But if a woman were going to focus on one color of the tartan, it would be the navy-blue or burgundy red.

David and Serene are announced with their titles, right before they walk into the party; Serene fakes a beaming smile showing off her look and glowing white teeth. Her sense of entitlement has her nose up in the air most of the time, like it is now with her arm wrapped around David's arm.

For the first time, David has been taking all this in and he sees her, as well as the other women he has dated, as they really are...*fake*. Bri was right; he is growing tired of the fake. He is wanting *real, he wants Bri*. He pushes those thoughts down for now, Serene was his date tonight; unfortunately, the harder he tried *not* to think of Bri, the more he did.

David looks around for The Inn's guests and only sees James with Katie. The first dance is about to start and then he hears the announcement of Lord Jackson Carlisle and Lady BriaLynn Harris. David watches them enter and can barely manage to keep himself composed. He refocuses and puts his left arm behind his back, raising his right hand up for Serene's hand, and she sets her left hand in his to walk to the dance floor.

Bri and Jack see The Duchess and Bri notices, "The way The Duchess just winked at you, I can't help but think...well," then she whispers to Jack, "*let's just say I'm suspicious.*"

"Full disclosure?" He quietly asks. Bri nods with an 'of course' look. "You *are* being set-up, *but not with me.*"

Bri gives him a questioning look, then shakes her head when she realizes he means David. "*OH no!*"

"OH, *yes!*" Jack grins.

She quietly replies. "Haven't you all been *paying attention*?! He's *not* interested in me and it's mutual because of his asinine behavior!"

"The funny thing is you haven't been paying attention!" He sees her eyes roll as she scoffs. "*Don't be that way!* You're in the thick of it, so you *can't* see it..." he grins, "*but you will!*"

She scoffs. "You're confused."

"But I am not, Gorgeous!" He chuckles. "I'm here to help my best friend take a chance! Although being with you now, if he lets you slip through his fingers," he gets close to her ear, "*I won't!*" He sees her shiver a little. "I'll chase you all the way to America if I have to!" He pulls back as he quietly laughs. He holds out his arm and she takes it.

When they had entered the ballroom, Jack was introduced as Lord Jackson Carlisle; and as they are walking to the dance floor, she gets a playful smile.

"Jackson, huh?" She smiles biting her lower lip.

"*Not* if you expect me to answer." He flirts back. "Then again, *maybe for you,* I'd make an exception. It does sound better in your accent." He grins.

She giggles. "Glad to hear it, since it's one of my favorite names." His eyebrow goes up in a questioning look. She laughs. "*I'm serious!*"

They have a moment holding each other's gaze dancing a waltz, then carry on a conversation as they dance. Bri finds Jack quite easy to talk to and he helps her to relax. It's a gift he has with people in general.

David has been keeping an eye out for Bri, trying to be inconspicuous, but isn't very successful. Serene is already suspicious, but it's when David had seen Bri when she first entered the ballroom that Serene's suspicions were confirmed. David sees Bri with Jack, and if David weren't already smitten with this American, he would approve of Jack with Bri. Serene wants to stomp this out before she loses her chance at becoming a duchess. Unfortunately for Serene, the cards were already stacked against her, long before David ever met Bri...even before Serene came through his 'revolving door.' Serene won't be staying because no woman that comes through his revolving door, or Jack's for that matter, ever stays long; they are never meant to. Although Jack sometimes has short-term girlfriends, any of the women coming through their 'revolving doors' are meant to revolve right back out the door again.

The Duke and Duchess have taken a position to watch The Duchess' handy work, as people come over to mingle with them. She clearly sees David watching Bri with Jack dance around the dance floor and David's agitation. Carlotta can't help being pleased with how things are going and Peter is chuckling.

Peter says to Carlotta, "I do have to say, those two do look magnificent together! One way or another, I think this lovely lady will be joining our family soon!"

Carlotta smiles and nods. "I think you're right...it'll be wonderful!" She continues to watch the three of them.

Jack and Bri look like a refined couple. Bri is so graceful; she makes anyone look good...but David wants it to be him.

Jack says to Bri, "You're great at waltzing! It's almost like you ballroom dance professionally."

"Ha-ha! Kind of!" She tells him about her job in DC. He holds her close, listening to every word, talking, laughing, dancing cheek-to-cheek. After a few dances, she and Jack take a break to get something to drink.

David covertly pulls Jack aside, "Why did you ever agree to be Bri's date? You and Maddy just broke up! You like your one-night-stands after a breakup; she deserves better!"

"Mother knew Maddy and I broke up. Since I didn't have a date, I was going to cancel." Jack tells him. "When she asked if I would take Bri so *both ladies* would have a date, I thought it could be fun, *and it is!*" He slightly tips his head in Serene's direction and a look on his face that reads, '*Really*?'

"I asked her weeks ago!" David tells him.

"If you weren't so bloody stubborn about admitting you really like Bri, it wouldn't matter who you had asked! As for a one-night stand, she *does* deserve better than that and do you honestly think I would do that to you?"

"No." David has a hint of a defying smirk. "Then that means I don't have to admit what *you* already know."

"Then I also know, *as do you*, she deserves *the real David* and not this," he gestures David, "whatever you call this to keep women like Bri away! Honestly, when your mother sent me a pic of Bri, I was in! It'll be your loss if you pass her up like a bloody coward!"

"It would've been bad form to cancel on Serene so late!" David replies, knowing his argument is weak. "The press would've had a field day, *especially since it's her family's business!*"

"*That's a load of rubbish and you bloody well know it!* Literally *anyone* would've been better than Serene! David, I love you, brother! But it needs to be said: *you're an idiot!*" Jack looks at Serene and back to Bri. "*I* can even feel the attraction and chemistry between you two!"

"Jack, I won't deny there's a strong magnetic pull with Bri! I even find myself thinking '*She's the one!*' The reality is she also lives in the US and I have to consider how that would work?!"

"Just more *idiotic excuses* because you're scared! Once you let her in, you'll never ask that question again! It really will be your *unbelievable loss* because if you don't chase this woman, David, I promise you, *I will*!" He is stern, with a hint of frustration. "I'll chase her all the way around the world if that's what it takes, because she's wonderful and fantastic! Consider yourself warned." Jack starts to walk away; irritated with his best friend's stubbornness!

"You'd do that to your best friend?!" David asks.

"Look!" Jack pivots back to him. "*She's amazing* and if we could clone her, I'd be all for it! IF you're going to wise up and not miss this 'once-in-a-lifetime' woman, I'll be your biggest supporter! *You know this*!" He smiles a smirk at David, gesturing with his head. "Until then, looks like I have the best-looking date of anyone here!" David absentmindedly nods as he stares longingly at Bri. Jack excuses himself. "Looks like I need to go rescue her from some piranhas." He pats David's shoulder before walking away.

David watches Jack walk up to Bri and puts his arm around her waist, pulling her close in a protective way. He hears a voice in his head agree with Jack...'*He does have the better date.*' In fact, he has with the most incredible woman David's ever met! His heart had never physically ached as it did right then. But none of it mattered if she was never going to speak to him again. He shakes his head; he has to get his mind off her and he goes looking for Serene.

Serene beams when she knows what David has in mind. She leads him away from the party to keep his attention fully on her and off Bri, but it doesn't work; he can't even kiss her. For the first time, Serene's use of her feminine body doesn't work on the man of her choice. She knows she needs to get rid of Bri and get David over this little crush of his...and *fast*!

Jack and Bri dance and mingle for a couple of hours. "Ms. Harris?" Says a familiar Spanish-accented voice.

Bri turns and is delighted to see a friendly face. "Countess!" Bri smiles as they kiss the air next to each other's cheeks. "It's so good to see you!"

"You, too! And who might this handsome man be?!" The Countess smiles holding her hand out to Jack as Bri introduces them.

"This good-looking man is Lord Jack Carlisle." She motions to Jack and then motions to the Countess. "Jack, this *stunning lady* is Countess Sabina Reyes."

"Ah, Lord Carlisle! I'm delighted to finally meet you!" The Countess smiles. "The Duke and Duchess are always raving about their sons and you're the only one I haven't had the pleasure of meeting yet."

"It's wonderful to meet you, too, Countess." Jack says as he bows some and kisses the back of her hand. "How did you lovely ladies meet?" He asks.

The Countess responds, "Oh, we first met a few years back in Washington, D.C. When someone important comes to town, Ms. Harris is one of the first to know." For the first time, Bri's last name doesn't feel right; '*Odd.*' She thinks to herself. The Countess continues, "A person quickly learns that she's the only person you really need on your side. She knows everyone and everything in town!"

"Gosh, I hope not!" Bri laughs. "There are answers to things I *never* want to know!" They laugh like there is a secret between them.

"Oh, Bri! I'll be coming to town in a few weeks. Would you be able to get me in front of that favorite senator of yours, um...?"

"Senator Jenkins?" Bri grins.

"Yes! That's it! Senator Jenkins!" The Countess replies.

"How much time?" Bri asks.

"Oh, I don't think it would even take an hour." The Countess says. "I was hoping to gain his support for a particular issue."

"Would he know the issue?" Bri asks.

"I'd be surprised if he didn't!" The Countess says.

"That's all I need to know. The less info up here to store, the better." Bri points to her head and they laugh. "If they have questions, they'll ask when they call to make those arrangements."

"I left a message for you with Amy and she said you were in the UK. It *could* wait until you get back, but his schedule may be filled up by then. You know it's earlier back there..." The Countess hints with a pleading smile.

"You're lucky I like you Countess, or I'd make you wait." Bri says with seriousness, but there is an obvious smile behind it.

"This is why you're the best!" The Countess says with a huge smile and squeezes her hand.

"Wait." Jack says, confused. "Today is Saturday."

Bri pulls out her phone. "The beauty of cell phones, or *mobiles*," she teases, mocking his accent, "I can send a text message and he can respond when he can, but at least this is in motion for The Countess."

"Making you the best!" The Countess adds.

David overhears and looks at Jack, who looks back at him, discreetly pointing to Bri and mouthing '*Amazing*!' Serene exhales in annoyance and glares at Jack, but he doesn't care.

Curious, David steps in with Serene. "Ah, Countess Reyes! So good to see you again!" David bends and kisses her hand.

"Lord Newhaven, so good to see you." The Countess smiles, but her smile drops when her eyes lock onto Serene.

"Countess, this is Lady Abr—."

The Countess has a bit of a scolding tone, "Regrettably, I do know who *she* is and where she comes from. Lord Newhaven! I'm disappointed in you. As smart and handsome as you are, you show up with someone from the bottom of respectability..." you can hear the snobbery in her tone as she looks Serene over, "it wouldn't have taken much to do better than this."

Serene's embarrassed and angry. "You can't talk to me that way! Look at you!" She gestures between The Countess and Bri, "You're standing here next to that-that, *nobody*!"

Jack takes a protective stance between Bri and Serene, while The Countess takes a stance next to Jack and continues addressing Serene. "That shows what *little* you know. Never mess with a woman who has *her* kind of connections!"

Bri keeps a straight face, but she is surprised by that comment. She has never thought about anything like that, let alone anyone who would do something...

Serene scoffs. "*Please*. Who could this *American* know?"

The Countess smirks a grin. "There are quite a few *around the world* who would snuff you out right now simply because you don't treat Ms. Harris with proper respect." The Countess looks to David, "Lord Newhaven, please keep your date away from me, *and* probably anyone else here who doesn't want to talk to the likes of her...*ever*." She turns her back to Serene and positions herself to keep Serene behind her and out of the group's conversation.

Bri feels her phone vibrate in her hand and sees the Senator is calling her. Bri steps back, pointing to her phone and looking at The Countess, who then knows the Senator is calling Bri directly. Bri tries to answer, but it's too loud.

> "Let me call you back in a little bit. I need to find a quieter place for this conversation." Bri tells the Senator, but she's unsure if he heard her or not.

"And that's not rude?!" Serene asks, pointing at Bri.

The Countess shakes her head and walks away. Serene watches Bri with disdain, the very woman who threatens the upgrade to her social status!

Later that night, Jack leads Bri upstairs to the loft that overlooks the ballroom. It's surprisingly quieter, which Bri appreciates while she waits for Jack to run to the restroom.

He says, "I'll take you outside for more privacy for your phone call when I get back." She gives him a small smile with her nod.

Since David is in there, Jack thinks she will be safe; but Bri soon finds herself with a small group of women she will refer to as 'vipers.' Serene, their leader, is seated with them and David stands behind Serene's chair, leaning against the wall. David's heart longs for Bri, but it's mixed with frustration. Bri has invaded his thoughts deeper than he knew, he couldn't do anything with Serene, not even kiss her...he didn't want meaningless anymore, but his mind fought his heart...he was terrified of getting hurt again, however, he is getting more terrified of losing his chance with her.

"*Oh look*," Serene's voice oozed with venom, "here's tonight's charity case The Duchess invited at the last minute." Turning her head upwards to David, "Isn't that right, *Dah*ling?" He stood there looking at Bri, his jaw clenching. "It looks like your mother did a fantastic job dressing up a commoner to pass as nobility!" She laughs and the other vipers join in.

Bri locks eyes with David, raising an eyebrow. Bri waits to see if he steps up and defends a guest, only he is waiting to see what she will do to handle herself. She reads his body language...and he isn't going to budge. '*Oh, heck no!*' She thinks to herself. In fact, while never losing eye contact with David, she stands and squares her shoulders as she walks straight to him. Jack walks in and quickly assesses the situation and backs out of the room; listening at the door to what Bri says to David...hoping she makes a breakthrough!

Standing in front of him, she crowds Serene, but she doesn't care. Serene doesn't know what to do, but she's thinking it's going to be fun to watch Bri's embarrassment and smirks to her groupies. Bri articulates every word for clarity when she speaks to David, stunning everyone around them.

"*Anyone* who would surround himself with vapid women, supporting their childish and bratty antics, is anything *but* a gentleman!" There are gasps around them. David goes to step forward to get Bri to back down...*She. Doesn't. Move.* He is stuck until *she* decides to move. When she sees his jaw clench more firmly shut, she knew she struck a nerve and that is *exactly* what she wants!

He glares, but she defiantly returns his glare. His voice is low in volume but there is *no* mistaking his anger, "Do you *really* know who I am?!"

She has a humorless laugh as she rolls her eyes and folds her arms. "*Do you?!*" She raises her eyebrow adding more defiance. Guests around the room are getting agitated with this American.

He gets as close to her as he dares to, the attraction is getting more intense now. He goes to say, "I'm—"

Bri cuts David off with a wave of a hand. An older gray-haired man, who is tall, thin frame seems fragile under the weight of his tuxedo, interrupts, "This man is of nob—" She cuts him off, too, with another hand wave. "Well! *I've never!*" The man grumbles to those around him. "*Just who does she think she is?!*"

She is still looking right at David. "*This* is between *you and me*...unless it's a problem for you?" She flicks her eyebrow up higher for a second. David doesn't say anything, not wanting to give her the satisfaction. "Your silence is *still* an answer and I'll take it as an agreement." Bri's eyes are still firmly locked with his. "Now, if that man were about to inform me that there's some sort of noble title you'll inherit," he gives her a smug look, "and one day you will be addressed as 'Your Grace'," he adds a raised eyebrow to his smug look, "then it's a shame because 'grace' is what you're *sorely lacking*, along with all the other words that describe a 'gentleman!'" She sees David shift, knowing she is getting to him and continues. "The last time I checked, pompous, arrogant, and conceited don't line up with the definition of 'grace.' Unfortunately, those words *pathetically* describe you!"

The word 'pathetic' strikes a nerve as it was supposed to do. Barely louder than a whisper so he doesn't lose his temper with her, he angrily says through gritted teeth, "How *dare* you!"

"How dare I *what*? How dare I stand up to you? How dare I tell you the truth? How dare I not tolerate being treated in any way, but with respect? Did you expect me to just sit back and keep quiet? Are you kidding me?! Wouldn't the horrible treatment of guests *your mother*, The Duchess, personally invites herself, be up there on a list of faux pas?! *And you*, being a member of her family, and *The Heir* no less, should *never* allow guests of *any* social standing be disrespected! *Period.* You're a cocky, pretentious, arrogant——." She clamps her lips down inside her mouth with her teeth, to stop herself from saying the swear word that pops into her head.

"No, *please* continue!" His anger seethed.

"Do you really want me to lower myself to speaking vulgar language?" She angrily glares.

He studies her, not sure what to say to that or anything else; he is too shocked, too stunned and angry by this point; *and* it was all said in front of guests! Bri turns on her heels and goes to walk out of the room...*determined* to get out of there, *fast!*

'*Oh, no you don't!*' David thinks to himself and goes after her. He could've thrown her out, he could've called security, or in some way he could've truly stopped her if he really wanted to, but he didn't. He grabs her arm, halting her and turning her to him.

"Oh, we're not done, *Ms.* Harris!" He not only sees her anger and frustration, but he now sees hurt in her eyes which surprises him. His heart squeezes and he holds his breath.

Yanking her arm back, "I think we're through making a scene, *Mister* Worthington!" He grabs her behind her jaw and pulls her into the most passionate, magnetic, all-consuming kiss of her life. She struggles for a few seconds, but soon he feels her arms wrap around him. She starts to melt into his arms and her arms hold him firmer. Serene is fuming angry. If she were a cartoon, her face would be red with steam coming out her ears and nose.

Bri pulls back, looking at him in confusion while shaking her head! '*What?! No!*' She scolds herself. '*I can't be attracted to him! Even if that was the best kiss of my life!*' Then she thinks to herself. '*Damn it!*' She comes back to her senses and sees the cocky look on his face; David knew he had her. She scoffs with disgust and pushes David away. His face falls when she turns and rushes out of the room...

Jack can barely keep up with her as she makes her way downstairs, through the guests, and out into the gardens before he gets her to stop. She takes a deep breath, blowing it out slowly, looking at him a little embarrassed.

"How bad was it?" She braces herself for his answer.

"Are you kidding?!" He laughs as he claps. "That was *bloody brilliant!* You're my hero!" He laughs as they continue walking. "There's hope for getting my best friend and brother back!" He takes off his jacket and puts it on her shoulders, then wraps an arm around her waist. "Why don't you return your call? I can give you some privacy."

"Privacy won't be necessary; you already know what this is about. It's not like it has to do with national security or anything like that." She smiles as she puts the phone up to her ear and winks. He smiles watching her walk onto the bridge ahead of him.

Jack can overhear the conversation and picks up on how much this senator likes Bri as a person. He steps back and looks him up on his phone and finds he is a powerful senator in America. He sees pictures at various events and some are of the senator with Bri, even the two of them with his wife at these events. He quickly sees Bri is no stranger to this world!

CHAPTER 7

Imperfectly Perfect Admitted Truths

Bri had left David standing in place as she ran out of the room; he could only watch her leave as he is too stunned to move. '*Damn*! *Why did I have to be so bloody attracted to her?*!' He thinks to himself and remembers the way she melted into his arms when they kissed...then the weight of what she had said to him sinks in, and he deflates...*finally* his walls crumble...

David always thought of himself as a gentleman: opening doors, offering an arm, kissing the back of a woman's hand...but now he understands why she meant all that was meaningless. When the time came to stand up and *be* a gentleman, demanding his guests treat each other with dignity and respect, he failed...*miserably*. It wasn't the title, the money, or his social class Bri saw...she saw *him*! The man he had become! However, at the same time *she knew* he could do better; she knows he could *be* better! He wasn't angry with her; he is angry and disappointed with himself!

When David thought of what Serene said to embarrass Bri, David's heart *hurt* for her and he scolded himself for allowing it to go uncorrected. When he heard Serene at this very moment saying more awful things about her, David puts a stop to it.

"Serene, stop talking!" He says firmly, turning to face her and she freezes. "You're embarrassing yourself, me, *and my entire family*! You don't get it! Ms. Harris is right! About ALL of it!" Everyone in the room is flabbergasted David agrees with this insubordinate American commoner! "She doesn't need a fancy title for everyone to see that she *IS* a better person than any of us in this room are right now, *even you*, Serene!" She gasps and so do a few of her friends.

Serene is irate. "You Bas—!"

"IF anyone is upset with her it's only because *she's right*!" He cuts her off. "She's holding us to the higher standards we placed upon ourselves, especially when we *are* stuck up and arrogant." He looks pointedly at Serene. "*Don't* forget who *you're* talking to, *Lady Abrams*!" He is very stern with a bit of irritation in his voice. He walks up to her. "I know *exactly* the type of women I date, so marrying you was *never* going to happen."

She is fuming as she shoots up. "*How dare you* lead me on!"

"*You* led yourself on!" David tells her. "I made it clear to you both times we had a date; this is *not* a relationship. *I didn't want to lead you on*! I knew my reputation, *but so did you*! I knew it was *never* going to happen, because I made a point to date women who were like Ava, so I *wouldn't* marry them."

"Then what do you call that poor excuse for a socialite?! That *American* no less!" She detests.

David doesn't hesitate, "My wife!" He sees Serene's mouth drop when he says, "And the future Duchess of Newhaven."

"*Oh please!*" She scoffs in disgust. She looks at him again and says, "You can't be serious?!" She is horrified. "You think you'll actually marry this woman?! She can't even *stand* you!"

A sly smile spreads across David's face as he thinks about the kiss. "Oh, I *know* I'll marry her!" David responds with confidence as he realizes, "She wouldn't have bothered to confront me like she did, if she thought it was a waste of time. She didn't address you about your behavior because she knew it would 'fall on deaf ears,' and that *would be* a complete waste of time." She glares in loathing. "Serene, our date is over." He takes a deep breath. "Now," he says as he straightens his tuxedo, "if you all will excuse me, I need to go apologize to that amazing woman - no," he stops briefly, "that amazing *lady*!" When he walks out of the room, the men and the women who weren't part of Serene's group, hung their heads a bit as humility sets in.

David walks with purpose back to the party to find Bri. He sees his parents, particularly his mother, who has an all-knowing smile. He gives her a faint smile as he walks up to her and his father.

"Mother...How much of this did you orchestrate?" He asks.

"Just enough to get the ball rolling." She pats his arm. "You arrived here Thursday speaking of an American, that a *Ms. Harris* caught your eye. I knew she was coming to stay at The Inn, but I also knew if I told you then, you would get in your own way. Your father and I hoped she would be the one for you, that maybe we would get our son back." Carlotta says smiling, affectionately touching his cheek. "We think she found him."

He holds his mother's hand and smiles sweetly at her. "I should be angry with you for meddling, but *she is remarkable!*"

Peter puts his hand on his son's shoulder and laughs, "I think you met your match, Son!"

"No doubt!" David laughs. "*She's the one...*I just hope I didn't blow it and I can still win her over." David says reluctantly.

"David, whatever she has gone through *in her past*, has her scared, too." Carlotta tells him. David hadn't considered that! She also says, "As perceptive as she is, she hadn't noticed the chemistry between the two of you. That's why your kiss surprised her more than anything else!" David nods as he remembers her face when she broke their kiss.

"Be prepared," Peter cautions, "she may want to run *from you*, David."

"I've been sensing that." David replies.

"From what we've gathered, she works with the elite. Mingling with politicians and dignitaries, seeing that they get what they need, but she doesn't take a lot of attitude from them either." Peter explains. "We've talked to quite a few people here who've met her in DC and hope to say 'Hullo' before the night's over. It takes a special person to run a tight ship at work and, as you've seen, she will go head-to-head with those that need to be set straight, but has the respect of each one of them, too." Peter smirks. "Just like you have for her right now." David agrees with a smile.

David tells them, "I didn't expect her to put a mirror up to my face..." He thinks about her feistiness and her sassiness. "Thank you, Mother, for meddling. *Truly.*" He hugs her and kisses her cheek.

She hugs him back excitedly. "You're welcome, Sweetie, and we love you." She also adds, "David, if she runs when you confront her, you might have to let her."

"What?! *Why?!*" He asks.

"Just make sure you're right on her heels." Peter tells him. "She may not run until her vacation is over," he explains, "using going home as the best place to break things off."

"Hiding behind distance." David adds as he listens.

"Right." Peter replies.

Carlotta gives David a soft smile. "While you've met your match, she needs to see from you she has met hers." She smirks, as does David with a nod.

"I'll keep that in mind." David says, giving her another hug. Carlotta points outside and smiles encouragingly. He hugs his father before he heads outside to find Bri and Jack.

Peter and Carlotta watch him as he walks towards the doors leading to the gardens. She asks Peter, "Is this *finally* happening?!"

He turns to her. "Lotti," he gestures the direction David took, "even if, for some unknown reason she doesn't want to be with him, she has set his heart free. And for that, I'm already grateful for her!"

Carlotta hugs him. "Oh, me, too!"

David finds his way through the garden, walking up to Jack and sees Bri on the phone. He overhears Jack talking to himself as he went from looking up the senator, to looking up Bri. He sees more connections to some powerful people around the world.

David comes up and stands next to Jack, who whispers, *"The Countess was right! This woman becomes more amazing by the second!"* He scrolls through more photos seeing people he knew and recognized. *"Wow..."* Jack exhales quietly, "she's definitely one-of-a-kind, David! Look at this!" He shows him the senator first. "She's on the phone to this guy right now for The Countess! This guy is *'The Senator'* in Washington and from what I've overheard," he throws his thumb over his shoulder towards Bri, "he genuinely likes her, just like The Countess. We were mingling when we were stopped by The Countess, who was looking *for her!* I'm wondering how many more would feel the same about her because," he brings up pics of her with various people, "some of these people are right inside," he points to The Manor. "Maybe she's met Herst already!" He is referring to their third 'Musketeer.'

"Mother and Father did say there are people here tonight who saw her and hope to talk with her this evening." David says, taking Jack's phone and scrolls, seeing the various people Jack's referring to. People who are more pompous and arrogant than he ever was, seem to be really smiling with her. These people have discovered what he and Jack were figuring out...Bri is incredible!

"She isn't a man-made diamond; she is that rarest and hardest to find diamond!" David quietly says.

"That she is!" Jack agrees.

Bri had finished her phone call and is looking out at the nighttime lighting glistening on the stream that flows under the bridge she is standing on. They see her wipe her cheek and David motions for Jack to walk up to her; he wants to listen so maybe he can come up with *some way* to make it right.

Jack walks up to her asking, "What's wrong?"

"Just coming down emotionally, I guess." Bri says, carefully wiping the tears away from her eyes.

When she takes a deep breath he asks, "Are you ready to admit to yourself you're in-love with David?" Jack bluntly asks.

Her head snaps to look at him in shock. "*What?*" She scoffs. "I'd ask how much you had to drink, but you've been with me so that leaves '*you're bloody mental!*" She teases with his accent.

He snorts a laugh. "Okay, if *you're* going to be stubborn about this, then let's talk you through it."

"No." She says.

He ignores that. "Friday, when you both met, it was passionately charged, to say the least."

Bri laughs a little in ridiculousness, "Ooo, wow, if that constitutes passion then there are *a lot* of people out there that I must be *secretly in-love with* given my job alone!" She rolls her eyes with another scoff. "Is that the best you got, *Jackson* Carlisle?" David's eyes go wide when he hears her use Jack's full first name.

Jack looks intensely at her, with a smile. "Okay, let's go back to earlier today. What happened this afternoon at the waterfall? We've taken girls up there at various times over the years, doing 'surprise dives' with some of them."

Bri closes her eyes for a moment and says, "It's stupid."

"Not if you're shaking from just the memory of it!" He hugs her with one arm. David feels even worse.

Bri inhales...then feels David's presence. "I have this stupid fear, David," she looks around Jack's shoulder in David's direction, "of not being able to touch the bottom in water, except in swimming pools." She explains. Part of David wants to go to her...but he didn't want to scare her away, so he walks to edge of the bridge. "In a pool, it's a given that there's a bottom, but in the ocean, you could be over a trench and *never* touch the bottom. I should've been fine, you never let go of my hand; but when a toe never felt anything, I *panicked*." She steps to the side to see David better. "I'm sorry for letting my panic get the better of me and slapping you across the face," she apologizes, and he can see the tears in her eyes.

Jack leans in whispering, "*And there's the proof.*"

She wipes her eyes again, before looking at him with confusion. "What are you talking about?"

"How did you know David was even here?" Jack grins. Bri doesn't answer, just slightly glares at him. "Now, I'd even wager, that you wouldn't have bothered with David this evening if you honestly thought he was just a pompous, arrogant twit." He smirks and looks intensely into her eyes. "You *know* I'm right."

"*Ugh,*" she waves her hand scoffing, "you *both* can go now!"

Jack chuckles a little. "*I'm going anyway* to give you two a few minutes to talk."

"I don't want to talk anymore!" She wipes another tear watching Jack walk over to David and shake his hand, hugging him with the other arm.

David whispers, "*I owe you one, Brother!*"

"Yes, you do..." he looks back at Bri with a longing he pushes out of his thoughts, while Bri is back to watching the reflected lights on the water once again, "but since she's one of a kind, that's not possible. *Don't screw this up!*" He says in all seriousness. "I meant what I said earlier. I'd fly around the world, and back again, if that's what it took!" He pats David's shoulder.

David gives him an appreciative smile, "Thanks, Jack." David pats Jack's upper arm before Jack walks back to The Manor. David slowly walks up to Bri. "Can we talk?"

She throws up her hands a little replying, "You both have gone and lost your minds completely!" David is trying to hold back a smile, but it doesn't work. "*Seriously*?! You think this is funny?! Why on earth do you even *want* to talk to me? Is this some sort of sick, twisted joke to you? You don't even *like* me!" She goes to walk away, but he steps in her way; she exhales in annoyance, "What *is it* with you?!"

David swoops in and cups her face, pulling her into a kiss, only this time she immediately melts into his kiss. David pulls their lips apart, still holding her firmly; he sweetly smiles, "You're *incredibly sexy* when your upset. Did you know that?"

She is baffled; most people would back down when she calls them out, but he doesn't. She looks away from him, asking herself, '*Why am I so attracted to him*?!'

"Look," he gently pulls her chin towards him so she looks at him, "you got your say in front of however many people, so the way I see it, the *least* you can do is let me have mine out here in private." He commands her gaze. "Isn't that what a *lady* would do?"

She raises her eyebrow and smirks with defiance. "I actually have the excuse of not having a title, so technically I'm not '*a lady*.'" She mocks his accent.

"Ah, but I told a whole room of people back there," he points towards The Manor, "that *you* don't have to have a title to prove you're a lady and you're better than the lot of us in that room!"

"Why would you say that?!" She asks.

There is a teeny tiny flower coming up through a crack that somehow catches his attention. As he picks it, he replies, "I may be all of the things you pointed out, *and then some*," he hands the little flower to her, "but *liar* isn't one of them." It's a sweet gesture and she takes the flower with a soft smile. He tells her, "I *honestly* meant it." She looks at it and it reminds her of a Forget-Me-Not flower. She isn't sure what kind of flower it is, but this act of sweetness goes to her very core and begins to work on her. She curiously studies him and he playfully adds, "I'll get my say one way or another, *Ms.* Harris. If you prefer I embarrass myself further, we can go back inside." He throws his thumb over his shoulder gesturing to The Manor. "The embarrassment being mine because you're absolutely right about everything."

"I know." She says looking back out to the water. He lightly chuckles and shakes his head. She takes a deep breath and exhales, "I'd also like to skip further embarrassment and drama *for both of us...*" she looks at him raising a playful eyebrow, "for now." '*Ugh, I can't be flirting with him!*' She scolds herself.

David quietly laughs. He smells her hair or perfume...maybe both? A scent he can imagine waking up to every morning for the rest of his life. He takes a deep breath. He is not fighting it anymore...he knows she is perfect for him!

David clears his throat and looks at Bri. "I don't know where to begin. 'I'm sorry' doesn't come close."

"No. It doesn't." She isn't going to make it easy on him, *nnnot just yet*. Serene's words playing in her mind, the waterfall, Artemis...but his kisses...'*wow....Stop that!*' She scolds herself again.

"First, about the waterfall, *I'm terribly sorry!* It was meant to be adventurous, not traumatizing." She gives him a small acknowledging smile. He takes a deep breath. "Up in the loft, you were right about *everything* you said tonight." His kind smile makes her smile in return, threatening to melt all of her defenses; it terrifies her, but she pushes it down to hear him out. He holds her chin with his thumb and forefinger, slowly leaning into kiss her, but she pulls away. He's confused, "Don't you feel this, too?"

"*Yes, I feel it!* I also want to be treated differently from any other woman you've ever kissed before, let alone the ones you had in your bed, like Serene!" She points out.

"Oh, trust me, Luv'..." he says with a hint of a playful smile, "you are!" His accent is more noticeable. David looks at her and goes to say, "I'm sor—." Bri cuts him off with her hand on his mouth.

"I promise you, David, I'm *truly* not trying to judge you for anything you may've done tonight, or any night for that matter! I don't want to know." She goes to the side of the bridge again saying, "You don't answer to me."

He stands beside her. "That's just it, Bri! I *want* to answer to you!" He looks longingly into her eyes. "I've kissed Serene in the past, but tonight I just couldn't! Believe it or not, I couldn't even kiss her because *it has been you* on my mind; consuming my thoughts since before we met, when I first laid eyes on you in the hotel lobby."

Bri laughs a little, "Technically, we were never *properly* introduced. I just logically deduced who you were in the stables."

"Let's remedy the introduction. Hullo," he holds out his hand, "I'm David Worthington and from the moment I heard your laugh and saw your beautiful face, I was hooked." He kisses her hand.

"BriaLynn Harris." She shakes his hand. "A pleasure to meet you, *Lord* Newhaven."

"I *never* said 'Lord,' Ms. Harris."

"That's your title, isn't it?" She asks. He gives her a 'come on now' look and she exhales, "Then *what* should I call you?"

"Like I said Friday, you can call me anything you like, although I've grown fond of *Mister* Worthington coming off these beautiful lips *when your being a feisty firecracker...*" David tucks a strand of hair behind her ear. "And I think I'll love the sound of 'David' coming off them." He winks. He takes her hand and carefully turns it to gently kiss the inside of her wrist, sending 'good feeling chills' up her arm which David notices her slightly shiver. He gives her a little bit of a smoldering look as he steps closer and wraps an arm around her waist. "I've *never* kissed anyone like that before." He tells her.

"I've never *received* one like that either." She softly smiles.

"Good." And he kisses her on the inside of her wrist again. "This place will be *only* for you." He runs his thumb in a small circle on her wrist, Bri's breath catches and she holds it. "I hope I'm not overwhelming you."

She shakes her head a little trying not to feel overwhelmed. She takes a deep breath, then refocuses the conversation. "You recognized me in the stables."

"Micro expression?" He smirks.

"Try obvious." She plainly answers, turning to lean against the railing. "You had said that I already blew you off, but by that point in the stables I had blown off the 'Mystery Stranger.' Why didn't you say anything?"

"Well, being turned down has *never* happened to me before!" He runs a hand through his hair, then leans down on the railing next to her. "It came as a surprise and was driving me crazy."

She smiles a little. "In my defense, I had no idea who you were," she leans over a little and lightly nudges him, "'*Mystery Stranger*.' For all I knew, you could've been the complete opposite of what you are."

He turns to her smirking. "And what's that?"

Bri studies him...part of her wanted to run, but she will be leaving soon enough anyway, as they make their way around Ireland before going back to DC. At some point, she and Katie will have to say goodbye to luxury and get back to the reality of life and responsibilities. But she does want to enjoy this time with him, right here in the present...

"Well, you could've been bald, smelly, overweight, and unrefined." She replies. "I prefer this version."

"Which is?" He urges her.

She quietly giggles. "*This you!*"

He stands up straight and gently pulls her to him. "Keep going..."

She bites her lower lip and smiles. "The handsomest man I've ever met, let alone has ever been interested in me. The way you look at me makes me turn around to see who is behind me."

David frowns a little. "*Why?!*"

"David, Serene is incredibly beautiful, which is why you asked her to be your date. She would be gorgeous if she wasn't such a snob. Me? I'm just your average girl who is anything but a beautiful model-type! Sure, I can be sassy; I'll put up with a lot but I *will* call people on their horrible behavior. Men overlook me for the gorgeous woman who *is* standing behind me; sometimes that's even Katie. She has had her share of incredibly good-looking men! She's beautiful and knows how to put on the charm, with the perfect amount of funny and the right amount of sass around men."

David smiles wide and beautiful. "You have *absolutely* no idea how gorgeous and sexy you are, do you?! Your sexiness is magnified when you're feisty, sassy, and an overall firecracker! Those men didn't pass you over for someone more beautiful behind you, they were intimidated by you!" He chuckles. "It takes a strong man—."

She rolls her eyes. "Most men hate that I challenge their very authority—." He puts his fingertips on her lips.

"No. Trust me. If that were the case, they would've sought to have you fired. Those are the ones who never engaged you because you threaten their delicate ego, their very manhood. The rest of them *engaged you* because they enjoyed the sexy show; Jack and James are the perfect examples! They stuck around the stables just to watch *you*!"

"Oh, please!" She rolls her eyes again. "They stuck around to watch me challenge their brother!" She looks back at the water.

David turns Bri to face him. Cupping her neck, he puts his forehead to hers, inhaling deeply and exhaling as he summons the courage to really open up to her. "At the risk of being too honest, too soon...I *never* wanted a serious relationship again, let alone get married again, after my ex-wife. I never wanted to be betrayed by someone I loved *ever again*, at least..." he lifts his head to look at her, "I *thought* it was love, but now I'm not sure what I felt with her." He stares into her eyes. "In order to never be vulnerable like that again, I needed to keep women at arm's length and date ones I'd *never* marry. I'd purposely pick ones who reminded me of my ex-wife in some way."

"*And now Serene makes sense*! I mean, I kept wondering about why you'd be with anyone like her because she's a *mean* snob, but now I get it. Wait. Your ex-wife is a mean snob?!"

"She definitely is, but she also knows how to be polite and conduct herself respectfully in public."

"Ah, two-faced." Bri adds.

He gives her a little embarrassed smile. "Was there a reason for these awful women? Yes. I know it sounds horrible, but they served a purpose for me. Only lately, I've been getting bored; even tired with meaningless sss, er, dates."

"You're starting to see what good guys eventually realize with women like that." Bri smiles as David looks curiously at her. "That under the hair, makeup, skin, and boobs, they're all the same! *Empty*!"

David cracks up laughing, agreeing with that blunt, but very true, statement. "Well, I thought about the woman I wanted to find, the woman I dreamed of, and after a while I started to convince myself, she didn't exist..." he caresses her cheek with his fingers, "*until now.*"

"*Me*?!" She scoffs and laughs. "I'm not *anyone's* dream! What you could be feeling is loneliness after all those narcissistic snobs, and I'm the first woman who is *real and genuine*, to pass through your life."

He says sternly, "I know *you know* this is more than that! You feel it right here, too!" He carefully taps her heart. "You just said you feel something between us, too, so *I* won't let *you* dismiss this!"

"Well, it doesn't matter what *this is* because, just in the physical distance of where we live, a relationship across the pond would be doomed." She takes a deep breath. "Then add the fact I don't put out without a wedding ring on my finger, would also put a strain on any relationship before it starts." *There,* she thought, *no sex before marriage should send him running for the hills*! She studies him to try to read him...

David knows she is trying to scare him away, which is also a version of running. Bri may have written a chapter in her book on running away, but he has written an entire collection of books *dedicated* to the subject. Waiting for marriage to be with her physically will be a challenge, *but she's worth it*!

He smirks. "If that's the case, then distance would be an advantage, don't you think?" He sees her surprised look. "When do you leave?"

"Um..." she shakes her head a bit, "tomorrow afternoon."

"No, no. To go back home?" He clarifies.

"In eight days."

He smiles a flirty smile. "Good! I selfishly want them all! I'll make sure Katie has visitation, so she won't miss you too much! I'll even ask James to keep her busy, which he seems to like anyways."

"I think they really do have fun—*Hold on!*" She shakes her head as she tries to gain control of her senses again. "David, I can't—."

There is a text notification on his phone, which he is relieved to break her train of thought for a moment. "Sorry. That's Jack's tone." He digs out his phone from inside his tuxedo jacket. "He's asking if we're going to come back inside. He wants more dancing with *his date*, and there are guests who keep asking for you." David smirks.

"*Me*?!" She asks.

David offers his hand. "Would you do me the honor of letting me escort you back inside?"

She smiles and takes his hand saying, "Enjoying a wonderful party and dancing the night away with two handsome men seems like a great way to end our last evening together."

"We have eight days." David reminds her.

She reminds him, "I never agreed to that. *I* have eight days left before *I* fly home." She explains. "I didn't get a chance to tell you, but Katie and I will travel around Ireland, then leave from Dublin when we fly back to the US."

"Bri, the flight itself would be of no concern for the two of you. I'd get you back on a private jet. The question is whether you'll change your plans and stay away from that wretched country to spend it with me?!"

"Wretched? Really?!" She's surprised. "Everything I've read and heard about Ireland say it's beaut—."

"In this scenario, it's the worst!" He grins.

"Ah, so in an everyday scenario it *is* beautiful?!" She confirms.

"I'm sticking with 'wretched' for this conversation." He remains adamant.

He is not sure how to keep her with him, but he *will* convince her, *or die trying*! He laces their fingers together and they continue to walk back to the party.

CHAPTER 8

Imperfectly Perfect End to the Night

David and Bri are walking back to the party from the gardens. He senses her nervousness as they get closer to the doors to go inside the ballroom. He stops and has her face him, but she speaks first.

"I suspect there are outside influences that will be *more* than happy to see us together?" She asks.

He smiles at her. "There is a reason Jack and I are best friends and brothers; the same reason my mother had him escort you tonight. My mother has been trying to set James, Jack, and me up for quite some time. So, before your arrival, I thought I'd mention to her I saw this fantastic American woman in a hotel lobby that very afternoon." Laughing to himself. "Well, she had figured out the 'fantastic American woman' I was smitten with was one of the ones coming to stay at The Inn."

"So, she enlists Jack's help to try to bring us together." She says.

"That, but more so because she knows Jack will tell me flat out what he thinks!" He starts walking with her again.

"And what did *he* tell you?" She purses her lips in a playful smile.

"That I'd be an idiot to let you slip through my fingers." He winks and kisses the back of the hand he is holding.

"*You would!*" She winks and he chuckles.

When they get to the doors, Bri notices David is standing a bit taller; there is even a bounce in his step. He smiles when he notices she is studying him, giving her a slight questioning look.

"What is it?" He asks.

She quietly giggles. "Your demeanor and body language have changed."

"I don't doubt that!" Putting a hand at the small of her back as they walk through the door. "I have the most beautiful woman on my arm!"

He gives her his best smile and she can't believe how it squeezes her heart. 'Ugh! Stupid heart.' She thinks to herself. 'I can't fall for him! Our lives are literally an ocean apart!' There is a happiness in his smile that she reciprocates, coming from just being with each other. They pause inside the door and he sees her staring at him again.

"So...is this the real David Worthington?" She asks.

"It is! And he's here to stay..." he lifts her hand, "with you..." bringing her hand close to his lips, "if you'll have me?" He kisses the back of her hand. His parents see this and hug each other, they're so happy the plan succeeded!

Bri can't help but wonder, "David, how can this work?!" He puts an arm around her. Bri sees Serene making her way towards them and she whispers, "Uh-oh."

David looks at her, then follows the direction Bri is looking. He sees Serene and shakes his head, scowling at her. She folds her arms and glares right back at him.

"Serene, I told you earlier, we're done." David says emotionlessly.

Jack comes up to David and Bri, quietly saying, "It's about time, Brother! I've got this!" He steps over to Serene.

Bri barely hears Jack telling Serene to leave her and David alone. He stresses David doesn't want to pursue a relationship with her. The sad look on Serene's face almost, almost, makes Bri feel bad for her. However, Bri does feel sorry for who Serene has become because she will never know real happiness, or true love, if she continues this way.

Bri's attention is brought back to David as he leads her to the dance floor. In a few swift steps they are lost in each other's arms and all seems right with the world, at least for the moment.

Bri inhales and says, "You smell amazing!"

He smiles and whispers next to her ear, "I've had that same thought about that with you a few times this evening." He feels her cheek move as she smiles. He kisses just below her ear, sending good chills through her body and warmth through her chest...to her heart.

Sadly, the dance ends all too soon. They go and mingle together.

In a group of people, Bri recognizes, "Sir and Mrs. Walker?"

Mrs. Walker turns around and smiles, "There you are, My Dear!"

"So nice to see you both!" Bri says as she shakes their hands.

"Ah, Ms. Harris. Looking more stunning than ever!" Sir Walker kisses her cheek. "We were *hoping* for a chance to say 'hello' this evening!"

Another gentleman approaches Bri. "Nice to see your pretty face here!" He shakes her hand and pats it with his other hand.

"Oh, Professor McDowell, you sweet talker!" She giggles.

Cullum McDowell tells the group, "One of my very favorite students!" Bri had greeted his wife while he spoke and more people were gathering around her and David.

"Morgan Townsend! What on earth brings you out here?" Bri asks as she gives him a hug. Then he stands next to her, putting his arm around her waist.

"Looking for you, Luv!" He teases, then looks at David. "Unfortunately for me, it seems I've been replaced by an improved model!" Both men laugh and shake hands. "David, you're a lucky man if you snatched this one up! There are some men in DC who've had their hearts broken, or egos deflated, by this one; then there are the few she has dated..." The Professor starts to say, but Bri discreetly shakes her head at him with David catching it.

"Oh, Professor, I think you and I will need to discuss all that later!" David teases Bri.

"*No, you don't.*" Bri tells them.

They mingle more, even with a group that Jack, Peter, and Carlotta were standing in. They were impressed that she knew so many of their guests.

Bri tells the group, "Prince Ramadan Cordova is going to be visiting the US next month and we're looking forward to his visit. I'm sorry to have missed your wife tonight." She looks around a bit in case she missed seeing her. "Will she be joining you next month?"

"She will! But she'll be upset she missed you tonight. Won't you join her for lunch when we come to DC?" He asks.

"I'd love to! I'll have Amy schedule something!" Bri says, taking her phone out and making a note on her calendar.

There is more dancing, even Jack steals a couple dances. As the party nears the end, there are a couple toasts before the last dance of the evening. Jack graciously gives up the last dance with Bri to David, who takes Bri out to the dance floor and he wraps an arm around her waist and holds her hand to his heart, dancing cheek-to-cheek. They dance without talking and just enjoy the moment, being in each other's arms.

When the music ends, he whispers, "*I don't want this evening to end.*" He kisses her neck.

She whispers, "*Unfortunately, like all fairytales, they all come to an end.*" She kisses his cheek.

She sees Serene approaching and uses her arrival to slip into the crowd that is preparing to leave for the evening. He goes to follow her, but Serene blocks his path.

He takes a deep breath. "Look, Serene, I'm sorry if you're feelings got hurt. I hope—."

"*Serene*, there you are!" Jack says, distracting her again.

David looks around for Bri but he can't find her. She had slipped out the back door unseen and follows the path she knows will meet up with the road that goes to The Inn. She pulls out her phone as she walks and notices there were a lot of missed calls, voicemails, and text messages. '*Odd…What's going on?*' She wonders.

The Duke and Duchess are standing by the ballroom doors to say goodnight to their guests; David, James, and Jack join them, to thank everyone for coming. After saying goodnight to the last of their guests, David looks around for Bri and sees Katie.

"Do you know where Bri is?" David asks her.

"I haven't seen her since I saw the two of you dancing the last dance together." She replies, looking around.

Jack is confused. "*Did she leave?*"

"She *thinks* she's going to run away from this." He snaps his fingers remembering he saved her number Thursday.

David texts Bri: "Where are you? Are you alright?"

Bri is silent for about five minutes, but it feels like an hour to David who is waiting to hear back from her.

David sends another text: "Talk to me, Bri. Please."

Bri: "Sorry, I was listening to voicemails from work...I'm walking back to The Inn. I'll see you tomorrow. Goodnight."

David reads it out loud, then says, "She can't walk there this late! She'll freeze to death or walk off a cliff!" He motions for a staff member and asks her to quickly bring a car around, he didn't care which one.

Jack is dying to know, "What happened to cause her to have a showdown with you again?" He's referring to the incident with Serene.

"She said nothing that shouldn't have been said." David slightly grimaces. "She put me in my place when no one else could...except family, which I haven't been listening to them."

"It just needed to come from a feisty gorgeous woman." Jack smirks.

David nods. "*Feisty is an understatement...*" he exhales a silent whistle, "she's a feisty firecracker!" He explains. "My behavior *was* appalling, and she told me I needed to hold *myself* to the higher standard we set for ourselves as 'gentlemen.'" He smiles to himself. "She flat out said that I wasn't actually a gentleman, that I lacked the grace it called for; in fact, I was the opposite! I remember pompous and arrogant being on the list." He quietly chuckles more to himself.

"And did you ever address those snobs?" James asks.

"Well, it took a minute after Bri left for it to all sink in. I set Serene and the rest of room straight! I told them that kind of behavior would no longer be tolerated. I told Serene I always knew what she was after, but it was never a possibility from the start; however, she also knew this because she knew my reputation. I was only dating one type of woman; one I would *never* marry." He laughs as he thinks back, "She asked what I would call Bri and I said, 'My wife and future Duchess of Newhaven!'" The family looks at each other with relief and excited smiles; Carlotta grabs Peter's hand with tears in her eyes. They know when David sets his mind to something, he doesn't stop until he has succeeded. He says, "The proverbial icing on the '*humbled* cake' for Serene was when I said Bri didn't need any title to prove she was better than all of us in that room, because she's already a lady!"

"*Agreed!*" Jack tells him.

James nods. "Proud of you, Brother!"

"Bri is the most amazing woman I've ever met!" He says, "She's not only gorgeous, but she's *bloody brilliant*, incredibly intelligent, *and her witty comebacks...*" he trails off exhaling with a soft whistle.

Carlotta asks, "Is Bri going to The Inn already?"

David nods. "I have a car being brought around so I can pick her up and give her a ride the rest of the way." They nod.

Katie says to David, "Bri's a hopeless romantic and encourages others to find true-love; sadly, she believes she has missed her chance at that kind of love."

David's eyes go wide. "Seriously?!"

"She thinks it's not in cards for her in her lifetime." Katie adds.

He tells those around him, "I'm trying not to scare her off, but once I know she's onboard, I'll take 'hopeless romantic' and romance her for the rest of our lives! I don't deserve her, but I'll spend the rest of my life showing her how wrong she is about true-love for herself. She'll know what it feels like to be loved, cherished, and adored! *Somehow*, I'll find a way she can be loved more than any other woman has ever been loved!" Carlotta gives him a hug! James and Jack are smiling.

"Go after her, David." Jack tells him, giving him a light push towards the door. Everyone follows David outside and he jumps in the car.

"David, she likes her alone time to think." Katie tells him. "She might not be happy to see you...she may even fight you—."

"*All Bri has been doing is fighting me!*" He says with a bit of exasperation in his voice. Carlotta snickers, as Jack, James, and Peter chuckle.

"*Can you blame her?*" Katie snips. "You haven't exactly been the most *charming*! Besides, she will push and push until she pushes you away. It's what *she does* to protect herself." Katie says, sounding oddly annoyed.

"She won't push me away; I won't let her." He says in all assertive seriousness. "In fact, I think it's time to return the favor and push back a little. It's time she realizes she has met *her* match!" He pulls away and heads towards The Inn.

As they watch David drive towards The Inn, James turns to Katie, "Are you going to text Bri the plans?"

"*Are you kidding?! Absolutely not!*" She doesn't recognize the jealousy she is starting to feel, not even when she is kind of hoping Bri will push David away completely and she gets her best friend to herself again. She wanted this trip to be about mending their friendship!

David looks around for Bri and begins thinking she might find relaxation with the crashing of the waves at the bridge to The Inn...he is right. There is a bench sitting off to the side of the road to overlook the waters out into the sea and it has a perfect view of a sunrise in the mornings. He parks then looks for tissues and finds them in the back seat. He quietly walks over to her, handing her the tissues. Her 'thank you' is barely heard over the crashing waves below.

"What are you doing here?" She asks louder to be heard.

"Making sure you're alright. May I sit?"

"No." She is quick to answer, which he was half expecting that and is prepared for the 'push' that comes next. "I'm leaving tomorrow and we had a wonderful ending to the night, David. Let's leave it at that!'

"*No!*" He firmly tells her.

She looks at him and he sees her annoyance. She says with exasperation, "We live in two *vastly different* worlds; *an ocean actually separates us*! That will make a long-distance relationship virtually imposs—."

"That's just it BriaLynn! It *can* work *if* we want to make it work...*if* you let me show you it can! We aren't in two different worlds." He points towards The Manor, "All those people who knew you, *proves* you and I are very much living in the same world!"

"No, David. I know how to *navigate* your world! There's a *big* difference." She studies him. "I don't understand why you're pushing this?! Up until a couple of hours ago, we couldn't stand being around each other."

He grins. "*Bri*, it's chemistry and a whole lot of attraction!"

She gives him an unbelieving look and says plainly, "Depends on the type of chemistry; lust can be pretty powerful in these situations, too."

"You know bloody damn well this is *not* that!" He says with conviction. "I've experienced those *fleeting moments* which is how I know this *isn't* lust *and I know* you feel that, too!"

She raises an eyebrow, "Oh? You know me so well after knowing me for what? *Five minutes*?!" She rolls her eyes and scoffs, folding her arms.

David takes a deep breath. He looks at Bri and smiles warmly. "I know you're trying to push me away." She breaks eye contact by closing her eyes and holding them closed. Then turns her head and opens her eyes to watch the moonlight on the sea as she listens to David. "If it were simply lust, you wouldn't waste your breath trying to push me away or try so hard to scare me away with 'wanting to wait until marriage' talk." She looks at him again. "It *doesn't* scare me! You don't realize you're worth *any* wait!"

David sees Bri shiver and she tightens her crossed arms across her chest to try to keep herself warm. He takes his tuxedo jacket off and offers it to Bri, as he sits down next to her. She gives him a small smile and takes it. She leans against him and nestles under his arm, using his jacket as a blanket, and he kisses her head. It was all so fluid, like they do this all the time.

A car David assumes is taking Katie and James back to The Inn passes by them. They continued to sit there for quite some time but he didn't care if the sun came up...he is right where he wanted to be for the rest of his life; with BriaLynn. He's not scared anymore...his heart feels safe with her.

Bri's eyes are tired and she is about to fall asleep. "It's late." She notes and she walks him to the car. The goal was to send him back to The Manor to go to bed and she will walk across the bridge to The Inn. She says goodnight and starts to walk away, but David stops her.

"David, it's late. You don't need to take me further; you need your sleep, too." He picks her up in a sweeping motion and carries her to the car, she instinctively wraps her arms around his neck. He sets her down on the passenger side and opens the car door. He motions for her to climb in and she does.

He leans down and says to her, "As tired as you are, I'd be scared all night that you fell into the unfriendly waters below, dooming us both."

She shakes her head as she softly laughs. "Both?" She asks as he shuts the door and watches him walk around to the driver's side and gets in.

"I'd dive in, too. Now that you brought my walls down, I won't be able to live without you." He winks.

Bri rolls her eyes, "*That's incredibly sappy!*"

"Perhaps, but romantics like sappy."

She has a faint knowing smile. "You spoke to Katie."

"I'll *never* reveal a source." He tells her and she smiles a little. "Besides, it's easy to deduce you're a romantic." He pulls up to the front door of The Inn.

She snorts a laugh. "How could you *deduce that* in the five minutes we've known each other and of that, we fought or avoided each other for four minutes and fifty-five seconds of it?!"

When they get out of the car, David comes over to her side. He comes right up to her and steps her back so she is up against the car. He has a determined look on his face. He leans in like he's going to kiss her and her eyes close, but he leans next to her ear.

"You're fighting to protect *your heart*." He hears her breath catch and that's all he needs to hear. "And just as you're in-tune with me, I'm trying to get in-tune with you." He rests his forehead to hers. "And I'll take whatever help I can to get there faster." He looks at her with a smile and winks.

David takes her hand as they walk into The Inn. They go up to her room, greeting the night staff along the way. She opens her door to find Jack is sleeping on the couch; Katie and James are in the adjoining room. Her empty bed is waiting for them. David stops Bri, pulls her out of the room and quietly shuts the door.

"I have a better idea, so we don't wake anyone." He says.

He takes her hand walks to the quarters James uses. When she walks into the room, she sees it looks like the overall interior design of The Inn. The gray stones look brighter with the crisp white accents and sheer white curtains, white linens and brown tones of the wood and furniture accent colors. There were fresh flowers on a rectangle table right by the door with an elegant mirror above it.

David takes Bri's hand again and leads her to the bathroom, where he grabs a t-shirt and pajama bottoms that tie at the waist from the closet. He comes back over and hands them to her, then pulls out a toothbrush still in the package from a drawer of the sink vanity, and he leaves the bathroom. He goes over to the bed where he takes the extra pillows off and pulls the covers back for her. He sits on the bottom corner of the bed to wait for her.

When he hears the bathroom door open, he looks up and is struck by how she is even more beautiful with her hair down and no makeup. He tells her to take the bed and he goes into the bathroom to get ready for bed.

After she had washed her face, Bri already felt better, but crawling into a bed and sleeping will be heavenly. She lays down and is comfortable; she is drifting off to sleep, when she feels David kissing her cheek. He goes to retrieve pillows and blankets to sleep on the couch but decides to grab a blanket and lay on top of all the covers, snuggling in with Bri.

He drapes an arm across her and she tenses for a moment. He whispers, "I'm on top of all your covers with my own blanket. I swear I just want to sleep next to you."

She exhales, too tired to move or talk, let alone argue. With a small 'okay' she sinks back into the pillow again and falls asleep; he gets comfortable and falls asleep not too far behind her.

CHAPTER 9

Perfectly Perfect Sunday Picnic

When BriaLynn wakes up later that morning, she is facing David who is still sound asleep. She sees the clock just behind his shoulder on the nightstand. If she gets up now and hurries, she could make it to church on time. She must have had clouds to walk on because she somehow made it out of bed without waking David.

After leaving a note for him, she sneaks up to and into her room. She throws in a dress, washes her face more thoroughly, then pulls her hair back into a ponytail and adds some earrings. She doesn't have time for makeup, but she can add powder in the car on the way over. She picks up her phone and finds her purse.

"Where are you off to?" Jack asks, rubbing his eyes.

"Church." She quietly answers.

"Do you need a ride?" Jack asks, barely awake.

"I can see if someone else who is already dressed can take me." She pecks a kiss to his cheek and something about that little cheek kiss tells him there could have been something wonderful between them. "I'm barely going to make it on time as it is."

"Paul should be down there since he was a driver for the guests last night. If he isn't, just text me and I'd be happy to take you. What's your number?"

She rattles the number off quick as she flies out the door, telling him, "Go back to sleep! I'll see you later?"

"Definitely!" He sends her a text so she has his number, too.

Paul happens to be finishing his breakfast and says he would be happy to drive her. He takes her out to the car and they get on their way. Thankfully, the roads aren't busy and they might be there a few minutes early.

Bri's thoughts go to David and how wonderful he was last night. She will text him later, but in the note she explained she was going to church; she doesn't like missing two Sundays in a row and since she missed last Sunday traveling and possibly next Sunday traveling, she didn't want to miss today if she could help it; she hoped he understood. She tells him what time she will be done, and she will see him afterwards.

Arriving at Church with not much time to spare, she tells Paul he is welcome to join her, or do whatever he needs to do until he comes back to pick her up. Paul reads a text from David asking if he could secretly pick Bri up.

Paul looks up at Bri showing her the back of his phone and politely refuses. "I was actually going to stay here and join you; I have a couple friends that go to this church. Unfortunately, something just came up." She nods with a little smile and quickly says she will see him later before she rushes inside.

David woke up to an empty bed and found Bri's note. He is fine that she wanted to go to church, but he isn't thrilled she left without waking him up to tell him; he will talk to her about that later. He looks at the time and texts Paul he wants to secretly pick her up, assuming he drove her. He is relieved when Paul texts he just watched her go into the building and was now going to go home, unless David needed him for something.

> David: "Enjoy the rest of the day and take the week off. I plan on spending it with Bri!"

> Paul is *thrilled* for David: "Thanks and have fun this week! Let me know if you need me."

David sends Paul a 'thumbs up' before he gets ready and makes his way downstairs. Everyone is curious where Bri is and he explains what he knows. Katie says more to herself that she forgot today is Sunday.

Inspired, David turns and asks the chef who is finishing up breakfast, "Would you be able to throw a simple picnic together for two?" James whistles with a smile.

Jack smiles as he asks, "What's the plan?"

He smiles and looks at Katie, "Winning the heart of a hopeless romantic." He winks and smiles at her, as he pops a couple of grapes into his mouth.

David finds himself wanting to be romantic and has all kinds of ideas of things to do over the course of their lives. He has never been this romantic before; it's kind of invigorating. David even calls over to The Manor to have his red convertible brought to The Inn.

"Where are you going to take her?" Jack asks.

David looks at Katie. "Isn't this trip about ancestry, too? Is there a place for Bri that she is wanting to visit where you two haven't been...a place you wouldn't mind her seeing without you?"

"I guess I could loan her out for the day." She teases as she brushes the crumbs off her hands. "She is dying to visit Dunfermline and I haven't seen any of my ancestors from there yet, just around Fife." David looks to James and Jack with the mention of 'Dunfermline.' Katie sees this and asks, "What? Didn't I say the name of the city right?"

David is quick to reply, "No, no, nothing like that. Dunfermline is common in royal and noble ancestry is all." That strikes a jealousy nerve with Katie that she pushes down. She *does* want to be happy for her best friend; she *needs* to make up for the horrible things she has done to Bri...*if that's even possible...*

When the picnic basket is finished, The Chef hands it to David. They shake hands as David thanks him and all the kitchen staff. He takes the blanket he is also being handed before he walks out of the kitchen and to the main doors.

Robert brought his convertible over and tosses David the keys as he walks in. David catches the keys and smiles. "Thanks, Robert! I owe you one!"

"Let me borrow the convertible sometime and we'll call it even!" He jokes.

"Anytime!" David sees a big grin on Robert's face. David nods as he puts his sunglasses on and walks out the door as Robert thanks him.

David stops in his tracks when he sees Serene in the car. His smile fades and he actually starts to feel sick; he doesn't want to deal with her anymore.

"What are you doing here, Serene?" He asks.

With a huge smile, she happily says, "I overheard you were planning a romantic afternoon and I was too excited to wait for you to come apologize and ask me to come with you, so I came over with Robert!"

"I have no intention of apologizing to you for anything, Serene." He says without any emotion and watches her smile drop. "Look, Serene, I thought I was clear last night: I'm *not* interested in a relationship with you."

She turns angry, "You mean you're still *more* interested in that *disgusting* American than in me...in *my* pedigree?!"

He says sternly, "I've warned you about speaking against the future Duchess!" He goes and puts the basket and blanket in the trunk, or boot as they call it. "Serene, do you even *hear* yourself? Your focus is on a pedigree, like we're some sort of breeding stock! Pedigree isn't what matters!"

She scoffs, "*What else is there?!*"

"Love."

With a sultry look, she shifts in the seat to sit more provocatively. "Oh, you know I can give you that, Da*h*ling." She runs her fingertips down her neck and her hands down her body.

David is not impressed. "That's lust, Serene, *not love*." He opens the passenger door. "Get out."

"But you love my body." She continues to run her hands over the upper half of hourglass shape.

"'*Love*' is an exaggeration." David says dully and Serene glares.

To David's relief, Jack comes out after he noticed through a window that Serene is there and quickly runs outside to the car. He reaches down and takes hold of Serene's upper arm.

"Get out of the car, Serene!" He pulls her out of the car.

David walks over to the driver's side and gets in, calmly saying to her, "We fulfilled that lustful want, only now I want more. I'm sorry, but that's something *you* can't give me. I wish you the best, Serene. I *really* do." He looks at Jack. "Please make sure she leaves the property; I want her gone before we get back!"

She is angry, livid even, but before she says anything, David is driving away. Serene says to Jack, "He won't find a better bloodline than mine! That disgusting American is going to ruin him!"

"No, Serene, *you* and *every woman before you* were ruining him! With Bri, we have David back! She'll even help him rise up to be the great Duke he's supposed to be, while prospering Newhaven!"

She scoffs again, "An American could never inspire such a thing when she can't appreciate our traditions!"

"Like you?" Jack mocks.

Her smug smile spreads across her face. "An American won't stand for the tradition of *him* having a Noble Consort."

"For the last few generations, it's been 'on paper' and nothing more, Serene." Jack plainly tells her.

"Not if *I* don't agree to those terms!" She smugly smirks.

"What makes you think it'll be you?" Jack asks.

"I'm the best choice, especially since he would be marrying an American who will be lucky to have even the *one* bloodline needed! Then there are the indiscretions our social class accepts, and that *bloody American* won't stand for those either!"

"Obviously, you've forgotten about Ava's affairs which doomed their marriage?" Jack snaps back. "He knows how it felt and he'll *never* put that heartbreak on Bri!"

She replies, "Those were indiscretions, not affairs."

"To David, it's all the same, Serene." Jack tells her. "Unacceptable."

Annoyed, Jack turns and leads Serene to the golfcart by her upper arm he was still holding. "Get in! I'm taking you to The Manor."

"Why?" She pretends to pout with her lip out.

"You heard David. You need to collect your belongings and go home." Jack says with a semi clenched jaw.

"*I don't want to go home yet!*" She actually pouts.

"Get in, or I will have security throw you out and we will send you your things!" Jack firmly tells her.

Jack's seriousness by this point *demands* obedience, so she gets in and stews as Jack drives, *neither of them saying a word*. He knows she is trying to recalculate her plans, but to her credit, she does go home within an hour with her 'tail tucked firmly between her legs.'

David follows the directions Paul has given him. He pulls into the parking lot of the church, and backs into a spot in the back row across from the entrance. He walks around for a short while, noticing how beautiful and peaceful it is, and the warm cloudy day just makes it that much more enjoyable. He makes it back to the car when people start coming out of the church. He leans against the car and patiently waits.

David is half sitting, half leaning against the front of the red convertible, with his legs straight and he has his arms crossed, looking relaxed. He is wearing a blue t-shirt that is just tight enough to see he is toned, with khaki pants and dark brown sandals. Bri is talking with some people as she walks out of the building, so she doesn't see David across the parking lot just yet.

The Bishop sees him first and smiles a knowing smile at her. "I think we'll be seeing more of you in the near future." She gives him a questioning look when he slightly tips his head to the side towards David in the parking lot.

Bri looks and her breath catches when she sees David. She can't help but light up when she sees him; his heart skips a beat at her reaction to him. She tries to push all these feelings down.

Bri looks from David back to The Bishop, "I'm just here on vacation, that's all this is...or rather, it's all it *can* be."

"No, My Dear, this is true-love blooming." He gestures slightly between her and David. "Trust an old man who has been around long enough to see couples come and go. *This* is the kind of love, true-love, that pulls two people together!" He gives her a knowing grin. "You just *lit up* when you saw him!"

The Bishop is a bit overweight with white hair and a few inches taller than her. His eyes are brown but are a bit gray with age. He wears a light blue suit and a yellow tie with his white dress shirt. He is a man who *exudes* fatherly love and Bri can't help but take what he says to heart.

He senses her shift in awkwardness and turns her to him. "I feel I need to say this, so please hear me out." She nods with kindness in her eyes. *"Trust the Spirit;* trust there's a reason for David *and* a reason for a connection with Jack." She is briefly surprised he knew about the connection with Jack; he is being inspired to tell her this. He gestures David. "Love like this is special and shouldn't be so easily dismissed. Even when 'I love you' may seem early to say, it can be *immediately* felt...no matter how hard you fight against it." He holds the top of her arms. "Bri, love follows no timeline, nor any set of rules, because *you know* who is really in charge!" She nods. "In fact," he smiles big at her, *"sometimes* He will break right through mortal rules and timelines!" He sees her eyes are a little teary and hugs her. *"Trust yourself!* Trust that you do know how the Spirit speaks to you."

She thanks him, then turns and walks towards David with a big smile on her face as she puts her sunglasses on. Bri notices there are people around her staring at them and smiling, but she sees David's eyes are locked on her.

"What do I owe such a surprise, Handsome?" She asks, coming to stand in front of him.

He stands up replying, "Do I need a reason to spend time with the most amazing and incredibly beautiful woman I've ever met?!"

"Flattery like that will get you *almost* anywhere, *Mister* Worthington." She smirks. Then they hear snickering from those watching.

David smiles, then cups her cheek, and lovingly kisses her other cheek. There are some 'aaaws' and various forms of things like, 'so sweet,' being said around them.

David winks. "Will you join me for a stroll and a picnic?" There are more sounds and whispers of approval.

"Sounds *lovely!*" She teases with his accent.

David opens the car door and when Bri is inside the car, he closes it. He goes around the car, waving to those watching them and he gets in. That's when it dawns on her! *They KNOW who he is!* Bri tries to cover her nervousness, but David sees it.

He kisses her hand, then simply says, "Don't."

"What?" She asks.

"Don't worry. *Don't* overthink this, Bri." He holds her hand to his chest. "Yes, they know who I am and, if they don't know already, they soon will, and it will be alright. Besides, from their comments, I'd say they liked what they saw. You'll find almost everyone will be supportive. I do get recognized, but it's *nowhere near* like it is for royalty or a big celebrity." He starts the car. "Anyway, it's the gossip magazines and such rubbish that want to spread horrible rumors and bad feelings; most people aren't like that, especially in Newhaven. It's like we're in our own little world out here, even our newspaper upholds their reputation as a *credible* news source and detests sensationalism for news."

"Good thing you know I don't read the gossip magazines and such *rubbish*." She teases with his accent again but makes a mental note to look into Newhaven's newspaper.

"I do! A *lovable* quality, truly!" David looks to see her smiling at him with loose strands of her hair blowing in the wind and winks. He thinks to himself, '*This is one of those moments when life is perfect*.' He laces their fingers together and holds her hand with their arms on the armrest as he drives.

Bri enjoys the wind blowing on her face, she only wishes it could blow her cares away. Once they arrive on the mainland, they drive for what she guesses is an hour once they leave the port in Edinburgh, but it didn't matter. They drive through some beautiful countryside and she feels an overwhelming feeling she just can't seem to shake...'she is home' and it isn't because of her ancestral roots.

"Where are we?" She asks, looking around for a sign.

"Dunfermline." David parks near Dunfermline Abbey Church.

She is confused. "Dunfermline?" She gets out of the car and leans against the side of it.

David comes around to her side of the car. "Katie said you have ancestors from here, but she didn't. I thought maybe it would be fun for you if we walked around and I told you some of Dunfermline's history, since Dunfermline is in my ancestral line, too. I hope that's alright?"

"If Katie said it was okay, then that's fine. I wouldn't want to hurt her feelings coming here if she had wanted to go." She explains.

He smiles in understanding. "What do you know about your ancestors and connections to Dunfermline?"

"Supposedly, I have connections to some important events that have happened in Scotland. While a blockbuster movie was made about one such time period, there are connections to the Scottish Prince Henry, along with Stirling Castle..." she gestures the town, "and of course there is the city of Dunfermline. Oh, and the county of Fife is also a common location. There is more that I can't think of right now, but I could look it up quick if you need me to?"

"That's a great start!" David is pleasantly surprised hearing her connections, particularly Stirling Castle, and even more curious about her ancestral tree with Prince Henry of Scotland. However, he knows his mother would have been all over it Friday, when she made the connection to the American he told her about, and one of the Americans staying at The Inn. Bri has said enough to make him think she might have more than the one bloodline needed so he can marry her; perhaps even a link to Scottish royalty which will go far with their Newhaven people, as well as Scotland. "Come then," he goes to the back of the car, "let's walk around the grounds that have been walked by your ancestors, and perhaps some of our shared distant ancestors!"

He grabs the picnic basket and blanket, but she offers to carry the blanket. He holds out his hand for hers and she takes it with a sweet smile. They walk around the Abbey and the grounds, or as it's referred to by the locals, 'The Glen,' while David explains some of the history and tells her stories that he has heard. She is taking it all in and finding that she loves listening to his accent, too...*maybe more.*

They find a place to lay their blanket down and have their picnic. They sit facing each other, completely relaxed, enjoying the fresh air and the delicious food. After a few minutes of quietly eating, David feels this is a good time to bring up last night.

"Do you want to talk about the texts, voicemails, and phone calls from last night?" When he started talking, she dropped her stare the blanket, so he knows she hears him; but she is silent longer than expected.

He is about to change the subject, when she says, "I guess I don't know where to begin."

"Well, let's start with the problem at work that's interrupting your holiday?"

Bri inhales and slowly blows out. "Basically, an ambassador is coming to DC and only ever wants to work with me...thing is, he's arriving Tuesday. He found out I was on vacation and is requesting I cut it short, even when he's told I'm overseas."

"*Wow.*"

"You've seen my assertiveness firsthand," she says and he quietly laughs, "only with this guy I've had to be that way more in the beginning. Now there's a special relationship between us I can't explain, other than there's a closeness, but it isn't romantic by any means." She looks out at other people walking in the distance. "He should've been happy I wouldn't be there because he'll be able to get away with a lot more. I'm the only one who can put my foot down with him." She inhales and exhales, then has a faint smile. "It's also hard to know the kind of week my people will have if I *don't* go back; yet they'll feel bad that I cut my vacation short, especially since—." She stops herself.

David cups her cheek on the other side of her face, to turn her face to him. "Especially?" He didn't know where she was going with that, until he sees her blush and look away. *Now he gets it.* "*Especially since* you met me and fell *madly* in-love with me!"

She looks at him, halfway laughing. "Wow! So sure of your irresistibility, aren't you?!"

"No, Love. *So sure* of our feelings for each other!" He says to her. "Selfishly, I want you to stay, but I do understand loyalty to your job and colleagues."

She's looking out across the park, "I do feel the pull with you, David, and it would be fun to see where this would go."

"*But?*" He encourages her to continue, to get all her reservations out so they can deal with them.

"I just keep thinking you don't need to be tied down to someone so far away. You should be with someone who *deserves* to be loved and adored by you, who lives *here*."

"Can't you see yourself living here?" He asks.

"I wish it were that simple, I'd move here in a heartbeat, but I have others to think about."

Suddenly, it hits David...she has kids! He smiles sweetly, "How old are they?"

She turns to look at him and sees his smile. "The girls are 16 years old...I couldn't move them from their dad and stepmom, nor their friends, this late in the game so-to-speak."

"And your ex?"

"Oh, he and I are great! We love each other as any family members do, but there was never any deep, abiding love because we were never in-love with each other. He was mad, angry when we first split up, but eventually realized what I meant when he met *his* true-love. We've always supported each other and our relationships with the girls." She takes a drink of water, then continues. "He's married to a sweet woman who I sincerely call my friend. I think the girls benefit by how well we all get along and support each other...I even support his wife's relationship with the girls; it's so *incredibly important* for kids to have as many *healthy* relationships with adults as possible."

David is quiet and Bri thinks she has finally scared him away with talk of two daughters. She braces herself for his rejection, telling herself, '*It really is for the best.* However, the rejection doesn't come; only he still isn't saying anything. She's puzzled and musters the courage to look at him. He is staring out at the landscape in front of them; he sees her nervousness out the corner of his eye.

He turns to her and she sees his face is full of so much love, her hand reflexively touches her heart; she can actually feel her heart expand for him. He squeezes her other hand a little. "Part of you is hoping you scared me away with the mere mention of kids..." he cups her cheek, "but you actually only made me see more of the depth of how *absolutely incredible* and *amazing* you are!"

"*What?*" She whispers as tears fill her eyes.

He firmly tells her, "*You heard me!*" He smiles. "You are the most heartfelt woman I've *ever* met!"

She shakes her head. "I'm not. I tend to be in my own world because I think about all the things going on at work and with the girls, but I also contemplate spiritual things, too. Which is why I prefer being alone when I can. I know that's selfish and it can make me seem heartless, perhaps even mental—."

"To someone who doesn't care enough to get to know you, *maaaybe*, but that's a stretch. It's more likely *they're* blind or mental!" He stands and helps her up, so they can continue walking around. "If I knew when I first saw you, what I know now, I hope I wouldn't have wasted *any* time being with you!" They walk into a wooded area with a small waterfall, flowering bushes, and lush trees all around them.

Bri looks around taking it all in. "This is beautiful, David!"

"Mother brought us here numerous times over the years when we were younger." He smiles. "James, Jack, and I, ran all over this place. This was a place we could go and just be kids. I had forgotten about it until it popped into my thoughts driving to pick you up this morning and thinking about past visits to Dunfermline."

"It's a beautiful memory." She tells him.

He smiles. "There's one more I'd like to add to this day." He holds her hands. "Last night, with Serene, part of the reason I didn't say a word was because of how sexy you were standing up to me, and the desire to kiss you was getting increasingly more difficult to resist."

She smiles with a twinkle in her eye. "Until you didn't."

"Which was a kiss I won't forget!" He grins. She purses her lips, trying to hide her smile, but it doesn't work. He taps her chin, "And you won't either..." He grins.

David wraps an arm around her waist and his other hand holds the back of her neck. He leans in and tenderly kisses her lips. This magnetic pull they have felt this whole time, has fireworks going off between them. Her arms wrap tightly around him and he deepens the kiss. They keep kissing each other until they have to pull apart to catch their breath.

"It feels *so* good to kiss you, and to be kissed back by you!" He winks.

"You mean like this?" She puts her hand on the back of his jaw and pulls his face to hers for another meaningful kiss.

He returns it and then smiles against her lips. "Yes, exactly like that!"

"And here's my apology for slapping you." She says. She first kisses the cheek she slapped, before sweetly kissing his lips.

"How about one more for good measure?" He taps his lips with his finger.

She smiles and leans into another kiss. He holds the back of her head to keep her lips locked to his, and he kisses her deeply, meaningfully...*lovingly*.

She pulls apart, smiling at him and teases, "It feels *so* good to kiss you, and to be kissed back by you!" He chuckles and taps another kiss to her lips before she wraps her arm around his and they turn towards the direction of the car, taking their time walking back.

When they get within eyesight of the car he asks, "Have you decided what you're going to do for work?"

"I have to think about everyone involved. While loyalty is a great characteristic, it can also be a negative one; I don't want anyone to suffer needlessly and this diplomat can be super difficult for *everyone* else. With me, he happily stays within the boundaries."

"Then we'll take you back." He says with a loving smile.

She is surprised. "You're going to drop everything to fly to DC for me—?" He kisses her. "Why did you do that?" She asks.

He smiles, "Did you forget what you were saying?"

"No. I remember Jack saying you were the CEO of the family's corporation. You can't just drop everything for me!" He tries to kiss her again. "Nice try." She raises her eyebrow expectantly.

He exhales. "Bri, a perk of being CEO is I *can* do just that! I can drop everything *for you* to be *with you*! I can fly you to me for a long weekend here, or we can meet anywhere!" He smiles wide, "*That's how I know this will work!*"

"That's going to get expensive! Last minute flights are *never* cheap!"

"Bri, it's not a problem. We have a private jet and we can book other flights if we need to." He informs her.

She rolls her eyes. "That sounds even *more* expensive!"

He smiles. "I plan on forever with us, so I will say this to you, money—." She covers his mouth.

"Stop. We don't know each other well enough for you to make that kind of a statement, let alone finish the next." She inhales deeply and refocuses. "Now, about that *one* flight. There's no need for you to arrange a flight. The Ambassador has already arranged a private jet at the local airport there in Newhaven to take me back to DC. Which reminds me, I need to talk to Katie and encourage her to finish the vacation. I also have to arrange my luggage from the hotel to be sent to The Inn so I have it to go back with me tomorrow." She looks at the time on her phone. "Although it may be too late for that."

She unlocks her phone, but David puts his hand on her phone saying, "Let me make those arrangements with the hotel, while you talk to Katie." He smiles. "Being a Worthington does have its perks."

"Hmm, is it 'Worthington' or is it 'Lord Newhaven' that has its perks." She teases with a light giggle.

"Both. What time in the morning?" He asks.

Bri has the phone up to her ear, calling Katie. She answers, "Thankfully the plane leaves at 8:00 in the morning." She talks to Katie, who says she will stay at The Inn and figure things out tomorrow.

She relays that to David and while she finishes her conversation, David arranges to have hers and Katie's luggage packed and brought over to The Inn later this afternoon. They will also be officially checked out of The Coriander Hotel. He hangs up and calls the local airport in Newhaven to arrange a detour of the flight in the morning. He walks back over to Bri and she is just hanging up her call.

He asks, "Not a morning person?"

"No. *I'm not*. However, I usually wake up neutral, so it's what happens in those first few minutes that tips me one way or the other. For example, when the girls were small, if they woke me up by crawling into bed to snuggle and watch cartoons, then it's a good mood; however, if I wake up to those same little girls fighting and crying...*nnnooot* so much."

He is laughing lightly as he opens the car door. When she is inside, he closes it, then goes around and gets in himself. "Now, Beautiful, we've been walking and talking for so long, is there something you would like to do, or go see?"

"It's Sunday." She simply says. He lifts an eyebrow before he pulls out of his parking spot. She smiles. "Easy, simple, and spending time with loved ones is best."

"Good to know and I think I can remember that. So back to The Estate for dinner?" He asks.

"Perfect!" She smiles.

Arriving at The Manor, David pulls around the fountain and stops in front of the main doors. He helps her out of the car, then pulls her close, wrapping his arms around her and kisses her soundly.

He takes her hand and goes to head inside for dinner, but Bri takes one step and stops. "David, I thought we were dropping the car off, then going to The Inn to eat?" She shakes her head saying, "This isn't right. I don't want to intrude on your family's dinner."

"Bri, I found out before I went to find you and Jack in the garden last night, my parents had watched last night's events with great anticipation. Normally, I would've been *furious* with my mother's meddling, but this time I was thanking her, *and my father*. Bri, it's been you my heart has been searching for all along..." he lifts her chin and smiles, "now that my heart's found you—."

She kisses him this time. "You're not finishing that sentence yet either."

Just then the door opens and Jack comes out with a big smile, looking as handsome as ever. "Come on in, Gorgeous! Dinner is about to be served. Oh, and bring that good lookin' guy, too!"

David chuckles, "See! I'm now just an afterthought!" Bri giggles.

Jack kisses her cheek, then shakes David's hand and they hug each other with their other arms. David takes Bri's hand to lead her inside and Jack follows. The three of them sit together at the table, across from Peter and Carlotta.

With everyone sitting around the bigger family dining table, there is a discussion about their afternoon. As Bri talks about her ancestral family tree, David looks at his mother who gives him a knowing look; confirming what he already knew, she was looking into Bri's ancestral tree.

They finish dessert with Bri and Jack getting ready to go to The Inn. David has convinced Bri to go somewhere with him before flying back to DC. Since they have to get up even earlier in the morning, David and Bri decide to say goodnight at The Manor.

David tucks a strand of hair behind her ear. "Until the morning?" She gives him a small smile and kisses him as she hugs him firmly.

Jack comes into the foyer and comments, "You two look like you've been kissing each other your whole lives!"

David smiles. "We're making up for lost time!" He kisses her again, dipping her and deepening it.

Bri smiles against David's lips. "My knees are going to give out completely if you kiss me like that again." He puts his forehead to hers for a moment, then kisses her cheek.

David walks out with Jack and Bri. She climbs into the front seat of the golf cart and David kisses her once more before Jack drives them to The Inn. Jack had volunteered to be the fourth player to play some card games with James and Amy.

Peter and Carlotta are inside the door when David comes back inside. "Dunfermline?" Peter asks with a smile. "Prince Henry?"

"Yes."

"You know what this could mean!" Carlotta's excitement is heard.

"That she may have *a* noble bloodline?" David teases.

"David, she *has to have* a bloodline connection if she has roots there. *However,* if she has as many ancestors as it sounds in Dunfermline, not to mention Stirling Castle, she could very well *be a Direct Bloodline!*" Carlotta says. "We'll know when the certification comes."

Peter adds, "Which means, protecting *her* bloodline with a Noble Consort would be required."

"She won't go for that!" David swiftly answers. "Besides, she can get pregnant, so we'll have babies..." He smiles at the thought of having a baby with her.

"Does she have kids already?" Carlotta curiously asks.

"Twin girls who are already 16 years old. That's one of her reservations about dating." David says.

Peter is puzzled. "Tell her we'll love them as the grandchildren they are!"

"No, it's not that." David tells him. "It's—."

It dawns on Carlotta. "It's that they're in school there and it would be cruel to move them from family and friends when they're almost off to a university!"

"Right." David says. "They go to school until they finish their senior year in high school, which is typically when they're 18 years old."

Peter says, "That's understandable *and workable*. David, she may not go for a Noble Consort, *at first*, but it may help the Newhaven people gravitate towards her quicker if she grabs onto a long-standing tradition. An American marrying an heir and accepting a tradition that's over seven hundred years old, would be a great way for them to get behind her as the American wife of 'The Heir to Newhaven.' They will embrace her when she is officially named The Duchess, because she has embraced *our* tradition, probably traditions by then." Peter pats his sons back. "Just think about it." David nods.

Jack and Bri arrive at The Inn and they all gather in James' room to play a couple of card games. They ended up playing many more hands, with Jack and Bri beating James and Katie at 'Hearts.' One of the rare games they lose is the last one when Katie talks Bri into 'just one more game.'

The guys walk the ladies up to their rooms and say goodnight. James and Katie say goodnight, then go into Katie's room. Jack and Bri hug at her door, with Jack kissing her cheek. He rests their foreheads together for a moment, feeling their chemistry.

He smiles. "Safe travels."

Bri hopes that if she focuses on work and squeezing David into her life, it will extinguish any spark of romantic feelings for Jack. '*I love David.*' She tells herself and then softly gasps thinking to herself, '*I love David?! How can I; it's so soon?!* She thinks about this as she gets ready for bed and remembers what The Bishop told her: '*Love like this is special and shouldn't be so easily dismissed. Even when 'I love you' may seem early to say, it can be* immediately *felt...no matter how hard you fight against it.*'

CHAPTER 10

Imperfectly Perfect Holiday...is Over

It's Monday morning and David is waking Bri by kissing her cheek. She smiles with her eyes closed, "I'm *really* liking this dream!"

David softly chuckles and kisses her cheek again. He slowly pulls the covers back, giving her a chance to stop him in case she isn't decent.

"Come on, Beautiful, we need to get going!" He softly says to her.

"OH, *NO!* Is this the dream where it *seems* like a great one, but somehow turns into a *bloody* nightmare?!" She lightly teases and pops her head up. "*Nnnooo,*" she drops her head back down, "*let me sleep, My Love...*"

Bri didn't realize what she had said, but David caught it. This helps confirm that the detour he has planned will have his desired result. *Now* he is *more* eager to get going!

"We have a sunrise to watch somewhere *not here*, before we go to DC." He whips the covers off this time.

"Seriously?!" She exhales with exaggeration. "Didn't we say goodnight a few minutes ago?"

"Funny," he says, "a minute from you feels like an eternity for me."

She scoffs, rolling her eyes at him, grumbling, "Good thing I'm too tired, or I might believe you...or I'm too tired to fight how attracted to you I am."

"Let's go with both!" He grins. "You're fighting me, but you're going to get up because you're curious."

"*Please,* no! Surprises before the sun is up, is just a cruel and twisted joke!" She looks at the clock. "It's only been a couple of hours!" Her voice is soft and cracking as she lightly whines. "Do you seriously know what time it is?! In MY time zone?!"

"I do." He says like it's no big deal. "You can sleep on the plane." Then it hits him. "*Wait,* a couple of hours?!" He asks. "How many card games did you play?!"

"I've made up my mind, Worthington! This isn't going to work between us! Two different countries, two different time zones, and mine's saying it's time for bed. Plus, you're a morning person *and I'm SO not...*it all adds up to this relationship being an *extremely* bad idea!"

Completely unfazed, but humored. "You're adorable."

"Go away!" She snips.

"Look, you promised me eight days *aaand* we're down to six; you can't have them back! And I won't let you take them back!"

Bri sits up and says, "No. I didn't, *Lord Newhaven!*" He cringes. "I turned you down." She gives him a smirk of satisfaction as she pulls the covers back up and lays her head on her pillow. "I think we're done here." She does a shooing motion with her hand as she closes her eyes and gets comfortable once again. "Have a nice life!"

"First of all, Beautiful," David has a cheeky grin on his face, "I've said before I prefer your lips calling me *anything* that's less pretentious, than you saying my title like that!" She lifts her head and gives him a smug look, then lays her head back down. He leans down next to her ear, "When we're married, I'll make you forget your own name and mine will be the only one coming off your lips."

"*Bri.*" She sasses back.

"We're not married yet, which leads me to my second point; now, listen up, *Cheeky.*" He yanks the covers all the way off and she inhales a sharp gasp. He crawls on the bed and has a hand on either side of her. "If you keep this up, I won't be able to resist you and *you won't* be able to resist me! It'll throw the whole 'wait until marriage thing' right out the window!" When she doesn't move, he adds, "It'll look something like this..." He slides his fingers under the back of her shirt and she rolls over. He's staring down into her eyes and smiles.

"Fine!" She slightly glares. "But for the record, if we don't wait until marriage, I'd end up resenting you and hating *myself* for it. It'd *seriously* doom us as a

105

couple." He gives her a smug smile of satisfaction that makes her physically push him back.

He helps her up. "Bri, I'm aware, *I promise you*! Which is why I'm respecting that," he smirks a little, "however, the more sass you give me, the sexier and more irresistible you are! *So, I need you to work with me*!" He chuckles, "You should also know you gave away some insights to help me fill in some of *your* puzzle pieces."

"Oh? And what would that be?" She asks, as she picks up her clothes she had laid out before going to bed.

"You *want* this relationship to work! *Admit it*! You see a future with me!" He handsomely grins at her.

"I admit nothing, *Mister* Worthington! And I most certainly *won't* tell you how good looking you are so *ridiculously early* in the morning either!"

"*Look who's talking*!" He laughs. "And there's that cheekiness I just said makes you irresistibly sexy!"

"Ugh. *Fine*. But this had better be *good*!" She motions for him to turn around so she can put her clothes on. "Or any visions of *any* future will burn away with the rising sun!"

"If it's good, will you promise me the next five days?"

"Technically I won't be on vacation anymore once I get back to work." She says reluctantly. "You can turn back around now."

He walks over to her. "Then let me date you and have whatever time it takes to win you over! Why are you being so bloody stubborn about the days?!"

Bri makes it a point to study David. In a blasé tone she says, "*Fine*. Deal." She waves her hand. "*Give it your best shot, Worthington*!"

"First, *answer the question*! Why were you refusing to let me have the time?" David asks again with a hint of annoyance in his tone that isn't lost on Bri.

"Honestly," her voice is soft and humbled, "I *hate* making promises I'm not sure I can keep."

That tugs at David's heart. He wasn't expecting that answer and he can definitely appreciate what she is saying, making him fall in-love with her once more. He steps closer to her with a loving smile.

"Since you're going back to DC and back to work, your time will be limited. You're going to have to squeeze me in if we're serious about this, *which I am*! I told you we can make a long-distance relationship work, but I *need* to know you're committed to this, too. For the first time in my life, Bri, I'm excited about someone, about you *and us*!" His smile is full of possibility, she finds she couldn't say 'no' to him even if she wanted to, but she doesn't want to.

She nods and he barely hears her whisper with a lump in her throat, "*Okay.*"

He lifts her chin a little to look into her slightly teary eyes and smiles sweetly. "How does a sunrise in Paris sound?" Her mouth drops a little. "We won't have much time, but if you like it, we can go back and spend more time there." Bri is staring at him. He gives her a raised eyebrow. "What's wrong?"

"Nothing...just trying to figure *you* out. There's the saying, 'If it's too good to be true, then it usually is.'" She notes.

David laughs. "You know perfectly well that saying *doesn't* apply here!"

"*I do?*"

"How quickly you forget setting me straight on my behavior and actions not even two days ago!" He reminds her.

She softly kisses his lips. "Of course I forgot! I'd never want to hang someone's mistakes over their head for the rest of their life." He grips her tighter and kisses her with his other hand holding the back of her head.

"See!" He grins. "You do see a future with me!"

"Shhh," she has a playful look, "*or you'll jinx it!*"

David chuckles as he watches her go into the bathroom to finish getting ready. She will skip the attempt at putting makeup on this morning having only a little sleep. It takes about fifteen minutes and they are on their way to the airport. Bri isn't sure if she will ever get used to private planes, but they *are* faster and that leaves more time for things, or places, like a detour to Paris with David.

As soon as they land in Paris, David has the staff prepare for the flight to DC. On their way downtown, Bri is busy watching the sights of Paris that she doesn't hear David right away.

He gently nudges her. *"Penny for your thoughts?"*

Bri looks at him with a mischievous smile. "Oh, I hope my thoughts are worth *way* more than a penny, but for you, they're free!" She winks. "Honestly, I'm just taking it all in! All the history! Like Napoleon and then my thoughts go to the French Revolution. Oh, then there's 'The Black Plague' that ravaged Europe..." She looks at him, her cheeks blush. "Sorry."

"Don't be!" He happily says. "Our shared fascination with history makes you that much more fantastic to me!"

"Ha-ha, if you were in here," she points to her head, "it may be the strangest place you'd ever visit!"

"You should be afraid I'd never leave." He grins.

She giggles. "When James drove Katie, your mother, and me over to the stables that first day, I was asking about the history of your family's estate. One of the first things I learned about 'James' brother' is his knowledge of The Estate's history. He said you were the one to talk to and would enjoy having a conversation with someone who'd appreciate its history."

"Unfortunately, *at that time*, I would've been suspicious of you and being set-up." He replies.

"Ha-ha! *Paranoid* is more like it!" She laughs and he chuckles in agreement.

The car service drops them off and they board a small tour cruise line that will take them along The Seine River passing various places like: The Notre Dame Cathedral, The Louvre, and of course The Eiffel Tower. They are on the top deck and David stands behind her, wrapping his arms around her as they enjoy the sights.

Eventually, David turns Bri to face him. He wraps an arm around her waist and his other hand holding her cheek. He kisses her slowly...tenderly, then moves his hand from her cheek to tangle in her hair, behind her neck.

He gently pulls away, "With your love of history, I wish we had time for more sites, but there's only time for one stop without being rushed." She smiles sweetly and nods.

David has arranged for them to be taken up privately to the top of The Eiffel Tower. Once they are up there, David explains what the different signs say that are in French as they look out to the various sites around the city.

He wraps an arm around her waist and he holds her hand over his heart. "I know it's crazy, but I feel I need to say something to you." She nods with a little smile and he continues, "I've never met anyone I've had these kinds of intense feelings for, let alone so immediately." She sees the loving look in his eyes for her. "I've been drawn to you since seeing you in the hotel lobby. And after the last few days, I now understand why men are so protective of the woman they love!"

"Why's that?" She asks.

"They're protecting their heart." He says and watches Bri's eyes fill with tears and her jaw shakes a little. He rests his forehead to hers for a moment, then after taking a deep breath to steady his nerves, he looks adoringly into her eyes, "I love you, BriaLynn!" She can barely breathe with the lump closing off her throat; it hurts when she tries to swallow it down. David squeezes her hand a bit, "It's been hard to fight these intense feelings I have for you. *Undeniable*, no matter how hard I fought them at first. That day in the stables...my heart was yours, but I was too terrified to admit it. When I briefly let you in and followed you to the waterfall, I ended up scaring you and I'm *deeply* sorry for that."

She puts her hand on his cheek that she had slapped. "I'm sorry for slapping you." He kisses her again.

He continues, "That night at the party, when you stood up to me, I realized you were seeing *me*! Not my title, not my social status, nor my money; you didn't care about any of that!" She is unknowingly shaking her head. "You held a mirror up to my face and I didn't like the reflection, I wanted to change it! I want to be a better person and to be the man I thought I was, but more importantly, to be the man *you* deserve by your side." He tucks a strand of hair behind her ear. "If I knew you would, I'd marry you right now!"

Bri's eyes and cheeks are wet. "You love me?!"

He beams. "Yes, *I love you*! And even though you don't see how incredible you are, I see it because *I see you*!"

Like a dam breaking, the tears stream down her cheeks as she holds her hand tightly over her mouth to try to hold her sobs inside. When she gets control over herself...she takes a deep breath. All of a sudden, she remembers, "Wait, *you* had these walls up because you *never* wanted to get marr—." He kisses her hoping she'd forget what he had said.

He tells her. "What *matters* is what I recently said in front of witnesses! I promised I'd spend the rest of my life proving to you how wrong you are about love for yourself. I'd find a way you can be loved more than any woman has ever been loved, *and* for you to be cherished and adored that way *forever*!"

She looks slightly to the side at Paris whispering to herself, but he hears, "*I just need you...*"

He kisses her fiercely, then rests his forehead to hers. There is a long silence before he pulls back again. He is *trying* to be patient...he sees her jaw shake, then looks into her wet eyes that are so full of love for him.

He hugs her and whispers, "*I know you love me...*" He kisses the curve of her neck. "But I need to hear it..." Bri's eyes close as she summons the courage to admit what has been in her heart, too. He looks at her and she blinks back some of her tears, but it pushes them out of her eyes and down her cheeks. David's hands cup her face to wipe her tears with his thumbs. "I see it, Love. *I've felt it from you*, just as you've felt it from me..." She nods as she inhales and holds her breath for a few seconds.

She slowly exhales to calm her emotions. "*I...*" She takes another deep breath and holds it a moment, then squeaks out a breathy, "I love you, too, David!" David is *thrilled* and with his hands still cupping her face, he kisses her fiercely again. When they pull apart, she smiles, the lump is her throat is fading and she says it again as if she has been set free, "*I love you*!" She takes a deep breath and explains, "I love you so much, it scares me, too, *mostly* in a good way. Part of me is waiting for this dream to end and I wake up because..." she holds her breath, putting her hand on his cheek, "because I haven't done anything to deserve your love...or to love you..." She kisses him gently.

They rest their foreheads together again and enjoy the *knowing* feelings of love flowing between them. Then he kisses her deeply and completely; there is no doubt in his kiss that he is *completely* in-love with her, and she reciprocates that wonderful feeling.

"Bri, I never wanted to fall in-love, or get married, again, *but I hadn't met you*! Now that I have, *this* is love and I want it all *with you*! To be part of *your family* with the girls, and their dad and stepmother; I even want babies with you, if that's what you want! To be perfectly honest, I'd want at least one with you to not only have an heir, but to have a baby with the woman I love!"

"I want all that with you, too, David!" She smiles so happily at him, but it fades a little.

"What is it?" He asks.

"Will we be able to get married? I mean, I've heard talk about ancestral lines and marrying an heir?"

He smiles. "Mother has already been looking into that and we don't think it'll be a problem with all your ties to Dunfermline."

"I need you to understand, if it comes down to it and I don't have the necessary ancestry to marry 'The Heir of Newhaven,' I—." He gives her a little more than a tap of a kiss.

"*Not* going to be an issue." David looks adoringly at her. He'll marry her, even if he has to give up the title to James. He shifts the conversation. "I've talked with you a little bit about Ava." She nods. "One thing that just occurred to me is how upset I was at finding out she had an abortion a couple of months into our marriage. I was so crushed...I should be ashamed that I'm now realizing that if we'd had a child, we would still be married and I would've missed out on this; *on us*!" He knows he would've been watching his best friend and Bri get married...Jack has been clear he would go after her if David didn't.

"David, can I say something about that?" She asks.

He gives her a small smile. "Sure."

"I'm going to say this, but we don't have to really discuss it if you don't want to." She sees him nod and continues. "You said it yourself, that she was *determined* to become a duchess. Seriously think about this: why would she have an abortion that would've solidified her hold on that title?" She watches him really think about that and she adds, "You know I firmly believe 'everything happens for a reason' and sometimes those reasons aren't seen without the hindsight of time." He agrees with that. "If she thought she could pass that baby off *as yours*," helping him understand it more, "she would've done just that and *never* would've told a soul differently." She sees it click in his mind...*the baby wasn't his to begin with.*

"DNA." David throws out there. Bri slightly furrows her eyebrows putting together what he means and agrees as he also explains, "It's something that's done nowadays. I believe even right there at the hospital after the baby is born. Our children will have to have it done, so it's 'proven.'"

Bri thinks out loud. "Then Ava knew this and—."

"Didn't want to have a baby that wasn't mine." He finishes her thought with an angry tone in his voice towards Ava and the situation.

"That baby wasn't the super glue she needed to the duchess title and she couldn't 'waste time' being pregnant with another man's baby; plus, think of *that* scandal!" Bri gets an annoyed look, "And to dismiss a baby like that seems so heartless and—."

"Selfish!" He helps.

"Well...yeah...*and* heartbreakingly sad." Bri adds.

He exhales some relief. "I'm so grateful to have you in my life! If you're right and 'everything happens for a reason,' then that means there's a plan in place for us."

She has a big smile! "I *guarantee* there's a plan for everyone! As for a plan for us, *that* remains to be seen." She winks. "Even our heartaches can be used to help us appreciate the blessings that come into our lives." She taps a kiss to his lips.

"If you truly believe that, wouldn't you believe *our* plan includes whatever's necessary for us to be together." He smirks.

"*Perhaps.*" She says coyly. "Relationships of all types and lengths are meant to grow and change us from the things we learn, *usually* about ourselves."

He's curious, "What did you learn about yourself from your marriage?"

She shrugs. "When Jeff was angry with me about something and in his worse possible mood, he'd tell me how uncaring, selfish, heartless, mental, and so on, I was." She stares past his shoulder. "I *learned* I didn't like how *he saw me*; I didn't like who I was through his eyes and nothing I could do or say would ever change that."

"What else?" He asks.

She looks at him and shrugs again, "Pick a word associated with those and add it to the list. It's all been said one way or another."

"I'm not doubting that, but there's something you're not saying...something that was the *most* hurtful." He says and gently pulls her chin for her to look at him. "In all of that hurt, there must be something more serious that cut the deepest."

"Why do you think that?" She wonders.

"Because whatever it was, it was the beginning of the end for you and your marriage?" She stares at his shoulder as that sinks in. He holds her jaw. "You can trust me. *I swear to you* this won't come back to haunt you, like I suspect you've been conditioned to expect."

She closes her eyes and inhales deeply, deciding at that moment to trust in his love for her. She looks at him, "Aside from not wanting to be married to someone who saw me in such an ugly way..." she pauses, "what cut me to my core is on particularly bad days he would tell me I was a horrible mother and how I didn't really love or care about the girls..." her eyes close again when she remembers the worst parts.

David studies her. "Talk to me..."

"I'm just trying not to play those worst moments in my head." She says with such sadness, he pulls her into a firm embrace.

He says in a soothing tone, "Oh, Love..."

She steps over to the side and looks out over Paris. "They'd have a screaming tantrum at the same time every night, screaming at the top of their lungs for thirty to forty-five minutes. If I tried to intervene to calm them down, then it would last a solid hour or more." She wipes her cheeks and looks back out at the landscape. "When they'd *scream* at the top of their lungs, I would step outside because at those pitches and my sensitive hearing, my eardrums would vibrate a static sound. If I'm exposed to that for too long, it triggers a migraine." She takes a deep breath. "It was the hardest time of my life and the most alone I've ever felt!"

"Motherhood is your 'Achilles Heel.'" He says and she looks at him again. "All the other things he said that were meant to hurt you didn't work, so he attacked you as a mother." He stands next to her but leans sideways to face her. "Honestly, Love, *that* was verbal abuse!" He sees her eyes go wide as she considers what he is saying. He continues, "When *you're* angry at someone, how often do you tear them down as a person, or a parent?"

She shakes her head. "I don't."

"Why not?" He asks.

She scrunches her eyebrows, "Because I don't *want* to hurt them," a lump closes off her throat and she forces it down, "I may be upset with something they did or said, but I don't want to belittle them and take their self-esteem away. I *try* to pick my words or bite my tongue."

"*Precisely!*" The anger in David's voice isn't difficult to pick up on. "Every time he cut you down, it was to *purposely hurt you.* That's all a reflection *on him!*" He takes a deep breath to calm himself. He pulls her chin to look at him. "The row in the stables and then at the party, well, everything you said was the truth. You were assertive, but you weren't being vicious."

She is surprised he said that and replies, "It kind of was!"

"No, Love. It was *all* true! Every word of it and it needed to be said exactly how you said it, because I wasn't listening to anyone else." He stands. "Let's look at it this way." He leans his backside against the railing. He reaches to turn her towards him. "They say kids are perceptive," she agrees, "so your daughters had to pick up on a time here and there when their parents were fighting." She nods. "What did you tell them?"

"What do you mean?" She asks.

"As beautifully as you navigated the divorce *for* your daughters, coparenting in friendship with their father and befriending the new wife; your compassion and kindness towards a man who crossed a line numerous times that *never* should've been crossed the first time is *astonishing*! It makes me wonder how you navigated those times when the girls overheard an angry tirade of his?"

She inhales, raising her eyebrows. "I had them remember how grumpy they get when they don't get a lot of sleep. Then I said when their dad doesn't get enough sleep at night, sometimes multiple nights, it all catches up to him and he gets *very* grumpy."

"*That* shows what a fantastic mother *you are*!" He holds her cheek. "He went after your very motherly spirit *intending* to hurt you!" She wipes a tear and softly nods, as she listens. "Love, *all of that* was abusive!"

She digs out a package of tissues from her purse. "David, I'm not blameless, *nor* completely innocent..." she wipes her eyes.

"*BriaLynn*, we're discussing a very specific piece of a complex relationship equation; not the entire marriage. I have no doubt you've looked back and analyzed the marriage; having come up with things you did wrong, that you should've done differently, and so on." She agrees. He smiles sweetly, "I'm sure you'll take what you've learned and apply it to our marriage; just as I will." She nods, then her eyes flick to him as it sinks in what he just said. He winks and tucks some hair behind her ear. "What I'm discussing right now is being a decent human being and having a basic code of honor which means you don't *purposely* hurt someone's feelings like children do. That leads me to ask, what kind of a person purposely hurts the feelings of someone they *should* at least care about because she's the mother of his children? A woman who goes out of her way to protect *his image* as a father with their daughters?!" He holds her hand. "Those moments they see or hear their dad yelling things at you *they know aren't true*, you were protecting them from having bad feelings towards their father. It definitely makes me wonder what morals this man actually holds true to?"

"It's said something like ethical and moral people know right from wrong; however, moral people actually *do* the right thing." She says. "I'd like to think Jeff felt bad afterwards. He always tried to be extra nice to smooth things over."

"But he never apologized." David states.

"Rarely and even then, some of those times not really." She tells him. "There were moments throughout our marriage I could see what a sweet man he could be, if only someone could bring that out in him all the time... I heard it said somewhere, something like, 'Men don't change. However, a man will change for only one person...the woman he loves.' *Oliva is that for Jeff!* The girls thought it was weird I was okay with Jeff and Olivia being together, which I am happy for them, but also happy the girls have seen it! For them to remember how ill-matched Jeff and I were, then see him happy with Oliva and *observe* the difference! Then they can take that and apply it to their own relationships as a tool to help them find their 'true-love.'" She sees him staring in awe of her. "What is it?"

"There are so many words that come to mind describing you. Amazing, incredible, unbelievable, but I'll go with *bloody fantastic and brilliant!* I'm glad Jeff's a changed man! I'd like to think that he's told Olivia every deep-dark secret and she's already pointed out how *ghastly* his behavior was! If she's as nice as you say she is, then she's already highlighted how good of a mother you really are!"

"You've never met the girls. For all you know, they could be spoiled and horrible." She tells him.

"It's based on what I know of you so far! There's *no way* they're ghastly, or even remotely close."

She laughs a little and asks, "You do remember we're talking about teenage girls, right?!"

"I do! I also think the moment they take a step in the 'ghastly' direction; you're nipping it!" He smirks. She rolls her eyes, but nods. "I'm guessing your divorce only had the expectation of coparenting and shared child support; you didn't ask for anything else."

"I shared a condo with Katie, eventually moving to the condo across from hers." Bri explains.

He softly chuckles. "You could've asked for spousal support and so much more, but you didn't. My divorce from Ava was the complete opposite! Shamefully, I was so angry with her and she was fighting so hard to keep her title that would make her duchess; it was horrible."

"She cheated on you the entire relationship, David. I don't think I would've handled it any better! I said this already, but I need to remind you that I'm SO *not* perfect!" She says.

"No, but just as you're excusing his *inexcusable* behavior away and giving him an out, your behavior will be forgivable and your flaws are going to be fewer with me." He smiles adoringly. "You see my flaws and love me anyway, I'm sure when I see yours, I'll love you anyway." He winks.

"Funny...I can't remember yours." She grins.

He chuckles. "Seriously, I've only seen flaws, stemming from your strengths We talked yesterday about loyalty being a strength and a weakness," she nods in agreement, "your independence is going to be one of those. Being nobility has it's perks, but one of the drawbacks is you're not going to have the same amount of independence as you once did. Your driver would be your security for the times you might need it, but we'll add a bodyguard when you become duchess, or sooner if need be." He sees her shift uneasily. "I'll want you to be safe at all times, but I also *never* want you to feel you have no control over your life either."

Her eyes are teary again as she finds herself thinking, '*I don't deserve him...*' Only now she knows she'll love him the way he *deserves* to be loved...*completely*.

Bri has gone quiet and David asks, "Are you alright?"

She looks at him and more tears make their way down her face. She kisses him fiercely. He wraps his arms around her and dips her back, deepening their kiss, then slowly brings her back up.

Bri rests their foreheads together. "My heart is full, David. The man I love just said he loves me AND he wants a future with me!" She cups his jaw and pulls him into another kiss, then throws her arms around his neck to hug him; he holds her tight and lifts her up off the ground and spins her around. "The whole point of our lives is to learn and grow from the various lessons we're given; avoiding those lessons, we cease to grow and learn. I'm dismayed and wondering how on earth I deserve to be matched up with someone who is so *bloody fantastically brilliant*?!" She teases with his accent and he chuckles. "I knew this love and happiness was out there, but to feel it and have it in my life?!" She can only whisper, "*I'm happier than I've ever been!*"

"Good!" He says with determination, as he looks into her eyes. "I plan on *keeping* it that way!"

She giggles. "You seem so sure."

"*I am*! You're so easy to love." He says and she shakes her head. "Your loving heart couldn't take Jeff's verbal abuse," he puts his fingertips to her lip, "no matter how infrequent those times were that you're about to say." She turns to the side and looks at the landscape as she tries to suppress the tears that keep coming. He steps in front of her again with a sweet smile, handing her another tissue. "These tears *also show me* you have a wonderful heart." He lifts her chin. "You don't want to call his words what they are, because you know how hurtful it would be for him to hear, let alone admit!" He pulls her to him and holds her. "It's okay to trust me. You're safe with me, I promise you." He feels her arms hug him tighter and he holds her firmer, staying like this for a couple minutes.

She places a kiss in the curve of his neck, then lifts her head to hold his jaw. "I love you." She kisses him in such a tender way, he *feels* loved. She gently pulls her lips from his and has a loving expression on her face. "All the terrible things that have happened in my life are worth it, because they led me to you!"

"They did!" He smirks. He kisses her one last time up in The Eiffel Tower before they leave.

On the plane, they settle in and get comfortable. She looks over at David who turns and winks with a smile. "All good?"

"Right now, everything's perfect...until we get to DC." She sadly says.

He gently pulls her in for a kiss, then smiles, "I really enjoy kissing you!"

She lightly laughs, "I *really* enjoy it, too."

Bri goes to the back bedroom and lays down on the bed. David checks on a few things with work, then he goes back to join her. They both sleep for most of the flight.

CHAPTER 11

Imperfect People, A Perfectly Divine Plan

Landing at the airport, David and Bri thank the staff before walking off the plane and down the stairs. The back door of the awaiting limo opens and a long-time friend gets out.

"Ken!" She runs up to him and throws her arms around him in a hug! "*It's so good to see you!*"

He chuckles. "I'm happy to see you, too, Sweetie!" He's like an uncle to her after knowing him for as long as she has.

Ken Thompson is a veteran detective with the DCPD and his job has crossed with hers a few times over the years. The effects of Ken's job have taken its toll on him. He looked like he was in his seventies when he was only sixty-two. He is bald on top and has a very thin layer of white hair around the rest of his head. He is overweight but his stomach doesn't hang over his belt much. When she looks into his eyes, she sees the stress of his job. He wears the same 'warrior armor' many police officers and law enforcement wear when working in this field, but he also knows when to take it off; a valuable trait to detectives when they talk to victims and their families, as well as witnesses.

Ken is a professional anchor in a city where ethics, values, morals, and standards seem to be rewritten daily. Ken and Bri trust each other completely and are very loyal; if they need something, *anything*, all they have to do is ask. They confide in each other personally, as well as being each other's sense of professional reasoning when emotions can make it hard to see what's right in front of them.

Ken knows how to profile people and he has taught her how to read people better, essentially helping her to be better at her job. Ken jokes that he helped her read people a little *too* well when she would see right through him. Then he would look around and realize the politicians and diplomats she works with and says, 'there is probably no such thing as reading people too well.' He manages to show up when she needs cheering up, which explains why he is here now.

No one knows she is traveling with someone, so after he hugs and kisses her forehead, he looks at David, then back to her with a smirky grin. Bri turns and holds her hand out to David with a loving smile for him. He takes it and as she gently pulls him closer to her, she introduces David and Ken. Instead of shaking hands, Ken gives David more of a fatherly hug.

Bri explains to David, "Ken and Henry, who you'll meet shortly, are always looking for that perfect match for me, but made me *swear* I'd never marry anyone I worked with." She turns to Ken and back to David. "Ken would use more colorful words when describing politicians and diplomats, but with me he tries to use words like 'weasels.' I'd have to remind him that he deals with the criminal side of things and contrary to popular belief, not 100% of politicians, diplomats, etc., are criminals!" She winks. "And yes, *some* diplomats will use their diplomatic immunity to their advantage. It's the criminal activity of these few when our professional paths cross." They get into the limo.

Once settled in their seats, Ken asks Bri with some disappointment, "Why are you letting Ambassador Lombardi bring you back here before your vacation's up? I'm sure this good-looking guy could think of a few things you two could be doing right now, rather than be here!" He lightly laughs.

David laughs and also recognizes the 'Lombardi' name; they've done business together through The Worthington Corporation. David has never met the guy personally, but thinks he is a decent guy from what he has heard...which is probably the case and why Bri is here. If he wasn't a decent guy deep down, there is *no way* she would have come back this early. She said it herself; the Ambassador would get away with a lot more if someone else caters to his every whim.

Ken saw David's face when he said, 'Ambassador Lombardi,' and asks, "Do you know him?"

"Our family's company has done business with him a few times." David says.

"Well, maybe that will come in handy, because our Bri here will need all the help she can get and," turning to Bri, "having David with you may be helpful, especially with his son coming!"

"What?!" Bri is horrified. "*Craaap*! I didn't know that!"

120

"I'm glad to see you unknowingly brought reinforcements!" He tips his head to David. He sees they are holding hands, fingers laced, and Ken smiles warmly, "I'm absolutely tickled for you Sweetie!" He gestures to their hands. "How long has this been going on?"

"Since Saturday night." She looks from Ken to David and smiles lovingly at him. He returns the smile and kisses the back of her hand.

"*Really*?! I swear you two seem like you've been together longer than that, just kept it on the *down-low*!" Ken says with a twinkle in his eye.

"One word, Ken," she says, "*whirlwind.*"

"I'll say!" Ken chuckles.

"Besides, do you really think I could keep something like this a secret for long? *Especially from you*?!" She looks at David, pointing at Ken, saying, "He's a bloodhound." She looks back at Ken, "The smile on my face alone would be hard to hide!"

"Well, love looks good on you, Sweetie!" Ken tells her.

"See!" She gestures Ken. "Most wouldn't have said 'love' so soon, but you caught it!" They all laugh.

David curiously asks, "What's with the Ambassador's son?" Ken and Bri look at each other with 'oh boy' expressions.

Ken explains, "Well, you see David, it's like this: The Ambassador gives his son *anything* he wants. About a year ago, the Ambassador had business in DC and his son wanted to tag along to see what the big deal was about the US, or DC, or whatever it was. Somewhere along the line, the Ambassador introduced his son to our Bri, and Antonio decided he had to have her."

David shifts in annoyance. Bri is a person, an amazing and beautiful woman he gets, but she is *not* a possession!

"The Ambassador is trying to help his son get what he wants...*Bri.*"

Bri sees David's uneasiness and explains, "David, you need to understand I've never wanted anything to do with Antonio since I first met him over a year ago! He's as narcissistic as they come, and I wouldn't be surprised if he were diagnosed with something else. I'm uncomfortable being around him; just the thought of him makes me sick. I'll try to avoid him like the plague. It's only bearable this time knowing you're here in DC with me." She squeezes David's hand with a little smile.

"I understand! Honestly, I don't mind men noticing your beauty; they can respectfully look all they want, but *absolutely no touching*!" He lovingly smiles. "What frustrates me is, well, all of what Ken said! Like you're some*thing* to be owned, a possession... I'll protect you, Bri, even if it means bodyguards, or hitting the Ambassador hard financially; whatever it takes."

"I hate to say it," Ken said, "but David has the right idea."

Bri inhales deeply and exhales looking out the window as the limo pulls up to the restaurant. She disappointedly sighs, "*Yeah...*"

Ken asks. "I can see about having protection assigned to you, too."

"I hope it doesn't come to that. With David here," she turns to David, "*AND,* if you're up for it, I plan on frustrating the heck out of any plans Antonio may come up with." She mischievously smiles.

"Oh-ho, I know that look!" Ken laughs. He says to David, "Best be glad you're on her side!"

David smiles wide. "Always!" They climb out of the limo and go inside the restaurant.

"What's your plan?" Ken asks.

"Take this man everywhere I can with me! Quietly showing Antonio I'm taken and not available for anything!"

"I'm there, Love!" David kisses her sweetly.

"Good, because if that doesn't work, I also plan on having to be blunt and assertive...prepared for the worst, while hoping for the best!" They follow the hostess to the table. "Once the Ambassador knows how I feel about David and with the connection the Ambassador and I have, he'll support *my happiness* over the fleeting feelings his son has for what he *momentarily* wants."

Henry and Maggie Bradshaw are waiting at the table when Bri, Ken, and David walk up. "Hi, Sweetie!" Maggie happily says.

"Have you been waiting long?" Bri asks, hugging her and Henry.

"Oh, not long at all." Maggie replies.

Ken shakes Henry's hand and kisses Maggie on the cheek. "Looks like our girl here brought her own reinforcements!" Ken turns and gestures to David.

Everyone looks to David who has a surprised look on his face. It was hard for David to get a good look when Bri was hugging them, but when they were talking to Ken, he saw them clearly. "Uncle Henry? Aunt Maggie?" They, too, are stunned.

Bri is confused. "What?" She watches Maggie rush to David and hug him tight, which he happily returns it.

Henry is right behind her with a hug for David. Henry is choked up as he says, "Good to see you, Son!"

Bri thinks back many moons ago and pieces things together, realizing now Henry and Peter had a falling out *decades* ago. "David's father is your best friend, *Peter*?! And *Lotti*, is your sister, *Carlotta*?!" Henry nods. She is still stunned, but she puts it on hold for a moment. "I need to run to the ladies' room quick. We can discuss this more when I get back."

"May I order you something to drink, Love?" David asks.

Her mouth is dry. "Yes, please. A mango-peach smoothie?"

"My pleasure." David smiles.

Maggie puts her arm around Bri saying, "I'll walk with you, Sweetie." They get away from the table and Maggie beams, "*You fell in-love!*" She happily hugs Bri just outside the ladies' room.

"I did!" Bri hugs Maggie back. "I'm still surprised how fast it all happened!"

At the table, Henry, who in a typical Henry-soothing voice, says, "David, I don't presume to know what went down with between you and your ex-wife, but I'm here if you ever want to talk because the effects of it can cause someone to lose their way." David nods a 'that's-the-truth' look. Henry sees his expression, "Then it's no surprise that meeting our Bri would help you get back on track." David's head snaps to Henry at 'our Bri,' and Henry explains how he met Bri at work, told Maggie she was the daughter they never had, and she met her and agreed. "Bri came over to our home one evening for dinner..." Henry chokes up.

"And stayed in our hearts forever!" Henry's oldest son, Joe, finishes his dad's sentence walking up to their table with his brothers Sam and Mitch. Joe hugs David, excited to see him, "It's been awhile, Cousin!"

"*Too long*, Joe!" David says, returning his excitement and he hugs Sam and Mitch. "This is fantastic! Seems like yesterday you, Jack, and me were traveling to each other's campuses to par—," he glances at Henry, "er, *study* together." The men all laugh.

Henry gives a knowing smile. "Maggie and I couldn't say much, when all of you were doing so well with your studies."

Joe tells David, "Bri has been a daughter and sister to our family for, well, forever now. As you already know, she went on a trip with Katie this past week." David nods and Joe continues. "Anyway, after I found out where they planned on going and Edinburgh being on the list, I mentioned to Dad how funny it would be if she and Katie ended up..." He trailed off and his head snaps to David, "Wait, how *did* you two meet?!" Bri and Maggie were making their way back to the table and Bri's breath catches when she sees David, so relaxed and a part of everything. Joe asks in an authoritative older brother tone, "What *are* your intentions with my sister?"

David holds his hands halfway up, surrendering. "The best ones, I swear!" Then he holds one to his heart. "Let's just say our first meeting was *educational*. Fact is," David continues, "she's a force to be reckoned with!" Joe knows the force Bri can be. "Then she had the audacity to stand up to me and call me out for my less than chivalrous behavior when I let my date get away with her bad treatment of Bri."

"Hold up!" Joe questions, "Bri is an invited guest to a party, who is insulted, and you did nothing?!"

Joe's annoyance is noted by David, who admits, "Joe, I was an idiot!" Joe takes that answer and relaxes. "Now, I'd be more *descriptive* if we were in private." David has fully redeemed himself now. "I should also tell you that she had me all twisted up and turned inside out. I was angry she called me out while in the middle of about two dozen people, but when she was finished and left the room, the weight of the truth in her words sank in." David had felt Bri's presence and stands up to say, "I told everyone she didn't need a title to prove she's better than the lot of us!" He kisses her cheek.

Bri tsks and shakes her head. "Not *better*."

The ladies hug Joe, Sam, and Mitch. Joe pushes Bri's chair in as she sits down and she lays her napkin in her lap again, then takes a drink of her smoothie.

David takes her hand and continues talking to Joe, while looking at Bri. "She was right about me not being a true gentleman, I was only acting like a gentleman on the surface. That I was quote '*sorely lacking grace*' and quote '*all the other verbs that describe a gentleman.*' She also told me that words like pompous, arrogant, and conceited, aren't in the definition of a gentleman either; there's more, but you get the idea." David smiles a teasing grin at her. "After an angry 'how dare you' from me, you launched into your finale and *WOW*! You were *ravishing*!" He runs his hand down her arm sending chills along the path, the sensation becomes so overwhelming that she clears her throat to snap herself out of it. David is enjoying how her body reacts to his touch. She looks around and sees everyone with knowing smiles; her cheeks get a little red. David adds, "Although I fought it at first, I've been drawn to Bri since I first saw her in the lobby of The Coriander Hotel. Of course, Artemis thinks he fell in-love with her first." David glances and then looks around the table at the confused faces and explains, "Artemis is my horse, well," he looks back to Bri, "only *now* I think he's devoted to Bri."

Bri laughs. "Well, in his mind he did *see* me first!" The table laughs.

David laughs. "With his temperament, he could very well decide you're the only one he's going to let ride him from now on!"

She playfully teases. "*You make it sound like I'll be in Newhaven on a regular basis!*"

"Bri, I know you're teasing, but in front of family *know this*: I *will* marry you very *soon*! Then, I plan to love and adore you, even spoil you, for the rest of our lives and in whatever comes after this life!" He holds her hand to his heart, "And I intend to keep my promise of finding a way you'll be loved more than any woman has ever been loved!" Henry and Maggie are fighting back their tears; Ken is, too.

Joe's eyes are a little moist, as he pats David on the shoulder. "Well, said, Cousin. She deserves it!"

Bri is staring at her silverware in front of her; there is silence for a long moment. "Bri?" He places a finger and a thumb on her chin to turn her head towards him. She pivots in her chair putting a hand on his knee and the other cupping his face, then lovingly kisses him. He smiles against her lips, "I like that answer!"

"I have no words, just more love for you, David!" She tells him.

"*Brilliant* answer, Love!" He is smiling adoringly at her.

She lightly taps his lips again and then gestures to Ken. "He's going to make you stick to your promise."

"Great!" David says, unfazed.

Bri giggles, wiping her eyes. "You don't understand."

Ken is sitting back in his chair, chuckling. "What she's trying to say is, I know some of the best forensic people in the world; if you hurt her, they'll make it look like you just dropped off the face of the earth!"

"*Really?*" David is intrigued.

Ken smirks. "If there's no evidence a crime was committed, no circumstantial evidence because it looks like you dropped off the face of the Earth, then how can one *prove* a crime actually happened?"

"Or which crime for that matter!" David adds.

"You got it!" Ken laughs. "And then, how does anyone know someone didn't just walk away from everything and disappeared on their own? Which someone has every right to do in this country."

"*That's fantastic!*" David laughs.

Their meals come and everyone starts to eat. Bri and David are so comfortable with each other, they let each other have a taste of their meal while following the table conversation. Henry, Maggie, and Ken watch the two of them; they're all so grateful to see Bri so happy and in-love!

126

David runs to the men's room and he stops the waiter on his way back. He has their bill and David pays for it. A few minutes later he joins the table again, overhearing Henry telling Bri, "...if you let this work, Sweetie, you'll have a *wonderful* life!" Henry kindly smiles and Bri nods, wiping a tear from her cheek.

Henry looks around for the waiter, "As soon as we get the bill—."

"I already took care of it, Uncle Henry." David says. "We can leave whenever we're ready."

Joe asks, "What are you doing in the corporation these days?"

Henry's the first to answer, "Peter retired from the company, making David the CEO, and from what I continue to read and hear, doing a fine job!" Joe gives Henry a curious look. "What? I stay up on what our family is up to, just not as closely as I had thought." He points his hands towards David and Bri.

"This all just happened Saturday, Henry." Bri said.

"After you said all that to him?!" Henry asks.

"After that kiss!" Maggie giggles.

Bri lightly laughs. "*I never said we kissed!*"

"Oh, it would be expected! With such charged up feelings, there *had* to be a magnetic kiss!" Maggie laughs.

"That kiss was fantastic and felt way better than being slapped!" David grins and winks at Bri.

"That's because *you made me* jump the waterfall with you! But you really should've been slapped for kissing me after I told you off for being a cad." She smirks.

"Good to hear it didn't go too far, Sis!" Joe teases.

"Like you should talk! You're the one who made out on your firsss—." She stops herself and bites her lips together inside her mouth as she remembers who is listening...Henry and Maggie.

"Made out with who?" Henry asks with a sly smile.

"I'm *not* finishing that sentence." She looks at Joe apologetically and he winks at her with a huge smile. "David, rescue me before I completely betray Joe's confidence! Please?" She asks. David stands up with her, chuckling.

Everyone thanks David for lunch as they make their way outside the restaurant. When Bri walks out the door, David falls in line with Bri's steps and holds her hand, lacing their fingers.

"Hey, do you think we could head to Uncle Henry's?" David asks.

Bri's heart sinks. She told him about her daughters, but they haven't had any detailed discussions about her kids. David kisses her hand and says, "I'm excited to meet your daughters!"

Bri stops cold in her tracks; David turns to her. Tears fill her eyes and she chokes up as she sees the sincerity in his eyes. "H-Wh..." She stands there, shaking her head as her tears threaten to spill over.

"It was mentioned," he gestures the restaurant, "they were at Henry and Maggie's house." David looks at her with compassion. "*And* there was some discussion about your daughters when we were in Dunfermline."

"A *mention*! We haven't really discussed them, or what it all means." She says.

David smiles at her and lifts her chin, as everyone else watches. "What's there to discuss? It's obvious that it means it's, 'a packaged deal,' for lack of a better way to say it."

Bri gives an airy, nervous laugh. "The discussion that somehow prepares you for the very real truth, *there's no way to prepare you for what you're getting into*." She takes a step back and David knows she is scared, but he lets her say what she needs to first. "The discussion where we talk about how their home, their school, *their life*, is here and I'm having a hard time imagining what life would look like with Newhaven thrown in." She keeps stepping back.

"Oh, Sweetie." Maggie quietly says. "Everything can be worked out more easily than you realize! *We'll help!*"

"Bri." David reaches for her, but she pulls back. He admittedly says, "I won't pretend to know what to do, but I don't think I could be in better hands. I suspect your daughters are fantastic *and* brilliant because you're an *amazing* mother." Bri scoffs, rolling her eyes and goes to say something, but he interrupts, "Please, let me finish." He knows her objection. "Bri, those girls have the best possible life in any situation where their parents are no longer together! Their parents support each other, as well as them, plus your friends with his wife and it makes this *so* healthy for them. Never do they have to feel torn, like they must choose a side, or hate someone. *Do you know how incredible that is*?! You two are their parents, and the stepmother and stepfather," he motions to himself, "are supporting roles." Bri gets mad at herself when the tears flow.

"David, it means the world to me that you would say all that." He smiles and kisses her cheek with so much love, it feels like her heart is melting into a puddle; she wraps her arms around his neck and hugs him tight. "*Oh, no!*" She gasps, releasing her hug. "I have to go check in at the office and make sure things are good to go with the Ambassador's visit. Then I should check in with the fundraising gala and see how they're doing getting things started."

David looks at his watch. "That seems like a lot to do with over half the day gone already. What can I do to help?"

"Right now, nothing." She smiles. "I just need a feel for where things are at, so I can get a plan forming for the week ahead." She explains.

"No worries, Sweetie!" Maggie says, then suggests, "Why don't the boys bring '*Cousin* David' over and we can introduce them slowly? We'll just see where the Spirit leads us and go from there!"

As strong in faith as they are, Bri trusts they'll do just that. She agrees, hugging everyone goodbye, only she kisses David with her hug.

CHAPTER 12

Imperfectly Perfect Long Overdue Reunion

Bri leaves in one of the cars to go to her office. She calls her assistant, Amy, who is already at the townhouse where the Ambassador likes to stay. Bri asks her driver to change course to meet up with Amy. She is helping Bri with the list of specifications the Ambassador and his family will need. There are dietary restrictions Chef André, the chef the Ambassador loves and who is also 'The Head Chef' at The White House, will see to the adherence of during their stay this week, and for the fundraiser event.

The Chef is paid ridiculously well for his time and Bri tells him with all sincerity, "André, you're worth *every* penny! I'm so grateful you're in this with us, *again*!"

"My pleasure, Bri! You shouldn't have to suffer alone." He teases and she lightly giggles.

When she bids him and the staff goodbye, she reminds them to call her with issues, especially if special requests get out of hand and those requests usually do with his son. "Enjoy the peace and quiet today, for tomorrow the real fun begins." She says with sarcasm.

Bri and Amy stop by The Embassy to see how preparations are going for The Charity Fundraiser this coming Friday night for 'The World's Children's Hospital.' This charity sends doctors all over the world to assist and perform procedures, along with advancing a doctor's learning. It's last minute since Bri just agreed to come back early from vacation, but it's also a way *to try* to keep the Ambassador's son in check since eyes will be watching and all news will be reported. Bri picks up tickets for herself and the family, including an extra one for David.

In the car, Bri calls the boutique she uses and asks Liza to pick out a dress for her. She has known Liza for a few years now and Liza knows Bri's style and preferences. Bri says she will get back to her with measurements for David's tuxedo.

> Bri: "I've requested a tux for you from the boutique where I'm getting my dress for Friday night."

David: "Isn't it considered bad form to ask someone out on a date by text message?"

Bri: "It's a double-standard, but I believe that's for a man pursuing the woman. (adds a winking face) Besides, didn't you agree to help in any way you could this week?"

David: "Touché!"

Bri: "If you don't want to go with me, I could see if Jack wants to escort me to another black-tie party. He looks really handsome in a tux, too!"

David: "NOT funny."

Bri: "I'm serious! He IS handsome in a tux!"

David: "He's NOT taking you!"

Bri: "You never said you would!" (adds a kissing face)

David: "The answer to spending time with you is always YES."

Bri: "Ooo, I love that answer! (a happy face) The boutique needs your measurements ASAP. If you're okay with my assistant, Amy, having your number, I'll have her get in touch with you."

David: "Absolutely! I'd like to have her number, too! I might enlist her help as we make the long-distance part of the relationship work!"

Bri: "She would! P.S. You're wonderful! Thank you, My Love! Love you! xoxo."

David: "Anything for you! I love you!"

"Amy, David's fine with you having his cell number, so I'm texting it to you as we speak." Bri says and presses 'send.'

"Don't you mean '*mobile*'?" Amy teases with a British accent.

Bri laughs. "He says it both ways because he was born in Scotland, went to boarding schools in the UK, then went to Harvard and Columbia."

At her office in The Executive Office Building, she is on the top floor, in a corner office. Her office has a view of The South Lawn of The White House. On tough days when she can use solitude, she looks out the window and can see some form of an illusion that she is not one of tens of thousands in the DC metro area at that moment. The building is old, but historically beautiful. It is a typical office with darkly varnished woodwork, including the wall paneling, and furniture. Yet, somehow, with her love of history, it suits her.

Amy sits at the round table in Bri's office and has her laptop open. She and Bri finalize the itineraries for the week, adding things on Bri's calendar that are mandatory and highly suggested by her boss, but Amy is focused on keeping a lot off Bri's schedule this week to prepare for the wake of chaos the Ambassador's son inevitably causes Bri and her team...*and* to help the romance between her and David.

"Bri, it's 3:00. Go home to your family and that hunk of a man who is *crazy* about you, *and rightfully so!*"

"You haven't seen him yet!" Bri laughs, but it fades when she tries to read Amy's face.

Amy had paused for a moment, then she pulls up a tabloid photo of her and David on a boat...their cruise down The Seine River in Paris. The headline: *Has This Scottish Heir and Billionaire Playboy Finally Found Love...Or Just an American Toy?*

Bri's mouth drops. "At least they don't know me, *yet*, but *craaap*...it's only a matter of time." Her elbows are on her desk, her hands holding her head. "What happens when they do—*the girls*?!"

"For what it's worth, kids tend to be 'off limits.' If they do capture them in a random photo, the viciousness doesn't seem to be heaped on them; at least with what little I tend read, I haven't seen any."

"Well, I guess we can be thankful they have at least a sliver of moral character." Bri sarcastically says.

"Mm-right...morals..." Amy is a bit more sarcastic.

Bri's phone chimes familiarly and Amy notes, "*Katie beckons.*" Bri has a bit of an eyeroll. Amy tells her, "I'm going to go back to my desk, and you need to get ready to leave...or I'll call David now that I have his number and have him kidnap you!" Bri giggles as she picks up her phone and reads Katie's text message.

> Katie: "We're in town! Since their hotel is close to our condo building, we can meet up!"

> Bri: "Not clear on the 'where'...condo or hotel. (winking face) Besides, I'm headed to the house, David is already there. Let me know which place and I'll text when we are on our way."

> Katie: "He's at the house with the girls? AND on his own without you?! Bri, I have to say, if you don't keep this guy, I'll drop you as my BFF!"

> Bri: "No you won't! You couldn't function without me!"

'*Sure wish she would lose interest in our friendship.*' Bri thinks, then scolds herself for wishing that; she needs to be a better person than that.

> Katie: "Too true, but I also think he's the one for you!"

Katie's envy of her best friend grows as she begins to wonder if Jack likes Bri. She is now focused on getting Jack to like her and forgetting about Bri. This annoys James; he isn't upset with Jack, because Jack *is trying* to rebuff her advances without being rude, but it's not working. In fact, it seems to be fueling her advances.

> Bri: "You 'think' he's the one???"

> Bri: [Photo] "The press doesn't know of me...*yet*...but it's coming. I just hope they respect the girls in this and keep them out of it."

Katie shows James and Jack the photo, watching Jack closely. When she sees Jack happily smiles, she wonders if maybe she is wrong about Jack having feelings for Bri.

> Katie: "Now we need time for some serious girl talk!"

Bri hasn't looked forward to that for quite some time...then again, she hasn't needed a 'girl talk.' Katie was the one talking during these 'girl talk sessions' and Bri has been fine with that.

Amy pops her head in, "Your car is waiting outside, but I'm to tell you Mateo will go back to being your driver tomorrow."

Bri smiles as she gathers her stuff. "Fantastic!" She doesn't bother taking much with her since her day will start earlier than usual tomorrow morning.

When Bri slides in the back seat of the car, she texts David that she is on her way to the house.

>David: "Can't wait! xxoxx"

>Bri: (she sends a smiley face and a kissing one)

A little while later, the car pulls up and David is waiting out front for her. He opens her door and helps her out, before wrapping his arms around her and kissing her passionately. A perfect moment that ends when a limo pulls up. It's Katie, along with James, Jack, Peter, and Carlotta.

Katie squeals and runs up to hug them both. "I'm so excited for you two!" *And* she is happy Bri isn't competition for Jack.

Henry had looked out the window when he heard the squeal and saw James getting out of the limo with Katie. He and Maggie come out to greet Katie and see their nephew, but find Peter, Carlotta, and Jack, too. They all look as confused as David did, especially watching Katie go to Maggie and Henry, being welcomed warmly. Bri and David walk over to Peter and Carlotta, David threading his fingers with Bri's.

His father is confused. "What's going on, David?"

Bri gives him a kind smile. "This was sort of a surreal moment for us earlier today, Your Grace."

"I think 'Peter' will be fine." He smiles, acknowledging their hands, and she smiles brightly at David.

Bri explains, "I've known Henry, Maggie, and the family since I moved out here to go to college and worked at his law firm. The new part for me is making the connection that Carlotta is 'Lotti,' Henry's sister, *and* you're his best friend, Peter."

Henry walks over and says, "It's been a long time." Then, true to Henry, he hugs Peter, which Peter hugs him back as tears threaten to fall from his eyes.

"Let's go inside." Maggie suggests, as she and Carlotta, who've already hugged, walk inside together with an arm around each other.

The Bradshaw's have a small estate themselves with a half-circle drive; smaller fountain and flower beds are in the middle section. Their house is considered a mansion, but compared to The Manor and The Inn, it's small. A white marble entryway greeted them with a staircase to the left and wrapping around to arrive at the center of the second floor in front of them. To their immediate right is a sitting room they gather in. A plush white couch and two loveseats, along with Bri's favorite overstuffed chair and ottoman. She automatically goes to it, and David sits next to her on the arm as she leans over and into him. She is surprisingly comfortable and at ease with David by her side. Jack sits on the ottoman, in the middle, so Katie can't sit next to him.

"David has been filling us in on The Worthington Corporation's newest ventures. I was just about to tell him before Bri arrived that the block where Bri's and Katie's condos are located, is owned by several investors. One investor went bankrupt and now they're having to sell. If your company's interested in adding it to its company's portfolio, it may be a rather promising investment!"

"I'd love to learn more about it! How about we come to your office tomorrow and talk about it?" David offers.

"Sounds great! I'll clear my schedule if I have to!" Henry says.

Peter just watches Henry...then says to Henry a little choked up, "How can you just act like nothing happened?"

"Peter, you and I have been best friends pretty much since the day we were born. We've been through a lot of good times together, made it through some bad ones, but my point is we make it through because we're family." Henry chokes back some tears of his own. "The only two people that are closer than you and me," he gestures in the direction of Jack, David, and Bri, "are David and Jack!"

Peter lightly chuckles. "And let's not forget Herst!"

Henry laughs, too. "Can't forget 'The Third Musketeer!'" Bri has heard a couple stories about their childhood and this guy has come into them quite a bit.

Peter clears his throat. "I said some *awful* things to you and our friendship stopped!" He looks over at Bri. "Seems the Lord is blessing us even when we're not looking." Peter softly smiles at her and she smiles in kindness; she feels David squeeze her shoulders a bit.

"All I remember is that it was hard for you to understand, but I felt that when you were ready, you'd reach out. Only now I'm guessing life with kids, businesses, Newhaven, *and plain stubbornness on both our parts*, played a large part." He looks at Bri, but still talking to Peter, "And as you said, outside circumstances were always in Divine play...perhaps even long ago."

Maggie laughs a little. "It *has to be* Divine intervention because how on earth did Bri and Katie end up on an island, *and* at The Worthington Estate of all the places, on their trip?"

"Isn't that the truth! Don't you think, Katie?" Bri laughs and Katie agrees. Bri tells them, "We were at The Primrose Café having hot cocoa and pastries, talking with the locals and *they* mentioned Newhaven to us!"

David scrunches his eyebrows together. "Was that the same afternoon I saw you for the first time in your hotel lobby?" Bri nods. Henry and Peter look at each other, Carlotta and Maggie look at them and each other; all of them are a little surprised.

Bri hears the girls splashing in the pool backyard and slips out to see them. When the girls see their mom, they wave and smile as she playfully and dramatically blows them kisses. The girls tell Bri about their wonderful day and how they "really like Uncle Joe's cousin and *your boyfriend*!" While it's a relief that the girls like David, Bri wonders how they will react when he is part of their immediate family and life would dramatically change?

Carlotta gets up and excuses herself, and motions for Maggie to join her. It's not too long before everyone is in the backyard, gathered around the pool. David takes Bri's hand and he feels her tense up.

"It's all good, Love." He whispers. *"They know I'm* crazy *about you!"* He kisses her hand, and they hear, *'aaaw,'* from the girls. David winks at Bri.

Maggie introduces everyone and one of the girls ask, "Is David going to marry mom?"

Carlotta glances at Bri with a knowing smile, then looks at the girls. *"We sure hope so!"* She looks back and sees Bri's teary look. She goes and stands on the other side of her, wrapping her arm through Bri's. "It's obvious you're their mum, they look *just* like you!" She turns to Bri. "And we're *thrilled* to be instant grandparents." Bri silently gasps. Carlotta asks with concern, "I hope I'm not making you uncomfortable?"

Bri shakes her head as she nervously smiles and quickly wipes her tears. She holds up the hand that holds David's hand, their fingers laced together. She smiles at David and assures her, "I think we're good. I'm just so amazed at how all this seems to be falling into place…it's kind of scary, but a *good* scary!"

David pulls Bri into a kiss and dips her. The girls giggle, *'ooOOoo'* and playfully make kissing sounds like little girls would, just to tease them. He brings her back up and they pull apart laughing, along with everyone else.

The girls get serious. Emmie says, "We're happy for you, Mom!"

Natty has a huge smile. "We really are!" Then she playfully smiles saying, "Now we'll really get to travel!"

The girls giggle with Bri laughing and shaking her head. David pulls her closer and she relaxes, exhaling with contentedness.

An hour later, Peter, Carlotta, James, Jack, Katie, David and Bri pile into the limo out front and head for the hotel. Jack, James, and Katie decide to hit the nightlife and Bri suggests that David join them since she has an early morning of being at the airport at 6:00 am. David is only interested in staying with Bri. Jack isn't excited about going because of Katie, so at the last minute, Jack changes his mind and decides to stay in.

Peter, Carlotta, David, Bri, and Jack have appetizers brought up to the luxury 2-bedroom penthouse suite. Peter sits next to Bri because he has something on his mind.

"Bri, I'm going to ask you something and I need you to be honest with me, *regardless* if you think it'll hurt my feelings."

Confused, she shifts to face Peter and hesitantly says, "*Okay.*"

"I have it on good authority that Henry confided in you about our falling out." Bri sucks in and holds her breath, unsure of what question comes next. "How much did Henry hate me for all the horrible things I said?" She shakes her head as he continues. "I never understood how he could walk away from his family, his home, *from his future*, all to go to America? Of course, my words weren't so mildly put." He looks down. "I felt so helpless...he was giving it all up, *everything*...and for what?!"

"*For* everything!" Bri blurts out.

He looks at her, a little hurt. "*For* everything?"

Bri puts her hand on top of Peter's and he sees a special kindness in her eyes. "When someone finds their spiritual path, they walk it *with the Spirit*. They'll leave everything, to *gain* everything...they learn to look at things, decisions, LIFE, from an eternal perspective!" She gives him a small smile. "Peter, he didn't walk away *from* you, he was walking *to* something bigger, something eternal. It wasn't about you or your family, but it had *everything* to do with following the guidance of the Spirit. Faith is knowing *and trusting* the Spirit *will* lead you to a better life than you could *ever* do on your own and, well, *that's worth everything!*" She glances at David, then continues. "There's a Divine Plan to get us on our 'spiritual path.' Henry's path brought him here. He has a successful law firm that provided well for his family, raised wonderful sons within a loving marriage. And *my spiritual path* needed to cross into theirs for several reasons." She lovingly looks at David and he winks at her. She looks back to Peter, "Had Henry and Maggie never moved here, it would've had a domino effect on other people's lives." She sees Peter nod as he takes in what she's saying. "One of the hardest things we mortals have a difficult time doing, is *trusting* the Lord *really does* know what He is doing, even if we don't understand *how* He will do it. As we learn to let go of the control we *think* we have, we eventually realize *we never had control*, only choices. Then we have to learn to make *better choices* so we can be blessed with *better consequences*."

That statement affects not only Peter, but also Carlotta, Jack, and of course, David. Jack and David already knew she had a strong belief system, but her faith is inspiring!

"I've never thought about it like that..." Peter admits.

"Another reason being that all these years I've been adopted into the family and it's like I've always been their daughter. *Now we know*, I *couldn't* have been born to them directly but I do belong to them." Her emotions start to bubble to the surface. She takes a deep breath. "Henry knows that even though you all may have been separated in mortality, families *are* eternally connected! Look at the emphasis on ancestry in Newhaven, the UK, Europe," she throws up her hands a little, "*all over the world!*"

Peter stands, then offers his hand to Bri to pull her up and into a hug. He fights back his tears and struggles to say, "*Thank you.*" He hugs her a little tighter and Carlotta hugs them both.

"Henry's the most loving, most forgiving man I've ever known, and he loves you all so much! He *never* lost faith in you, or your friendship!" Bri adds. "You know as well as I do, this is all 'water under the bridge' to him." Peter nods and hugs her a little longer, patting her back in a loving fatherly way.

He holds her face. "Thank you, Bri." He turns to Carlotta and wraps an arm around her as they walk into their bedroom.

Jack and David watch Bri. When she turns around, she scrunches her eyebrows together and asks, "What?"

"That was amazing!" Jack replies.

David adds, "We're just in awe of you, Love. You really are incredible!"

David, Jack, and Bri talk about everything and nothing for hours. Bri's eyelids are getting heavy and she can't believe the time. David wants Bri to stay but she has to start work in a few hours and she needs her clothes and toiletries. David smiles and points to her luggage they brought back with them and her clothes are back from dry cleaners, hanging on the hook above her luggage. She agrees to stay so she can get more sleep, rather than spend the time traveling back to her condo.

David says she could have his bed; he'd take the foldout the couch. She shakes her head and says, "I will sleep on one of the couches. Really, its fine."

"I *will be* sleeping on a bed!" He gestures to the couch.

Bri raises her eyebrow. "I still see a couch." Jack lightly chuckles.

"Et tu, Jack!" David teases him.

"What can I say?" Jack shrugs. "She's prettier than you!" Bri giggles and winks at Jack.

David exhales and says, "If I pull out the bed, will you be satisfied?"

"Yes!" She happily replies.

He shakes his head, laughing. "For as exhausted as you are, how do you still have a sense of humor?!"

"*Believe me*, it's a short window *and it won't last long.*" She informs them.

He pauses as he looks over at Jack and both say, "Noted." Jack takes the throw pillows and throws them at Bri.

She throws one at each of them. "You both are lucky I'm too tired to throw them back very hard."

David is yanking the bed out while Bri grabs extra blankets and pillows. Then she grabs her toiletries bag and pajamas on her way to the bathroom. When she is finished and David is getting ready for bed, Bri sneaks to the pull-out-bed and crawls in, asking Jack not to say anything. He quietly laughs.

She is just about asleep when she hears David's protesting. He crawls over to her. "I will carry you to bed." He smiles against her cheek, then kisses it.

"I'm *in* bed! Just snuggle with me." She grabs his hand and wraps his arm over her. "We're out in the open and Jack is on the other couch; plus, you'll be on top of the covers again."

"Now this I can approve of but let me grab a pillow and another blanket." He replies.

Her "...*kay*" is barely audible. By the time he gets back, she is asleep.

He gets comfortable snuggling with her and places a kiss on the curve of her shoulder. It isn't long before both men are also asleep.

CHAPTER 13

Imperfectly Perfect Spontaneous Date

Bri's 4:30 alarm goes off and she quickly shuts it off. She goes to slide out of bed without waking David up, but he holds her tighter.

"You're *seriously* not thinking of sneaking away again?" He asks.

"You make it sound selfish! Obviously, my alarm woke you up, and probably Jack, too! I'm trying to let you two sleep because this is too early for *normal* people to be awake!" She tells him. "Besides, I'm just going into the bathroom to get ready for work, I'm not *leaving*."

"For a non-morning person, you're pretty awake and sassy." Jack notes from the other couch.

"Just because I don't *like* getting up early, *Mister* Carlisle and *Mister* Worthington, doesn't mean I won't. I have a job to do and it requires an even earlier wake up time this morning, I just don't have to like it." She tells them.

"Oh-ho, you *are* annoyed this morning." Jack notes without opening his eyes.

David looks from Jack to Bri confused. "Why?"

"I didn't *want* to wake you and yet here we are." She says a bit grumpy.

"Lucky for you, I *am* a morning person. Jack and I are up around this time *normally* to go workout."

"Yeah! In *your* time-zone!" She retorts. "This is even earlier than that!"

He runs his hand through her hair to the back of her neck pulling her close, but just before he kisses her, he adds, "This is how I want to wake up in the mornings with you from now on." He presses his lips to hers. "I also plan on waking you up like this, too..." He kisses down her neck.

"Mmm, I *could* get used to that...it'd be hard *not* to be in a good mood waking up to that and such a handsome face." She sweetly kisses him. He smiles, giving her one last peck before she gets up and goes to get ready for work.

When she is about ready to go, she comes out to the living room. David and Jack are dressed to go workout. David has a pastry and a glass of milk waiting. She eats it while scanning her schedule.

David walks over to her as she says, "I'm free at 11:00, so if you want to do lunch—."

"I'm there!" He quickly replies. "I'll text later for an address."

"Text both Amy and me. I should be in my office, but she'll respond quicker if I can't." She stops and turns to Jack. "If you're not busy, you're welcome to come." She smiles at him.

He wants to join them, but he needs to keep distance between Bri and his heart as much as possible. "James wanted to go see The Lincoln Memorial and I'm not sure where else."

"Okay. Have fun!" She tells him.

She finishes her pastry and throws her purse over her shoulder. She texts Amy quick about The Duke and Duchess of Newhaven being in town and needing to ensure their security, including David's, with the various agencies in town.

She tells David and Jack, "Amy will make the arrangements. Plus, you'll have a little security this point forward, and your parents may have additional security added to what they already have, but the specifics are up to those agencies."

"That's not necessary." David tells her.

"Actually, it *kiiind* of is. Technically now that your parents are here, you're on all the various law enforcement agencies' radar, of sorts...not to mention any enemies," she cuts him off knowing what he's going to say, "both known *and unknown, Mister* Worthington."

"Ah. So, we're a responsibility." David teases.

"Let's just say our professional paths are crossing, nothing personal." She grins and kisses his cheek.

He grabs her and kisses her firmly. "I guess I never thought about paths crossing professionally, but it's *always* personal, Love."

"I never think about it either. I forget your 'heir' because I love *you*, and I've been too wrapped up in *you and us*, that I forgot this is part of your life."

He puts his forehead to hers. "I like the sound of that."

"Of what?" She asks.

"That you see me for me, *and* you're wrapped up in *me and us*! Only I'd say all this is now a part of *our life*."

"Don't you mean our *lives*, plural?" She asks.

He shakes his head. "No. Marriage will combine *our lives* into one, side-by-side paths."

Bri puts her purse down, wraps her arms around him and kisses him with all the love she can. "I always see you! Not only are you the man I love, but when I see you, I see the man who loves me!"

"Oh, I do love you! Don't ever doubt that!" He smiles and kisses her once more before she leaves.

She takes her purse and goes to the door. She opens it and pauses, turning to them with a mischievous smile. "Keep in mind I have the authority to ask for even more security to be added to yours, so behave yourselves!"

They both chuckle. Jack throws a pillow at her saying. "*Now* you've made it tempting ditch security altogether!"

"*Ooo*, that sounds like a challenge, *Lord Carlisle*." She laughs. "Don't make me teach *you* a lesson when you were learning so well *by observation*!" She smiles with an over exaggerated wink as she shuts the door and the guys chuckle some more.

She goes down to the small entourage in front of the hotel that is going to the airport to pick up the Ambassador and his family. She is dreading the Ambassador's son's arrival.

Waiting out on the tarmac, Bri talks to the staff and prepares them that this may be a tough week. They all need to stick together and remember to laugh and joke when they can, but certain jokes need to remain private. They all agree and fist bump each other, including Bri.

They all watch the plane land and pull into position. The door opens and the stairs come down to sit at the edge of the red carpet that is rolled out to the limo. Ambassador Giovanni Lombardi is the first one off the plane, followed by his son, Antonio, and the Ambassador's wife, Callista.

The Ambassador has a Mediterranean look of short, dark brown hair, deep brown eyes, olive skin, a goatee, and a wonderful smile with white teeth. He is fit, just like his wife and son. His son, Antonio, is a younger version of his father, except Antonio is completely clean shaven and his smile isn't genuine. The Ambassador's third wife, Callista, may look like a 'trophy wife' with her beautiful petite figure, clothes tailored to perfection, long dark brown hair, dark brown eyes, and olive skin; however, she is *genuinely* nice and kind.

They walk up to Bri, and greet her with a kiss on both cheeks, and duck into the awaiting limo. Bri slides into the back seat of leading car with her driver, Mateo, driving. The entourage heads to the townhouse where the Ambassador and his family will be staying for the duration of their visit.

At the townhouse, Antonio gives Bri a gift. It's a beaded necklace that looks similar to a Catholic's Rosary Beads, only it is called *Komboloia*, or 'worry beads,' if Bri remembers the meaning correctly. Callista steps in and says they, as a family, want her to have them and hope they don't offend her; they hoped it would show they respect her, as well as her faith and spirituality. With that, Bri accepts the personal gift from Callista, and also the Ambassador; Antonio is *not* happy.

They freshen up, before the Ambassador leaves with Bri to go to The Embassy to begin his workday. Antonio is expecting Bri to keep him busy, but Bri has other things to do.

"We can go to lunch!" Antonio suggests.

"No. I have things to do and I already have a lunch date." Bri says.

"What about me? I came all this way to spend time with you. Don't blow me off for that joke of what you Americans call a 'pretty boy.'"

"If I would've known from the beginning you manipulated all this to get to me, I would've saved everyone the headache. We go over this every single time you're here, Antonio, and my feelings haven't changed; they *won't* change!" Bri states.

"I'll work to change your mind and I'll start by coming with you." He firmly tells her.

"*No!*" Bri is not fooling around. "Antonio, I love that 'pretty boy.'" She picks up her bag. "I have work to do and I don't have time to entertain you." Bri leaves before Antonio can protest.

Once at The Embassy, she sees the gala preparations are coming along superbly and she couldn't be happier! She tells her staff so, and thanks them all for their attention to the details, especially on such short notice.

"You're all an exceptional group, and I can't thank you enough for all you're doing for this event!" Bri sincerely raves.

In the car ride to her office building, she texted Amy about gift cards for all the staff this week. She returns a text with a 'thumbs up.' When they pull up to the office building, she sees David is outside waiting for her. Her face lights up when she sees him, and so does his for her. He helps her out of the car and gives her a sweet kiss on the lips.

"You're a wonderful sight!" She says, relieved to see him.

"My father and I just finished up with Uncle Henry for today and I want to take the woman of my dreams to lunch!" He happily smiles.

"Sounds great! If we run up to my office, I can gather my things and we can head over to my place, or out to Henry and Maggie's, for the rest of the day."

He laughs a little. "If gathering a few things means I have you all afternoon," he wraps his arms around her, "let's go get them!" He kisses her again.

While David waits for Bri to gather her things, he quickly arranges a flight to New York City. He remembered her saying she had never been there and that someday she wanted to go sightseeing and go to a Broadway Show.

David stays in the hallway and manages to arrange all that. He texts Amy enlisting her help with hotel rooms at The Plaza Hotel, or penthouse with two bedrooms; plus, they would also need a set of clothes and toiletries. She gives him a 'thumbs up' to his text.

David walks into Amy's office which has her desk on one side and a small reception area on the other. One has to walk between Amy's office area and the reception area to get to Bri's office. He slips Amy a credit card with a smile and mouths 'thank you,' before heading into Bri's office. She happily nods back with a knowing smile.

Bri finishes gathering her things and he takes her computer bag to carry out to the awaiting car. "I have a little change in plans." He playfully smiles.

"Oh really? And what might that be?" She smiles curiously.

"I'm whisking you away to 'The Big Apple!'"

"*Mister Worthington! Are you planning* another *romantic getaway?*"

"If you're up for it?!" He chuckles.

"I really shouldn't because of work, *but...*" she bites her lower lip with a smile and a desire to go.

"I promise I'll have you back to work in time for your first appointment in the morning!" He crosses his heart. "You can work on the plane and I'm sure Amy can handle it, should something come up."

Amy smiles at Bri. "You are going, one way or another!"

Bri laughs, "*I am?!*"

"Yep! I'll have Ken arrange a police escort, handcuff you if comes to that, whatever it takes; but *you* will *be on that plane!*" She stands and walks over to Bri getting serious. "Bri, you *finally* have the love you deserve and a man who is *crazy* about you *and* being *super* romantic right now! Don't ruin it for yourself, *nor* for that wonderful man!"

Bri smirks at David. "She *maaay* have a point..."

"May?" David teases back and she giggles.

"The jury is still out on your wooing techniques, although you are off to a great start with Dunfermline and Paris!" She winks and he is chuckling. She has a big smile and tells him, "Let's do it!" David happily smiles.

As they walk over to Amy's desk, he covertly takes his credit card back. He briefly holds it up mouthing 'thank you' again, while Bri hugs Amy goodbye and thanks her for being such a great friend.

Bri and David leave the office to go out to the car where Antonio watches them from a corner of the building. He is clinching his jaw in irritation as he watches them and he sees David kiss Bri before they get into the back seat of the car. He watches them as they pull away from the curb; he never loses and he isn't about to start. Mateo is happy for her and smiles to himself thinking he wouldn't be surprised if they eloped!

Before she knew it, David is showing Bri around New York City. The Statue of Liberty, Times Square, and Wall Street are all amazing to see as they discussed the history about them. He took her to a high-end clothing store for an evening dress for her and a new suit for him for their night seeing a Broadway Show. It is late into the evening before they arrive at the famous Plaza Hotel.

The Lord Newhaven entourage arrives and employees were addressing them as Lord and Lady Newhaven. When Bri goes to correct them, David gently lays his hand on her arm and she stops, not saying anything. He continues registering for their Penthouse Suite.

When they are taken up to their room, she whispers in his ear, "*Why couldn't I correct them?*"

"Why bother?" He lovingly smiles. "You will be soon enough!"

"You're persistent!" She tells him.

"No, Love," he wraps his arms around her, "I know I love you and you love me. *Aaand* I know you see us married, too, so I'm just keeping *our goal* in sight!" She lightly snorts a laugh.

David insisted Bri take the bedroom with a rooftop patio. Bri tries to hide her nervousness as she walks to the railing to look out over Central Park. However, when David gets close to her, he can sense it.

"Bri, don't." He says. "Please don't be thinking how you're going to push me away." He turns her to look at him. "Talk to me. We can work through whatever it is you're feeling."

"I'm not so sure what to think, or how to feel." She looks back out at Central Park and the various lights that illuminate it in the darkness. "You're used to all this! *I'm not!* I've built my career dealing with people who live like this *and expect all this!* And now..."

"*And now*, you'll build *your* life in it *with* mine!" He says.

"That's easy for you to say! You'll go back to Edinburgh and Newhaven, but I'll still have a job to do here in DC! Not to mention, your spending money on me that I'm not entirely comfortable with and the more you spoil me—." She closes her eyes and keeps them closed for a few seconds, while David patiently waits, and she tsks herself, too emotional to speak.

"Bri, look at me, Love." She hesitates a moment, but she does. "First. I understand you aren't comfortable with spending money that might be tied to The Worthington Estate, or Newhaven money in general, which just makes you more duchess material than you know; but it also goes to show you how alike we are." He tangles his hands in her hair. He smiles sweetly, hoping it will help put her at ease. "I'm not only the CEO of The Worthington Corporation, but I've made money in countless business ventures with the best business financial guru and genius there is, who happens to be my best friend and brother, Jack." She has a small, surprised look on her face. "His name should really be 'Midas' because his golden touch on anything and everything he's involved with becomes gold! I wasn't surprised when he hit the trillion mark a few years back and has drug me *willingly* with him; *he's that good!*"

She playfully smiles. "If you're selling me on Jack, you're doing a *great* job!"

"Ah, Love, only if you weren't already madly in-love with me." He kisses her with a little more than a tap. "Second. I'm sorry to say, but when you said you love me, too, you sealed your fate to me." He smirks as he wraps his arms around her waist.

"You *never* said I'd be doing that!" She says, keeping a serious poker face. "I take it all back!"

He looks at her just as seriously. "Not a chance in—!" She kisses him and unknowingly moans into his kiss, which starts to heat things up, so he quickly pulls their lips apart.

He exhales a whistle. "The way you moaned..." He rests his forehead to hers, working hard to quell some of the most intense desire he has had for her yet.

"If it's any consolation, I'm right there with you." She says with her eyes closed, foreheads still resting together. She holds her breath and after a minute, she exhales slowly. "David, I'm afraid..." she looks at him, "you have my heart, and I couldn't take it back if I wanted to!"

David ha a heart melting smile, "*Good*! You'll *never* get it back!" He kisses her again.

"Seriously though, if you keep this up, I'll expect you to spoil me all the time." She tells him.

"Not 'if,' Love." He holds her face and lovingly smiles. "I plan on spoiling you for an eternity."

She smiles sweetly, "Thank you, My Love! This was a *perfect* afternoon and evening!" She taps a kiss to his lips.

"My pleasure!" He kisses the inside of her wrist. "But if we were married, this night would end *more* perfectly." He playfully grins.

"For the record though, you don't have to go all out all the time, like today. Romance to me includes a text or a call during a busy day; or a walk together," she touches his face, "or even a tiny flower." She is referring to the teeny tiny flower he gave her that Saturday night they were in the gardens.

"How about we get ready for bed and sit outside for a while?" He suggests to her.

"I'd like that, but it's getting late and I was up early, so I'm not sure how long I'll last." She gives him a little smile.

They get ready for bed and snuggle in on a lounge chair. She feels so relaxed with David, so at home with him, she easily falls asleep. David carries her to bed and covers her up. He goes to his bedroom so when he gets up to go exercise in the morning, *his* alarm won't wake her up.

CHAPTER 14

Imperfectly Perfectly Alarming

The next morning is Wednesday, and Bri wakes up to David kissing her shoulder, then down to her neck. It took her a few seconds to remember where she was. She turns to him and puts her finger up for a 'just a sec.' She quickly runs to brush her teeth and when she comes back, she gets in the exact same position she was in.

"Good morning, Handsome!"

He softly chuckles. "Good morning to you, too, Beautiful! You're happy this morning."

"Of course! I'm with the handsome man I love and adore. The sun is shining!" She giggles. He loves the sound of her laugh.

"It's still early for many people," he gives her a pointed look, "especially those who aren't morning people!"

"Then I guess it's waking up to being kissed by the man of my dreams!" She hugs him, tucking her nose into his neck and inhaling. "You smell good!" She says and kisses the curve of his neck, just above the collar of his white t-shirt.

"I took my shower after I went to the hotel gym." He pulls back to look into her eyes, "I was hoping to order breakfast while you were in the shower and we can eat before we leave?"

"I think that can be arranged." She kisses him quickly then heads to the bathroom, grabbing her clothes along the way. "Surprise me, but nothing fancy; no sauces." She is answering his question about what she wanted for breakfast before he even asks it.

They eat breakfast and David asks how things are going for the fundraiser. She is pleasantly surprised things are going smoothly with only minor glitches here and there. She looks at his face and reads that isn't all he wants to know about.

She smiles with a knowing look. "You're wanting to know about Antonio."

David gives her a little smile. "I trust you! I'm just wanting to know how he's treating you and your employees."

She smiles sweetly. "Thank you. Yesterday morning I told him that I had a lunch date, that my feelings towards him hadn't changed, and they never would. I left before he could object to anything, but I probably should've stayed because he was ill-tempered after that. His father heard about it right before I did and stepped in for me."

"Maybe he'll back down?" David asks.

Bri shakes her head. "He'll have more tantrums to throw before the week is out. Unfortunately, they'll be louder with you around." She snorts a laugh as she remembers, "He refers to you as 'pretty boy.'"

David chokes a little. "I'm going to have to resist the urge to ask if he has a crush on me."

"Resist." She plainly responds. "*That won't go over well.*"

"You're probably right." He replies. They gather their things and leave for the airport. He gently grabs her arm to stop her. "*Please* be careful. Let me know if you need me there. I can stand in the hall, sit in a chair in the reception area, or in your office. *Whatever you need*, just let me know."

She smiles. "Thank you. That means a lot." She gives him a sweet kiss before she walks to the door.

When they have boarded the plane and settled in, David asks Bri what she has planned for the day? She tells him Amy has her light on appointments today.

He asks, "Are you available for lunch?"

"*Well*, I'm booked. That's my longest appointment of the day! It's with this *hot* guy I met across the pond last weekend."

For a brief moment, David wasn't sure where she was going, but then he grins. "Oh?"

She smiles. "Nnnhnnn."

He encourages her, "Tell me about this dashing gentleman who has put such an exquisite smile on your face!"

"He's the kind of man a little girl wishes for before blowing out the candles on a birthday cake!"

"I'm going to need more *specific* details." He kisses the inside of her wrist and up to the inside of her elbow.

Bri lightly laughs. "Shouldn't I keep *my* birthday wishes to myself?!"

"Ah, but your wish has already come true, hasn't it?" He handsomely smiles.

"How so?!" She smirks.

"You have him right here next to you!" He gestures.

"Really? I didn't see Jack anywhere?!" She teases and he tickles her. She kisses him, before getting a little more serious. "Seriously though, My Love, the man next to me is not only the hottest guy I've ever met, but he's also brilliant, funny, sweet, not to mention charming, and a *true* gentleman." She winks and hugs him. He kisses her shoulder and her eyes close as she feels the sensation he gives her with his kiss. "He's quickly becoming my best and greatest friend." Bri holds his jaw. "The best feeling in the world is loving and adoring him so much and feeling his love for me in return! It all makes my heart melt and my knees weak!" She gives him a firm, meaningful kiss as he embraces her a little tighter.

David rests his forehead to hers, "I *definitely* feel your love! I'm glad you can feel mine." She nods. He holds her hand, his fingers laced with hers, to his chest. "You're my best friend, too!"

She smiles with a twinkle in her eye, "I'll settle for being second to Jack and this '*Third Musketeer*.'" He chuckles and they kiss meaningfully before having to buckle up again.

He gets a playful grin on his face. "Once we become *intimate*," he kisses the back of her hand he's holding, "you'll *definitely* be closest to me."

She softly laughs. "I guess I can't argue that!"

When David drops Bri off at The Executive Office Building, he's going to run to Uncle Henry's office again and then be back later for lunch. He offers to escort her to her office, but she tells him the sooner he gets his business done, the sooner he comes back to her.

"Got it! I'm leaving now, but *not* without this..." he pulls her in for a kiss and a hug before releasing her. He watches her walk up the stairs and into the building before he leaves for Uncle Henry's law firm.

Bri beats Amy to work, but Antonio is somehow in her office. *'That's weird. My office should've been locked.'* She thinks to herself. Antonio had watched the kiss from the window and is still standing at the window when Bri walks in. His face shows his frustration, but he motions to the six vases of lavender flowers that are native to his home country, Reñiato.

"Thank you, Antonio, but I can't keep these for my office. I only accepted the beads yesterday because they were given at the townhouse *and* from the family, *in private*, but even that was pushing it. These are here, in my office, it's 'against the rules,' so-to-speak, for me to personally accept them." That's a big part of it; however, the rest of the truth is that they are from him *and* she can't stand the scent of lavender by itself! The scent has to be mixed with something stronger, like peppermint, for her to even tolerate the smell. "We try to spread the gifts around to public spaces for *all* to enjoy because all of us government employees serve the public. It's weird, but someone could say it's a 'bribe' somehow, then things could get complicated for serving your family in the future."

"We wouldn't want that." He forces a smile, which comes across creepy.

"Thanks for understanding." She takes a deep breath and wonders how she will put a stop to his advances...

Before she can say anything, Antonio asks, "Do you want to go to breakfast?"

She wants him out of her office and a busy public place *is* better to talk. Something about him makes her *extremely uncomfortable*...so much so, her skin crawls, but she manages to resist the urge to shiver.

"There's a coffee shop around the corner where I'll have a smoothie and you can have whatever you'd like. We need to have a serious discussion, Antonio." She tells him.

She doesn't understand why that comment makes Antonio happy? '*Ugh!*' She thinks to herself. She wants to talk to him so she can make it clear that the two of them are *never* going to be a couple!

Amy walks in and says, "Hi!" She stops when she sees Bri leaving with Antonio and has a questioning look.

Bri tells her, "We're going to the coffee shop. I'll text you in a few."

Amy nods in understanding. "The one around the corner with the smoothies?" She wants to be sure.

"That's the one!" Bri replies. Amy nods and gives a little wave as Bri walks out behind Antonio, shutting the door behind herself.

At The Coffee Shop, Antonio insists on ordering and paying. She relents, but she plans to watch him carefully to make sure he doesn't do anything to her drink; she wouldn't put it past him.

Bri texts Amy and David together letting them know she is at The Coffee Shop so she's in a busy place when she lets Antonio down a little harder. David says that if she needs him to text him. Amy basically said the same thing, and she is not afraid to send Ken and his partner in to rescue her with DCPD reinforcements! Bri smiles at that.

She watches Antonio when his name is called, all the way over to the table. He sits across from her and gets comfortable. He reaches for her hand, but she pulls away.

"This *isn't* a date, Antonio."

"Why not?" He is disappointed. "We like each other, no?"

"No! *I keep telling you*, I'm *not* interested. And now I'm dating someone."

Antonio's eyes show annoyance. "Long distance relationships never work, so why not cut him out." She knows he means, 'cut him loose.'

"I never said it was long distance."

"I've seen the articles." He arrogantly states.

Bri is assuming he is referring to the gossip columns. "First of all, you're being hypocritical wanting a relationship with me when you live in a different country *further away*! Long-distance relationships don't work *long-term* when neither person is willing to make necessary sacrifices to make it work."

"I'm already making the sacrifice in our relationship." Antonio states.

"*We don't have a relationship!*" Bri says firmly, trying to keep her anger in check.

Antonio ignores her. "I'm already moving here. I'm buying a place in 'The D.C. Gardens Complex!'"

Bri's face loses all color from shock. "*What?!*" The 't' is enunciated.

"Living closer, we can spend more time together." Antonio smiles.

"*HHHooow* did you know where I live?" Bri asks with panic setting in.

"I hired what do you say...private investigator?"

"Antonio, I'm NOT okay with this! This is stalking and you've violated my privacy on *so many levels!*" She needs to get out of there, so she stands up and grabs her purse.

"Where are you going? We're not done!" Antonio's confused and starting to get upset.

Her voice volume is a little louder, but she isn't yelling, "You had *NO right!*" He shifts, getting ready to stand up. "*Don't get up!*" She tells him. "I'm freaked out right now, Antonio! Stay down, or I'll *make you* stay down!" He starts to laugh as he rises a little from his chair, but abruptly stops when she raises her eyebrow and pointedly glares at him. He slowly sits back down in his chair showing her he is going to stay sitting. Bri puts her purse on her shoulder and is about to step away, when she turns back to ask, "Was your father okay with this?!"

"He paid for it!"

'*Of course, he did!*' She thinks to herself, rolling her eyes. "Stay away from me, Antonio! I mean it! Stay.*Away!*"

He yells after her, "I *will* have what I want, Bri!"

Once Bri is outside, she calls Mateo and asks him to pull the car around for her in front of the office building. Then she calls over to The Embassy to make sure the Ambassador is there and asks them to let him know she is on her way over to talk with him; she knows he will wait, even if he has an appointment. She walks to Mateo and the car, hoping to calm her nerves just enough *not* to punch the Ambassador in the face. She has never done that before, but she didn't know if this would be the first time, or not.

After reading Bri's text, David wraps up his meeting with Uncle Henry as soon as he can and rushes over to her office building. She isn't back upstairs yet, so he goes back outside to wait for her on a beautiful day. He is descending the outside stairs of the building when he sees Bri walking up to Mateo and the opened back door of the car. He runs to catch up, calling after her. Mateo sees him and Bri hears him just before she places her foot inside the car.

He could see she was incredibly angry and goes to ask, only before he says anything, she abruptly puts her hand up to cut him off. "David, it's rare I'll ever ask this, but *not* a word right now! I need to stay angry. I promise you'll understand why if you come with me, or I'll explain later, but I need to leave *right now*." He goes to grab her hand and she pulls it back. "No. You'll calm me down and trust me, I *need* to stay angry. So, either get in and keep to yourself, or I'll meet you wherever when I'm done." She gets in the back seat and slides over for him to choose. He is curious and gets in, honoring her request by keeping to himself. She texts her boss briefly of the situation.

David sees they have pulled up to an Embassy. He gets out first, then Bri. She does accept his hand to help her out but she quickly lets go. Mateo closes the car door and then waits patiently by leaning against the car and pulls out his phone, but a friendly security guard comes up and starts to chat with him.

When Bri walks in, she asks where the Ambassador is? He has been waiting for her and someone runs to get him. The people there have never seen Bri angry like this and it's unnerving for some of them. The staff watches the scene between Bri and the Ambassador play out.

The Ambassador walks to Bri with his arms stretched out, happy to see her. "Bri! To what do I owe—"

"Cut the crap, Ambassador!" She tells him. He is stunned to silence; David and the staff have mouths that drop open; they can't believe what they're hearing. "Did you, or did you not, hire a private investigator so your son could stalk me?!" She doesn't give him a chance to answer. "Are you *out* of your *mind*?! I thought we respected each other, Ambassador?!"

"We do!" He quickly chimes in! He wants to calm her down, he doesn't like seeing her angry, *especially with him*!

"Really?! Your son knows where I live, and you're buying a condo *right there*! This crosses a *huge* line, Ambassador! I can't express to you how *violated* I feel right now!"

"Bri, I promise you I had no idea! I'm so sorry!" The Ambassador says remorsefully. Bri's about to forgive him, but she wants him to say more before she does. He explains, "Antonio said he wanted to go back to school and get his masters. He thought looking into places and areas close by school would allow him to walk to school, and walk wherever else he needs to go, without having a car service all the time. He also wanted to be close to The Embassy for when I travel back and forth. That's what he said this private investigator was for; to figure out options. Unfortunately, you never crossed my mind. *Only recently*, he mentioned his continued interest in you; *that's why we came back*! That's why I insisted on you cutting your vacation short, to help him either win you over, or help him move on." He looks at her.

Bri's eyes fill up with tears and the Ambassador approaches her, putting her hand between his hands, patting the top of her hand a couple times. "I promise I'll get to the bottom of this. I've begun the process of buying a condo in this 'Gardens Complex,' but I will see what I can do to back out of the purchase."

David steps forward. "Sorry to interrupt, Sir, but I may be able to help with the condo." He offers a hand to the Ambassador to shake and they do. "I'm David Worthington."

"Worthington? As in 'The Worthington Corporation' in Scotland?" He asks.

"Yes, Sir." David respectfully answers.

"Ah, yes! I know your father, Peter! Our companies have done business together a few times."

"We have, Sir. Right now, I'm finalizing paperwork for the corporation to buy the entire block 'The DC Gardens Complex' is on, which means—."

"You're the one I would talk to about withdrawing my purchase." The Ambassador says to David.

"Exactly. Look, it seems to me you two have great respect for each other and I believe you when you said you didn't know what your son was really up to. Let's just stop the paperwork and refund your money; no penalties and both sides will just walk away."

"I don't want to be unfair to you, David, or your company; this is business. Let's set up a meeting to discuss that piece further." He looks back to Bri, whose hand he is still holding. "In my country, lying is one of the worst things you can do. It's right after murder and assaulting women and children. Antonio lied to me numerous times to accomplish all this. He *will* answer for it!" His angry tone is noted.

"Thank you, Ambassador, this means a lot to me!" She squeezes his hand and pleads, "*Please*, just keep him away from me and from The Embassy, because I need to be in and out as we get closer to Friday night. I get he might attend the fundraiser Friday night, *but that's it.*"

"He *won't* be attending." He gives her a small, apologetic smile. "I can feel your hand trembling! I'm sorry, Bri. *Truly.*" With kindness in his eyes, he smiles sympathetically. He whispers so only Bri can hear, and David since he is standing right there, "*Bri, you know how special you are to me?*"

She nods. "I do." She gives him a faint smile. David is curious about that but he will ask her about it later.

"*Please try not to be disgusted with me when I tell you this.*" He continues to whisper and she nods. "*I will protect you at all costs. Do you understand?*"

"I do, but..." She starts to shake her head quickly, but he hugs her tight. When they pull apart, she wipes a couple of tears and says, "Thank you and I'm sorry for coming in here and—."

"You have *nothing* to be sorry for! Coming in here like you did was understandable and I'm grateful our audience, both seen *and unseen*, stuck around to hear it all." He lightly laughs. "Perhaps next time, though, we can talk more privately?"

160

She hugs him again, then she sees Callista who smiles remorsefully and apologetically. She whispers to the Ambassador, "*Give Callista a chance, love might surprise you again!*" When they pull back, the Ambassador gives Bri a faint nod, then Bri goes over and hugs Callista, too.

Bri walks back over to David and the Ambassador as the men shake hands. It sounds like they made plans to meet about the condo purchase, or rather *un*-purchase now. One more tight hug from the Ambassador and she walks out of The Embassy holding hands with David; he laces their fingers together. David doesn't break the silence on their ride back to her office, so she can sort through things in her mind.

David and Bri pull up in front of her office building. Mateo puts the car into park and goes to get out but before he does, Bri asks him to give her and David a few minutes and he nods in acknowledgment. He gets out of the car and goes around to the back of the car where he half sits and half leans against it to give them privacy, but she can knock on the window to get his attention if she needs him.

Bri turns to David and when she looks at him, her eyes fill up with tears. When the words don't come, she pulls him into a kiss. He doesn't miss a beat and pulls her as close as he comfortably can, deepening their kiss. She feels so much love for him *and from him*. He hugs her as she relaxes in his arms and with the emotions from everything that has happened, tears begin to flow down her cheeks. He feels her trembling because she is really scared and his heart breaks for her; he wants to fix everything for her.

"It's okay..." He holds her tighter.

"Don't let go!" She hugs him tighter, too. "Not just yet."

"I won't!" He continues to hold her firmly. "I'm not going anywhere."

"I think I'm starting to believe that."

"Hey, hey, now," he pulls back a little, "starting to?" He gently teases her.

"Well, no, not 'starting,' sorry. Bad choice of words there." She digs in her purse for tissues to wipe her eyes and face.

"I think I can let that slide, considering." He smiles and runs his hand to the back of her head. "Let's get you inside."

They climb out of the car. Bri thanks Mateo for waiting and he replies, "Not a problem." He waves to them, then goes to park the car until she needs to leave again soon.

David walks Bri up to her office. She tells him, "I've had this feeling that something bad is going happen and I can't seem to shake it."

He stops on one of the landings and looks at her. "With Antonio?" She nods. He suggests, "Then let's get you bodyguards! Better yet, we say there's a 'family emergency' and take you back to the UK!"

She laughs a little. "How do I explain *that* when I'm not from the UK?" She cups his cheek with her hand. "Thank you for the thought. Antonio will be leaving Saturday and I can relax then!"

Inside Amy's office, Bri sees she has re-homed all but two of Antonio's vases of flowers so far. David sees the flowers and asks Amy, "Who's the lucky guy?!" When her eyes flick to Bri, he knows. He asks with annoyance towards a man he has never met, "How many did Antonio send?!"

"Six, I think?" She looks at Amy with a questioning look.

Amy confirms with an agitated, "*Yyyep!*" She is annoyed for her boss, who has grown to be her closest friend.

"All the same?" He asks Bri.

"All lavender, which is great!" Bri plainly replies.

David's jaw clenches and they realize he doesn't know. Amy tells him, "Bri *hates* the smell of lavender!"

David looks at Bri and she is giving him a small smile; relief shows on his face. Bri walks up and wraps her arms around him. "Admit it, *Mister* Worthington! You were worried just a *tiny* bit!"

He wraps his arms around her replying, "I'll only admit that you will *always* have me, Love...if you want me?"

She is starting to feel better and teases, "You're growing on me!"

Amy snorts a laugh. "You two are so cute together!" She smiles. "Now," Amy clears her throat to get back to business, "Mateo will take you for your dress fitting and David for his tuxedo fitting. I guess everything arrived right away this morning and if they need to make adjustments, they will have a little more time to make them."

Amy asks about Antonio, and Bri gives her the story quickly as they waited for Mateo to text when he is out front. Amy then asks, "What's the Ambassador going to do about it?"

Bri lightly shakes her head replying, "He said he'd take care of it."

"What does that mean?" Amy asks.

David is also curious and adds, "What did the Ambassador mean when he said, '*at* all *costs*' earlier?"

Bri grows quiet as she looks away from them, somewhat lost in thought. She explains, "It means he'll protect me to the death of himself or Antonio, *or both*." Amy and David look at each other with surprise and concern.

David replies, "Don't get me wrong, I'm glad he's on our side, but why is he so committed to you?"

"Yeah. I've wondered that, too, Bri." Amy adds.

She looks at both of them. "The Ambassador confided in me after a particularly frustrating um...*discussion*, we'll say. First off, he was still married to his second wife, but they would divorce shortly after leaving DC that time. I wasn't backing down because he had treated the staff unbelievably rude with language that I won't repeat, and some was in his foreign language I couldn't repeat, but it only seems logical it was just as foul. Anyway, he had said some horrible words directed towards me, I said he was a despicable human being and if he ever talked like that to me or the staff again, I'd 'blacklist' him. When I started to leave, he yells something to the effect of 'Don't you walk away from me, Maya!'"

Amy gasps, "He called you his wife's name?! Er, wait..." She remembers that wasn't his previous wife's name. The text came through that Mateo was out front, so Bri tries to finish quickly.

"I stopped in my tracks because his wife's name *wasn't* Maya. I turned and looked at him; he hadn't realized his mistake and tells me that I could leave only with his permission because he's '*The Ambassador*!' I said I wouldn't stand for the verbal abuse, nor would I force anyone else to endure his mistreatment! Telling him goodbye, I left, even with him yelling for me to stop again." She takes a deep breath. "The Ambassador called my boss to apologize, but the Ambassador suddenly realized I never said anything to him. My boss was a little disappointed that I hadn't because, from what the Ambassador had told him, it was disgraceful. I agreed but felt there was more to it than just a selfish, self-centered, entitled diplomat wanting his way, and not caring how he treated people; *that wasn't his first visit*. My boss understood my reasoning, but made me promise to loop him in next time there was a problem *with anyone*. My boss said he would always support me." Bri takes a deep breath. "Now, the next day, a Friday I believe, Amy set up a luncheon at The Embassy with the Ambassador."

Amy adds, "*After* he apologized and said he owed Bri a much more detailed apology, *in person*."

"He did. While I was uneasy about going, I'm glad I did because he opened up, perhaps more than he should have, but I think he was lonely and needed someone to talk to. I eventually asked about Maya and he explained Maya, his first wife, would walk away from him when he was being downright rude. It angered him, even though she had every right to do so. I still remember his loving smile to his day as he talked about her." Bri smiles in fondness. "He said Maya was the love of his life and I reminded him a lot of her. But there was sorrow when he told me she died giving birth to Antonio. The Ambassador sees Antonio as a part of her and he spoils his son to try to be a good father, thinking it somehow honors Maya."

"So, Antonio's the way he is *out of guilt*?!" Amy asks, slightly appalled.

Bri gives Amy an understanding smile. "I think it's also motivated by a deep love for Maya, not realizing it has been detrimental to Antonio in the end...*at least until more recently*. Now, more than ever, the Ambassador has to face the fact that his son is something like a narcissistic sociopath, or whatever the diagnosis. No parent, who is truly trying to do their best for their children, dreams their child will one day end up like Antonio has become! I believe the Ambassador pictured his grown son differently than who Antonio is today. Most parents want their children to be well-rounded, loving, and giving; to find love and be happy, successful...the Ambassador is no different. I do feel

164

for him as a parent and wish things were different for him and Antonio." She pauses and takes another deep breath. "Anyway, the Ambassador asks for me because I remind him of Maya. His wife Callista, as far as I know, has no idea and I would *never* want her to find out the Ambassador is still fanning the flame for his first wife. Bri reaches into her purse and pulls out a box. "Antonio tried to pass this off as his gift, but Callista said it was from all three of them." David and Amy look at what is inside.

"This is beautiful!" Amy gasps. "It's handmade!" She says, reading the informational card that is tucked in the box with it.

David has been really listening and is admiring the Ambassador through Bri's eyes. He quickly understands, "These are really from the Ambassador, aren't they?!"

"The Ambassador has never outright said it's a gift from him, but these are 'worry beads,' or some would call them 'prayer beads.' The Ambassador and I have had many personal talks about spiritual things and we have a mutual respect for each other's beliefs and deep spiritual roots. Callista is not stupid and she sees there's a fondness between us, but I try to make sure she knows it's sweet and nothing more." She tells David, "Just like I need you to know."

"*That's why* you hugged her before we left." David follows along.

"Right. I hope it helps her to know it's only friendship, that's it. Just as I hope you do, too!"

"I do, Love." He kisses her temple.

"Well," she continues, "the Ambassador would know about spiritual things and he would also know I couldn't necessarily accept a personal gift like that straight from him. He probably thought I would feel better at accepting this gift if it was given from both he and Callista." Bri looks at her watch...

She and David rush out to Mateo. Amy texts Mateo that they are on their way, then she calls the dress shop. David and Bri apologize to Mateo; he isn't bothered by it, just worried about getting her to her appointment on time.

Mateo jokes, "It's part of my job description!" David and Bri lightly laugh as they get into the back seat of the car.

CHAPTER 15
Imperfectly Perfect Faith

David and Bri get to the dress shop only one minute late, which is a miracle this time of day. David tries on his tuxedo and only a couple of alterations are needed. Everyone that is going to the event with Bri was in earlier for their fittings; Amy had picked up the extra tickets for Bri for them.

"Looking good, Handsome!" Bri says smiling and biting her lower lip.

Bri tries on her dress and it doesn't need any alterations. She won't let David see her dress until Friday night.

"Ugh! You tease! You saw me in my tux, so it's only fair..." He says with pleading eyes.

"Yeah, but I've seen you in a tux already." Bri giggles through the curtain but cracks the top of it to look at him and adds, "Think of it as building up the anticipation!" She gives him a little flirting wink.

He gets close for only her to hear, "*IF* I could have my way with you afterwards, anticipation is great! Since we're waiting..." he gives her a sad look, "...you're going to hit me with your gorgeousness all at once, like last Saturday, and it's utter torture!"

She gives him a playful, but thoughtful smile. "I didn't know you liked me then, so that doesn't really count."

"Take pity, Love!" He pleads.

She exhales. "*Alright*...but just this once!"

David laughs. "Oh-ho, so I'll have to make sure I marry you *before* we have another black-tie event to go to!"

"A wedding usually *is* a 'black-tie event!'" She has a cheeky grin.

"Right, but I'll also get to have my way with you that night!" He grins while she giggles. He studies her; she may be more ready than *she thinks* she is ready to get married. He steps back from the curtain so she can step out of the dressing room.

He smirks. "Once again, I'll have the most stunning date on my arm!" He kisses her hand and the ladies gush with audible 'aaaws.'

She whispers, *"Technically, I was on Jack's arm that evening."*

"He escorted you for *me!"* He steps closer. *"Why is it, the cheekier and sassier you are to me, the more I want to drive* you *crazy with desire?"* He runs a finger down her arm, leaving a trail of goosebumps.

She bites her lower lip, smiling as she lifts her eyebrows and shrugs before ducking back into the changing room. She says loudly, "Maybe you need to re-channel your energy and thought processes!"

He laughs. "That's *not* going to happen!"

While Bri is changing, David arranges for the dress and tux to be delivered to the hotel penthouse where they will be getting ready that evening. He secretly tries to pay for everything, including those going with them, but finds out Jack already did; so, David adds to the generous tip Jack has also already given them for their rush.

Back inside the dressing room, Bri changes and has the strangest feeling of being in danger, but brushes it aside as being paranoid. She hears the place go silent and comes out of the dressing room to find extra security, a few familiar faces. She knows who it is, then it's confirmed when her boss comes through the front door.

She grabs her phone in a slight panic, looking at it as she says to him, "Did I miss something, Sir?"

"No, no, Bri, everything's fine. I talked with the Ambassador and he has talked to his son about staying away from you; there was even a threat or two he gave his son." He gives an 'eek' look but doesn't say anything more on that. "I was worried about you and told the Ambassador that I didn't trust his son and we needed to protect you. He agrees and is allowing a couple of Secret Service Agents be added to his detail without his son knowing. Also," her boss points to the front door as someone walks in, "Bri, this is FBI Supervisory Special Agent Oliver McMasters. He volunteered to be assigned to you, for as long as you needed, because of the Ambassador's son. Now, I called a few people and they suggested we do this to keep you safe, so please don't fight his."

"I won't." She quietly says.

Her boss does a double-take in surprise. "*Wow*! You really *are* scared?!"

"When I was in the dressing room, I felt like I was in danger," the ladies in the shop are confused until they hear Bri say, "which is ridiculous to think back there." She puts her things down in a chair. "I'm trying to push that aside and not be neurotically paranoid."

Everyone watches Bri, but McMasters starts to carefully look out the windows. He has been around long enough to know to take victim's instincts seriously, even when they tend to brush them off. McMasters then steps over to shake her hand and she takes that moment to introduce David to her boss, The President of the United States. David had wondered if this was The President when he walked in, but he is surprised Bri never mentioned who her boss was before; *then again*, it does go with what he knows of her already...she wouldn't show off who she has met or knows, let alone who she works for. She respects a title and a position, even if she doesn't always like the person holding the title or position. Besides, she wouldn't have necessarily wanted people to know she reports directly to The President of the United States, particularly those who are most difficult to please.

McMasters turns to Bri and locks eyes with her to make sure she hears him. "Ma'am, *please* don't push your instincts aside! Those instincts, the little hairs on the back of your neck that stand up, the feeling of dread and such, are all there to keep you safe; so, whenever you feel them, *I need to know about them*! Let me check them all out because I don't want you to brush them aside when we can use them to protect you."

Bri softly replies, "Alright, Agent McMasters."

"Please, just 'McMasters,'" he gestures, "let's sit."

"Well then, 'Bri' will do, McMasters." She smiles.

"Bri, I don't want to scare you more, but you need to understand this can go one of two ways: we hope he gets frustrated and leaves well enough alone." McMasters explains, inviting David to sit next to her with a hand gesture, which David does, while McMasters pulls up a chair across from her. "It's important for both of you to know how bad this could also get. Given his history of what happens when he doesn't get his way—."

"You mean he throws a tantrum?" Bri plainly asks.

"*Exactly*! In this situation, though, it could get ugly. He went to great lengths to learn everything about you, to live close to you, and to get you back here early from your vacation. We did talk to the P.I. and he looked horrified when we told him what happened. He said he had no idea and believed Antonio was trying to find his girlfriend's long-lost sister, and that his girlfriend wanted to live closer to her sister. He asked if we would give you his apologies and he would destroy everything he's already gathered. I said we wanted it all and *we* would destroy it. Which he did hand it all over and he let our computer specialist wipe off your files from his laptop."

"I never blamed him." Bri says. "He's a victim, too! This is all on Antonio!"

McMasters agrees. "I've already briefed Lord Newhaven's detail before I came inside."

"Please, 'David' for me, too." David says to McMasters, who nods.

"David has an agent assigned to him and he's been briefed because Antonio sees David as a rival and he's ultimately in danger, too!"

"Oh my…" she covers her mouth with her hand. She removes her hand and says, "David, *he's right!*" She stands up and steps around McMasters; she is panicking. "You shouldn't be here! What was I thinking having you come with me on Friday?! You *have to* go back to Scotland! You can't stay here!" Tears start to stream down her face and one of the ladies hands her a tissue. "This morning, I watched Antonio like a hawk when they gave him my smoothie, because I think he's capable of *anything*. And if he's capable of anything with *me*, then it isn't a leap for him to do worse *to you!*"

David walks over to her, she goes to back away when he gets too close, but he takes her into his arms and hugs her close. "I love you!"

"*I know!* Which is *why*—."

"*Stop it, BriaLynn!*" He firmly says and she freezes. He pulls back and holds her face in his hands. "You need to hear me, because this is the only time we will *ever* have a discussion like this. I'm *NOT* leaving. I'm not going to leave you behind to face this lunatic, nor any other mental person, without me!"

"I couldn't live with myself if anything happened to you, especially *because* of me!" She tells him.

"Don't interrupt me!" He sternly says. "I hear you AND McMasters! I know I'm in danger, *but so are you*! Even more so after you rejected him again this last time!"

"I do want you with me, but I need you to be safe!" She replies.

"*I need you safe* and I *need* to be here!" David says sternly.

"David—."

"*You heard me*! No! I'm not going to let you push me away! I'd be out of my mind with worry every single minute, of every single day! Being here, helping you, supporting you, this is where *I'm staying*! Would you do anything different if the situation were reversed?!" Bri peels her eyes from his and looks at the floor so David can't read her face, but he doesn't need to...he knows. "You'd do *the exact same thing*!" She nods as she fights not to cry, until he pulls her to him and wraps her in a tight, comforting hug. He feels her wrap her arms around his waist and she quietly cries.

There is a whisper of a plea, "*I don't want anything to happen to you, David*," she looks up into his eyes, "*if it did, I'd never forgive myself*."

He keeps one arm around her waist and looks at her. He tucks a strand of hair behind her ear before wiping her tears with the back of his forefinger. "There would be nothing for you to forgive, because you couldn't push me away, even though you tried!"

"Then maybe we should break up." She says flatly. "Maybe that would cool all this all down with Antonio as well!"

"No! *Absolutely not*!" He gives her a determined look. "Staying is *MY* choice, *not yours*! I *choose* to be here because *I love you*! This is no longer up for discussion, or this will turn into a huge fight and I *don't* want to fight with you. Okay?" She can only nod because of the lump in her throat. He takes her hand and laces their fingers, then holds them up saying, "We're in this *together*!" He kisses the back of her hand and then leads her back to where they were sitting. "McMasters, please, say all of it. We can only make informed decisions if we're actually informed."

"Well said." McMasters agrees. "If this gets bad, being informed could keep you *both* alive! If it goes as far as Antonio taking Bri," he looks at her, "trust yourself! Play along if you must, stall him as long as possible for us to get to you."

"*Never* go to a second location!" Bri remembers.

"I'm glad you've paid attention to Ken over the years." Bri is not surprised he knows Ken, she gets that a lot, but she is surprised when they know her. "Ken thinks the world of you! I'm starting to see why." He lightly smiles. "I know more of his advice will come to you, if the situation calls for it." Bri agrees. McMasters turns to David. "It's also important for you to play along. Deny feelings for Bri; or tell him he's the better man and you will 'bow out' of the relationship; whatever it takes until we get there, or you can flee, *or somehow defend yourself.*" The door opens behind Bri and David, McMasters acknowledges the gentleman.

"I should be heading back to the office." Her boss says. He shakes everyone's hands, but hugs Bri. He asks McMasters to keep him personally updated, then walks out the door and into his entourage; most of the security leaves with him.

Everyone else leaves and goes to Bri's office building and David walks with her and McMasters to the outside stairs into the building. David stops and says he'll be back in about an hour. After a quick kiss he watches Bri and McMasters go into the building. David walks with his security guy to an awaiting car.

Up in her office, McMasters looks everything over and gives it the 'all clear.' He tells Bri, "I'm going to go check the other offices of this floor to get a feel for the people and the layout." He pulls out his phone asking, "What's your number?" She gives it to him and it's what he has; he sends her a text for her to have his number. He tells her, "*Don't* leave this office without me." She nods.

When she turns to go to her desk, McMasters goes out and starts walking the hall, checking the offices and rooms on her floor, making note of the empty ones. Bri gets to work focusing on her to-do list. About an hour later, Amy went to the break room so she could be back before Bri leaves. Bri is just finishing up some things to wrap up for the day when Antonio walks in.

Bri looks up from her desk and freezes. She manages to pull her thoughts together and unemotionally asks, "What are you doing here, Antonio?"

"We need to finish our discussion from this morning." He says. Her phone rings, it's someone from The Embassy staff. He angrily snaps, "*Don't answer it!*" She slowly shows him she is 'ending' the call to send it to voicemail. He walks over and touches her face with his hand, but she pulls away.

"I thought I was clear this morning, Antonio." She softly reminds him.

He grabs her hair at the back of her head and jerks it; she lightly gasps. "Bri, it doesn't matter what you say, I *always* get what I want." He looks at her with a coldness in his deep brown eyes, making them look almost black. He pushes her head forward as he releases her hair.

She stops herself from rolling her eyes. "Well, you're just going to have to back down because my answer is 'no' and it will always be 'no' because *I'm not interested!*"

"I *want* you!" Antonio wraps a hand around her upper arm and jerks her up. "And I *will* have you!"

"Antonio, you're hurting me!" He squeezes harder. Bri inhales through her gritted teeth. She struggles through the pain to ask him, "Could this be that you just want what you can't have? When you get what you want, you always get bored and lose interest. It'd be the same here, Antonio! There's *nothing* special about me!"

He is not really listening. "My Father *will* force your hand!"

"No." She jerks her arm free. "He won't." She rubs her upper arm, but she can feel a dangerous evil has come over him. She tries a gentler approach, almost pleading with him. "*Only because I'm not worth all this*, Antonio! No one is worth all this...*effort!*" She adds, "*Certainly not me!*"

She walks to her office door, but as she starts to open it, he grabs her upper arm again and he slams the door with his other hand. He yanks her to him and says in a low, gruff, angry tone, "*Break it off with him!*" She was going to confess her love for David, but she can't open her mouth to say anything more. It's like her jaw was locked shut. "*Do it tonight*, or *you will* be sorry!" He sneers low and forcefully.

David bursts through the door and yells, "GET YOUR HANDS OFF HER!" David grabs Antonio and punches him. Antonio stumbles back a few steps and cowardly runs out of the room, holding his face.

McMasters is working his way back down the hall when he hears the commotion and comes running. Sadly, Antonio had already slipped into the nearby stairwell. David goes to run after him, but McMasters stops him and has him go back to Bri while *he* gives chase.

Back in Bri's office, David hugs her. "Are you alright?" He doesn't let her see his worried face. She nods with her head on his shoulder, his hand is on her head, hugging her close.

He moves to hug her around her upper arms and she squirms in pain. He lets go and pulls her sweater down to push up her short sleeve. He finds a red handprint and the start of an awful bruise forming; he starts to clench his jaw in irritation.

She gently pulls her arm away. "Can we leave?" She asks as she pulls her sweater back up over her shoulder.

"What happened?" He asks.

"Antonio was trying to make it clear he wants me, and he wasn't giving up; that he's essentially going to win." She rolls her eyes. "I tried to convince him that I wasn't worth all this; *no one is*! And maybe this is just about wanting what he can't have..."

He kisses her temple. "Gather what you need, we'll leave as soon as McMasters get back."

"I'm right here." McMasters says. "We can leave whenever you're ready." While Bri grabs her things, he explains that Antonio was finally arrested when they found him in his hiding place but says his arrest won't help. "Even though he doesn't have Diplomatic Immunity, he'll more than likely make bail without any kind of record, and this could make him even angrier."

"Make bail?" David swears under his breath. "And asking the Ambassador to leave him in jail would be asking too much." Bri reluctantly agrees.

174

As Bri looks at him and McMasters, a peace comes over her and she calmly, but firmly, tells them, "I'm as sure as I'm standing here that both of you will do *everything* in your power to protect me; *however*, you're both *human*. My *faith* knows the Lord has a plan for everyone, even me. You both need to know that *if* this ends in my death, it's part of *His plan* and there *is* a reason for my death!" She locks eyes with David and asks him, "Do you hear me? It's important you know my faith is in *His* Divine Plan; whatever it brings and wherever it leads!" She steps over to David who's blinking back tears at the *thought* of losing her. "My faith in His plan has made it where I could imagine there were pieces put into play years, *centuries*, ago in preparation for us to be brought together. Which means, I still have hope there's more to our story than this." She lovingly smiles with tears and kisses him tenderly. She steps back and says to McMasters, "I need you to know, too, my faith is in His plan and whatever happens, *it's what's meant to be*! If I die, it's my time and there's *nothing* anyone can do to stop it, *not even you*."

McMasters is a bit choked up, too, but nods. He clears his throat, "I can't see what good can come from having faith in all this, if it ends in your death?!"

"The answer to that question would come to you, McMasters, but not necessarily right away. I'm just preparing for the worst, while hoping it never comes to that either. I know the Lord can bring about good from very bad situation, even if it's simply for you to know where my faith lies." She gives them a kind, small smile. "*Look*, I trust you both will do what you can, but we are all given our free will to make choices, good or bad, *even Antonio*. And this will all end however it's meant to end!"

After they all had a minute to collect their thoughts, they left for her condo. They pull up in front of the building and go inside, but she begins to feel a sense of dread that only gets worse as they make their way up to her floor. The elevator doors open and they step off, but she freezes.

She turns to McMasters and David. "Something doesn't feel right. It could be I'm still unnerved that Antonio knows where I live."

"We'll pack up a couple bags and go to the hotel." David suggests.

"I can stay with Henry and Maggie." Bri says. McMasters takes her keys and opens the condo.

"Let me be clear, Love," he enunciates, "*not.leaving.my.sight*! Unless it's into McMasters care." He taps a kiss to her lips.

McMasters had stepped inside her townhouse to look around. He comes back out a few minutes later. "Prepare yourself. Someone has broken in."

"*What*?!" She asks.

"I called Ken and he's on his way."

Bri shakes her head in disbelief. "I don't want to go in there at all."

Just then, they hear a ding and Katie comes off the elevator. Each floor of this particular building has two condos; Katie has the two-bedroom condo on one side of the floor, while Bri's condo has three bedrooms and has two-thirds of the floor. Katie asks what's going on and Bri tells her.

The elevator dings and it's Ken and Bill, with a few CSU people. The stairwell door opens and it's Katie's 'friend' from 'once upon a nightmare.' Bri goes white and looks to Katie, who shrugs. The guy sees Bri and as he registers who he's looking at, Bri punches him and he stumbles back, swearing as he grabs his nose. Everyone's eyes just about jump out of their heads at what they saw Bri do! Then, when Katie's friend slowly gets back up, they are shocked once more when Bri gets close to him to knee him in his groin. Katie yanks Bri back and goes to the guy's aid, as he writhes on the floor in pain and holding himself.

Katie looks back over her shoulder, glaring at Bri. "*You* should be arrested for this!"

Bri gives her a cold glare as she plainly says, "*Really*? You're going to defend him after what he did–*after what you both did*?!" Bri motions between her and the guy asking, "What the hell is going on, Katie?!"

"What happened to forgiveness, Bri?!" Katie bites back, then takes a look at this guy's bloody nose.

"*What happened to remorse*?" Bri snaps. "Didn't you learn *anything* from what happened?!" Katie glares more at her.

The guy has an obnoxious smirk on his face, even with a bloody nose, and there is a muffled, "*I sure did*!"

Bri's anger is written on her face as she starts to lunge forward to punch this guy again, but Bill pulls her back. "Whoa there, Sweetie!" With Ken, David, and Bill being the only other witnesses, Bill's the first to say, "Right now, he just tripped and fell into a wall..."

They hear a muffled, "*A wall?!*" The guy holds his bleeding nose again.

Katie angrily exhales, "Ken! You need to arrest her for assault!"

Ken looks at Katie, "If I'd known Bri was going to do that," pointing to the guy's face, "I would've helped! If Bill says he ran into a wall, I'll back that up! And if David knew *why* Bri did that, well, you best get him into your condo and lock the door, *or we'll be covering up a homicide next!*" Ken gives Katie a stern look.

Katie angrily looks at Bri, then helps the guy into her condo and locks the door. Bri, Ken, and Bill look at each other in understanding, except David; only he will ask Bri about it later.

McMasters had joined them a minute ago when Ken was talking to Katie. They, along with Bill, David, and Bri, talk for a few minutes about everything that has happened with Bri's condo. Bri will have to go through and take an inventory of sorts, but it doesn't have to be right this minute. Ken tells her to go to Peter and Carlotta's hotel penthouse and he'll send additional men there. He'll call Henry to let him know what has happened.

"Can't I just stay at Henry and Maggie's, *with David?*" She asks, remembering what David just said. "I have things already there."

"Believe it or not, the hotel will be easier because all we're doing is reinforcing the security already in place with Peter and Carlotta staying there." Ken informs her. "Rather than starting from scratch."

"Alright then, I definitely don't want to make more work. McMasters, we'll need to make a stop or two along the way so I can buy some things before we go to the hotel."

"I'll let my people know." And he slips downstairs since Ken and Bill were with Bri and David.

On their way out of the condo building complex, Bri asks Ken, "Would you call and have the locks changed, then lock it up for me *before you leave*? No one but you gets the key, not even Katie. *No.One.*" Ken nods and hugs her before she leaves.

Walking to the awaiting cars, David asks, "What was that about?"

Bri says to him in the back seat of the car. "It seems Katie is rekindling old *friendships...*" She watches out the window. "Let's just say this all has to do with the strain on Katie's 'BFF' status with me and Ken is right..." she looks at him and he studies her, "you would've *at least* made him *wish* he were dead..."

David's eyebrows slightly go up, and while he is intrigued, he lets her leave it there for now. He doesn't want to push since she has already had a rough day. He kisses the back of her hand and he hears her faintly wince in pain. He delicately lays her hand on his thigh and carefully splays her fingers out but doesn't say anything. He lets her have some quiet for a few minutes.

David and Bri, along with McMasters and the security detail, go into some shops in a mall for her to buy a few things, but her toiletries are still at David's hotel so she won't need much. David wanted to buy her everything, but Bri refuses.

"No, David. I can do this."

"Bri, I want you to know, I'm here and I'm *not* going anywhere! *Ever*! I love you and *I will* take care of you. I want to show him I'm not going to be scared off." He holds her unhurt hand, lacing their fingers and holds them up to remind her, "Together!" She nods.

She pulls his tie to bring him in for a kiss, but pauses. "I love you, too, David!" He smiles, then he kisses her. "But I'm still buying!" He goes to say something, but she covers his mouth. "*No, Mister Worthington.* Either you let me pay for my own things, or we break up right here, *once and for all. NO joke.*"

"You're being impossible!" He tells her.

"Only when I have to be..." She winks, then completes *her* purchase.

David steps to the side and tells McMasters he wants to buy her a luggage set before they leave. He wanted to secretly do it, so McMasters arranged for a couple of people to go with David.

They meet back at the cars; David has one of the guys put the luggage into the trunk while he slips into the back seat with Bri.

"All set?" David asks.

"I think so! I almost forgot about a pair of shoes."

"'A' pair?" He asks confused.

"I guess you haven't realized I'm *not* a typical woman." She smirks.

"Oh, I caught onto that at the stables with Artemis, Love." He grins.

"Good! Then it shouldn't surprise you too much that I don't *love* shoes. At most, I *may* have roughly a dozen, give or take. But I have some in my suitcase, so I should be fine." She says and he chuckles.

They arrive at the hotel and everything is brought up, even the luggage he bought for her. "David! You didn't!"

"I believe the correct answer would be, '*David, you're the most wonderful man I've ever known, and I love the luggage! Thank you so much!*'"

"David," she walks up to him with a smirky, but more smoldering look, putting her hands on his chest saying, "you *are* the *hottest* man I've *ever* met *and dated*, and I *thank you* from the bottom of my heart for the luggage and *everything* you've done, continue to do, and *will* do for me! *I absolutely adore you!*"

He has a hand on her lower back. "Even better!" He smiles and tugs her closer. "I'll need a kiss for it to be perfect." He says with a playful grin.

She lightly laughs. "Good thing I strive for perfection." She curls her hands around his lapels and pulls him into another kiss.

"Mmm...Now that's *beyond* perfect!" He says against her lips. He taps a little kiss before he pulls back and looks at the hand she punched the guy with. "Do you need some ice for your hand?" He asks as he gently moves it to see if maybe something more needed to be done. "Maybe we should get it x-rayed, or at least wrap it?"

She closes and opens her hand a few times. "Surprisingly, it's not as sore as it should be for as hard as I punched that b—er, jerk's face!" She gives an 'eek' for her almost slip.

Peter and Carlotta come in with Henry and Maggie. The ladies go right to Bri and hug her, making sure she is alright. Then they all go to the dining room downstairs. Peter rented out the whole restaurant for a few hours so they could eat, keeping Bri as safe as they could. David and Bri fill them in on everything with Antonio.

Peter suggests they take Bri back to Newhaven on Saturday. "That's sweet, but I have the girls Saturday and through next week, but I'd also have to be back to DC first thing Monday morning."

"What about the girls with all this?" Carlotta asks with concern for them, making Bri's heart grow more for her. "Are they safe?"

Henry answers. "We've hired two people to be with them at school and the school has been great. They know it's precautionary but they, too, want to help just to be sure; plus, we want to make sure no other kids are hurt in the middle of all this either. They're staying with their dad and stepmom this week, so they're as safe as they can be."

Bri tells Carlotta, "We feel that if they're not near me, they will be safer; but the security helps put a mother's mind at ease. I honestly think he is so focused on me; he doesn't really consider them at all. So, if they are at their dad's house, that's probably enough for Antonio to leave them be...*we hope.*"

"Like you'll magically forget about them." Jack throws out there.

"Right." Bri shakes her head at the ridiculousness that she could ever forget about her kids!

They wrap up dinner and say goodnight to Henry and Maggie. Bri and David sleep separately, David insisting Bri take the bedroom. She doesn't argue this time and she can sleep a bit knowing David and Jack are on couches right in the next room. Bri cracks her door open and smiles when she sees Peter and Carlotta have done the same with their door.

CHAPTER 16

Imperfectly Perfect Lunch Date

Thursday morning comes fast. David and Jack are already down in the hotel gym. Bri takes her shower so they can have it when they come back up. By the time she is ready, they are still not back. She checks in with McMasters who knows she has an early meeting with her boss and says they are waiting out front. Bri left a note for David to check in with her, but she needs to be at The White House for a meeting.

> She adds: "P.S. BTW – Technically, I'm not slipping out while you're sleeping." (winking face)

When she arrives at The White House, she is brought into the Oval Office by The President's Secretary, Patty, who also has a mango smoothie for her from Chef André. When The President comes in from a different door, he sees her with the smoothie and chuckles, shaking his head.

Bri smiles with confusion. "What's so funny this morning?"

He gestures the smoothie. "That proves what I've heard about you and have seen for myself since day one."

She laughs and teases, "Wow...you got all that from a mango smoothie?!"

"Chef André, who is cooking for Ambassador Lombardi this week, *for you*, had that smoothie sent up knowing you were here this morning." He laughs. "You're very intelligent, Bri, so you know not everyone is going to like you, but I can guarantee almost all of them *at least* respect you." He sits down in an armchair next to Bri, who is sitting at that the end of the couch. He pours himself some orange juice and grabs a muffin. "Bri, I need your help with something, and it needs the finesse that only you can give."

"*Ooo*, sounds interesting!" She smiles.

"You mentioned Monday that you were wanting another position and frankly, I don't want to lose you. It'd be a shame not to utilize your talent, let alone lose it altogether! Plus, finding people in this town you can trust is hard to come by, as you're also fully aware." She nods in full agreement. He shifts more towards her. "Bri, I want to channel your expertise! You see, I need the

182

various law enforcement agencies to come together and support each other. We need to be united as a country *and* in law enforcement, so we need them to work together. Somehow, we need to get the FBI, CIA, Homeland, and so forth, working together as one big, *united team*. Right now, everyone wants 'dibs' on various cases, to take credit for big shake downs, or they're focusing on issues that don't matter as much as finding the kidnapped, chasing down a murderer, shutting down a terrorist group, a trafficking ring, or *whatever* criminal activity."

"There's a huge political wheel and everyone wants to be the one with the most power." Bri notes and he agrees. She asks, "How would this work?"

"I'd have all the Directors report to you."

Bri almost spits out her smoothie. "What?!" She coughs into her napkin. "I'm *so* not qualified—."

"Calm down a minute." He says with his hands moving up and down a bit.

Bri raises her eyebrow with 'calm down' and gives him a look as she teases with a hint of seriousness, "Are you sure you want to go with saying 'calm down' to a woman?"

He chuckles. "Good thing you're in a better mood!"

"Right!" She giggles a little, taking a bite of a croissant.

"First of all, you're *qualified* to see patterns! Second, you're *qualified* to see when things aren't working! Third, you're *definitely qualified* to give these people 'what for' when they act like childish adults! *You've nailed me a time or two*!" He laughs. "Do I need to mention your degree and graduating with top honors *makes you qualified*!"

Bri studies him for a minute, thinking. "Sir, with all honesty, the only way this will work is from the inside out."

"What do you suggest then?" He curiously asks.

"Agencies all reporting their cases to one person is great, but to see patterns, I'd have to know what every team, of every department, of every agency is working on or assigned to. That's going to require a *huge* amount of '*finessing*' because they would *need* to see I'm *not* a threat, Sir."

"Why would they think that?"

"It's human nature. When they think they're 'reporting to me,' they think their boss is no longer 'The President of the United States.' In their mind, they've just been demoted, or knocked down a level or few, on 'the flow chart,' then I'm coming in and discussing, *maybe even challenging*, what each department is working on...well, IF we do this, and for the record I do agree with your goal, we first need to sit the directors down and hear their objections because we both know they will have them, *and lots of them!*"

"Fine. Done. How does this afternoon sound? I'd say tomorrow morning, but with the fundraising event that evening, I want to keep that clear for you if we can." He calls Patty in and talks with her about scheduling a meeting with everyone, "being here is mandatory, unless physically out of town."

"I appreciate that, but if tomorrow works better, it will be fine." Bri says.

"Focus on this afternoon!" He tells Patty.

"Amy will reschedule anything if necessary." Bri adds.

"Amy is wonderful to work with! The problem lies mostly with a couple of the directors and not wanting to free up their schedule so easily." Patty notes.

"Sounds about right. They have to put on a show of importance, even for The President." Bri replies. Patty nods, then goes back to her desk.

"Well, I think we can pause our discussion for now, so you can start thinking about the meeting this afternoon." He says.

"I also have a few things to untangle this morning for Friday night, too." She tells him.

He walks Bri to the door and pats her on her mid-upper back as he opens the door for her. Bri leaves and walks with McMasters and another agent back to her office across from The White House.

Bri gets back to her office and Amy has already been in touch with Patty, but Bri fills her in on the specifics. "Wow! How are you going to accomplish that by this afternoon?"

"I'm not sure, but I have a few ideas. I need to put them together and handle a few things for the fundraiser yet." She walks into her office and Amy follows her.

"Where is your to-do list?" Amy asks with a bit of a commanding voice.

"In my binder." Bri answers.

"Let me see it." Amy holds out her hand waiting. Bri's phone rings and she hands Amy her binder as she answers her phone. Amy knows if Bri hasn't taken it out, her agenda is in the front, which it is, and she takes it out.

Amy whispers, "*Let me knock what I can off your list.*" Bri mouths a 'thank you,' to Amy; she smiles with a nod and goes back to her desk to work.

Bri gets off the phone and pulls up a presentation document on her laptop and begins putting her ideas together. A few hours later she is finishing up when there is a knock on the outer office door. Bri hears David talking to Amy as he makes his way to Bri's office.

"Hullo, Beautiful!"

Bri looks up and beams, "Hey, Sexy!"

He walks around her desk to give her a 'Hello' kiss. "'Sexy' is you!" He grins. "Especially with this whole overworked look you've got going on right now!"

She snorts a little laugh, "This whole 'stressed-out' messy look?!" Bri rolls her eyes. "My hair isn't in place, there are pieces hanging down; my face looks stressed and my clothes aren't crisp-looking anymore, which is sad because I have a presentation this afternoon. Yeah," she has an expressionless look on her face, "this is *real* sexy..."

"You forgot to mention the glasses your wearing." He winks.

She rolls her eyes then looks at the clock. "It's lunchtime already?!"

She inhales deeply and exhales while she saves her work. She uploads the file so she can access it for the meeting later. It's set for 1:30 in a conference room back over at The White House.

"If you need to finish, I can go pick something up or have something delivered; we could even go somewhere close by if you need to be back right away?" He suggests to her.

"I didn't do very many slides, I just wanted to get some points across. That made it easier for me to whip through it and finish. I've uploaded it, but saved it," holding up a thumb-drive, "*and now...*" she smiles as she gets up, "we go to lunch." She slides the thumb drive and her laptop into the bag to bring it all with, just in case she can't access the uploaded file.

"What are you hungry for?" He asks as they pass Amy's desk.

"Hold up!" Amy tells them. "Chef André had some questions and I said you have a lunch date, then a meeting at The White House. He said if you two didn't mind being taste testers for lunch, not too many couples can say they had an exclusive date at The White House!" Bri laughs and looks at David.

He says with a playful smile, "*That would be pretty smashing!*"

She smiles back. "I guess Chef André will have a couple of taste testers for lunch." She kisses his cheek. "Thank you."

"For what?" He asks.

"For helping with the fundraiser preparations Amy and I are trying to tackle!" Bri smiles.

He smiles lovingly, cupping her cheek. "*Happy to, Love!*"

"Great!" Amy says. "I'll call over and let them know you're on your way and walking over should give them enough time to finish up anything if they need to." They thank Amy and lace their fingers together as they walk over.

When they enter The West Wing, they make their way to the kitchen with Bri saying 'Hello' to a Congressman, a Senator briefly stops, and a couple Cabinet members; she introduces David to all of them. The last person they run into is the last person she expected to see when they were almost to the kitchen; her favorite senator and it's obvious to David that the platonic feeling is mutual! Senator Jenkins gives her a great big hug and Bri introduces him to David, mentioning they were on their way to a lunch of taste testing with Chef André.

Senator Marcus Jenkins puts an arm around her upper waist and tells David, "There are some men in this town who've tried to land this woman! You're a lucky man, David!"

"That's what I've been told!" David smiles and winks at Bri.

Bri blushes a little. "You're exaggerating, Senator."

"*Not really*, you just don't notice because you're so focused on your job." He grins. "Look, I just came down here to say hello to my niece who just started working here and now I have to get to a lunch appointment myself." Marcus smiles as he gives Bri a kiss on the cheek. He shakes David's hand again as he says goodbye. "See you both tomorrow evening!"

They wave and say goodbye, then Bri takes David to the kitchen and she explains that Chef André will want honesty. "He's good about when someone doesn't like something. He just makes a note as to why they don't and moves on to the next thing."

In the kitchen, Chef André and his staff have a small table with two chairs set up. The table is covered with a white tablecloth and two full place settings on the table with red napkins. There is a small, clear vase with a single red rose in the middle of the table for the finishing touch.

"Oh, Chef André, this looks lovely!" Bri sweetly smiles.

He kisses her on both cheeks and in a French accent that's not quite so strong as one might expect, he says, "This is our way of thanking you for having lunch with us!" He looks at David and goes to shake his hand. "And just who's this handsome man for our beauty?" Bri introduces them and Chef André introduces his staff before he motions for David and Bri to sit.

For the next hour or so, Chef André and his staff present an incredible array of samples that look amazing. Most of the samples were delicious, a couple were bland, and a few were not so good. Chef André made his notes with their comments and thoughts. He lastly made a dessert, his signature tiramisu, and it was '*to-die-for*.' David tells Chef André he would hire him in a heartbeat if he ever wanted to move to Newhaven! Chef André said he would love to be a guest chef the next time their chef goes on a vacation, handing him his card. David takes it and says he will remember that!

After thanking Chef André and staff, David and Bri leave for the conference room where her meeting will be. She gives him a little tour but tells him she will see about a better tour another time.

"What do you think of your visit to DC so far, *minus Antonio*?" She asks.

"Right now, I'm amazed at how much more incredible you get!" He stops and faces her. "And I think you will make a *fantastic* and *brilliant* duchess."

She rests against the wall and folds her arms. "You assume I would give all this up to play 'Duchess' to your 'Duke?'"

"Play?" In a swift movement, he is in front of her with a hand on the wall next to her, his other hand holds her cheek and he kisses her firmly, passionately. He pulls their lips apart and has a knowing smile. "Knowing what I know so far about you, you will take it *very seriously!*"

She sees someone out of the corner of her eye and turns her head to see the Ambassador standing with The President's Secretary, Patty, who is trying to hold back her excitement for Bri.

David and Bri go a little red. "Sorry," Bri says as they stand up straight, "we got caught up in the moment." Bri looks at David and says, "I'm going to make a very official introduction since Patty likes to know the details because of her position." David nods. "Mrs. Patricia Miller, *this* is David Worthington, The Marquee of Newhaven. Lord Newhaven, The President's Secretary, Mrs. Patricia Miller."

"Please, call me Patty, Lord—."

"Then I insist you call me 'David,'" he slightly bows, kissing the back of her hand, "please." Patty nods. David then shakes the Ambassador's hand, "Good to see you again, Sir."

"Likewise, David!" He smiles, shaking his hand back. He looks at Bri and says to her, "I didn't know how serious this was." He tells David, "You're a lucky man."

"That's what I keep hearing," David looks at Bri, smiling with love, "and I *completely* agree!"

"You wear love well, Bri." The Ambassador says, with Patty happily agreeing, then he hugs Bri. "I have a few things I need to do for the fundraiser, at Amy's request, because you had something come up." He looks at the conference room she is standing next to.

"Right! At 1:30 and it's..." she looks at her watch, "1:20! Oh, gosh, I need to set up. It was good seeing you both." The Ambassador nods and bids them farewell before he goes his own way.

"What's on the agenda this afternoon with your presentation?" David asks.

"A meeting to try to accomplish the impossible." Bri answers.

"*That's* an understatement." Patty sarcastically adds. Patty offers to help, but there is really nothing she can do. Patty says her goodbyes before she goes to her desk.

David walks into the conference room with Bri to wait for his security detail to come for him. When they arrive outside, he gives her a quick kiss before McMasters walks him to the exit.

CHAPTER 17

Imperfectly Perfect Presentation

At the meeting, the conference table is filled with agency directors along with Cabinet members like The Secretary of Defense and The Secretary of the Navy. The President is the last to join the meeting.

"Ladies and Gentlemen, let's get started." The President starts off, walking over to Bri. He begins to explain what he would like to accomplish, but it's not going over very well.

"Mr. President, may I?" Bri asks and he motions for her to take over.

"Okay, I know by the way you're all shifting in your chairs, this doesn't make you happy." Bri starts.

"Yes, I—."

"Please, Mr. President, let me." She says with a kind smile, then looks at the group. "Everyone, please don't think of this as anything negative. You're still going to continue reporting to the same person and only to me *for this project*. If we take a step back and look at this objectively, I think you'll see what this really is about; *our* goal."

A slide pops up: 'War Room,' and it does exactly what she hopes; *it gets their attention*!

"We're essentially creating a virtual 'War Room.'" They sit up and lean in closer to the table. "I'm not going to insult any of you and say that I'm even remotely qualified to do your jobs *and I don't want them*! You couldn't pay me enough either!" There was light laughter and chuckling among them. "I *do believe* I can create a place, a 'War Room,' where we can join as a united front against all enemies here in the US, *and* internationally. What this means is I need to know what each team of each department is working on in each agency, to see if patterns or duplicity exist."

The next slide reads: 'We are *ALL* fighting the same battle...A battle against evil!'

Bri tells them, "We want to create a world that's at least a little bit safer to hand over to our kids and our grandkids." Flipping through more slides, she continues in her presentation: "President Lincoln paraphrased Matthew 12:25 saying, 'A house divided against itself cannot stand.' He was referring to freedom and how freedom for one can't exist with slavery. Today, I'd say 'freedom' can't exist until we embrace everyone. Black, Hispanic, Asian, White, purple aliens with yellow polka-dots." There is a little more laughter. "'Lady Justice' needs to be blind, but law enforcement needs to embrace *everyone* to be united. Keep that in mind when I ask, 'What happens when we're *not* united together?'" She looks around. "*Evil wins!* The phrase, 'Divide and conquer' is what Matthew 12:35 essentially means and that has definitely been the case with all of the agencies working separately. The only way to kick evil where it counts, is to *be* united!"

She goes on. "As a member of the public and a government employee, it does my heart good when I hear of 'multi-agency cooperation!' When forces of good work together, less evil slips through the cracks. When people get wrapped up in the politics, territorial jurisdictions, or whatever it may be, even fighting over which agency gets credit, *our focus is lost!* Aren't you all tired of fighting each other?! I mean seriously, wouldn't it be nice to not only *act* like you play on the same team, but actually *BE* on the same team? When you work together, *that's* when the magic happens; true miracles take place when everyone stops tripping over egos!"

She continues through her PowerPoint as she speaks and finally gets to the last slide. "At the risk of sounding like a cliché, help me to assist all of you in the *very real* fight against the evil forces threatening our country, our people, and our colleagues; *just look around!* I'd bet there isn't anyone in this room we wouldn't fight to protect!" She watches them look around and give friendly nods to each other. "So why not fight to protect each other *now* and take more of an offensive stance?!" She sees their surprised looks. She goes on, "I swear, I'm *not* the enemy and I'd think most of you know my reputation; I like to make rational people reasonably happy." She sees some of them nodding. "I've worked with some of you, so please, work with me to accomplish this *huge* task, and help the others to trust me as well."

Homeland's Director looks around as he asks, "How do you suppose we do this, Ms. Harris?"

She explains. "I'm going to create a database, a spreadsheet of sorts, that any one of you can open up to look at what cases are being worked on by any team in every agency. I want us to create an environment of working together where we can agree on the rules and procedures, penalties for egos, pooling resources and applying them where it's *most* effective. Maybe there's a case that a CIA team has been dealing with, but their skills are better used for a different case they didn't know about in a different agency and can tackle it more efficiently because of *their* expertise. Perhaps, a team with members of various agencies is what it takes to take down a trafficking ring. There have been times when a case that has been years in the making, is foiled by a different agency's team because of an entirely different case; who knows, maybe a fresh set of eyes or few could help that case greatly?! A database like this could alert the agency directors of the investigations so they could talk about the best way to handle *both* cases. Gone are the days of saying one case is more important than another; *everyone* works hard on the case they've been given and no one has the right to say otherwise to get the upper-hand! The possibilities with a database like this would be endless; *if everyone works together!*"

She shuts off the slide show and addresses them. "Here's where I could ask what your pros and cons are, but I'm hoping you'll ponder on this; I mean *really* consider this *working*! Let this all sink in and between now and end of day Monday, you can email me your comments, questions, and concerns. My only stipulation is this: you can*not* send me a whole list of cons or a whole email on why this won't work. Every single one of you knows this *can* work, *and will work*, IF you all cooperate and see me as an ally, like a partner in crime-fighting. Does that much seem fair?"

There's silence for several *long* seconds or so, when The Secretary of Defense comments, "Bri, if I had to work with anyone to accomplish this huge undertaking, I'm glad it's you! You have our," he gestures to the other members who are present, "*full support!*" Bri looks around and sees nodding, although a few of them are not very convincing.

"That means a lot to me, Sir. Thank you!" She says as she shakes his hand. He looks at the others as he addresses them, convincing them to give her a chance and for them to talk to their people about cooperating. The rest of them shake her hand and some half hug her before leaving. Her boss is still there, and she says to him, "Well, let's hope I can do this because if I can't, I'll *need* to find a new job!"

"Bri, this will only fail if *they* don't cooperate." He simply states.

"True. That's why it'll be fun to make sure they do!" She grins. "They can either cooperate, or I'll have to hound them, and no one wants that! *Not even me!*" They laugh. Then she tells him, "I'm *really* excited about his project!"

"I can tell!" He chuckles a bit. "That's another reason it'll work with you at the helm!"

"Let's pray that trust isn't misplaced..." She says with a nervous look.

"It's not." He replies as they walk out of the conference room together.

They say goodbye in the hallway, shaking hands and he shakes McMasters hand, who was outside the conference room while Bri was in her meeting.

"Keep up the good work trying to keep her safe!" The President says before leaving with his Secret Service detail.

"Thanks, Mr. President." McMasters replies.

Bri heads to her office over in The Executive Office Building with McMasters by her side. She gets to her office and sees David relaxing as he waits for Bri, chatting with Amy.

"How did it go?" Amy asks as Bri bends down to kiss David a 'Hello.'

"I'm hoping good. They have between now and end of day Monday to email me with their questions, concerns, and comments, but they *can't* send me just a con list or an email of only why they think it won't work; they have to have something positive to say or recommend."

David remembers her project that starts next week. He can see how excited she is about doing something that's not just 'glorified babysitting,' as she calls her current position. He starts to wonder if she can be mobile with it.

"Is this something you have to do by going from one building to the next or can you remotely work on it, too?" He asks.

"Oh, most of it will be from my computer inputting the information into a database." She offhandedly says. Noticing David's relief, she walks into her office saying as he follows her, "David, this is why long-distance relationships are hard; we both have jobs to do."

"I know. I just want to know if you can fly to me occasionally. If there's a party, it'd be nice to bring you; but if you can't, you can't."

She gives him a slight sad look, "David, I refuse to pick up my life and move for a boyfriend. I'm sorry." She looks down at the paperwork on her desk.

He asks, "How about moving for a husband?"

She is still looking at the papers but doesn't hesitate, "*In a heartbeat!*" Then she realizes what she just said and looks up. She smiles, biting her lower lip, and walks over to him with a playful look. "I'd definitely work something out with *whomever* that might be."

He wraps his arms around her. "That's all I need to know, Love."

"What? That I'd move wherever for the man I marry? Or are you *assuming* that's you?" She teases.

He holds her firmer. "Oh, I *know* it will be me!" Reminding her, "I've been told you've already turned down everyone in the city—."

She laughs out loud, "*Not* everyone! *Not even close!*"

"Just about!" Amy pipes in from her desk.

"Hey! Whose side are you on?!" She says loud enough for Amy to hear.

He lovingly smirks. "*Ours!*"

Bri grins back and raises her eyebrow. "Until she remembers I can fire her *at any time!*"

Amy snorts, "*You'll just rehire me tomorrow!*"

She says to David, but loud enough for Amy to hear, "Training a new assistant *would be exhausting!*" She teases.

"Love you, too, Bri!" Amy says.

Bri giggles. "You *are* the best, Amy! And, yes, I do love you!"

David chuckles and refocuses their conversation. "If you are telling me the truth and you love me..."

"That's kind of right!" She teases him, then adds, "I love *and adore you!*"

He cups her cheek and kisses her. "Now we're getting to the truth!"

"What do you mean?! Everything I said *is* the truth!" She replies.

Amy asks from her desk, "Mateo is out front to take you to The Embassy."

"Thank you!" She says in Amy's direction, then turns her head back to David, still in his arms, "I'm headed to The Embassy for an hour."

"Amy mentioned that." He replies.

She moves to wrap her arms around his neck. "I want to make this trip short because there is this *fantastic*, good-looking man I'm head over heels in-love with that I want to spend more time with!"

David raises his eyebrow with a smirk. "Is this me? I can't be sure because of what you were say—." She kisses him fiercely and he deepens it.

"You tell me." She playfully smirks.

He winks. "If it's only an hour, maybe I'll hang out and wait."

"Yeah?" She says with an excited smile. "In that case, there's a coffee shop down the block from The Embassy that I've heard is rather good. You're welcome to come in but honestly, I'd rather walk around for an hour for the scenery or to people watch, *maybe a little bit of both*, on such a beautiful day like today." She suggests.

"I'll figure out something, maybe see where Jack ended up."

"Amy, David is going to hang around and wait for me at The Embassy. Would you let McMasters and the others know?"

"Sounds good!" Amy smiles wide. "This way you'll have more incentive to leave on time, *or* preferably earlier yet." Bri lightly laughs.

David and Bri meet up with McMasters in the hallway, right down from her office door, then they all go outside. Mateo waits by the car and when they get closer, he opens the back door for Bri and David to get into the back seat.

The Embassy isn't that far away from Bri's office. They pull up to the front and climb out. David kisses Bri's cheek before watching her go inside. A security guard smiles at her and then waves to David in acknowledgment before David walks down the street in the direction where Mateo says this coffee shop is located and his security guard says he knows where it is.

David arrives at the coffee shop and places his order. He sits at a window counter and texts Jack and James. When his drink arrives, he walks around and comes to a small park. He finds a bench to sit down. Bri was right, it *is* a beautiful day; perfect if she was there with him. Jack texts that he is close by and will meet up with him in the park.

Inside The Embassy, Bri is answering questions and moving things along. The staff seem to be in good spirits, but there is stress in the air as the event was a little over twenty-four hours away. She helps with a few extra things to move everything along.

She types a text to David letting him know she is about ready to leave, but before she could send it, she is grabbed and yanked into a room. She stumbles before regaining her footing.

She turns around and gasps, "*Antonio!*"

Antonio had pulled her into a study of sorts; it only had a couch, a chair on each side, and a large, round coffee table. He was angry with her, livid. '*McMasters is never far...*' She thinks to herself. '*He should be here any minute!*' She tries to think of a way out of the situation.

Antonio says with anger and frustration, slapping her across the face, "*I told you to break up with him!*"

She places her hand over her cheek, stunned and frozen. She knows he is too irate to see reason, and anything she says, even if innocent, could make him angrier. She notices it feels like her mouth is locked up again, glued shut. '*Perhaps Divine intervention is helping me keep quiet?*' She thinks to herself.

Antonio's rant continues, "Then I hear you're in The White House making out with this guy for all the world to see, like some—!" The word he uses is in his native language, but it isn't much of a stretch to discern what the equivalent word would be. Grabbing her upper arms to force her to face him, he continues to yell, "*How dare you do this to me? HOW DARE YOU KISS HIM*

IN FRONT OF PEOPLE!" He screams. "*You filthy——!*" And more words in his native language pour out. He goes to backhand her, only she moves her head back, which infuriates him more to 'seeing red.' He pushes her to the floor with all his rage and might, only she isn't balanced on her feet enough and she hits the side of her head so hard on a marble coffee table going down, it knocks her out. He kicks her a few times while she is unconscious, calling her more vile names in his native language. Scared he will get caught, he stops and quickly sneaks out the way he came in.

David is sitting in the park with Jack when he felt Bri is danger right before the assault even began, but it's interesting that even Jack feels it. They didn't say anything, they didn't have to! One look at each other and they immediately start running towards The Embassy, David's bodyguard right behind them. When they get there, they are stopped by security. David waves over the familiar guard who saw David arrive with Bri.

David frantically says, "Something's wrong with Bri! *Please*, let us come in and check with you!"

The security guard tells the other guards, "We can let them through, they're with Ms. Harris."

The guards apologize as they let David and Jack inside the gate. They run inside with the guards. David and Jack step inside the large open square foyer where the whole second floor above them is open and people can look down onto the first floor. Someone comes to the above railing shouting for the guards to begin a sweep for the Ambassador's son! David's and Jack's hearts sink. The guards run upstairs with Jack, David, and bodyguard right behind them; they begin searching the rooms.

When they get to the room where Bri is at, they see McMasters squatting down over her, while on the phone with 9-1-1. McMasters stands and turns to see David and Jack rushing over.

Stepping aside, McMasters tells them, "She is unconscious, but breathing." They are on each side of her and drop to their knees.

"*What happened?!*" David asks.

"We don't know exactly. Someone said they saw Antonio slipping out a back door. I immediately went to look for Bri and found her like this!" McMasters anger towards Antonio is clearly heard.

Bri starts to stir and she sees Jack first because of how she is lying on the floor. She gives him a faint smile, then she turns and sees David, giving him a small smile. Bri tries to speak, but winces in pain and holds her head.

Jack quietly tells her, "Shhh...Help is coming." He gently runs his fingers through her hair on the top of her head.

David sees her eyes close. "No, Bri! Stay with me! Squeeze my hand and let me know you hear me! Please, Love!" She can't squeeze but manages to move her fingers. "That works! Stay with me!" He lightly kisses her cheek, Bri hisses softly as she loses consciousness again, a tear trickles down her temple.

The paramedics rush in and tend to her. When they have her on a gurney and wheel her out to the ambulance, they want David to follow them to the hospital. He won't hear of it and climbs in; Jack tells him he will text everyone from the car.

Jack runs out to Bri's car and slides in the back seat of the car Mateo is driving, it's parked out front of The Embassy. Jack quickly explains everything to Mateo and he wastes no time making his way to the hospital; almost catching up to the ambulance. Jack begins the task of sending a text to Amy, Henry, Maggie, Joe, Carlotta, Peter, James, and Katie.

Jack: "Bri is at the Hospital. We'll explain more when you all arrive."

Jack hopes no one will ask him questions by text. And all the responding texts were forms of, 'On my way!' That is...*except one.*

Katie: "I can't make it but keep me posted!"

Katie heads to her next meeting after she sends her text to Jack. This only added to the disgust he has been starting to feel with her, but he doesn't exactly know why; call it intuition of what he will learn, about what happened between Bri and Katie... *What he does know*, is Katie's 'BFF' is in the hospital and she can't be bothered?! '*What a piece of work*!' He thinks to himself.

198

In the waiting room, a nurse comes out and asks David if he is Bri's husband. "Not yet." He replies without a second thought. He looks at her expectantly, waiting to hear an update on Bri's condition.

"I'm sorry, Sir, but we have to wait for her family to arrive. Our clinics show a 'Henry Bradshaw' and a 'Margaret Bradshaw' as her 'emergency contacts.' Do you know if they're on their way?"

"They are, but can't you tell us *anything?*" David asks.

"I'm afraid not, Sir. It would be a violation of federal law for patient rights *and* against hospital policy for me to give either of you that information without approval. We have to wait for her next-of-kin to arrive to—."

David throws up his hands and snapping, "*What does that bloody mean?!*" Jack puts a hand on David's shoulder and David quickly catches himself with the nurse. "My apologies."

The nurse has a small compassionate smile for David. "I understand it's hard not knowing and if I could..."

David nods, then his face drops as he takes a deep breath. "All I know is the woman I'm madly in-love with and want to marry, is hurt, and considering her going in and out of consciousness, she must've received a significant blow to her head."

"That's a good assessment." Detective Stevens tells him after he and his partner, Detective Brooks, overhear him. "From what Special Agent McMasters has gathered so far, The Embassy staff and visitors say they heard angry shouting and a smacking sound, then a loud thud as something, *or someone,* collapses to the floor. They heard some grunting sounds before it was quiet again."

The detectives see the fury in David's eyes when he says, "It was the Ambassador's son, Antonio."

"Did you see him?!" Stevens hopes.

"No," David replies, "but he has been infatuated with her for some time and has been harassing her since he arrived here in DC!"

"We were told he and his family arrived Tuesday morning for the week?" Stevens asks.

"Yes." David answers.

David starts to pace and asks, "Where is Uncle Henry or Aunt Maggie?" Jack shakes his head with an 'I don't know' look.

It isn't much longer when both families and their friends, like Ken and Bill, walk in about the same time. They gather around David and Jack to listen to David answer more questions.

Stevens asks, "Do you know what happened when the Ambassador and his family arrived?"

David exhales out loud, thinking. "Bri has been organizing a charity fundraiser for tomorrow night." He looks horrified.

"What is it?" Detective Stevens asks.

"She has felt like something bad would happen!" David exhales in frustration. "Why didn't I just take her away?!"

Maggie hugs him. "She wouldn't have left."

Henry had gone up to the check-in desk to let them know he and Maggie are there and would like an update. He also says, "David can have whatever information he needs, whenever he wants it."

"Actually," a nurse comes out to the waiting area, "Ms. Harris just updated her records. I was just coming out to get a David Worthington and a Jack Carlisle for her."

As David and Jack walk up to the nurse, the doctor comes out and explains to everyone, "She has multiple bruises on her abdomen and a concussion and we'd like to keep her overnight just to be safe and if all goes well, we will release her in the morning."

The doctor said Bri could have visitors and he would leave the length of their stay somewhat up to her. David and Jack go first since she asked for them. When she sees David walk in, her face lights up and tears fill her eyes.

"David, I'm so glad you didn't go back to Scotland like I was insist—."

He gently covers her mouth with his fingertips. "*I'm* relieved I was already here or it would've been the longest flight of my life! How are you feeling?" He asks as he sits on the bed next to her and carefully hugs her.

She smiles a little. "I'm sore, but good considering." He rests his forehead to hers and she says, "I love you!"

He smiles. "I love you, too!"

Bri pulls back to see Jack in the doorway. She smiles sweetly, reaching out to him with her other hand. He comes over, taking her hand, and sits on the other side of her bed.

"Thank you for being there for me and David."

Jack gently squeezes her hand with a smile, secretly pushing his other feelings for her down. He is grateful there are light taps on the door and the detectives, Stevens and Brooks, walk in with Ken, Bill, and McMasters behind them. They came to find out what happened from Bri and she tells them.

With what she is telling them, there are only four people who would've known of the kiss, two of them being Bri and David, another The President's Secretary, and the only other one would be Antonio's father, Ambassador Lombardi.

"I truly feel the Ambassador didn't mean any harm to come to me. In fact," Bri states, "it would make more sense if he said something to Antonio to try to deter his son from pushing his obsession."

David agrees. "The Ambassador is fond of Bri and *it would* make more sense that he was trying to get his son to leave Bri alone."

After they finish asking their questions, Stevens and Brooks wrap up their notes. They give Bri their business cards in case she remembers anything else and wish her well. She thanks them and they say goodbye. McMasters, Ken, and Bill walk them out to give Bri time with David and Jack.

Henry and Peter arrange for a private room for Bri so David can stay with her. Jack had gone back to the hotel with James to bring back some things for them. Jack walks in with her new bag that goes with the luggage set David had bought her. He has a change of clothes with basic toiletries for both of them. Jack kisses her on the cheek and they both have a small moment that David notices. He realizes his best friend doesn't just have feelings for Bri, but '*He's in-love with her*!' David isn't mad or upset. '*Who could blame him? Jack freely bowed out so I could be with her, the whole time being honest that he would go after her if I let her go*!' He is sad that Jack will never find another woman quite like Bri. '*Jack has always been the better man and this proves it*!'

Jack clears his throat and says he will visit in the morning. She smiles softly and thanks him for the bag and he nods. He waves to David as he shuts the door behind himself. David hands Bri her phone so she can read texts and listen to messages; he says he'll be right back.

David runs after Jack. "Jack, hold up!" Jack stops and inhales, holding his breath as he faces David. "Jack, if anyone can understand falling in-love with her, *it's me*!"

Jack is silent a few seconds before he says, "Please don't make me say it." He has a sad pleading look for his best friend. "I just need to lie to myself for a little while..."

David gives him a brother's hug. "Thanks for being here."

"*Always.*" Jack says, hugging him back. He leaves for the hotel and David returns to Bri's room for the rest of the night.

Bri had responded to her boss that she is staying in the hospital overnight for observation and should be released right away in the morning. She still plans to attend the fundraiser tomorrow night.

Her Boss: "ONLY if the doctor approves!"

CHAPTER 18

Imperfectly Perfect Nightmare

Friday morning, Bri is released from the hospital. Her bruised cheek is barely noticeable, but makeup and nighttime lighting that evening will cover it up completely. The bruises on her torso were a different story. She was black and blue in a few places on her abdomen, plus her upper arm was still bruised from Antonio grabbing it when he was in her office Wednesday afternoon.

David takes Bri to the penthouse suite where she takes it easy the rest of the day. Amy handles a lot of the minor issues that pop up. There are couple things that Bri is handling, but she is able to do them over the phone and with her laptop at the dining table. Jack and David are working on their own things at the table with her.

That evening, Bri gets ready for the fundraiser, Carlotta and Maggie have come into the room to help her. Bri walks out of the bathroom and the bruise on her upper arm is partially seen and out of a mother's concern, Maggie lifts the sleeve. She and Carlotta are alarmed.

"Don't worry," Bri explains, "the glove will cover it." And she shows them.

"Well, from what injuries we know you have, can we assume this is a sample of what's on your abdomen?" Maggie asks, giving her a 'the truth' look.

Bri nods. "I'll show you both tomorrow if you'd like, *if* we can temporarily forget and enjoy the party?" The ladies give her motherly, loving smiles and careful hugs, before going out to the living room.

James and Katie arrive from her condo, dressed and ready to go, with Amy arriving right behind them. She offered to go with Jack, as friends, when she picked up on how he feels for Bri last night at the hospital. He is such a nice guy that she just wants to help him out, which he appreciates.

Bri puts her shoes on and grabs her purse. She steps into the living room and locks eyes with David, whose breath catches at the sight of her, but so does Jack's and he looks away. Amy notices and wraps her arm around his and squeezes. When Jack looks at Amy, she winks at him and he smiles. Katie is irked when she sees what looks like an intimate secret between them and now erroneously assumes Amy's going after Jack.

Jack whispers down into her ear, "*Thank you for understanding.*"

"*No problem.*" She whispers back. "*Friends help friends out!*" He smiles as he softly pats her hand.

David walks over to Bri and takes her hands. "How is it you look more and more beautiful every day?" He kisses her tenderly, 'aws' from Maggie and Carlotta are heard. Jack was thinking the exact same thing, but he really is happy for David and holds no hard feelings towards his best friend. Jack knows Bri will be deeply loved and treated like a princess; that's all that matters to him.

"Are you ready?" Bri asks David.

He is surprised. "I should be asking *you* that question!"

She laughs. "I've done these enough times it's just another event." She gestures to Katie. "When I drag Katie with me, she seems to make the best of it! *I* need to be more like that!"

Katie smiles at Bri as her heart softens a bit for her friend. She wishes she could get rid of these feelings of jealousy, but it won't be long before they creep back in.

"Well, I don't want to ruin your casualness, but this will be the first time we're going to be introduced together." He smirks at her. "The press will now know who the stunning woman is in my life, so," he gives her a pointed look, "*are you ready?*"

She feels a moment of panic. "No." She says flat out, but catches herself, "*Sorry.* I shouldn't have said it like that; that was too honest."

"Yes, it was honest. I want you to *always* be honest with me. I never want you to hold back something important, even being nervous or uncomfortable." He wraps his arms around her.

"So, all the cards on the table?" She asks.

David raises an eyebrow and then he remembers what that expression means. "Right. No tricks, no games, no lies or secrets; everything out in the open so we can deal with what we need to." He holds up her hand he is holding, their fingers laced, and reminds her, "Together." Then he kisses the back of it.

"Okay." She takes a deep breath. "David, I love *you*! Not your title, or your social status, nor your money, or anything like that; *however*," she stresses, "I also know that to love you, I have to accept that you're an heir. With that title comes a place within the elite upper-class society where you're bound to your obligations as '*The Heir to Newhaven*.' I love you and no matter where you are, that's where I want to be; even if it means accepting a title and the social status *to* be with you."

'*She's ready*!' He thinks to himself about marriage and smiles knowingly. "And tradition?"

"I apologize if this is too simplistic, but isn't that what being an heir essentially is...*tradition*?" She asks and there is chuckling around them.

"Yes. But the specific traditions can vary from duchy to duchy, connected to other traditions, and wrapped up in the duties of the duchies." He says.

"I'm intrigued, but we'll table this for now. David, I couldn't support you, nor support you as The Duke, if I didn't figure out a way to accept what comes with the job, so-to-speak." She tells him and he hugs her, glancing over her shoulder at his parents, who are smiling and nodding in approval of the answer.

"I love you so much, it takes my breath away!" He smiles.

She looks at his parents and back to David. "Why do I feel like something's up–No, we don't have time to get into it." She dismisses it for now.

She kisses him one last time before they all file out of the penthouse and into the elevator; all on their way to the awaiting limos that will take them to The Charity Fundraiser at The Embassy.

The arrival at The Embassy is a *much* smaller scale of the red-carpet glamour one would expect at an awards show or movie premiere. There are the social elites, politicians, diplomats, dignitaries, fans, press, and the public wanting to see who is arriving. The announcement of their limo is "The Duke and

Duchess of Newhaven" with Peter and Carlotta getting out first and after a few seconds or so in between, David and Bri climb out of the limo; the other couples in the limo behind theirs join them.

Peter and Carlotta are announced before entering the ballroom, and the doors open for them to walk in, then close behind them. David and Bri step into place and he winks at her.

Then the MC's voice is heard saying, "Ladies and Gentlemen, David Worthington, The Marquee of Newhaven, accompanies Ms. BriaLynn Harris," the doors start to open, "our organizer helping the Ambassador put this evening's event together with her amazing staff!" There is applause.

As they walk in, Bri whispers to David, *"No pressure."*

"No worries, Love!" He says looking around, "This place looks *fantastic!"* The ballroom had the elegance that looks like something one would find inside a royal palace.

"That's because of the *amazing people* who put a lot of extra hard work into it this week to get it ready on time!" She tells him.

They find their table, which has them sitting with the Ambassador and his wife, Peter and Carlotta, The President and First Lady; there are two more place settings, but she isn't sure who they are for yet. This table arrangement was not like this as of yesterday when she last saw it.

"Bri! David! So glad you're here and you *both* could join us this evening!" The Ambassador says, shaking David's hand and giving Bri a gentle hug. He whispers, *"Thank you for coming tonight; it means a lot to me you came!"*

She nods as she blinks back tears saying, "Of course, Ambassador! I wouldn't dream of missing this night, even if I had to sit all evening."

He chuckles. "I hope you don't mind that I changed up the seating arrangement a bit."

"Not at all! You *are* the host!" She replies with a smile, then she takes her seat David has pulled out for her.

The event gets underway with dinner courses, dessert, dancing, mingling, and a silent auction that ended at ten o'clock that night. Those who had winning bids were announced shortly after. David and Jack each anonymously match what the charity raises from everyone else's bids, tripling their overall donations number.

"We've raised the most money at this event than any other event so far this year!" She smiles at David and kisses him. "You and Jack didn't have to donate that much money!"

"You bring me to a charity event that you're behind and you can count on me making a sizeable donation, Love! If Jack is also there, we both usually split the matching of the donations that have been raised. Tonight, we decided we would each match the donations raised to encourage more positive press towards you, and ultimately us." He smiles and kisses her again.

There is more dancing and mingling. Bri dances with David, then he asks Bri to ask Jack for a dance and he asks Amy...David is testing a theory.

Bri winds her way to Jack and he sees her walking up to him, his heart flips inside his chest. She asks, "May I have this dance, Lord Carlisle?"

He can't help himself; he has a big smile. "The pleasure is all mine, Lady Harris." He slightly bows and kisses the back of her hand.

"Stop that and dance with me." She softly giggles.

Jack follows her to the dance floor and takes her in his arms. He is so relaxed with her; he holds their hands to his chest. They dance in comfortable silence for a while before he says, "You're so happy and in-love with David, somehow it makes you even more beautiful."

"I have so much love for him, my heart overflows and I don't know what to do with it all!" She tells him with their cheeks still snuggled in.

David is watching this and sees how much his best friend loves Bri. Jack has never been like this with anyone before! Jack and Bri's dance is ending and there is a moment they look into each other's eyes and feel their connection, along with the chemistry and attraction.

She smiles sweetly at him. "I think we can both say we feel something and if we met first, WOW..." she inhales deeply and exhales slowly, "but maybe we're just like those fabled 'star-crossed lovers' fated to always wonder what could've been?"

Jack steps back with a small smile, as he acknowledges what she said. "You're probably right." He kisses the back of her hand. "Until next time."

Bri is approached by a congressman and asked to dance, which Jack takes that opportunity to slip off the dance floor. Before the congressman can dance with Bri, someone from the staff urgently comes up to her. Bri has been dealing with minor issues like this all night, running here or there on occasion; she wasn't usually gone long...*until now.*

David asks Jack about Bri and he tells him the little he knew about the dance with a congressman. They find the congressman who tells them she had an urgent matter she went to tend to. David and Jack then go and find McMasters, who starts searching while Jack and David search for Ken, then all of them frantically join the search.

Minutes earlier, Bri was on her way back to the party when she was grabbed from behind, with a hand going over her mouth to keep her quiet. She's forced into a room where Antonio shoves her down *hard* to the floor.

He quickly pulls a gun and angrily says, "Be quiet!" He hopes to keep her from screaming.

Bri glances around and sees she is in the main floor library. Antonio had pushed her down so hard that, with the bruising she already had from when he kicked her numerous times yesterday afternoon, she is hurting. He motions with his gun towards the back door of the library, before pointing it back at her.

"You're going to stay quiet and we're getting out of here!" He tells her.

Bri knows if she goes to a 'second location' with this volatile man, she multiplies her chances of dying. She needs to stall him until someone finds her. She struggles to get up but manages to steady herself with her hands on the ground, tucking her legs underneath her, and her feet flat on the floor.

"The worst thing I could do is leave with you!"

She is about to push up to stand, but Antonio angrily kicks her; this time she hears and feels ribs cracking, maybe even breaking. She gasps with the sharp pain, grabbing her side. In that moment, she can't breathe because of the pulsating pain through that side her ribcage. Eventually, she *has to* breathe, only it's difficult. Bri sees someone out of the corner of her eye, but she doesn't look because she doesn't want to give it away to Antonio. She continues to talk to Antonio to keep him focused on her, hopefully allowing whoever it is to figure something out to help her.

As she starts to stand up again, she says, "By not wanting to stay here, you've inadvertently told me you're *too afraid* to stay here. You feel you have a bigger chance of getting caught *here*! Going somewhere you feel more comfortable is a dangerous move on my part, so I won't be going anywhere with you! *Here*, I might have the upper hand. If you kill me, you'll do it here!" She is standing and looks him right in the eyes. "Because *here*, there is a greater chance you'll be caught!"

She has seen enough in her peripheral vision by this point to know it's McMasters in the room with her. McMasters is trying to come up with a plan to gain control of the situation, but in each scenario, she could easily wind up dead. Bri sees anger and hatred in Antonio's eyes, but there is an evil in them, as well.

Antonio yells, "You—!" It cuts off because he punches her back down to the floor and she doesn't hear anything because of the pain.

Bri can taste blood in her mouth and her cheek is numb. As the feeling comes back, it tingles into a throb; the blood taste goes away. Antonio catches a glimpse of McMasters' reflection in a window and he yanks Bri up by the hair to use her as a shield.

Holding his gun to her head, Antonio tells McMasters, "Toss the gun over here and get back, or she dies!"

"She dies, *you die*, Antonio!" McMasters threatens with his gun pointed straight at him.

There is a momentary standoff but when McMasters sees Bri flinch as Antonio pushes the barrel of the gun harder into her temple, McMasters relents, sliding his gun towards Antonio, but making it so it didn't go all the way to him. McMasters partially puts his hands up, slowly moving back a step. He is still trying to figure out a way to gain the upper hand, but if there is one that keeps Bri safe, it eludes him at the moment.

Antonio tries to pull Bri towards the back door, but Bri fights him. "No! *I'm.not.leaving!*"

She doesn't make it easy for him, continuing to frustrate him. McMasters thinks if she keeps frustrating his plans, then it just might create enough of a 'window of opportunity' for him to help her.

"Do you really want me to hurt you?!" He yells pushing the gun into the painful side of her ribcage, causing her to inhale sharply through her gritted teeth and hold her breath.

She struggles, "*You're hurting me anyway!*"

Ken comes in with Jack and David right behind him. Antonio slightly turns with Bri, keeping McMasters in view while telling Ken, "Drop it and slide the gun over here, or she's dead!"

Ken looks at McMasters and complies with the demand. Ken, David, and Jack partially hold up their hands, too, trying not to make the situation worse. They quickly take in the scene and see Bri has been hurt because of the dried blood under her nose; plus, she has to be hurting from yesterday when he attacked her. Both Jack and David are livid, but they keep their cool. They are all trying to come up with some way to get Bri, *and everyone else*, out of this alive.

"You'll either come with me, Bri," Antonio says, "or I'll shoot your cheating lover!" He is now pointing the gun at David and gripping her hair tighter, causing her to grimace.

For the first time, Bri's fear briefly shows on her face for everyone else to see, but Antonio. He is enraged with anger and David is in the room with them, which makes Antonio *more* dangerous, if that is even possible.

He sneers, "*At least I won't have to worry about you two going behind my back anymore!*"

"No, Antonio!" Her tone pleads with him.

"Then let's go!" Antonio demands.

"No!" The pain causes her to inhale sharply and tense up.

"You would rather stay *and watch him die*, than to leave with me?!" He aims for David again, laughing a humorless laugh. "Fine by me!"

"Shoot me!" Jack blurts out.

Antonio glares. "Why?"

"Bri and I are the lovers, not her and David. David stepped in to try to divert suspicions and, well," he looks back to David, who has his eyebrows furrowed, "it worked a little too well."

"Prove it!" Antonio says.

"What?" Jack asks puzzled. "*How?*"

"Kiss her!" He tells Jack.

"Kiss her?!" Jack is surprised.

"As my father said about their kiss," he gestures David and Bri, "'a kiss can never lie!' If you're lying," he gestures for Jack to move closer to Bri, "you'll both die!" He points his gun at David, keeping a tight grip on Bri's upper arm and watches them closely.

Jack walks to Bri and she wipes her face the best she can. He makes sure her eyes are focused on him. He gently cups her face with his hands, but instead of a tender and sweet kiss, he purposely captures her lips in a heated, passionate kiss that sears into her heart. The pain she feels temporarily goes away as she focuses on Jack and their kiss. He gently pulls their lips apart and she is leaning into him. He has a ghost of a smile going up into his eyes. And now, David knows more than ever, just how serious Jack was about not letting Bri get away if David had let her slip through his fingers that Saturday night.

Antonio yanks Bri to him and she cries out in pain this time. Jack yells, "*YOU DON'T HAVE TO BE SO ROUGH WITH HER!*" In one movement, Antonio points the gun at Jack and shoots.

For a split-second Bri freezes in shock, then she screams, "*NNNOOO!*"

Ken holds David back from tending to his best friend at that moment. "*Wait!*" He sternly whispers to David, "*Assess is best!*" He repeats a line he has used in training other officers. *"Take a brief moment to assess the situation, or risk more people getting hurt! What happens if you or I are hurt?! Who's going to be left to help and take Antonio down?"* David nods.

Bri notices Antonio is turned just enough, giving her an idea. She gives McMasters a look that says she is going to try something. McMasters watches her carefully seeing her make a fist and as she raises her arm up, he is ready to leap into action, and he does when she plunges her elbow into Antonio's ribs with as much strength as she can muster.

It's enough for Antonio to gasp and hold his own breath, loosening his hold on Bri so she could twist out of his grip completely. She rushes over to Jack.

Antonio struggles to yell at Bri, "YOU'RE DEAD—!" McMasters tackles him to the floor and David jumps in to help McMasters when he sees Jack being tended to and Ken rushing over to them, too.

Jack is shot in the upper left shoulder. Bri tries to rip his shirt but doesn't have much strength, but Jack manages for her. She is able to get a good look and it looks like the bullet went straight through. She takes her gloves off, rolls them up and applies pressure with them, locking her arms into place, which she hopes will be enough to at least slow down the bleeding.

Her eyes are filling up with tears and she looks down into his eyes, her lower jaw shakes. She can barely whisper with a lump in her throat, *"Jack!"* She shakes her head as the sobs try to come to the surface and she works to push them down.

"Ah, no, it'll take more than this to keep me down, Gorgeous." He cups her cheek. "I'll be fine. *You'll see.*" He smiles sweetly.

A shot rings out, jarring them back into their reality and her urge to cry disappears as a panic takes over when there is another shot. She frantically looks in the direction where the shot came from. Antonio is holding his gun tight, while struggling with David and McMasters on the floor. Antonio keeps squeezing the trigger and she knows one of the bullets hits Ken when he grabs his mid-upper arm.

"Ken!" Bri watches helplessly as her hands are holding pressure to Jack's wound. "Hold this!" She puts Jack's hand on his wound. "I'm going to check on him, but I'll be right back!" She tells him and Jack nods. She notices her body's almost numb from the pain, so she's able to stand without too much of a struggle.

Ken quickly tells her, "I'm fine! Just a flesh wound!" He motions with his bloody hand, "Get back down!"

Her attention briefly goes to the struggle David and McMasters are having with Antonio. He is still trying to pull the trigger and manages again. David gets one more punch in, his hardest one yet, before Antonio finally releases the gun and David pushes it out of Antonio's reach. McMasters goes to flip Antonio and David helps. David then presses his knee into Antonio's back, so McMasters can handcuff him. Bri is amazed at how everything happens so fast, yet in slow motion.

The Ambassador comes in and sees his son being handcuffed. He sees Ken and Jack, but when he sees Bri standing with blood on her face, hands, and the front of her dress, his anger turns to rage against his son. His son's terrorizing ways have gone too far and it needs to stop. He picks up the gun David had slid out of Antonio's reach. The Ambassador, an expert shot, sees an opening when McMasters and David are on either side of Antonio. The Ambassador aims with precision and pulls the trigger. Everyone looks in horror in the direction of the gunshot, then they see the Ambassador standing there with smoke in front of him, as he slowly lowers the gun he just fired.

David and McMasters quickly catch Antonio as he collapses and guide him to the floor. With a bullet through his heart, Antonio's eyes were open, fixed and dilated; death was instantaneous. McMasters feels for a pulse at his neck, just to be sure...nothing.

Bri is in shock. Antonio is dead and all she keeps thinking is, '*It's over...it's finally over...*'

David turns to her, but she gasps, "Jack!" They look over at him and see Ken is already putting pressure on Jack's wound.

"I think most of the bleeding has stopped." Ken continues to hold the pressure. "We're not taking any chances! You're not getting up until the paramedics get here!"

David walks over to Bri and he doesn't hear the Ambassador telling him to, "Lay her down on the floor!"

Bri looks at David with an emotional smile, but it slowly fades. "I don't feel so well...I think I'm going to throw up." There are beads of sweat on her forehead as she holds her stomach.

"It's over, Love." David hugs her close.

Jack heard the Ambassador and props up on his elbows to look at Bri. Her hand leaves fresh blood on the back of David's shirt. David steps back and Jack sees the front of David's shirt also has fresh blood on it. His eyes flick to Bri's dress that's a darker red.

When the light reflects off the wetness, Jack is terrified. "*David*!" Jack points to her abdomen. "Bri's been *shot*!"

The Ambassador is at Bri's side and repeats, "Lay her on the floor!"

David and McMasters horrifyingly see her abdomen. Everyone sees the blood collecting on the front of her dress where she was wounded. She touches her stomach and sees the fresh blood on top of the dryer blood on her hands. David sees the fear on Bri's face when she instinctually knows how bad it is. Her knees buckle and David quickly catches her.

"David, the Ambassador's right! We need to lay her on the floor, she's losing a lot of blood by the looks of it." McMasters says.

David does what he is told with his heart pounding in his ears; he and McMasters lay her down. He tries to stop the bleeding, taking his shirt off to apply more pressure to her wound. The Ambassador goes and collects a bunch of books to stack on the floor to elevate Bri's feet.

Jack tries to get up to help, but David stops him. "Jack, stay there and be still, *please*! I can't lose her *or you*!" Jack hears the panic in his voice and does as David tells him. He sees Bri's hand and scoots around to hold it. Jack prays...then prays more *and harder*.

David had ripped Bri's dress where the bullet made a hole in her dress so he could apply more direct pressure to her wound. McMasters is talking on his phone to arrange for the paramedics to come in through a side door of the library to keep party guests and gawkers out of the way. David is holding pressure, but Bri is still losing a lot of blood, *fast*.

"David," Bri hoarsely speaks, "I—."

He cuts her off, "Shhh, save your energy, Love."

She raises her hand again, but instead of reaching for David's face like they thought, she points to her wound; some would say instincts kicked in, but Bri would say it was the Spirit.

"If you don't pinch off this artery, I'll bleed out before the paramedics ever get to me!"

They look up and out the windows where they see flashing lights. They could hear the sirens of the ambulance, it's like the ambulance is on top of them. There is such a seriousness to Bri's voice that Ken pulls out a pocketknife and hands it to David. David snatches it from his hand without a thought of anything else, not even cleanliness, and he makes the wound a little bigger. Thankfully, she still didn't feel anything. The bullet comes out easier than David expected and somehow, with Divine help, his fingers manage to reach in and pinch off the major source of the bleeding.

"*David...*" Bri says with a whisper, her fingers lightly touching the bottom of his chin. She has a little smile before her eyes close and her arm drops to the floor.

Ken feels for her pulse. "She's unconscious, but still alive." David's mind is spinning, but he holds onto that; *she is still alive*!

A few minutes later, the paramedics come rushing in after McMasters waves them to the door. "She's over there!"

They ask everyone to step back, but immediately see why David doesn't. They check her over and prepare her to be moved. Making an odd judgment call, they didn't want David to let go of his grip, *if* he could manage to hold on until they got her to the surgeon. The blood was like a glue on his fingers and he tells them he would be fine. The paramedics pray she doesn't go into cardiac arrest as they rush Bri to the hospital, or they'll have to rethink things.

Another set of paramedics would load Jack on a stretcher and have Ken ride with him. That ambulance being only a few minutes behind the first one.

As the hospital staff rush out to meet the first ambulance, it's all so surreal for David. He is in awe of how quickly they all work, *and work together*, so effortlessly, that in the blink of an eye, the nurses are covering him the best they can with a gown, hat, and so on, before they go into the operating room they've prepared before Bri's arrival.

The operating doors open and they all rush in. The surgeon takes charge as they hurry and prep Bri for surgery.

"Can I have your name, Sir?" He asks David, but David's watching what they're doing to Bri that he doesn't hear the surgeon.

The surgeon looks at a nurse who tells him, "It's 'David.'"

"David." No answer. The surgeon says it again with a little more urgent force, "*David!*" David's head snaps to the surgeon. The surgeon, through his mask, explains, "David, a couple of these guys are going to pull you away when I tell them to, but first I have to have a look at what we're dealing with." David watches as the anesthesiologist intubates Bri, noticing how gray she looks and what that means...he can no longer hold back the tears.

"David." The surgeon says.

"David?" A nurse pats him, then points to the surgeon.

David apologizes, "Sorry."

"David, I promise I'm going to do everything I can for your wife, BriaLynn!"

"Bri." He smiles at her, never correcting the surgeon calling her his wife because in his heart she *is* his wife.

"I'll do everything I can for Bri and so will everyone here, alright." The surgeon explains. David glances around seeing everyone agreeing and he nods. "David, we're running out of time! I need to make this cut bigger so I can put clamps on either side of where your fingers are. If your squeamish, we can put up a makeshift curtain of sorts to block your view." David shakes his head. The surgeon continues, "We'll moisten your fingers to help you let go, but *only when I tell you to*. David. It's *critical* you focus on me right now!" David nods, locking his eyes on the surgeon.

David watches the surgeon as he makes the incision bigger. He hears the surgeon talking about what he sees and asks for what instruments he needs.

They make sure David's fingers are moistened, then the surgeon pauses to address David.

"We're ready, David! Are you?" The surgeon asks.

David gives him a fast, solid nod, as he struggles to say, "*Yes.*"

"Alright David, let go." The surgeon acts fast and without looking up again he says, "We'll take it from here, David." The gentlemen pull David back and then out of the operating room.

Another nurse is waiting to strip him out of his gown, hat, mask, and so on. Right before the door closes, they hear, "*We're losing her!*"

David is pulled over to the side to move completely away from the door as another nurse rushes out to go get more blood. With the door open, he hears the surgeon say, "That's it! Stay with me, Bri!"

The nurse tries to lead David away, but he goes up the glass windows on the doors. He whispers. "*Fight, Love!*" He peers through the window, praying she is given the strength to fight *and live.* "*Please, God, help her through this! I swear I'll do everything I can to make sure she is loved forever!*"

"You can't stay here, Sir," a soothing voice is heard, "and we should get you washed up."

"I don't care about that." He absentmindedly stares at his hands and shirt, but he allows her to lead him away from the operating room. She goes to help him wash up, but most of the blood is on his clothes. The nurse then escorts him to the waiting area.

As he walks over to his family, there are gasps from various random people in the waiting area when they see his clothes with all the blood on them. His family hopes he has news, but he doesn't. They take in the blood on his clothes and the enormity of Bri's wounds sets in. All they can do now is pray and wait...

CHAPTER 19

A Perfectly Perfect Miracle Needed

McMasters had called Henry at Ken's request, who rounded up those at the party and texted everyone else. When David had walked into the waiting room, everyone stood up hoping to hear some news from him. He shakes his head, sitting down and taking a few deep breaths.

David asks his father, "How's Jack?"

"They're working on him, but the bullet went straight through and they expect him to make a full recovery." Peter tells him. "Are *you* hurt, David?"

David thinks as he stares down at himself, "...*This is all Bri's.*" He hears Sam, the youngest of the Bradshaw brothers, swear under his breath.

The middle brother, Mitch, asks what everyone wants to know, "*What the hell happened tonight?!*"

"Yeah! Wasn't there enough security?!" Sam asks.

Joe gives his brother a 'come on now' look, "You know how Bri feels about people wanting to commit a crime."

Sam reluctantly replies, "They'll find a way."

"Right." Joe says. "She could've had all the security in the world, guns could be outlawed, but she would say this guy would've found a way to get to her, after buying a gun out of the back of some guy's trunk somewhere."

David gets up and paces to try to calm himself, as more questions surround him and swirl in his mind. McMasters and Ken tell the family what they know, which is all David knows.

Peter walks over to David, "What can we do, Son?"

"*Pray!*" He replies, watching Henry join them. "Pray like you've never prayed before!" Tears start to fill his eyes again, "Bri was already crashing when I was leaving the operating room!" Carlotta gasps.

Maggie half pleas, half cries, as she looks up, "Oh, please, God! *NO!*"

David falls apart, "*Oh, God...she can't die!*" Peter pulls him into a hug and Henry hugs Maggie and Carlotta. They listen to David, "She has lost so much blood!" Henry's jaw trembles and tears fall from his eyes. David gestures his shirt, "This is *all* hers! I keep asking how she can possibly survive losing so much blood?! Her dress is worse than this!" He gestures himself again.

"A miracle." Henry states. "We pray for a miracle!"

"*And* to feel like we're doing something, we can all go donate blood, whether we're a match or not; to appreciate those who have already given their blood!" Peter says and everyone agrees. He looks at his son who is truly sick with worry; his eyes are red from tears, as she tries not to cry. Peter had only seen his son like this once before, when he and Jack were younger and Jack was sick in the hospital. "David, I'm sure Henry and the family know more than we do, but from what we've seen already she's strong-willed when she has to be, *and* she loves you. *Which means she will give it her best fight!*"

David nods as he stares into space, tears streaming down his cheeks. They all sit down together.

"Dad, I've *never* seen *anyone* look like she did! When they put the breathing tube in, she was lifeless! *She looked gray.*" David struggles with his emotions.

Henry and Peter look at each other with fear. They look to Ken, who nods they were thinking correctly.

Carlotta asks, "What does that mean?!"

Maggie looks at Ken. "Spit it out!"

Ken answers. "There's no easy way to say this...people will say gray, but the color is 'ashen' and it's the color people have when they're dead or dying."

There were audible gasps and a few other 'No's!' There were sniffles around them and lots of silent prayers. David looks upward and keeps praying His plan *isn't* her death.

A nurse comes out and says the surgeon, Dr. Lucas, will be out shortly to speak with them. Unfortunately, the doctor isn't out right away for an update on Bri's condition, but one does come out and speak to them about Jack. The bullet went clean through and there is no permanent damage. Carlotta goes to see him while everyone waits for Bri's surgeon and finds Jack sleeping comfortably. Carlotta is surprised she makes it back before they find out anything about Bri's condition.

It's almost an hour before the surgeon finally makes it out to them. Dr. Lucas apologizes, "I was on my way out here when Bri went into cardiac arrest again. We have her stabilized once more, *for now*; but honestly, I'm not sure how much more her body can take. Shocking one's heart takes its toll on the *entire* body." Maggie sobs and Carlotta holds her hand as the doctor continues. "I'm not going to sugarcoat anything for you, folks; it just *doesn't* look good. She has multiple rib fractures and a couple of broken ribs. In fact, one broken rib barely missed the heart, another broken rib made a small puncture in her lung. This tough woman was already internally bleeding *before* she was shot, and she is *still*...fighting." The surgeon surprises himself when he gets a little choked up and he clears his throat. "There is a *significant amount* of blood loss." He looks at David being covered in Bri's blood and so do the others. "Blood clots are also a concern we'll be watching for. I do feel that the damage to the organs won't have much, if any, permanent damage, *if* she survives this ordeal, and it's a big 'if.' We did induce a coma for the swelling of her brain. She has a pretty big bruise on the side of her head that our records show she received last night, but tonight's battle aggravated that." He looks around asking, "Please tell me they caught the bas—," he catches himself, "the *despicable* human being?"

"He's dead." McMasters matter-of-factly tells the surgeon.

"Well, at least he won't be a threat to her anymore, if she makes it through this." He looks around and the surgeon has a great deal of compassion for all of them. "Look, I just want to prepare you the best I can for the very grave condition this woman is in. The next 24 to 36 hours are crucial. I'm afraid of giving you false hope. We were able to stop the bleeding and repair the damage, she is healthy and strong. It looks like there are a lot of people here for support that she can draw strength from; *she is going to need every bit of it*." The surgeon looks at David. "I don't say this to scare you, but out of respect for any religious beliefs, you'll want to arrange a vigil, last rights, prayers, anything, because this will take *nothing* short of a *perfect miracle* for her to survive!" There were more gasps and cries.

David couldn't breathe! He paces, then punches a hole in a wall before dropping to his knees. The tears had been pouring down his cheeks, but the lump finally wins out and he sobs. All he could think was: '*Lord, I didn't let her slip through my fingers, how can You let her slip from my grasp now?!*'

The surgeon squats down to look at David's hand. "This should be x-rayed."

"*I need to be with Bri!*" He adamantly states.

The doctor tells the nurse to wrap it and immobilize it, he'll address the x-rays with David a little later. The nurse goes over with a tray and sits next to David, who is still on the floor, but now sitting against a wall. He lets the nurse take care of his hand, but he is in a daze and staring through the floor.

Peter and Henry go to him and hear David say more to himself, "I finally have the woman of my dreams, but I could lose her to a nightmare?!" His head tips back against the wall and looks at his father and his uncle. "*Why?!*"

Henry tells him, "David, we haven't lost her yet and miracles *can* happen, *but you have to find your faith*! Until then, lean on my faith," he gestures Maggie and his sons, "lean on all of ours, even Bri's!"

Joe sweetly smiles through his tears, "She has more faith than most of us combined!" They all smile and nod in agreement.

Henry smiles at David, "You have to have some idea of how much faith Bri has; she practically wears it on her sleeve!" David nods, remembering what she said to him and McMasters in the dress shop. Henry adds, "It's going to take all of our combined faith to pray for this 'perfect miracle!'"

The doctor hears them talking and tries hard to push down the lump in his throat again. He takes a deep breath, exhaling slowly. "If you want, I can take you all with me to the ICU waiting room since I need to check on her again anyway. For a little while, I ask one visitor at a time in her room." They all nod.

When David's hand is all wrapped up, Joe helps him up. Then they follow the doctor through the twists and turns, with an elevator ride somewhere in the middle of all that, to the ICU.

Carlotta went to break the news to Jack. She walks in and he turns his head and sees her walk in. He teases, "I thought you forgot about me..." He trails off when he sees her face and his eyes fill with tears. "Oh, Mother," his jaw shakes, "tell me she didn't die!"

"It doesn't look good, Jack." Carlotta softly says to him, having difficulty saying that out loud. Like David, he falls apart. He looks up at the ceiling as his eyes fill with tears, his free hand goes to a fist, then he brings it down hard on the bed. Carlotta hugs him.

He is wiping his eyes. "How's David?"

"The same as you, so he needs you," she touches his cheek like a mother would, "just like you need him." He looks at her and she gives him a 'come now' look. "You're both in-love with the same woman." Jack looks at her with a guilty face, but she gives him a little understanding smile. Jack doesn't deny it, just gives her a little smile. "If anyone should feel guilty, Jack, it should be me. The two of you are so alike, I should've expected you both could've fallen for her that night. I should've asked James to take her—."

"Stop, Mother." He gives her a faint smile. "I wouldn't change a thing," he squeezes her hand, "*really*. She's an incredible woman in so many ways, in every way that matters! She's helped me to *feel* what true-love is and I'll be forever in-love with her...I'll just have to figure out a way to love her at a respectable distance." Carlotta knows something he doesn't *yet*.

Carlotta pleas, "Promise me you won't do anything crazy to force yourself to move on *too* quickly." He knows she is referring to the risk-taking adventures, like skydiving and swinging across canyons, he has done in the past when he is working through something.

"This love *is* the real deal, Mother, I have no desire to do anything risky." He gently pats her hand asking her, "What did the doctor say?"

"I wish there was an easier way to say this." Carlotta's eyes fill with tears. "The surgeon said he wasn't going to sugarcoat anything, and believe me, *he didn't!* And neither will I because you need to hear it all, too, but it'll be hard to say, so bear with me." Her jaw is shaking. Jack nods in understanding, trying to brace himself. Carlotta clears her throat. "He first apologized for being about an hour late because Bri went into cardiac arrest, *again*. What hit me was when he said she was stabilized 'for now' and he wasn't sure how much more her body could physically take of being shocked." Jack exhales slowly to push his emotions down so he can listen. "She had multiple rib fractures; a couple were broken where one almost pierced her heart, but another one made a small puncture in her lung." Carlotta smiles tearfully. "He noted she is one strong woman!" Her smile fades, but she recovers. "She has—."

"No, Mum," Jack squeezes her hand a little, "whatever you're not saying, say it, or *you are* sugarcoating."

Carlotta is reluctant, but he is right. "The surgeon believes she was bleeding internally *before* she was shot. Knowing you and David, you would blame yourselves for not getting there sooner, but—."

"I kissed her..." Jack says to himself, replaying it in his mind.

She is confused. "What do you mean?"

"Antonio had a gun pointed at David because of his relationship with Bri *and would've shot him.*" He gestures himself. "I wanted to throw him off, so I said David was covering for me. Antonio told me to prove it by kissing her, so I did...it wasn't difficult to prove my feelings for her."

"Nor hers for you for it to be fully believable." Carlotta adds with a sweet understanding smile. "Now, what does a kiss have to do with her broken ribs—Oh, no, Sweetie! She *wasn't* internally bleeding because you kissed her."

"He yanked her back to him and she cried out briefly, right before he shot me..." Jack tells her.

"Oh, Jack." She affectionately rubs his uninjured arm a little bit.

"What else did the doctor say?" He wants her to continue.

"He was able to stop the bleeding and repair the damage to her organs. He doesn't think she'll have much for permanent damage *if* she survives. Now Jack, he stresses '*if*' because she lost a lot of blood and they're worried about blood clots as well." She thinks for a moment. "They put her in an induced coma because of brain swelling, so he stressed the next 24 to 36 hours are the most critical. The little hope he could give is that she is strong and healthy, plus she has lots of people here who love her. The last thing he said, was to encourage us to call a pastor, or hold a vigil, or..." a sob slips out and she needs a moment.

Jack squeezes her hand for support and whispers, "*A priest for last rights?*" She nods. David and Jack have friends who are Catholic so they know that last rights are only administered shortly before it's believed someone will die.

Jack gets a little frantic and starts to fumble with his covers, "I need to get to David! *To both of them!*"

A nurse walks in and explains he is going to be taken to a private ICU suite they've prepared. "The Duke of Newhaven arranged for Ms. Harris to have a large private room, so you'd be able to recover in the same room with her; making it easier for the family to be with both of you." The nurse starts to get him ready to change rooms. Jack sees she is working at a good steady pace and he is grateful for that.

David had followed the surgeon into the private room Peter arranged while Bri and Jack were still in surgery. The rest of the family waits in a waiting room the staff have set-up them. The room is more like a private corner of the floor considering it needed to be an ICU room for Bri. They also had to have extra space between Bri and Jack for the staff to do what they needed for both of them.

The surgeon gently talks to Bri. "I brought someone for you, Bri." They hear the heart monitor skip a beat. "Interesting, I haven't told you who it is yet." He smiles and turns to David, pointing to the monitor for David to see before it slides off the screen. "See that? Her heart just skipped a beat and that's for you, David." He smiles and David has a ghost of a smile. "*That's* a visible sign of love right there." He pats David's shoulder a couple times. He then checks on a few things with his patient, makes some notes, and clicks his pen before hooking it to his front pocket. "Now, I'm going to let you two have a little time together." He lightly squeezes Bri's hand. "Keep fighting, my friend." He softly pats her hand.

"Can she hear us?" David hopes.

"I'm not sure, some do. I'd like to believe she does. Besides, it can't hurt." He smiles.

David gives him a small smile through his tears and nods, then watches the doctor leave. David can barely breathe, his jaw shakes as he fights the lump in his throat; she looks so fragile hooked up to everything. He is afraid to touch her, yet he wanted to hold her; *no*, he wanted to trade places with her!

He noticed her lips had no cuts on them. When her nurse walks into the room, he asks, "Would it hurt if I gently kissed her lips?"

She smiles sympathetically. "Well," she looks, "a tender kiss from our significant other when we've been through something horrible, may be just what we need; any pain would be worth it."

David gives the nurse a little grateful smile, then turns his attention back to Bri. He gently taps her lips, then whispers in her ear, but the nurse overhears, "You can't leave me, Love! *Please*! Stay with me! And I'll marry you as soon as you say 'yes!'" He kisses her again and he sees a tear slide down her cheek.

The nurse takes a tissue and dabs it. "I want to take that as she heard you or, at the very least, she knows you're here and that's very important, too!" The nurse says to him as she pushes a chair over to David for him to sit.

"Thank you." He says as he sits down. He holds Bri's hand, praying and praying with all his heart that she makes it through.

A little while later, David hears something outside the door and gets up to see what is going on. He sees they are bringing Jack to the private suite. David goes out into the hall to hug his best friend and brother.

"She looks so fragile, Jack."

"She's a fighter, David!" Jack clears the lump in his throat. "We'll be a strength for her and be here for her!"

David nods and takes a deep breath, wiping his eyes. David moves so the nurses can bring Jack in. David walks in behind them and sees Bri's heart monitor do the same thing it did for David. Everyone is so busy getting Jack situated, they never see David snap a quick photo of it.

When the nurses leave, he goes to show Jack the picture of the heart monitor, but Henry and Maggie knock to have a few minutes. This is the beginning of visitors cycling through; the oddest were her parents. One could see they cared, but there is a feeling underneath it all that gave David and Jack pause; it is a feeling that something about her mother isn't genuine.

CHAPTER 20
Imperfectly Perfect Choice

That evening, Bri's parents went back to their hotel. Henry, Maggie, Peter, and Carlotta are with David, Bri, and Jack. Henry is holding Bri's hand and feels the Spirit deeply.

He leans into her ear and whispers, but everyone can hear, *"BriaLynn, you need to heal and gain your strength, because there's a life for you that won't be conventional, but it will be* wonderfully extraordinary!" His eyes fill with tears. *"You still have more children waiting to come to you, to be loved and raised* by you." A tear rolls down his cheek. *"You'll do a great work for your countries and for* your *people...with your blood, even* royal blood...*there are three lives to be lived simultaneously."*

David and Jack look at each other, confused, but absorb the words. While Jack is stuck on 'three lives to be lived simultaneously,' the part that sticks with the others is 'royal blood.' They look at each other and nod. Carlotta sits next to Jack on his bed as Peter turns the chair to face them and has David sit in it. Peter sits next to Carlotta at the foot of Jack's bed, Henry stays holding Bri's hand sitting next to her, while Maggie sits at the foot of Bri's bed, next to Henry.

"David," Peter says, "we were going to talk to you about this when we were flying back home, but since circumstances brought us here, this actually might be a better time."

Carlotta explains, "Ava has been working with Serene on a mission to change the law to say you can't marry *any* American." David shifts in annoyance. "As you know, I already hired researchers to research Bri's family tree. David," she smiles, "they've found what we suspected..." David's eyes dart to his mother and he studies her.

Jack asks, "What did you suspect?"

Peter smiles at Jack. "That she *is* a 'Direct Bloodline.'"

Carlotta smiles at David then tells Jack with Maggie and Henry listening, "We figured with Bri's strong ancestral ties to Scotland she'd *at least* have one bloodline, but when we heard about Dunfermline we started to wonder if *maybe* she might be a rare 'Direct Bloodline.'"

Jack looks up at the ceiling and exhales. He thinks to himself, '*Of course she would have lots of royal blood! She's the perfect woman!*'

"After everything that has happened, Mother, if she didn't even have one bloodline—."

"There's no need to think that way! She *is* a Direct Bloodline! Which means having a 'Noble Consort' will fall to her, with your approval, *or choice*." She slightly tips her head in Jack's direction with a knowing smile; Jack is still looking at the ceiling lost in his own thoughts.

Henry and Maggie smile at Bri and then each other. Bri *couldn't* have been born to them because she needed a specific ancestral tree...a 'Direct Bloodline' lineage.

David smiles big. "I couldn't agree more, Mother! That'll be the best fit for *all* of us, *if* I can get them onboard with it."

"*Don't you think Jack will agree to it?!*" Carlotta whispers.

"*No doubt!*" David quickly answers as he looks at Jack still staring at the ceiling, then Jack looks over to Bri. His mother looks at Jack when David says, "He's in-love with her, Mother." Jack looks at David, then everyone else, a little embarrassed.

"Don't be embarrassed, Jack." Peter says. "We've *all* seen it."

"*Great...*" Jack says sarcastically.

Carlotta smirks. "Yes, he's in-love with her." Jack gives her a little glare. "Question is..." she turns back to look at David, "will Bri *want* to do this? We know her heart could *easily* love you both and have plenty of love for a house full of children!"

David chuckles at that. "The real concern is whether Bri will agree to do this the way tradition calls for, rather than it being 'just on paper.'" David looks at Jack with seriousness. "There's a connection between you two that's only stopped because of her relationship with me."

Jack's eyes get teary as he hears what David is saying and he looks back up at the ceiling again; a tear slipping down from the corner of his eye. "I can't go there," Jack says, then looks at Bri again, "not yet."

"Well, then, let's help her get stronger and then work at getting her onboard with this." Henry chimes in. "She has an extraordinary life *to begin!*" He looks down at her, gently patting her hand, then he kisses her forehead.

Peter states, "If she is an American marrying an heir to a duchy, the best way for her to gain the support of our people, of the UK, would be to—."

"To grab onto a seven-hundred-year-old tradition!" Carlotta finishes with a huge smile at her husband. She looks to David and whispers, *"Knowing you, David, you'd marry her right when she woke up!"* He nods. *"Which means you need to start the discussion of a Noble Consort with her right away, to give her time so she won't feel trapped, or boxed into a corner. She loves you and there's a connection with Jack that sounds like she won't be able to ignore once she gets past the initial shock of what a 'Noble Consort' would mean for her, and for all of you."* David nods in understanding.

Peter stands up. "It's getting late." The four of them say their goodbyes to Bri, Jack, and David, before leaving for the night.

James had made a run to the hotel to grab a change of clothes for David and some toiletries for both Jack and David. James was glad to be doing something, *anything.* James is upset with Katie because she has been showing so much interest in Jack, it was embarrassing at the fundraiser. He is disgusted with her that she wasn't more supportive of Bri in the hospital. After Bri came out of surgery, Katie wasn't in Bri's room five minutes before she wanted to leave. James hugs both David and Jack before leaving for the night. Katie wants him to come stay at her condo, but he decides to break things off with her instead.

When David returns from getting ready for bed in the bathroom, a nurse has a sheet, pillow, and blanket on the recliner that she laid flat for him. This thing doesn't look comfortable, but it's better than a straight back chair or the floor. David settles in and they talk for a bit, but Jack purposely doesn't talk about anything special before they both get some sleep.

It was a long restless night for Jack and David, but Bri made it through without crashing and that is something they would hold onto, they hope she *will* come back to him...to them...

It has been two days since the attack and Bri is slowly, but steadily, gaining ground. Dr. Lucas feels it is no longer necessary to induce a coma, so they took her off those drugs and now they watch to see what happens...*and pray*. David tells her to take all the time she needs, as long as she comes back to him, *preferably soon*, to spend the rest of their *long* lives together.

At some point, during the time she is in a coma, Bri found herself in a sort of 'spirit limbo.' She is in a darkened room where she is surrounded by a deep, dark blue color, not quite black. A glowing beam of bright white light pours down over her and she feels so much love within it. She sees a slender woman appear before her, dressed in a white dress that seems to glow because of the brightness of the white color. She has brown hair, hazel eyes, and a lovely smile that goes up into her eyes.

"BriaLynn, don't be afraid. My name is Jessica and I'm a messenger sent to be your guide."

"My guide? Am I dead?" Bri asks, more curious than scared.

Jessica steps closer and begins to explain, "You've been what we call, 'touched by death.' What this means is, you're going to be given a choice: you can choose to stay and become a messenger like me; *or* you can choose to go back and 'live a *wonderfully extraordinary* life.'"

Bri looks around and whispers to herself, "*Henry?*" Because she hears those last words said in a sort of echo of Henry's voice.

Jessica continues. "*However*, if you do choose to go back to mortality, the lasting effect 'death's touch' will have on you is the ability to see spirits, as well as developing abilities you can't possibly begin to imagine for yourself without being overwhelmed." She also warns Bri, "Should you choose to go back with this gift, the power and abilities you'll develop, will also require a great price *and* a great responsibility that very few people can handle. One reason being they haven't discovered, or they haven't accepted, *perhaps both*, that there is a *very real power* in *pure* love. That's the kind of love that will help you use your power *responsibly*."

"How's that?" Bri asks.

"By understanding everyone has 'free will' or 'a right to choose for themselves.' Right or wrong, good or bad; you *can't* take that choice away from *anyone*." She stresses. She sees a hint of a panicked look on Bri's face. "It sounds like a great undertaking, *and it is*, but you know you wouldn't have been given this opportunity if we didn't think you could handle it. However, this decision to go back *must be* yours," she emphasizes, "because of the price to be paid."

"Price?" Bri repeats. "You mean knowing there will be times when I can somehow intervene in a situation but can't, because there's a choice someone has to make?"

Jessica adds. "There's a choice someone has to make *first, before* you can intervene. And to do that requires the purest of love *you do* possess! This will help you to *let* someone make their choice. There will also be a great lesson of love later on." Jessica watches her try to process what she is saying. "You can also choose to stay, to be a messenger like me, and no one will fault you for that choice."

"I can't leave David." She smiles as he comes to mind. "He's many of the reasons I'm still alive!" She pauses, closing her eyes and senses, "*And Jack?*" She whispers, then gives Jessica a questioning look.

"Yes." Jessica answers. "Your mortal journey will be one that's unique *to you*. It'll take you down paths and open doors you *never* would've imagined were there! The good you'll do, your children will be a part of your legacy, and all will come together to create an extraordinary life, and you will live in eternity with all *three* of your husbands."

"Wait. *Three?!*" She shakes her head in disbelief. "I can't go back just to lose David! Then somehow find love again, only to lose them, too! *Maybe I should rethink this!*"

"Bri, no one said anything about losing David." She replies.

Bri says with a face to match, "I'm confused."

"You won't remember everything we discuss here right away, but I'm planting seeds so we can talk about these things along the way. You'll marry David and accept Jack as your Noble Consort, which is another marriage. Your lineage will also attract the attention of The King and after some time, you'll agree to become *his* Royal Consort, a third marriage." Jessica sees Bri's eyes go big. "We can see the past, present, and future, which is how we know what you'll decide. *However*, when you go back, you'll still need to make that choice for yourself, so you can't remember this conversation until *after* you make *your choice*."

"H-*Hooowww* do I do that exactly?!" Bri asks, trying to push away the overwhelming feelings.

"By looking at this as a tradition used to protect the most royal blood and, in this situation, that's your blood! You'll have more children that'll have half your blood, ensuring these descendants will have a strong *royal* ancestral lineage, and thus, strengthening these lineages for generations to come!" Jessica explains.

"No pressure!" Bri lightly laughs, but there is a nervousness to it.

"Bri, David will insist that you do this *for* love. Jack is already in-love with you. You're *just about there* with Jack and once you allow your heart to open up to him, you'll get there *instantaneously*." Jessica smiles. "When Jack kissed you, it was real for him, but it was also *very* real for you, too."

Bri touches her lips at the memory. "*It was*." She whispers to herself, then she thinks of David and feels guilty.

"You feel guilty because you haven't considered the circumstances that led to the kiss in the first place." Jessica reminds her.

Bri thinks for a moment. "Antonio was going to shoot David..."

"Right. Jack shifted Antonio's focus to him." Jessica replies.

Bri gasps, "But then Jack was shot!"

"He survived and he will be fine." Jessica informs her, then smiles compassionately at her. "Bri, you have so much love to give. Now that your heart has been opened by loving David, it'll become natural for you to love Jack. Your love for Jack won't take any love away from David, nor does loving David prevent you from loving Jack completely. Their love will make your love grow and you'll be able to love The King, which all three will make your love grow immeasurably and you'll have more than enough love to love your children."

232

Bri's eyebrows raise. "I think you're expecting a lot from me!"

Jessica has a marble bench appear and they sit. "Bri, you've known for a long time that you have more love to give."

"I just couldn't unlock it." Bri replies.

"But that wasn't actually the case." Jessica states.

Bri thinks about that and is surprised by the answer that comes to her. "David! He is the key!"

Jessica smiles. "Right." Then she shifts their conversation. "When you wake up from your coma, you will have weeks of recuperating, giving you lots of one-on-one time with David *and Jack*. It's like a condensed courtship in that amount of time. Unlike your time with The King, which will take a bit more time because you're both busy, and he will work hard to shield you from The Queen Mother."

Bri's eyebrows furrow. "Why?"

"Let's just say your relationship with him will be your most difficult in various ways, but your relationship with him will make you feel complete because of all the love you have in your heart." Jessica says.

"I understand David's support of Jack, they're like this," she crosses her fingers, "they're this tight! But why The King?" Bri asks.

Jessica replies, "David and Jack have known The King since they were kids. They know he needs your love to help him heal from the effects of his childhood, which you'll do and ultimately helping to heal his family in the process. You'll need to remember, *'Things aren't always as they seem.'* You'll bond with The King in a way, like no one else, not even Jack or David, but you won't love Jack or David any less. *However*, you need to trust your sensitivity to the Spirit and let it guide you; even if you, or others, think it's trusting the Spirit *right into danger!*" Jessica smiles with kindness. "How about a glimpse into your future?" She gestures to the other side of the bench. Bri turns her head as Jessica says, "This is your son with David, who will be born first of your children waiting to be born to you."

Bri stands up as she watches him appear. Standing before her is a young man who looks a lot like his father with the deep brown hair, right down to the same navy-blue eyes he and his father share with his grandmother, Carlotta. Bri reaches up and touches his face, her eyes fill with loving tears and she feels her heart swell with love for him.

"You look so much like your father!" Tears fall down her cheeks. "What's your name?"

He looks at Jessica who tells him, "She can at least know while she's here."

He smiles proudly, "Jackson Christopher Worthington, but you'll call me 'Jacks.'" He hugs his mother. "Oh, Mum, I know you're nervous, but don't be! The things you accomplish will be nothing short of amazing! I'm so proud to be your son! Not only for all the things you'll accomplish for Newhaven, and even our country as our Queen, but because of your *greatest gift*!"

"My greatest gift? What would that be?" She wipes her cheeks.

"A true mother's love. The love I feel from you right now; it's the very first thing you've ever given me and it's the purest love of all..." he touches her face and she sees David so clearly in him. She hugs him again, surprising herself at how much love she already feels for this young man; she can *feel to her core* he *is* her son! "That pure love, Mum, will be the love that helps to heal the deepest wounds in Uncle Jack and even deeper wounds in Uncle Herst."

She's stunned and can only whisper, "Uncle *Herst*?" She thinks of the stories Jack and David have told of their childhood and teenage years. They seemed to almost always include Herst, 'The Third Musketeer.' She asks, "If 'Herst' is 'The Third Musketeer,' then that makes Herst..." her eyes get big as she makes the connection.

"The King." Jacks smiles wide.

"*Herst* is '*The King*'...How did I miss that?!" She asks herself, then to Jessica and Jacks, "How is all this going to work *and* for me to be taken seriously?!"

A smile spreads across his face as he smirks, just like his father and his Uncle Jack. "You'll see! I don't want to spoil the journey of getting there!"

Bri laughs but freezes when it dawns on her. "Hold on and back up! *Queen*?!" She steps back, looking from Jacks to Jessica, shaking her head. "How's that possible?" Her mind is spinning. "I thought I'm to be his 'Royal Consort?!'"

"This falls under what I said earlier; that doors will be opened to you that you never knew were there!" Jessica gives her a caring smile. "Bri, you'll soon learn that your ancestral tree makes you a 'Direct Bloodline.' This is incredibly rare, because while you're connected to many of the European countries' monarchies, some of those monarchies your connected to no longer exist. Your blood will be sought after, your life will be in peril at times because of it, but your ancestral blood will open doors for you that wouldn't have been opened any other way. I don't want to say anymore and overwhelm you further, hindering your recovery. I'll visit you along the way to help and you may call for me any time you need me. I can't say this enough as you move forward in your mortal life: *trust and follow the Spirit.*"

Bri nods with a smile, but it fades as she feels a strong sensation. "I think I need to go back...*is that right?*"

"Only you would know." Jessica answers, smiling a kind smile.

Bri looks at Jacks. "Thank you for letting me see you!"

Jacks smiles sweetly. "You'll see how we all love your hugs because we will feel so safe in your arms, so..." he cups her cheek, "*loved!*"

"Because you are!" She touches his face again with an emotional, loving smile. "I'm really looking forward to seeing you again, *my son...*" He smiles at his mother.

Then everything begins to fade away...it's time for her to start waking up.

CHAPTER 21

The Perfectly Perfect Miracle Indeed

It has been three days since the shooting. David is sitting in his usual position next to Bri's bed; he sits facing the wall with his feet propped up on the upper end of her guardrail. He is holding her hand and dozes off to sleep. It takes him a second to come out of his light sleep and realize Bri's hand is moving inside his hand. He pulls his feet down and sits straight up in his chair, staring at her hand when it twitches again.

"What's wrong?" Jack asks. He had been sleeping, too, and rubbing his face to wake up more.

Tears filling his eyes, David tells him, "Her hand! It moved, Jack!" David looks at her face and her eyes struggle to open. "She's waking up!" David says, as he stands up to get closer to her face.

Jack has been moving around for a couple of days now, so he gets up and shuffles his way over to the other side of Bri's bed. He holds her other hand close and watches her face; he fights back tears of his own.

Her eyes open and she sees David smiling, who softly says to her, "Hi, Love!" He kisses her hand. "Welcome back!" Bri looks around, taking in her surroundings.

She says to David and Jack in a froggy voice, "You act as if I died!" They see a flicker of a teasing smile. David kisses her forehead, closing his eyes and the tears slide down his face; he is relieved and overjoyed.

Jack chuckles. "Glad to see you're still cheeky as ever, Gorgeous, but let's not joke about death just yet."

"Too soon?" She winks at him.

"Just a tad." Jack grins, holding up his finger and thumb less than an inch apart. She sweetly smiles, but it fades.

Her eyes get teary when she remembers, "Can I at least say I'm glad *you* didn't bleed to death last night?"

Jack smiles, stroking her hair. "Me, too! Only that was a few days ago."

"*What?!*" She whispers in shock. "*All that took a few days?*"

David studies her and asks, "What took a few days?"

"I guess it must've been a dream..." She looks from David to Jack. She remembers only a picture of her son with David and that's enough for now. "David..." she looks at him with so much love, his heart squeezes for her, "thank you for trusting me and pinching off that artery. I know it must have been hard, but if you hadn't..." she chokes up and her jaw shakes as she tries to quell the sobs.

"Honestly, it was surreal! But having you wake up makes it all worth it!" David says, kissing her lips again. Jack strokes her hair on her head and kisses her temple.

The nurse comes in and brightly says, "Bri! It's so good to see your lovely eyes! These fantastic men, *and fantastically good-looking men might I add,*" she says that last part in a loud whisper, "have been a nervous wreck waiting for you to wake up!"

Her nurse, Sasha, is a beautiful, curvy Black woman with a fun personality. Her humor makes people laugh and laughing is *great* therapy!

She gets close and with more loud whispering, "*These two are of that rare breed of men, the* 'best of the best' *of the good ones! We do need to talk later cause I'm going to take one of them home with me, but I'll make sure to leave yours here with you...*" she pauses, "course my husband won't approve of being upgraded." David and Jack laugh and shake their heads. Sasha winks and smiles at Bri who giggles a bit, but winces from the pain. "Ooo, sorry, Honey, but at least I can give you a dose of pain meds since it's time." She tends to Bri's pain right away.

David is concerned. "Where does it hurt?"

"*Everywhere*...I feel like I've been hit, then backed over, *by a dump truck!*" She barely gets out without squeaking because of the pain.

"That's from what Dr. Lucas and the on-call staff had to do to fight to keep you alive, Honey." Sasha sympathetically tells her.

Bri's eyebrows scrunch together. "Does that mean what I think it means?"

"Honey, you coded numerous times and it was getting to the point we weren't sure if the last time you coded *would be the last time*." She explains. "People assume when someone codes and we shock their heart, it's just the heart—."

Bri's voice is breathy, "But it's felt through the entire body!" She squeezes David's and Jack's hands. "But I never would've guessed it would hurt like this *three days later*?!"

David looks at her with tears in his eyes. "After you were in surgery, Dr. Lucas sent a nurse out to say he'd be coming to talk with us, but it would take an hour because you had coded *again*."

"Actually…" Sasha hesitates a moment, "she coded a few times then, but Dr. Lucas," she looks at Bri, "wasn't going to give up on you if you were still going to fight; nor did the family need to know the number of times you actually coded that night."

Bri looks at them compassionately, "I'm so sorry you had to go through that!" She pulls David closer to hug him, and she hears him take a deep relaxing breath. Bri looks to Jack and squeezes his hand.

Jack kisses her hand. "We try not to think about the various ways it could've been horribly worse!" Bri nods a little at that.

Sasha walks over to Jack after changing out his bedding. "Let's get you off your feet, Handsome. Just because you're moving around better, doesn't mean you should overdo it either."

"Yes, Ma'am!" Jack teases back with a salute.

"Oh, you can give me attitude, but best remember I know how to *inflict pain*!" Sasha raises her eyebrow and looks pointedly at Jack.

Jack whistles. "Point, set, match, Nurse Sasha!" He bows his best with his one arm in a sling.

"Mm-hmm, now that's more like it!" She laughs.

"You just wanted me off my feet to have access to my body," Jack teases and Bri snorts a laugh.

Sasha laughs, "Oh, we'll get to that soon enough, *Baby*, but you need to be *all* healed first!"

Bri and David are laughing, but Bri is holding her abdomen, with a mixture of tears from their banter and the pain.

The next few weeks are long and hard for Bri as she recovers in the hospital. David and Jack spend most of their time with her, switching back and forth for showers or to take a walk and get some fresh air. They were keeping up with their work by laptop and phone. The men worked from the desk in her room and an extra bed table. As she got better, she wanted to dive into her new project to keep from going stir crazy, but she wasn't able to do much more than set up a template.

Jack had been released already and today he has a meeting he scheduled in town with a client who came to see him. David used this time to talk to Bri about her bloodlines. He sits on her bed next to her, pushing her work away that is on the bed table.

"Love, there's something important we need to discuss." He says and she gets worried. "To marry an heir, you already know you need to have a bloodline to do so."

She gets disappointed. "And I don't have one."

"On the contrary!" He tells her. Her eyebrows go up and then furrow a bit; she doesn't understand. "There's a possibility of four and I have three. Four occurs when one is born *from* a Direct Bloodline; or *being* a Direct Bloodline."

"So, I have two or something?" She asks, trying to follow along.

"Love, Jack and I have always felt you were a rare kind of woman and the fact that you're an *actual* 'Direct Bloodline,' only proves it." He smiles at her.

"What does that mean exactly?" She wants to understand, although there's a sense of familiarity in this topic of conversation.

"It means that your blood is more valuable and in the rules of 'Royal and Noble Consorts,' *yours* is the bloodline to protect." He elaborates, "For over the past seven centuries, 'The Noble Consort' has been mostly for The Duke of Newhaven to ensure children, particularly a male heir, to carry on the title with the strongest royal bloodlines. You'll be the third duchess to have 'The Noble Consort' to ensure *your* bloodline continues on in our children."

"I don't think I'm following." She starts to say.

"You're trying, but you have an American view that's getting in the way." He gives her a little smile. "In Europe, and other countries around the world, royals and nobles would have consorts to have more chances of having a *male* heir. This is a long-standing tradition that, if you accept having a Noble Consort, our Newhaven people, even the UK, will gravitate to you and support you, an American, marrying 'The Heir of Newhaven.'"

He sees her absorbing this, then she innocently asks, "I don't recall a consort for your father?"

"For the past few generations, the noble consorts were only on paper with timelines established for an heir to be born. For my parents, it's more if something happened to my mother, his named 'Noble Consort' would have thirty days to dissolve any marriage and enter into a marriage with him. Then an heir would need to be at least 'on the way' within two years. But it was all nullified when James was born." He squeezes her hand. "For this to work with us, *we* need to do this as it was always intended to be done." He gives her a compassionate look. "I'm telling you this now because I want to give you some time to think about it, but I plan on marrying you as soon as possible once your released from the hospital. I didn't want to propose, to have you accept, then drop this on you."

She is staring down towards her knees. "Just who am I supposed to marry?" She asks, but her head springs up looking at David when she realizes, "*Jack?!*" He nods. "But isn't that dangerous? You're best friends, *brothers*, and if you guys get territorial—."

"*Never* going to happen." He says with conviction. She goes to argue, but he stops her. "Bri, Jack and I are close because of what he went through when we were sixteen. There's nothing that can come between us because we both have a brotherly love, honor, and respect for each other. The only one close to that is Herst, who you haven't met personally yet, but I'm not sure if you've met professionally in DC?"

"I remember some stories you two have told with Herst in them." She grins. She goes to ask about professionally, but David keeps the conversation going.

"I don't say any of this lightly and with anyone other than 'The Musketeers,' it'd *never* work. I trust them with my life, I trust Jack will love you *almost* as fiercely as I do!" He winks and she smiles sweetly. "The only piece to this is whether or not you can truly love him in return? Otherwise, without true-love between both of you, *it most certainly won't work!*" He watches her for a moment. "Let's just leave this here so you can get used to the *idea* of a 'Noble Consort,' alright?"

She nods with a small smile and he kisses her. David knows Jack can handle himself and trusts his charm will win her over.

While Bri has physical therapy, David tells Jack that he explained things to Bri about having a 'Noble Consort.' He also asked that she think it over. Jack is holding his breath, hoping Bri would agree to David's plan.

At one point, when David steps out for a conference call, Bri and Jack focus on getting to know each other more, but they never discuss The Noble Consort. Jack explains how he grew up as one of the Worthington's because his father had his heir in his brother, and Jack was the 'spare.' After his mother died, his father remarried and that relationship was even worse with marriage; they couldn't stand to be in the same room. Fortunately, his stepmother was cordial with him and his brother; she wasn't motherly, but she was at least friendly with them.

"Oh, Jack that's awful! I just can't imagine. I mean, none of us kids are close to my parents, or each other as a group, but I don't think I can recall any of us feeling disposable..." She squeezes his hand, holding his gaze.

David has come back and is listening at the door to see if there is something he can use to help bring the two of them together. If Bri agrees to this, things would be fitting together like he has been feeling they should.

"It's fine, really. The Worthington's were *always* there for me and they still are. I grew up wishing I were an orphan and could be adopted by them and be 'Jack Worthington.'" He tells her and her heart squeezes. She repeats, '*Jack Worthington*' in her mind...there is something familiar about it...

"No, I get it." She says. "It's like the Bradshaw's. I didn't know them in my childhood, but I'm grateful they adopted me as an adult! There were areas I still needed to grow up in, even things I needed to change about myself, my way of thinking on certain things to gain perspective and understanding. They also helped me to see my soft heart wasn't a bad thing, like I grew up being told it was and that I needed to 'toughen up.' Henry and Maggie helped me to see that it's quite the opposite! Although, I do get frustrated at times when tears come so easily! Henry and Maggie are more my parents, with Joe, Mitch, and Sam more my siblings, than any of my blood-related family! I never understood the saying, 'blood is thicker than water' because I never saw any sort of 'strong family bonds' growing up. What the Bradshaw's helped me see is that *love is thicker than blood*; it's the strongest bonding agent there is!" Jack smiles in agreement, as he stares off into the distance. Bri uses that time to change the subject.

"Okay, *Mister* Carlisle," she grins and he laughs, "are you ready for a *very important* question?"

"Ask me anything!" Jack tells her and David listens carefully.

"Have you ever been married or have kids?" She smiles her simple, 'Mona Lisa Smile,' but it's brighter and playful than that.

He laughs a couple times. "No and no." He goes to leave it at that, but she looks at him expectantly and sweetly. He explains, "I've always had fun with ladies. I get annoyed at the world's view of beauty! I want *all* women to feel beautiful *because they are!*"

"It's what makes you special, Jack. *We ladies* can feel that from you." She smiles a little wider.

He winks at her. "Anyway, the ones I'd go out with, we'd have a great time. The ones I slept with, well, it was better with some than others..."

"So, no marriage *because*...you were having too much fun?" She asks.

"I never fell in-love until...." he trails off. He is staring out the window at this point, so she doesn't see the panicked look on his face at what he almost blurted out.

Gotcha! David smiles to himself. He can help Bri connect the dots to that later. For now, he walks in to save Jack.

"Hey there!" David says, walking up to Bri and giving her a soft, gentle kiss. Jack exhales in relief at the interruption and quickly goes to the door.

"What's up?" David asks, watching Jack fly out the door.

"Oh, he's running, before he talks about his *really deep* feelings." She grins, then it slowly fades as it sinks in. Her eyes flick back to David. "He said he's never been in-love *until*, then he stopped." She looks at the door as she pieces it all together.

He tucks some hair behind her ear and turns her chin to him. "*That's* what I've been trying to tell you..."

"It's just, well, everything you were saying was kind of overwhelming." She replies.

David smiles lovingly at her, but before he responds, the Ambassador comes to see her. '*Perfect*!' He thinks. '*Now I can chase Jack down.*' David shakes the Ambassador's hand and then steps out to give them privacy; he goes to find Jack and have a serious conversation with him. Jack avoided this conversation before she woke up, in case she didn't make it.

The Ambassador had been personally calling to check in at the nurses' station periodically; the nurses had permission to give him information on her condition. The Ambassador has paid for her and Jack's hospital bills and would pay for any lost income; he did the same for Ken.

The Ambassador sits in the chair next to her bed and holds her hand. Their conversation starts off simple enough, but eventually the Ambassador brings it to the night of the shooting. He goes to apologize to Bri, but she talks first.

"Ambassador, I'm so sorry for your loss, regardless of what else happened that night." Bri says with pain and tears in her eyes *for* the Ambassador.

He clears his throat, "Bri, *I'm* sorry! I feel this is all my fault! I made it clear I'd help set up the right conditions, like coming to DC, hosting a ball, and so on. I also told him that no one can force the heart, which I thought he understood, especially after I had explained how in-love with David you were and are." He looks at Bri for a long moment. "Can you ever forgive me?"

"There's nothing to forgive. *You* didn't hurt me. You said it yourself; you can't force people to love, but you also can't force them to make the right choices. He chose his actions, and *he* owns those, *not you*!"

Tears fill his eyes, and he squeezes her hand a bit. "You really are a special lady! Maybe more special than my Maya."

"*Oh no!* The love you two share makes her more special to you than me!" Bri tells him, not wanting him to lessen his feelings for Maya.

"Is it alright if I come back to see you before I fly back home?"

"I'd be offended if you didn't." She smiles softly at him. He chuckles a bit as he squeezes her hand again before leaving.

Jack replies to David's text that he is up on the roof. It isn't hard to find his best friend; he is looking out towards the National Monument in the distance as David walks up to him.

"How much of that conversation did you hear?" Jack asks David, his eyes still looking out at the view.

"Not much, but it was enough." David looks at Jack with a compassionate smile. "Look, I actually came to talk to you about *being* her Noble Consort." David leans against the railing, but still facing Jack. "I think we could both have a wonderful marriage with this incredible woman we're *both* madly in-love with. While I have *no doubt* she is in-love with me, I think love between you two is right there, unless I'm *completely* misreading things...Am I?"

Jack shakes his head and looks at David. "No. It's there." He takes a deep breath and exhales. "I don't think she knows it."

David hands him his phone with the picture of the heart monitor. "This is Bri's heart monitor and if you look right here," David points, "you see that her heart actually skips a beat. The surgeon noticed her heart did that when I first walked in with him and he pointed it out to me. Jack," he waits for Jack to look at him, "this is her heart skipping a beat when *you* were first brought into the room with her!" Jack is stunned; he looks back down at the picture on the screen. When Jack hands David his phone back, David puts a hand on Jack's shoulder. "Honestly, knowing you'll love her like she deserves to be loved, is the only way this *can* work!"

"I know." Jack agrees. "*And she has it!*"

David tells him, "She is worried we'll be jealous of the other," Jack scoffs, "and she *will* worry about you being pushed aside when she and I are in our official duties. Of course, we know your personality isn't one to let you be missed," Jack softly laughs, "but at the same time you're happy to let others have the spotlight."

"*That's the truth*!" Jack chuckles. "I have enough spotlight with work."

David nudges the side of Jack's arm. "Seriously though, Jack, we both also know Bri has such a big heart and so much love to give, neither of us will feel like we are lacking love from her!"

Jack agrees. "Her love for you already overflows..."

"Question is..." David turns to his friend again, "will you stand with us at the head of *our* family," he gives Jack a tearful smile, "with a stronger bond than we already have?" Jack also chokes up and David asks him, "What do you say, Brother?"

Jack smiles. "I'm in! *If* she'll have me!"

"Alright then, I'm going to need to propose to her so she will let herself open that door." David replies.

"*You can't possibly be nervous*?! You know she'll say yes!" Jack says.

"But that was before all 'The Noble Consort' talk." David gives him a nervous look. "What will trip her up is having two husbands because for an American—."

"That's a big no-no for them." Jack finishes.

"Right." David says. "But if you remember when we were just about to leave the hotel for The Charity Fundraiser that evening, she also knows traditions come with marrying me." Jack nods. "Plus, I want to be married right away, possibly putting the wedding a week from when I propose, which could scare her, too." Jack takes a deep breath.

David pats Jack's shoulder and goes to leave Jack to his thoughts. "David," Jack says with gratefulness, "thank you! I don't think I could be so generous with such an incredible woman."

David stops and looks at him baffled. "Jack! *You already have been*! You helped me see what I'd risk losing if I didn't stop being an idiot and you were already falling for her by that point." David gets choked up. "Plus, you took a bullet that was meant for me!" He takes a deep breath. "No, Jack, you've *always* been a better man than I could ever be, and I can only hope to one day become half the man you are!" They hug and pat each other's back.

"With Bri being the greatest gift, the greatest bless..." Jack trails off as he remembers what Henry was saying to her that first night. "What Henry said that night...if she agrees to this, we know what he meant." He is implying their 'third musketeer.'

David nods. "But that's for a different time." David clears his throat. "See you back downstairs?" Jack nods, then he looks out at the horizon again.

On his way back to Bri's room, David reflects on the last few weeks or so. It's been roughly a month since he first laid eyes on Bri in the hotel lobby. Three of those weeks she has been in the hospital and David has gone from hoping to having a future with her, to *knowing* he will; *if* she says, 'yes.'"

CHAPTER 22
Perfectly Perfect Proposal

The day Bri is released from the hospital is one of the happiest days for David and Jack since she was shot, although when she woke up after three days is right at the top. The families want to be there when she is released, but David and Jack convince them to hang back, they didn't want to overwhelm her. The Bradshaw's and The Worthington's all wait for them at the Bradshaw's house. Bri's parents, particularly her mother, wouldn't stand for it and she goes to the hospital anyway. Unfortunately, by the time they arrived at the hospital, Bri, Jack, and David had already left.

Bri's mother calls and her yelling can be heard by Jack and David. Jack takes her phone. "Martha, I'm sorry we already left, but had we known you were coming we would've waited. Why don't you come out to the Bradsh—." Martha refuses. Jack says some more things to smooth it over in true Jack fashion. Bri found her heart squeezing for him when he handed her phone back with that signature smile of his.

The Bradshaw's have Bri's room ready and all her things, along with David's and Jack's, were brought over from the hotel weeks ago. They also hired a physical therapist and have worked out a schedule for the girls to see their mom in the hospital, then at the Bradshaw's. When the car pulls up with Bri, David, and Jack, the whole family is there. The Worthington's all came back last night to be here today for Bri. She was emotional and grateful for their support and hugging everyone.

David caught his mother before she goes out to the back patio with the others. "Did you get it?" He asks with excitement and a huge smile.

"Yes!" She quietly laughs. "And your design is stunning, David!" She pulls out a velvet ring box.

"Thanks for your help with this!" He kisses her cheek. He hands it back to her asking, "Can you keep this for just a little longer today?" She nods and puts it in her purse, before setting her purse back down.

They all spend a quiet evening talking and having dinner before heading to bed. David isn't ready to leave Bri's side and he asks her if they left the door open, could he sleep on top of the covers? He just needed to be with her.

She reaches for his cheek and smiles. "At some point we *are* going to have to sleep separately."

"We just won't be starting tonight." And if David has it his way, they'll be married soon enough.

Jack offers to sleep on the couch in her room. They take him up on it and while David is in the bathroom, Bri makes Jack a bed on the couch. When she finishes, she stands back up and sees him smiling.

"I seem to be making a habit of sleeping on the couch." He winks.

She smiles, "This one is more comfortable than the others and the hospital beds." She pecks a kiss to his cheek.

David comes out of the bathroom and Bri grabs her pajamas to go in next. Jack and David watch her, with David whispering to Jack, "*She just might be coming around to the idea...*" Jack nods in agreement.

That night, David's in a real bed with the woman he loves right next to him. David sleeps hard for the first time in weeks.

The next morning, David had fallen back to sleep after he and Jack went to exercise and showered. Bri wakes up and sees David on his back with his head turned towards her. She leans in and carefully kisses his lips since she hasn't brushed her teeth yet. He starts to kiss her back and rolls her over so she is on her back. She covers her mouth and slips into the bathroom to brush her teeth.

She comes back and slides back into her spot. "Good morning!"

"It's a great morning!" He cups her cheek. "This is a *much* better way to wake up!" He smiles.

"Agreed." She grins.

Bri tries to get up, but David won't let her. He pulls her back into another kiss. When he lets her up, she goes to get ready for the day.

At breakfast she mentions needing to call Amy for a car and asks if someone would go with her to work. She had to take care of a few things Amy is waiting for her help on. It wouldn't be much more than a couple of hours round trip.

David is confused. "I planned on taking you, Love."

"David, you and Jack could use a break from taking care of me and entertaining me." She has a little bit of teary eyes. "You both should go *do* something today." David sees she thinks she is a burden to him and doesn't want to be.

"You're not a burden." He tucks some of hair behind her ear. "I'm in this, Love!" He laces their fingers together of the hand he is holding and kisses the back of her hand.

She has a lump in her throat and her jaw shakes, making it difficult to say anything. She wraps her other hand around the back of his neck and pulls him in for a kiss. He holds the back of her head to hold their kiss a bit longer.

"How about we bring Jack along," she smirks, "to *entertain* you?"

Jack grins. "That can be arranged!"

Later that morning, they arrive upstairs in her office building. Jack and David walk around while Bri goes through her paperwork and mail, then helps Amy with the tasks that need her attention. David and Jack run into Senator Jenkins who takes them on a small tour over at The West Wing; he needed to drop off something. They run into The President who shows them The Oval Office while Jack and David tell him how Bri is doing.

Bri sends David and Jack a text that she is wrapping up, to give them time to get back to the office building from wherever they were at.

> Bri: "I'm about done, so we can leave whenever you two get back to my office."

Jack sends her a 'thumbs up' while David and her boss are talking. The three men step outside where an aide walks David and Jack to the crosswalk that leads to The Executive Office Building across the street. They thank the aide, then walk over to Bri's office. Bri has her things in a chair at Amy's desk while she waits for Jack and David. When they come back, they tell the ladies where they were and how they ended up there. Bri smiles as she pulls out her phone and sends 'thank you' texts to Senator Jenkins and her boss.

At the Bradshaw's, the girls are enjoying the pool and the adults are having tea and lemonade outside. Later that afternoon, Bri has her physical therapy appointment outside. Then that night, they go to bed early. Jack sleeps on the couch again so David can sleep next to Bri.

The screeching of the obnoxious alarm clock the next morning wakes Bri. While she typically wakes up neutral, that specific alarm sound could drive the most pleasantly dispositioned person to commit murder. She buries her face in her pillow, wondering why she ever agreed to get up so early *again*?!

With her eyes closed, she turns her head and says, "Didn't we break up the last time you woke me up early, *Lord* Newhaven!"

David softly chuckles. "Note to self, *and Jack*, this beautiful woman is *still* not a morning person. *However*, the formal way she addressed me is *far* too pretentious, *especially for her!*"

She exhales loudly in frustration. *"I'm thinking we need to officially end this!"* She rolls away from David and gets comfortable again.

"Oh, no, no, *no*. It's time to get up, Beautiful. We have places to go today!"

The look on his face is an excited pleading, making her heart melt. "Alright *Lord* Newhaven, *this better be good!*" She says with all seriousness but lets him help her up. She points her finger at his chest, "Or—*."

He kisses her quiet, then kisses her jawline back to her ear. *"I'm hoping to take your breath away!"* He whispers in her ear and hearing her breath catch makes him smile.

She pulls back and looks at him with her brown eyes, so full of teary love. "You already do!" She gives him a sweet smile and he taps a kiss to her lips.

David turns around as he tells Jack to stay where he is, he already has his back to them, so Bri can get dressed. She lets them know she is dressed as she walks to the bathroom. She brushes her teeth, then fixes her hair, adding a few curls. She sees David in the mirror, standing in the doorway.

"Seriously, David, it's barely the start of a new day, most would say this is *still* nighttime! Want to explain to me how we're going to make a relationship work when we're not even close to waking up at the same time, then what happens when we're in *different* time zones?!" She asks.

David walks over reminding her, "You gave me your time since we came to DC and you're *not allowed* to take *any of it back*, let alone break up with me!"

"Oh, really?" She raises her eyebrow watching him step behind her.

He wraps an arm around her, looking intensely into her eyes through the mirror, making her a little weak in the knees. She turns to face him and he passionately kisses her, running his hand down to her bum. When he squeezes his hug a little more, she feels so much desire from him and for him, it's all she can do to pull their lips apart.

"Wow!" She fans herself and clears her throat. "Keep kissing me like that and we'll both go mad with desire and living in our own tortured Hell!" They hear Jack snort into a laugh.

"Then maybe we should get going!" He suggests.

"And where's that?" She asks as they walk to the bedroom door to leave. "Are we eloping?" She snickers.

He whispers in her ear, as he opens the room door, "*I do have forever in mind, Love!*"

He laces his fingers with hers and they walk to the awaiting car out front. She loves that he is always holding her hand with their fingers laced together. When they are riding in the back seat, she lays her head on his shoulder and rests her eyes.

David had asked all the staff on their flight to help keep their destination secret. He planned every detail while he was by her bedside in the hospital and he is fairly sure she will accept his proposal, *but* the 'wild card' is Jack being 'The Noble Consort.' He will wait as long as she needs, but *prays* she will agree to the date he has been planning. A flight attendant tells them they are about a half hour from landing, so the window shades need to be closed.

Once landed, David asks Bri to put a blindfold on; she complies. He helps her to the car, and she slides into the back seat. The driver knew in advance where to go and pulls away from the plane. They drive into the city and park the car.

David helps Bri out of the car and she can smell fresh bread in the air. They step into an elevator and ride it all the way up. He walks her over to where he told her he loved her for the first time and takes her blindfold off for the big reveal.

"The Eiffel Tower?!" She's surprised. "I should've known with the wonderful smell of fresh bread in the air and the long elevator ride!"

"I love seeing you this happy!" He hugs her from behind and looks out at the view with her. "The sunrise and being in Paris are symbolic..." He leaves it at that and she lets him. She smiles as she reaches up to cup his cheek.

He walks around to face her. "While you were in the hospital, Uncle Henry and I would have some deep spiritual conversations. He and I would even have those while my parents were there to listen, then we all had some nice open discussions; even Jack joined in!"

"That seems about right for Jack."

"It does?" David asks.

"He and I have had some really deep spiritual conversations also." She says, looking at David confused. "You haven't?"

"Shamefully, no. I assumed he wouldn't want to talk about those kinds of things because of his mother..." David trails off for a moment, then continues. "I understand more of *why* Uncle Henry made his decision all those years ago, and I'd like to think my father does, too. It's different, but I would've given up *everything*, even being The Heir, without a second thought to be with you!"

She shakes her head. "David, I'd never want—." She starts to say, only he kisses her quiet.

He rests his forehead to hers. "I know. I also know that it's necessary to have faith in His plan for each of us. While I'm working on that, I know you are very much a part of that plan for me. Spending all this time with you, I'm even more convinced you're the one for me!" He reaches into his pants pocket and pulls out a velvet ring box saying, "I love you more than I've ever loved *anyone*. This may be cliché, but it doesn't have any less meaning for me: you *are* the love of my life! I love you now and I'll love you for an eternity." He goes back to explain, "I said earlier that the sunrise was symbolic, and it is because it marks the beginning of a new day, *and today*, I'm hoping, is a new chapter in our relationship and lives..." He goes down on one knee and as he opens the box he asks, "BriaLynn Harris, will you marry me?"

Bri holds her hands up to her mouth as she inhales a soft gasp. She is staring at a one-karat diamond ring in a white and yellow gold setting. It has a gold Triquetra on either side of the round diamond, and a pattern of stretched-out Triquetras in white gold goes around the rest of the band. She watches him take it out of the box.

"I had it made just for you and Mother brought it with her!" His excitement can be heard and seen. "I was going to have a larger diamond put—."

She shakes her head, taking it from him and looking at it closer. "*It's beautiful!*" She whispers.

He shows her the engraving and says it, "*Tá mo chroí agat!*" Directly across is its meaning, "You have my heart!" There is a Claddagh etched in between each end of the sentences.

Bri has tears in her eyes and she is trying to swallow the lump in her throat. She takes a deep breath and exhales slowly as he slides the ring on her left finger. He now knows, *without a doubt*, she is going to say 'yes,' or she never would have let him put the ring *on* her finger.

She is trying to come up with something more eloquent than 'yes,' because he is so amazing, so wonderful, and she loves him deeply. "*Hmmm*, I have to come up with a big word, that *small one* just won't do..." She teases him as she gives a dismissal wave.

The seconds of silence feel like hours. "That little *three* letter word will do nicely, Love..."

"*Shush*, I can't think of a great word with interruptions. How about..." she taps her chin.

He groans in a plea, "*Briiii...*"

"Will '*absolutely*' work?!" She smiles the biggest and happiest smile he has ever seen on her!

David is just as happy as he jumps up, cups her face, and says, "I love you!" He pulls her lips to his and kisses her fiercely. He wraps an arm around her waist and the other hand around the back of her neck, kissing her deeply and passionately. He kisses her again and again, then picks her up and twirls her around.

She puts her hands to his cheeks. "I love you, too!" She bends her head down and kisses him passionately again as he slowly sets her down.

"A quicker answer would've been less torture, Love." He smirks, kissing the ring on her finger.

"I'll try to remember that for the next time you ask me to marry you!" She teases, smiling happily and so full of love.

With their foreheads together he reminds her, "I believe I have five days left."

She giggles. "Sounds like you have some ideas for those five days."

"As I said earlier, I only have forever in mind!" He says.

She lightly shakes her head in confusion asking. "Okay?"

He is hopeful when he says, "Our wedding!"

She pulls back in shock. "What?! Are you—I can't poss—?" She is too surprised to find the words to make a coherent sentence.

"Bri, the scariest time in my life..." he chokes up, "was that night you were shot; *you almost died!* All that blood...*your gray color!*" He takes a deep breath to push back more tears. "The worst part was leaving the operating room and hearing words that I won't soon forget, 'we're losing her,' and knowing what that meant. All I could think was, '*How could I lose you?!* I just found you!'"

Bri's eyes fill with tears. "I'm so sorry you had to go through that, David." She wraps her arms around his neck and hugs him.

"I did find comfort learning from Uncle Henry about the purpose of life. What felt even worse," he tries to swallow the lump down and looks at her, "was you could die, and we were never married." He tucks some flyaway strands of hair behind her ear. "I want to be your husband and I want you to be my wife." He holds her hand up, lacing their fingers and says, "Together, through eternity."

She kisses him, hoping he can feel her love. "I adore you, David!"

"I adore you, too, Love!" He kisses her once more and deepens it. Finally, they pull back slightly out of breath.

"We've only known each other a month! *This is insane*!" She says.

"In that month, we've done a lot of talking. Talking that would've been spread out across a lot of months!" He tells her.

She lightly laughs, then she thinks back, "We haven't had our first fight!"

He rubs his cheek. "Oh, I think we got *those* out of the way in the beginning!"

She scoffs. "That was *before* we began!"

"We *began* with the texting outside The Coriander Hotel, Love." He gives her a grin because he knows he has her! "What do you say? Will you marry me Saturday and become who you were always meant to be...*my wife*, the true Mrs. David Worthington and the future Duchess of Newhaven?"

"David, I need more time to plan a wedding!" She looks at him and sees the expression on his face. "*You already planned the wedding*?!"

"Nothing that can't be changed if you hate it, but I did a lot of it while you were in the hospital. I had to do something to keep me busy, *besides work*." He grins with a wink.

"I highly doubt we'd have to change anything since you have fantastic taste! In fact," she teases, "I bet we could get married right this second and it would be perfect!"

"Not perfect, *but*..." He sweetly smiles and she giggles.

"If you and I are there with close friends and family, it's already perfect!" She replies. "It's all we really need."

"Touché." David laughs and his heart squeezes that much more for her. He taps a kiss to her lips. "I just wanted to show you how serious I am about the promise I made to you; that I'd marry you as soon as you were released from the hospital! I didn't pick out your dress or bridesmaids dresses; tuxes will have tartan squares or coordinating color squares for the pockets." He is so happy and excited. "What do you say?!"

"I say this is crazy! *I'm crazy* for even considering this! I won't tease you again and make you wait any longer for my answer. I'm so crazy in-love with you, *Mister* Worthington! So 'yes'!"

"Yes?!" He wants to be sure he heard correctly.

"Yes, I *will* marry you this Saturday!" Bri tells him. "And I'm so confident you won't have to change a thing and you can keep it all a surprise!"

David picks her up, twirling her around again as he kisses her, but he sets her back down as gently as he can when he faintly hears her grimace in pain.

"Sorry, Love."

"*Completely* worth it for these..." She pulls him into another deep and passionate kiss.

"Then the nurse was right." He says.

"About what?" She asks.

"When I first saw you after your surgery, I asked the nurse if I could kiss you. There wasn't any bruising or scratches on your lips, so I thought *maybe*." He tells her. "She said having a kiss from a significant other is worth any pain."

She smiles and nods. "She's right!" They kiss for little longer, before they need to leave.

In the car, David sends a group text to all their family and friends, also including Bri on it.

"Bri said 'Yes!' AND pack your bags, we're getting married this coming Saturday!"

There are lots of congratulations and 'we love you' texts that come back to them. Katie's text is only a 'congratulations.' A bit disappointing to Bri, but also telling.

CHAPTER 23
Imperfectly Perfect Noble Decision

They spend the rest of their trip at The Palace of Versailles. They walk around and find a garden bench, tucked away from people. They sit, but they are turned towards each other to talk better.

David takes her hand. "We need to discuss something important right now. I know you're marrying me for me and not for the title of 'Duchess.'" She thoughtfully nods. "And I know, *you know*, that by saying 'yes' to marrying me, you also agree to certain *requirements*."

She nods. "I do." Taking a deep breath to steel her nerves for talk of a Noble Consort. "Marrying you means Jack will be my Noble Consort..."

"I've given this *a lot* of thought, Bri. Please hear me out." He squeezes her hand a bit. "I know there is chemistry between you and Jack, and it's been there from the beginning." He pulls up the heart monitor picture and explains. "When the surgeon first brought me to your room, he showed me your heart monitor and how it 'skipped' a beat for me." She smiles as he points to what he's talking about.

"*That's incredible!*" Bri says with amazement.

"Bri, this is a picture of the second time the heart monitor skipped a beat..." He smiles when she looks at him. "I quickly snapped this picture when Jack was first brought into your room."

Her mouth drops in disbelief. She whispers a barely audible, "*What?*"

"I also know Jack has been in-love with you and has been fighting it because you're with me. *And* I know that, had I been stupid and let you slip through my fingers, *he wouldn't have*. On top of all that, I also know he will *never* find another woman like you!" He grins and she rolls her eyes with a slight smile. "Most importantly, Love, you have so much love to give that you can *easily* love both of us and we'd be very fulfilled in our relationships with you! Above all," he lifts her chin to look into her eyes, "I know, *without a doubt*, that in order for this to work, you *both* have to be *in-love* with each other."

"David, I'm *NOT* the sharing kind, and there is absolutely *no way* I'd ever agree for you, or Jack, if it goes that way, to be with another woman–er, consort!" She states.

"I know!" He laughs.

"If you know, then what would've happened if you would've been the one with the consort, knowing I wouldn't sign up to share you with another woman! Seems hypocritical of me, don't you think?"

"Love, it would've been 'on paper' like the few generations before me. Plus, one rule is the spouse has to approve." He smiles. "One thing is for sure; my heart *isn't* as big as yours and there is room for *only you!*" He lifts his eyebrow as it occurs to him, "Aren't you the first one to say, 'everything happens for a reason?'"

"Trust me, *that has* occurred to me." She admits. "History always shows male royals and nobles with consorts, but what has also come to my mind with 'everything happens for a reason,' is that a woman with the consorts *may* make more sense."

"*Intriguing.*" He says. "Explain that."

"Take financially. A male having the consort, or in some countries it's consort*s*, would be one source of income spread out over two or more households. However, a woman with the consort, or consorts, there would be *multiple sources of income*, like yours and Jack's, pooled together to take care of *one family*. Then timewise, workaholic men can continue to be dedicated to their careers, splitting family time between them."

"And not feel guilty because we'd know you're being taken care of when you're not with us."

"Right." She notes, "And in more medieval times, more than one protector of the family and lands."

He kisses the back of her hand and she smiles, but he still senses her uneasiness. "Love, could it be that you're looking at this as unfair because you're looking at it from a sexual view?" He asks, watching her think about that and adds, "But, if you look at it from a view of adoring love..." he pulls her chin to look at him, "*your* heart can love us both individually and completely, making it *completely* fair!"

"How can you say that?!" She asks as tears leak down her cheeks and she wipes them away quickly.

He puts his hand on her heart. "I feel it from you!" More tears run down her cheeks and he holds her face. "Love, I *know* he loves you and you know it, too! The question is: would you be able love him?" He sweetly smiles, "*Perhaps you already do...*"

"I've never let myself 'go there' because I love *you* and *you* have my heart!" She tells him. "I swear—.'

"I know, Love. I never doubted your feelings for me, or your faithfulness. Try to see this with Jack separately." He suggests and she gives a little nod. He taps a kiss to her lips and holds her hands. "Jack is the greatest man I know, Bri. Truth be told, he's a better man than me, always has been. I've told him as much throughout the years, reminding him of that fact not too long ago."

"I doubt 'better than,' but I do see he is absolutely wonderful, just like you!"

"Love, he needs to be loved *by you*! You're the only woman in the world who can, and will, love him the way he deserves to be loved. He needs someone who will protect his heart and *genuinely* accept his love in return. *That's you*! I believe in your love for me and I know you believe in my love for you!"

She grins. "*Absolutely*!" He winks with a loving smile.

"He should be in your heart, Love. Protected by your love and free to love you, rather than keep it bottled up inside." He rests their foreheads together.

She sweetly smiles. "In order for me to give you an answer I do have a question, just to be clear."

"Of course!"

"What do you see happening in his relationship with me?" She asks.

"Love, you would essentially be married to both of us. I want you to develop a relationship with him, as you have and continue to do with me. It would be two marriages side-by-side and you with *all* your children in the middle." He cups her cheek. "They're a part of you and we'll love and take care of all of them because we *deeply* love their mother. Plus, we love each other as brothers and best friends, so we will love each other's children as our own as well!"

"I keep thinking," she chokes up and takes a deep breath, "this seems like we're asking for trouble!"

"Jack and I are as close as brothers can be, closer than James and me! We've always supported each other over the years and our 'rivalry' is fun competition in the moment, but we don't 'keep score' because we don't want to." He squeezes her hands. "I think the three of us have a shot at having two wonderful marriages and a stronger friendship than ever before!"

"I'm still having a hard time believing this will work because of the whole 'male testosterone' thing. The male ego being so fragile, it's the cause of a lot of crimes!" She says.

"This isn't like that, I *swear* to you, Bri! Jack and I *know* we wouldn't be in competition for your love, because we know you have more than enough to love us *individually*!"

"How can you be so sure?" She asks.

"I'm sure, as long as we keep respecting each other, first and foremost." He smiles. "You'll fret about the relationships and fairness, until you start seeing what I've been saying, *and* what Jack will tell you." He taps a sweet kiss to her lips, then a smirk spreads across his face. "Call me crazy, Love, but I believe you when you say I have your heart."

"Good!" Her voice cracks and her eyes are teary. "*Because you do!*" She wipes her eyes with her fingertips.

"Great!" He kisses the back of her hand. "Then what will you do when I say *I want* Jack in your heart, too?" Her mouth drops. She is lost for words and clamps down on her lips inside her mouth, glaring at him; he softly chuckles.

"And what does Jack say about all this?!" She asks. "He has to have some reservations about all this?"

"*Nope!* Not one!" He looks at her with a knowing smirk. "Bri, why do you think he spent so much time with you in the hospital?"

She smirks back telling him, "He's *your* best friend!"

"If that's all it was, he would've traveled back and forth, making the best of meeting up with clients in New York and Boston. *But he didn't.* After he was released, he would only meet with his top clients who had to come to DC, *and* they met close by the hospital."

She kisses him tenderly. "*If* we do this, there has to be some added rules..."

"Alright." He listens.

"I don't have all of them, so some might come as we would go along. One rule *has* to be 'what goes on behind bedroom doors, *stays* behind bedroom doors.'" She tells him.

He nods. "What else?"

"Marital beds are to stay 'sacred,' so-to-speak." She says.

"Good. And?"

She looks so lovingly at him. "*You're* running this ship, so in a way you're the captain and Jack would be the first officer. *You* dictate how this goes! If this ever gets called off in any way, shape, or form, I need you to know, David, *I pick you!*"

He kisses her and smiles. "*I swear to you* it will *never* come to that! Besides, it's easy to say that now, but when you finally open yourself up to love Jack, it wouldn't be!" He smiles and taps another kiss to her lips, then he grins, "For the record, you're the admiral!"

"Me?! What? *Why?*"

"I want you to live your life *with us in it.* Most importantly, it'll always be *your* body, so *your* rules!" He smiles lovingly. "That's why any rules you set; we will agree to."

"Thank you for that." She taps a firm kiss to his lips. "Now, when would this 'Noble Consort' thing go into effect, or whatever?"

David lightly laughs. "Essentially, the day before we're married, so Friday, there would be paperwork that we three would sign. The paperwork for 'The

Noble Consort' would say when we're officially married, you would essentially be married to Jack as well."

"Seriously, though, the media and press will crucify us, *ME*!" Bri says, which causes David to laugh hard.

"*If* this was America, but I'd think feminists would come to your defense, because as you noted earlier, noble and royal *men* typically have the consorts!"

"*There may be truth to that...*" Bri admits.

"In Scotland, the UK, and well, *all through Europe*, we love our old traditions; the older the better. Our public in Newhaven will embrace something that hasn't been done in centuries, of a Duchess, *or future Duchess*, having a Noble Consort." Bri lifts her eyebrow; he chuckles a bit. "Like I said before, a *Duchess* having a Noble Consort hasn't been done in centuries. Plus, the people will embrace you because you are a rare 'Direct Bloodline.' As cold as it may sound, they know it means an infusion of various monarchies into the noble lineage of Newhaven and ultimately the UK. The best part will be that their future Duke is fully supportive of your marriage to The Noble Consort and seeing all three of us happy together will only help to solidify their *excited* support of *you*."

"Aren't we stacking the genetic cards against our children?" She asks.

"I can see why you might think that, but the 'Direct Bloodline' markers go back far enough to ensure genetics aren't an issue like that." He replies.

They stand up and he cups her face. "If you're truly considering this, talk it over with Jack. If you say you just can't do this, I promise you, I'll drop this whole thing and only ask for this to be 'on paper.'"

"Which means?"

"If anything happens to me, then Jack would step in; but again, it would still be your choice. The 'on paper' means I support it."

"David, it's you. I need you to know that! I will *always* choose you, the man who has my heart!"

"That's because you wouldn't let yourself fall in-love with Jack *because of us*." He says. "But when you do, and your love for him grows deep, you will be grateful you will *never* be asked to choose."

She shakes her head. "David, this strong bond we've had since we met, *proves* you're the anchor, *my* anchor! An anchor can mean many things, but spiritually it represents love, hope, faith, and trust. All of which keep us committed firmly to each other, in the craziness of life." She kisses him firmly, passionately, and deeply. "I love you, David!"

"I love you, too!" He kisses her and hugs her. "I like that description of an anchor." He says. "I really think the three of us could be *incredibly happy*, but it's your happiness that matters to both Jack and me." He smiles and caresses her face... "Did you know Henry felt inspired to say some things to you that first night you were in the hospital, even though you were in a coma."

She shakes her head. "What did he say?" She has so much love in her eyes for him, his heart melts.

"Keep looking at me like that and I'll see about giving you the world!"

"Oh, *Mister* Worthington, it isn't just because of this pretty face," she points to her face, "you love me, so you already want to do that!" He chuckles and nods. She sits back down and has him sit next to her. "Please, David, tell me what Henry said."

"This may put pressure on you, and I don't want to do that! I want this to be *your* decision; it *needs* to be *your decision.*"

"David, didn't you say Henry was inspired?" She asks and he nods. "Then it's important for me to know because that was an inspired message *for me*. Besides, you're the one who said, 'everything on the table so we can deal with it,' remember?"

He exhales a small laugh. "He told *you* that you needed to heal and gain your strength because, while your life won't be conventional, it would be '*wonderfully extraordinary!*'" They say the last two words in unison as she somehow remembers them being said to her.

He is confused as to how she knew, but she encourages him, "Keep going."

He thinks for a moment. "You have children who need to be born *and loved by you*. You'll do a great work for your people and countries, with your blood *and* with royal blood. Oh, and he said there are three lives to be lived simultaneously."

"Royal blood meaning being a 'Direct Bloodline?'" She asks.

He shrugs, "Maybe." Although he thinks it might have to do with Herst, he keeps that to himself for now. He asks her, "Are you alright?"

She inhales and then exhales a 'whew' look with her eyebrows raised. "Too many thoughts going through my head, just trying to sort them all out."

He takes her hand and he starts walking around again. They walk in comfortable silence for a while. She keeps thinking of *'wonderfully extraordinary.'* He stops and she realizes he was saying something.

"I'm sorry." She apologizes.

"What had you so deep in thought?" He asks.

"Ever since I woke up," she continues in their walk, "I've felt like there is this amazing dream I had, only I can't remember it." She gestures her head. "It's right there, *I feel it*, but I can't quite grab hold of it. I have a picture, but that's it. Then when you said, 'wonderfully extraordinary' it's like I had already heard it in Henry's voice." She stops. "I sound crazy—."

"You're not crazy." He says.

She taps a kiss to his lips. "Enough of that for now. When are we supposed to decide, or move ahead, or *whatever?*"

"Go to Jack and see, but before Friday." He gently kisses her lips. "Open yourself up to him and I have a feeling your heart will do the rest!"

She smiles. "I guess it's back to the real world?"

"Well, I'd love to take you to Newhaven, but you and Jack need some time. I have a couple of last-minute things for the wedding and I need to take care of some 'fires' at work." She is quietly staring out into the gardens they came from, but at a downward angle. "What is it?"

She holds her eyes closed for a moment. "Ever since the night when your parents' party ended and I had a barrage of missed calls, voicemails, and texts, I was feeling tired. Yes, I have a knack for handling difficult people with influential positions, but all I kept thinking Saturday night, and especially spending time with you on Sunday, was that a huge part of my job was babysitting the worst of those influential people. I don't know if I said it, but thank you for that Sunday in Dunfermline, *really*."

"You don't have to thank me! Spending time with you was, *and is*, a *completely* selfish act!" He grins and she giggles. He tells her, "If you want to quit——."

"I did, until, well, you've been talking about marrying me for a while, so just the other day I was pondering: *could I quit my job*? But now that my boss asked me to do this special project..."

"And you'd like to see it through?" He asks with a sweet smile.

"Yes! Unfortunately, it won't be done by Friday. We're bringing all the agencies like CIA, FBI, Homeland, and so forth, to have a 'one stop war-shop' of 'good versus evil,' and trying to use each agency's expertise, accordingly; sharing info, working together...ah, it would've been *SO* great! I'm just sad I won't see this through."

"Hold on!" His Scottish accent strong with that phrase.

Bri can't help but giggle. "Your Scottish accent just then was pretty heavy, not to mention *very* sexy. It's also very soothing to my soul..." then she closes her eyes to hear more.

"Alright," he chuckles, "but the feeling is mutual."

"Me? *I'm* not the one with a Scottish-English accent." She grins.

He kisses her, then smiles and says against her lips, "Yours just adds to your gorgeousness!" He kisses her again before pulling back and getting serious. "Love, no one said you have to quit, at least not right away! Your duties later may be such, you won't have time to dedicate to a project like this for a different country, but you can right now!"

"What?" Her eyes fill with tears.

"Love, there's only one thing I want more than anything in this world!" She gives him a confused look. He smiles, "*You're happiness!*" He holds her cheek. "Your face lights up with excitement when you talk about this project! How could I *not* want you to see this through!"

Bri grabs his jaw and fiercely kisses him, then she hugs him saying, "I love you so much, David!"

"I love you, too!" He laughs. "If memory serves me correctly, you're able to work from your desk, right?"

"*Riiight...*" She looks at him a little suspiciously with a smile.

"I'm hoping we can work something out for you to have an office at The Manor, or better yet, there *and* at The Worthington Corporation with me?!"

"I think if I had my laptop since it's secured and working with IT to secure Wi-Fi in both places, we *may* be able to..." She says as she considers her options. "My loyalty to my job and coworkers won't be pulling at me like they have been. My loyalties have shifted and they're to you first."

"As are mine to you." He adds.

"Ha-ha," she laughs with tears, "I kind of got that feeling when you haven't left my side! And Jack, well, if Jack and I do this then he's up there on my list with you! The girls, and future kids, are a 'no brainer'. *However*, within reason, marriage coming first ultimately benefits the kids; it adds to their stability."

She kisses him and he returns it. He puts his forehead to hers, letting the love pass through them that they feel for each other...Lots of love that is almost overwhelming. It's all this love she feels from him that has her love overflowing...David is right, she *will* be able to *easily* love Jack!

He pulls his head back. "Let's get you back, so you can fall in-love with Jack," she snorts a little laugh and he winks, "*and* so you can organize things to work remotely as soon as you can." He kisses her one last time before walking to their awaiting car.

They go to the airport where they say goodbye for a couple of days. Bri tells him, "Maybe it's for the best we're flying our separate ways." He looks at her puzzled; she giggles. "This was the perfect day and now I'll be dreaming of how wonderful the wedding will be, but with you around it would be *much harder* to stop thoughts of the wedding night."

His eyes have a hint of desire in them. "I can *definitely* relate! The more I love you, the more I want to be *very* intimate with you."

"That's the *only* good thing about the miles! It'll help keep these feelings suppressed for a little while longer!" She smiles softly. "Remember, David, you have my heart. I love you!"

"I love you!" He kisses her one last time, before she boards the plane.

He sees her wiping tears as she sits by a window. They wave as the plane pulls away and he watches it take off. He gets into a car that takes him to another plane to fly back to Edinburgh. David texts Jack quick.

> David: "Meet Bri when her plane lands. She's nervous about how all this will work between the three of us."
>
> Jack responds: "Text me the info and I'll be there!"
>
> David: "Sent."
>
> Jack: "Safe travels, Brother!"
>
> David: "I will, knowing our girl is safe with you!"
>
> Jack: (thumbs up emoji)

CHAPTER 24

Imperfectly Perfect Love

Bri takes the time during her flight to think about Jack being this 'Noble Consort' and if it could work. She thinks about what David had told her about Henry, and what he said that first night she was in the hospital. She also wanted to talk to Jack because she does feel a connection with him. When David told her Jack was already in-love with her, which Jack almost admitted to her when she was in the hospital. It all makes her think there *may be* a real chance this could work...

When Bri's plane lands, she gathers her things. She steps off the plane and sees Jack waiting for her. She was unprepared for an overwhelming sense of love for him in that moment; *'instantaneous'* coming to mind as she puts her hand over her heart. He smiles seeing her smile with her hand over her heart.

She descends the stairs down to the tarmac and walks towards Jack. She takes in that he is looking handsome wearing a polo shirt, khaki shorts with sandals, and a beautiful smile, all while standing next to a sporty blue convertible. The similarity of this picture brings to mind David's red convertible he drove to take her on their Sunday picnic.

Something comes over her...*is it love*? She walks right up to him, drops her things, and wraps her arms around his neck as she kisses him fiercely. She feels his arms hug her tight as he returns the kiss. A hand goes down her bum, then deepening their kiss more as he partially dips her back and holds her there. They stop to catch their breath for a moment and smile as they look into each other's eyes.

"Well, *Mister* Carlisle, am I right in assuming David sent you?"

"You'd be correct." Then he grins. "Although I wasn't expecting this!"

"Neither was I!" She smiles and pulls him into another kiss.

He slowly brings her back up and rests their foreheads together; his hands resting on her hips. "I knew there could've been something between us, but...*WOW*!" He kisses her once more, then releases her. He bends down to pick up her things for her. "Are you taking any pain meds?" He pops the trunk and puts her things in it so nothing blows away.

269

"*Ha-ha*! I've been off those things long before I was released from the hospital!" She informs him.

"Double-checking." He smiles wide tossing her the keys, then he goes over and opens the driver's door for her.

"You want me to drive?!" She asks with a huge smile.

"I do! Now get in!" Jack smiles back.

She squeals a little in excitement as she gets in; his heart feels good seeing her excited like this! He shuts her door, then goes around and gets in on the passenger's side.

"What do I owe this fun little ride?" She asks.

"Well, David said we should *talk* and see where things go." He smirks. "*Although,* I am *partial to your deviation*." He has a heart melting grin on his face and adds, "Take me somewhere we can talk, Gorgeous!"

Bri texts Henry and Maggie to ask if the beach house is rented and she gets a response right away that it's open. She drives that direction and they enjoy the nice drive to get there. She slows down as she drives through town.

Jack asks, "Where are we?"

"We're passing through the town that's before we get out to Henry and Maggie's beach house." She replies. "It's kind of private with the various dunes and hills along the beach."

They pull into the driveway and up to the house. They walk up to the door and there is a box with a key locked inside it. She puts in the code to get the key, then unlocks the door and puts the key back in the box to be locked in. He follows her inside, all the way to the back and out the patio doors. They walk out to the beach together and to the edge of the waves washing ashore.

"Why are you so willing to jump right into this, Jack?" She asks, watching the waves and the water.

He turns to her, then he turns her to face him. "Bri, you're the most amazing woman I've ever known *in my life*! I never thought one woman would capture my heart because I enjoy being around women. I figured I'd be a bachelor for life. Getting to know you and seeing how incredible you are, I fell fast! That Friday with Antonio and the aftermath, I couldn't deny it anymore. That kiss might've been a show for Antonio, but it was very real for me, Bri." He holds her cheek. "I think it was for you, too." She nods. "When David would discuss with me that he wanted me to be your 'Noble Consort' and for both of us to be married to you..." He exhales slowly.

Bri asks him, "Was I the one you fell in-love with when we were talking that day in the hospital."

"Yes." He is relieved finally be able to say it out loud.

"Aren't you afraid of being pushed aside as David and I are thrust into the Newhaven spotlight?"

"*Not at all!*" Hi quickly replies. "I grew up knowing my older brother and David were the heirs to the family titles. The *enormous difference* is The Worthington's treated me as family regardless; but to my 'birth family,' I was disposable. *Never once* have The Worthington's ever made me feel less than their son! Your relationship with David will be different than your relationship will be with me, and I'm *more than okay with that, Bri!*"

"Yeah, but—."

"In a world of duties with the duchy, along with society parties, fundraisers, and craziness, I think you could, *and can*, find some sort of 'normalcy,' and," gesturing the direction of the convertible, "*even fun!*" He grins. "And maybe a little more time just being yourself." He holds her hands. "Don't get me wrong, I'll have my own fancy parties and dinners to attend, but—."

"It'll feel like I'm there as your wife and not a soon-to-be duchess?" She tries to finish his sentence.

"*Not exactly.* For fancy parties and dinners, you'll be both. People will know *my* wife *is* the soon-to-be-duchess and will expect you to also dress the part."

"What does that entail?" She asks.

"For you to look extra gorgeous, if that's even possible!" He winks. She goes to ask something more, but he puts a finger to her lips and looks at her with so much love, her breath catches. He says, "I don't know if I could be as great a man as David! If I caught you first, I would've convinced you to elope with me right then and there!"

Bri giggles. "You probably would have, or shortly after!" She tells him, "David thinks *you're* a better man than he is."

"I know, *but he's wrong.*" He runs his hand in her hair. "Bri, when you were walking towards The Inn that night of The Black-Tie Party, David made a promise before he came and found you." He holds her hair out of her face. "Did he ever tell you?"

"I'm not sure, he may have...hum a few bars!" She winks with a sweet smile.

He lightly chuckles. "I remember him saying he'd find a way you could be loved more than any woman has ever been loved and adored!" Bri's eyes fill with tears as she remembers him telling her. Jack goes on to say, "Bri, you fill him with so much love that he feels you're overflowing with it and it'd be so easy for you to love another! Then both David and I could love and adore you, helping him to keep his promise!" He looks at her and notices she's holding her breath. "*No, David is* definitely *the better man*! He has proven that with you!"

"Jack, I can't let you into my heart," she says and he is confused...until she tells him, "I can't '*let you in*' when you're already there."

He laughs and shakes his head. Jack takes Bri's hand and goes to walk along the beach some more, but she doesn't move.

"What's wrong?" He asks.

"That's it? I just say you are already in my heart and then nothing?!" She goes from exasperated to a bit disappointed, "*Honest*—."

His lips crash into hers as he cups her jaw and she holds his forearms for a few seconds, before sliding her arms around his waist; losing herself in their kiss. He wraps an arm around her shoulders and her back, so her head is nestled in the curve of his elbow.

Jack gently pulls his lips from hers and smirks. "Better?"

She smirks, "Can we do it again?" He doesn't waste any time and kisses her again. It's when she is about to moan into it, she pulls their lips apart again. "*Wow!*" He gives her a smoldering look with his smile.

They hold hands and walk down the beach some more. They talked a lot about him when she was in the hospital. She asks for a bit more detail about his degrees and career. They talk about his going to Columbia University and getting his bachelor's and master's degrees. He loves working as a Business Finance Manager for an international investment firm; with David, The Worthington's, as well as The Worthington Corporation, are all his clients. He also likes that he can travel anywhere.

He asks about her degree in criminal justice with a minor in psychology. He then asks her about her dreams and she said she needs new dreams, because she had given up on true-love being in the cards for her.

"*Obviously*, I was wrong about that..." she looks him up and down and she winks at him, "*twice over!*" He chuckles.

They leave things as they are. Jack wants to give her some time to think and process everything.

CHAPTER 25

Imperfectly Perfect Fatherly Discussion

Bri has been wrapping things up with her liaison job in DC. Her boss is ecstatic about the news of her engagement and sad he will eventually be losing her. For now, he approves of her dual citizenship and working remotely on the project he has given her and traveling to DC, as necessary.

Bri meets with IT to figure out how to best carry out working on this project. A place at The Manor would be nice, but they also prepare an office at The Worthington Corporation Business Complex. David has been incredibly supportive and has arranged an office for her on the upper floor with him that is not being used. His assistant Mary has been working with her on the phone, as well as the IT guys that have flown to the UK to secure her offices there; Gabriel, one of Carlotta's assistants, has helped with securing Bri's office at The Manor, while David's assistant, Mary, is helping with the office at The Worthington Corporation.

Bri has been working with Amy to get her up to speed with everything. She encourages Amy to apply for her job.

Amy shakes her head. "I like making things happen and not having to deal with difficult and horrible people face-to-face on a regular basis." Bri laughs, nodding in agreement. "Besides, James and I have started seeing each other and, I don't know, it feels...permanent. Is that weird to say?"

"Not at all! I can definitely relate!" Bri laughs a little. "I'm so happy for you both!" Bri has tears. "Both of you deserve to be happy and my vote is forever with each other!"

"I hope so! He's a really great guy!" Amy smiles.

"Because his parents raised him right, just like David and Jack!"

Amy laughs and agrees. "They seem like you'll have the best in-laws!" Bri agrees. Amy changes the subject. "Did Katie talk to you after she dropped by?" Bri's eyebrows come together and she shakes her head. "You went down to Parson's office with Carlotta and Jack was waiting here."

"I didn't even know she came by." Bri states.

"She gave off some strong vibes towards Jack." Amy says with her eyebrows raised. "*Un*-com-fort-*abllle*!" She enunciates and stresses.

"Really?" Bri gives an eek look.

"James broke up with her because she wasn't taking their relationship more seriously and she has been making the moves on Jack. Not to mention her lack of concern for you in the hospital." Amy says disappointedly. "It's weird she would show up *here* to specifically see Jack. Unless she was hoping to 'steal him away,' or something?"

"It is odd...almost stalkerish..." Bri notes. "Besides, she never came to see me while I was awake in the hospital, not sure about when I was in the coma. She's colored 'jealousy green' and there's a good chance she'll start using drugs again, if she hasn't already..." she thinks back to seeing her outside her condo and punching that guy. "The last time she combined drugs and alcohol she set up that crime against me...well, perhaps there's an added 'pro' to a 'pro-con list'...*moving away from her?*"

"Jealousy can bring out the ugly in anyone, but what she did to you...there aren't strong enough words for how awful that was. The fact that you're still friends with her shows what a forgiving heart of gold you have!" Amy states.

Bri thinks about that. "I'm not sure I'd say 'forgive' as much as she doesn't want to admit what she did and I haven't wanted to face it either." Bri gives her a sad little smile. "'Avoidance' might be a better word."

"Well, when she came here, she came on embarrassingly strong to Jack!" Amy *gives her* an 'eek' look.

"The only time she's 'not herself' is when she's 'Drug Addicted Katie.'" Bri is saddened.

"It would explain her behavior better, but so would 'the green-eyed monster.'" Amy says.

"Drug addiction can cause promiscuity, which 'Drug Addicted Katie' usually jumps on the first person she *knows* will have sex with her. Which makes it odder yet she would come here for Jack because I don't think she and Jack have ever had—."

"No, we haven't!" Jack answers after overhearing the last part of their conversation when he is walking in. "A drug addiction wouldn't completely explain her coming on to me like she did."

"Your sexy handsomeness?!" Bri teases and Amy snorts a laugh.

He smirks and walks closer to her. "My handsomeness wouldn't be responsible for drug addiction." His hand grabs her bum and tugs her to him; Amy raises her eyebrow. "I'd be involved in the physical activity to help detox." He teases.

"Ooo, so true! But it *could* be responsible for driving women mad!" She giggles.

"I prefer the phrase, 'drive them wild.'" Jack winks and swats her bum playfully before grabbing another box to take down to the car. Bri looks to Amy, whose eyebrows are raised with this interaction.

Bri smiles. "After all this time working together, going through the crap I went through with Katie, you've easily become my best friend."

Amy gets a little teary-eyed. "You're mine, too!"

"I'm curious what your opinion is on something that's a secret between David, Jack, The Bradshaw's, and The Worthington's. James knows, but if you two are just getting your relationship started—."

"He may have been playing it safe, considering he just got out of a relationship of sorts with Katie." Amy adds.

"Right." Bri tells Amy of her ancestral lineage and 'The Noble Consort' and how David wants it to be Jack and why. When she finishes, she looks at Amy, "You've been so quiet...do you think this is a bad idea?"

Amy smiles. "Bri, I agree with them!"

Bri has a surprised look, "You do?!"

"I do! Which all that also explains his touchy-feely-ness on your butt just now!" Bri giggles and nods. Amy also tells her, "It's been clear since you all met, Jack's been secretly in-love with you, which is why I offered to be his date that Friday night for the fundraiser." Amy gives Bri an encouraging look. "If anyone can pull this off, it's you!"

"I hope so! But that would mean my friendship with Katie would be——." Bri starts to say.

"Bri, your friendship with Katie was over the moment she *conspired* against you!" Amy firmly states; Jack listens by the door for a moment. "Her ass should've been locked up in jail for years, hell, *locked up still*, for what happened that night!" Amy takes a deep breath. "Sorry. I push all that aside for you when she's around but I'm with Joe! We both loathe that woman! And it's obvious you haven't told David or Jack because they would somehow loathe her *way more* than we do!"

Bri hadn't noticed until now that she had a couple tears streaking down her face. Amy hands her a tissue and Jack uses this time to walk back in, but he is texting David at the same time.

> "What's the story behind Katie and Bri? What I overheard between Bri and Amy sounds like something really bad happened, so bad that Amy and Joe loathe Katie, but no details."

Jack points to another box and Bri nods. Amy smiles, "Dang, girl! Two *incredibly* good-looking men...you better get used to never being able to walk again!" Amy laughs.

Bri giggles as she winks at Jack. "I have a feeling they're amazing in the bedroom in their own fantastically good ways!" Jack chuckles as he walks out of the office.

Bri goes over and hugs Amy. "I need to get going." She is grateful Amy will still be her assistant through this project, along with the person who takes Bri's position. "With any luck, *you'll* be moving to Newhaven in the not-*too*-distant-future! *Regardless*, we need to stay in touch though."

"Of course!" Amy replies. "How many mere commoners, can say they're friends with, even texting and conversing with, a real-life Duchess?"

Bri rolls her eyes, "I'm not a Duchess yet and it's just a title. I'm still going to be me, Amy."

"Yeah, but with a title, you can do so much good with it, *making a bigger impact*! You're going to be in a position to make a *real* difference, Bri, to *real* people!

It's huge even if it's only for one person, but we know it'll be more; *so many more!*" They hug once more. "See you Friday!"

Bri thanks her for everything and, with a few tears falling down her cheeks, tells her to, "Keep being awesome!"

All her boxes are in the awaiting car outside, thanks to Jack. Bri looks at her office and out the windows one last time, before she leaves. Amy walks her to the elevator and gives her one more hug. They wave as the elevator doors close. Bri says goodbye to the security guards she has known for some time.

Jack and Carlotta are patiently waiting by the car, enjoying the beautiful day outside. Carlotta wanted to see where Bri worked and Bri had arranged a tour of The White House for her and Jack, which Bri joined them until she had to be in a meeting. She would meet back up with them after her meeting and take them to meet Chef André. She had permission to show them The Oval Office before they left The West Wing. Afterwards, they went over to pack up her office.

As Bri walks up, Carlotta and Mateo are talking while Jack is texting David.

> David: "I'm curious about that, too. All I know is there's a guy we saw in her condo building. She punched him and kneed him between the legs. He has to be involved because Ken told Katie to get this guy inside her condo before I found out what was going on and there would be a homicide to cover up."

> Jack: "Daaamn...Let's ask her about this *after* the wedding, unless it gets brought up sooner."

> David: "Agreed."

Carlotta, Bri, and Jack climb into the car and Mateo takes them to the Bradshaw's. Her condo has already been packed up and the boxes sent to Newhaven by one of Carlotta's assistants, Gabriel. He has offered to be Bri's assistant in Newhaven and will work with Amy to coordinate DC things with her schedule; *if Bri approves* and Bri *definitely* does!

They pull up to the Bradshaw's and they go inside after she hugs and says goodbye to Mateo for now. Bri relaxes for a little while, trying to process everything. She asks Henry to talk and they go into his study. They sit on the couch and he leans forward, patting her lower knee with a fatherly smile.

"I can't tell you how good it is to be sitting here with you again, Sweetie!" Henry tells her.

"Me, too!" She smiles through her tears. "David told me what you whispered to me that first night when I was out of surgery. Do you think that applies to Jack being The Noble Consort? Something about three lives lived together at the same time?"

"The Spirit was the strongest I've ever felt that night, Bri. It's almost as if something more spiritual was going on at the same time, but of course I couldn't see anything."

Her mouth drops a little as she starts to get a strong feeling. "Henry, I thought what happened was a dream, but maybe..." she thinks hard about it.

"Maybe you had a near death experience instead?" He thinks out loud and she considers it. He asks, "What happened?"

She closes her eyes and thinks..."I can only remember being in white light and feeling deeply loved." She opens her eyes and sees Jessica had appeared in the room with her and Henry, startling Bri.

Henry looks in the direction Bri is looking. "What's wrong?"

"*Jessica?*" Bri asks, confused how she knows that. Jessica nods. Light from Jessica's hands goes to Bri's forehead, which Henry sees part of Bri's forehead glow.

"*Amazing!*" He exhales in awe.

Bri looks at Jessica. "I had been 'touched by death' and I had a choice whether to come back or not?"

Jessica kindly smiles. "Yes. Only coming back comes with a price."

"Price?" Bri asks. She looks at Henry. "She's telling me that choosing to come back, comes with a price."

Jessica tells her to tell Henry, "He was inspired to tell you all those things and that your life will be *wonderfully extraordinary.*" Henry hears this and tears fill his eyes.

Bri tells him, "I heard those two words in your voice, as a sort of echo, during that time, too!"

"You did! Because of how eternal time and mortal time work, it lined up these occurrences to overlap at that moment." Jessica tells her and Bri relays that to Henry. Jessica goes on to explain one of the prices of 'death's touch' is prohibiting her from getting in the way of a person's freedom to choose, but giving her great power and abilities. "Which ones and to what degree, only time will tell."

"Something about a real power in pure love?" Bri wonders if she's recalling correctly. "And that my mortal journey is *unique*..."

"Yes. And Amy's right! You will accomplish so much good with your marriages." Jessica tells her and Bri repeats it back to Henry.

Bri thinks out loud, "Something about three..."

"Three?" Henry asks. "*Of course*! And royal blood!"

"What do you mean?" Bri asks.

"I felt your blood was important with the Spirit specifically adding 'royal blood' and then there was mention of 'three lives living concurrently.'" Henry recalls as he thinks back.

Bri starts to remember more and looks at Jessica a little surprised. "I was told the third marriage will be the most challenging...but we'll bond like no one else?" Her eyebrows furrow together. "What does that mean? David explained how he picked Jack because he trusts Jack will love me; that none of this would work with just anyone! Who's royal that David would trust as much as he trusts—what's his name?...'Herst'...I think..." Henry's face is surprised. "What?" She asks.

"Sweetie, in all the stories Jack and David would've told you, I would've thought there would be a connection that 'Herst' is a nickname, short for Heathherst." He explains.

"*Waaait a second*!" She stands up and walks around behind the couch talking out loud. "*The* Heathherst's? As in *The* Royal Family?!" She looks at Henry who nods, then she looks at Jessica.

"Specifically, *The* King." Jessica smirks.

"Waaait. Wait. Wait. *This can't be right*! He's married!" Bri exclaims more in disbelief. "And by all accounts, Queen Genevieve is a really nice person!"

Jessica calmly speaks. "Things aren't as they seem to be, Bri. Your love will help heal him, *and his family*. Just remember to trust the Spirit to guide your footsteps." Jessica glances to the side, listening, then back at Bri, "I need to go." Bri nods in understanding and they say goodbye.

Bri rubs her head. "I think I'm getting a migraine."

Henry smiles standing up and walking over to Bri. "One step at a time, Sweetie." He holds her upper arms. "You need to take your 'American glasses' off and view this from Newhaven's point of view." She leans against the couch to listen to what he's saying. "Bri, your people will look at you taking on this tradition as you wanting to ensure the bloodlines for Newhaven. David wants to do this so Newhaven, your people, will support his wife, an American, to one day become 'The Duchess of Newhaven,' because you honored such an *important* tradition, *and you're a Direct Bloodline*."

"David said this has to be for love with Jack, or it won't work." She tells him.

He cups her cheek. "He's right. David and Jack are both *really* good men, Bri. Do you think Maggie and I would entrust you with just anyone?" He chuckles and she does, too, shaking her head. He tells her, "Continue with your relationships with Jack and David. Focus on what's right here and now. We don't know when Herst will fit into this." He rubs her upper arms a little, "Okay, Sweetie?"

She takes a deep breath, nodding, "Okay..."

"I'll tell you this just for reference," he smiles, "David, Jack, and Herst grew up together, with Seth, James, Abagail, *and Genevieve*. Queen Genevieve and Seth have been a couple since they were teenagers, and from what I understand they're still a couple with the support of The King."

"So that's possibly what Jessica meant when she said 'things aren't as they appear to be.'" She says.

"Could be..." Henry nods.

She takes a deep breath and exhales. "I have this image of a son with David in my mind's eye. I saw him, too, during this *near death experience*."

"Hold onto that, Sweetie." He pulls her into a hug. "This will be a wonderful beginning for you and we're all excited to see how this falls together over the years to come!"

After supper that evening, Bri goes up to her room for a hot shower. She is working on forgetting how 'Herst' will fit into this and focusing on David and Jack. She gets out and sees a shirt of Jack's hanging on the closet door. She picks it up, holds it to her nose and inhales, closing her eyes as she takes in the smell of his cologne. Memories associated with smells are a powerful thing, especially for her since her senses seem to have been heightened since her coma. She puts it on and remembers dancing with Jack, his kiss before he was shot...She finds herself thinking of the memories that flood her mind and how she has so easily fallen for this wonderful man. There is a knock on the door, but she didn't hear it. Bri hears a text notification that is Jack's chime and she smiles, picking up her phone.

Jack: "Do you know how extremely sexy you are in my shirt?!"

She freezes and looks up at the reflection in the mirror; Jack is leaning against the bedroom door frame, arms folded, with love and desire in his eyes. She goes to speak, but he holds his hand up as he shuts the door and walks over to her.

"You can wear *any* shirt of mine, *anytime* you want!" He folds his arms around her and kisses her passionately. She breaks the kiss and walks over to the couch. She falls into a sitting position on the couch. Jack walks over to Bri and sits down on the coffee table in front of her. "Now, about you and me...what do you think?"

She raises her eyebrow. "I've been *more* forthcoming than you, Jack*son* Carlisle!" He is a tad surprised. "Something David and I promised that I want that same promise here! Let's promise to *always* be honest with each other, Jack. No tricks, no games, *just the truth*."

He tangles his hands in her hair. "Always!" He pulls her in for a tender kiss, but it instantly goes hot and passionate the second their lips touch; their chemistry is undeniable.

Jack is now on his knees, leaning against her knees, and has an arm holding her tight at her waist. The other hand is still tangled in her hair, but he moves it to the back of her neck to keep their lips pressed firmly as they kiss. One of her hands is on his jaw, the other in his hair on the back of his head. They're both out of breath when they pull apart.

"*Now* I'll say what we *both* need to say out loud to each other." Jack gives her a pointed look.

Bri's mouth is close enough to his that he could feel her breath on his lips as she asks, "And what might that be?"

He tugs at her waist. "We want each other, I know you want me just as much as I want you!"

She rolls her eyes. "Be serious!"

"*I am!*" He runs a finger down the middle of her lips. "This chemistry, this passion, I haven't experienced anything quite like it!" He smirks. "*Because* I love you!"

She holds his jaw and captures his lips with hers, kissing him fiercely and her legs wrapping around him. His hands go to his shirt she has on and starts to unbutton it; she quickly grabs his hands.

"Jack, wait a second." She gasps a deep breath.

"What's wrong?" He asks. "David..."

She shakes her head. "It's not what you think. I won't do this outside of marriage." She adds, "It's been *really* difficult for David and me, too, but he's honored this request because he also knows if we cross that line—."

"You'd hate him for it...and me if *we* cross it..."

"*I'd hate myself*, more than either of you." She says, resting her forehead to his. "Want to argue lust isn't a part of this?"

"Bri, it isn't that lust isn't there," he looks her into her eyes, "because there's *lots* of sex in our future." He winks with a smile and she shakes her head softly laughing. "It's way more than that, *it has to be* in order to make us stop." He looks lovingly in her eyes. "Something really special, Bri!" Jack kisses her again and back along her jawline to her ear. "You're so beautiful in so many ways which only makes you more incredibly sexy and irresistible, but you're right." He sits back up on the coffee table.

She clears her throat and takes a deep breath, exhaling slowly. "*Jack...*"

He gives her a loving smile. "I was in-love with you since The Black-Tie Party that Saturday." He kisses the back of her hand. "I never wanted to say it out loud, because then it would be real and I was scared it would make it that much harder to get over you and move on. I thought this, us, was never a possibility." Jack strokes her cheek with the back of his fingers, then kisses her sweetly. Looking at her once more and holding her gaze he tells her, "I love you, BriaLynn!" Her eyes lose a few tears. "I've *never* told a woman I loved her before...because I've *never* fallen in-love before you." He rests his forehead on hers again.

Bri lifts her head, lovingly smiling at him. "I definitely feel and have felt the chemistry we have for each other!" He smiles an incredible Jack signature smile. She gives him a tender kiss.

Jack slowly kisses his way back to her ear; she moans a little. "*Briii...* You're not playing fair!"

She lightly giggles. "I prefer to look you in the eyes for what I'm about to say next." She feels him smile against her neck and then sits back to look at her. "I love you, Jack!" Both Jack and Bri are teary-eyed. "I *really* love you!"

"I *really* love you, too!" He says with his eyes leaking tears that he quickly wipes away and clears his throat. He cups the back of her jaw, kissing her passionately and it makes her knees a little weak.

"It's weird...while I'm nervous about all this, I'm also excited to have you and David in my life!" She smiles sweetly. "I don't know how I can love you and David as much as I do, *but there it is.*" He chuckles. She has a serious look on her face, but there's love in her eyes for him.

"Ever since meeting you, I don't want anyone else. Katie has come on to me *numerous* times, but I just couldn't take her up on it for a few reasons." He holds her face and grins with a gleam in his eye, "You're it, Gorgeous! If you want me, you've got me! You're the only one I want! Like David, I'll wait as long as it takes."

Jack kisses her, dropping to his knees, leaning against her knees, his hands feel all her curves on the sides of her body. When his hands start to travel up her thighs, he stops himself halfway as she breaks their kiss.

"For future reference, this is all *super* sexy. Can we pick up where we left off at a later day, on whatever couch, when we can finish with some fireworks?" She playfully smiles.

"You're on!" He smiles and stands up, then pulls her up to him. "Goodnight, Gorgeous! I love you!"

"I love you, Jack!" She taps a kiss to his lips. "Goodnight, Handsome, and sweet dreams!"

"I'd say 'only if you're in them' but after tonight..." he wraps an arm around her waist, "I think my sleep needs to be dream*less* for now." He smiles big and kisses her cheek, then swats her bum as he goes to the door. She quietly squeals and laughs. He winks as he shuts the door.

After her hormones calmed down, she started thinking about the events of her life, let alone in the past few months. She thinks about David and that he has been in Newhaven with his dad and James. He plans to fly to DC Thursday evening and fly back with everyone Friday morning. *Tomorrow*, she will hatch a plan with Jack, Carlotta, and Peter, to surprise David at his office before he flies to DC.

CHAPTER 26

Imperfectly Perfect Preemptive Strike

When David had first gone back to Scotland after proposing, he went straight to his office at 'The Worthington Business Complex' to put out some work fires. After one meeting, he walks into his office and there is a fire-starter herself, his ex-wife, Ava Warwood.

His voice takes a disgusted tone. "What *do you* want? *Wait.*" He stops. "*How did you even get up here?!*"

"I have my ways." Ava walks up to him.

David knows it wasn't his assistant Mary; she can't stand Ava. The receptionist in the main lobby has a crush on David, so it's doubtful she would help Ava, but it may not be entirely out of the question; Ava is a master at manipulation!

Ava's hands go to David's chest and she moves them upwards to feel his toned pecs. "These never get old, *Dah*ling! I wish more guys cared about their bodies like you, Jack, and James, even Herst!"

He has to put his laptop bag and jacket down before he can take hold of her wrists to stop anymore of her unwanted touching. "You're touching what belongs to my fiancée."

He despises her more than he ever thought he could! It's disgusting that she thinks he would be interested in sex with her after *everything* she has done to him; *after everyone she has slept with*!

"Oh, come on *Dah*ling, for old time's sake." She barely gets to her toes to try to kiss him, as he pushes her away.

"Don't! Whatever you are selling, *Ava*, I'm *not* buying." He walks over to his desk and looks through his mail. He tells her assertively, "That ship long ago sailed *and sunk*, it'll *never* come around again."

"No need to be rude!" She shuts the door, purposely not locking it. "We were perfect for each other and *you know it*!" She starts to unzip her dress.

"Stop it, Ava!" He says to her. "We were a match in social class, that's it! Or you wouldn't have slept with every guy who would have you!"

"You say that as if I didn't have any standards!" She saunters over again.

He replies, "More like *they* didn't have standards."

She wasn't paying attention to what he said. "Maybe none of them were exceptionally good in bed, but this American woman can't be better than me..." she goes to put her hands on him again but he grabs her wrists before she does.

"Touch me again and I'll no longer conduct myself as a gentleman, Ava!" He lets go of her wrists and they drop down.

"You're seriously going to stand there and tell me she's better in bed than me!" She scoffs. "After all the things we've tried?!"

He continues looking and opening his mail, unphased. "I'm not going to justify that with a response, Ava."

"*You haven't slept with her yet?!*" She says in shock and laughs.

"Ava, I'm not discussing that level of intimacy about her with you, or anyone else for that matter!"

"Right. But—."

"*But nothing!* She is *not* a topic I ever want to discuss with you; *she's off limits.* You and I are *never* getting back together and," he blurts out, "I won't sleep with used goods!" He sits at his desk and docks his laptop.

Her face gets a seething look and anger takes over. "You BAS—."

"*SO,* then," David cuts her off, "*why are you still here?*"

She chooses to ignore him again and regains her composure. "We need to join our families together again. We'll give Newhaven the surge it needs!"

He furrows his eyebrows. "What surge?"

"Come on, David, don't be idiotic, *Dah*ling. Newhaven's heir and wife back together, all warm and cozy, starting a family." David can't help it; he bursts out laughing again. She gets angry. "Why are you laughing like some mindless twit?!"

"*Because*," he laughs, "this is all about *you*! You're *actually* pregnant and you don't know who the father is!" He laughs harder. "You're trying to avoid the bigger scandal!"

"Why do you keep laughing?!" She angrily asks. "You were upset when I had an abortion and now...what?!"

"It *finally* occurred to me that I was an idiot for thinking that other baby was mine in the first place! Bri helped me realize if that baby was actually mine, there would've been *no way on this earth* you would've given up your claim to 'The Worthington Estate,' *or Newhaven*! But you knew it wasn't mine and you couldn't be pregnant with someone else's baby and you'd only risk your figure with an heir." He takes a deep breath. "I do thank you though, for proving once again Bri's faith in 'everything happens for a reason' is well placed."

"What do you mean?" She's confused.

"You were a *dreadful* mistake I had to experience to learn from!" He replies and she glares. "BriaLynn is the *true* Mrs. *David* Worthington! She's the woman of my dreams and our children will have an *incredible loving mother*!" He looks her straight in the eyes saying, "The *most* qualified to become the next 'Duchess of Newhaven!'" He folds his arms and leans back, "*Nothing* you're offering interests me and I'm not so daft to screw up everything with her, *like you did with me*! Besides, Jack would have a go at me, *and I'd deserve it*!"

She asks with nastiness, "What makes that *American* so special?!"

He scoffs. "*Besides the fact that BriaLynn isn't you*?!" Ava glares daggers this time. He asks, "Or how about when we're at a party, I know she hasn't slept with even a fraction of the men in the room?!" She scowls as he tells her, "Ava, you don't want a husband; you want a title!" He waves towards the doo telling her, "Go sniff around some other poor, unsuspecting chump because that isn't me anymore!"

Ava's red with fury now. "Do you really think you'll have the support of the Newhaven people if you marry that-that, *American*?!" She sneers. "*You will actually self-destruct this time*!" A wicked smile spreads across her face. "But your

288

loss would be *my* gain, because if you're family loses the duchy, the titles would go to my family."

"If you honestly thought that, then you wouldn't be here trying to seduce me and sell me on this mess of your life. Besides, you forget that it would all go to James first."

"We both know he doesn't want it." She retorts.

"He may not want it, but he *hates* you more than I ever have for what you did to me, *and tried to do to our family*! He'd accept the title just to stop your family from getting their hands on it!"

"Still, it'd leave *you* nothing when your American tramp slinks back home." Ava smiles evilly.

He stands up and leans forward saying with a cold seriousness, "First of all, *watch your tongue when you speak of my soon-to-be-wife*, your *future Duchess*!" He says in a tone she knows not to mess with.

"My apologies." She says through gritted teeth.

He goes to his bag again and pulls out some magazines he picked up to show Bri. "Second, I already have everything with her! You see," he shows her the cover of a magazine and a newspaper lifestyle section, watching her face drop, "she's becoming more popular than you *ever* were, or ever could be, because *she actually has a heart*! She has a lot of supporters that *genuinely* like her *and we aren't even married yet*!" He smiles at a picture of Bri.

She sees his face and detests, "Americans liking an American who steals a title, isn't really newsworthy. That's the stuff for those rags!"

"Look closer! Her supporters are international because of her job in Washington, D.C." David tells her.

Ava couldn't believe her eyes! One of the rags is the tabloid Serene's family owns! "I'm going to have a word with that bi—.

"BElieve it or not," he purposely interrupts again, "Bri doesn't even follow this stuff; *it's not important to her*! *Proving she gets it*!"

"If she really 'gets it,' then she *would* care about what people are saying! Gossip columns are always so fickle."

"She cares more than you ever did about *people*, she just knows how the media works. Now," he gestures the door again, "if you'll *kindly leave*..." He says in the same serious tone she heard when he had told her he *knew* she was cheating their whole relationship; the same tone that told her he was never going to budge in their divorce *and* she did sign a prenup. The last thing he stripped her of was his last name...and he is so glad he did now that he is marrying Bri.

She is furious! "*This isn't over!*" She puts her clothes back on.

"Knowing you, I don't doubt that. *Just* so we're clear, it's *been* over for me. Security will be notified to call me directly should you ever come back into this building. Ava, Bri has shown me there *is* love to be had! She's not only naturally beautiful, but her heart is the biggest heart I've ever known."

She half laughs. "What do you mean, 'naturally beautiful?'"

"Look in the mirror..." he smirks, "*you* won't see it." She glares. "Bri's the genuine article! She's not high maintenance! She uses makeup to highlight her beauty, not to use it like a mask!" David takes a deep breath. "For the first time I see you and all the women before Bri for what you *all* are: pathetic, plastic, and *sadly* miserable." Ava is fuming, but he continues, "I don't hate you, Ava...I guess I feel sorry for you, like Bri does. You don't know what love is, nor how good a relationship can be when two people are in-love with each other. If you did, you'd seek after love, rather than titles, money, and social status." He smiles thinking of Bri again. "Bri is sincerely grateful for anything big or small done for her! A simple gesture will move her to tears..." He thinks of the tiny flower he gave her that first Saturday night in the gardens.

She says with disgust, "*Weepiness isn't considered a good quality in a duchess!*"

"The world is changing, and I don't think people want to see two stoic vessels of leaders walking side by side, emotionless. Yes, certain situations call for it, but only a few of them. I think what the public wants to see on a regular basis is their married leaders happily in-love with each other. Even simple, *but genuine*, gestures of love like holding hands as they walk side by side; or an arm around the other as they stand next to each other; even a smile to acknowledge they see the one they love." There is a pause as he smiles at the

290

thought of Bri. "I've *never* been this happy, but I never knew it was possible either! Not only do I love her, but she loves me *for me*! A title and being heir aren't on the 'pro' side of a 'pros & cons' list, *nor her goal*, Ava, but she is aware that marrying me means there's a title for her and she'll happily learn what will be required of her *because she loves me*." He walks her to the door and notices she never locked it; he knows she was hoping someone would walk in on them, perhaps Bri. *Ava really is a sad, pathetic, clueless socialite.* He thinks to himself. He tells her, "I will offer you a friendly warning."

"And what's that?" She says with a sarcastic undertone.

"*Make no mistake*, what I'll do is bury you and your family in a mountain of legal trouble if you push me too far, or even think of hurting Bri. Am I understood?" He stares her down.

"Fine." She rolls her eyes to brush him off.

He firmly grabs her upper arm. "My father will be more than happy to push from his side of things, too!" David tells her, pushing her towards the door. He grabs Ava's jacket to her dress and purse that are right there, shoving them to her; he doesn't help her with her jacket.

She yanks them out of his hands and snaps, "Let's hope *you* don't regret this!" She is just outside the door and putting her jacket on.

He refers to a page from Bri's playbook for inspiration. "Regret what? Shutting this all down before your venom infects my life again, or worse! It infects my fiancé's life! Nope, I'm good." He says without emotion. "You and Serene are your own worst enemies...think about that, Ava." He swipes the door shut and locks it, so she can't come back in to say anything more. She does try the door, but angrily exhales as she stomps off.

He stands at his door, listening for the elevator. Once he hears the elevator ding, and a minute passes for her to be on it, he unlocks his door. He then goes to his desk and calls Bri to let her know what happened. He knows Ava is going to hit the tabloids to get back at him. He is only worried about how Bri will react to it.

> "Thanks for letting me know, My Love, and I think I have a plan to thwart her efforts." She tells him.

> "Like what?" He's curious.

"Nope. Better you don't know until—." She stops herself. "Hopefully I'll get this done tonight yet."

"What are you—." He tries to ask.

"Gotta go! Love you!" She tells him.

He barely gets, "Love you, too," out before she hangs up.

David smiles, shaking his head a little at his phone. '*I adore that woman!*' He thinks to himself as he digs in and buries himself in the work that has piled up some. He has the word 'Macushla' come into his thoughts again; he has heard it over the years but couldn't remember what it means. He makes a note to research it later. Right now, he needs to send emails to his employees who covered for him while he was out and will cover for him during his honeymoon. He also had Mary arrange gift cards to be delivered by the end of the day. He thinks back to what Bri said during one of their long talks, 'Loyal employees will do almost anything for their boss, as long as they feel appreciated and they don't feel taken advantage of.' He hopes emails and gift cards, which he pays out of his personal account, will help them feel appreciated because he does appreciate them!

Back in DC, Bri is on the phone to the few reporters she trusts. In DC, they are hard to come by, so she has always kept them close. She explains the situation and how she needed 'The Love Story of David & Bri' or 'A Scottish & an American Love Story' something catchy, to draw the people on both sides of 'the pond.' They all agreed to meet at the Bradshaw's for an exclusive to help Bri get ahead of David's conniving ex-wife and possibly the so-called ex-girlfriend; plus, their hatefulness at her being an American is insulting to all Americans, even them. Bri wanted these articles out that evening, which was *almost* impossible, but time was of the essence.

Keith, Larry, and Marie were all gathered in the Bradshaw's sitting room, getting comfortable. Bri picked her favorite overstuffed reading chair and ottoman. She explains she wouldn't use the ladies' names because if they retaliated, they would name themselves.

Marie smiles. "Calling themselves out...good play!"

"Right! So, if I slip—."

"We heard nothing!" Keith says and the others agree.

Bri begins to tell them *almost* everything...from how they met and how she stood up to David, to how furious he was until it all sank in with David admitting to the room full of people, she was right. She leaves out the part where he says she doesn't need a title to be better than those people in that room. The reporters were recording the interview but taking notes at the same time. She didn't hold back about her attack; that David and Jack spent every moment at the hospital with her, and how Jack fits into all this. However, she doesn't tell them about Jessica and her 'near death experience.'

Bri tells them of David planning his proposal and their wedding while she was in the hospital. He proposed and wanted to marry as soon as possible. Now they are only days before the wedding and David's ex-wife is still trying to get her claws on David's title before he remarries. Bri explains the events of the afternoon and the ex-wife's desperate attempt to do whatever she can, even seduction, right up to the very last moment. It wouldn't surprise her if she teamed up with David's ex-girlfriend, well, ex-*date* is more accurate, and they try to stop the wedding Saturday. Bri feels they should be pitied really; Larry says Bri is a better person than most people would be.

The reporters ask for pictures and Bri texts David asking for pictures from their relationship so far; she will combine them with her pictures. He texted all the pictures he had on his phone of her. She had tears at ones he had taken when she didn't know he was watching, including ones he took when she was in the hospital.

> Bri texts David: "Do you have a habit of taking pictures of a woman's backside?" She snickers to herself.

She sends some of the pictures to the reporters, making sure to keep ones back she wants to keep private.

> David: "Only of the most gorgeous woman I've ever met!"

> Bri: "How would I know?!"

> David: "Anytime you want to look through my pics, you'll see you're the only one starring in my personal photos."

> Bri: "Hmmm..." (adds a thinking emoji)

David: "It's true! I deleted everything when I kicked Ava out and I never took any pictures of the women between her and you because I knew none of them would be staying."

Bri: (sends a kiss emoji)

Marie puts her things in her bag and walks over to Bri. "We've gotten to know each other over the years and we have respect for each other. I've never seen you mean; assertive, yes. I've seen you stand up to a dignitary treating staff horribly, even sticking up for a reporter," she gestures to herself, "but assertive in such a way that's still respectful. If you need my help, I *want* to help you." Larry and Keith both said they would like to as well.

Bri's eyes fill up with tears as she hugs and thanks each of them, knowing her trust wasn't misplaced. She walks them to the door saying, "Saturday may be short notice, but you can be added to the guest list, if you think you can make it. Think of it as a follow up for your readers, *and* you'll witness something 'out of the ordinary' for Americans, and something for Newhaven's history books."

"History in the making?" Larry chuckles. "You can count me in!"

"I wouldn't miss it!" Keith says.

"My Editor would think I was crazy if I missed it and I'm sure I'd be fired!" Marie laughs.

Bri giggles. "Okay, I'll get you all on the list with a plus one." They smile and hug her one last time.

She waves as they get into their cars and drive away. She pulls her phone out of her pocket as she shuts the front door.

Bri: "I have three names to add to the guest list." Winking face.

David: "Care to share?"

Bri: "And ruin the surprise? Not.A.Chance!"

David: "A hint?"

Bri: "All will be revealed in this evening's magazines and newspaper editions."

David: "This late in the day! I can add this to your never-ending list of talents!"

Bri: "Some talents will be discovered *after* we're married. XOXO" (winking and kissing heart emojis)

David: "Vixen! XXOXX"

All three articles came out and told the narrative of David and Bri's love story. Marie liked her "*A Scottish & an American Love Story.*" Keith went with, "*Finding Love Across 'The Pond.'*" Larry went a little closer to home, "*D.C. Sweetheart Finds Love.*" For the first time, those three worked together to use the same info, but divided up everything to make their articles unique enough for someone to read all three and gain more insights; they even shared the pictures the same way. They sent over the first printings to the house, courtesy of their editors.

Bri sends all three huge 'thank you' texts telling them the articles were better than she could've hoped for and they were all awesome journalists! She ended with she looks forward to seeing them this weekend. They all would respond within the hour with versions of 'you're welcome' and they 'look forward to Saturday, too!'

Bri texts David and Jack the three articles from online, but no response from either one yet.

CHAPTER 27

Imperfectly Perfect Ruined Surprise

David convinces Bri to have an office at The Manor and at The Worthington Corporation, partially for the selfish reason of having her near him all day when she is working. There is also a practical reason that having an office in the city would be good for various meetings and functions as Marchioness and when she eventually becomes a duchess. Maybe it didn't matter, but there wasn't pushback from the IT guys when they secured both office locations.

David also has Mary hire an interior designer who would use 'The White House' and 'Americana' as a theme for Bri's office, but some authenticity is a must. Mary found one designer from London, Sophie Taylor, who meets with David and shows him sketches of what she came up with.

"These are perfect, Ms. Taylor!" David happily says.

"Oh, I think she'll love these!" Mary adds.

"Please, call me Sophie."

"We'll stick with formalities for now." He simply states. "Will you be able to finish by Friday?"

"I should be able to have it done by early afternoon that day." She says but thinks she could be done by Thursday afternoon; only she wants to be prepared for something unforeseen.

"I'll throw in a bonus in if you have it done before I return Friday, by noon?" He checks his watch, "Please excuse me, I have a conference call. I leave you in good hands with Mary." He gestures to Mary and then leaves the conference room.

Sophie watches David leave the room. "Is he seeing anyone? Rumor has it, he likes to rotate through the ladies."

Mary smiles. "He's getting married Saturday to a wonderful woman and he wants this to be her office."

She exhales. "I should've guessed he'd have someone."

Mary turns to her. "He's *really* in-love with Ms. Harris. He's been by her side since they met and through her almost dying."

"Oh no! That's horrible! Her almost dying that is." She clarifies, Mary nods with an understanding smile.

"I haven't met her in person yet, but we've spoken on the phone. I've *never* seen Mr. Worthington *this happy*! Anyone that could pull him out of his shell *and the rotation of ladies*," Mary smirks and Sophie laughs a little, "well, she's fantastic! I do look forward to meeting her! This is the first time they've been apart and it's to finalize plans for the wedding *he's* planning for her."

"He's planning the wedding?! Aaaw, that's so sweet!" She is enthusiastic. "Okay then, let's get this office decorated for her!" She jumps up and starts explaining to Mary, "I did research and made some phone calls on the train ride up here, so I just need things brought in and with any luck, all should come together rather nicely even with an unseen hurdle or two."

"Let me know if you need anything." She says. "You may use Ms. Harris' desk in her office."

"Thank you!" Sophie replies as Mary walks her down to Bri's office.

Bri wanted to surprise David for a change, so she worked with Jack, Carlotta, James, and Peter to fly to Edinburgh on Thursday. Bri and Jack fly together and it's during this time Bri starts to think about how it feels right being with Jack, just like it does with David...like the three of them were always meant to be...*except*...she keeps feeling something is *not yet complete*. She ponders on it as she draws a Triquetra that keeps popping into her mind, helping her to open herself up and think...

Jack looks over and sees some of her many doodles. "Ah the Triquetra." His accent is very heavy on the 'E' sound at the end of the second syllable. "One of the more recognizable Celtic symbols, although more people associate it with other religions and beliefs."

"Which tells me there is truth behind it. Do you know what the original Celtic meaning is?" She asks him.

"A Triquetra, Trinity Knot, Love Knot, and so on, are made without any breaks." He explains.

"Like a circle without and end; an eternal representation?" She asks.

He nods. "It was adopted by Christianity around the *fourth* century, I believe, to represent the Father, Son, and Holy Ghost, but prior to that, these points have been associated with terms used with the Claddagh and other symbolism: eternal love, loyalty, trust, unity, fidelity, and friendship. It's also the basis for a motherhood knot, too."

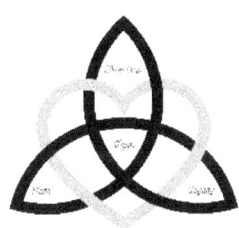

When she moves her arm a little, he glimpses something in her other sketches. He gently moves her arm more and sees she has drawn a heart through all three loops. He watches her write *faith, loyalty,* and *friendship* inside each loop and *love* in the very center of the heart, which is also the center of all three loops...then she tries a few other ways, but she always keeps *love* in the center.

"Appropriate," he points to the heart, "considering you fill each of us with so much love."

"Thing is," she looks at it, "I don't know what this mean? If this represents the three of us, then maybe it means love connects us?" She exhales. "I feel like I'm missing something..." She continues to stare at her paper, taking in what Jack said about 'each of us.' Then 'Herst' comes to mind and she recalls the memory with Jessica...how she will feel complete with Herst...she barely whispers, *"The Third Musketeer,"* to herself; too quiet for Jack to hear.

He smiles at her staring at her drawings. "I think you're the only one who can answer what it means."

Bri stands, holding her hand out for him and he takes it with a smirky smile. She goes into the back where there is a bedroom. She has him lay down and she snuggles in with him. She looks up at him with so much love and wonder.

"I'm amazed...I don't deserve David! And now you?!" She shakes her head as tears flow; she buries her face in his chest. He hugs her tight, kissing her head.

"I'm not *that* special! I certainly have my flaws!" He says.

She smiles. "No, you're not perfect, but you most certainly *are* special to me!" She kisses him firmly. "I love you!"

"I love you!" He kisses her once more before they nap for a while.

Bri and Jack make it to The Worthington Corporation just before 1:00, a half hour earlier than expected. Jack drops her off and he goes to his office ten minutes away for a little while. Bri walks into a modern open lobby that looks clean and bright with all the windows. She looks around and starts towards the elevators, but she is stopped by the receptionist.

Bri smiles. "I'm here to see Mister Worthington. I was told I could—."

There is a slight look of disgust on the receptionist's face. "*You've* been misinformed." The receptionist says to her. "*Everyone* must check in with me! *No exceptions.*"

"My apologies," Bri looks at her name on the counter, "Ms. Wilson." Bri says nicely to try to smooth things over.

The receptionist scoffs and rolls her eyes. She picks up the phone and calls up to David's office, speaking to Mary.

> "There's someone here *insisting* to see Mr. Worthington, but his schedule doesn't show anything this afternoon...right," she gives Bri a snotty look, "that's what I thought. *Thank you!*"

The receptionist stands and says in a snotty tone to Bri, "As you're perfectly aware, *you* don't have an appointment. Mister Worthington is headed out of town soon, so you'll need to leave and make sure you have an appointment *before* you return."

Bri's eyebrow raises, this has already gone too far. She sternly states, "I never said I had an appointment. I was told by *his father*, The Duke of Newhaven, to just go up." The receptionist rolls her eyes again. "You didn't tell Mary *who* was here to see him because *you* never asked. Mary would've told you to let me come up because she *is* expecting me!"

"Having a tone like that with me *won't* get you up there. If they were expecting you, I'd know about it! I don't need to ask your name, because I don't care;

just because you know his assistant's name, doesn't mean anything." She glares at Bri as she looks her over. "Take your services elsewhere!"

"My services?" Bri asks, then she realizes Ms. Wilson is implying Bri is a prostitute. "Whoa. You need to stop—."

"I'll *stop* when you leave! *Your kind* isn't welcome here!" She is glaring at Bri then looks at the security desk and waves a guard over, then folds her arms. "Now, *leave*, or security will throw you out." Bri rolls her eyes.

The security guard approaches and Bri sees people staring. She looks at the guard and says, "Please give me a minute and I'll clear this up." The guard nods and leans against the reception desk to wait.

"*What?!*" The receptionist starts to raise her voice. "*No!* I want her OUT OF MY LOBBY!" Now everyone is staring.

Bri opens her phone saying to the receptionist, "This isn't *your* lobby." She puts the phone up to her ear.

The receptionist glares at Bri, then at the guard. He tells her, "She's not hurting anything and if she's going to get this figured out, I'd rather let her and *not* lose my job."

"Mary, this is Bri. I can't seem to get past Ms. Wilson."

"That was you? I was wondering. My apologies. I was in the middle of something and didn't see the time until now. I'll be right down!"

Mary quickly calls down to the security desk to figure out how big of a problem this has become.

She asks a guard, "*Is there an issue going on down there?*"

"I'll say! Ms. Wilson's calling a woman a tom," in other words a prostitute, "and says Mr. Worthington didn't have an appointment with her and now she is trying to have George throw this woman out!" The guard notices, "*Oh!* Mr. Worthington is walking over to the reception desk now."

"I'm on my way!" Mary hangs up.

David's face lights up seeing Bri. He doesn't say anything, he grabs the back of her jaw and kisses her fiercely. Ms. Wilson is sick to her stomach and the guard is relieved he didn't throw this woman out!

David pulls their lips apart with a smile. "I love this!" He kisses her again. Mary walks hurriedly up to them. David turns to her, "Mary, this is my beautiful fiancé, Ms. BriaLynn Harris!" Ms. Wilson deflates.

Mary happily smiles and shakes her hand saying, "I'm so happy to finally meet you, Ms. Harris!"

"Likewise!" Bri says with a smile.

"My apologies." Mary starts to say.

"It's fine." Bri tries to smooth everything over; she just wants to move on.

"What's fine?" David asks looking from them to Ms. Wilson and the guard. "What's going on? What was with all the commotion that caught everyone's attention, including mine?"

Mary looks at Ms. Wilson. "Why didn't you tell me it was *Ms. Harris* who was here to see Mr. Worthington?"

Bri answers, "She didn't know my name." She is trying to diffuse things.

"You could've offered it!" Ms. Wilson snaps trying to defend herself, not realizing she is making it worse. Bri is trying to keep her out of trouble. Ms. Wilson looks at Mary. "You could've called or emailed me that you were expecting her!"

David scolds her, "*Ms. Wilson.* I don't like the disrespecting tone towards my assistant *or* my fiancé!" He then asks her, "As soon as you knew, why didn't you call Mary back?"

"I didn't know she was anybody until you-you *kissed her!*" She stumbles with a faint hint of irritation in her voice.

"Ooo, now that's not very honest, Ms. Wilson." Bri interjects. "I had pointed out right away you never told Mary who I was because you never asked. Do we need to go into what came after?"

She glares. "That I was going to throw you out for causing a scene?" She scoffs. "You *Americans* are all so alike."

Bri's eyebrow raises. David goes to defend Bri, but Bri puts her hand on his forearm. "Is that how you want to play this? Because, My Dear, that scene goes something like this: *you* are an embarrassment to this company for the way you treated me, an American, *and* anyone else you've discriminated against, or even accused of being a prostitute!"

David tries to keep his voice volume low, but his anger wins out, "SHE WHAT?!" He gets angrier just looking at Ms. Wilson.

"What's more, you insult Mr. Worthington by accusing a woman coming to see him of being a prostitute, which is wrong on *SO* many levels!" Bri tells her. Ms. Wilson hasn't considered that until now and glares at Bri more for embarrassing her. "You also pointed out that 'my kind' isn't welcome here. Did you mean a woman coming to see him, prostitutes, or Americans?"

Ms. Wilson is embarrassed and looks at David. "I'm sor—."

"Shut it, Ms. Wilson!" David's voice booms and Ms. Wilson shrinks back. Normally, David would be more discreet, but after hearing Ms. Wilson call the woman he loves a prostitute; he is *beyond* livid! He angrily whispers, "*You were addressing my fiancé!*" He pauses for a moment. Bri doesn't need to be here for what comes next and he wants to spare *her* any more embarrassment. David looks at Mary. "Would you take Ms. Harris upstairs for me?"

"Certainly, Mr. Worthington." Mary replies. She addresses him formerly when they are not upstairs.

David turns to Bri. "I'll be up in a few minutes?"

Bri looks at Ms. Wilson. "I wish this would've gone better than it did." She turns to Mary who smiles at her, gesturing in the direction of the elevators; Bri walks with her in that direction.

Mary and Bri are walking to the elevators and they hear David saying to Ms. Wilson, "You should be ashamed of yourself for making *anyone* feel like they are less of a person, regardless of who walks through our doors!" Mary and Bri step into the elevator. David is saying to the receptionist, "This is a global company and we welcome *everyone*..." then the elevator doors close.

CHAPTER 28

Imperfectly Perfect Office Reunion

Mary and Bri ride the elevator to the top floor and when the doors open, they step off into a beautifully decorated office reception area with Mary's desk in front but off-center. The walls are painted a cream color against the darker wood of her desk and accent wood, which somehow makes it seem cheery. Maybe that is also because there are fresh flowers in a vase on a table and green plants in various places, which would make any room feel happier.

The elevator dings again and David walks out. He thanks Mary and informs her that Ms. Wilson no longer works for them. He takes Bri's hand, leading her to his office and his phone starts ringing.

He holds a finger up. "My apologies, Love, but—."

She smiles a little. "It's fine, David, answer it!" He winks at her.

"Herst! Sorry about not calling on time, there was an urgent matter I had to take care of!"

"Oh? What was so urgent?" Herst chuckles.

"The love of my life came to surprise me!" He says and Bri quietly giggles as Herst laughs.

While they talk for a few minutes, Bri walks over to the doors that lead to a patio, and steps outside. She looks around at the beautiful city, the cars, buses, the people walking around. She takes a deep breath and just enjoys the peacefulness. Eventually, she hears the call end.

"Thanks, Herst! I appreciate that and we'll see you all Saturday!"

David hangs up and joins Bri on the patio. He sees her hand wipe what he assumes are tears. He comes up behind her to gently turn her and sees he's right. Not saying a word, he cups her face and kisses her with all the love he can. He doesn't let go of her, nor does he release the kiss until he feels her relax in his arms.

When she does, he holds her firmly and looking into her eyes he smiles lovingly. "Hullo, Beautiful. What do I owe the pleasure of seeing your *gorgeous* face earlier than expected *and here*?"

"Well, I wanted to surprise *you* for a change, but failed..."

"Oh, I'd consider it a success!" He smiles a big, happy smile at her, then goes to kiss her some more, but she doesn't allow it.

She tsks. "How can you say that?! I couldn't even make it to the elevators!"

"That doesn't count!" He replies.

She rolls her eyes and steps back, out of his arms. "When Serene had a disdain for Americans, I just thought it was because her insecurities made her a pathetically sad, mean, and spiteful socialite, using anything as a negative against anyone she sees as a rival...but now?" She stands looking out again. "*Now*, a receptionist is showing a disdain for Americans and I find myself wondering if I'm kidding myself that I'll *ever* be accepted, let alone supported, as your partner in *running* Newhaven?!"

"Bri, it's simple—."

"No! *It's not*!" She faces him again.

"*Yes, it is*, Love!" He says. She scoffs and rolls her eyes. "There's the eye roll of defiance!" He exhales in frustration and folds his arms. "*Do you love me?*"

"Of course, but—."

"No, BriaLynn. No 'buts,' just 'yes' or 'no.' Do.You.Love.Me?"

She folds her arms to mirror him and gives him a defiant, "*No.*"

He raises his eyebrow and gives her a look of: '*This isn't a joke!*' He tells her, "*Don't* lie to me and *truthfully* answer the bloody question!"

"Ugh. Fine. *Yes.*" She answers with a flourish of her hand, rolling her eyes.

"Do I still have your heart?" He asks her with a firm voice, so she'll answer honestly. She can only nod because of the lump in her throat, and he can see the tears welling up in her eyes. He softens his demeanor a bit.

He gently holds her upper arms and tells her, "Don't you see?! Just as I have your heart, Bri, *you have mine*! I need you to know that you mean *everything* to me, because you *are* everything to me!" He goes to hug her and while she doesn't back away, she shakes her head. "I'd even give up *everything* for you!" He lifts her chin. "Even being——."

She softly cups her hand to his mouth. "*Don't* say it! I've come to terms with this being a part of your life, David. Besides," she lets her hand drop, and gives a hint of a smile in her eyes, "I kind of figured that would be the case, some time ago."

"Yet here we are?" He innocently states.

"David, I don't doubt you love me! I don't doubt Jack loves me! You both want to see me happy, as I want both of you to be happy, too. So, when I hear that you're willing to do anything, or give up everything for me, it tells me that you also trust in my love for you, and that I would *never* ask you to do anything, nor give up something *so important*! David, being *willing* to do whatever it takes to be with me is incredible to me, because I've never had someone love me like that before! In turn, I love you too much to ever support you giving up what you've been preparing your *whole life* to do! Something *I know* you'll be *great* at!"

He lovingly smiles. "This is another moment I just fell in-love with you again, BriaLynn Harris!" She smiles through her tears. "To have you believe so much in me! That's," he chokes up, but pushes out, "*a remarkable feeling!*" He kisses her fiercely.

She barely whispers, "*I love you, David!*" She kisses him again.

"You also need to understand that just as much as you're marrying *me*, Love, I'm marrying *you*. I'm not just saying it for romance, Bri; you really are the woman of my dreams!" He smiles softly, then he rests his arms on the railing and looks out. "Not too long before we met, I was getting bored with the women coming through the, as you call it," he uses air quotes, "'revolving door.' Any time before this, I never would've allowed myself to dream of a happy marriage, but by this point my heart was wanting real. Those dreams were simple, where I'd come home to a loving wife, we'd have a family dinner and later we'd relax together watching a movie, or read in bed before going to sleep..."

Bri quietly responds, "Sounds perfect."

David turns his head to her and smiles. "You are!" He caresses her cheek. "Bri, while her face wasn't completely clear, the rest of her was, but I have known it's you since I first saw you!" He stands up straight, turning to her and he kisses the back of her hand, then holds it to his chest. "Bri, I can already sense part of you wants to run, but I won't let you run, Love. It's *far* too late for that!"

She doesn't say anything, just raises her eyebrows a little surprised. Jack has made his way up to David's office and David can see him in his peripheral view. He moves his hand so only Jack sees his finger for 'just a sec.' David wants Jack to listen because he might have something to add.

David takes both of her hands. "Bri, the stereotype of Americans is they don't appreciate history or traditions. It's assumed they'll 'tear down the old and build new.' This stereotype is something I considered with you and our tradition of having a 'Noble Consort.' At first mention of it, I foolishly said you wouldn't go for it. That Americans usually frown upon anything that goes against their conventional. But when I thought of Jack and his love for you, and how easily you love, I started to realize you *could* do this *for love*. I'm glad I was right." He is still holding her hands and gently pulls her arms for her to come closer and when she steps forward, he knows she is not wanting to run anymore. "You're getting used to the idea of taking this huge step outside your comfort zone."

She grins and teases, "It's not *that* huge. Have you two looked in the mirror?!" David chuckles and Jack quietly laughs to himself.

"*There you are, Love...*" David smiles. "This grand gesture with Jack on your part will go further than you can realize at the moment." He takes her left hand and laces their fingers. "Together." He kisses the ring on her finger. He tips his head down to catch her gaze. "Please, say you'll marry me, Saturday?"

Her eyebrows come together. "*What?*" She's caught off guard. Once it sinks in, she says, "*Oh, David——.*" She just hugs him tight. "*I might've wanted to run,* but *never permanently.*" She looks at him. "I'm sorry for that...for letting that woman get to me. Truth is, *you've got me,* and I'm afraid you're stuck with me forever." David smiles and he cups her face again as Bri says, "I love you so much, David."

He kisses her, then rests their foreheads together. "That's a relief! It'd be a shame to cancel the wedding now!" She snorts a laugh and he can't help but laugh, too. He tangles his hands in her hair and kisses her firmly again.

When they pull their lips apart, she grins, "You're forever stuck with me, too, Jack!" She had also seen him earlier in her peripheral vision.

Jack walks out onto the patio smiling at her. "There's no one better we could be stuck with," he kisses her cheek, "and to love."

She puts her hand on his cheek and smiles so lovingly at him, his heart melts. "I'm surprising myself at how much love I have for both of you and it's only growing!"

Jack taps a kiss to her lips. "It doesn't surprise us!" David shakes his head.

"David," Bri has an apologetic expression, "about downstairs...I'm sorry if I overstepped."

He shakes his head. "Bri, I'm just glad *I* could defend you, *although you were doing a great job!*" He tucks some hair behind her ear. "Being the CEO, I have to insist anyone who comes into our company be treated with respect. Most importantly, to set the precedent that *you will be treated with the respect* as the future 'Duchess of Newhaven!'"

She shakes her head. "As *you're wife*...the wife of the CEO." She looks down to hide the tears in her eyes and his heart squeezes at her response.

He lifts her chin with the side of his forefinger. He sees her emotions and lovingly looks at her saying, "I know you've been in situations where it's been just you against some horrible people, and you've fought *beautifully* well. But I swear to you Bri, Jack and I are working on making sure you're never alone in situations like that again." Jack agrees.

She scrunches her eyebrows together. "How?"

"Later." He smiles sweetly.

They hear someone clear their throat behind them. They're thinking it's Mary, but when they look it isn't her.

"Ah, Ms. Taylor," David says waving her over to them. "This is my beautiful fiancé, BriaLynn Harris and my best friend, Jack Carlisle. This is Ms. Sophie Taylor, an interior designer here from London who's been decorating Bri's new office."

"What? David! *That's crazy!*" Bri gives a surprised soft laugh. "I just need a desk to work from, with all the necessary computer security measures, that's it." He gives her a 'don't you know by now' look as he kisses the back of her hand. "Can I see it?!" She excitedly looks from David to Sophie and back to David.

"*Not* unless Ms. Taylor is done!"

"Well, actually I was stopping by to tell you I *am* done." Sophie smiles at Bri and finds she is starting to like her!

Bri shakes her hand. "First, my apologies on my manners. It's really nice to meet you!" Bri tells her, then asks excitedly, "I'd *really* love to see it!"

Sophie looks to David, who says to her, "Well, Ms. Taylor, you've done the work, and I haven't seen it finished yet, either. Will you do the honors?" He waves his arm towards the door.

"It would be my pleasure, Sir!" Sophie smiles wide.

Bri lightly claps. "Yay!"

Sophie smiles and leads the way straight down the hall, to the corner office that is opposite David's corner office. "Would it be too much to ask for you to close your eyes?" She asks Bri, who smiles and closes her eyes. Sophie opens the door and David guides her by the upper arms into the office. Sophie waits for David and Jack to stand beside Bri, then she tells Bri, "Nooow...*Open!*"

Bri looks around the office and gasps, "This is *wonderful!*" Bri turns to David. "This isn't the small office I asked for," she gives him a doubtful look. "This isn't right. What will your employees think?"

He laughs as he wraps her in a hug, kissing her temple. "One of the countless reasons why I love you!" He looks into her eyes. "I'm hoping you'll love it so much you'll continue to use it *long* into the future. As for employees, not many of them will be up here, let alone on this side of the floor, and I highly doubt they'll even care. Plus, I put you on this side, so my work craziness doesn't distract you. Most of my senior staff is on the floor below us, except a couple and they're on the same side as my office."

"Well, being away from craziness would be helpful!" Bri teases.

David lightly laughs, then says, "Ms. Taylor, why don't you tell Bri about the things in her office."

But before she could, something catches Bri's eye. "*Oh my gosh*, is that an old map of Washington, D.C.?!"

"It is!" And Sophie begins to explain the various things in the room. An antique chair that could fit in with The White House décor; a white porcelain bust of George Washington; a picture of Abraham Lincoln; and a framed copy of JFK's 'Inauguration Speech' and 'Inauguration Program' with his picture being sworn into office.

"What's with the empty frame?" Bri asks, pointing at the wall.

"I also have one on my office wall." David says. "Our wedding photo will go into them in the next few weeks." Bri lovingly smiles at him.

Sophie excitedly jumps in with, "Congratulations!" She has a genuine smile. "You two are just so lovely together. I wish you both all the best, with years filled with happiness and joy together!"

"That's so sweet of you to say. Thank you!" Bri happily smiles.

Sophie motions to a picture. "This picture of an empty Oval Office arrived by courier this morning from The President! Your President! *Of the United States*! I'm surprised he even knew or cared." Sophie smacks her hand up to her mouth in shock, then slowly brings it down, "I'm *so* sorry, I didn't mean it like that!"

Bri smiles at her. "It's okay, really. I know what you meant. The President is my boss, but not many know that. My guess is he had conversations with David to arrange this gift." She gives him a questioning look.

"He did! He asked if we'd reserve space on a wall for a framed picture and gave me the dimensions. This is what he sent."

"That was so nice of them to do!" Bri says.

"Them?" Sophie asks.

"He and his wife." Bri answers and Sophie nods with a smile that had an 'ah, of course' expression.

The bookshelves have old leather-bound books, some of them early editions, but a couple first editions; one of them being the Charles Dickens' classic, 'A Tale of Two Cities.' There is also a globe from the Civil War era; models of The White House and Air Force One, along with a bronze eagle.

"This is all so beautiful, Ms. Taylor! Thank you so much!" Bri gives her a hug. Bri turns to David and hugs him. "Thank you, My Love!"

"*Entirely my pleasure!*" He hugs her back firmly.

Sophie adds, "Normally clients have me stressed out in short notice situations, but this was really fun to do!"

David laughs a little. "I'm glad it wasn't too much pressure!"

"It helps when her taste is simpler and classier, rather than over the top." Sophie smiles.

Mary comes in with a box she gives to Jack. David says to Mary and Sophie, "Let's go to my office for a few minutes and then Mary can walk you out, Ms. Taylor."

"Sounds great!" Sophie picks up her things, then says goodbye to Jack and Bri. The three of them leave, giving Bri and Jack a moment.

Jack walks with the box to her desk and puts it down. "Open it!" He smiles with such a look, she couldn't say 'no' if she wanted!

Inside the box, Bri finds a mini sandbox and she smiles wide. "A Zen Garden! Jack this is *perfect!*" She hugs and kisses him. "Thank you!"

He wraps her in an embrace. "You're very welcome!" He kisses her again. "It's not exactly perfect with your décor." He gestures around the room. "I saw this and thought it would be perfect, but maybe I should rethink that."

"Ah, but it is perfect! I'll show you." He helps her take everything out of the box and she places it on her desk where she can easily reach it. She finishes messing with it and says, "Perfect! Perfect gift, perfect spot..." she taps a kiss to his lips, "a perfect representation of you!" She has an excited smile on her face, "Don't you see it?!" He struggles as he stares at it and the room. "Jack! *You're* my Zen in this crazy world! I can go crazy or relax, or somewhere in between! But you'll be there for my mental break when I need it, or is it 'mental break*down*?'" She teases.

Jack kisses Bri and hugs her. She sees David at the door and loosens her grip. Jack chuckles and she looks at him apologetically.

"It does my heart good to see this working, Love!" David says walking to her. "Bri, you'll see this will be fine in front of each other. The only time we'd purposely remove ourselves is to give the other two time alone, like I just did so Jack could give you, his gift."

Jack jumps and looks at the time. "I need to return a phone call, or it'll be too late to do so today. *And* the two of you can have a moment together." Jack winks at Bri and ducks out. Jack's talking on his phone walking down the hall, his voice fading completely as he walks into David's office.

"Thank you for this and, well, *everything!*" Bri pulls David into a passionate kiss; he returns and holds her firmly.

"Saturday night can't come soon enough!" He says, trailing his fingers across her collarbone and he smiles as he watches her shiver a little bit.

Bri clears her throat, "What happens now...it's 3:00, isn't it?"

"It's 3:30 actually." David says, looking at his watch. "Well, we can leave now and get to the airport, where we fly to DC. Then we could all have breakfast together in the morning before returning."

"*Or?*" She asks, knowing everyone is coming here.

"*Or* we take our beautiful fiancé to dinner and then we get her settled into her new home. Then tomorrow we can get her dress and bridesmaids dresses—."

"Oh, the bridesmaids' dresses will be coming from DC. Maggie has seen to the fittings for the girls and will make sure the dresses come with them tomorrow. *My dress* is in the works. In fact, isn't Paxley on the way to Kingsbury, then The Manor?"

He lifts an eyebrow in curiosity. "It can be."

"Then if we stay in the city, we can go to the island in the morning and make two stops along the way to The Manor."

"I'm intrigued! But first, let's talk more at an early dinner, if you're hungry?" He suggests.

"I'm starved actually." She says. "The time change and jetlag…" David holds her hand while they walk to his office to grab his jacket, wallet, and overnight bag. Bri grabs her purse and sweater as Jack walks in from the patio. "Oh no!" She snaps her fingers. "I didn't plan on staying here tonight, so we have to go to The Manor this evening, well, actually my things are at The Inn."

"It's fine, Love. We'll get it worked out." He sweetly assures her.

They walk to the reception area and David talks it over with Mary. He asks her to send Bri's things from The Inn to his townhouse.

Jack jumps into the conversation. "David, your townhouse is packed up and movers are coming in the morning. Why don't you two stay with me at my flat? I won't be moving up until next week when you two are on your honeymoon."

David looks at Bri. "It's up to you! Honestly, I don't care what we do, except I refuse The Manor." She sees David's surprised look. "I want to be married before I sleep inside the walls of The Manor." David is pleased she wants to make The Manor special.

Mary says she will have Bri's things sent to Jack's flat. David thanks her and they say goodbye to Mary, before leaving in the elevator.

When they are about to get off the elevator, David feels Bri starting to hesitate. They step off the elevator and David pauses to whisper to her, "*I need you to walk with confidence, Love. I need you to walk like you're* the wife *of the CEO of this company. Will you do that for me?*"

She gives him a little smile and whispers back, "*I can put my 'game-face' on.*"

David holds up their hands with their fingers laced. "Together." She nods.

Jack is on her other side and winks at her. Then the three of them walk through the lobby and out to the car. David tells Paul which restaurant, as Jack and Bri get into the car. Once they're on their way, Jack is curious to hear what happened, and David wants to know what happened from the beginning.

Bri shakes her head. "It's over, let's just leave it at that."

"She was *incredibly* disrespectful! We can't just leave it at that!" David says.

"Yes, BUT she could've been rude because she was annoyed with women trying to go up and see you all day—."

"No way!" He cuts her off. "That's not even *close* to correct!"

"How would you know if she's sending them away *before* they even make it to the elevator?!" She asks.

David and Jack start to laugh and David responds, "There's truth to that *theory*, but that's all it is, Love. These women don't follow me to work."

"I did!" She says.

"You're not just any woman either, Bri. Remember, I had what you call, '*the revolving door of women.*'"

Jack grins at her. "And you also said that 'under the hair, skin, makeup, and boobs, they were all the same.'" Paul laughs out loud, but coughs to cover it, although he believes that is a true statement!

David smirks at Paul, then continues. "As you're *all* well aware, those women were more wrapped up in themselves, with shopping and beauty appointments, than to come to what they feel is the boring business district. Besides, Bri, I *preferred* it that way. I didn't want attachments."

She looks at him and replies a little frustrated, "*Fine*. You *may* have a point."

"Glad to hear it, even with the frustration in your tone." He taps her chin with the tip of his finger.

Bri inhales and exhales some of her annoyance and frustration before she lays it all out for them. Jack and David were nodding as they listened, but their jaws were still clenching throughout and by the time Bri is done explaining everything that happened, they are both *furious*.

"You should've *called me*, Love!" David tells her.

"That *definitely* would've ruined *any* surprise!"

"Not necessarily. It was still a surprise you were in the lobby!" David replies. "And Mary will email a picture of you tomorrow so *every employee* will recognize you!"

She shrugs. "I could care less if someone recognizes me or not..."

"It was her rudeness." David and Jack both say simultaneously.

"Right. Although, I'm still stunned being called a prostitute! I've had men make passes before, mostly when they're drunk, but still..."

"*That's when you've noticed.*" The corner of David's mouth slightly lifts in a smile. "You think because those other men were drunk, those passes were less genuine. I think some of those men felt they needed a bit of 'liquid courage,' you might say."

"*Riiight*...I'm to be flattered by a man who needs the mind-altering effects of drunkenness to find me *attractive enough* to see if I'm willing to jump into bed with them?" Jack and David chuckle.

David notes, "Alright, *you* maaay have a point, although it could be they were lacking confidence, and wanted—."

"Okay, Love, I'm going to stop you right there, because this will just keep circling around sex." Bri tells him.

"Rather than a relationship." David adds.

She nods. "Now, if this drunkenness were to ask a woman out on a date, getting drunk first is not the best approach, but I can see the nervousness behind taking that first step. But a drunk man approaching me, or any other woman, for just sex is *insulting*."

"I can definitely see that." David then confesses, "I'm guilty of that myself."

"Me, too." Jack reluctantly admits.

She smirks. "I said all those women coming through your 'revolving doors' were the same underneath the hair, skin, makeup, and boobs, but I never said they were smart. *They probably thought it was all the same thing because they lack the self-respect to know the difference* and require better *from men!*" The guys agree as they softly laugh as they pull up to the restaurant.

Jack asks David, "You fired that woman, right?" David, even Paul through the rearview mirror, sees the pained look on Bri's face.

David replies, "*Rather quickly.*" Bri's eyes close and she holds them shut for a few seconds. "Bri, *as a gentleman and CEO*, I needed to make a stand for the mistreatment of our visitors, as well as my wife! Especially in front of those who witnessed the interaction between you two!"

"Using my own words against me may not be in your best interest, *Mister* Worthington!" She says. "However, 'wife,' *is* a nice touch."

"Not against you, Love. *Never* against you!" David smiles.

"I'm sad that she went too far. I even tried to help her save herself, but I couldn't and *she* got *herself* fired." She gives a little reluctant smile as they nod. She quietly asks, "Can we drop this now and talk about happier things?"

David kisses her hand. "*Of course.*"

Jack smiles. "Like the wedding?" Bri smiles happily in agreement.

They get out of the car and Bri says, "I'll stand by you both, even if I don't agree, as long as you've *respectfully* heard me out."

"Thank you, Love." David replies. "We'll do the same, too."

Jack nods. "Absolutely!" Then the three of them go inside the restaurant.

After dinner they go to Jack's flat and watch a movie. She wants them to take the bedrooms because, "I'm a handful of hours behind you right now. I can read for a while or watch the *telly*." She teases with their accent.

"I'm not doing anything less than what's chivalrous." David smirks.

"This is different!" She tells him.

"Please, don't fight me over being a gentleman, Love." He lovingly smiles. *"Especially with you."*

She grins, "But it's what brought us together!"

"That's when I had forgotten how to be one! Now shut it and let my chivalry *keep us* together!" He says with a playful mad face.

She giggles, "Alright." She kisses David, then walks over to Jack. "Considering you haven't had time to prepare, are there going to be things in your bedroom belonging to a female *friend* of sorts?"

He playfully smiles. "I dare you to find something!" She studies him for a few seconds before he asks, "What?"

"Just trying to discern if it's confidence, or you're being overly cocky." She replies.

David chuckles. "Love, here's the deal. We've admitted our doors were revolving doors, but with that also means no one *stayed* around to accumulate things. They were rarely brought here or to the townhouse. It was usually a hotel or their place so *we* could leave when *we* wanted to."

"Interesting answer..." She replies.

David steps closer. "It's just the truth."

"That's why it's an interesting answer, *Mister* Worthington." She holds his jaw. "We're all capable of lying to each other, *if* that's the type of relationship we want to build. Only, I don't think any of us want lies and secrets between us." The guys shake their heads.

They get Bri all situated in Jack's bedroom. Jack walks over to her and kisses her sweetly goodnight. They say, 'I love you' and kiss once more.

David comes in next. "Goodnight, Love. I'll see you in the morning." He wraps his arms around her. "I love you!"

She smiles lovingly at David and hugs him back. "I love you, *Mister* Worthington!" He kisses her firmly before he and Jack leave the room. She crawls into bed and reads until she is tired enough to sleep.

CHAPTER 29

Perfectly Perfect Wedding Dresses

The next morning, Bri wakes up to David sitting beside her and running his hand through her hair. She groggily says with her eyes still closed, "You're so lucky I love you..."

"That's the understatement of the century!" He chuckles and kisses her cheek, then whispers, "*Blessed is more like it!*"

"That answer helps your cause, *Mister* Worthington." She admits.

"Good! Then get up! We'll need to leave here soon and head home. You can shower before we leave, but *only* if you get up now." David tells her, swatting her bum on top of the covers.

"Ugh..." She turns up her nose at the time and asks him with a hoarse voice, "Do you know how much sleep I've gotten in *my time zone?*"

He rests his hand on her covered bum and kisses her shoulder. "I'll make it up to you on our honeymoon, I swear, and maybe even an early bedtime tonight, scratch that—."

"The engagement party..." She moans, rolling out of bed. "Calling *everything* off sounds so much simpler right now!" She says, shuffling to the bathroom.

David laughs, throwing a pillow at her backside. "Oh, Love, you ran out of time for that the moment you said, 'yes,' to marrying me."

"Ah," she turns and says with a smirk, "but I *didn't!*" She is referring to the 'absolutely' she gave him. "Besides, we aren't married yet, so there's *always* time!" She sticks her tongue out a little as she shuts the door to the bathroom.

He laughs and yells, "Just take your shower, Cheeky!" He walks up to the door. "Don't forget to wash off the sharper sassy and feisty!"

To herself she says, "Make me!"

He barely hears her and replies, "Gladly! Sunday morning, Love! Now, get busy, or I'll have to make it sooner and come do it myself!" She smiles, shaking her head.

Bri is half-awake when she climbs in the shower, so it takes her a minute to realize that one of them already had her shampoo, conditioner, and body wash in the shower. When she gets out and grabs the towel, she sees a dress hanging on the hook underneath it. She's not sure who got it for her, because both guys have great taste, as this dark burgundy-red dress proves it once again. She feels the fabric and it feels incredibly soft and comfortable.

When she finally comes out of the bathroom they are waiting with her pastry and milk. "Thank you." She smiles. "Thank you for the soaps and dress as well." She takes a bite of her pastry. "I would've used Jack's soaps because I didn't think about those and I do have clothes in my suitcase." Bri kisses David soundly, then steps over to Jack and hesitates but he understands.

Jack sweetly smiles. "We're a bit fond of your soaps and how good you smell. As for the dress, I picked it up a couple of days ago thinking it would look good on you and it looks *fantastic!*" *He* kisses her.

She smiles and looks down at herself. "I have to admit, this dress is *super* soft and comfortable! I should have you both pick out my clothes more often!" She winks as she goes to take a bite, but Jack steals the bite; she giggles shaking her head. She sits between them on the bed.

"What time are your appointments on the island?" David asks her.

Bri looks at her watch. "I said I'd call this morning, which I have their personal *mobile numbers,*" she teases with their accent, "but what's the earliest time we can make it out to Paxley?"

David replies, "An hour would be the best and it could be earlier, but typically, it's 35-45 minutes to get to Paxley—."

"Depending on the ferry." It dawns on her. "It's what Nicholas from The Coriander Hotel told us for our first visit to the island. If my sense of direction is correct, the hotel isn't that much further away." She points in the direction she thinks the hotel is in.

"Ah, your sense of direction would be correct." David remembers fondly, "Where I first laid eyes on the most beautiful woman I've ever seen!"

"Hnnn…" She smiles. "Do you have things to do here this morning or—."

"All on the island." He smiles.

"Great! I'll make those appointments and aim for first thing." Bri winks and walks over to the window to make those calls.

The guys talk between themselves when she is on the phone. They discuss rings and the design used. David says if he wants to, Jack can add a wedding band to her left finger.

David grins at Jack, "Herst is interested in Bri being his Royal Consort."

"That doesn't surprise me!" Jack grins. "She *is* one of a kind!"

David agrees. "That she is!"

"She never mentioned meeting 'The King of the United Kingdom of Provinces' before…then again, she hasn't really said who she has met over the years either." Jack comments. "It was pretty fantastic when we met her boss after she was released from the hospital and seeing The Oval Office. I was *still* in awe when Bri arranged a little tour for Mother and me at The White House. The people Bri knew just in the halls! No one famous, just that they knew her and they didn't just wave in passing; *they actually stopped and greeted her by name!*"

David nods. "Given that, it isn't much of a surprise if she doesn't remember everyone she has met either." They quietly laugh.

Jack asks, "When are you going to tell her?"

"Herst wants me to wait until we've both had our honeymoons with her." David says. "He and I will talk more when I get back and you two are on yours."

"Good idea." Jack replies. "It may be too much as it is with the wedding and a Noble Consort, then to ask her to *consider* being The King's Royal Consort is another." He hesitates. "Then again, she may be upset that we didn't tell her earlier."

"I think she is accepting this more and more as a way of life for aristocracy and tradition." David tells him as they watch her talk on the phone. "I feel she will have time after the wedding to get to know Herst. It won't be as short of a timeline like this has been."

"But there is a timeline?" Jack whispers.

"Something like a year-and-a-half, give or take." David replies. "She'll come around for this, too, especially if she knows this will elevate the entire Worthington family, to a point."

Jack looks from Bri to David. "On the flight here, she was drawing the Triquetra and wanted to know the meaning behind it. She said she couldn't help but feel there is a missing link. She had determined for herself that the three points represent faith, friendship, and loyalty. Then the heart she drew through all three loops represented love. However, she also said she felt there was something she couldn't quite see yet. Perhaps Herst *is* the missing link for her?"

"Maybe..." David considers it. "Before I talk to her about it, I need to know if you are okay with this, Jack?" David asks. "She would be splitting her time three ways."

"The workaholics we tend to be means the time we'll have with her will be quality time. Only I'd ask the time in between not be too long, though not too short with her either...no shorter than three days if we can help it."

David nods. "Maybe we should talk to her together about this."

"Just name when and where." Jack replies, then looks at her. "Can you imagine how wonderful The Royal Heir will turn out having *Bri* for a mother?!"

David smiles as he watches her. "Her love alone will end the cycle of ruthless rule and loveless parenting."

Bri is finished making her appointments and turns back around. She sees Jack and David are still sitting on the bed, until Jack's phone rings. He goes out of the room to answer it.

"We're all set," she says and Jack hears her before he answers his phone, "and we have a little over an hour to get there. They want me to come in a half hour before they open, even though I said it could wait and no one had to be in early."

She leans down to kiss David and he pulls her down onto the bed and she squeals with surprise; he pins her down with one leg on top of her. They get quiet when he puts his forehead to hers.

"I wish I could find the words to express *all* the love I feel for you!" He says.

"I do!" She runs a hand into his hair. "I'm surprised at how much love I feel when you hold a kiss on my cheek, too."

"Well, that's why I hold a kiss there! But, come Saturday night..." He runs his finger down her jawline.

"I'm trying not to be nervous. I know might sound crazy, but after everything you've done for me and for us, I just don't want your expectations to be so high that—."

"These aren't expectations," he interrupts, "*it's love.* And the love we have for each other means *physically* it's always going to be—."

She puts her hand over his mouth. "Don't say it! *Don't* jinx it!" She looks at him with so much love, all he can do is smile and kiss her. Then she suggests, "Now, let's change the subject."

He lightly laughs. "One last thing. I want you to know I'm fine if you and Jack find a moment to be *together* tomorrow after the ceremony."

"Then that's all we'll say on the subject." She nervously says.

He taps a gentle kiss to her lips, but she wraps her arms around his neck and deepens their kiss. She pulls back before she moans into it.

He gives her a knowing smile, then refocuses their attention. "About your wedding dress..." He helps her up. "Wait. Let's pause that until we get going." They gather their things and the three of them go down to the car. "Tell us more about your dress, Love..." David and Jack shift to face her as they talk.

"I apologize if I should've talked it over with you first, but I was inspired to reach out to local dress shops on the island. I sent pictures, measurements, and instructions for what I was looking for. They had until 10:00 Wednesday night DC time, to send me sketches of what they could come up with. I hoped someone would get close, and I'd work with the designer to make any changes, only...." she trails off to blink back tears, "the perfect dress was sent to me by a designer in Paxley, who has been working hard since to have it ready by Friday." David and Jack are stunned. Bri holds her breath because she can't read if their expressions are good or bad.

"*Wow...*" David says. "I knew you were brilliant, but I'm what we call 'gobsmacked,' Love! *That's impressive!*"

Jack laughs. "Proving once again you're *bloody brilliant!*"

She mentions, "I can't take credit for it since I was inspired." She excitedly tells them, "I'm glad you two are okay with this because there is a reception dress I love that is coming from Kingsbury!"

David chuckles a little and kisses her temple. "More than okay, Love! Now I can't wait to see them!"

"Oh, that *will* be tomorrow! *Don't even try to sweet talk me into an early viewing, Mister Worthington!*" Bri says rather adamantly that he raises his hands partially up to surrender. She looks to Jack with the same sternness, "That goes for you, too, *Mister Carlisle!*"

Jack puts his hands up in a surrender, too, saying, "I wouldn't dream of it!"

They finish their ferry ride in more lighthearted conversation.

David, Jack, and Bri visit both shops on their way to The Worthington Estate. At their first stop, David asks to meet the designer and their staff, but that she can talk to them first to make sure the dress is hidden.

"No." She says.

"Love, *I swear* I won't even try to sneak a peek!" David tells her.

"*Oh, I know!*" She quickly replies. "Because you're *not* going inside that shop!" She points her finger. "Don't think for one second I don't know what you're going to *try* to do!" She holds his hands. "Listen to me David," her eyes are moist, "you've done so much for our wedding, on top of running a company, *and* while being by my side at the hospital—." She chokes up and inhales deeply, then she exhales shakily. "I can't thank you both enough for being such a strength for me! And Jack, before we went down this road, you were still there for me when it had to have been so hard for you to do."

Jack is a little emotional whispering, "*SO worth it!*"

She sweetly smiles, then turns back to David. "You have planned *every* detail and all that's left are the dresses. The least I can do is pay for the dress, well, dress*es*, for *our* incredibly special day, David Worthington!"

"Bri, those dresses are being *made...*" David hints at the price.

Jack picks up on it and gets an idea. "Let *me* pay for them!" He knows David will be more comfortable with that, rather than Bri paying for custom made dresses. "*My* gift to the wedding that will marry the two of you and essentially me with the girl of *my* dreams!" He has a huge smile on his face.

Bri's mouth falls open...then she barely whispers, "*Jaaack...*" She slowly shakes her head, lost for words.

He cups her cheek. "*Please*, let *me* do this for all three of us!" He pleads.

"*Swear to me* that David *won't* pay a cent, er, whatever the equivalent money is here. *Noth-ing!*" She looks at him.

Jack looks from her to David with a grin. "*Deal!*" Then he hooks his pinky finger with hers. "I swear!"

She looks at David and he puts his hand to his heart. "*I promise I won't interfere.*"

Bri hugs David. "Thank you!" Then she hugs Jack. "Thank you!"

Bri goes into the shop first to make sure neither of them will see the dress. The dress is being worked on in the back of the shop; she'll find out the other dress is in a back room and already out of sight.

While they wait, David says, "This whole wedding is my gift to her, for the gift to love her forever, *and* for her taking a chance on a long-standing tradition! You're very much a part of all of this! Thank you, Brother, for doing this with us!"

"*It's me who's grateful!*" Jack happily replies.

David and Jack talk to both designers in private, Jack writing bonus checks for them and all their staff's hard work. Jack also wanted them to send any bills directly to him, giving them his business card. David goes to a local bakery near each place and has some goodies sent to the shops.

Once all is squared away with her fittings, she slides into the car with David and Jack. David watches her for a few minutes before she looks at him with a questioning look.

David smiles. "You're amazing, brilliant, and *incredibly* beautiful!"

She gives David a loving smile. "*We're* amazing! You're both incredibly intelligent, sexy, and devastatingly handsome!" She winks. "AND *I'm* the one blessed to love you both and be loved *by* you both!" She leans over and David meets her lips for a tender kiss. "I adore you!" She looks into David's eyes with so much adoring love for him and he also has that same look for her. She looks at Jack and is so choked up she can barely say, "I adore you, too, Jack." She needs a moment to quell her emotions so she hugs him a minute, then she taps a kiss to his lips.

When they turn on the road leading to The Worthington Estate, Bri watches the familiar woods go by, then the black iron fence comes into view and it's all decorated with green garland that will be decorated with fresh flowers tomorrow morning for the wedding. Turning onto the drive, the gates have beautiful green wreaths with the fancy W's in the center; they, too, will have fresh flowers in the morning.

Bri looking out the windows of the car saying, "David! This is all so wonderful and beautiful!"

"Mother has the green thumb!" He replies. "You should see the back gardens when she's done!"

"Can't wait!" She beams.

"Ah, but you'll wait until you see it walking down to the wedding ceremony tomorrow." David tells her.

She gasps, "*Why?!*"

"If I have to wait to see your dresses, then you should wait to see the gardens!" He says.

"Hey now, it's *tradition* for the groom, well grooms," she winks at Jack, "to wait to see the dresses!"

"It doesn't *have to* apply here." He teases.

"*Like hell it doesn't!*" She is quick to respond and they are both a bit surprised by her reaction. She asserts, "Tra-di-tion! Isn't that the reason behind having a Noble Consort?! And isn't there a *tradition* of the groom not seeing the bride's dress before the wedding, *nor the bride before the wedding* on the actual wedding day *for that matter?* Do you *really* want to argue with me about how certain traditions would or wouldn't apply here?! Besides," she asks, "is it too much to ask for both of you to wait to see me all put together with the dress, hair, jewelry, and so on?"

"I suppose not..." David looks at Jack, both half smiling. He tells her, "We concede, Love." David kisses her engagement ring on her finger. "Have you picked out jewelry for it?"

"Not yet. I asked the designers to bring some choices that day. Why?"

"Mother will have some ideas, if you don't mind her help?" He suggests.

"That would be wonderful!" She smiles happily.

"I will text her and ask about it." David says.

"I'd love that, but only if she has time." Bri replies.

Jack chuckles, "Bri, she will be *thrilled* to do it!" David nods as he types the text. Jack adds, "Mother will work her day around going to see those dresses!"

David presses 'send.' "She never had a daughter and I can guarantee she will be excited at the chance to share her pieces with you!" Jack agrees. Bri thinks back to the Black-Tie Party when they all first met, and the jewelry Carlotta had her wear; she smiles to herself looking out the window again.

As the car comes to a stop in front of The Manor, she asks, "Do you think I could go to The Inn and freshen up?"

David reaches up and tucks her hair behind her ear. "You're not staying at The Inn, Love. I want you here, in the residence that will be ours come tomorrow night."

She shakes her head, "But that's——." He covers her mouth with his fingertips.

"I don't want you anywhere else. I know what you said about not staying at The Manor until we're married, but can you *slightly* bend on this, the night before our wedding? I've never lived in these quarters, so these truly are *ours*! *Please*," he kisses the inside of her wrist, "do this for me."

"Okay."

He hugs her and starts to say, "Macu...." Then trails off.

She doesn't quite hear him. "What?"

He shakes his head and climbs out. He will explain 'Macushla' *at* the wedding. He helps her out and kisses her once more before he goes inside, leaving Bri with Jack; he walks around the car and up to her.

Bri holds out her hand to Jack. "Walk with me?"

"I'd love to..." He smiles as he takes her hand.

She looks at The Manor. "I'm assuming somewhere in this massive house we could get lost for a bit?"

He chuckles. "We could!"

He takes her inside and they walk around for a while, content to be together. They find a bench and she has him sit, but she straddles him.

"*Bri*..." Jack gets a playful grin.

"I'm doing this to have your undivided attention, maybe the next time I'm straddling you we'll have some physical fun, *but not now*. So, focus" He guides her to sit down with his hands on her hips.

She cups his face and looks at him so lovingly, the desire to take things further fades. It's just her and him in this moment. "I don't think I ever said thank you for agreeing to be 'The Noble Consort.'"

"*Your* 'Noble Consort' and *only* yours!" He sweetly smiles.

She kisses him firmly. "Thank you, Jack, for doing this with me, *with us*. My heart has fallen for you and would've Saturday if David weren't in the picture. I'm so blessed to have David's love, but to have yours on top of it?" Her eyes are teary. "While David is a *huge* blessing in my life, *you are a blessing's gift!*"

"No, Bri, I'm the one blessed! I never thought I'd get married, let alone getting married to someone as amazing as you, but here we are!" She kisses him passionately, but abruptly stops. She rests their foreheads together and blows out her breath. He smiles and says, "I feel it, too, Gorgeous!"

She smiles. "I know." She sits back. "I should probably tell you that David said if you and I wanted to... 'be together,'" she uses air quotes, "he said he was fine with it."

He tangles his hands in her hair. "Bri, tomorrow is your day with David."

"I understand why you might feel that way, except this marriage will also bind you and I together, too."

"I appreciate what you're saying," he smiles, "but I want you two to have tomorrow and your honeymoon. We'll have our time when you get back!" Jack kisses her and smiles. "I love you, BriaLynn."

"I love you so much, *Jackson!*" She grins with teary eyes, then she chokes up and she pulls him into a hug. She rests her forehead to his. "Just as much as I can't wait to be married to David, the same goes for you."

He looks at her so lovingly and smiles. "I know." She giggles and he taps a kiss to her lips. "Trust me, I'll let you know when I'm feeling neglected before I'm *very* neglected." He winks. She giggles again and kisses him once more before they go to find David.

CHAPTER 30

Imperfectly Perfect Prenup

David is showing Bri the gardens before lunch. "Your mother has *really* outdone herself! These gardens are breathtaking; almost like stepping into a fairytale!" David is still holding her hand as they come to the all too familiar bridge and stops.

David smiles adoringly at her. "These gardens *are* stunning, but I have a feeling they won't compare to your exquisite beauty that'll be highlighted tomorrow in your gorgeous dress and veil." He kisses her firmly and it gets more heated.

She pulls away abruptly. "Wow!" She inhales deeply and holds her breath.

"My sentiments exactly." David rests his forehead to hers.

She playfully smiles. "What makes you think I have a veil?!"

"Tradition." He smirks. "*Aaand* I might've seen it written down with some notes. No pictures or peeking, I promise." He holds up his right hand.

"Thank you for your honesty. I'll give you a little insight. The edges of the veil," she holds up her engagement ring, "have the same—." He surprises her when he kisses her. She smiles saying, "Maybe I should tell you more if that's the reaction I'm going to get!" She teases.

He holds her jaw. "No, you were right! I *want* to see you all put together tomorrow, *veil and all*, because that's the way *you* want me to see you. I'm thrilled you're adding touches to it that are traditional *and personal to us!*"

"I can't take all the credit. All I did was tell the designer I wanted to put some traditional touches on it, but also our own. I showed him my engagement ring." She looks down at her ring. "He said he had an idea and suggested using it on the edge of the veil."

He hugs her and catches the scent of her shampoo. "You smell good." He steps back. "We need to go take care of a couple of things today yet. Let's go back inside."

"Is everything okay?" She sounds a little concerned.

"Everything is fine." He smiles. "I promise."

"Then just a couple more minutes?" She asks with a small, sweet smile.

He lovingly smiles at her, wrapping his arms around her while they watch the stream flow towards and under the bridge. A few minutes later, she takes his hand and they start walking towards The Manor. They get to their quarters and he has them sit on the couch.

"In a couple of hours, we'll have paperwork to sign, and 'The Noble Consort' is part of it."

"What kind of paperwork?" She asks. He shifts a little to face her better and takes her hand. She reads his body language. "A prenup?" He looks at her with a guilty expression. "David, it's fine. I get it, *I do*." She sees the relief in his face and oddly it irks her. "*You're relieved*?! *Seriously*?! What did you think would happen?! *We've been over this*!" She angrily exhales. David is surprised.

She is more upset than she normally would've been if she didn't unknowingly have 'wedding nerves.' Before David can calm her down, there is a knock at the door and Bri goes to answer it.

"*Jack*!" She says with annoyance. His eyebrows go up with the tone of her voice. She tells him, "Maybe you can explain to *your* best friend here why I may be upset he was nervous to talk to me about signing a prenup!" She pushes past Jack and leaves. She hears Jack say, "What the..." before the door closes a bit hard, but it isn't slammed.

Jack folds his arms and says, "You *know* she would sign any kind of a prenup to marry you without a second thought, because she just wants to marry *you*! Secondly, we both know *that prenup* will do what the previous one with Ava did not: you will take care of her and *her* children, it's just the title won't be hers. Which makes this more 'Newhaven business,' so all you needed to do was hand her a damn pen!"

"*I know*!" David exhales in frustration at himself. "Can I plea 'temporary insanity' or something?"

Jack lightly laughs. "Well, that plea might actually work with her!"

"And a correction, Jack, she wants to marry *us*!" David states. "I don't know why, but my mind went to thinking 'if we have to redo paperwork, we may be cutting it close'...*idiotic* should also be the plea!"

"She won't insist on changing anything, unless it's to have you pay her *less* in a divorce." Jack sits next to David. "Then you both would be at a stalemate because *you'll insist* she is provided for, *and she will insist* she can take care of herself."

"You seem pretty sure of all this!" David slightly grins.

"*I'm as sure as you are*! I'm in-love with our 'feisty firecracker,' as you call her!" He nudges David.

David chuckles and stands up. "I'll have you sign the paperwork at 3:00 with us. I want the paperwork to at least be outlined as we sign because, as my mother warned, I don't want her to be surprised about anything after we're married and she somehow feels trapped."

"I hadn't considered that!" Jack says.

"I hadn't either! It was Mother's advice. We want her to feel in control of her life and her body, which is why we agree to her terms."

"Terms?" Jack asks.

"You two didn't get that far?" David asks.

Jack shakes his head. "Just no sex before marriage and all this is legal."

David explains, "There's only two others at the moment. One, she wants what happens behind bedroom doors, to stay behind bedroom doors..."

Jack nods in agreement. "And?"

'The marriage bed is sacred,' which means we won't have sex in each other's bed we share with her. I think the 'behind bedroom doors' is to say she won't talk about the physical intimacy with the other and we shouldn't talk about it between us either." David thinks back, "You know, we've ended up dating the same woman before because of our 'revolving doors,' and I don't recall ever asking..."

Jack chuckles. "I haven't heard any complaints either!"

David laughs. "From my view, Jack, we'll both have our own relationship with Bri; building our lives side-by-side with her and raising our family together, with all her beautiful children." Jack gets a little uncomfortable. "Yes, Jack! Yours, too! You need to open up with her about that, so you'll relax...but if *that* doesn't work, she and I will work together to convince you!" David teases a little, but he's also serious. "Are we good?"

"*Are you kidding*?! I don't know how I will ever repay you for the gift you've given me, Brother!" Jack inhales and exhales slowly.

"That's easy!" David grins and Jack furrows his eyebrows in a questioning look. "*Love her*!" David tells him.

"I'll love her *forever*!" Jack replies.

David pats Jack's shoulder one more time, "I know...even if you didn't marry her." Jack agrees. David takes a deep breath. "Right now, I need to go find Bri and apologize for my 'temporary insanity *and stupidity*.'" Jack chuckles watching David leave.

David goes up and down the hallways, checking rooms, and decides to try a different corridor. Eventually he spots her in unfamiliar territory for her. It's not that she couldn't be down there, it's just that there is really no reason for her to be there.

"What's down here?" He asks.

Bri reluctantly admits, "I took too many turns to keep track of and I got lost."

David empathetically smiles. "I've done that *countless* times."

"Yeah, *when you were four years old*!"

"*I still get turned around*!" He smiles reaching for her, but she steps back.

"*Don't.* I'm still angry with you!"

He gives her a 'come on now' look. "Angry?"

She rolls her eyes a bit. "*Fine.* I guess getting lost has downgraded it to '*very annoyed.*'" Mocking his accent. David snorts. "It's not funny!" She tries to say seriously but halfway laughs.

"Would it help if I came to apologize and plea '*temporary insanity* and *stupidity*' with you?" He asks.

"*Perhaps...*" Bri looks at him considering his question, trying to hide a smile but not hiding it well enough.

David gets closer and lifts her chin. "My uneasiness you picked up on was me thinking about the paperwork. If we needed to change anything, it would cut the timing close of everything, especially the wedding. It was stupid," he rests his forehead to hers, "and I'm sorry." She closes her eyes and places her hands on his waist.

She tips her head back a little to look at him. "I'm sorry I overreacted. You're under more pressure than me with planning our wedding *and* running a company! *I should be fine.*" She holds his cheek. "You definitely can use the 'temporary insanity,' but mine is more like *plain mental.*"

He snorts a laugh. "Nothing like that! You've been through a lot and then getting married in a matter of days from when you accepted my proposal; not to mention packing up and moving to a different country!"

She has a small smile and looks at him adoringly. "Then *we've* been through a lot!" She kisses him tenderly and hugs him close. His arms wrap around her, but when she kisses below his ear, his arms hug her tighter.

He says in a low husky growl, "*Careful...*two can play this game and torture ourselves for the next twenty hours or so..."

He feels her smile against his neck, then she places a kiss there. She moves up and kisses his earlobe. He knows this hallway is rarely used so he quickly turns her, stepping her backwards and against the wall; he pins her there. He runs his hands over the sides of her body. Her hands run up his arms and stop at his upper chest. His hands are at her lower ribs on each side, but he doesn't cross the line of her personal space that he is not allowed in...*yet*. He tangles a hand in her hair, while sliding his other hand down to her bum, kissing her fiercely and passionately, then up her jawline to *her ear*.

He whispers, "*Vixen!*"

She exhales a faint laugh. He feels her hands at his waist as he kisses down her neck, back up her throat, then captures her lips in an incredibly passionate kiss. This is a kiss that sets their lips on fire, causing her to unknowingly grab hold of his belt, by slipping her fingers just inside his waistline. This causes him to grab her wrists and break their kiss, whispering just the 'fff' of a swear word against to her lips. He rests his forehead against hers as he continues to hold her wrists, their arms hanging down.

He faintly whispers as he exhales, "*I want you...*" He sucks in his breath and holds it.

David doesn't move except to rub his thumbs over the soft skin on her hands and wrists; they stand in silence as they both try to regain control; these are some of the most intense feelings he can ever remember having! They both know that if they pushed it a second longer, they might have hit 'a point of no return' of sorts.

"I owe you an apology, David. You've been holding back to keep us waiting until we're married...I'm sorry for pushing it, but thank you..." He lifts his head to look at her but he sees her look at him with teary eyes. She tells him, "Thank you *so much* for keeping our relationship beautifully special."

She kisses him firmly, but lips closed, then she hugs him, tight. He hugs her back and his love grows more for her, because seeing her sincerity helps him push down the rest of his intense feelings for her.

"This isn't all your fault, Love. We *both* got carried away." He looks at her with a loving smile. "Thank *you* for making it worth it!"

"Ha-ha! You don't know yet if it's worth it!" She winks with her adoring smile. "*You* have to be the strongest man with the strongest willpower I've ever known!" She cups the side of his jaw and holds his cheek to hers. "Truly, thank you, My Love!"

"Like I said, you're worth it and I know because of our love and these feelings, it will be worth the wait!" Kissing the inside of her wrist. "Did you think we were lacking in the passion department?"

"Honestly, since the weekend we met, I knew it was there and I just thought you had it locked up tight. I *now know* you've been suppressing a *major* fiery inferno inside you! That kiss had me feeling things I've *never* felt before!" She exhales fanning herself, "Wow!"

He chuckles, *"That's a great way of wording it!"*

"I'll make it up to you tomorrow!" She looks at him with so much love in her eyes, his heart melts once again.

He smiles back. "Just let me have my way with you tomorrow night and we'll call it even!" He says and winks with a playful smile.

"*Ooo*! Can't wait!" She grins.

He kisses her with a little more than a tap, then says, "I don't mean to be rude, but I do need to check my watch because we have to sign paperwork at 3:00." She nods. He looks down and sees it's, "2:53." He takes her hand and laces their fingers, lifting her chin with his other hand to ask her, "I need to know straight up if you're okay signing—."

She holds her hand over his mouth. "I'm fine signing a prenup and whatever goes with it, David. I see this as something I have to do in order to marry The Heir to Newhaven," she sweetly smiles, "because I want to marry *you*, *Mister* Worthington."

"Not a 'pro' or a 'con' on your list." He says.

"*Precisely*!" She teases with his accent. He softly laughs. "David, it is what it is." She shrugs a little.

"Thank you." He smiles appreciatively at her.

"For what?" She smirks. "For helping you see how lucky you are to marry this, what was it you call me...a 'feisty firecracker,' is it?"

He cups her cheek, "For making me the luckiest man on earth to *marry* this 'feisty firecracker!'" He sees her smile. They walk quickly to his father's study.

Everyone is waiting when they walk in. There are knowing smiles when Maggie and Carlotta see Bri's hair is still a little messed up. Carlotta walks over and she runs her hands through Bri's hair to fix it. She pats Bri's arm and Bri gives her a small smile, before Carlotta walks back over to stand next to Maggie again.

As Peter welcomes everyone, Henry steps over and quietly whispers to David, "*Didn't go too far?*"

"*No, Sir.*" David whispers back.

"*More difficult?*" Henry asks.

David takes a deep breath. "*Yes, Sir.*"

Henry quietly comments, "Good thing the wedding's tomorrow?"

David raises his eyebrows and replies, "Or we'd elope tonight!"

Henry quietly laughs. "Probably best you won't see her after the party tonight *and* she walks down the aisle."

"Good point!" David is *slightly* relieved at that truth!

Peter handed the attention over to someone who speaks to everyone present: Peter, Carlotta, Henry, Maggie, James, Joe, Sam, Mitch, and of course Jack, Bri, and David with two attorneys, also called barristers or solicitors. The Bishop from Bri's church is also there, he is officiating the ceremony tomorrow, and there is another person, someone from Parliament, but Bri only caught, *Sir* someone?

This is the gentleman explaining, "Lord Jackson Carlisle is be listed officially as 'The Noble Consort,' with approval of all parties and it will become an additional binding agreement and vow upon the marriage of David Worthington, The Marquee of Newhaven, The Heir to The Duchy of Newhaven,' to his betrothed, BriaLynn Harris, a Direct Bloodline. The ancestral lineage of The Direct Bloodline is certified with His Majesty King Lawrence's seal and signature; and is registered with The Royal Records." He happened to look at Bri and thought she may not understand all that, so he kindly says to her, "Basically, it reads you will be in a bond of marriage with Lord Carlisle at the time you are married to Lord Newhaven, and your Direct Bloodline Lineage has been certified." Bri nods in understanding. The gentleman continues, "Is there anyone who needs clarification, or objects, to anything?" Everyone shakes their heads and says 'no.' "Good. Now, Ms. Harris, there is also the prenuptial agreement that I'll let Mr. Lewis explain."

"Right." Mr. Lewis steps forward. "This is a prenuptial agreement between you, Ms. Harris, and Lord Newhaven, but also with The Duke and Duchess of Newhaven—."

"Wait, wait, wait." Bri says. Jack and David smile as does everyone else who personally knows her. The attorneys, or barristers, and the gentleman from Parliament, on the other hand, freeze. "I'll sign it, but we don't need to discuss what basically comes down to, should David and I—." She surprises herself when a lump in her throat blocks her words. She swallows hard and takes a deep breath, rewording what she couldn't say. "Basically, if we were no longer married, I have no rights to the title, or anything associated with the title." They nod. "That's *exactly* as it should be."

The attorneys and the gentleman from Parliament look at each other, then look at her with pleasantly surprised smiles. "Alright." Mr. Lewis says. "But I do have to tell you that while it's binding on this day," he points to the paper, "you have thirty days to have your own solicitor look this all over and we can make any changes, upon the agreement of all parties."

"I understand, but it won't be necessary." She knows Henry will look it all over, if he hasn't already.

"I'd like to advise you to reconsider." He urges her. Everyone else smiles knowing what's coming next.

"Mr. Lewis, I appreciate the gesture, but if you look around at those in this room, they all probably have a knowing looks on their faces. That's because they know how I feel about all this. I love David, I'm marrying *David*! I also recognize that there are things that come with marrying him that would make a lot of ladies jump for joy, like a title; not me. *However*, because I love David and he's an heir, I'll do my best in the titled role this will place me in. If we should get div..." her jaw shakes as she fights back the tears. Bri is standing between David and Peter; David squeezes her hand as Peter fatherly hugs her shoulders.

Mr. Lewis clears his throat. "I see this is hard for you and it's hard to imagine the worst-case scenario."

"*Second* worst-case scenario." She politely corrects him, to which he thinks for a moment and realizes she is referring to David's death. He politely nods in agreement.

"If I may, let me just ask those witnessing," he looks at everyone, "do you witness her agreement in understanding that her title and future title won't leave the family under any circumstances?" Everyone present nods. "Now, I need signatures from the parties," he says as Bri, David, and Jack, are all handed a pen to sign with. "Jack and David, we'll have you both sign them first, because you'll sign roughly the same way every time, a little less confusing. Ms. Harris, you'll sign a couple different ways in preparation for tomorrow and your future role. Don't worry, we'll walk you through your signatures when these gentlemen are done. After you three have signed, Their Graces will sign."

She nods. "Thank you."

While she waits, Peter whispers, *"Thank you for loving our sons. Just so you know, you are well provided for in the prenuptial agreement because we know you're marrying our sons for love."*

Bri pulls back shaking her head. "No, no, no. It should say everything goes back to the way it was, and if there are children, coparenting."

Mr. Lewis overhears that last part. "If you want to change something before the wedd—."

"No! *Absolutely not!*" David stops signing and stands up to face her. "Bri, I love you! We all do! This *is* the prenuptial agreement, and I *won't* change a thing! I know you won't insist on more money; children are accounted for, as are your needs are *more than* adequately met. I won't sign anything less, nor will you insist on more money," she shakes her head, "this would put us forever at a full-stop!" He pulls her to him. "Forget the prenup and just stay focused on what's really here." Giving her a determined look, her eyes locked with David's. "We have all kinds of support around us that will help us if we lose our way, even if it's to kidnap us and take us to counseling!" He looks at The Bishop who softly laughs with the others, then looks back at Bri. "Just sign these documents, then forget about them; marry me and Jack tomorrow, and I promise *everything* we've talked about *will* fall into place and all this will remain a formality forever!"

She smirks and David's eyebrow raises, bracing for her cheekiness. She tells him, "I plan on all this paperwork being null-and-void anyways."

Mr. Lewis goes to object, but Jack smiles and holds up his hand, whispering, "*Wait for it...*"

Bri grins and looks from David to Mr. Lewis. "It becomes null-and-void when we *never* divorce, right?" Everyone bursts out laughing.

David holds the back of her jaw and kisses her fiercely. "I love you!"

"I know! And my prize is you! Then there's Jack..." she looks around David at Jack, "he's the bonus prize!" She smiles at Jack and he winks back.

She looks back at David and he says, "Say it! Say you'll sign now and marry us tomorrow!" She has a twinkle in her eye and a sly grin on her face, holding his stare. He pleas, "*Briiii*...we've tortured ourselves enough for today, don't you think?" He lifts an eyebrow to her. "Take pity, Love!"

She giggles. "*Alright*, I'll sign and marry you, *and Jack*, tomorrow, if you meet me at the specified location in the gardens and time!" David hugs her.

Jack hugs her next and whispers, "*I'm not perfect but I will learn to love you perfectly*—."

"*Jack, no one is perfect*! Let's look at this as we're...imperfectly perfect *together*!" She adoringly smiles at him.

"I love that!" Maggie smiles wide and Bri winks at her.

"I love you, Jack! And there's a whole lot of love in my heart for you both!" They both hug her in a group hug, then they get back to signing paperwork.

Once everyone has signed, Bri makes her rounds hugging Peter and Carlotta, then Henry, Maggie, and the others. She shakes the hands of the barristers, and the gentleman from Parliament who she had caught the name of a little earlier, Sir Williams. She hugs The Bishop before they all start to leave. Bri asks Henry, Maggie, Peter, Carlotta, Jack, and David to hang back. The others walk the guests out.

"Jack, I know you'll see this as the wedding anniversary for David and I." She says to Jack and he agrees. "So, before you and I go on our honeymoon, I want you and I to do something special to mark *our* day."

"*That's a wonderful idea*!" Peter happily approves.

David smiles. "I think that's a great idea!"

They all discuss some ideas, but Bri isn't set on any of them. "Nothing fancy or big; it can be something just between Jack and me, as long as it's special for us." She cups his cheek.

Carlotta starts moving everyone to the door saying, "I think we should give Jack and Bri a moment." They file out of the room, with David being the last to leave, he playfully smiles and makes a point to lock the door behind before he shuts it.

Bri smiles, shaking her head. *"That best friend of yours!"*

Jack chuckles. "That *fiancé* of yours!" He looks at her with so much love that her heart squeezes.

She looks into his eyes. "I don't *ever* want you to feel less—."

He gives her a soft kiss. "Being with you is *never* 'less' of anything, Bri!" He runs the back of his fingers up her cheek. "Your face is so soft..." He runs his fingers across her collarbone, "and across here..." then runs them down her arms, causing a trail of goosebumps. He leans into her neck and inhales the scent of her perfume. "I'll mark *our day* any way you like, but as I've said, I'll let you know if I need anything, or *lack* something," he grins, "just as David will; but *you* have to do the same and let us know if something isn't working, or bothering you, or whatever!"

"Like wanting to mark our day with something special?" She grins.

He chuckles. *"Precisely!"* He kisses her hand. "I love you, Bri, and I want to say that to you every single day for the rest of our lives, even if it's in a text!" He wraps his arms around her. *"Aaand* of course, I want to explore every inch of your body." She feels his arms tighten around her.

"The feeling is definitely mutual!" Bri kisses him, her arms slide up his back, taking in his toned back muscles.

He deepens their kiss and she moans into it. He kisses back to her ear, *"Brrriii..."* he moans as he nuzzles her cheek.

She pulls back and looks at him with desire and compassion. "This is close to the line David and I were *dangerously* on the verge of crossing earlier, so we need to tread carefully."

Jack looks at her, "Focus on you and David, enjoy tonight, tomorrow, *and* the next two weeks. *I promise you*, I'm happy for my best friend marrying the woman of his dreams, just like he's happy I'm marrying mine! You'll be glowing in happiness and love, *making your gorgeousness that much more exquisite!*"

She feels so much love for him. "This is an important day for David and me, but also for you and me as well! I promise to be *mostly* in the moment with David, *if* I can be in the moment with you every now and then."

"*Deal.*" He kisses her one last time. "We need to get going so we can get ready for the party!" He walks her to where they part ways, going in opposite directions of the hallway. They look back and wave to each other before Jack turns a corner.

CHAPTER 31

Imperfectly Perfect Engagement Party

Bri is almost to the door of her quarters with David, when a familiar woman appears before her. Bri stops in her tracks.

"Jessica? What are you doing here?"

"Hello, BriaLynn." Jessica smiles kindly.

Bri nervously smiles back. "Is everything alright?"

Jessica gives a kind smile. "It's nothing like that. I know you're focused on David and Jack tomorrow, and you're trying so hard not to think about being 'The Royal Consort.'" Bri nods. Jessica explains, "I just need you to keep an open mind when David introduces you to *Herst* tomorrow, *after* the ceremony, rather than seeing only 'The King.'"

"Keep an open mind about the 'Third Musketeer' will make us 'The Four Musketeers?" Bri asks and adds a sarcastic, "*No pressure.* Why wouldn't tomorrow need more pressure?"

Jessica gives her a compassionate smile but keeps their conversation moving forward. "Do you remember what we discussed when you were with Henry in his study?"

"I do." Bri replies. David thinks he hears her in the hall. He walks to the door of their quarters and listens for a moment...He hears her say, "That I've been 'touched by death.'" His mouth drops open.

"And you *chose* to come back to your mortal life." Jessica tells her.

"I also remember with that choice comes a great price." Bri replies.

David doesn't feel right listening anymore and steps away from the door. He walks back to their bedroom thinking about the 'touched by death' he heard and what that could've meant? He asks himself, *Who was she talking to?*

Jessica sees Bri's worried face and steps closer to her. "I know you're nervous, perhaps scared, because you're in 'uncharted waters.' While you rightfully believe 'everything happens for a reason,' also keep in mind you wouldn't be asked to do these things if you couldn't handle it! This includes loving David and Jack, and eventually Herst." She takes Bri's hands and tells her, "Love magnifies others, but it also magnifies itself within each person. You know this because you feel your love magnifying with Jack's and David's love for you!" Bri nods. "Their love causes your love to grow exponentially and you'll *easily* be able to love Herst."

Bri quietly remembers, "'Instantaneous' was used regarding falling in-love with Jack...*and it was*! Now I'm remembering *'three...to be complete?*'" Her eyebrows are scrunched together as she looks at Jessica. "Is that right?"

"You'll *always* have your freedom to choose, Bri." Jessica states. "Just as every other person does."

"Meaning I could choose not get involved with Herst and I won't be penalized for it?" She asks.

"You won't be punished, if that's what you mean." Jessica replies. "But you're perfectly aware that all choices, good or bad, also have consequences, good or bad."

Bri agrees with that. "True. And we can't choose the consequences of those choices either...like not choosing Herst and the possibility of feeling like I do now, that something is missing."

Jessica softly smiles but doesn't say much about that; the real significance of her choice will come to her. "Trust in your connection with the Spirit to guide you, Bri." She reminds her, "Have faith and trust, all is as it should be..." Jessica waves as she fades away.

Alone in the hallway, Bri stands still for a moment to collect her thoughts before going to get ready for the party. She walks into her quarters and into the bedroom. She freezes when she sees David...her eyes travel down his bare chest and sees his lower half wrapped in a towel. For the first time she sees exactly how toned this man is. *Daaamn*! She thinks to herself and starts to feel *very* inadequate at that moment.

"I thought we could get ready together for tonight." He smiles handsomely watching her stare as she bites her lower lip. "*Bri?*"

"What? *OH!*" Bri shakes her head and clears her throat. "Yeah, that's fine." Now making a point to avoid looking at him at all.

He chuckles. "Something you like?"

"*Ooo yeah!* But now who's the vixen, *er,* whatever the male version would be?" She asks.

"Sounds like you want me *almost* as much as I want you!" He chuckles.

"Right now, with you only in a towel, I'd say you've tipped the scales in *my desire for you!*" She asserts. "Or have you forgotten the hallway incident a little while ago?"

"*No way!*" He pulls her to him. "How could I?!" He runs a hand down to her bum. "That was flaming hot!"

"I'm about ten seconds away from dropping your towel, so I need to go jump into an ice-cold shower and try to get ready in a short period of time." She taps a kiss to his lips before she goes into the bathroom. He chuckles as he watches her.

When she comes out, she puts on his super soft robe. Then she dries her hair and puts curlers in before putting her makeup on. She looks over as she finishes her makeup and winks at David; he is buttoning the last two bottom buttons on the white dress shirt for his tuxedo. He already has his dress pants on and his black-tie lays around his neck.

"Only you can make this robe look incredibly sexy!" David says as he smiles and wraps his arms around her.

"Careful, there may be no stopping if we start again." She quickly hugs him before she slips into the closet to get dressed. She comes out and she sees he is smiling, biting his lower lip. She says with surprise, "*You peaked?!*"

"I couldn't help myself!" He grins.

"I would've hoped you could, because after seeing all that," she gestures his whole body with her finger as she draws an oval shape in the air, "I can't even *begin* to compete!"

"*Are you serious*?! From what I just saw, you're sexy as hell! AND your body is so incredible—.""

She puts her hand over his mouth, "*Stop right there*! First of all, if you're about to say because I gave birth—." He moves her hand and kisses her deeply.

"Love, a woman's body *is* incredible! And yes, one of those reasons is because those bodies can make a baby, *another life*! It's no surprise that yours was overachieving making two *at the same time*!" She can't help but snort a little laugh at that. "*I can't wait* to have a baby with you! *I can't wait* for you and Jack to have one! And from what I did catch a glimpse of, *I can't wait for tomorrow afternoon*!""

"Afternoon?" She laughs.

"I'm thinking we're both going to have a more difficult time after the ceremony." He has a sexy grin spreading across his face. She lightly laughs and nods in agreement. He cups the back of neck, then kisses her but keeps it short to be able to stop. When he pulls back, he sees her face and he wonders if he can bring up what he overheard. "Can I ask you something?"

"I don't know...I mean," she playfully grins, "it's not like we've seen each other naked!" She winks and he chuckles. "Seriously, My Love, you can ask me anything." She says as she continues to get ready.

"I heard what I thought were voices in the hallway a little bit ago and when I went to check it out, I could only hear your voice?" He watches her stop what she is doing as she considers what he is saying.

She quietly replies, "I'm not sure if you'd believe me...you may think I'm really crazy and decide not to marry me tomorrow."

At first, he thinks she's joking, and chuckles a little, until he looks at her again. David takes her hand and has her sit on the bed. He goes to sit on the bed next to her, but instead he decides to kneel in front of her.

He takes her other hand to hold both of them. "I *swear* to you, I'll *never* think you're mental and I *will* marry you tomorrow, *if* you meet me at our agreed time and place." He winks as he brings her hand up and kisses her ring; she softly giggles.

"Alright...I was talking to a spirit." She says it fast and holds her breath.

"I'm going to need a wee bit more than that, Love, because as old as this house is, I'm sure there are *loads* of them!" He says so matter-of-factly it catches Bri off guard. She hugs him tight. "Whoa, I'm all for this, but I'd *really* like to hear more." They hear Jack chuckling as he comes and sits next to her on the bed. David cups Bri cheek, "I *need* to know what 'touched by death' means? I'm trying *really* hard not to panic."

"*Clearly,* I was missing an interesting conversation! Catch me up..." Jack says with concern.

"We don't have a lot of time for this since we have a party to go to." Bri starts to say.

"Then talk fast!" Jack replies.

"Jack, David overheard me talking in the hallway a little bit ago to Jessica, a spirit messenger." She watches Jack's face and when he isn't freaked out either, she continues. "When I was in a coma, I was with Jessica during those three days where she explained to me that I had been 'touched by death' and that I had a choice: I could stay and become a messenger like her—."

"*Die?!*" David is alarmed by that thought he was even closer to losing her than he thought.

"Yes, Love." She touches his face. "*Obviously,* I didn't pick that choice." She winks, getting a small smile from him. He stands up and pulls the armchair over in front of her as she goes on, "My other choice, *and clearly the one I chose,* was to come back to mortality. Now, that may sound easy and simple, but *nooot* exactly. Don't get me wrong, coming back to you was a 'no brainer' *at any cost*." She says.

"'*Any* cost?'" Jack asks. "What cost?"

"I was told choosing to come back would come with a gift of being able to see spirits, along with having powers and abilities, of sorts." She tells them. "But there is a cost, or a price. I don't know what that would be yet..."

"Powers? Like magic?" Jack asks.

She shrugs a little, "The extent of these things will manifest itself over time. I was also told there was a great responsibility that's attached, because not many people can do whatever this is ends up being and they haven't understood there is a very real power in *pure* love."

"A bit cryptic, don't you think?" Jack asks.

Bri giggles. "She didn't want to overwhelm me."

David asks, "Do you see many ghosts?"

"I haven't, at least not knowingly. She's been the first, *that I know of*, since I woke up from the coma." Bri answers.

There is a knock on the main door to their quarters. Jack checks his watch, then says, "I hate to break this up, but we have a party to go to!"

David clears his throat. "Love, you don't have to choose me all the time, or feel bad for spending time with Jack tonight. This is time for all of us to have fun and celebrate!"

Bri's eyes fill with tears. "I'm still flabbergasted at your amazingness!"

He hugs her and whispers, "*You really don't see it, do you?*"

"See what?" She gives him a confused look.

"How amazingly fantastic and incredible *you are*, not to mention gorgeous and sexy!" He kisses her with so much love and passion her legs physically get weak and he helps hold her up.

"David," she says breathless, "kiss me like that again tomorrow night, or any day after that when you want a sure way to get me naked. Until then..." She fans herself and exhales out loud.

He slowly releases her so she can regain her footing. "I'm torturing both of us, Love. My apologies."

"*Never* apologize for showing me you want me! Just as I imagine the same goes for you?" She grins.

"*Oh, it does!*" He smiles wide.

"Let me finish up; give me three minutes." She says as they hear Jack welcome Amy, James, and Katie out in the living room.

Bri rushes to take the curlers out of her hair and styles it. She puts her shoes on, then grabs her purse and phone. Out in the living room, Bri can sense the tension between Jack and Katie, and now Katie's tension is also directed towards Bri. In Katie's mind, Bri can't have Jack and Katie *will* win him back!

Bri knows jealousy and envy are used interchangeably, but they're actually inter*linked*. They both compare their lives and focus on what is lacking in them; both are based on low self-esteem; and their pride gets in the way of rational thinking. Eventually, they cause that person to push everyone away because they express these feelings through the 'ugly green monster.' Their insecurity and lack of self-esteem isn't always about looks, but it could be a specific person, lifestyle, career, friends, and so on. As for Katie, her jealousy and envy, on top of their already strained relationship, has Bri starting to wish Katie wasn't there at all.

David turns to Bri and says, "You're stunning as always, Love." Jack agrees and kisses her cheek. Katie doesn't realize her scoff wasn't that quiet.

"Thanks! You both are incredibly handsome!" She smiles wide and looks at the others. "You all look wonderful!" She hugs James and Amy, but when she hugs Katie there is a coldness between them.

David holds his arm out for Bri to take and she loops hers in his. Katie thinks Jack will pair off with her, but he purposely takes Bri's other hand walking down the hallway. Katie stays close, just in case he changes his mind.

Everyone is in the cars and on their way to the party the executives at The Worthington Corporation wanted to throw for them this evening. David said it wasn't a Bachelor or Bachelorette party, but he didn't think Bri would mind, which she didn't mind at all. Before heading inside the venue, David lets everyone go inside without them. David reaches into his pocket and pulls out a small velvet box that's flatter than a ring box.

He hands the box to her with a smile. "Open it." She smiles with a questioning look as she opens it.

 Inside she sees a gold brooch with a smaller heart sitting nestled inside a larger heart, the hearts intertwined at the top. The bigger heart having a crown on top of it; the base of the crown lined with tiny rubies, emeralds, and sapphires with a little larger square diamond in the center, turned for a diamond-shape-look.

"David, it's beautiful!" She looks even closer and sees the same stretched out Triquetra design etched into the smaller heart as she asks, "What's this for?"

"I'm hoping you'll indulge me on some Scottish traditions."

"I will, as long as you tell me about them." She smiles adoringly at him.

He smiles and holds out his hand for the box. "May I?"

"Please!" She hands the open box to him.

He takes it out of the box and explains, "This is a 'Luckenbooth brooch.'"

"Mmm, I love that word in your accent." She grins.

He chuckles. "I had your *Luckenbooth* brooch made in yellow gold because of the family tartan colors." He lovingly looks into her eyes. "This brooch is typically given by the groom to his bride-to-be before the wedding, as a symbol of his love and commitment to her. It's later pinned to the baby blanket of the couple's first born for good luck. In our case, good luck to the addition to our family." He turns the pin over to show her the engraving on the edge of the larger heart: *Tá mo chroí agat!* And its meaning on the other edge: *You have my heart!*

Her breath catches and a hand goes over her heart as her eyes fill up with tears, "David, I..." She shakes her head, too choked up for words. She looks at her engagement ring and remembers it has the same inscription inside it.

He sweetly smiles at her. "I'm happy you made the connection with your engagement ring." When he's done pinning it on her, he lifts her chin. "I don't want you to ever forget." She shakes her head. He cups her face looking into her eyes, she wraps her arms around his waist and kisses him. He deepens the kiss as he wraps his arms firmly around her. When they step back a half step he explains, "Not to ruin the moment, but full disclosure: I did do this once before but looking back, I just went through the motions. In fact, she hinted on liking two hearts side-by-side overlapping with a crown essentially over both hearts. I did as she asked and figured they were all silver, so that's what I did for her ring. She never complained about the silver; however, she said she hoped there would've been a diamond sitting where the hearts overlapped. Anyway, I doubt anything would ever be said but if it was, I didn't want you to be surprised."

"Thank you for telling me." She has a small smile. "David, for the record, I love this! I look at the smaller heart and since I gave you my heart, it looks like your protecting it. My heart is in good hands."

"Always, Love!" He kisses her. When she tightens her hug around his waist, he deepens the kiss a bit. "We should probably go inside."

"Considering we're the guests of honor?" She giggles lightly. He puts his hand on the small of her back as they walk into the building.

Everyone seems nice and genuinely happy to meet her. There is lots of toasting and they have sparkling nonalcoholic champagne there for her that tastes fantastic. David did his homework and found terrific tasting champagne and wine that wasn't alcoholic but wasn't juice either. *Who knew there was such a thing?!* She thought to herself, taking a drink.

The employees toasted their boss and "The Happy Couple!"

Peter steps up to a microphone to make an official toast. "I'd like to propose a toast. Bri, you have been such a light of love to our family. We've enjoyed seeing David love you and you reciprocating that love..." His eyes are teary. "Loving you has been *so* good for him (*'and the company,'* someone yells), that too," he chuckles and lifts his glass in that person's direction. "David, your greatest accomplishment won't be this company, although I'm so enormously proud of you as the CEO! No, your greatest accomplishment will be to love Bri and *continue to earn* her love in return!" He looks to Jack who nods knowing that means him, too; Peter raises his glass to him. He turns to Carlotta. "I'm blessed everyday this beautiful woman still continues to love me." He swallows hard pushing the lump down, "Love is everything!" Peter kisses Carlotta's cheek. "And David, your mother and I have been so happy seeing Bri become *your* everything! And Jack, we're so proud of the incredible man you are and your decision to settle down as The Noble Consort! We know you and David are in the best hands," he looks at her, "Bri's heart!" He looks at Jack again, "Thank you for going on this journey with them and with us! We love you, Son!" He raises his glass, smiling through his tears, "May you three be blessed with many happy years together!"

"Here, here!" The crowd says together.

David and Bri take a sip from their flutes. Then, being careful not to spill from their glasses, David wraps his arm around Bri's waist as she wraps her free hand around his back of head and he kisses her firmly. Cheers and whistles come from around them. Then they both raise their glasses to Jack and wave for him to join them, which he gladly does!

Bri says, "To the amazing and handsome Jack, for jumping into this with us..." she puts a hand to his cheek, "with me!" He gives her a little more than a tap of a kiss.

"To Jack!" Everyone cheers taking a drink. Everyone, that is, except Katie...

Others go up to give various toasts. When it seems as if everyone has taken their turn that wants to, David takes Bri's hand and leads her onto the stage and up to the microphone. He wants to make the last toast of the evening.

"I'd like to thank all of you for not only coming tonight, but for being the best work family I could ever hope for! Your support as my father retired has meant a lot to me and still does! There are a lot of things Bri has said since we met that has had me thinking," he looks at her, "*and learning,*" he winks at her and she knowingly smiles; there is some chuckling as he looks out at everyone again, "but one thing I'll share with you now is she believes if employees know how much they're appreciated, the more successful a business is. I hope to do a better job of showing my appreciation for all of you, because I do!" The employees clap and cheer. "To my parents, whose love and support has been a strength in my life, something your sons, and now daughter, can count on...much like devising a plan before the woman of my dreams slipped through my fingers." He looks at his mom, "I love you, Mother!" There's laughter from the crowd.

"We love you, too, Sweetie!" She tells him.

David looks at Bri. "To my bride and very soon-to-be Mrs. Worthington... *Thank you* for snapping me back into reality! By holding up a mirror to my face, you inspired me to be the man I should've been, the man *I want* to be," he hugs her with his arm around her waist, "a man who loves you with all his heart!" 'Aws' from the crowd. He kisses her with a little more than a peck, then lifts his glass, "*Tá mo chroí agat*! And you will *always* have my heart, Love!" Bri pulls his jaw in for a sweet kiss.

"Cheers" and "here, here!" Come from the guests.

Later that night, Bri is nestled in the back seat tucked under David's arm, holding Jack's hand. David wants to snuggle with her all night, but he wants to honor the tradition of not seeing the bride before the wedding on their wedding day...*although this time of night may rival that a little*. They pull up to the main door of The Manor and he helps her out of the car, then hugs her goodnight. Carlotta, Maggie, and Katie are waiting for Bri on the stairs because for this night only, David is going to The Inn with James, Amy, and Jack. Some guests have already arrived and the others will arrive tomorrow throughout the morning and early afternoon. The four of them will be in James' quarters, and as soon as he is ready for bed, David is all but passed out on a couch when his head hits the pillow. All his wedding planning is complete, and he had handed the reigns over to his mother and a wedding planner so he could focus on Bri and enjoy their wedding day tomorrow.

Inside The Manor, Katie asks Maggie, Bri, and Carlotta more about Jack. Maggie tells her he has agreed to become Bri's 'Noble Consort.'

"What does that *mean* exactly?" Katie asks.

Carlotta explains, "It's a seven-hundred-year tradition in which Bri will be the third Duchess in that time to be married to 'The Duke of Newhaven,' and simultaneously married to 'The Noble Consort.'"

Katie's nose turns up. "And you agreed to this? *With Jack*? David's best friend?" Bri nods and braces herself for, "*Are you crazy*?! Aren't you worried about male competition, to say the least?!"

"Katie," Bri tries to help her understand, "there are things that come with marrying David and having Jack as 'The Noble Consort' is one of them. I'm starting to realize the relationship these two have are as close as two brothers *and* best friends can be. The love and support they give each other is inspiring and I only hope that *I* can measure up to them!"

Katie scoffs. "You won't! *You can't*! You're not experienced enough for David, let alone both!"

"Well, thank you for your support." Bri says with tired sarcasm. "I'm headed to bed." She hugs Maggie and Carlotta goodnight. She starts to climb the

353

stairs, then stops and turns to Katie. "You know, Katie, you really have no place to talk considering *our past!*" Carlotta looks to Maggie, who holds her finger up for just a minute while they listen; she'll tell Carlotta later what she knows. Bri adds, "No one, *especially Jack or David*, could *ever* top that!" Bri reads her face. "No, I didn't tell them, but I won't lie if they ever ask me about it either, but it's only a matter of time." She starts back up the stairs and adds as she walks, "The wedding *can go on* with or without you there..."

Unfortunately, this will eat away at Katie for some time to come. She had been dreaming of marrying Jack so she could stay in Bri's life like she desperately wanted to be. The four of them closer than ever, mending the break in her friendship with Bri; only now it looks as if Bri will never forgive her. For Katie, she is thinking she is on her way out...unfortunately, she can't see *she already* is *out*; she has been since that night Bri refers to as 'once upon a nightmare.' Only neither of them wanted to see it.

After getting ready for bed, Bri falls asleep quickly and in rare form, she is actually grateful morning comes just as fast.

Maggie and Carlotta are in Carlotta and Peter's quarters with Peter and Henry. Both Peter and Carlotta are wondering what happened between Katie and Bri.

"If we tell you what we know, it may make having Katie here for a few days after the wedding much more difficult." Henry warns.

"We've had years of practice to put aside the horrible things we hear." Carlotta says.

"If I can make it through various socials without sloshing Reginald Carlisle, especially when Jack was in and out of hospitals, I'd think I can survive making nice with Katie for a few days!" Peter tells them.

Maggie gives him a reluctant look. "Don't be so sure..."

Peter looks confused. "How bad was it?"

Henry says, "Bad is tame and horriffic isn't even close."

He looks at Maggie and then at Peter and Carlotta. They explain the events as they know them and say they are letting Bri tell David and Jack when she is ready. They don't think she has yet, or Katie probably wouldn't be here at all...at least not staying in The Manor.

"Had we known, she wouldn't be on the island at all!" Peter replies with anger for Bri.

Carlotta puts her hand on his arm. "It's Bri decision whether to remain friends with this woman. If she decides to cut all ties with her, *then* you can ban Katie from the island." He knows she is right and nods. "For now, we all have to push aside what we know and make tomorrow the happiest day it is meant to be for our sons, our new daughter, and all our family and friends!"

CHAPTER 32

Imperfectly Perfect Wedding Day

The day of the wedding couldn't have better weather! The sun is shining bright with scattered clouds here and there; there is a nice breeze blowing, but not with any force to be a nuisance. The Manor is a buzz of clinking glass and metal, along with other bustling noises of the staff, and the additional hired staff, making wedding day preparations.

The exuberant designer, Julian, is waiting in the dressing room when Bri walks in. "Oh *good!* You're *finally* here!" He claps his hands together and holds them there! "I'm *SO* excited to dress you up like a *real-life* doll in my very best *EVER* creation!"

"*Oh my gosh, he's* SO *fun!*" Amy says, enjoying Julian's flamboyant personality and excitement.

Antionette and Nicole do her hair and makeup first, while Julian keeps them all laughing. He still has them cracking up and Antionette is trying to say, "You'd better stop or we'll 'ave to do zee hair and makeup all *over* a-gain!" But they still manage to do a fantastic job.

Carlotta comes back after tending to a few things. They have just finished putting Bri's dress on and Carlotta smiles at her. "You look stunning, Bri!" She steps back and takes in the dress now that it's on Bri and says, "Julian, I think we picked the right jewelry to make this dress perfect!"

She goes to the safe and pulls out a simple chipped diamond tiara, an heirloom for Bri to wear with her veil. "Since you're marrying 'The Heir of The Duchy of Newhaven,' we need to add this." She hands it to Julian, who adds it to her veil.

Bri smiles sweetly. "Carlotta, I'm marrying David, your son. He being 'heir' is, well, like a side note, really. And then there's Jack! Trust me," she lightly giggles, "*I'm the one coming out* way *ahead here!*"

"That's why Peter and I adore you!" She says with a trace of tears of love in her eyes. "It does a mother's heart good to hear you say that! Knowing you *genuinely* love my sons."

She is holding Bri's hands as Julian finishes with the tiara and veil. Then Carlotta steps back and her hands clasp together near her mouth. "Bri, you're going to take both of their breaths away!" They all agree!

Julian adds, "You really are A *vision!*"

"At the risk of sounding similar to a movie line," Bri says looking in the mirror, "I do feel pretty." They all snicker at the movie reference.

Bri's wedding dress has simplicity to it and yet has intricate details the closer she looks at it. It was a full-length light ivory satin gown with short-sleeves and a unique V-neck. From her chest to her hips, it's not tight, but fitted, then the satin fabric flows the rest of the way to the floor. The skirt is 'open' starting on the left side, showing the family tartan colors; like an 'exposed layer.' The edge of the dress, along with the edge of her veil, has the matching stretched Triquetra symbol to her engagement ring.

"I know The Worthington's have a family tartan," she gestures her dress, "but I was thinking it was different than this one?" Bri asks. The Worthington's tartan color has a navy-blue base color with stripes of thicker burgundy red, thinner stripes of golden yellow, and pin strips of white and black.

"We combined yours and ours to make our *new* family tartan!" Carlotta says.

"*Really*?! How did you find mine?" Bri is very curious as she looks over the colors closely and sees there are quite a few colors.

This tartan also has a base color of navy-blue; along with crisscrossing thick stripes of burgundy-red, royal-blue, emerald-green; thinner stripes of golden yellow, black, and red; and a thicker pinstripe of white. Where these colors intersected in various places with each other, she could see purple, sky-blue, green, pink, and gray...there may be other colors.

Carlotta explains, "It took some research, but we tracked *them* down. You have connections to a few tartans. Peter and I decided to combine them, getting a mixture of all the colors used in most, if not all, the tartans of Scotland. Considering not all of our people here in Newhaven were actually born here, we thought this would be a clever way to include *everyone's* ancestry in Newhaven and Scotland!"

"*This is amazing!*" Bri says in a loud whisper looking down at the tartan piece to her dress.

"Time for something old, something new, something borrowed and something blue!" Katie purposely interrupts. "Something old," she points to Bri's head, "but you don't keep that, so it goes under 'something borrowed.' However, Carlotta does have the something old for you, too."

 Carlotta takes the velvet box she took out with the tiara and shows Bri the diamond necklace set. "This was something I wore when I married Peter. I always hoped to have a daughter to pass this down to, but it just wasn't in the cards...*until now*." Tears fill her eyes, and now Bri's eyes get teary, too. "I've seen you stand up to David when he needed it the most, seen your relationship blossom into something so special and beautiful. *And* to have so much love in abundance that you can fall in-love with Jack and love him so much, all three of you shine! It really does this mother's heart good knowing both Jack and David will be loved as they should be." Carlotta carefully touches the bottom of Bri's jaw with her fingertips. "Now, we're blessed with an instant daughter *and two granddaughters!*" She smiles wide. "I'd say not having a daughter to raise has been *more* than made up for in our lives!" She holds out the necklace to Bri. "I'd like to pass this necklace from me to you, my wonderful daughter."

Bri smiles, letting Carlotta put the necklace on as she puts the earrings in. After Carlotta has fastened the necklace, Bri hugs her.

"Carlotta, *I'm the one who's honored*. You've raised three *amazing* men! I'm blessed beyond measure and *so much more than I deserve!*"

"*That's for sure.*" Katie slips in under her breath. Bri pretends she doesn't hear her and Carlotta does the same out of respect for Bri; this is her day.

"Thank you!" Bri says to Carlotta and hugs her. "I'm touched and honored to wear such a beautiful necklace set."

Katie clears her throat. "We all thought it'd be fun for you to have a tartan garter in the new tartan colors!"

Bri takes the garter and looks at it closely. "This is *great* you guys!"

"One for David to give away," Amy hands her a second, "and then one for him to admire later!" Amy gives her a saucy wink and Bri giggles. Katie rolls her eyes; she is also jealous of Amy's growing friendship with Bri.

"Now, we did 'old & new' with the necklace and garter, the tiara is borrowed, and now...blue." Katie gestures to Amy.

Amy opens a shoe box. "I found these in DC, I only wish I had the thought to have a pair made here in Newhaven." She reluctantly says, looking at Julian who shoos her a '*that's okay*' dismissive wave with a big smile.

Bri happily tells her, "Amy these shoes are *fantastic*! And do I dare say, they look comfortable, too?!"

"They are! Put them on!" Amy says excitedly. "Maggie helped me with them!"

Bri notices a coin on the bottom of the shoe, tucked up under the arch of the shoe so it wouldn't bother her when she walks. Maggie sees her looking at it and explains, "It's the old saying you know, but with a Scottish twist: 'Something old, something new, something borrowed, something blue, and a sixpence for my shoe!' The sixpence coin is for good luck!" Maggie giggles.

"That's cute!" Bri says as she puts them on. "I love them!" She hugs Amy and Maggie, thanking them.

There is a knock on the door. Maggie opens it; it's Henry coming to get her and he sees Bri. He comes around and takes Bri in. Everyone steps out, giving Henry, Maggie, and Bri a moment alone.

"Bri! You look absolutely stunning!" Henry's eyes have tears.

Bri says to them, "I want you both to know how much I love you two, how much I love Joe, Sam, and Mitch."

"Shhh. Stop that now, or you'll be a mess before the ceremony even begins. You've *always* been a part of our family and you always will be, Sweetie." Henry smiles. "Saying you're the daughter we've never had isn't something that's just frivolously said; *you* are *our daughter*!" They wipe their tears with a tissue. He takes a deep breath. "As you've already figured, your parents couldn't come on short notice. David wanted me to tell you beforehand, but I said you'd be—."

"Thank goodness!" Bri is relieved. She realizes she cut him off and the three of them softly laugh knowing he knew she would be relieved. "I have all the family I need with the girls, the family who adopted me, the family I'm marrying into, the person officiating, and of course having David and Jack there would be helpful." She grins.

He chuckles. "This *is* a happy day, and we don't need anyone giving off bad feelings!" He says.

"You *may* want to talk to Katie then. She has been upset since finding out I'm essentially marrying Jack, too...well, before that, when she tried getting Jack, and he turned her down each time. Then she finds out about 'The Noble Consort Clause' so-to-speak and, well..."

"I'll have a chat with her." He tells her. "But jealousy runs deep with pride and it gets tricky. I'll see what I can do." He holds her hands, "I know it's been hard for you to accept, but maybe you two aren't going to patch things up. *Maybe* it's time to consider that your life is meant to move forward *without her in it.*"

"*Unfortunately*, I've been thinking along the same lines with her." She smiles genuinely and sweetly. "Thank you." She hugs them before they leave.

Jack had waited out in the hall when he heard Henry and Maggie in the room with her. He overheard talk of Katie, which peaks his interest again, but he'll ask Bri about it some other time with David. Henry and Maggie come out into the hallway.

Maggie hugs and kisses his cheek; Henry shakes Jack's hand, hugging him with the other. Henry tells him, "Be prepared," he smiles as a proud father, "she's absolutely stunning!" Jack happily smiles and pats Henry's shoulder before walking into the room.

He looks at Bri just as she comes completely into view. His breath catches and he pushes it out. "*Bri!*" He has a huge smile and his eyes are teary, too. "There isn't a word that can describe you right now! Breathtaking? Yes! Stunning? Absolutely! Then there's incredible, extraordinary, astonishing, and mesmerizing that describe you as well!" She giggles, warming his heart.

 Jack reaches into his pocket and pulls out a handkerchief that's wrapped around something. As he unwraps it, he says, "I know David gave you one last night, but this was my mother's and I want you to have it. She received it from, Uncle Max, her lover, not too long before she died." He shows her a Luckenbooth, but it's a simple, beautiful, imperfect silver heart, with something written on the front. Jack reads it aloud: "*Of eternal joys, I choose you!*"

"Jack!" She is only able to whisper. "It's——." She 'tsks' in frustration with herself for not having enough control over her emotions to speak a sentence.

Jack lifts her chin and she sees he also has tears in his eyes. "Bri, I wanted you to have this Luckenbooth right now, because you need to know when you're out there today *and every single day*, I *choose* this! I *choose you*! US!" He gestures with his hands saying, "This imperfectly perfect, crazy, untraditional for tradition relationship!"

She grabs a fresh tissue and dabs her eyes saying, "*Jack, I choose you, too!*"

"I know that!" He smiles lovingly. "I wouldn't be here otherwise!" He winks.

"*Touché!*" She giggles. "Thank you, this is beautiful *and perfect*! I know just where to put it!" She hooks it to the tartan part of her dress, next to David's. She then looks up at him, "I love you, Jack!" She holds his cheeks. "I really, *really*, love you!"

He smiles with tears, "I *really* love you, too!" He kisses her cheek. "I'd kiss you proper right now, but——."

Before he can object, she gives him a fierce kiss, full of love for him. "I don't have lipstick on yet." She playfully grins.

"In that case..." he kisses her again.

He rests their foreheads together for a minute before they need to get going. She checks her makeup and adds lipstick. Jack smiles and kisses her cheek before he helps her pull down her veil. He hands her the bouquet of red roses David has in the dressing room for her.

He holds his left arm out to her. "Shall we get us all properly married, Gorgeous?" Jack's signature smile is somehow bigger and brighter.

She takes his arm. "It already feels like it's been too long!" He agrees.

Jack walks with Bri out of The Worthington Manor and into the gardens, over a familiar bridge to some *almost* hidden ruins all covered with ivy. Inside the ruins is an open room where the ceremony will take place. There is an archway set up on a platform, rows of chairs facing it, with an aisle down the middle. David has red roses in arrangements around the room, but he went light on the flowers knowing she likes a simpler, more elegant look. The vines outside have grown inside and up the walls to the edges of what would have been the ceiling. All of this would fit an outside American wedding venue, but it has a Celtic and Gaelic feel that is intimate and very romantic. It's perfectly perfect!

CHAPTER 33

Imperfectly Perfect Wedding Ceremony

David put a note in the wedding program that says Scottish and American weddings traditions will be mixed into the ceremony, along with a couple of their own. The procession is led by David, who wants to look back, but for Bri he'll wait for the moment she wants to first be seen...about to walk down the aisle. David is followed by both of Bri's daughters, as her Maids of Honor; then James as Best Man. Jack, being 'The Noble Consort,' will stand next to James, closest to David, once he has escorted Bri down the aisle.

 When everyone is down front, David stands at the other end of the aisle with a clear view. The guests stand as Jack and Bri step into place at the end of the aisle, David's mouth slightly opens and his hand goes to his heart. Jack squeezes Bri's arm in a little as they begin their walk down the aisle. There are 'aws,' 'wows,' and whispers of 'beautiful,' and so on. When David and Bri make eye contact, tears fill her eyes.

Reaching David, they both are lovingly smiling at each other and Bri sees his eyes are teary, too. David shakes Jack's hand and hugs him. Jack places Bri's hand in David's before going to stand next to James. David helps Bri up onto the platform to stand next to him.

 "Wow, My Love!" Bri grins. "I didn't think you could get any better looking, but here you are!" She smiles wide.

He shakes his head as he holds her arms out to take her all in. "*You're absolutely stunning,* breathtaking, exquisite, perfect, *all these words*, yet none of them by themselves describe you, and all of them put together is only a start." He tenderly kisses the inside of her wrist. Seeing the sweetness, there are more whispers and 'aws' coming from their guests. He smiles when he sees the tiara. "Fitting, since you look like a fairytale princess right now."

She lightly laughs. "Then that makes you 'Prince Charming' right now."

The Bishop begins speaking, first to the guests, "Please be seated." Then to Bri, "*And here we are, Darlin*'..." He winks at her and smiles a happy 'I told you so' smile. She can't help but giggle with her nod. David smiles, but he is a little confused as he looks at them.

Bri explains to David, with everyone listening, "Do you remember that Sunday when you were waiting for me in the church parking lot to take me to Dunfermline for a picnic?"

He smiles. "I'll *always* remember our first date."

"Outside the door of the church, The Bishop saw you waiting for me first and said something like—."

"'I have a feeling we'll be seeing more of you in future.'" The Bishop repeating his own words from that day.

"You were right!" She admits and there are a few guests who softly laugh.

"To be fair," The Bishop says, "you knew it, too, even if you weren't sure how it would come together yet." He looks to David and Jack with smiles. Then he looks out to the guests. "Your Majesties, family and friends, true, adoring love can be instantly felt by the heart, but it can take longer for the mind to get onboard...a lot of those times, it's the people around you who see it first." He gestures to the family who nod, while David and Bri smile at each other. "On behalf of the family, we thank you all for being here to share this *wonderful* moment in their lives. David chose the ceremony to take place in the gardens because it was on the very bridge we all crossed over to get here today, where they *finally* opened their hearts to each other. Although, it wasn't too far from here where their love story dramatically began to unfold when they first *met* in the stables. Now, I've been informed that David's horse, Artemis, thinks he was the first to fall in-love with Bri and it really was 'love at first sight' for him, but may I suggest no one tell Artemis that David has married *his girl*, or there may be some sort of duel at dusk."

"Well, he is a handsome boy!" Bri smirks. Guests are chucking, as are those who remember their little row in the stables quite well.

The Bishop continues, "Weddings are a great time to contemplate on what love is and the love we have in our own marriages and relationships. Remember, just as there are no two people who are *exactly* alike, no two relationships are exactly alike either. *Please* don't ever compare your relationship to someone else's relationship; it's not fair to you or to them. What *is* the same, is that for love to begin, it requires both people to let their guard down and be vulnerable to the other person; not only to let oneself love the other, but to accept *and thrive* in the other person's love *for them*. True, abiding love helps the loved one feel safe to be who they are without fear of judgement or rejection. There's no longer a risk of being vulnerable; they don't ever have to pretend to be someone they're not, nor hide things about themselves. In true, abiding love, each person can be their individual self; being unconditionally loved *and accepted*; flaws and all! That love makes coming together physically for the first time, and every time after that, much more meaningful." The Bishop looks at David and Bri. "Loving someone unconditionally *and being loved unconditionally*, well, *that's* the greatest love there is!" David and Bri smile in agreement.

He says to the guests, "Let's get some business out of the way, so we can move on, shall we? This is where I ask if there is anyone here, who has *just cause* why this couple should not be joined in holy matrimony, let them speak now, or forever hold their peace."

Bri feels a blanket of peace come over her as she hears 'wait' come into her mind, right before she hears Ava and Serene shout, "*We do!*" Katie's ears perk up and she fills with hope that this 'farce' will be called off!

Of course, there are gasps, then disgusted scoffs when The Bishop asks for them to step forward. Bri turns to see the snobby sneers on Ava's and Serene's faces, but she catches Carlotta's wink to David.

David whispers to Bri, "*Don't worry.*"

"I'm not." She smiles at him and he softly chuckles.

She keeps composed and glances at family; her eyes catch a glimpse of The King. He tips his head to her with a kind smile and she gives a sweet smile in return. The Queen is next to him, while his brother is on the other side of The Queen, and next to him is his and The King's sister.

The Bishop asks with an authoritative tone, "What reason do you have why these two should not be joined in marriage?"

Ava holds up a piece of paper that looks like some sort of legal document. "He can't marry this commoner, this...*American*, because old bylaws state that an heir to a royal or prominent noble duchy has to marry someone with at least one royal bloodline and there *has to be* a 'Noble Consort.'"

"*And* nothing has been released as to who 'The Noble Consort' is to Lord Newhaven!" Serene says with a bit of frustration.

David glares at Serene and Ava. "*Then you two haven't been paying attention!*"

"All we've heard is disgusting rumors proving Americans have no idea what they're talking about." Ava snaps.

Carlotta interjects, "May I?" She looks at The Bishop.

"Oh, by all means, Your Grace." The Bishop partially bows, as he gestures for her to stand next to him, then he takes a half-step to the side.

"Thank you." Carlotta smiles, then looks at Ava and Serene. "We figured you two would have a last desperate—."

"We are *not* desperate!" Serene snaps.

Ava tells her, "We're just motivated to save The Duchy from an *American disaster!*" Ava waves her arm towards Bri. David's jaw is clenching; Jack and James are shifting their stance in annoyance.

"Yes, *you are* desperate, and before you rudely interrupt *again,*" she put up her hand in a stopping gesture to Serene, "as *The Duchess of Newhaven,* I'll *kindly* remind you to remember your place."

Both nod with a slight curtsy, and say, "Yes, Your Grace."

"Now, we figured there would be a last, desperate attempt to stop David from marrying BriaLynn, so I have something to say to *everyone.*" Carlotta speaks to The Bishop, "Yes, the bylaws do state what they're claiming about a bloodline, and as you know, we've already established everything with the help of our barristers." The Bishop agrees and she continues. "What these two haven't learned, and perhaps neither have some of our other guests, is that Bri, herself, *IS* a Direct Bloodline!" Gasps from a few guests and total shock for Ava and Serene; they are frozen knowing what that means. "In fact, her ancestry can be tied to monarchies throughout Europe, some of which no longer exist!" While The King knew Bri was a Direct Bloodline because he had to officially sign the paperwork to certify her lineage, he has taken a keen interest in the details and listens closely. David looks at The King and they slightly nod to each other with faint smirks. Carlotta adds, "From Newhaven's perspective, Bri has strong ties to Scotland!" She looks at Bri. "Scotland's in your blood, Sweetie, and your blood is *thick* with royalty, *even lost Scottish royalty!*"

Bri's mouth drops open a little; she didn't know *that*! She has the words 'royal blood' come to mind, connecting them to her conversation with Jessica and Henry. Then yesterday, Jessica told her to stay open when it came to '*Herst*,' rather than saying, '*The King*.' She glances at Henry, who gives her a reassuring nod, but she forces herself not to look at The King.

Carlotta explains more to Ava, Serene, and their guests. "In case you've forgotten what that means, it technically means *David's blood* could be considered too 'impure' for *Bri's* ancestral heritage; she's *too* royal." Bri's shocked by that statement, but Carlotta is also setting the stage for The King and his upcoming request for Bri to be his 'Royal Consort,' which Herst catches. "Her being a Direct Bloodline makes her the 'golden ticket,' with liquid gold in her veins." She winks at Bri, who faintly smiles back. "Serene," Carlotta addresses her, "this also means 'The Noble Consort' is for her, *not David*." Carlotta turns to David, but still speaking to the guests, "*Lord Newhaven* has asked *Lord Carlisle* to be BriaLynn's 'Noble Consort' and *both* Lord Carlisle and BriaLynn have accepted." David waves Jack over and David steps to the other side of Bri so she is between them.

David addresses everyone. "The three of us discussed actually taking on this historical tradition to the extent of what it was intended to be: two marriages occurring at the same time." There are actual cheers and applause, which also stuns Bri. David pats Jack's shoulder. "I couldn't think of anyone better than my best friend and brother, Lord Carlisle, to love Bri as deeply as I do."

David hugs Jack, then Jack kisses the back of Bri's hand before stepping back to stand next to James. David steps back into place and faces Bri. He holds out his hands to her and she places her hands in his, lovingly looking at him.

Ava and Serene are still shocked. "Wait. *Wait*!" Serene asks, "Doesn't David have three bloodlines? How—."

"*No*!" All eyes are on Bri. She isn't angry, but very stern. "Stop this! *All of it*! I don't care to hear any more about this right now. I'm grateful to share ancestry with the wonderful people of Newhaven, Scotland, the UK, and even Europe! But right now, in this moment, this is *our wedding*. Nothing else matters!" She looks to David, who smiles at her, as do Jack and James. Bri then looks at The Bishop with a pointed look to continue.

Before The Bishop can, David lifts her hand to his mouth and says, "Now there's the proof, Love!" He kisses the back of her hand, while she and The

Bishop give him a puzzled look. "The *proof* that you're so much better than I deserve! It's in your very DNA!" Bri's eyes tear up, shaking her head.

The Bishop lightly laughs, as he gives David an approving nod. He then asks Ava and Serene to either take a seat peacefully, or quietly leave. They slither back to their seats and quietly sit back down, their heads hanging low; they don't want to embarrass themselves any further.

The Bishop says, "Now Bri, I need to ask, *for the record*," she nods in understanding and he asks, "do you want to proceed with the ceremony to marry David, which binds you to Jack as well?"

"More than anything!" She smiles through her tears at David and Jack, who both nod in agreement. "*BUT* I do have one request..." she smirks to The Bishop, "whatever you do, *please* don't repeat your previous question!" She looks out at the guests and tells them, "You are *all* held to the part that goes, 'forever hold your peace!'" There is some soft laughter and chuckling, but there is annoyance from Katie, deflating with disappointment once again.

The Bishop continues, "David, would you like to say a few words to Bri."

David nods and smiles handsomely. "BriaLynn," he holds her hands and rubs her knuckles with his thumbs, "seeing you in the lobby of the hotel that Thursday afternoon, started a battle between my mind and my heart. I heard your laugh, seen your smile, and then your accent did me in! It was all I could do to get myself out of there, because my heart was hooked." There are some soft laughs. "Had I known you were coming out to The Estate that next day, I would've tried to avoid *everything*, including the stables, which coincidentally was the greatest day of Artemis' life!" There is more laughter. "This powerful, commanding steed became a different horse with you! He's sweet and gentle, not to mention making such a connection with you, he lowers his head just so you'll rest your forehead to his; something he has *never* done with anyone else, *not even me*! That horse fell head over hooves for you that day!" They hear snickering and chuckling around them. David clears his throat. "That moment in the stables was far from my greatest moment, but you held your ground. Unfortunately for me, there would be an even lower moment, my lowest as a human being, *and as a gentleman*. However, like the lovable, cheeky beauty you are, you stood up to me; you forced me to see the horrible truth of the man I had become. You didn't back down because *you knew* you were right; you also knew *I knew* you were right. I stand behind my words that night, that you didn't need a title to show you were better than those of us who were in the room with you that evening!"

368

"No. *Not* better than—."

"Yes, Love, *'better than'* and no interruptions from the enchanting bride!" He grins and kisses the back of her hand. Bri softly laughs, as do some guests. "Bri, *you* woke up my heart! The feisty firecracker you are, broke through my walls." David's eyes tear up. "You're an incredible, *amazing* woman, and you keep proving how phenomenal, how *bloody brilliant* you are!" He takes a breath and slowly exhales; he is overwhelmed with his love and emotions for her. "*You're so much more than* I *deserve!*" Bri smiles sweetly shaking her head, he smiles back. "You inspire me to be a better man, the kind of man deserving of your love!" There are very audible 'aws' around them.

Bri's jaw shakes. "Oh, David!" She chokes up. "*You're* wonderful *and* amazing! If I didn't feel you were a good man on the other side of those walls, you know as well as Jack and I do, I *never* would've bothered, but the four closest people in your life are your *greatest* supporters, or is it conspirators?" She teases and hears their family laughing. "David, if you weren't a wonderful man, *they* wouldn't have conspired to begin with." She turns and winks at Peter and Carlotta. "With that, it was easy to read you had been hurt pretty badly; people who are blindsided by hurt usually do have the thickest walls around them..." a tear escapes her eye and she quickly wipes it.

David takes another deep breath, exhaling slowly before he says, "The *worst* day of my life was when you had been shot!" There were quieter surprise reactions from the guests. "The sheer panic of so much blood and needing to stop the bleeding, or you would bleed to death; to feeling so helpless watching the doctors and nurses in the operating room working fast to save you; to the air being taken out of my lungs when the surgeon came out and said we *still* had to prepare for the worst. It was during this time when the love of my life is fighting for her life against *impossible* odds, the doctor said you needed nothing short of a 'perfect miracle,' I realized that, even though I was powerless, the Lord wasn't!" Bri shakes her head. "A perfect miracle did happen because *here you are*..." a lump closes his throat.

"Here *we* are!" She smiles with tears and winks at Jack, who smiles with his own tears.

David looks up for a moment to blink back more tears. "The whole time you were unconscious in the hospital, I promised you that if you came back to me, I'd marry you straight away. So, it goes without saying that one of the *happiest* days of my life was when you said '*absolutely*' to marrying me!" He grins. "I couldn't marry you soon enough! In many ways, I already felt you were already my wife, except one." He glances sideways at The Bishop and The Bishop chuckles. The King catches that and is surprised, *curious*, by the possibility they have waited until they are married to be intimately together.

"I have to admit your outlook of 'everything happens for a reason,' and applying it to any situation, was a little frustrating, *at first*, because of the events going on that would lead to you being shot. However, when you explained that it's because there is a lesson to be learned by someone or multiple people, it was then I understood. One lesson I learned was about faith. I've learned so much about faith just being with you, but my own faith was tested when you were in the hospital. *However*, it was also strengthened in a lot of ways during that time too! I'm grateful for your faith, especially the faith in us, *in me*." He smiles sweetly. "I wish I could promise we would always have sunshine and rainbows, but you know as well as I do, life isn't meant to be easy."

She gives him a loving look. "Because like sunshine and rainbows, there has to be rain in between them."

He chuckles and nods, so do others, then he continues. "This past week I kept hearing a word pass through my thoughts. It's a word I've heard over the years, but it's been long enough I had forgotten about it. That word is 'Macushla.' It comes from another word literally meaning, 'vein of my heart.'" He smiles through his eyes that are wet with tears. "You *are* the love of my life, the vein of my heart that keeps my heart beating, my reason for living. I'm *so* blessed to have your love, but I'm even *more* blessed I get to love you!" He reaches up under her veil to wipe her tears with his thumbs. "I'm so blessed to have you as my wife, the rightful woman it should be." He kisses the back of her hands.

Ava is finally starting to understand why her marriage didn't work...the underlying reason she cheated on such a great guy... she worked her own agenda and never bothered to fall in-love with him. Now she is seeing how easy it could've been and the big mistake she has really made...

"Because you're my '*Macushla*,' my love for you gets stronger every minute of every single day, *because of your love for me*. I now understand why I had to go through all the other relationships I did, that they were necessary for many reasons; the biggest reason," he squeezes her hands, "so I'd appreciate what we have, where we're going, and how much fun we'll have along the way!" He grins and she smiles in agreement.

"*Lastly*, and most importantly, thank you for *loving me* and inspiring me to be worthy to stand by your side." He laces his fingers with hers and holds them up. "Together, we'll make it through anything that comes our way! Together, we can, and will, do great things!" Her mind flashes to the time in her coma and hearing she would do 'wonderfully extraordinary things.' David concludes. "I love you, Macushla! Now and forever."

David's eyes have tears, he is emotional and so is Bri, but there were also tears in their guests' eyes. The King is stoic; however, he feels his heart beginning to crave love like that and *be* loved like that...

"Wow..." Bri tips her head back trying to blink back her tears. She exhales slowly to steady her nerves. "David, I didn't have the kind of walls up you did, but I would describe what was around me like a bubble within a bubble. We all live in our own little bubbles, but I added an extra layer. I closed myself off, convincing myself that I missed my chance at this kind of love. I accepted it and tried to enjoy life for what it was for me...then *you* happened." He has a small, soft burst of laughter through his tears. "I was in a bubble where I still interacted with people, had family and friends, and I was really good at my job; life was good. This bubble kept anyone from getting too close; but then, *there was you.*" She grins. "When I wanted time to myself, I didn't want anyone coming in and taking that away...it was *my* space. But. *Then there was you.*" Tears fill her eyes again. "You didn't take anything away; you were there *with me.*" He kisses her hand, then rubs her knuckles with his thumbs. She exhales slowly, her lower jaw shaking. "Going back to what The Bishop spoke of earlier about true-love." She looks at The Bishop. "My apologies if I don't remember word for word." She looks back at David. "True-love creates an environment with no secrets, no games, and most importantly, *no judgements!* When I called your behavior out, it wasn't to judge you; I was wanting you to face it! Now, I know you remember that I had some very descriptive words that night." She has an eek look. "There was conceited, pompous, arrogant, cocky, pretentious—."

"Oh, Love," he grins, "I *do* remember and I *clearly* recall you said 'arrogant' twice that evening." He teases and some of their guests laugh.

"Well, that's because it encompassed words like egotistical, opinionated, condescending, and words I couldn't use because they were *un*ladylike."

"All true, but we could be here all night if you continue with that list." He says. "There is more light laughter from their guests.

"*My point is* I would like to replace those words with charming, patient, amazing, caring, phenomenal, and another 'amazing' for good measure." She playfully winks and other guests chuckle. "You *are* an honorable man, a true gentleman with a heart that loves, and I know," her lower jaw shakes, "you love me *fiercely*, because *I feel it from you!*" She squeaks that last part out, then sucks in her breath and holds it a few seconds to push her emotions down; he nods as the tears fill his eyes. "I also said you were lacking 'grace' at that point, but now you have 'grace' in abundance!" David chokes up and looks down, tears escaping down his cheeks. Bri adds, "I know I'm safe mentally, physically, emotionally, and spiritually with you. I hope you know what a *precious gift* that is, David!" Her voice cracks and squeaks even more, she cries a little as she wipes her eyes with one hand.

David looks at her. "It's how I feel with you!" She gives him a teary nod.

Bri swallows again. "Looking back, what amazes me is I found myself letting you in my bubble without even thinking twice about it. It felt...*familiar somehow*. It wasn't until later that I realized you had become 'home' to me. Home is where someone should be comfortable to be their true self; home is that place you long to be when you are away from it; home is where love thrives. David, you're *all of that* for me!" She barely gets that last sentence out before she drops her head to pull herself together enough to continue. "You make me feel adored, like I'm the most important person in your life—."

"*Because you are!*" He interjects.

"Ah, but it's me who is honored..." she can barely whisper, "*to have your love, your heart.*" She continues to struggle to say above a whisper, "The love I feel from you, and for you, is deep and, like yours, *incredibly fierce!* It's something I never thought I'd ever experience in my lifetime..." Her tears drip down her cheeks. "What's amazing to me is, here I was, living a plain old ordinary life, when something *extraordinary* happened...*you!*"

David's jaw shakes as he smiles with so much love, bringing her hand up to kiss the inside of her wrist. She puts that hand to his cheek, smiling through her tears; but when sobs threaten to take over, she has to look down again. She inhales and holds her breath for a few seconds, then she shakily exhales.

"To be married to the man of *my* dreams; I'm *so* deeply blessed, David. We're two imperfect people, who somehow fit perfectly together...yet more 'rightly perfect' with Jack." Bri isn't bothering to fight back the tears anymore and neither is David, but Jack feels it, too...especially when Bri holds her hand out to him. "Jack, I know you wanted this day to be for David and me, but you're very much a part of this and if you, David, and our guests will bear with me just a few more minutes, I have some things I need to say to you." Bri smiles at Jack, then at David. He smiles as he steps over to stand next to James, patting him on the shoulder. "Jack, there's no doubt between the three of us, that had things gone differently that Saturday night, we would've ended up together; consensus being we would've eloped." Jack, David, and James lightly laugh. Bri tells Jack, "You have a *wonderful* talent of making anyone who is in your company feel special and important! I feel those things with you, too, but there is an extra energy when we're together. I almost feel like I could *fly* when I'm with you, because your passion and excitement is invigorating!" She quickly wipes a tear tickling her cheek. "As I keep saying, David is a blessing, which makes *you* a blessing's gift!" She swallows hard. "My love for you is separate from my love for David, but it's tailored to, and for, *you*." She winks. "I'm really looking forward to building something with you and for the three of us to be a family! You're home to me, too, Jack! And I also feel safe *on every level* with you; that's another *amazing* gift!" She squeezes his hand. "I love *you*!"

Jack inhales, then exhales, "*Oh, Gorgeous!*" He blows out another breath. "You're not only gorgeous and funny, but you're also a little cheeky with a *whole* lot of sass! Above all that, *you're bloody brilliant*! I love watching people realize they've underestimated you." Bri rolls her eyes. "*Aaand* there's the sass!" He points to her eye roll! He squeezes her hands. "Bri! Who did your boss turn to organize *all* federal law enforcement cases?!" The King's ears perk up because he heard the US is doing something like that, but he had no idea she was behind it. "Who did dignitaries, diplomats, and probably *every bloody world leader* call when they need something in DC? *You*! As smart as David and I are, it was only going to be *you* to be able to keep us *both* on our toes, because *you're used to keeping multiple people on their toes at once*!" He goes on to say, "Not only do you make life interesting, but *you* make life so much more enjoyable ad worthwhile!" He gives her a huge smile. "The love I have for you, Bri, is stronger than I've *ever* felt!" His voice catches, a hand goes to his heart, and his lower jaw shakes just a touch. "You had me from that first Saturday!" He holds her hands firmly. "With all that I am, with all the love that I have, Gorgeous, you have me, now and forever!" He kisses her hand. "I love you!"

Bri touches Jack's cheek saying, "Good! I'm keeping you!" He chuckles as he takes the hand on his cheek and kisses the palm of it.

Jack hugs David as they trade places again. Except for maybe a few people, there isn't a dry eye among the guests.

The Bishop reaches into his pocket and hands the three of them a tissue. "I was so wrapped up in listening, I forgot about these." He smiles and gives them a minute to compose themselves. Bri sees something out of the corner of her eye, behind The Bishop's shoulder. She looks and sees a familiar face...*her son with David!* She looks at him with a mother's love and her son smiles back at his mother. The Bishop moves the ceremony forward before she sees there are two other children who are just behind The Bishop.

"Well, then," The Bishop dries his eyes again and clears his throat. "David and Bri have chosen to incorporate the tradition of 'Handfasting' into their ceremony. While the wording has been changed to reflect their beliefs, they hope it still shows respect to the tradition as a symbol of their commitment today." The Bishop addresses them, "David and Bri, right now, as you seek to marry each other, it's important that you understand marriage from a realistic perspective. There will be times when one of you is upset with the other, times when your both upset with each other at the same time. It's imperative for you to focus on your love and *why* you love each other, *trusting* the love the other person has for you, and keeping an eternal point of view during those unhappy times. Do that, and those unhappy times will just be bumps on an overall happy road together, *for both couples.*" He looks at Jack, who nods.

The Bishop looks at David and Jack, "David, Jack, never *ever* stop dating this woman! As you continue to date her, it's just as important to make sure you continue to woo and to romance her, because she'll respond in kind. For those times you do have disagreements, keep in mind if you fight to win, *no one does*; choose to be happy by focusing on the other person's happiness, *especially* from an eternal view. In simpler terms, 'choose your battles.'" He looks at Bri. "Something I'm sure you're all too familiar with as a mother." He tips his head to her daughters, as Bri gives him a small smile. "Bri, always keep an open heart, even when you're fighting. Never let *their* wooing go unnoticed and always accept going on a date, *when asked.*" He looks out at the guests. "I say it like that because some men think an always standing date works, that it's 'good enough,' but then they're upset when their wife doesn't show up for their standing date when they're fighting. 'Good enough' should *never* be a description in your marriage! To settle with 'good enough' means you've stopped trying, stopped progressing! When someone stops trying, love fades away and eventually dies. Also, keep in mind that it's difficult to stay mad at the one you love when you're kneeling in prayer together, praying

374

for each other. Never skip those prayers out of anger or hurt feelings, and let the Spirit do its work; maybe, *and perhaps especially*, let the Spirit work on yourself."

The Bishop is about finished wrapping with the tartan strips, but motions for Jack and has him stand on his other side, closest to Bri. "The vows you *three* make today will keep you all bound together, through your lives forever. David, Bri, and Jack, as your hands are bound together, so are your lives in *boundless* love for each other." The Bishop finishes wrapping the strips.

"These strips only symbolize the bond. The actual binding comes from keeping the vows you make to each other. The fate of that bond is *forever* in *your hands*." Gesturing their bound hands. "Like a beacon of light, so shall your love be for each other; *if* you hold onto one another as you make your way through this mortal life together."

To the guests, The Bishop says, "May they continue from this day, in love and kindness towards each other, nurturing the true, abiding love between them. Thus, creating a firm foundation to be a place of comfort, healing, guiding, protecting, and most importantly, growing in that love for one another, their family, and raising children *together*." The Bishop felt the need to stress that, not knowing it's something The King makes note of; his mother is pushing *her* plan for The King to have a baby with the 'Direct Bloodline,' and 'His Heir' will be raised 'properly' by his mother...something The King *does NOT want*.

The Bishop unties their hands and sets the tartan strips aside, keeping Jack right there with them for the next part. "David and BriaLynn, please take each other's hands once again...David, do you take BriaLynn, to be your wedded wife; to have and to hold from this day forward, for better, for worse, for richer, for poorer, in sickness and in health, to love, to honor, and to cherish, now and forever?"

With so much love in his eyes he says, "*I do!*" He smiles beautifully.

"BriaLynn, do you take David, to be your wedded husband; to have and to hold from this day forward, for better, for worse, for richer, for poorer, in sickness and in health, to love, to honor, and to cherish, now and forever?"

Bri's heart is just as full, "*I do!*" She smiles lovingly back at David.

"Jack, I want to include you in this part because this marriage binds you to Bri." The Bishop states. David opens his hands and Bri takes Jack's hands.

The Bishop recites, "Jackson, do you take BriaLynn, to be your wedded wife; to have and to hold from this day forward, for better, for worse, for richer, for poorer, in sickness and in health, to love, to honor, and to cherish, now and forever?"

Jack's eyes are teary as he smiles, "*I do!*" He gently rubs her knuckles gently with his thumbs and she squeezes his hands, smiling through her tears.

"BriaLynn, do you take Jackson, to be your wedded husband; to have and to hold from this day forward, for better, for worse, for richer, for poorer, in sickness and in health, to love, to honor, and to cherish, now and forever?"

Bri can barely speak, "*I do!*" Jack kisses the back of Bri's hands, then he turns and steps back next to James.

The Bishop looks at James. "The rings, please." James hands The Bishop two bands, one for Bri and one for David, which match the same design on her engagement ring. The Bishop holds his Bible out for David to take her ring. "David, repeat after me..." He does pause at certain times to help David.

"I take you, BriaLynn, to be my wife. This ring is a symbol of my eternal love and undying devotion. I vow with all that I am, and all that I will ever be, as your husband, to be by your side and that I will *always be* your faithful partner. BriaLynn, when you look at this ring, let it remind you of our love, my faith in our strength together, and my promise to learn and grow with you. I am *honored* to call you, *my wife*." David stresses 'honored' and adds, "I love you, Macushla!" David tears are running down his face.

The Bishop smiles. "Slip the ring on her finger."

David first shows her it's engraved: *Macushla, eternally yours*. He pushes the ring onto her finger. He takes both her hands in his and gently squeezes them, kissing her rings on her finger. Bri loses it and she turns her head away from David, he squeezes her hands for support; but it's harder not to cry because she feels so much love from this amazing man, it makes her cry more! With a tissue in her hand, she cups her mouth and cries.

"We're almost done," The Bishop calmly says, handing her more tissues, "but when you're ready." She nods and then sees their son again, with another young man and young woman with him. A hand drops to her lower abdomen because she feels a strong motherly connection to them, adding to her tears. Jack sees this and looks in the same direction and when he doesn't see anything, he knows she must see something.

She lets go of David and steps away, her back to the guests to wipe her tears and take some deep breaths, praying in her mind to have help pulling herself together.

Her other son whispers, "*We love you, Mum.*"

"We're sorry if we upset you." Her daughter sweetly adds. She gives them a tearful, loving smile, and discreetly shakes her head.

David has taken this moment to collect himself, too, because he can feel her love just as strongly as she can feel his. Bri takes one more deep breath and exhales very slowly to summon the courage to step back into place. She takes David's hands again inhaling, but she holds it. Then, looking at him for a second, he winks to make her smile, which she does, as she turns to The Bishop and nods.

He holds the Bible out for her to take David's ring. "BriaLynn, repeat after me." The Bishop also pauses at various moments for her to easily repeat.

"I take you, David, to be my husband. This ring is a symbol of *my* eternal love and *undying* devotion. I vow with all that I am, and all that I will ever be, as your wife, to be by your side and that I will *always be* your faithful partner. David, when you look at this ring, let it remind you of our love, my faith in our strength *together*," she winks and he nods, "and my promise to learn and grow with you. *I am honored*," she squeaks a little, "to call you, *my husband*." Tears still streaming down her face, Bri says, "I love you, My Love!"

The Bishop smiles. "Slip the ring on his finger."

She shows David the engraving on his ring, which she had asked James to do for her and he was happy to do it for her. It's engraved in French for sentimental reasons behind Paris.

David reads it aloud, "*Mon coeur est à vous*" and looks at Bri knowing its meaning, but he says it so everyone would know, "*My heart is yours!*" Which is also engraved across from it, with a Triquetra Heart symbol in between the phrases. David smiles through the tears in his eyes, clearly choked up and barely holding it all together. She inhales again and holds her breath to stop herself from crying.

The Bishop continues. "With your love and the vows made today, I now pronounce you, 'husband and wife!' *David*," The Bishop smiles, "you may kiss your bride!" He steps back to give them space.

David smiles and is filled with incredible happiness, joy, and love, as he lifts Bri's veil, but pauses as his breath catches...he exhales slowly taking her all in this close. He steps inside the veil with her and his hand goes to his heart.

"You literally take my breath away, Macushla!" He says to her and they can hear 'aws' and such from their guests.

She laughs through her tears. "I'm a mess!"

He wraps an arm around her waist. "It only adds to your *exquisite* beauty!" He smiles as he puts his other hand on her jaw; her arms wrap around him, too. "I love you, Mrs. Worthington," he smiles, bringing their lips together. It's a tender and sweet kiss...*at first*...then it becomes fierce. He wraps his arms around her so he can dip her back, adding romance to their kiss. There were whistles and cheers.

After David brings her back up, he says against her lips, "*I've been looking forward to doing that!*"

"Feel free to kiss me like that *anytime!*" She giggles.

"Gladly." He winks and mischievously smiles, dipping her into a kiss again.

David lifts the veil up and over to the back. Then holds her neck and kisses her fiercely once more. He smiles and turns to Jack, but neither of them has to say a word. Jack goes up to Bri and wraps her in an embrace, kissing her firmly and passionately. He runs a hand down to her bum and pulls her closer for a few seconds, then releases her. They rest their foreheads together a moment to catch their breath.

"I love you!" Jack tells her.

"And I love you!" She replies.

David smiles at his now daughters and asks them to come up with them. Jack stands next to him while Bri watches whatever David and Jack have planned.

"Having your mum in the hospital was hard and terrifying for all of us, but we know it was hardest on the two of you. We can appreciate the blessings during that time even more, like getting to know the two of you. I hope you believe it when I tell you that Jack and I love you both!" He gestures to Jack, then James, along with his parents in the front row. "We *all* do!" The girls smile and nod.

David tips the gold with silver rings out of their velvet bag, "These gold rings have The Worthington 'W' on them, along with the golden Newhaven 'N.' This symbol is recognized here and throughout Europe and a bit around the world." He points to his lapel where he has a pin of the same thing, except his has a coronet, or crown, on top being The Heir to Newhaven. "We want you to have them and wear them because both of you are, and forever will be, a part of our family and we want you treated that way!"

He hands a ring to Jack and they each put a ring on one of the girls' right-middle fingers, but it's blurry for Jack and David since their eyes are a bit teary. Then the girls tightly hug each of the guys and kiss their cheeks; then they hug and kiss their mom before hugging the rest of the family.

Jack smiles at Bri, pulling her to him and kisses her sweetly to more cheers and whistles. Jack and James step back as The Bishop steps forward again.

"Ladies and gentlemen," he gestures, "Mr. and Mrs. David Worthington!" Cheers and clapping come from the guests as the happy couple kiss.

David and Bri couldn't be happier as they halfway jog down the aisle, hand in hand, on their way back to The Manor. Giving them a head start, Jack and James escort Emmie and Natty back to The Manor a few minutes later. David and Bri had stopped on the bridge for a couple of pictures.

"I've *never* been this happy in my life, David! Thank you!" She kisses David deeply and fiercely.

He whispers, "*If you keep kissing me like that, we'll have to sneak away for a while.*" He looks at her with love and desire in his eyes.

"Promise." She bites her bottom lip with a playful grin.

He laughs and says, "For the record, *I've never been this happy before either*! Unfortunately, it's not possible to make you as happy as I am, because I'm in-love with you, the most incredibly intelligent and most brilliant thinking, not to mention the most stunningly beautiful woman on the planet!" He lifts her up and twirls her around as she happily smiles.

"And you're all that in masculinity AND you fill me with so much love and joy, my heart is about to burst! That's not even factoring Jack into all this! So, *I* surpass your happiness level!" She laughs.

"Proving you have more than enough love for me and," he points, "Jack!" Jack is walking up the path to The Manor and they all stop on the bridge. David tells them, "You two should have a moment." David walks the rest of the way through the gardens with Emmie, Natty, and James.

"I love you!" Jack says as he wraps his arms around Bri.

"I love you!" She smiles. "I was just telling David I'm so happy and excited, I could burst!" Jack kisses her firmly, but it's Bri who deepens it.

"I'm supposed to make *you* melt!" He smiles adoringly.

Bri giggles, but her smile freezes a moment when she sees her three children's spirits again, standing behind Jack. He sees her face and asks, "What is it? What do you see?" He turns and looks where she is looking.

Bri smiles through tears. "I see three of my children who haven't been born yet, standing before me.''

"Really?! Yours and David's?" He asks.

Her son with David says, "Don't tell him too much, Mum. 'To everything there is a season...'"

Bri smiles at him, "'...and a time to every purpose under the heaven.'" Bri finishes one of the famous sentences from Ecclesiastes in the Old Testament.

"But..." her other son has a twinkle in his eye, "it doesn't mean you can't tell him what you already *feel*. It'll mean more than you know, and he'll explain it later to you."

Bri smiles a loving smile at him, then to her other two children. "I can already *see* which one of you has Jack for a father!" Jack stares at her and tears fill his eyes, he tries to blink them back but one escapes down his cheek.

"We just wanted to see the beginning of our family." Her other son says. "We love you, Mum!" Then the other two say, 'I love you.'

Wiping her cheeks, she tells them, "I love you all, too!"

"We'll visit again soon!" Her son with David tells her.

Bri nods in understanding. She blows them a kiss as they wave, then all three disappear. She takes a deep breath as she turns to Jack. And she tells him what they said. He is speechless. He *hoped* to have a child with Bri and here she was, *seeing* the proof they *do* have one. He hugs her and then he pulls back to kiss her.

After resting their foreheads together for a minute, Jack kisses her again before he leads her up the trail and around the corner to where David is patiently waiting. David carries her red-rose bouquet and holds her other hand as they walk to the luncheon for them, and their guests, on the back patio of The Manor.

CHAPTER 34

Imperfectly Perfect Wedding Luncheon

David, Jack, and Bri reach the back patio for the reception. Bri had never really paid attention to how big the patio was because they only use a small section regularly. There are tables set up to hold the smaller guest list for lunch, with the wedding party sitting on one long side of a rectangular table, and their guests sitting around the several round tables. The girls hug their mom, being excited and happy for her. They also hug David and Jack again before they all find their seats; David and Jack sit on either side of Bri. However, before she sits, David kisses her...cheers come from their guests as well as the staff, both regular and the additional ones for the day.

She lovingly looks at him. "I love you, *Mister* Worthington!"

He smiles beautifully. "I love you, *Mrs.* Worthington!" He kisses her again, dipping her back.

Jack pulls out her chair and pushes it in for her. He kisses her cheek, then takes his seat next to her. They hear clinking coming from Carlotta's fork tapping her glass.

"Hullo, everyone! I hope you'll indulge a proud and happy mother, *and now* grandmother." She lovingly smiles to the wedding party table. "Bri, I can't express to you the love and gratitude Peter and I have *for you!*" Her voice cracks. "We love having you in this family and we've come to adore you ourselves." She wipes a tear on her cheek as she turns to their guests. "I came across a quote this past week and I can't tell you who said it, but I kept thinking about it as we prepared for this *joyous* day. Then watching all three of them, throughout the ceremony, this just fits. It goes: '*In the eyes of a groom, you will see a bride's true beauty!*'" She turns to Bri, "While you looked stunning upstairs right before the wedding, seeing how our sons look at you, it was plain to see how true that statement really is!" David kisses the inside of Bri's wrist. Jack kisses her cheek again. Bri mouths, 'Love you,' to her in-laws as she wipes her eyes. "We love you, too, Sweetie!"

Peter stands next to Carlotta and adds, "David and Jack, I want you to know The Bishop is right!" He lifts his glass to The Bishop. He looks at David. "David, you learned early on, and mentioned to me, that Bri is so easy to love; she's the kind of person who will genuinely love any small gesture because of the thought, *or love,* behind it!" Peter addresses both Jack and David. "All these things you do are sweet to watch, but also *necessary* to continue because she will notice when you *stop* doing them. Watching you three love and adore each other, taking such care and concern over each other's well-being, is *really* beautiful. As Lotti said, we've grown to adore you ourselves, Bri, and have thought of you as our daughter and granddaughters long before this day; however, we're *overjoyed* it's official! To our daughter and granddaughters, welcome to our family!"

"Here, here!" The guests cheer.

"P.S." Carlotta beams, "The girls and I are wanting babies added to our family! Lots of *gorgeous,* beautiful babies!" The guests laugh. Bri smiles and winks at her.

She playfully whispers to David, "*Which we'll practice over the next two weeks to perfection!*"

He smiles at her with a look of desire, whispering back, "*I'll be there!*" He kisses below her ear and hears her breath catch. "*Plus, I have a few thoughts on how we can practice...*"

She softly giggles, "I don't doubt that!" She turns to look at Jack and winks, because for a little while she and Jack share a secret, the secret of her seeing their future children on the garden bridge.

Jack leans in closer, "*You* are so good for the soul!"

"Me?!" She's surprised.

"Just as you said you feel like you can fly when we're together, you're just as much a good feeling to *my* soul!" Her heart melts. She holds his cheek and kisses him.

After the meal is served and finished, the guests make their way back to their rooms, or go on excursions for a couple of hours. The wedding party and families take formal pictures and Bri is grateful to have Annette and Nicole help her redo, fix, and touch-up things at various times.

When they wrap up the formal pictures, Jack comes up and says to both of them, "I had the second dress taken to your quarters so Bri could *comfortably* change there," he whispers between them, "figured David could *help* you." He winks at her, patting David on the shoulder, before walking away leaving the two of them alone. Bri lightly laughs.

David looks at her with a playful smile. "Be right back."

He goes to the photographer and arranges to meet up near the stables in a half hour after Bri changes into her other dress. David comes back over and takes Bri's hand, then they go up to their quarters.

David gets to their door and opens it, but he sweeps Bri up in his arms. Her arms wrap around his neck and they kiss as he carries her over the threshold. Once inside, he kicks the door shut with his foot. He slowly sets her down as they continue to kiss, and he holds her in his arms. He pulls back and looks lovingly into her eyes as he sets her down.

"I want you, Bri, but part of me wants to wait when we can take our time and make the first time really count since we've waited this long..." he thinks out loud, "but the other part of me can't stop thinking about you and..." he exhales stepping back with his eyebrows raised, looking her over.

"I know what you mean, but can't we look at it as a *preview* for tonight." She bites her lower lip as she smiles. She sees him struggling, so she decides to take off her dress and turns around pointing to her back, "Help me? It's what we came up here for; we still have photos to finish up and Artemis to see." He reaches for her dress and helps her out of it. He carries the train as they go to the closet to hang up the dress. She smiles at him when she sees he is watching her closely. "You have about ten seconds to decide–*OH!*"

David pulls her close, grabbing behind her jaw, capturing her lips in a heated kiss. They both work fast to get his tux off before she playfully pushes him to sit in the chair.

After, he smiles at her. "You are incredible! I'd stay like this forever, but we do have prior commitments. If we hurry, we won't be late." She kisses him firmly before getting up.

Bri quickly goes to the closet to put her reception dress on. She walks out of the closet backwards asking, "Will you zip me, please?"

He chuckles. "This was the excuse of our escape, was it not?"

She grins. "Well, now it's not a lie!" He zips her dress up and Bri tells him, "Okay, close your eyes before I turn around." He complies. She looks in the mirror to check herself, then stands in front of him. "Open!"

He smiles a wonderful smile. "Your first dress was phenomenal, and now this?! WOW! It *almost* rivals the first!"

She lightly giggles. "*Almost?*"

"Bri," he holds her left hand and holds her jaw with his other hand, "seeing you that moment, *veil and all*, you were in *all* your exquisite beauty as *my bride!*" He kisses her rings. "I can't begin to describe to you the feeling of that moment! I planned all of this for the woman of my dreams and imagined that moment *a million times*; however, none of those imagined moments came close to the real thing!" His eyes water. "I've been in awe of you since I first saw you at that hotel, hooked since *before* you called me out at the party, and completely yours after you did." He clears his throat. "I have more love for you than I've ever loved anyone else, and at that moment, seeing you at the end of the aisle is a moment I'll *never* forget! It was the moment you stepped out of my dreams and into forever to be my wife!"

"*Wow!*" It's all she can say before she hugs him and kisses him more fiercely than ever! She tells him, "You could've used that in the ceremony, too!" Her eyes leak more tears and she kisses him with all the love she can. Then she looks into his eyes and beams. "I love you."

He smiles back. "I love you, too!" He rests their foreheads together and they soak in their love for one another. "We're going to be late. Are you ready for more pictures and then the party?"

"*I can't wait to see what else you planned!*" She has a huge smile.

He lightly laughs. "Hopefully, it meets your approval."

She puts her hands on his jaw, which he likes when she does that. "David, this has been the best day and the most perfect way to officially start our lives together! I know whatever comes next will be just as amazing as everything has already been! From the bottom of my heart, thank you *for all of it!*"

"I live to see you smile at me like this, to know I put it there." He says touching her lips with his finger.

"My cheeks hurt because I'm so happy!" She massages them with her fingertips.

"Shall we?" He asks and holds his hand out for her to take.

David and Bri descend the grand staircase and go out to the stables. They run into The King outside. "Herst!" David says and they hug while Herst tells him congratulations. David then turns to Bri. "Bri, this is—."

"The man who is truly honored to meet the woman who has singlehandedly broken the heart of nearly every woman in Europe by taking David *and* Jack off the market!" He smiles, then bows a little and kisses the back of her hand.

Bri quietly laughs. "I'll gladly take the blame! However, either you're giving me too much credit, or their 'revolving door' spun much faster than I realized!" She winks at them with a smirk and they laugh.

Carlotta's standing with The Wedding Planner and calls for David. Before he excuses himself, he says, "Herst, take good care of her while I'm gone!" David smiles and kisses Bri's cheek. He pats Herst's upper arm once before walking over to his mother.

"My pleasure!" Herst says holding out his arm and asks, "Where to, Darling?"

"We were headed to the stables to see Artemis for some pictures." She says as she takes his arm.

"Really? With the dress and dust, not to mention a spirited animal, it seems risky for a fantastic dress." He replies.

"Don't worry," she has them walk that direction, "he isn't David's horse when I'm there." She smirks.

"So I've heard!" He grins. "This is something I do want to see!"

They walk in, petting some of the horses walking to Artemis' stall. The staff see them and go to address 'The King,' but he shakes his head; he is just Herst right now. They come to where Artemis should be, but he's not there. His stall door to the outside is open so he can freely come and go. A newer staff member goes to fetch him, but Bri stops her.

"No need to get him, he'll be coming along." Bri smiles. "He is somehow in-tune with me and knows when I've come to see him—Oh no! I forgot a carrot!" She is disappointed with herself.

"I can get you something!" The staff woman holds up a finger in a 'just a second' gesture. Bri smiles in acknowledgement.

Artemis is in view trotting up to his door. When he's closer Bri exclaims, "Hi, My Handsome Boy!" He neighs some to greet her as he walks in. "I've brought someone to meet you!" Artemis walks over to her and gently lowers his head to her so she'll drop her forehead to his and she pets his face and neck. He lifts his head and looks over to her friend. "Artemis, this is King Lawrence. Can you bow down to him like a gentleman's horse, please?" Artemis sniffs him a little, before he steps back and this giant, beautiful black stallion bows down to *The King*.

"Your Majesty, this is *My Artemis*." Bri happily says with a big smile.

"Artemis, you *are* magnificent!" He says in awe of him.

The woman from the staff comes over and hands Bri a few sugar cubes. Bri hands one to The King so Artemis will eat from his hand.

Bri tries to think back. "I don't recall if we've already met in DC."

He is a little surprised. "We have!" He's not sure how to take that she has forgotten they have met.

She gives him an apologetic look. "My apologies if you're offended, Your Majesty. In my job, the ones I got to know well tend to be the problematic ones. In a way, not recalling that we met is a complement."

He softly chuckles. "From that perspective, I'll give you that." He pets Artemis some more. "That would mean you know my mother."

She sucks in her breath petting Artemis' neck. "Ooo, *quite* well, on the back end. I usually deal with the trail of problems she leaves in her wake." She realizes she overstepped. "Sorry, that was—."

"Truthful?" He pointedly looks at her, but with a knowing smile.

"Well, yeah," Bri starts to say, "but—."

387

"Bri, er, may I call you Bri?" He asks and she nods. "Bri, we aren't in front of the public, we are just two people having a friendly chat. I want you to be honest with me, just as I want David and Jack to be, even blunt if necessary. My mother is a huge pain in the *aaa—as you well know.*" He corrects himself.

Bri quietly snorts a little laugh. "I do and I agree."

"If you would've said how nice or how wonderful my mother is, I would've known you were lying, *or* tried to figure out what my mother wanted from you." He tells her.

Bri's eyebrows raise, "That'sss kind of...well, *sad.*" He studies her and she asks, "What? Do I have dirt on my face, or something?"

"What? *Oh, no!* Sorry. There is something about you that makes me want to tell you everything, yet at the same time—."

"You want to run and hide?" She playfully smirks.

"Yes, *and* not exactly." He says.

"Wow! Vague, much?" She teases and he laughs. She does note, "You do seem different right now, not so *stoic.*" She tells him as she pets Artemis' neck.

"Really?" He is surprised, but he does feel comfortable with her.

"You're more relaxed and personable here. In photos, you look so..." she thinks hard and senses there is a loneliness underneath. She tries to come up with a different word, but can't think fast enough...

He watches her and smiles knowingly, "It's alright, Darling, you can say it."

"*I don't know about that...*" She smirks and teases, "you could order me to be locked in your dungeon and it would be pretty sad if you sent me there on my wedding day!" She giggles and he chuckles.

There is a moment where they stare into each other's eyes; it's a connection of sorts that has Bri thinking about what she has learned already about him...and about being open. Just as he is about to say something, they hear David, "I thought maybe you would get a head start coming in here."

This breaks Herst's moment with Bri for now. Bri lights up when she sees David, intriguing Herst as he watches their interaction between each other.

She says to David, "I did, My Love! His Majesty was so wonderful to escort me in here to see *My* Artemis." David laughs shaking his head a bit.

David goes over to Artemis and pets him. "No hard feelings marrying your girl?" David asks. "I promise to take extra special care of her!" Artemis does something he's only done with Bri. He lowers his head for David to put their foreheads together. David's stunned, but he rests his forehead to Artemis' and whispers, "*Thanks, Big Guy!*"

Bri walks over and puts her forehead to the side of Artemis' head; David wraps an arm around her waist. For Artemis, there seems to be no hard feelings and he seems to be happy David will 'take extra special care of *his girl.*'

Bri lifts her head and whispers to Artemis, but loud enough for the guys to hear, "*Promise not to go* too *easy on David...*" Artemis nods his head. "That's my handsome boy!"

Bri kisses his nose one more time before the three of them go out to the photographer who has set up just outside. He has already taken some great candid shots of the three of them with Artemis, and a couple of shots earlier of Bri with Herst and Artemis.

CHAPTER 35

Imperfectly Perfect Wedding Celebration

That early evening, Bri waits with David at the closed ballroom doors after everyone has gone in before them. Bri looks over and sees a woman she would *swear* is a spirit, but she couldn't be sure until David followed her line of sight and asked what she is looking at. The sandy-blond haired woman glances over at Bri, smiling at her and Bri smiles in return.

David wonders if she is seeing a ghost and whispers, *"Seriously, Love, who do you see?"*

"I'm not sure who she is." Bri replies.

He looks at her. "You seem so calm when you say that."

She looks at him with a sympathetic look. "David, if this bothers you, I can keep it to myself, but this *is* the result of my *choosing* to come back..." she puts her hand on his cheek, gently reminding him, "to come back to you..."

"I know and it doesn't bother me. I just wish *I* could see what you see!" He tells her.

She softly laughs. "All I see is an extra person every now and then, not an entire room full!"

David goes to say something, but Gabriel, Bri's new assistant, tells them it's time to go into the ballroom. They face the doors again and David holds his arm out for her, then she wraps her arm around his.

They hear a male's voice speak, "Your Majesties, Your Graces, *ladies and gentlemen*, please welcome Mr. and Mrs. David Worthington, The Marquee and Marchioness of Newhaven."

Gabriel ducks to the side, as the doors open with the clapping and cheering from their guests getting louder. David sees her nervousness, but she covers it like a pro with her beautiful smile.

The same voice says, "Lord and Lady Newhaven, on behalf of everyone here, we would like to congratulate you both and we welcome you, Lady

Newhaven, to your new home here in Newhaven, and to your new country!" Everyone claps and welcomes her.

David had grabbed flutes of sparkling nonalcoholic champagne, handing one to her. "To my beautiful bride!" He taps her glass, and they drink.

"Here, here!" Their guests cheer.

David whispers in her ear, *"May she never regret marrying me."* Kissing her cheek. *"I'm sorry for not warning you about how we would be announced. Forgive me?"*

She turns and sweetly smiles. "David, your *always* forgiven but there's nothing to forgive, My Love. I was only overwhelmed with the enthusiasm." Kissing him tenderly. Setting their glasses down, he takes her hand, leading her to The King and The Queen; Jack comes up to the other side of Bri. The same voice says, "Your Majesties, The Marquee and Marchioness of Newhaven, and her Noble Consort, Lord Carlisle." David and Jack bow, while Bri curtsies to them.

After congratulations are given, Jack stays back and talks with Herst, and his sister, Princess Abigail, along with Queen Genevieve and Herst's brother, Prince Seth.

David leads Bri to the dance floor and borrows the microphone. He begins to explain, "I have a confession to make, *Mrs. Worthington.*"

Her eyebrow raises as she lightly laughs, "Oh *really?*"

"I gained access to your phone while you were in the hospital." He explains.

"Maybe you should explain *how* you got into my phone *before* I gave you the password?" She playfully replies and there is chuckling around them.

"I'll *never* reveal my sources that help me to romance you! Or in this case, adding a piece to our wedding." He grins and she softly giggles. "I wanted to study your music to try to find the perfect song; one you knew and I could get familiar with for our first dance with you as my wife."

Her eyebrows go up and she exhales saying, *"You could've found a few!"*

He raises his eyebrows and smiles. *"Oh, I did!"* There is more laughter. "I noticed you have a playlist with songs from just about every genre, spanning numerous decades." She smiles as she nods. "There were songs from 1940s bands, songs by Elvis Presley, which 'Love Me Tender' is a classic." She agrees. "A more recent would be 'You and Me' by Lifehouse."

"Another great song!" Bri smiles.

"Some of the ones I found will be mixed in this evening, but I just didn't feel any of them say they were 'our song.' So, I went back to your list of playlists and I see there's one in particular that had only a few artists. I figured these must be your favorite artists. I went on a mission to find a song from this playlist to be our first song at our wedding." He cups her cheek. "I found out why George Strait is called 'The King of Country Music' *and* why he's a favorite." She nods, thinking about which song he might have picked. He says, "There were a couple songs I was going back and forth on until I stumbled upon one towards the bottom of the alphabetical list."

"Which one is that?"

"I wanted one that wasn't too common for the first dance, although those are fantastic." He takes her hand and with a loving look tells her, "I went with, *'What Do You Say to That?'*" He asks, "Do you remember the lyrics enough to know which part might've jumped out at me?"

Her jaw shakes and she quietly answers, "There are *two* lines that come to mind..." she inhales and holds it a couple seconds before saying, "but the whole song fits us as a couple."

He smiles and nods through his tears. "Your memory is better than mine because I can only think of one line at the moment."

"All those songs you went through," he nods, "well, almost all of those lyrics, if not all, are stored right up here." She points to her head.

"*Seriously?!*" He's surprised. "There's got to be *thousands and thousands* of songs in there!"

She giggles out loud. "*Not quite that many*, but I guess it's a gift that once I learn the lyrics of a song, they are there to stay!"

"Alright then," he is curious, "what two lines are you thinking of?"

She smiles. "The first line that comes to mind is part of the chorus: 'Love was never really love without you...'" Her eyes fill with tears.

He caresses her cheek. "That's the one I'm thinking of and I'm sure I'll agree with the other one you're thinking of, *which is?*" He wipes her tears that spill out of her eyes with his thumb on one cheek and she quickly wipes the other cheek with her fingers.

She is overcome with emotions, but manages to tell him, "*My heart knows this is real at last...*'" There are audible 'aws' around them.

His emotions overwhelm him, too, so he can only nod and whispers, "*So true!*" He hands the microphone back before walking with her to the middle of the dance floor as the song begins. He holds her close.

Bri whispers in his ear, "*For the record, I'll never regret marrying you because I trust you'll never do anything unforgiveable!*" She feels his arm around her waist giving her a squeeze of a hug.

At some point other couples join in, but they are too into each other that they don't notice right away. She is lost in how they dance so well together. He kisses her lips, then down her jaw and neck.

"*You're so amazing!*" David whispers, then kisses just below her ear, before pulling back to look at her. "This whole night is a continuation of celebrating you," a tap of a kiss, "of us," another tap of a kiss, "of me convincing this *incredible* woman to marry me and to go on this adventure with me," another kiss, "and making me the happiest man alive!"

Bri's arm tightens at his shoulder as she hugs him, resting her forehead to his. "Flattery will get you just about anywhere with me, *Mister* Worthington."

He is softly laughing, "Is it flattery if it's true, *Mrs. Worthington?*"

She kisses him, then looks at him with so much love. "I love you, David!"

"I know!" He winks and she quietly giggles. "Just as I love you, Macushla!"

As the song ends, David soundly kisses Bri again, dipping her before bringing her back up and ending their kiss and dance. David places her hand in Jack's and goes to talk to Herst standing a few feet away.

Jack wraps his arms around Bri, both smiling with so much love, their hearts squeeze for each other. She runs her hand into his hair at the back of his head. "I love you, Jackson Carlisle!" She grins.

He holds her firmer giving her a look of disapproval of using his full first name but smiling, "I love you, *Gorgeous!*" He leans in and kisses her, then he rests their cheeks together.

"If this is any indicator of how life will be with both of you, being loved and adored, and feeling it this deeply..." she looks into his eyes, "I'm *beyond* blessed!" She kisses him again.

"*We're the ones who are blessed.*" He holds her close. They dance, feeling their love between them until the song ends.

In between mingling with their guests, they dance with parents, family, and various guests. One particular guest, The King, asks Bri to dance.

"May I have this dance with the beautiful bride?" He asks with his hand out. Bri smiles and accepts.

On the dance floor, Herst wraps an arm around her waist as his other hand holds their hands out from their bodies; her free hand goes up to his shoulder. She can tell that he is also built, only slightly bigger than David and Jack because he is a bit broader in the shoulders.

Dancing in his arms, there is a sense of power coming from him that she associates with him being king, yet there is something else she can't quite put her finger on. She feels how her body flows with his; *it's effortless.* She loses herself in their dancing so that when the music ends, she is slightly startled when he dips her back.

He smiles down at her and her heart squeezes for him, catching her more off guard. He slowly brings her back up and whispers, "*Are you alright, Darling?*"

"Yes." She nods with a small, nervous smile.

He studies her. "You're not being completely honest with me."

She is intrigued he is starting to read her so well, not really knowing her. Then again, being a 'Musketeer,' should she really be surprised that he can?

"It's more that I'm not being *completely open* with you." She replies.

His eyebrow flicks up a little in curiousness. "*Why's that?*"

"I don't know you very well, Your Majesty."

"We'll remedy that in the future. What else is there?" He asks.

"*It's personal?*" She says more as a question.

He studies her eyes. "If you want me to answer that, you'll have to give me more information."

"No." She simply answers.

He teases, "*I could get you to talk!*" He says and she raises her eyebrow again. "As it was said earlier today, I would hate to throw such an exquisite beauty in the dungeon on her wedding day, *or any day for that matter!*"

"I hear these words, yet there's..." She starts to feel...

"*Like?*" He questions.

"Oddly, that you would never hurt me." She gives him a questioning look. "Why is that?" She looks intensely into his blue-green eyes, but breaks the intensity saying, "I'm guessing it's because of David and Jack."

Herst could also feel his attraction to her intensifying. "*That's definitely true,*" he holds her firm and the powerful feeling she feels from that grip doesn't go unnoticed by her, "I'm hoping we can become friends, too, Bri."

"You assume a lot, *Your Majesty.*" She fails to completely hide her smile.

"You'll learn soon enough...I *always* get what I want." He smirks as if to challenge her.

She raises her eyebrow; she has heard that line not too long ago from Antonio; however, coming from Herst it's different...somehow challenging her to surrender herself to him... "*Your Majesty,*" she says in his accent, but with a snobby tone that makes him cringe, much like David does when she uses his title with the same snobby tone, "there's a reason David and Jack call me a firecracker!" She gives him her own challenging smirk.

He studies her some more and he sees what David and Jack were trying to tell him; the sexiness they were talking about with her. She isn't afraid to challenge him and this *fascinates* him. He is both intrigued and scared...it's like she can see right to his very soul.

When the song ended, Jack had made his way over to them and Herst is relieved to see him; he is starting to feel *really* exposed to her. She goes to curtsy, but he stops her.

"Please, no more of that today. This is *your day*, and now I will leave you with Jack." He kisses her cheek.

"Thank you for the dances." She says and he smiles with his wink. He pats Jack's shoulder, then slips through the crowd.

Bri happily smiles. "Hi, Handsome!"

"Hi, Gorgeous!" He says hugging her.

Herst goes to find one of his 'party regulars' that attends various parties with him. His parents had been pushing him to make one of these ladies 'The Royal Consort,' but now that Bri's lineage has been made known, his mother is pressuring him, to pressure The Worthington's and force their hand, which actually forces Bri's hand. He has talked with David and Jack about his mother's agenda and he *doesn't* want that! David made it clear that if Bri is pressured, she would definitely shut it down and never agree to being 'The Royal Consort.' Above everything else, in order for any of this to work, David stresses with him the same thing he stressed with Jack and Bri: it *has to be* for love! *Both of them* have to be in-love with each other, or David won't support it and neither will Jack.

David told Herst with their last discussion, "Technically, Bri is still a US citizen and will have dual citizenship, at least until her project for her boss is done." He smirks. "Your mother can't insist you force her hand because—."

Herst got a smirky smile of his own. "She is first and foremost a US citizen!" Herst will remember that for when his mother gets pushy again!

It's his mother's fault he is even in this situation with The Queen and his brother. Queen Genevieve fell in-love with Herst's brother Seth while they were all in school together; she was fifteen and he was sixteen. Jack, David, and Herst were about two years older than Seth and James, with Genevieve being a year younger yet and the same age as Herst's and Seth's sister, Abagail.

The *arranged marriage* forced Herst and Genevieve to marry, but Herst has always taken care of his brother and sister since they were kids. He told Seth and Genevieve to continue in their relationship and went as far to make Seth *her* Royal Consort. It's unorthodox for both a king and a queen to have consorts, but he didn't care and no one challenged it because the lineage would still be the same for their children. Herst would seek a Royal Consort for love...*although that's been proving to be more difficult when he factors in his mother.*

Herst finds Eloise, his 'party regular' tonight, and she is *all over* the guy she is dancing with. Prior to today, he would've been jealous enough to go up and purposely interrupt, to 'mark his territory' so-to-speak. But now? He decides not to even mess with it and goes outside to clear his head and think...

After Jack and Bri dance, they mingle their way through their guests, making their way to David. He sees Bri and smiles as he watches her walk up to him.

"Hullo, Macushla!" He smiles adoringly.

"Hi, My Love!" She smiles as her heart squeezes for this wonderful man.

She happens to see Herst come back inside and she sees him walk over to a woman Bri doesn't know is Eloise. Jack had noticed at the same time David did and made a comment about the 'party regular.' Bri asked what they meant and David whispers in her ear. Bri just nods an 'Ah' and moves on to mingle with more guests and family.

They mingle for a while before David takes Bri back out on the dance floor. Herst watches them, as do the other guests, who clap and whistle when the song ends with David dipping Bri into a passionate kiss once more. Herst is taken back when he begins to feel the need to run...*right* to *her*!

Jack dances with her next, holding her close. David dances with Amy, and James politely dances with Katie.

"*You're absolutely breathtaking.*" Jack whispers in her ear. He feels her cheek against his, lift in a smile. "As happy as you both look, it does my heart good to see you look so radiant."

She looks into his eyes. "I'm only radiant because of the love I feel from, *and for*, both of you! I love you, Jack!"

"I love you."

She is relaxed in his arms, just as she is with David. Jack and David are both 'cut from the same cloth,' but there are enough differences that she knows they're cut from *different corners* of that same cloth...which means Herst must be from a third corner.

She pulls back her head and gives him an understanding look. "Jack, if you need a *date* tonight—."

"Don't." He holds the back of her jaw and kisses her. With a determined look, he says, "*Never* say that to me again, please!" He says firmly. "It will *never* happen, and I need you to keep your standards as high with me as they are with David."

She smiles. "*Oh trust me*, I will...it's just that right now—." He puts his fingertips on her lips.

"No, Bri! You'll feel different in a couple weeks! Remember, *I chose this* because I choose you *and us*!" He kisses her again. "I also want us to...*consummate* when you come back from your honeymoon with David. We'll make up for lost time later and it'll be more special for us!"

Katie hears that part and smiles to herself. She thinks it'll be easier to get Jack into her bed with Bri gone on her honeymoon! David comes over and smiles at Jack and Bri. David hugs Jack before Jack disappears into the crowd. Katie follows him as he goes to get something to drink. She starts putting the moves on him; he ignores her and starts a conversation with Seth and Genevieve.

Bri and David mingle with more guests who offer congratulations and well wishes. They continue mingling until Bri's asked to dance; the gentleman introduces himself as Richard McCleary. Bri accepts and walks to the dance floor before David sees who she is dancing with...a womanizer, *only sleezier*.

Richard McCleary begins to talk about himself, talking up his 'conquests,' and Bri recognizes this type of a man; he oozes 'womanizing sexual prowler.' She is confused about that and all his 'escapades' because this man isn't much to look at. He is just an average guy with brown hair, basic brown eyes, she assumes he is the same height as her because she is wearing heels and is a couple inches taller than he is. She didn't get it...there isn't anything special about him at all! He doesn't even a 'ladies' man' kind of charm that can charm any woman they want.

Bri becomes *extremely* uncomfortable. When he whispers sexual things he wants to do, *she shuts it down at once.* "Look, Mr. McCleary."

"Please call me Richard."

"No. *Mister McCleary*, the more you flirt with me, the more it repulses me!" She tells him.

His smile drops has an annoyed look on his face. "I'm only flirting...*Reeelax...*" She feels his hand traveling downward and he has a crooked, smug smile.

"Stop!" She firmly says, although not too loud to make a scene; however, it does catch David's eye, and Jack has been watching.

When she goes to step back from Richard, he grips her tighter. "Not so fast, Luv...this song isn't over!" And he wants to give ample time for the two of them to be photographed together.

"It's *Mrs. Worthington* to you! You have some nerve, *and on my wedding day!*" She stands stiff and doesn't move to dance. "If my theory is right about your womanizing ways, I want to vomit from the images you just told me about and all the women's bacteria that are floating around in your mouth; *not to mention any STI's!*" She can't help doing a small gag reflex but manages to catch it in the beginning and stops it, but her body still shakes in revulsion. "And you *conceitedly think* every woman would be flattered by what you're offering, or why else approach a happy bride *on her wedding day*?!" She looks him over, "Then again, how many women really do take you up on your offer? Typically, the people who brag the most are usually the ones going home alone the most." She sadly whispers, "*Is that you?*"

"*Now who's insulting whom?!*" He angrily shouts, his face going a bit red.

"*It's the disgusting truth!*" She snaps. "No self-respecting woman wants the bacteria and potential viruses you're offering!" Stepping back, Bri shudders more. "*No* thank you! Not *ever!*"

Richard reaches out to grab her, to salvage what he can of his reputation, but it's Herst, very much as 'The King,' who grabs Richard's wrist. "I believe

Lady Newhaven has been trying to rebuff your advances, even though a bride shouldn't have to! So let *me* be *very* clear!" Herst looks at him with a cold, steely look so Richard knows, "Leave The Marchioness alone!" He leans in so only Richard, and inadvertently Bri can hear him, too, "Touch her again, *family or not*, I'll cut your hand off, or worse, right where you stand. Am *I* understood?"

Richard's 'way with the ladies' makes sense now! He is related to 'The King.' Bri also feels her being a 'Direct Bloodline' also plays into his advances with her somehow.

Richard's jaw is clenched as he replies, "*Yes, Your Majesty.*" He has turned several shades of red by this point with the crowd gathering around them. Bri is feeling that power from 'The King' she sensed earlier, which intrigues her more than it scares her.

Herst sternly tells him, "*Now* apologize *to Lady Newhaven for your rudeness*, you *revolting* prat!" Herst lets go of his hand and Richard apologizes. When he leaves the dance floor in a huff, there is soft clapping of approval.

Herst turns to Bri and asks, "Are you alright?"

She gives him an appreciative smile. "I'm fine. Thank you for the rescue. Although, I'm curious as to why you rescued me to that extent?"

"He's a bloody—!" He stops himself. "He never should've been such a problem for you, *especially tonight* of all nights."

She studies him. "There's more to it..."

Bri feels from the Spirit he has already spoken with David about her being 'The Royal Consort.' Maybe Richard knows this and was trying to 'beat The King,' to try to feel superior? It's obvious Richard feels inadequate and uses his connection to The King to fill that void of sorts.

Herst nervously looks away and sees Jack and David. They were going to intervene but stopped when they saw Herst grab Richard's arm. They let 'The King' handle it to avoid making it a bigger scene.

David asks, "Bri, are you alright?"

"Yes." She replies. "Hopefully, that guy doesn't react like Antonio did."

"Antonio?" Herst looks concerned.

"The incident with Antonio, well, that's when we almost lost Bri." Jack says, giving Bri a small smile.

"I don't think it will come to that because where Antonio was too aggressive, *Richard's a bloody coward.*" David tells her.

"*That's the truth!*" Jack states and Herst agrees.

Bri involuntarily shivers. "Men like that get uglier and uglier to me." She turns up her nose. "*Repulsive.*" Jack pats David's shoulder and he walks away with Herst. Bri realizes she had caused a scene and is upset with herself. "I'm so sorry, My Love."

David pulls her to him, so they can dance while talking. "It's okay. *You* didn't cause the scene." He nuzzles her and hugs her, then kisses just below her ear.

Sensing Bri's uncomfortableness, David kisses her lips passionately and she smiles against his lips. "Are you trying to take my mind off what happened, or have me thinking naughty thoughts of you and us?" She grins.

"*Both!*" He smirks. "Is it working?"

"*Almost...*let's try another kiss and see!" She flirts. He smiles into another kiss.

When the song ends, Bri and David were going to get something to drink when Katie comes over; it's obvious she has had a lot to drink. "It'sss *toasssting tiiimmme!*" She does a flourishing gesture to the waiter with champagne flutes. Bri and David look at each other, not quite catching the slurred words.

The waiter tells them, "I think she said, 'It's toasting time?'"

"Ah." Bri says and David nods.

CHAPTER 36

Imperfectly Perfect Wedding Toasts

"Please gather around! It's time to toast the happy couples." The MC says into his microphone. "Now we're doing this *a little* Scottish style, but mainly the awesome American style, which is anyone can toast with good spirit, and to offer their well wishes. *However*, starting things off is Best Man, James! *You're up, Mate!*"

James walks up on stage to the microphone. "Good evening, everyone! Growing up with David and Jack I learned a lot; some good, some not so good, and a few...well, *those* I'll take to my grave." He lifts his glass to David and Jack. Laughter comes from the guests; while David and Jack, who are standing on either side of Bri, nod and raise their glasses back to James. "Since Bri entered their lives, my brothers have taught me by observation an important *double* lesson: true, adoring love *is real* and it's *that* love that brings joy to life!" A tear falls from Bri's eye as she nods. "Bri, there aren't words to describe the love and gratitude in *my* heart for you! You really are an incredible, loving woman, who loves David and Jack with a love that's amazing to watch. You bring Jack and David so much happiness, I can finally let go of my guilt." He is referring to telling David of Ava's unfaithfulness. "I love you three and here's to a long and happy life together!" He lifts his flute a bit higher.

The guests say, "Cheers!"

When James comes off the stage, Jack hugs his brother, then James hugs Bri and kisses her cheek. Then he steps in front of David.

David tells him something else he has learned from Bri. "We own our own actions and decisions. You don't own Ava's affairs! Those are on her! If you knew but never told me, *that* would've been on you." He holds his brother's shoulders with a look of brotherly love. "*And*, if you *hadn't* told me, I would've missed out on Bri!" David hugs his brother. "Thank you!"

James hugs his brother back, getting choked up, but tells him, "I love you, Big Brother!"

"I love you, Little Brother!" David pats his brother's back.

Bri's stomach twists when she hears a drunken, "*Hellooo* evvveryone! I'm Katie Barnesss, bessst friend of the *briiide*. Watching David with *Briii*, I better understand what Bri meant when years ago you said, 'love is a verb.' She had learned in colleggge that love is the vvverb that proves the truth in 'I love you.' Exammmple, being at the hossspital every day while the one you love is recovvvering. It's no matter how intimidating David may seem, it's standing up to him when he's being an absssolute basss—er, jerk."

Bri's head drops and the side of her hand goes to her forehead, like the brim of a hat. "*Oh my gosh, this is mortifying!*" She whispers so only David and Jack hear her. "*It's an embarrassing train wreck!*" Bri's eyes close.

Katie goes on. "The act of love causssing Bri to jump into a noblllle role because sheee can have a 'Noble Consssort' and steal *my man!*" Bri brings her hand down and nervously looks around. She sees Jack quickly going through the crowd, towards the stage.

"David, this has been a perrrfectly beautiful wedding; really, evvvery woman's fairytale dream and *morrre*. You know jussst how special Bri is and hhhow lucky you are to havvve herr in your life. I'd tell youuu not to screwww it up, that Bri hasss such a forgiving heart, but sssince you already treat herrr like a queeen, I think you're prettyyy goldennn."

"Cheers." David raises his glass to her, hoping to end her toast.

Just as the guests are about to join him, Katie starts talking again. "*Unlike meee*, her bessst fffriend, screws up and sheee can't find *an ounce* of forgiveness fffrommm this woman! *I guess* forgiveness hasss to be fffforrr someone she'sss crazy in-love with…riiight, Briii?" She looks at Bri, then takes a breath. "Tooo Daviiid, Briii, and *my Jaaack* sheee stole from mmmeee; congratulllations and you thrrree can go to hhh——." Jack jerks the microphone away.

"Hull—ooo, Ladies and Gentlemen!" Jack says, wrapping a hand around Katie's upper arm and pulling her back; she stumbles that first step. "Most of you already know me. I'm David's better looking best friend and brother, Jack." He winks at James, who is chuckling and shaking his head. Jack quickly whispers into Katie's ear, "*Casually walk off this stage, or I'll embarrass you worse than what you just did to Bri!*" He lets go of her arm and continues on with his toast. "David and I quickly became childhood best friends, and we were inseparable and indestructible, or..." smirking at Carlotta, "maybe that's DEstructive?" She nods and laughs with Peter, as the other guests laugh, too. "Anyway, with long-term friendship comes highs and lows, but we never really had friendship lows..." he looks and sees Katie hasn't left yet, so he gives her a taste of his threat, "unlike a different friendship that seems to have gone from a low, to completely wiped out tonight with one being stupidly sloshed at her best friend's wedding!" She glares at him and he looks back at the guests. "David and I were always best friends, and as our parents say, 'Thick as thieves.'" He lifts his glass to Herst, "Even our King was part of our shenanigans being one our 'The Three Musketeers.'"

Herst raises his glass back. "My best memories are with my best friends and fellow 'Musketeers!'"

Jack chuckles in agreement. "I've been so blessed to be a part of The Worthington Family growing up and being raised by the greatest parents a kid could ask for!" He gets choked up but manages to lift his glass to Peter and Carlotta and they raise them back with tears in their eyes.

"We love you, Son!" Peter says and Carlotta blows him a kiss.

"To find out Bri was a Direct Bloodline was a surprise for about *two seconds*, then it made sense that this amazing woman has connections to all kinds of *royal families*! When David approached me with his plan for me to be 'The Noble Consort,' that he wanted it to be the way it was always intended to be, I was *stunned* to say the least. You see, Bri, David's probably told you more than once that you're the woman of his dreams..."

She turns her head to David, smiling, "He's mentioned it," there are 'awes' from various guests and Bri looks back at Jack, "*and so have you!*" She winks and he chuckles.

He has an incredible smile and says to Bri, "I knew anyone would be so *unbelievably lucky* to love you and *incredibly blessed* to be loved *by you*; but to marry you?!" He exhales a 'whew.' "Now here was David, offering *me* a chance at this same dream!" He looks at Bri so lovingly. "When a fantastically brilliant woman walks into your life, *hopefully* you have a best friend who'll tell you you'd be an idiot to let her slip through your fingers, right, David?" He grins and their guests chuckle.

David chimes in, "And *you* would've been the biggest idiot to let this *incredible woman* slip through *your* fingers, *because you knew better!*"

Jack smiles adoringly at Bri. "Which is why I said I was *all in*, Gorgeous!" There are more 'aws' from the guests. "Bri, loving you, and being loved *by you*, are feelings I can't describe." He holds his hand to his chest as Bri is walking up on stage; Katie had already slinked off. "You have my heart." Bri joins him. "Bri, your love is inspiring. It proves how even imperfect people can be perfectly *and divinely* matched!" He lifts his glass, "Now it's been said that 'love is insanity that marriage cures,' because real and true-love does heal!" He looks out at the guests. "And Bri's heart can heal *the deepest* wounds!" He looks at Herst, then back to Bri. "May you and David be happier every new day than you were the day before!" He hugs Bri close with one arm and smiles wide saying, "I know I am!" He taps a kiss to her lips. "To David and Bri!"

"To David and Bri!" The guests concur.

He puts the microphone back on the stand, then kisses Bri firmly, dipping her back. There are whistles and both Bri and Jack smile against each other's lips looking happily into each other's eyes as he brings her back up.

"I love you, Bri!" Jack tells her with his heart melting smile.

"That's *fantastic news* because I have all this love for you, Jack!" They sweetly kiss and there are more 'aws.' He shakes hands with Henry who has come up on stage next. Henry kisses Bri's cheek and hugs her before she steps off the stage with Jack.

Henry is emotional as he steps up to the microphone and smiles. "If there is *any* scenario where this," he motions all three of them, "could go down in the history books, I'd say you three are well on your way! As you two have discovered, Bri is so incredibly loving and while your love for her will grow, you *haven't* seen anything yet! Wait until you see her fall in-love with her babies..." he chokes up, holding his hand on his heart, "*it's a beautiful sight.*"

He clears his throat. "Good evening, everyone, I'm Henry Bradshaw. My relationship to the couple is quite unique..."

Katie winds her way to Bri, her hair and clothes are slightly disheveled. "What diiid I mmmiss?"

Bri looks over at Katie and sees she's waving to the waiter with her fingers as he smiles at her. Bri holds back an eye roll and refocuses on Henry.

"I'm *also* the groom's uncle, although we didn't piece things together until Bri had introduced us to the new man in her life." He chuckles with the people in the room. "We couldn't be happier they found one another. David, Jack, you're wonderful men and even better ones since you've found her!" Jack happily nods in agreement.

David looks to Bri and lovingly says, "I *completely* agree!" He kisses the back of her hand.

"To Jack, Bri, and David! May you rise to your best selves because from where we're all standing, the love you have for each other makes the other shine! May that love bless you as you grow in love and happiness." He lifts his fluted glass. "Here's to a very unique, but *wonderfully extraordinary life* together!" He winks at Bri and she lifts her glass to him.

"Here, here!" Is echoed.

Now, it is Peter's turn. He hugged Henry on his way to the microphone.

"Thank you all for being here. Being the Father of the Grooms," he looks at Jack and David, "I feel I need to say a few more words. Bri, you're a wonderful woman, mother, and no doubt you'll be a wonderful wife because of how much you already love David and Jack. Lotti and I are convinced *no one* could love them the way you do!" He talks to the guests. "It was Bri who hit David with the reality of who he had become with his proverbial walls up. She managed to do the impossible and had him bring those walls down so he could be the man, and heir, he is meant to be, but lost sight of. David, I've always been proud of you, yet *somehow*, I'm even more proud of the man you've become with Bri by your side!" He takes a deep breath. "Now Jack, you've always loved women and thought loving one would be a disservice to the rest."

"That's because I hadn't met Bri yet!" Jack smirks. There is quite a bit of laughter around the room.

"Ha-ha! Proving my next point." Peter says. "While loving all women can be a great gift, you've seen, *and felt*, that loving one, incredibly special lady with all your heart, is so much sweeter." Jack lifts his glass to Peter and kisses Bri's cheek. "Bri, we'll forever be grateful for you!" He genuinely smiles with tears in his eyes, making Bri somehow tear up more.

"Bri, David, and Jack, you're terrific individuals, but more amazing together! I have an immense amount of love and respect for each of you. True-love is the most beautiful, most precious *and priceless* gift there is! Love brought me together with Lotti, brought two sons into the world, and we raised *three fantastic sons* within that love. Love brought David and Bri together, as well as Bri and Jack, and in front of us today they made promises and vows founded in that love, with faith." He takes a deep breath. "Bri, we're honored you're our daughter and we're excited to have granddaughters to spoil!" Peter smiles at the girls. "Here's to your lives together being full of love and laughter, making it joyful with so many more good things to come!" Raising his glass. "To Bri and Jack! And to Mr. and Mrs. Worthington!"

"Here, here!" All the guests say.

Bri goes up and hugs Peter, whispering, "*You're behind these wonderful men! With all my heart, thank you for setting an amazing example for them!*" He hugs her tighter, then kisses her cheek.

Bri steps up to the microphone. "I hope you'll bear with me a little more today. First, I wanted to thank all of you for coming. Less than a week's notice from when I accepted David's proposal, then to this *perfect* wedding. I want to thank you all for your love and support as we begin uncharted territory, even if we do live in more modern times." She hears light laughter.

"To our parents...you've loved us, prayed for us, fought for us, fought *with* us, then prayed *more* for us, pushed us, hugged us, and were there for us whenever we needed you, *and you still are!* There is no way to even begin repaying that, but you have our love and *deepest* respect and gratitude." She catches the tears about to fall with her fingertips.

"Repay us with *more* grandbabies, Sweetie!" Maggie says this time, with Henry's, Carlotta's, and Peter's enthusiastic agreement; everyone else cheers.

She giggles. "We'll get to that soon enough, I promise! Now, to our siblings...we love you and thank you for being there. No matter how difficult life may be, we know you'll be there just like you know we'll be there for all of you." She looks at Joe. "Like with a middle of the night c-*call*—." She squeaks choking up, managing to whisper, "*I love you!*" Joe mouths, '*Love you!*' She nods and inhales deeply.

She takes a deep breath and smiles as she looks at David. "It still amazes me when I think of you, *David and Jack*, that things will just come to mind. Just now, part of the Song of Solomon from the Old Testament went through my head and I think it sums it up quite well for how I feel for the both of you. It's been a while, but I think it's the...*fourth* verse of the...*third* chapter, I believe, and it goes something like: 'I found him whom my soul loveth: I held him and *wouldn't let him go*.'" She chokes up again, whispering, "*Dang it!*" She 'tsks,' "*So* close." David and Jack get choked up.

She inhales and exhales slowly. "Jack, I'm not sure if you know what David said to me about having a 'Noble Consort,' and it being you?" Jack shakes his head. "David, do you remember?"

He smiles wide. "*Oh, I do!*" She laughs and waves him up; he happily joins her on stage. He explains looking at Bri, "I said to you, 'Call me crazy, but I believe you when you say I have your heart."

"And I said, 'Because you do!'" She adds with a loving smile.

David smirks. "To which I said, 'Good! Now, what will you do when I say I want Jack to be in it?!'" David smiles at Jack and they hear 'aws' around them. "*That's when I knew I had her!*" Bri softly laughs. Jack has tears in his eyes and smiles as David looks from Jack to Bri and mischievously smiles. "There was an unspoken, '*Checkmate!*'" Their guests chuckle.

Bri looks at Jack. "And yet, even with that 'checkmate,' *I* still won!" She smiles as her jaw trembles a little. "I still have *no idea* what I did to have an incredible and wonderful man in my life," she smiles at David, then turns to Jack, "*but two?!*" She can barely get it out in a whisper as her tears flow.

Bri looks out to the guests. "You all have made me feel like a princess today and I thank you for that. David, I can't express my gratitude enough for putting *all of this* together. You never cease to amaze me. I love you in countless ways, My Love, *you do have my heart*..." she trails to a whisper, then swallows hard to push the lump down. "Jack, you're truly in my heart and I love you more for how committed you are to me and how both of you..."

she is so choked up, she holds her hand to her mouth hoping to keep her sobs contained inside her, but she can't finish.

David hands her a tissue and pulls her closer to him. "You've done beautifully, Love, but would you mind if I take over?" He asks so he can rescue her. She shakes her head, handing him the microphone; he kisses her temple and clears his throat.

"Good evening, everyone. I agree with *my wife*..." He smiles at Bri. "It feels *so* good to finally say that!" She nods, still emotional. David continues, "Thank you all for coming and making this day special for all of us. With only a handful of days to put the final touches on this wedding, a huge thank you is extended to all who worked, and are working, to make this day come together in the way I hoped for this wedding," he looks to Bri, "and ultimately, for my bride." He pulls her closer and kisses her cheek. "Knowing how spiritual my wife is, I actually came prepared today." He playfully grins. "Proverbs 31:10-11, do you know it?"

"Not off hand, but I might recognize it if you hum a few bars." Bri replies and there is light laughter around the room.

"Well, I did change a couple words to fit you: 'When one finds a virtuous woman, her price is far above rubies.'" He places her hand over his heart, "'The heart she gave her husband she does safely entrust with him, and he shall take care not to spoil.'" As he expected, she has no words; she just hugs him. "Bri, you have my heart, *and Jack's*," he kisses the inside of her wrist, "and there is a lot more love to come!" She doesn't catch that he is also referring to Herst. "Macushla, I made a promise, *with witnesses*, that first Saturday night. You see, I promised I'd find a way you can be loved more than any other woman in the world. With Jack's love, he's helping me fulfill that promise!" He lifts his glass to Jack and Jack lifts his back. He turns back to Bri, looking at her with so much adoring love. "I'm thrilled to finally call this magnificent and gorgeous woman my wife!" He looks so lovingly at her. "Bri, as we all know, this day wouldn't have happened without you."

"*Nnnooo*, I'm pretty sure you and tradition had a hand in it!" She smirks, gesturing to him and Jack. He chuckles with everyone else.

"I'm talking about your heart, *Macushla*. You're a source of great love and support for me, and for Jack; for all those you love and care about. What you're referring to, well, that's still you and taking a chance on me! On all this!" He cups her cheek. "Most importantly, *thank you* for loving me and Jack the way that you do!" She kisses him fiercely, then hugs him for a long minute, as people lift their glasses to them, then take a drink.

Jack brings a chair over and takes the microphone. Before he can say anything, Bri tells him, "I'm so crazy in-love with you, too, Jack." She kisses him fiercely, only he deepens it as he dips her.

Jack says to the guests, "It's time for the bride to show us *a little leg!*" There is lots of cheering and whistling.

David pulls Bri into a hug and turns her back to the guests. He starts lifting her dress at her bum, bringing the bottom hem up almost to her knees. She shows off her blue shoes and the coins on the bottom. David flirts with her, and kneeling in front of her, he uses her dress as a shield the view of his hands running up her leg and above her knee.

"*Careful...*" she lifts an eyebrow with a smirk, "paybacks, Love..." There is chuckling and snickering around them.

David, keeping his eyes locked with Bri's eyes, slowly tucks his fingers inside the top of the first tartan garter he comes to, then slides it slowly down, taking his time to feel her soft skin along the way and leaving a trail of goosebumps behind. He takes her blue shoe off to slide the garter all the way off.

She says only loud enough for David to hear, "*That* was *incredibly* sexy!"

"For me, too, Love!" He winks.

She kisses him and they laugh as they hear more whistles. Now that they were married and have been together physically, she feels the depth of the fierceness in his love for her *and* their magnetic bond. David no longer needs to suppress it all or hold it back, within reason.

Cheers and applause come as David shoots the garter out into the group of men for one of them to catch. David and Jack's friend, Cullen, tries to catch it, but it hits Herst in the chest and he catches it before it drops to the floor. The guests cheer louder for The King, some of them have begun to wonder if he has his eye on Bri for 'The Royal Consort.'

David sees a second garter and motions to Jack, who smiles. When Jack squats down, Bri whispers, *"How do I keep this one for a keepsake?"*

He lovingly smiles and says, "I got you covered, Gorgeous!"

Jack lifts her dress, just above the garter. He caresses his hands up her legs, kissing her knee. He slides his fingers inside the garter and slowly pulls it down her leg and slides it off.

Jack stands and walks over to David saying to everyone, "I think the groom should wear this one!" Jack puts it on David's upper arm for him to wear, saying so only David can hear, *"She wants one as a keepsake."* David winks at her in understanding, while their guests cheer and laugh.

Next, Bri tosses her red rose bouquet and Amy catches it. She is excited and James goes over to her and dips her into a kiss, adding more excitement and romance. Bri, Jack, and David cheer as they watch. The woman who has become Bri's best friend is in-love and Bri is *ecstatic* for her!

With Bri by his side, David addresses the guests, "From the bottom of my heart, I want to thank all of you for celebrating with us! Let us have three final dances for the evening. For those leaving The Estate, we will have people drive you; for those staying, you will be taken to The Inn from here."

Jack takes the first of the last three dances, offering his hand to Bri and helping her down off the stage. He leads her out to the dance floor and holds her close. As they dance, he quietly tells her, "For the record, I'm never letting you go now that I have you in my life! I'm so grateful to be in your heart; *that's* priceless." He kisses her tenderly.

"Yes, David has my heart, but I picture you both right in the center." She wipes a tear, as her jaw shakes. "I just feel so loved by you and David, but so undeserving of all this." She gives him a sweet loving smile.

Jack takes her hand he is holding as they are dancing and lays it over his heart. Tapping his forefinger lightly on the back of her hand, "Do you feel this?!" He asks. She nods. "My heart *only* beats for you! I never wanted to get married, but my heart fell for you; and when David finally opened his eyes, I politely bowed out. I tried to let go of these feelings I have for you, but my heart was yours *and always will be!*"

"I love you, Jack! And I can't wait for our honeymoon either!"

"Me, too!" He chuckles. "But enjoy your time with David!"

"Oh, I will! Just like when we're together, I'll enjoy it, too; like this dance." She playfully smiles. "I had forgotten there were other people around us." He holds her tighter. "Jack, are you sure you're going to be okay?" She asks, then apologizes. "My apologies. You asked me not to—."

He kisses her with so much love. "I'll be fine. I'm a big boy and not some hormonal teenager, although," he playfully smiles, "I'll be in touch with him in two weeks!" She giggles. "I love you, Gorgeous!"

"I love you, Jack!" As the song ends, she kisses him firmly and he returns it with an embrace.

The King and Queen leave social engagements during the last dance, ahead of crowds for security reasons. Herst comes over and hugs Jack, then Jack kisses Bri's cheek before disappearing into the crowd. Herst twirls Bri once, then steps close to her and they begin to dance.

Jack makes his way to Maggie and asks her to dance, Peter and Carlotta are on the dance floor and Henry is nursing a sprained ankle. Maggie is delighted to dance with Jack again. David hangs back and talks to Henry until the final song plays.

On the dance floor with Jack, Maggie says to him, "It does this mother's heart good to see you all so happy and in-love, Jack!"

"She is an incredibly special woman!" He smiles sweetly. "I never knew it was possible to love someone like this!" Maggie hugs him.

Herst has Bri in his arms, dancing in silence. She feels so protected by this man, so *invincible* with him, but she doesn't really know why. He does some fancier dance moves with her and she never misses a step. The song ends and David makes his way over to them.

Herst kisses her cheek, whispering, "*Until we see each other again, maybe in a month or so.*" He smiles and then kisses the back of her hand. He shakes David's hand and hug each other with their other arms.

David leads his wife in the last dance of the evening. He dances a few steps, twirls her, then brings her in close. After a couple more turns, he laces their fingers and brings their hands to his heart. He kisses her, smiling against her lips when she moans in approval.

He kisses his way back to her ear and whispers, "*I want you, Macushla.*"

Bri smiles and whispers, "*I want you, too, My Love.*" He kisses her in the tender spot below her ear, he feels her shiver and smiles to himself. She does feels him smile and warns him, "*You better stop, or we won't make it upstairs.*"

"That would be quite the show!" He quietly chuckles.

"Or a way to clear the room!" She jokes, then gets serious. "I know I keep saying this, but thank you for this day, David!"

"Seeing you this happy makes it all worth it!" He replies.

She has a playful look. "Let me have about a five-minute head start. I want to put on something that's '*for your eyes only.*'" She bites her lower lip.

He gives a low growl next to her ear. "Alright, but I can't guarantee a *full* five minutes though..." She laughs and kisses him deeply; he dips her a bit.

The song ends and she slips through their guests to go upstairs; speaking to only those that notice her with quick phrases of, 'Thank you for coming!' She sees Jack on her way; he smiles.

She goes up to hug him once more and whispers, "*I'll see you in the morning.*"

He kisses her and squeezes her bum, pulling her closer to him. "You can count on it, Gorgeous!" He watches her go upstairs until she disappears.

When he turns around, he jumps a little; a drunk Katie is right there, two inches from his face. "Feeel like annn after partyyy for twooo?" She asks with her lips puckered out, trying to kiss him.

He stifles the urge to laugh at the ridiculousness of it, *of her and how she looks*! "*Never.*" He removes her hands resting on his chest. He matter-of-factly says,

"And you're drunk." He has never slept with a woman this sloshed, nor does he want Katie in that way. It's been Bri and only Bri since he met her!

"*Commme onnn.* Davvvid and Briii are onnn their way to sommme action. Amy hasss sunk herrr claws into James, so heee's going back to The Innn with herrr." She hiccups.

"Katie, you won't find anything here either."

"*Don't* beee like thaaat!" She falls into him and he steadies her, keeping her physically at arm's length. "I caaan taaake your mind offf...OH, and the thiiings *we* could do that Bri doesn't dooo and sommme 'Miss Goody-Goody' wouldn't even knnnooow about." She stumbles to the side.

"Tread carefully, Katie." Jack warns.

"*I'm* just sssaying, I cannn helllp you forrrget all about her tonight."

"*I would never want to forget about her*!" He snaps. He takes a deep breath, exhaling with agitation. "You may not think my being 'The Noble Consort' means anything, *but it does*!!"

She scoffs and rolls her eyes, "Oh, *come* onnn!" She tries to bat her eyes, but she is so drunk, she squeezes them shut a few times instead of fluttering them. "She doesnnn't even haaave to *know*; it'll be our *little* sssecret!"

He is getting more annoyed. She is supposed to be friends with Bri, *best friends*, and yet she is being relentless in her pursuit of him.

He plainly says again, "Katie, you're drunk."

"*S.S.Sooo*?" She asks as she stumbles into him again; she is not letting Jack put distance between them. "Bri neeeds to share. It'sss a preschool lllesssonnn!"

"Well, the basic preschool lesson *you're* forgetting is not stealing what *isn't* yours." He says and she rolls her eyes. "And we both know if I were that stupid to do anything with this," he moves his hand up and down to gesture her, "you'd be the first to tell her *just to hurt her*! I can't figure out why you're so determined to hurt her?! She's done nothing to you, but you on the other hand—."

Katie may be drunk, but that comment makes her angry. "*I* don't knooow what she'sss told youuu, but *everything* that hhhappened that night, *she was into!* She neeever stopped *any of it!* Afterwards, she was *ashamed* of herself annnd doesn't waaant to admit *she* was veeery much a part of *it all!* Blaaaming me and *MY* boyfriend, but not herself! Oh *nnnooo!* Nooow I asssk *you, how isss that fair?!*" Jack knows she is lying because it doesn't line up with what he already knows of Bri; and what little he knows of Katie by her own admissions. Katie's demeanor changes to more of a seductive approach and she tries flirting with Jack again, only more sexually this time.

Jack has no intention of sleeping with her, nor anyone else for that matter. He is essentially married to Bri and even though she has tried to give him a 'free pass,' he meant what he said; he isn't interested in sleeping with anyone else. But the gentleman that he is, he doesn't want anyone to take advantage of Katie, or any other woman, especially in this drunken state. With Katie this way, the trick will be how to get her to her room safely *and keep her there!* He looks around and sees Stephen, a longtime staff member at The Manor, and waves him over.

"Yes, Lord Carlisle?"

"Would you see to it that Ms. Barnes gets upstairs to her room safely?" Jack asks him, telling him where her room is. Richard McCleary hears this and sneaks up a back way.

Katie scoffs. "I'mmm going with youuu! We have mmmore..." she stumbles again, "goood times *to haaave!*"

"You know what? You should go change out of your dress and into something more...*comfortable*—." He forces himself to say while trying hard *not* to turn up his nose.

"*Ooo!*" She happily smiles and walks to the stairs.

Jack says to Stephen, "Make sure she gets there safely and she stays there. She is incredibly sloshed and we don't want her around someone who might take advantage that; *nor do I want her to come looking for me!*" Stephen nods. Jack adds, "*And we* definitely *don't want her drowning in the fountain out front either!*"

"No, we *definitely* wouldn't want that either! As far as getting her safely to her room, consider it done, Sir. I'll lock her in her room and sit in front of her door the rest of the night if I have to!" That would have made it impossible for Richard to get to her that night if he hadn't snuck up to her room to wait.

"Thanks! I owe you one!" Jack tells him.

"Nah, not necessary. Happy to help ensure someone's safety!" Stephen says as he goes to the stairs and catches Katie stumbling forward. He rushes up to her and steadies her as they walk up the stairs together.

"You're a good man, Stephen!" Jack waves to him.

"See you soon, Jaaack-eee!" Katie says, puckering her lips and kissing the air.

He stops himself from doing a full body shake at the sound of his name. He focuses on helping Henry upstairs to their room, which is across the hall from his room.

It was close to ten minutes when David finally made it upstairs. Bri has already changed into a long white chemise style nightgown and matching robe, she took her hair down and touched up her makeup, even added a touch of perfume.

"Wow..." He smiles with desire walking over to her, he is carrying his jacket and he tosses it on the chair. "I think it's clear by this point that no matter what you wear, you take my breath away..."

He cups her face and kisses her passionately, as she begins to pull out his shirt and unbuttons it. He takes his cufflinks off and sets them aside. She pushes his shirt off his shoulders, and he tosses it on the chair.

She smiles playfully as she runs her hands up his chest. "I think it's clear by this point that I'll never tire of this!" He chuckles softly.

When she goes to his belt, he takes her hands in his and looks into her eyes as he kisses her rings. "Love, will you let me take my time with you?" He cups her face. "I want to get to know every inch of you." She bites her lower lip and smiles. He kisses his way to her ear. "I love you, Mrs. Worthington..."

Afterwards, they get comfortable in bed and David shuts the lights off after setting his alarm on his phone. She catches a glimpse of the time.

"*How early*?!" She asks.

"We have a honeymoon to start tomorrow! So yes, *early*..." he informs her, and she gives him a fake glare. He chuckles, wrapping his arm around her and snuggling up with his wife for a while.

"This day was perfect!" She turns on her back. "Thank you."

"And it's ended perfectly..." He kisses her, then he sees her playfulness.

"*Or has it*?" She kisses him passionately.

"Weren't you just complaining about getting up early?" He asks.

"Right." She rolls him on his back and lays on top of him. "But we won't be getting up early if we never go to sleep!" She teases. He matches her playful smile and pulls her into another kiss...

CHAPTER 37
Perfectly Perfect Beginning

They are dozing off to sleep when David's alarm goes off. He fumbles for his phone and turns it off. He rolls over to wake up his wife, kissing her shoulder and up to her neck.

He kisses her cheek when she says with a froggy voice, "It's still dark out..."

"I'll make a morning person out of you yet!" David tells her.

"How *dare* you say such an *awful* thing to me, *Mister* Worthington!"

He is laughing. "The feistier you are Mrs. Worthington, the sexier you become." His hand travels down to her sheet covered bum. "And now," he squeezes, "I can do something about it!"

"Well, then, expect a whole lot of sexy!" She sasses back.

He chuckles as she turns to face him. She pulls him into a passionate kiss and he moans in approval.

They start kissing heavily when he quickly pulls back realizing, "Are you trying to seduce me?"

"Is it working?" She playfully smiles.

"*It would*, but we have a plane to catch *for our honeymoon, Mrs. Worthington!*" He smiles brightly, making her melt.

He is so excited about it; she decides to put aside her feelings for early mornings. "Well, since you did such a *phenomenal* job with planning yesterday, I guess I *could* tagalong and see what my wonderful husband has in store for our honeymoon!" She smiles and her eyes sparkle in such a way that makes *his* heart melt.

"What is it you say to me? 'Flattery will get you anywhere,' or something?"

"Yes, but it's, 'Flattery will get you *almost* anywhere!'"

He laughs. "Well, with me, flattery will get *you* anywhere...but *only you!*"

"*ooOOoo, fantastic answer!*" She says with a playful giggle.

He kisses her again and pats her bum saying, "Let's get going!"

They get up and take showers, their bags are already packed; she shouldn't be surprised by that, but it's almost like magic that it's hard not to be surprised. He is dressed and sitting on the bed when she finishes getting dressed. She says she just needed to do her hair and throw a little makeup on. When she goes to brush her hair, he comes up behind her and hugs her. Looking over her shoulder in the mirror. "No makeup."

She laughs. "Wait....*you're serious?!*"

"Love, the first time I saw your face at the concierge desk, you didn't have makeup on, and you were the most beautiful woman I had ever seen! At the stables, I had a closeup of you not wearing makeup; you were *gorgeous* and had me all tangled up in knots!" She lifts an eyebrow. "Please?"

"For the record, I did have a little makeup on for my own confidence."

"Will it take long? I only ask because everything that can go to the hotel from the airport needs to be packed away in our luggage."

"Done." She says. He looks at her with his own raised eyebrow. She laughs a little. "I was putting the little bit on as we were talking." She winks and hands him her makeup bag. "Will you tuck this away in the suitcase and I'll finish my hair?" He nodded thinking she'll probably be done with her hair by the time he puts this bag in their luggage. "Done!" She announces. He chuckles to himself.

The family is having an early breakfast and when Bri walks in, the men stand for her. Jack comes over and kisses her, saying, "Good morning, Gorgeous!"

She smiles lovingly at him and hugs him. "Good morning to you, Handsome! Hmmm, I need another word since I also say that to David." She thinks about it as she sits down.

Jack grins. "If he's 'handsome,' then allow me to take 'sexy!'" Everyone laughs.

They all sit and talk while they eat their breakfast. Afterwards, Bri and David hug everyone and says she will send pictures; Maggie hasn't been to Paris '*in ages*.' Jack walks out with David and Bri to hug and kiss her once more before closing the back door of their car. Bri and David wave to Jack from the back window and Bri sees Katie watching expressionless from her bedroom window. '*Is that the Richard McCleary guy*?!' She asks herself but brushes it aside. Bri acts like she doesn't see Katie at all. She has been feeling in her heart Henry is right, that her friendship with Katie is over, but neither one of them wants to admit it. And after last night, she is starting to think there isn't too much to salvage.

David whisks his wife away to Paris to finish watching the sunrise from The Eiffel Tower. He is hugging her from behind. When the sun is completely above the horizon, he reaches into his pocket and pulls out a small velvet box, then he hands it to her.

She is surprised. "What's this?" She asks as she turns to face him.

"Open it and find out, Macushla!" He excitedly says.

"David!" She softly gasps. "*They're beautiful!*"

"Your worth is even far beyond rubies!" David says.

Bri is staring at a pair of diamond studded earrings. The intricate design of the setting holding the stone to the stud post, is the same stretched out Triquetra design that matches their rings.

"Well? Put them on!" He happily encourages her.

She closes the box shaking her head. "David this is too much, I don't deserve these, especially after everything you've already given me and done for me! There's *no way* I can come close to giving you anything close to this in return." A tear skips down her cheek. "And I should've gotten something for—."

"No, Love! If we keep score, it's me that would come up short!" He lifts her chin with his thumb and finger. "I'd give you the world, even the moon, if I could!" He kisses her. "Please, *Macushla*," he opens the box for her, "wear them for me, *just out of love*..." He is so happy and she doesn't want to disappoint him.

She gives him a small smile as she dries her cheeks. She takes out the pair she already has on and puts in the new ones; he closes the box with her old ones inside. She tucks her hair behind her ears to show him. He is smiling with so much love for her, her heart squeezes for him.

"Perfect." He hugs her. "I'm overjoyed to *finally* be married to you, BriaLynn Worthington!" He smiles sweetly at a memory that comes to mind.

"What?" Bri notices.

"I was just remembering when I first saw your name and number on a piece of paper, I had 'BriaLynn Worthington' go through my mind that Thursday and I was frantic to push it out *and keep it out.*"

"And yet, *you still texted me!*"

"Trust me, I know how mental it was, especially knowing what I know now..." He kisses her firmly. He rests his forehead to hers and whispers with determination, *"There aren't words to describe how much I love you!"*

"I feel the same way, My Love!" She says, as they stand with their foreheads still resting together, soaking in their feelings for each other.

"You have so much love to give that it's once again like an overflowing fountain!" He lovingly looks her in the eyes. A gift comes to her mind, but she studies him trying to gage whether he can handle it or not. He sees this and asks, "What's going through that beautiful brain of yours?"

Her eyes get teary. "There's a gift I *can* give you."

"Macushla, you and your love, *loving you,* are *priceless* gifts! That's what I've been try—."

She covers his mouth with her hand. "It isn't an object, but maybe something you would like to know ahead of time."

"Well, considering the timeframe, you can't know you're pregnant yet."

"Funny you should say that because it's related." She tells him. His eyebrows scrunch together as he tries to figure out what she means. "I've seen *our* son." She tells him and she watches David as his emotions overcome him.

"*Our son?*" He can barely speak. "*How?*"

She smiles so lovingly with her teary eyes and she cups his cheek. "I first saw him when I was in the coma, but then I was given those memories back *after* I accepted your proposal and the tradition of a 'Noble Consort.' *Oh, David,* does that young man look like his dad!" She wipes her cheeks. "The second time I saw him, he was standing behind The Bishop at the wedding ceremony and then his two *siblings* joined him. That's when I became the most emotional. The last time I saw them was on the bridge with Jack, right after the ceremony."

"Oh, *wow*, the questions! First, did Jack see them?!" He hopes.

"No, but he heard me talking to them and I told him one of them was his child, it was hard to miss *those* features!" She grins.

"So does he have a son or daughter?" He asks and Bri gives him a smirking nod. "Ha-ha!"

"I *purposely* haven't said." She doesn't say anything about the third child and David wonders if this will be a child she has with Herst, but he's not ready to have that conversation with her yet.

"Did *our son* say anything to you?" He asks.

"Yes." She replies. "I've spoken with our son more than the other two." He tucks the loose strands of her hair behind her ear. "When they were there on the bridge with Jack and me, I was warned not to say much because *our son* reminded me, 'To everything there is a season' but with a twinkle in his eye like his dad and Uncle Jack get, he also hinted that I could tell Jack what I felt and that *one* of them was his child; the resemblance was too obvious."

David smiles. "That had to have meant so much for him to hear!"

"He was speechless." Bri's emotions are getting the better of her and it frustrates her. "*Ugh!* For years, I get teary eyed for things, but since the coma, it feels like I've been getting emotional quicker and it's getting so *frust—*."

"You're empathic, Bri!" She hears Jessica's voice say, before she appears.

"Bri?" David asks with his eyebrows scrunched together.

"You feel so much for people, or with them, sometimes both. Right now, you're feeling yours *and* David's emotional states that it's overwhelming your senses. Don't worry, you'll eventually get a handle on it." David looks to where Bri is looking and Jessica smiles. "If he would like, I can show myself to him, but you have the power to make it where he can see me, or anyone else you see."

"*I do*?! How?!" Bri asks her, but puts her finger up and asks David, "Do you think you could handle seeing Jessica, My Love?"

"Yes! *Absolutely*!" He enthusiastically answers.

Bri looks back to Jessica and asks, "How do I do that?"

"Do you remember being told you have power over spirits?" She asks Bri.

"Kind of, although I'm not sure what that means." Bri admits.

"Well, with that power, you have power over me." Jessica tells her and Bri is surprised. "It will get easier for you to do this, even becoming second nature; for now, I want you to look at David and think about your love for him. Think about how much you want him to see me because you want to share this with him, out of love..." Bri concentrates on that...then Jessica says, "Hello, David."

David sees Jessica for the first time. He smiles, "It's good to see you and meet you!"

"It's good to be seen." She lightly laughs. "Now, Bri, as I was saying, your emotions are such that you've *always* been empathic to a degree, only now it's growing. This is necessary to control your power, rather than your power controlling you."

David is curious. "What power, may I ask?"

"*Power over the dead*?" Bri asks with confusion in her voice.

"You're developing your power over *spirits*; there is a difference. We'll get into that later. Right now, David is able to see me because of this power, this gift, *and* your love for him." Jessica explains. "David, you and Jack will want to help her," he nods, "and the key to her power is love. You and Jack are closest to her, but you're not yet complete." David thinks of Herst, but questions that when Jessica asks, "Bri, do you remember?" Bri nods. "David, your love and Jack's love will help fuel her love to grow; however, *your love* will keep her anchored, yet free; while Jack's love will give her normalcy, yet spontaneity."

"It's what Jack said when we were talking about the chaos of titles and the duties that come with them. That, in the craziness of it all, I didn't want him to feel pushed aside."

"And he said he wants to be the 'normal relationship' of sorts." David says understanding Jack's thinking.

"'The calm *in* the storm.' A place for me to 'recharge,' so-to-speak." She says and he nods. "Yet, I'm sure there will be times he will try to talk me into ziplining through the rainforest with him!"

David laughs. "He's done that! But that was after a breakup of one of his longer short-term relationship a few years ago."

Jessica smiles. "He will be that 'calm in the storm.' He will help you re-center yourself, like re-magnetizing a compass; to find the courage to take '*leaps* of faith.'" Jessica says to David, "Your love will keep Bri 'anchored' when others would be consumed by the power she has been given over spirits. However, the love you and Jack give her will be freeing so she can do the *extraordinary* work she is meant to do!"

David wraps his arm around Bri's waist and says to Jessica, "I'll see what I can do."

Jessica quietly laughs. "I know she's in good hands. Until next time." Bri nods as they watch her disappear.

"She disappeared from both our views, right." David asks.

She giggles, "*Yes.*"

She kisses him before walking to the elevator. He asks her to pose with him for an official picture with The Eiffel Tower in the background.

"This will go on our various official social media pages."

After the pictures are taken, they climb into the car to go to the hotel. David shifts to face her. He runs his hand into her hair and rests it at the back of her head; his other hand rests on her thigh, as he leans in and kisses her. The car pulls up to the front of the hotel and they pull apart when they feel the car come to a stop.

When the driver gets out, she says to him, "I want you, David!" Then she bites her lower lip.

He gives her a smoldering grin. "I know, and trust me, I want you, too!" The back door opens and he says, "Let's go!"

Bri and David walk into their hotel, hand in hand with their fingers laced. They check-in and head up to the penthouse suite. They step into the elevator and Bri stands against the wall on the side as David stands in front of her and presses their floor number. When the door closes, he cups her face and kisses her; their passion ignites as he pins her with his body against the wall. Luckily, they go straight up to their floor with no stops in between.

Inside their room, they pick up where they left off in the elevator. He pins her to the wall again and they passionately kiss some more. She untucks his shirt, but before she can unbutton, there is a knock on the door; their luggage has arrived. They lightly laugh and while David answers the door, she starts exploring their suite.

A few minutes later, David finds Bri out on the balcony looking out at the city and The Eiffel Tower. He hugs her from behind and kisses her neck.

"This is like a two-floor *apartment*..." She notes.

"I did it this way because it's more private, and after being intimate with you already," he smirks, "I'm glad we have the added privacy..." She bites her lower lip. He sees her nervousness from the side and tells her, "Ah, no, Love!" He hugs her tight and playfully grins, "That's a great thing!"

She snorts a little laugh and turns to face him. She raises her eyebrow and teases, "Speaking of privacy, I haven't explored the bed–OH!" David scoops her up and takes her up to the bedroom loft.

That evening, they discuss what to order for room service and Bri goes back out to the balcony and watches the things happening around them. The balcony is made of cement, so she's able to walk out in just David's dress shirt and no one can see below her shoulders. David comes out and hugs her from behind again.

She smiles. "I love you, *Mister* Worthington."

"I love you, *Mrs. Worthington!*" He smiles. She turns her head to kiss him and he kisses her tenderly.

"I knew we spent a lot of time in bed, which I'm *not* complaining, just an observation—."

"But it's hard to believe the sun is setting already?" He sweetly smiles and she nods.

David comes around to the side of her, keeping an arm around her waist. They stand together in comfortable silence for a little while. She kisses him, passionately, and he deepens it.

When room service comes, they sit at the table on the balcony. They don't sit across from each other, but perpendicular to each other to enjoy the view as they eat. They are both hungry and eat for a few minutes with innocent small talk, but after a little while the conversation tip-toes around Katie. David looks at her, wondering if he should ask.

He has a hesitant look on his face. "Can I ask you a question?"

Bri smiles so kindly. "David, we're married, and I don't think there is anything that should be off limits between us if we truly love each other, *especially* since we *have* seen each other naked now." She winks.

He softly chuckles. "*Good point!*" He looks her over. "And with *raving reviews!*" David gives her a smoldering look. "Why do you think we've spent so much time in bed?"

Bri clears her throat and fans herself. "We need to change the subject, or our dinner will get cold!"

"Alright. *Katie.*"

"Well, that's definitely going to be a mood killer..." She says matter-of-factly.

He is surprised. "Jack and I were going to wait until the honeymoons were over to ask, and if you want to wait until then I'll understand..."

Bri shrugs. "I was never really sure when to talk about it, so I just felt the time would be right when you or Jack asked me."

He reaches over and puts his hand on top of hers. "You and Katie don't seem as close as best friends should be..."

She snorts a humorless laugh, *"That's an understatement."* She begins explaining, "It feels like a lifetime ago. She and I were the best of friends and I even moved back in with her when my marriage was ending. She was still in the condo where she and I lived when we were in college. Little can be hidden when you're roommates and Katie had started using drugs again."

"Again?! That's awful! Around the girls?" He asks.

"No, because *at first*, she was just a weekend user and wouldn't touch anything if the girls were going to be around. Then she would just stay at her boyfriend's place. I would talk with Maggie about it at lunch one day, then she talked with Henry that evening. We agreed that when I had the girls, the three of us would stay with them."

"Good plan, but that's not what caused the rift." He says. "Not with your big heart. It had to be something *huge*."

She gives him a weak smile. "When they say you're dealing with the addiction and not the person, they're right..." Bri had stared out at the landscape, lost in thought.

David gently squeezes her hand, bringing her back. "Then what happened?"

Her response is more robotic. "Nothing."

David could tell it was more of a generic response. "Love," he gently takes his fingers to her chin and turns her head to face him, "talk to me."

"I'd rather not talk about it on our honeymoon." She quickly tells him.

"No, Bri. That's just, oh how do Americans say it...a cop-out. Besides, if you don't want to tell me—."

"I will. I—."

"Just get it over with, Love. Obviously, it still hurts, so the sooner you put it out there, the sooner we can do whatever we need to do to help you truly move forward this time."

"You know, I *really* hate it when you have a point!" She glares.

"No, you don't." He replies. "You're getting scared about having to face whatever she did to you again by telling us."

She exhales, "I just wish I didn't have to relive it again with Jack later."

"Hold on." David grabs his phone and calls Jack.

"Jack! Bri wants to tell us about what happened between her and Katie, but she didn't want to repeat it to you later. Do you have some time?"

"I'll make the time!" Jack replies. "Give me five minutes!" He hangs up.

CHAPTER 38

Imperfectly Perfect Ultimate Betrayal

Jack is in a dinner meeting with a client and a couple of people from his team. Jack has them wrap the meeting up while he goes to his car for an important call. David gives him a few minutes, then presses a few buttons and gets the video call set up so Jack can see Bri.

"How's that?" David asks.

"Fantastic! *Hullo*, Gorgeous!" He smiles and sees the top part of David's shirt she has on. "'*Sexy Gorgeous*' is more like it!"

"Hi!" She says with love in her eyes for him. "You sounded a little more British than Scottish just now." He lightly chuckles.

David quickly catches Jack up with the little bit already discussed and then they look to Bri to continue. "Just to warn you both, your feelings for Katie will go *far beyond* hatred. Yet, you'll love Joe more for being there right away for me; as well as Ken, Bill, and the family."

"Now we're even more curious!" Jack says.

Bri takes a deep breath and begins to explain the whole horrible sequence of events. "Katie's boyfriend had been making moves on me for some time. I'm not sure if you know the expression, 'He's a dog!' Although it isn't much of a leap to guess."

"We're aware." David replies.

"Katie was 'Drug Addict Katie' by this point and she didn't believe me when I told her to keep her 'pimp boyfriend' away from me. *Nooot* the best choice of words, which ticked her off and she told me *I* was the one out to jump into bed with him! He eventually convinced her to have an 'open relationship' and I guess one day they made some sort of deal: me for drugs."

"Was this guy her dealer?" David asks.

Bri nods. "Katie tried to convince me to help her out and no one would ever know. I said it's sad she refuses to see he doesn't love her and once he gets bored with her, he'll drop her! In fact, him wanting an open relationship already pointed he was bored with the relationship; he was just wanting to conquer the challenge he thought I was...I tried to stress with her that I was merely a conquest."

Jack thought back to the night of the wedding when Katie was trying to sleep with him. The things she was saying to him...this was the pivotal point in the dooming of their friendship.

Bri goes on to explain, "After he found out from Katie about my 'no sex before marriage rule,' his *sole purpose* was to get me to break that rule for him; like he was some 'stud.'" Bri rolls her eyes. "Katie thought what I said about him and their relationship was funny and for some crazy reason, she tells him! She didn't understand that it challenged his manhood, his 'machismo,' and her laughing about it only fueled it."

"Or did she?" Jack throws out there.

There is silence as Bri takes that into consideration. David gently pats her hand and her eyes flick to his, giving him a faint smile.

"Well, now this guy knows I've figured him out, so he knows he has no 'game,' and with Katie laughing at him because he has no chance with me, this all infuriates him. He would *scream* at me that night with vulgar and demeaning words," she has a humorless laugh, "and Katie was furious with me that her boyfriend was so upset! I didn't know at the time that Henry and Maggie were in the process of buying the condo across the hall from Katie for me and the girls; they thought it would do the girls and I good to have a small move." Bri smiles at that. "Anyway, one night, Katie and her boyfriend came to the condo and they were as nice as could be. To keep the peace with Katie, I played nice and hung around to eat pizza while we watched a movie, but I'd go to my room when he puts on a 'skin flick' to watch." She tries to think as she tells them, "I'm still fuzzy on the details; *I have no idea how they drugged me!*" A tear trickles down her cheek. "Anywhere else, I would've been *super* careful...it never occurred to me that Katie would actually set me up!"

"Oh, Love..." David says, holding her hand again, bracing himself for whatever comes next.

"What did they do?" He asks and holds his breath.

"Like I said, the details are still fuzzy..." Bri closes her eyes trying to remember. "It's bitter-sweet, I guess." She inhales deeply. "I do remember I kept pushing away his advances, as I stumbled into my room, only to pass out. My memory skips to a flash of being handcuffed to my headboard and then another flash moment when her boyfriend says something to Katie to anger her. Another flash is a few seconds longer where he is taking his clothes off and I was able to look around to see where my phone and keys were, hoping I'd remember when the drugs wore off." They continue to listen, but it's hard for Jack and David to stomach. "Then I passed out or blacked out completely; I'm not really sure. When I finally came to, I wasn't handcuffed anymore and had a sheet over my midsection. I slowly sat up, looked around in a streetlight lit room and saw Katie's clothes next to a pile of used condoms on the floor." David pulls his chair closer and hugs Bri. "It's when I stood up, I really felt how *sore* I was. I stared at the disgusting pile on the floor...I just couldn't form a thought. I couldn't imagine what they did, nor what Katie's role was?!"

"Self-preservation, Love." David rests his forehead to hers.

She nods. "It took a minute, but I remembered my phone. I texted Joe to simply 'pick me up out front' and he never questioned it! I swear that man grew wings and flew there!"

> "So that's what you meant in your toast about middle of the night phone calls." Jack notes and Bri nods wiping her eyes.

Her jaw shakes so she takes a deep breath. "I turned off my ringer and snapped a few pictures before I dropped my phone in my purse. I found sweats and a t-shirt and worked through the pain to get them on. I snuck to the kitchen for plastic baggies and individually bagged the condoms. I figured I'd talk to Ken later that morning, but I needed to get out of there. When I came back to my room after returning the box of baggies to the kitchen, I saw their phones on my dresser. I felt strongly I needed to take them and I dropped them in my purse. I had a grocery bag to put all the bagged condoms in and tied it." Her nose is turned up in disgust. "I slipped on sandals and pulled out my phone to see where Joe was at; thankfully, he had just texted he was out front and I slipped out of the condo. I wasn't expecting Joe to be at the front door. He hugged me and asked what was wrong. I said I'd explain when we were in his car; I just needed him to drive me away from there. He would tell me later he was thinking it was just a BFF spat. He knew about everything up until that moment and was already annoyed with her. When I explained what happened, maybe with an extra detail or two I'm not

431

remembering now, I'm not sure...Joe had pulled up to the ER at a hospital within Ken's jurisdiction."

"Good!" David says and Jack was grateful for that, too.

"I didn't want to go in, but Joe sternly and assertively told me that friends, let alone best friends, would *never* set the other one up; they couldn't even fathom taking any part in it!" Bri wipes a few more tears. "I could either walk in on my own, or he would carry me in, kicking and screaming, if need be, because, at the very least, I needed to be checked out."

"And you went in." David says.

"I did. The drugs had worn off enough that I knew he was right." She replies and David kisses her hand. "When the nurse had taken me back to do a rape kit, Joe called Ken and Henry. Joe figured I'd swear him to secrecy, which he would be right, so he needed to call them *before* I did that. Ken and his partner, Bill, were on-call that night as it was, so they were already on their way to the hospital because the hospital had called in about a rape victim...they just didn't know who it was yet. Joe would walk Ken and Bill back to me. Ken didn't——." Her voice cuts off from the lump in her throat. "Ken didn't say a word, he just hugged me tight for the longest time while I cried; Bill would read the hospital notes. When I had stopped crying, Bill traded places so he could hug me while Ken read through the notes. Ken looked at me in shock and asks in disbelief, "*Katie?*" Henry wondered what Katie could have done... Ken didn't want me to have to rehash everything, so he handed Henry the report. While Henry reads, I remembered to pull out the grocery bag of used condoms in baggies and handed it to Ken, as well as my phone with the pictures I took. Then I gave him their phones asking if he could have someone look to see if there were any pictures of me on them and delete them if there were." Bri holds her breath for a moment. "Henry would hug me and I cried hard. He felt bad that he didn't wake Maggie and have her come with him; Joe told him to come to the hospital but nothing more. When Henry did call Maggie, she came as fast as she could! She would hug me in a protective, motherly hug, and I cried the hardest yet..." She looks out at the city lights. "When I was dressed again, Ken would tell me that with all the physical evidence, the rape kit, and all the photos, the police were on their way to the condo to arrest them before they were even out of bed that morning."

"Oh, Love, I wish I knew what to say..." David says slightly above a whisper.

"There's nothing you can say, My Love." She squeezes his hand a little before she continues. "This was back when most people didn't lock their cell phones and anyone could access the information, or pictures, on them. I'm grateful he didn't give me any diseases or infections, probably because he used protection, which most likely prevented pregnancy, but they gave me pills to make sure."

"Good!" Jack says and David nods, clenching his jaw as he stares at the table.

"I do have moments when Katie is around, where something she does or says will trigger a flashback and catch me by surprise, but I've managed to push it out."

"Please tell me this sick bas—er, snake, went to jail?!" David asks.

"AND Katie! *Damnit*! She was supposed to be your best friend, but screwed you over, and for what?! Drugs? And she had the audacity to tell me—." Jack stops himself as he feels his blood starting to boil.

Bri and David don't know about Katie's attempts to have sex with Jack at the wedding, nor what she said about that horrible night to him, but Bri catches that he didn't finish his sentence.

"The audacity to tell you what?" She asks. "I know you wouldn't sleep with her so does that mean she made more desperate advances with you?"

"Sorry. My anger got the better of me. I should've stopped—."

"Jack, it's okay. I know the anger is *towards her*." She says with a little smile. "I'm assuming she kept trying to seduce you the night of the wedding?" He nods and she rolls her eyes.

"She was really sloshed by the end of the night." He chooses not to tell her what Katie said about that horrible encounter, not just yet, and Bri lets it go.

She clears her throat a little and continues with her story. "Yes, charges were filed. The rape kit had DNA from both of them, linking them to the crimes. Back then, I could've had the charges dropped and boy did they try every way possible to get me to drop them; her boyfriend focusing on having me drop his charges, while Katie was working to have me drop both of their charges. Around that time, in the US, they were working to take pressing charges out of the victims' hands so they can't be persuaded, *or intimidated*, to drop the charges of a crime." She takes a deep.

"I'm pretty sure they have something similar to that in the UK now as well!" David says.

"Well, both of them agreed to their own plea deals, with one of the stipulations being they each have to walk through the crimes." Bri quietly cries for a minute and David hugs her. She takes a couple of deep breaths. "I couldn't listen to it all and asked Henry and Ken about it later. I guess the condoms I collected were only a fraction of what they used that night." She tells them, "Whatever drug it was, get this..." she has a humorless laugh, "*they didn't even know what it was!* They were told a person wouldn't remember a thing later." She slightly dry-heaves when her mind goes to the bacteria and bodily fluid. "There is something I can't bring myself to ask her...she knows how sensitive I am to a lot of medications, what if I would've died?"

"Deep breath, Macushla." David rubs her back and she does take a deep breath. "Look at me..." When she does, he tells her, "Deep down you already know that answer, *or you would've asked.*"

She shakes her head, and it tells them she still isn't ready to admit it yet. She moves on. "Katie's sentence was lighter than her boyfriend's and I'm still not sure what to think about that. But Joe and I worked hard to get her into rehab and off drugs. She was angry when I moved out and into the condo across the hall, she didn't understand right away, but she eventually came around that I couldn't put the girls at risk. Bri wipes her cheeks with her napkin. "Katie refuses to see she didn't just break my trust and friendship, she *obliterated* them. I wanted to pretend it never happened, but her recent actions make it glaringly obvious it's envy and jealousy, which led to a rage against me. The more comments she makes and the things she does, like acting out and sleeping around with anyone who would have her at the reception—."

"Wait a second. *Our staff* was sleeping around while they were paid for a job?" He asks, a little annoyed and upset.

"Look, David, let's just chalk it up to the staff being on a break and let it be just that. I don't want to put a stain on that day with the embarrassment of your wife's *so-called-best-friend* 'acting with conduct unbecoming.' *Please, My Love?*" She has a pleading sadness in her eyes.

"*For you.*" David kisses her temple.

"We can also assume that it was probably the temporary staff because your longtime staff would be more loyal and devoted than to do something so reckless." Bri says.

"Good point." David replies.

"Katie doesn't know *I'm glad* she isn't with James *and thrilled* he's with Amy! Unfortunately for her, my loyalties shifted away from her at the time of her *ultimate betrayal*, only to shifted again so my loyalties are now with you two."

"And safe." Jack smiles sweetly at her.

She gives him her own sweet smile. "Amy and I became closer and I've only recently realized Amy has really been my best friend for quite some time now...I'm hoping she and James do get married because it would be nice to have her here permanently!"

David smiles. "James and Amy *are* getting pretty serious." He remembers and asks, "When we were at your condo with McMasters, Ken, and Bill, that first week in DC, was that Katie's old boyfriend who came off the elevator and Ken noted, after you punched this guy and kneed him between the legs, that there would be a homicide, *by me*, if Katie didn't get him into her condo and lock the door?!"

"Yes." Bri states.

"What the—?!" Jack stops himself.

"*Uncle Henry was right*! The smug look he gave you, I would've jumped in and at the very least, broke every bone in that swine's face!" David admits, inhaling sharply and holds his breath to calm himself. Bri gently taps a kiss to his cheek.

"Maybe I should've taken two minutes to get to the bottom of what was going on right then with Katie..." Bri explains. "Maybe I could've—."

"The bottom of a situation that had to do with this same boyfriend of hers who raped you multiple times, *with her help*?!" Jack asks, then blows out a long whistle. "Bri, she's *not* your responsibility!"

David says, "That explains why you wanted the locks changed on the condo and were adamant she didn't have a key. It seemed like there was something more to it, but I forgot to ask you about it."

"Honestly, Love, I don't know if I would've told you then or not. There was a lot going on with Antonio and the fundraiser, plus we just met and, well, I just wanted to spend time with you; I wouldn't have wanted to relive such a dark time when we were just getting started." She gives him a little smile. "Well...that's everything...that I can remember at least." She says to them and takes a deep breath and exhales.

"One more question, Bri?" Jack asks.

"Alright." She replies.

He curiously asks, "Did this guy spend *any* time in jail?"

"Yes, but I don't remember how many years because he was paroled for 'good behavior.'" She rolls her eyes.

"Would've been nice if it was more?" Jack comments.

"Yes, it would've but then there would've been a trial and being the 'Liaison Officer,' I didn't want everyone knowing the details of what happened to me; *I didn't want to know all the details of what happened to me!*" She answers. "With Katie and her boyfriend having to walk through what they did in detail; Henry somehow got those records sealed."

"Well, thanks for telling us. She leaves tomorrow and I only have to avoid her one more day, so I won't say anything you might regret—."

"I don't really care if you say anything at this point." She sits closer to the screen. "I'm just sorry she's there at all."

"Don't be. Like I said before, I'm a big boy. I'll be fine." Jack tells her. He sees the sadness in her eyes. "Just forget about her and enjoy your time with David in France!"

"I'll always worry about you, Jack, just like David. It comes with loving you!" She smiles.

Jack and Bri say 'I love you' before they all say goodbye.

Bri and David finish their meal and David shows her their dessert. She laughs, "I love it! A simple cupcake! How did you manage..." she gasps, "*Mister Worthington*! Did *Lord Newhaven* make a special request?!"

"I will *not* reveal my secrets!" He takes icing from the cupcake and puts icing on her lips and kisses her. He playfully grins, "Are you up for some fun?"

"I am, but after we finish this fantastic cupcake!" She scoops some icing on her finger.

He grabs her wrist and puts her finger in his mouth, then sucks the icing off it...he smiles seeing her face. "The cupcake is yours to eat, but the frosting..." he stands up and pulls her to stand up with him, wrapping his other arm around her to hug her close, "now that's mine to do with what I want!"

"I'm intrigued." She kisses him, then he scoops her up to carry her to the bedroom for the rest of the night.

CHAPTER 39

Perfectly Perfect Paris Honeymoon

The next morning, David asks if there is anything in particular she wants to do. She rolls him over and looks down into his eyes.

"*You* look like a man with a plan..." She kisses him. "*Count me in!*" He laughs and playfully slaps her bum.

They get ready and, as usual, David is ready before Bri. He uses that time to make an appointment before their reservation, plus he has a specific dress sent to their appointment, along with a suit. When Bri comes out with her purse, he smiles lovingly at her.

"You're as beautiful as ever!" He kisses her sweetly.

She smiles adoringly. "Thank you, Handsome!"

He takes her hand and they walk into the hall; David has arranged to meet up with their own security at the elevators. Bri does a double-take and her mouth falls open.

"McMasters?!" She says surprised. "It's *so* good to see you!" She hugs him. "What brings you here?!"

"*Your husband!*" McMasters chuckles a little as he hugs her back.

"David?" Bri asks, still pleasantly surprised.

David explains, shaking McMasters' hand. "He was *going to* retire but hated the thought of sitting around all day collecting dust."

"So, you think we'd be more exciting?" She giggles, "Let's hope not!" The elevator doors open, and they get in.

"Well, I was wanting to retire, but not completely. I was looking into doing security for a business. I got to talking with David, er, Lord—."

"Our first names are fine, McMasters. It's only at official engagements *you* may want to go formal but to tell you the truth, the fact that you're protecting my beautiful wife," he looks at Bri, "that's *always* going to be personal and never 'just business.'" He gives her a peck on the lips before the elevator doors open.

As they walk through the lobby, Bri wants him to finish his story. "McMasters, you got to talking with David *and...*?"

"He and I got to talking when you were in a coma about retirement. He asked if I'd ever consider moving to Newhaven?" McMasters replies.

David says, "I asked him if he'd consider working for us, being in charge of *your* detail?" McMasters is also aware of the interest in Bri as The Royal Consort, but that David and Jack haven't talked with her about it yet. "McMasters said his wife wants to do some traveling and I said she can travel with him when we travel, whenever she wants, and if there's somewhere she wants to go while he's away or they want to go together, we'll help with those arrangements as well."

Bri smiles wide. "*She* must've agreed to the terms because here you are!" He laughs and nods. "Wait." She wonders, "How does this work, exactly?" They walk out front and David has her slide into the short limo.

When they are all inside the limo, David explains on their way to their first stop. "Right now, I have McMasters strictly for you and will drive you, as Paul does for me." David holds her cheek, "Anywhere, and I mean it, Love, *anywhere* you go, *he* goes! You two will develop your relationship where he is first and foremost more loyal to you than to anyone else, *including Jack and me.*" He looks to McMasters, still talking to Bri, "And that's okay! That's how it's supposed to be." McMasters nods in agreement. "You'll get so accustomed to him being there that you'll feel weird if he takes time off and someone is else is there in his absence."

"So right now, Paul is more loyal to you than me?" She asks.

"*That's just it*, my wife is becoming more loved by our staff than me, so Paul is probably more loyal to you already!" He laughs and kisses the back of her hand. "That's okay, too!"

The car door opens and they are in front of a store, 'La Bijouterie.' A few people stop to see who is climbing out of the limo and Bri is still focused on the building, she doesn't hear them say her name at first.

Eventually, she hears, "Lady Bri!" She looks and sees four ladies wave and Bri smiles, waving back at them. They snap a few pics and off they go. Bri feels David take her hand again, lacing their fingers together.

"David, what does, *La Bijouterie*, mean?"

"*La Bijouterie* means 'jewelry store.'" He replies.

The meaning doesn't sink in right away. "Wow! I love how it rolls off your tongue." She smiles wide.

He quietly laughs and they go inside. They walk up to the counter, as 'jewelry store' sinks in. There is a man and woman waiting for them.

"Ah, Lord Newhaven! And zeest must be your bride, Lady Newhaven!" He bows slightly from the other side of the counter. "Monique will take you in zee back and 'elp you weeth your dresses."

Bri looks to David and he says, "Before you say a word, will you please indulge me, the man you love?"

"*Ooo*," she playfully glares and points her finger upwards at him, "*SO* not playing fair!" Bri says this while the others snicker. "I could throw that back and say *because you*—."

David kisses her, even deepening it as he dips her a little. He keeps her there until he feels her relax in his arms, then brings her back up. "*Because you love me*, you won't throw any words back at me right now." He winks.

She tells him, "I'm starting to not like you!" She tries to hide her smile.

"No." He says in a bit of a commanding voice, "What you don't like is *me* having the upper hand."

Bri smirks. "Oh, I don't mind you having the upper hand," she leans in and his arm hugs her firmer as she whispers in his ear, "*as long as you're on top*."

His breath catches and he smiles playfully at her. "How do you do that?!" She raises her eyebrow. He holds her tight against him saying, "*Take back* the upper hand?!"

"A gift!" She lightly giggles. "Just leveling the playing field."

"Leveling?! Ha, ha! *No bloody way!*" He rests their foreheads together. "You're too fantastic for that to *ever* happen!"

He takes her hand, as they follow Monique to the back. Monique shows them fruits, breads, cheeses, and champagne, which she mentions is the nonalcoholic brand David requested.

"This champagne tastes amazing!" Bri exclaims. "It reminds me of what we had at the wedding."

 "We did have this at our wedding, Love!" David smiles as she looks at the logo on the bottle, trying to read the slogan quietly to herself. David reads it out loud for her: "Vigneto Toscano: Una Relazione Amorosa con l'uva."

"How is it I look at that and see 'foreign language,' but hear it from your lips and want to swoon?" She grins. "What does it mean?"

He lightly chuckles. "Tuscan Vineyards: A Love Affair with Grapes." He hears Bri repeating, 'Vigneto Toscano,' to herself. He whispers, "*Sounds beautiful from your lips, too.*"

Bri tries on a fun, mauve-pink, knee-length, short-sleeved chiffon dress David had arranged to be there. While she re-fixes her hair and adds matching shoes, what she wore to the store is boxed up to be sent to the hotel with anything else they buy. They added a square and a pin-striped tie to David's suit that matches the same mauve-pink color of Bri's chiffon dress.

 David has Bri close her eyes as Monique helps put in her new earrings and he puts on the necklace for her. She looks in the mirror and has tears in her eyes.

"David," she lightly touches the necklace around her neck, "these are absolutely stunning, but—."

"No, *Love*. No, 'buts'..." He cups her cheek. "Hearing you like them makes me *very* happy, so add 'thank you' and it will do my heart good!"

She hugs him tight and he hugs her back just as tight, lifting her a bit off the floor. It is a diamond necklace that has her thinking of snowflakes with a bigger 'snowflake' cluster in the front and the snowflakes taper down in size as they go to the back; each earring has one snowflake cluster.

She whispers, "*I'm still not used to being spoiled, especially with this much money, but...*" he sets her down, "*thank you.*" She smiles.

He holds her face. "You've been mistreated for so long with words, actions, or both, by some of the people who should've cared most about you, your feelings, and your well-being. *That's all over*! You're loved, Macushla! And that's how you'll be treated *for the rest of your life*! And forever into eternity!" He grins and she lightly giggles.

She looks around as she says, "I'm *really* not comfortable with all this, David."

"Would it help if I said my business finance manager suggested it?"

"May—*waaait a second*! No!" It clicks who his finance manager is. "*Jack didn't tell you to buy all this*," she gestures herself, "*and whatever else your concocting in that brilliant brain of yours*!" She points to the counter where the jewelry is laid out. David smirks with a 'wanna bet' eyebrow lift. "*Ugh...*" Not wanting to argue, she concedes and plainly asks, "What else are you going to buy?"

"That's the spirit!" He leads her over by the hand, not seeing the reluctance on her face. "We all think navy and royal blue are two of your colors, but the reds and darker pinks are, too." He looks her over and smiles. "So, we've matched up some pieces with dresses. First, Mother sent The Newhaven Tiara and Necklace to The Royal Jewellers to be cleaned, tightened, reinforced, etc., and whatever else is needed."

 The Newhaven Tiara has different sizes and shapes of diamonds, rubies, emeralds, with a focus on sapphires; a large oval sapphire sits as the focus at the center of the tiara. The necklace set looks like one V-shape cluster of pieces, roughly the same size of diamonds, emeralds, rubies, and sapphires; a smaller oval sapphire sits at the center of the 'V.' The matching earrings have a cluster of the same thing as the necklace. They each have a small oval sapphire at the center and surrounded by a cluster of diamonds, emeralds, and rubies.

"Here's one possibility to go with that jewelry." David points to the dress.

Bri walks over to take a closer look at the dress they just laid out for her. The dress is a navy-blue, short sleeve, full-length gown, with it loosely flowing from the curve of her hips to the floor. He smiles when he sees he is right about the dress.

"The little bit darker pink dress is a favorite and it matches the necklace that I saw and I said to myself, 'That's *Bri's* necklace! *And see*," he moves the necklace next to her to show her in the mirror, "those earrings can work with this as well."

"These snowflake-looking ones?" She asks touching her ears and looks in the mirror...then she agrees.

 The necklace is made of a long cluster of diamonds in a curvy-V shape of sorts, one-inch wide, with a large emerald-cut pink sapphire gem dropped down from the middle. He has a huge smile and she thinks, *He really is enjoying this.*

The dark pink dress has cap sleeves, a straighter neckline, and it fits to her figure. David sees her looking at another necklace that would also match nicely, maybe better, with the neckline of this dress. He holds it up to the dress for them to have a better look and everyone agrees that it works better with the dress. It has ovals of darker pinks, squares of lighter pinks and orange, and small, round diamonds sparsely mixed in. If she heard correctly, they are all lab-created sapphires and diamonds.

"You have amazing taste, too, Love." He smiles. "I love the colors and I think you do, too!" He has a knowing smirk on his face.

"I do love color in many things! Let's hope my taste isn't as expensive as yours!" Bri nervously smiles.

David whispers a reminder of what he hopes she needs to hear. "*Our* assets are well into the trillions. Liquid is in the millions and it wouldn't take much to replace any liquid funds if I needed to. Jack has much more because he's *truly brilliant* with money." He pulls back and asks, "Does that help, Love?"

She shakes her head exhaling, "*No!*" Her eyebrows come together and she asks him, "How can you be so calm? Do you do this sort of thing so often that you're used to it?!"

"This is my first time *and I'm really having fun!*" He gives her a genuine and beautiful smile. "*Breathe, Love.*" David whispers near her ear.

There is a knitted navy-blue dress the store sends over thinking it's more casual, but it would look great with her body shape; they were right. It has a cowl neckline, which happens to be one of her favorite necklines, and it's in quite a few things she wears, as well as V-necks.

"I do love this..." Bri says to them, turning different ways in the mirrors.

"This more *simple* necklace of channeled square-cut sapphires with diamond haloes would go nicely with this." David suggests.

She shakes her head laughing, "'Simple,' *you're cute.*"

"Love, perhaps *your* 'simple' needs to change." He smirks.

"*Not a chance!*" She defiantly replies. "*Yours* needs to simplify!"

"*Not a chance in Hell!*" They chuckle and he moves on. "So, we have a couple of balls coming up. The tradition of going to a formal dinner at The London Palace is one I'd like us to start with. It's called The Stately Dinner where members of Parliament, along with the governing members of all the duchies, such as dukes and duchesses and their heirs. It will help familiarize you with people we will be working with." He explains. "The second one is our Halloween ball of sorts, it's called 'The Midnight Ball.'"

"Does the ball start at midnight?" She wonders.

"No, it ends at midnight." He answers.

"Ah, so we really should end the party a little early, so the 'Cinderellas' of the evening can make it home before their carriages turn back into pumpkins." She then playfully adds, "But they better bring their own prince!" She grins.

"Oh? Why's that?" He is being coy.

She teases back, "Jack's taken, *of course!*"

He steps closer with a smoldering look, running his finger across her collarbone. "Is that your *only* answer?"

She has a flirty look. "Well, you're *definitely* taken!"

"*Much better!*" He slides his hand around her waist.

444

She leans into his ear and whispers so low she can't even hear herself whispering things that are '*for his ears only.*' She hears him hold his breath and feels his arm hug her closer.

He clears his throat and gives her a smoldering smile before leaning in and whispering, "*Vixen,*" in her ear and she bites her lower lip. He gives her a pointed look. "*No more stalling* and back to the task at hand."

"*Oh, of course...*" she says with a little sarcasm.

He lifts his eyebrow, then pulls her close. "We *want* to buy these things for you, Love."

"You and Jack are coordinating this?" She rolls her eyes and says with more sarcasm adds, "*Great,* something to look forward to with him..."

"Well, I'm afraid we wouldn't look *a fraction* as good as you if *we* wore these pieces!" He teases and everyone around them lightly laughs.

She scoffs. "*You're* being impossible."

"I know." He happily grins.

"Do you buy all your jewelry here?" She asks.

He gives her a '*you should know by now*' look. "Before you, I bought the occasional gift over the years, usually for Mother's birthday but sometimes for Christmas and a few things for Ava; *nothing like this.* Ava has her own collection she is *really* proud of and usually brags about it to anyone who will listen." He notices they're alone and tells her, "Herst is into jewelry designs. I asked him to take a look at your engagement ring sketch and he made it at The Royal Jewellers for you. I also explained what I wanted for the wedding bands and it all turned out beautifully!"

She lovingly smiles as she looks at her wedding set. "*I wholeheartedly agree*! He did a wonderful job!" She adoringly looks up at him. "I love them!"

"I'm hoping more of your pieces will come from his designs." David says.

"Well, since he is king, I can find relief that he's probably too busy to make too many pieces." She smirks.

"*Don't be too sure*. It's cathartic for him." He kisses her, then grins when something else comes to mind. "I could also say this is all an investment."

Bri rolls her eyes. "These aren't what I can wear every day, so it seems like a waste for any kind of *investment*." She teases with his accent.

"They're meant for you to wear when it's expected, like a ball or a public appearance." He tells her.

"What does it matter if I wear them just being somewhere—*OH*, because that's what the public expects of their Duchess, which will one day be me!" She says with a small, embarrassed smile.

"Right! But they do expect to see fancier jewelry during the day from ruling duchesses of prominent duchies, and of course royalty. So, while they expect to see more impressive pieces on you, soon-to-be a prominent duchess, it would be bad form to see it on the ladies down through the noble titles, including duchesses that aren't ruling a duchy either." He kisses her temple sweetly. "Now, 'The New Year's Holiday Party' is another ball. The dress is still in the works, but I have a picture of a colored drawing." Bri's mouth falls open as she looks the details over.

The short sleeve ballgown is a V-neck of lace over the top of a sweetheart neckline of the bodice; lots of sequins and rhinestones cover the dress from the bodice and around her hips, scattered in a whimsical pattern all the way down and there is a rhinestone belt around the waist. The color of the bodice is lilac from the top and through her hips, then it gradients to darker shades of purple, to an *almost* black with the darkest purple at the bottom.

"*David...*" She whispers but goes quiet.

He sees her holding her breath and smiles. "It's beautiful, isn't it?"

Bri shakes her head, whispering, "*Stunning...*"

"It'll be stunning with you in it!" David says. "We don't have jewelry for this yet..." He sees Bri's nervousness. "*Love?*"

She can barely whisper, "*This is all too much...*" She swallows, handing the picture back. "*it's overwhelming...Please.*" She shakes her head, wiping the corner of her eye before a tear escapes.

David gives her a compassionate look, "Monsieur, let's just box these up." David motions what they've already talked about. The gentleman also looks at Bri with compassion and nods with a kind smile.

While David signs for everything, Bri catches her breath and goes to talk to Monique. "Would you be able to do something for me, well, for David from me? Would you be able to engrave something on the back of his watch before you're done with it?" David is having his watch annually cleaned and looked over while they are in Paris.

"*Why ov' course!*" Monique happily replies. "What would you like eet to zay?"

Bri says, "*Mon coeur est à vous!*"

"'*My heart tiz yours!*'" Monique excitedly whispers. "*That tiz beautiful!*"

"Oh," Bri quietly says, "and please add a wavy dash with 'Macushla' after it."

"Yes, Madam." Monique smiles as she makes a note of it.

Bri goes to hand Monique her bank card, but she lowers Bri's hand. She explains how they do engravings at no charge for pieces bought in their stores, but with the purchases today, even if the watch wasn't purchased from this store, they still wouldn't charge anything for the engraving.

Bri smiles. "*Merci!*" Monique smiles and nods before she walks away. When Bri looks back at David, he is walking over to her with an adoring look and taps a kiss to her lips.

They all say goodbye, with David and Bri thanking them for their help. They walk out of the store and climb into their limo that has been waiting for them. They pull away from the curb and David sees Bri staring out the window.

"Hey," he takes her hand and gives it a squeeze, "is everything okay?"

She looks at him and smiles. "Just thinking about a set that was made with black and white diamonds."

He gestures towards the store. "We can go back and—."

"*No!* No, no. It's not that! It just gave me an idea about a 'black and white' themed fundraiser." She tells him.

He smirks. "Sounds like that necklace set *inspired* you."

"*Don't get cocky!*" She sternly tells him.

"I'm only pointing out that buying jewelry doesn't *have to be* a stressful event." He smiles. "Oh, but for this fundraiser there will be *no* auctioning off dates! Because if I'm taken for the Cinderellas, you're *definitely* out of the running for *any* bidders."

"Just make sure you or Jack are the highest bidder!" She teases.

"*You're not even on the auction block!*" He looks at her with love and desire.

"And I'm *very* happy *not* to be!" Bri winks.

"*Fantastic* answer!" He grins.

"Seriously though, I'm not exactly sure why, but I keep thinking, 'It's not all black and white.' Then I'm thinking about a fundraiser to help victims or their families...or something that helps with second chances...I'm still brainstorming." She looks at him with an excited look. "*What do you think?*"

"I think I'm married to an incredibly brilliant and beautiful woman, whose intelligence is the only thing that rivals her beauty; but *nothing* surpasses her heart!" He sweetly says. "I'm confident that whatever you come up with will be perfectly brilliant!"

"Yeah, but for what foundation or charity? There are so many to choose from!" She says.

"I have no doubt you'll figure that out, too!" He smiles.

They pull up to a beautiful theater and get out of the limo. David holds Bri's hand, fingers laced, as they walk inside. There is an orchestra gathering and The Maestro comes to greet them. He and David speak French to each other and Bri looks around noticing they are the only guests. The Maestro greets her in English and bows a little as he kisses her hand before she and David make their way upstairs to their balcony seats.

Once sitting in the balcony, Bri and David get comfortable. She looks at him and asks, "What's this all about?"

"Jack and I have known The Maestro for years. His orchestra has played in some of the most well-known operas and in famous opera houses all over the world. I'm not a huge fan of the opera singing, but I can appreciate a good symphony, or few; and if I had to guess, I'd say you would at least appreciate the talent that's gone into them as well."

"Oh, *absolutely*!" She smiles.

"I can look into an opera if you'd like..."

"You mean you'd suffer through for me?" She teases with her hand up to her chest and batting her eyelashes.

"*Yes*." He grins. He holds her hand on his thigh, rubbing his thumb back and forth over her soft skin.

She giggles. "Thank you for the thought, but honestly, I like maybe one opera song out of fifty. I have sensitive ear drums, which makes for great hearing; *however*, a lot of high-pitched notes can be physically painful to my ears. I wish it weren't like that because I do appreciate the fine arts...I just have to appreciate some of it from afar." He smiles in understanding. They listen to the various symphony arrangements until intermission. "David, is this a dress rehearsal?" She wonders.

"It's a performance for my beautiful wife, The Marchioness of Newhaven."

"So, the dress and suit were for this?" She asks.

"This and where I'm taking you for dinner."

She smiles with excitement, "*And that is*?"

"*Another surprise*." He smiles so adoringly she leaves it at that.

She leans into his ear and tells him, "*Keep smiling like that and I'll melt into a puddle right here*." She kisses his cheek. She sits back down as the intermission ends and the orchestra begins again. When the orchestra finishes their performance, she asks, "Can we go down there and thank everyone?"

"I think they would appreciate that." He says.

They are on their way to their dinner reservation. It's starting to get dark outside and Paris starts to take on a magical feel once again with all its lights. David purposely keeps her distracted so that when they pull up and climb out of the car, she doesn't notice where they are. As she looks around, she sees steel beams and thinks it's odd, until it clicks.

"The Eiffel Tower?!" She excitedly looks up.

"Is this okay?" He asks. "I would've brought you to the restaurant the other times we were here, but the timing never worked out."

"David Christopher Worthington," she wraps her arms around him, "you know I'd be happy being *anywhere with you*, even on a deserted island; though," they step into the elevator, "I do have to say, I love this idea!" She kisses him with a tenderness that squeezes his heart for her. "I can't describe to you how I've felt all day today...so overwhelmed at times, undeserving all the time!" The elevator dings as it slows down. She looks lovingly at him. "But deeply loved and adored by my handsome husband *all the time*."

"Because you are!" He winks as the doors open.

They're seated at a table for two with the best view of Paris in the restaurant. Bri hears, "Lady Newhaven," and sees the chair is pulled out for her.

"Merci." Bri says. The man smiles and bows his head just a bit.

David discusses how they serve dinner since their menu is more laid out, rather than having all kinds of choices. They eat their courses watching the city lights get brighter the later it gets in the evening.

On their ride back to their hotel, they're seated comfortably in the back seat. "This was just wonderful, My Love." She kisses his cheek. "Another perfect day with you!" She smiles.

"I have a few ideas for an absolutely perfect night!" He grins.

"Can't wait!" She bites her lower lip.

Their first week flew by! Their time is filled driving around and sightseeing, or taking a train to see more of France, not to mention lots of time in their hotel room as the honeymooners they are. On their last day, David asks if there is anything Bri would still like to do?

"I don't know...we've already done what I wanted, and so much more!" She playfully asks, "Want to know what my very favorite thing to do with you is?" She sees a smoldering look on his face and she giggles, "*Outside of that!*" He cups her face and she tells him, "*Just* being *with you!*"

"So, if we found a local deli and went to a park to eat, reminiscent of our first date in Dunfermline..."

She lightly giggles. "I'll love it! Then we can come back here and *stay in*?" She gives him a kiss before getting up.

David props up on his arm and watches her get ready. He is sitting on the bed by the time she comes out in her new coral dress and the snowflake-looking diamond jewelry set. She sees him watching her, smiling to himself.

She asks, "What are you smirking about this time?"

"That I was right! Diamonds make you shine that much brighter!" He answers. "*And* I'm thinking about how *I'm* the luckiest man in the world!"

"You're a handsome charmer, you know that, right?" She asks. "And *yes*, you are lucky!" She leans down to kiss him. "Now, you need to get ready, too!" She knew David had been up before her to get his exercise routine in, then showered before she woke up. He snuggled back into bed with her for a while. He kisses her once more before standing up, then going into the bathroom.

It doesn't take long for him to get ready. He is putting on his watch and it slips. When he catches it, he sees something etched on the back of it. He flips it over and reads:

"*Mon coeur est à vous ~ Macushla.*"

David's a little teary-eyed when Bri walks out of the closet with her shoes; she sees he has seen her surprise and is walking over to her. "I know it's your favorite, and I probably should've asked before I had it engraved—." He kisses her fiercely, holding her jaw.

"I love this and I love that it's on the back of my watch I wear all the time!" He kisses her again and hugs her. He says determination, "*I love you*!"

"I love you, too!" She says returning his hug and kisses him again.

He reaches down and picks her up, so she wraps her legs around him. They kiss passionately as he takes her to the bed...

CHAPTER 40

Imperfectly Perfect Jump

When they fly home, David gives Bri a medium sized velvet box. She pauses before she takes it from him.

She suspiciously asks, "*What did you do,* Mister *Worthington?*"

"Open it and find out." He handsomely grins.

She opens it to find the black and white necklace set she had seen in the jewelry store that one day. She stares at it for a long minute... She can't believe it's the right necklace set!

"H-How did you know which set?" She looks at him with her eyebrows scrunched together, "I *purposely* never gave you any details..."

He smiles. "I have my ways." He kisses the rings on her finger. "Love, the inspiration it gave you was beautiful! How could I *not* buy it for you?!" He gestures the set telling her, "They *earned* the right to be part of your jewelry collection!" She snorts a little laugh, rolling her eyes.

Bri gets up and straddles him to hug him firmly. "I love you, David!" She kisses his neck. "Part of me wishes you wouldn't spoil me so much, but *all of me* loves you anyway."

He lightly laughs and she feels him hug her tighter. "Well, *get used to it*! I plan on spoiling you forever, *Mrs. Worthington!*"

She sits back and smiles with teary eyes. "I love you, *Mister* Worthington!" She kisses him fiercely and hugs him again.

"*I love you,* Macushla!"

When they pull up to the front of The Manor, David gets out of the car first, then helps Bri out. The family, including Amy, were waiting out front for their arrival. They hug and greet everyone, with Bri looking for Jack in between; trying not to be disappointed when she doesn't see him.

Bri asks David, "Where's Jack?"

David smiles. "He's in his quarters waiting for you because I didn't want you holding back when you see him because of me." He kisses her hand and smiles, tipping his head towards The Manor. "Go on!" She kisses him firmly before she goes inside.

Jack knew he missed Bri, but he didn't realize how much, until the moment when she walked in. He stands up, as he takes her in; his emotions fill his chest and his heart squeezes. Her heart flips in her chest when she sees him, she all but runs to him, throwing her arms around his neck, and he catches her in a hug; they kiss each other fiercely. He deepens their kiss, making her weak in the knees.

When they pull apart, they are out of breath. Jack smiles wide. "Hullo, Gorgeous!" David walks in and Bri freezes.

"Love, this is why I picked now to walk in. You're still getting comfortable and it's okay, but we want to help you be as comfortable as we are with all this. Jack, kiss her again, will you?"

"Gladly!"

Before she could protest, he dips her back as he plants another steamy, passionate kiss on her lips. She couldn't help but melt and return the kiss. They pull their lips apart and smile at each other as Jack brings her back up.

David says, "That doesn't bother me, Love!"

"I'll try to get more comfortable quicker." She sweetly smiles.

Jack says to David, "I think it'll be good when all three of us are together more often." David agrees.

There is a knock on the door and David answers it. Peter, Carlotta, Amy, and James came to chat. They talk about France and the places they saw. Then Bri tells them she is surprised anyone would have recognized her, but a few did here and there.

Peter explains, "From Newhaven, all the way through Europe, the majority of the people are thrilled to see a traditional 'Noble Consort,' *and that it's a man.*" Peter chuckles...then he explains further. "I think our people like knowing that Jack, as 'The Noble Consort,' would step in as 'acting Duke,' if you will, should anything happen to David; until his heir is able to assume the title." Peter looks at Bri, "While they do support your marriage to David, you're still an American and it could take some time for them to *completely* embrace you, *although*...with all this support already, it wouldn't surprise me either if they embraced you sooner, rather than later!"

"We also released which tartans your connected with to help our people, and those with lineage in Scotland, make a connection with you...a Direct Bloodline." Carlotta tells her. She also hopes it will help Bri gain support to be 'The Royal Consort,' but she doubts Bri will have too many problems because she is a 'Direct Bloodline.'

Bri walks over and sits in her favorite type of chair. It's a super comfortable overstuffed chair, much like the one at Henry and Maggie's house, and in her quarters with David. Jack was on a mission to get one for her while she was gone; it's actually more comfortable than the others.

Jack is watching her. "Are you okay?"

"I'm fine." She smiles sweetly. "I was expecting to be hated by most of the people for either being an American, marrying David, or having a Noble Consort; *even all the above*. To know it's not as bad as I prepared for it to be, well, it's a relief to say the least. While I *may* be overly sensitive about Jack and me, I also feel this," she gestures them, "will be 'normal.'" She smiles at Jack and David. "*I'm definitely getting the best part of these relationships!*"

Jack laughs. "No way!"

David walks over and cups her cheek, "Bri, you have so much love to give because of your *amazing* heart! Once you and Jack focus on the two of you over the next two weeks, and we all move further on our parallel paths, you'll see...we're definitely getting the better end of the relationships!"

"*Agreed!*" Jack chuckles. "I *know* our hearts aren't as big as yours *and* there's only room for *just you* in them!"

"That's what I've been telling her!" David replies. "This only works because of love and family." He gestures to the room, and they all agree. "Jack, we'll go and take care of...*some things.*"

"*Wooow...*" Bri looks at David. "I guess there *is* something you're horrible at!"

455

David looks at her with a raised eyebrow. "What might that be?!"

"*You're a* horrible *liar*, Mister *Worthington!*" She grins.

David chuckles. "I love you!" He leans down and kisses her cheek.

"I love you, too!" She tells him and watches him as he leaves with the others.

Jack walks over and sits in front of her on the ottoman. He gives her the 'come hither' with his forefinger.

"*ooOOOoo...*" She smiles and puts her feet on the floor, then scoots to the edge of the chair. "Are we going to pick up where we left off in DC, when I was sitting on the couch and you were on the coffee table in front of me?" She playfully asks, holding his jaw and kissing him fiercely before he could answer. Their passion is red hot from the second their lips touch. She moans into it... He quickly pulls back smiling.

"Let's go for a walk!" Jack suggests and stands up. Bri's face has a moment of confusion; she wasn't expecting that! "I need to say some things to you *before* the clothes fly off because," he gives her a smoldering look, "I don't know about you, but I'm not far from doing just that!"

She gives a small burst of laugher. "That was *kiiinda* the idea!"

Jack chuckles, offering his hand to her. Bri takes his hand and stands up. He recommends to her, "You may want to change your clothes to a t-shirt, shorts, swimsuit underneath...*or not*. That could be optional!" He shrugs with a mischievous look, as they walk to the door.

She curiously smiles, but she has learned from David these last two weeks to just go with it. She goes to change her clothes when they get to her quarters with David. After she finishes putting her tennis shoes on, he takes her hand and they head out back, walking into the gardens. Bri is thankful she had shoes on for hiking since they were making their way to the waterfall. Jack wants to climb it with her, but he isn't sure how she feels about it because of what happened the last time. He is relieved when she just starts climbing; he starts climbing up right behind her.

They get to the top and she says, "This is as far as I go!" She implies she is not jumping off, as she cautiously looks over the edge. She turns to Jack, who takes her hands in his and pulls her gently to him.

"Bri, we wanted to do something that would mark *our beginning of forever*." She nods with a small smile. "Here we are, *just you and me*, Gorgeous." He smiles adoringly. "I hope you see my eyes are *wide open*! While you and David are out in the public eye," he tangles his hand in her hair and holds her jaw, "I hope to be the place you can relax and recenter yourself...*or* be adventurous, 'throwing caution to the wind.'" She sees Jack drop down to one knee and she holds her breath. "BriaLynn, will you make *this day* our day to begin *our* wonderful life together; to go wherever this crazy adventure leads us?"

Her eyes fill with tears and she excitedly smiles, "Yes, Jack!" She pulls him up and into a hug, then kisses him as he swings her around. He rests their foreheads together and they soak in their love for each other.

He pulls back with a nervous, yet loving smile on his face. "Now, *don't freak out*," his Scottish accent was heard in that, "but I want to jump this waterfall *with you!*" She shakes her head and her frantic look wrenches his heart, but he doesn't let her say anything yet. "*Hear me out...please.*" She gives a little nod. "I swear I *won't* do a 'surprise dive.'" He sees her relax a bit as he pulls out a bag from his pocket. "This is for our clothes and shoes so we can toss the bag down over there; the ladies seem to like having dry clothes to put on." Bri faintly smiles in agreement. "Just as David didn't, I won't let go of your hand and I'll be there to pull you up!" He gives a playful smile. "Honestly, I think I have a chance you'll do this with me, because now you know what to expect." Bri's eyes narrow at the edge of the rock, as she considers it. Jack starts to strip down some. "I'm going to do this! And I'm *really* hoping I won't have to do it alone..."

"*I don't know...*" she mischievously smiles, "I'm *really* liking this view!" She flirts looking him over and he chuckles walking over to her.

He takes hold of the bottom of her shirt. He slowly lifts, waiting for her to stop him, but she doesn't. She raises her arms and he lifts it up, never looking away from their gaze until he pulls the shirt over her head.

He watches her as she hooks her thumbs inside the waistline of her capris, pausing when she sees Jack's face. "In touch with your teenage hormonal self already?!" She giggles. "You look like you're about to see the girl you like in a swimming suit for the first time?"

"Correction," he grins, "*the girl I love...*"

She raises her eyebrow. "You know, I'm not so sure you can handle this!"

"*Risk it!*" He tells her, as he waits with her shirt in his hand. She takes off her capris pants, and he exhales a whistle seeing the whole tankini. He smiles wide. "*That's my girl!*"

She lightly laughs, throwing her capris at him. He puts their clothes and shoes in the bag and closes it, then walks over to a spot where he drops the bag so it lands on dry ground below. He turns back to Bri and looks her over.

He sees she is nervous. "You're *gorgeous!*" His desire for her is clear. He holds out his hand as he steps to the edge of the cliff; the water is coming out of the side of the cliff between the rocks, just below their feet. "Standing here on the edge is where we're at now," he holds her hand tight, "but jumping into this marriage *with me*, I promise I'll love you, cherish you, and adore you every day, now and forever!" He holds her face and passionately kisses her.

"I may be crazier than I thought because, I believe you and I *want* to jump off this cliff with you, Jack!" She nervously wipes a tear. "I already feel like I can do anything with you..." She peers down the waterfall. "It seems like I'll be testing that flying-theory..."

He laughs. "Crazy *can be* freeing!" She rolls her eyes, but she is smiling as she squeezes his hand; he grasps her hand firmly. "On three. One...two..." She jumps before 'three' with a squeal! Jack was actually expecting that from her and is a split-second behind her.

They hit the water and true to his word, Jack never let go of Bri's hand! He pulls her up and close to him. She is so exhilarated that she throws her arms around his neck and kisses him passionately, as she wraps her legs around his waist. He swims over to the side of the rock wall behind the waterfall and presses her against it, so he can hold her up and kiss her some more. The exhilaration from jumping, being with Jack, and how adventurous she feels with him, she wanted to go all the way with him right there.

Tucked behind the waterfall and out of view, she whispers to him, "*I don't want you to stop, Jack, but we don't have any protection!*"

Jack pauses and looks her in the eye. "Bri, it isn't necessary and I'll explain later." She scrunches her eyebrows, but she decides to trust him and not overthink it. She kisses him passionately...

Afterwards, he kisses her face, then whispers, "*I love you!*"

She lovingly caresses his face. "I love you, too!"

He sweetly kisses her once more before making their way out of the water. They find a spot to lay in the sun to dry off some before getting dressed. After a while, Jack sits up and digs in the bag with their clothes and shoes. He secretly pulls something out of the pocket of his shorts. He turns to sit the opposite way and helps Bri to sit up so they can face each other.

He cups her cheek and smiles at her. "My heart is overjoyed and so in-love with you, BriaLynn!"

"Hnnn." Bri smiles. "My heart overflows with love for you!"

He taps a kiss to her lips. "While you were gone, I tried to come up with something official, but the waterfall kept popping into my head. Eventually, I realized," he gestures the waterfall, "this would be perfect! The perfect place for us!"

"It is!" She agrees. "The official part was the wedding a couple of weeks ago. For us, I like the intimacy in this."

He smiles *so* lovingly at her, her breath catches. He tells her, "You've already classified our relationship as a special blessing, very near and dear to your heart, which is *exactly* where I want to be!" He is teary-eyed as he tucks a strand of hair behind her ear and he recites:

> "*You are the sun in my mornings, the moon of my nights,*
> *and your love draws me to you, like a beacon of light!*"

Bri's emotions sneak up and overwhelm her. She manages to whisper, "*Like a lighthouse...*"

Jack hears her and smiles. "I love that analogy!"

"Then maybe you'll like that Jessica, the spirit messenger, also compared your love for me to a compass and the re-magnetizing of that compass—."

"Like being able to recenter yourself...to be able to find your way again." He says and she nods. "I do like that!"

With teary eyes, her lower jaw shakes a little bit as she tries to stop the sobs that threaten to erupt. She looks down and wipes her eyes. She looks at him and notices he is holding something.

Jack shows her a beautiful wedding band with a design that's different than her wedding set. It has two hearts linked, creating an infinity symbol in between each set. Small stones were placed in the middle of the infinity symbols, and in between each set of hearts. The stones are arranged in a simple pattern with a small sapphire or a small ruby in the middle of the infinity symbol, and a bigger diamond in between each heart.

On the inside of the ring, he has it engraved with: '*Mo chridhe leatsa gu bràth*' And its meaning is across from it, '*My heart is yours forever.*'

She can barely whisper, "*Jack!*" She covers her mouth and cries. He hugs her close to comfort her. Eventually, she gains control again and tells him, "*I love you so much, Jack!*"

Jack takes her left ring finger and slides his ring up against her set from David, he kisses them and says to her:

> "*I vow as your husband, to cherish you as my wife, forever; to be your best friend, partner, and lover. And as our love between us grows strong and sure; the bond it creates will forever endure.*"

Bri's tears drip down her cheeks. She hugs him as she cries. He hugs her close in a tight embrace.

She rests her forehead to his. "I want to put that one, and the other one, in my journal, so please tell me you have it written it down somewhere!"

He laughs. "I had to write them down to memorize them. I looked at some of the best wedding vows and blessings for inspiration and wrote these just for you."

"For us." She softly kisses his cheek. "Jack, this is perfect! I just wish I would've known so I could have something more to say." There are more tears as she realizes, "*I don't have a ring for you!*"

Holding up his forefinger he says, "I got a matching pair, minus the stones for mine."

She wipes the tears from her eyes and takes the ring. She wishes she could've had it engraved, but she'll think about that later. She puts it on his left ring finger saying:

> "*When you see this ring, think of me and my promise to love you, adore you, and be there for you; like a lighthouse beacon, I'll be there for you even in the darkest of times, always and forever!*"

"You didn't need any time! That was perfect!" Jack kisses her. She hugs him a little tighter and he feels her shiver with the gentle breeze. "Let's get back; the hike will warm us up!" She agrees.

They get ready to go back, double checking that they have everything. Jack takes her hand until they get to the narrow part of the trail, then he walks behind her, but moves beside her again when the trail opens back up. Jack texts David when they're about two-thirds of the way back.

When they reach the old ruins, the same ones Bri and David had their wedding ceremony at, David is waiting, along with Peter, Carlotta, James, and Amy. They all hug them.

David smiles lovingly. "I think whatever Jack's idea was, *worked!*"

Bri smiles with tears. "*It was perfect!*" He kisses her.

They all walk around to the front of The Manor where a car is waiting. Jack tells Bri, "I can't be away from my job for two *full* weeks, like I'd like to have with you, but my clients are way too whiny and needy for me to be away *that long*." Jack winks at Bri, who softly laughs.

"Hey now!" David jokes being offended.

Jack explains, "I wanted no work interruptions for the first week; *however*, I do have the second week as a 'working out of the office for the week,' so we can do things in between in Rome and around Italy, maybe Greece?"

461

"Rome?!" She excitedly smiles. "That sounds wonderful! I think we'll make some great and lasting memories in Italy!" She wonders, "Isn't Reñiato over there?" She thinks about Ambassador Lombardi and Callista, wondering how they are doing.

Jack smiles apologetically, "We may not have time for that one." She smiles and taps a kiss to his lips.

"You two will undoubtedly have a great time!" David says. He hugs Jack goodbye and kisses Bri in a held goodbye kiss. "Try to *enjoy* picking out some more jewelry, Love."

She gets a little payback, "I think I'll have more fun picking out lingerie to wear." She mischievously grins.

He drops his hand down to her bum and pulls her closer. "*Vixen!*"

"Ha-ha! Paybacks, Love! You tortured me with the expensive jewelry, it's only fair I get to torture you with thoughts of me—." He kisses her firmly.

"Point taken, Macushla."

She smiles behind pursed lips. "See you in a couple weeks?"

"You can count on it!" David gives her a big hug. "I love you, Macushla!"

"I love you, My Love!"

Jack and Bri get into the back seat of the car; David shuts the door behind them. Bri turns and waves to David and the family from the back window. When she turns back around, she sees Jack watching her.

She asks, "What is it?"

He smiles, "It's okay if you're going to miss him, I hope part of you missed me—."

"*Oh, I did!*" She tells him.

"Just as long as missing the other one doesn't have you *missing out* on being in the moment with the one you're with." He runs his finger down her lips, down her throat, and down to the tip of her V-neck shirt. He smiles to himself when she shivers.

"No worries there!" She happily smiles. "I'm really excited we're spending time together!"

He has a smoldering look in his eyes. "I'm excited to show you Rome and spending lots of time with you," running the tips of her fingers between his lips, "being naked."

He smiles his best smile, and she melts. She taps a kiss to his lips and looks at him lovingly. He traces the side of her face with his finger.

"You and David are so incredibly wonderful! I'm still getting used to how supportive you both are of each other and your relationships with me!"

"Take all the time you need, Amore Mia." He replies.

"*Amore Mia?*" She thinks about how 'amour' means 'love' in French, so she wonders, "is that 'My Love' in Italian?"

"It is! Amore Mia is the feminine form of the Italian 'My Love.'"

"Ah, making you, Amore Mio?" She smiles.

He chuckles. "I also like 'Inamorata' for you, too!"

"*Ooo*! What does that one mean?"

"Sweetheart or..." he leans into her ear and whispers, "*Lover.*"

As he kisses down her neck she asks, "Do you both know French and Italian? Greek?"

He smiles against her neck, then taps another quick kiss there before pulling back. "We do. David loves Rome and Italy, but *loves* Paris and France, and wanted to share those with you. Mine is the opposite. I love Paris and France, but *really love* Rome and Italy, even the Mediterranean, and I wanted to share those with you! It's like Mediterranean water flows through my veins!"

"Kind of like when I hear people who visit, or move to, California or Hawaii say that the ocean has become a part of their 'life force' in a way?" She smiles.

"Exactly!" He grins.

They arrive at the plane and board. She uses the restroom, and he has a mango smoothie waiting for her when she returns.

She smiles and sits. "*Thank you for this!*" She takes a drink and does a double-take at Jack watching her. "You're staring pretty hard there, *Mister* Carlisle."

"*Can't help it.*" He tangles his hand in her hair. "I'm trying to memorize every gorgeous detail about you." He kisses her firmly. Then they get comfortable before they take off.

Once airborne, they discuss Katie for a few minutes. He tells her exactly what happened the night of the wedding. "...she was *so* drunk; she was stumbling *up the stairs!*" Bri's eyebrows shoot up. "Maybe I shouldn't have tricked her into going to her room thinking I would join her, I don't ever want to give someone false hope, but..."

"Jack, *she was drunk*, and men *have* taken advantage of her in that state when I'm not around to prevent it. Thank you for being the wonderful gentleman you are!" She smiles sweetly. "I didn't say anything to David since I didn't want to spoil the honeymoon and then I forgot about it when we were talking about it before. I could swear it looked like that Richard McCleary guy was with Katie, watching out the window when David and I left for our honeymoon a couple of weeks ago."

"James and I looked up at the same time and saw her there before she ducked out of the window, but I only saw her." He shrugs.

"If she cared to ask, I might care enough to explain more in depth how all this came together with you, David, and me. *Sadly*, she would rather play the jealousy card and be angry..." She reads his uneasiness. "What did she say?"

He shakes his head. "It was when she was drunk and I refuse to give it any more thought right now." Jack holds her face and firmly tells her, "*You know* you're *not* responsible for *any* of *her* choices."

"*I do.* It's just so hard to watch." She gives him a faint smile.

"It is, but at least you won't be right there to see it, or be in danger of her hurting you again, not to mention the girls." He tells her.

464

"True. But she isn't done. Her job has her traveling, so she'll make it a point to keep poking." She tells him.

"*Why?!*" He asks. "You'd think she would be too busy, or at least get bored."

"I think she doesn't want to be forgotten." Bri simply replies. "Her dad ran out before she was born. Her mom died of a drug overdose when Katie was a teenager, and she was in and out of various foster care homes until she 'aged-out' of the system. In a way, she is *desperately* trying to prove she matters, when, in her whole childhood, she never felt like she did."

Jack is surprised. "Well, she's not going about it the right way!"

"*No*, but she's not thinking rationally either, is she? She's jealous of my life," she gestures him, "and she wants what we all want." He is trying to think what that is... She holds his cheek. "To be loved *unconditionally*." He nods, taking her hand from his cheek and kisses it. "She's hoping this will all fall apart, so she and I are somehow on equal ground again. Jealousy only pushes people away. *I've been wanting to put more distance between us*; however, if I do that, it could very well send her over the edge and into old habits..."

"*She's already back to them!*" Jack states.

"Okay, *deeper* into old habits then." She corrects herself with a faint eye roll. "What people don't understand is that Katie's jealousy has everything to do with her insecurities. She *knows* what she did ruined our friendship, yet both of us both haven't been ready, or willing, to face that this friendship may be beyond repair." She takes a drink. "Granted it was 'Drug Addicted Katie' which is why I remained friends, to a point, but I can only do that to a point; *no matter how much I try to lie to myself*. She has never talked about it with me. She goes out of her way to avoid talking about it, because I think one of the scariest things for her is to *admit to herself* what she did to me...she would have to confront the monster she became when she was on drugs."

"Could it be that *maybe* you remain friends to a point is because you feel responsible for her?" He asks. "That you'd feel guilty if she turned to drugs completely if you turned your friendship away?"

She thinks about that. "I don't know...*maybe*...but then again, isn't she already making the choice for me?" She shifts to turn towards him more and changes

465

the subject. "I remember discussing your parents and brother, but tell me more about your mother?"

"Amore Mia, you should know by now that I, *like you*, like to live in the present and focus on where I'm going. I can appreciate the past, with all its twists and turns, but I never stay there for long."

She touches his cheek with a loving expression. "I was just hoping to appreciate the woman who began shaping you."

He smiles. "I want to enjoy the people who matter in my life. Most importantly," he lifts her chin slightly, "*you*."

"*She* matters, Jack!" She sweetly asks, "*Please?*"

"My mother died when I was six, so my memories of her have faded. I can barely keep what she looks like from disappearing completely, but I try to remember the last trip she, my brother, and I went on; we went to the Mediterranean. She met up with Uncle Max, which come to think of it, she had my brother and me with, so that probably wasn't the best—."

"Stop. Jack, remember your mother for the goodness she instilled in you *and a love for the Mediterranean*." She winks with a little smile; he gives her a faint one back. "I'm not condoning an affair, but I refuse for it to be a consideration as to whether she was a good person, let alone a good mother, *especially* when we factor your father and his mistreatment of you, *and ultimately his treatment of her*, into this! She did a lot right with you because of the love you have for me!" A tear drops from her eye and Jack's jaw shakes.

"How can you say that?" He is choking up and has to force out, "*I was six!*"

She runs her hand into his hair. "You've said it yourself, Jack, that your father had very little to do with you, except the very few times during your childhood he needed to make an impression of a 'happy family' socially." He nods and she continues. "If I remember correctly, it has been said our 'love-map' is essentially written *by the age of six* and sometimes as late as eight. It can change over time as we learn what love means to us, but we can talk about that more some other time." She squeezes his hand a little. "What matters here is that, through the most critical time your 'love map' was being formed and initially shaped, *your mother* was *beautifully* responsible for it!" She holds his jaw wiping a tear off his cheek with her thumb. "I'm *incredibly* grateful for what she instilled in you. It was a great foundation for Peter and Carlotta to build on!" She leans in and kisses him meaningfully.

"I love you..." Jack tells, then keeps kissing her to avoid talking about it any further.

Their plane lands and they have a nice ride to a picturesque hotel with gardens all around. He carries her across the threshold of their suite, and she looks around while the luggage is being dropped off. She is out on the balcony and, being on the top floor, admiring a breathtaking view. He walks out, wrapping his arms around her and she hugs him back.

"I can see why you love Rome!" She kisses him deeply, then rests the side of her head against his. "This view beats out some of the ones in France, but not all of them..."

"It's so much better being here with you!" He admits.

"Good answer, Amore Mio!"

He smiles. "Let's go have a nice dinner, then I'll show you around a bit..."

"*Ooorrr*," she starts to unbutton his already untucked shirt, "we can stay in and make a whole day of all that tomorrow." She bites her lower lip.

"Not sure about *all* day..." He scoops her up and she happily squeals. "I have naked plans every day for the next two weeks!"

"Sounds fun!" She kisses him as he carries her inside.

CHAPTER 41

Perfectly Perfect Roman Honeymoon

Over the next few days, Jack shows Bri around St. Peter's Basilica, The Colosseum, The Roman Forum, The Pantheon, The Catacombs, they even threw a coin into The Trevi Fountain. Jack made a point to share a romantic kiss or few throughout their sightseeing. There is a marketplace they have visited a few times. On one of those visits, they shared an authentic Italian pizza and, on another visit, they had spaghetti and lasagna. Today, Jack has brought her to a jewelry store and they are stuck outside the door because Bri is refusing to go inside.

"No, Jack! David did this a few weeks ago and it was hard for me! Everything was beautiful, some stunning, and a few were even exquisite, but it was hard on my heart knowing he was spending such a *ridiculous* amount of money *on me*! No, Jack! *I'm* not *going in there*!" She defiantly folds her arms. "*You can't make me*!"

Jack puts his hands on her upper arms. "Amore Mia, do you think I haven't done my research?"

Bri lifts her eyebrow. "*Research?*"

He tells her, "I spoke with David about the details of your trip to the jewelry store." She glares. "I wanted to be prepared in case you refused to even go inside!" He gestures to the door. "For the record, *that* is the *only thing* we discussed in detail."

"*For the record*, I trust you'll both honor 'the behind bedroom doors, stays behind bedroom doors' rule, so it never occurred to me to question it."

"We do, *for you*." He playfully tells her, "I have a feeling if he and I compared notes, you would reap the benefits."

"Wouldn't that take the fun out of *learning* about each other?" She asks.

"Touché, Amore Mia. Now, I'm going to do this for you, *AND* I've already picked some pieces out. All I need *you* to do is slide your gorgeous self into a dress, or few...However, if you make me do this on my own, I swear I'll buy the most expensive, gaudy jewelry I can find!"

She scoffs, "*No you won't!* Not the gaudy kind!" She argues. "You have *great* taste and you wouldn't be able to bring yourself to buy anything gaudy!" She smirks. "It would blemish your record, *and ego*, for 'great taste!'"

"*Which leaves expensive...*" He says with bold determination.

She gives him an exasperated look. She rolls her eyes saying, "*Fine...*"

He puts his hand on the handle of the door and holds out his other hand for her to take. "*Please?*" Hoping she can't resist his plea.

With a pained expression she asks, "You're really going to do this?!"

"If *I* don't, then David and I will coordinate without you because we both feel that you, a soon-to-be duchess of a prominent duchy, should have a start to a *fabulous* jewelry collection." He knows, as David does, that if she becomes The Royal Consort, Herst will personally add to her collection. He and David don't want to take away from that, so this really is a start until she makes her decision one way or the other.

"You know there's *already* a jewelry collection for 'The Duchess of Newhaven.'" She smirks, "Carlotta had me wearing some already."

"As you know, there are pieces that stay with 'The Duke and Duchess of Newhaven' titles, it was part of the paperwork you signed the day before the wedding." He says.

"The paperwork stating that the pieces stay with the titles." She finishes.

"Right. And David and I want you to have *your own* pieces." He opens the door. "Shall we?" He offers his hand again.

She rolls her eyes as she takes his hand. "Did you think about needing a bucket?" He pauses inside the door and gives her a confused look...he looks at McMasters who shrugs an 'I don't know.' "Ah, then you *haven't* thought of everything!" She whispers closer to them, "*What do you have for me to throw up in when it gets overwhelming again?*" Jack and McMasters quietly chuckle.

They've walked into a beautiful Italian two-story jewelry store. Giuseppe, the owner and store's namesake, is waiting for them with a big, happy smile.

"Lord Carlisle! Lady Newhaven! We're so excited to have you!" He shakes Jack's hand and kisses Bri's cheeks. He looks back at McMasters. "We'll be temporarily closing the store," he gestures to the store's security guard who is already locking the front door, "and another guard is at the back entry that is also locked. *Please* relax and enjoy refreshments." Giuseppe motions to the little table. "Hugo will keep you company." McMasters nods a 'thank you' and introduces himself to Hugo.

Giuseppe leads them to the counter where he introduces them to Vincenzo, and two ladies walk up to Bri. They are introduced as AnnaMaria and Giuseppe's wife, Valentina. They will be helping Bri try on the dresses brought over from Valentina's dress shop.

Jack explains, "I want you to try on the dresses. Most of these will be red to find one for the night I hope you'll accompany me to a work event."

"*Ooo, I'd love to*!"

He smiles. "The other dress will be for 'The Sweethearts Ball.'"

"This 'Sweethearts Ball' is for February I assume?" She asks, surprisingly lacking the emotion he expected.

"Yes." He turns her head and studies her face for a moment. "Seriously?! *You*, the '*I'm a sucker for romance*,' doesn't like Valentine's Day?!" She shrugs.

"Valentine's Day has never really lived up to the hype for me..." she says as she tries on the first dress. "Valentine's Day has become a day for people to spend too much money on an overly priced paper card and chocolates that barely get ate because most of them are disgusting. Then roses are *normally expensive* but just for that 'special day,'" she rolls her eyes as she uses air quotes, "they're marked up to *outrageous*! Plus, the roses don't last long unless someone pays an *obscene* amount of money for *possibly* better quality, and that's only if you know where to go for those! All to show someone 'love' by going bankrupt?! *Pleeease*!" She rolls her eyes again. "Shouldn't wives get better gifts from their husbands, if they are truly in-love with them, that require more effort like jewelry, a day at a spa, or a vacation? Although, husbands would have to plan ahead and most of them don't, which is ridiculous nowadays with electronic calendars and reminders! But *why wait for a commercialized so-called-holiday to do any of it*?! Wouldn't you want them to feel loved and special throughout the year?"

Jack holds her upper arms. "Take a deep breath, Amore Mia. I get your point; that any gift for someone has the potential to be a huge waste of money—."

"*And* disappointment *on both sides* of the gift!" Bri adds. "The kind of disappointment that can lead to hard feelings and even resentment because of expectations! The gesture of anything can be really sweet if expectations are realistic! It's just sad that the price tag for any of it is *insane* and all to be *assumed* it's in the name of 'love.' Real, true-love is a *verb*, not a price tag!" She goes back into the changing room. "One could argue giving a gift is an action, but so is sex, which is often *expected* on that day, too, especially with jewelry and of course lingerie! We could talk ourselves in circles when we factor giving gifts with the *expectation* of sex; kind of zaps romance out of it, don't you think?"

"Not if two people are truly in-love..." He gives her a loving smile. "Bri, I'm just gobsmacked, *dumbfounded*! It makes me wonder what happened in your past relationships to make you so jaded with Valentine's Day?! You have the biggest heart of *anyone* I know, with so much love and faith, *it's inspiring*; so it's *unreal* you *hate* Valentine's Day!"

She steps out. "I *hate* it's an expensive and commercialized day. *Where's the real love in all that*?!"

Jack holds the back of her jaw. "It's going to be my mission to make you one day *love* Valentine's Day, Amore Mia!" He smiles and kisses her deeply. "I love you!"

"Mmm..." she smiles. "I love you, Amore Mio!" She smirks, "But I'd lower that task to the bottom of your 'bucket list.' And don't get your expectations up *at all*!"

He winks at her and gets back to the task at hand. He holds out her arms, "*I'm loving* this *dress*!"

It's a red V-neck dress with a little bit longer short sleeves, a layer of lace on the top half of the dress and chiffon from the waist down; there is a satin belt and a removeable rhinestone brooch on the left.

Bri turns to look from different directions in the mirrors. "I do, too!"

"Perfect for the work party!" Jack suggests.

Valentina says she loves it, too, and hugs Bri from the side. Bri smiles at her before she goes and takes it off. She hands the dress to AnnaMaria through the curtain and puts on another dress.

The next series of dresses are a bit of a workout, but Bri manages to find one for The Sweethearts Ball. The dress was a short-sleeve, dark red burgundy ballgown with rhinestones and sequins scattered throughout the sweetheart cut satin bodice, the ballroom skirt was smooth satin from waist to the floor.

She sees two other dresses that catch her eye, and she asks to try them on; they are more than happy to have her do so. One is silver with silver sequins on top and chiffon from the upper waist down; the other is a turquoise chiffon; she loves both of them.

Bri does something she never has before, saying, "I'll take both!" Then she goes to get dressed again.

She walks over to the dresses that are laid out with the jewelry suggestions for them, but as David suggested, they leave the jewelry boxes closed. She goes up to 'The Sweethearts Ball' gown first and before she opens the jewelry boxes for it, she asks if there is a heart-shape or shapes among it. They shake their heads.

"I want something fitting," she sweetly smiles, "something heart-shaped." She is inspired and whispers to Jack, *"Maybe the 'Third Musketeer has an idea?"*

Jack is surprised. *"How did you—?"* He chuckles. *"Right. David told you."*

"He *may* have mentioned it..." She grins.

He lightly laughs. "We can look into it." He studies her for a minute.

"What?" She asks, looking down at herself.

"You have hope for Valentine's Day!" He tells her.

"*Of course, I do*! I have you and David, *and true-love*!" She is quick to reply. "Your goal is to have me *love* Valentine's Day; I have *hope* that I'll *tolerate* it because I love the two of you. I'm happy spending it with either of you, or both of you with a bowl of popcorn and a great movie of *almost* any genre; or whatever is planned! There." She grins at him. "Expectations *managed*!"

He snorts a laugh, shaking his head. "Let's keep going, Gorgeous..."

 She steps up to a box containing 'The Newhaven Tiara.' "This makes it seem like I'm 'The Duchess.'"

Jack comes up beside her and puts his hands on hers. "This is 'The Newhaven Tiara' that *Mother, The Duchess*, lovingly sends to go with your dress for the party." He says, leaning in and whispers, "*Bri, this comes with the role you married into with David, just like I've married into.*" He gives her a loving smile that drops when he sees her frowning.

She quietly and sternly tells him, "*You*.are.*not*.a.role!"

"Sorry, Amore Mia, I didn't mean it like that!" He turns her to face him. "What I meant is, when we both agreed to this arrangement, we knew there were expectations for you, as The Marchioness of Newhaven, *and* when you become The Duchess of Newhaven." He sees her face change to irked. "Talk to me, Bri."

All she says is one word, still looking at the tiara, "*Arrangement.*"

He kicks himself in his mind. "As Americans say, I just keep shoving my foot deeper into my mouth." He puts his hands on her upper arms. "Can we erase all that and start over?" He asks, taking a finger to her chin, lifting up for her to look at him. "I'm sorry, I keep saying the wrong things when I'm just trying to say—."

"There are certain things we *accept* because they came *with* the marriage." She finishes and he nods.

"*For me to be with the love of my life*, she has a title and responsibilities that come with her." He rests their foreheads together. "Are we good?" She gives him a little smile. She lifts her head and taps a kiss to his lips. He smiles wide, holding her arms out. "This dress is fantastic, too!"

"Yeah, it's a favorite!" She admits. Then she remembers to ask a question from before. "What's the company event we're going to while we're here?"

"This party is given to the top producers of the company every year. We'll already be at the venue, which makes it easier for McMasters." He starts to explain, watching her look around. He looks over to where she is looking. "You found something?" He smiles.

"I did!" She said pointing to a necklace that would match the turquoise dress she is getting perfectly.

AnnaMaria also sees where she is pointing. "That's perfect! *Oh*! We have shoes to match, too! *Valentina*!" She goes running off...

The necklace was made of square-cut dark blue quartz and emerald-cut turquoise quartz. The same color of turquoise gems, with dark blue and silver shapes are on the thin straps of the shoes. The ladies show Bri and Jack, and he sees she likes them.

"Ladies, wrap them up, please! She'll take them!" Jack says to them, smiling at Bri. Before she can say anything, he kisses her soundly.

"You're *incorrigible*! You know that, right?! *Both of you*!" Bri states, trying not to smile, but he sees the twinkle in her eye.

"I'm thinking maybe David was on to something when it comes to colors in the jewelry." He asks about a necklace for her silver-gray dress.

"No, no!" She tells them. "The snowflake looking diamond necklace set we got in Paris will work *perfectly*!"

"I'm starting to think you don't want another necklace set." He says, moving to stand behind her, gesturing a few options.

"*I swear* the one I have will work the best! It's back at the hotel and I'll prove it later!" She turns to look at him. "Besides, *what on earth* would I do with another expensive set? It isn't *practical*!"

Giuseppe interrupts. "If I may, Lady Newhaven." He gestures to himself with an Italian accent. "Unless you were raised in Europe, it's hard to understand that your people will see the wealth that you wear and associate it with Newhaven prospering. It all works together to show a couple of important points; first, that Lord Newhaven was right to pick you!" He smiles. "Second, the three of you will help Newhaven to prosper and flourish!"

"He's right!" Vincenzo adds.

AnnaMaria also chimes in. "My degree is in World History. It's often talked about how kings, dictators, emperors, and so on, parade military strength and their wealth as a visual for people 'to see' how strong they are as a leader and a country. They knew visual displays of wealth when one rules a kingdom is imperative to their survival as a ruler."

"You all make a great point." Bri admits. "They did march their militaries and spoils of war right down the street, in the heart of their capital!"

 "I managed to find a unique piece, but with Vincenzo's and Giuseppe's help!" He opens a small velvet box. "This large amethyst is believed to have been a gift from a king to the woman he loved and adored." He kisses her sweetly. "Interesting..." he takes a closer look, "one might expect the heart to be a ruby."

"Oh, I don't know..." Bri says, pondering.

He sees her thinking. "Bri, if you say purple is the color of royalty—."

"I was just thinking about how an *amethyst* is associated with the chakras and spirituality. The seventh chakra," she points to the top of her head, "is believed to be a connection of one's spirit with the Spirit, God, the Lord, or whatever higher power someone believes in. To give a gift like this, one could believe that *this man* really did love her on the deepest level."

Jack smiles and points saying, "It definitely is a gift to the woman *this man* loves and adores!" She sweetly kisses him.

"I can't imagine a ruby this big but I'd imagine any gemstone this big would be incredibly rare...how many karats is this amethyst?" She asks.

"Barely over 100 karats." Giuseppe replies.

Bri's mouth drops for a moment. "That also has to be *incredibly expensive!* There can't be too many of these larger-sized amethysts in the world."

Jack replies, "Just one." Bri's eyes get big looking at the brooch and she quickly puts it down on the counter as if it were on fire. Jack softly chuckles as he wraps his arms around her in a hug. "One-of-a-kind, *just like you!*"

 When everything is boxed up, including a pair of diamond earrings that were pear shaped diamonds haloed with teeny tiny diamonds, dropped from a diamond cluster; Jack pays and signs various places on the paperwork. The jewelry, clothes, and accessories will be delivered to the hotel tomorrow.

Jack does carry one velvet box with him and hands it to Bri. "Would you slip this into your purse, but promise me you won't look at it *yet?*"

He looks at her with a knockout smile, she smiles in agreement and opens her purse for him to put it in her purse himself. As they leave the store, having thanked everyone, they climb into their car.

Jack asks, "Where would you like to eat?"

Bri smiles playfully, "In our room," she leans and whispers in his ear, "*dessert first.*" She hears him moan a low growl as he shifts in his seat.

When the car pulls up to the hotel, they get out and Jack takes Bri's hand. He walks with such long strides, she has to almost jog just to keep up. "Slow down a little Amore Mio, I don't want to sprain or break an ankle."

Jack stops at the elevator, wraps an arm around her waist and presses the button with the other hand. "Sorry, Amore Mia," he kisses her, then kisses his way back to her ear as other guests approach the elevators and he whispers, "*I can't stop thinking about you wearing* only *what's in that box!*"

"*Looks like I will have all the control.*" She whispers back.

The ding for their elevator chimes and they get on. They make a few stops as the elevator climbs its way up to their floor. Once inside their suite, they put their things down and she wraps her arms around Jack's waist and his go around her shoulders.

"Thank you for spoiling me, even though I had to work through the feeling of wanting to throw up with so much money spent on me." She has a tear escape down her cheek.

"My pleasure, Gorgeous!" He kisses her passionately and hugs her tighter. He gently pulls their lips apart and he sees her eyes are closed a few seconds longer. He taps another kiss to her lips and they smile lovingly at each other.

He walks over to her purse and takes out the velvet box. He hands it to her with a smoldering smile. She smiles and bites her lower lip, taking it and going to the bedroom.

When she steps out of the bedroom wearing the necklace set and a shirt of his, he has a smoldering grin walking up to her. He passionately kisses her, reaching down, lifting her legs up to wrap around his waist, then walks over to the couch...

That evening, when Jack crawls into bed, Bri snuggles into him with her head on his chest. "Jack, can I ask you something."

He laughs a little. "Yes, Amore Mia, you can ask me anything." She goes silent, but he can feel her drawing softly on his chest. He looks down and lifts her chin, so he sees her eyes. "*Anything*, Amore Mia!"

"If you aren't ready to talk about it with me, it's okay..." She takes a deep breath and exhales, remembering the comment after they had jumped the waterfall. "Why didn't we need protection in the water, but we've been using it since?"

Jack realizes he had forgotten to discuss this with her. The significance is how much she really does trust him because she is just now asking.

"I apologize for not talking to you sooner." He explains. "Other than David, James, Carlotta, and Peter, I went through it privately. The reason why I can still have children is known by even less. I've *never* told anyone outside them, certainly not any of the women I've dated."

"Jack, if you——." He puts his fingertips on her lips.

"You have *every right* to know and I should've told you before we got married. I need to tell you...it's important."

She puts a hand on his cheek, "Talk to me. I love you and nothing you say will leave this room, nor will it make me love you less. In fact, I have a sneaking suspicion I will love you more." She sweetly smiles.

He hugs her firmer as he stares at the ceiling. "As you know, I had cancer back when I was sixteen."

She hugs him with her arm on his chest. "I wish I was there with you."

He clears his throat. "I was stage two almost stage three, because I kept denying anything was wrong before mentioning something to Carlotta. Like a mother, she *flew into action* and made appointments with the best specialists. Peter and David went to as many appointments as they could. Some of the treatments made me so sick, I just wanted to die." Her eyes fill with tears as she pictures a blond haired, blue-eyed, sixteen-year-old Jack, in a hospital room and sick with treatments...

"No child should ever wish they were dead, nor wish they were never born." She said, not knowing he had wished he was never born, until David and his family unofficially adopted him. "I'm assuming they encouraged you to plan ahead for children in the future?" He nods. She has tears and tries to hide her sadness, but he senses it.

He rolls them over, so he is looking down into her eyes. "It's been, what? Like twenty years?! I'm fine, I just can't father our beautiful child the 'fun way.'" He winks.

She brings his head down to rest against her forehead. "I don't care *how* I conceive our baby; I just can't ever imagine you not here with me." He lifts his head and looks at her. He sees so much love and affection in her eyes for him, he kisses her.

She wonders, "Purely informational, is there no chance naturally?"

He tells her, "I don't remember the percentage, but to me it might as well be zero. At the time, I was just a kid and it didn't matter. Now, I'm glad I let Carlotta convince me to plan ahead! She also made sure that I understood that it *wasn't zero* and if I wasn't going to wait until I was married before having sex, I needed to protect myself; and I always did, *except once*," he caresses her check, "with you."

"This is why you were so emotional when I told you I saw our child at the ceremony, and again on the bridge!" She says. He tears up at the memory and she hugs him tight. "You worry that there might still be a problem?"

"With me or storing it this long; now I know I don't need to be!" He smiles sweetly. "Amore Mia," he taps on her heart, "I'm so lucky to have a place in here; for your heart to have so much love that it can fill David and me up separately *and completely*!" He holds his breath to push down his emotions. "I love you, BriaLynn!" Her hands are on his cheeks and he kisses her with so much love.

"I'm in-love with you, Jack*son*!" She snickers when he gives her a look.

"Don't make a habit of that..."

"Jack, I'm *very blessed* to love you and David and to have you both love me!"

He kisses her deeply, his hands traveling her sheet covered body. He takes the sheet and pulls it up over their heads. She giggles, and it makes his heart feel good...

As they lay in bed, she tells him, "Goodnight, Amore Mio! I love you!"

"I love *you*, Amore Mia!" He kisses her fiercely, before they get comfortable and fall asleep for the night.

CHAPTER 42

Imperfectly Perfect Honeymoon *Crasher*

Over the next couple of days, they enjoy being together, not only in their suite, but around Italy. They get back from a country drive and Bri changes into a dress shirt of his and her lounging pants. She is taking off her jewelry when she sees the necklace set Jack had her take with her when they left the jewelry store. It's just a whole lot of diamonds, in various sizes, clustered together; thicker in front and tapers down as it goes around to the back. There is a row of pear-shaped diamonds on the bottom edge, with one in the center that is a little bit bigger than the others, and the rest taper down in size as the row moves to the back.

She goes out and sits on the couch. "Question."

"Alright." He sits down next to her.

"This necklace and earring set," she gestures herself and sees the playful grin, "what else did you have in mind for them to be worn with?"

Jack shrugs. "*Whatever you want!*" He leans back. "Anytime I see those I'll be thinking it's the best eight hundred thousand I've *ever* spent, *because* of how good they look on you and," he gives her a smoldering smile, "the memories associated with them!" Bri smiles, then it fades as the amount registers.

"*Hold up!* You spent over three-quarters of a *mill...*" she trails off in shock.

"Hey, hey, hey! It's an——."

"*Investment?*" She rolls her eyes. "I swear, I might actually scream the next time I hear that!"

She looks away because she is also frustrated that her eyes are getting teary. All of his money, and all of David's money, that was spent on jewelry, *for her*, makes her feel like it was all '*wasted.*'

Jack hugs her. "David told you money is nothing to worry about!"

"It helped *a little*, but still, it's altogether adding up to be more than I'd ever earn in my lifetime!"

"It wasn't that much, Amore Mia. Would it help to know I'm well into the trillions with money and assets?" He asks her.

She snorts a humorless laugh, "Not anymore! Not after all that you bought!" Bri says, pointing to the necklace set she has on for him.

Jack chuckles. "What's a few million?" She glares. "Bri, the only way I'd even feel it is if all that was spent was in the *billions* and it *wasn't even close to one*! Besides, these will be listed as an asset *I can assure you*!"

She studies him, then sternly tells him, "*You lied.*"

His eyebrows shoot up in surprise, "*How so?!*"

"You said if I *didn't* go into the store with you *then* you would find the most expensive——." He kisses her with a long, passionate, and loving kiss that she melts into. He doesn't pull apart until he hears her moan into it, then slowly pulls their lips apart. "If you and David weren't very good at that, it wouldn't work so well!"

He just smiles with a knowing look, taking her hand and kissing her rings. "Bri, it wasn't the most expensive piece in the store, I swear to you!" He pulls her into his lap and holds the bottom of his shirt she has on. "That would cost *millions*, and more than likely, it was *gaudy*!"

She scoffs and rolls her eyes. "This *has to be* the most expensive of anything I have!"

"Like I said, *best money I've ever spent*!" He grins, tangling his hand into her hair, pulling her into another passionate kiss...

They find a movie and lay on the couch together. Bri sleeps for a couple of hours next to Jack. When she moves, she is facing Jack and he watches her for a moment before he kisses her softly to slowly wake her up. Bri starts to smile with her eyes still closed.

BAM! BAM! BAM! The loud banging on the door of their suite causes Bri to gasp out loud, as they sit straight up.

They hear, "JACK CARLISLE!"

Bri falls back on the couch asking in a raspy voice, "Is *that* who I *think* it is?!"

He angrily whispers, "*I'll handle her!*" He gets up and grabs his pants, putting them on quick. He takes the shirt he was wearing, and the one of his that Bri was wearing, and tosses them in the chair. "*You* are going to stay *just like that!*"

Her mouth drops and she looks down at herself. "*WHAT?!*" She whispers. "*WHY*–er, ugh!" She exhales shaking her head. "*How does she know we're here, let alone what room?!*"

He zips up his pants. "I don't know, but I'd love to get my hands on whoever's responsible!" He angrily goes to answer the door.

"*It's about time!* Where's Bri?!" Katie snaps.

He doesn't let her in. "What the hell are you doing here, Katie?!" Jack says with annoyance, but the anger is just underneath.

Katie pushes past him. "Bri doesn't respond to my text messages or answer her phone—Oh..." she stops midsentence when she sees Bri on the couch, holding a blanket up to cover herself. Jack can't help but have a smug smile because her shock was the intended result. Katie gestures her saying, "David can't seriously be okay with the two of you—."

"Watch it Katie," he stops her before she can be crude, "or I'll actually throw you out!" Jack warns.

"No, Sir!" McMasters walks in the open door. "*I'll do it!* She lied to me!" He looks apologetically at Jack, "She said you were expecting her *and* she knew your room number."

Jack tells McMasters, "I don't blame you." He asks Katie, "I *am* curious how you got the information in the first place?!"

Katie is somewhat ignoring him, still staring at Bri, pushing down her anger and jealousy that is threatening to explode. "I tried to get a room on this floor, but they're all booked." She continues to talk as she looks around the main room. Bri texts David about Katie and asks if he booked the whole top floor they were on. A minute later her phone lights up...

David: "No, Jack already had. I was in a meeting and just read James' text that he messed up and told Katie the hotel, but he's not sure how she found out the room number; *he doesn't even know it!* He double checked to make sure the top floor you're on was booked, then went ahead and booked floor below when he heard Katie was going to Rome. He feels absolutely terrible, Love!"

Bri: "Well, she's here and I'm wondering why she even wanted to come to Rome in the first place, let alone to our hotel room?!"

D: "I just texted James and he should be there any minute to run interference for us. I think he asked Amy to fly in and join him with running that interference with Katie until your honeymoon is over."

B: "I can't believe this! She's being rude and obnoxious because she says she needs to talk to me?! Ugh!"

D: "Love, have you considered that maybe you're the one who's changed?"

B: "Gee, thanks." (she adds a sarcasm face)

D: "Seriously! Your heart is so loving, so accepting, and forgiving, but you're intolerant of horrible behavior in those you know can do better. And when she fails to even *try* to do better, you unknowingly put more and more distance between the two of you."

B: "Possibly..."

D: "Let me call James."

David calls James, who is almost to the door of Jack's suite. James knocks on the now closed door and McMasters lets him in. James puts David on speaker.

David's stern voice is clear, "Katie, *you've overstepped!*"

Katie raises her voice, "She's MY best friend and I have every right to warn her, you bast—."

"NO!" He sternly interrupts. "She's MY wife! *She's Jack's wife!* And at this moment, I'd wager Jack and I are better 'BFFs' than you *ever were*, but I'll let her clarify your relationship with her. For now, you have *no* business being there!"

Embarrassed, Katie glares at Bri. "*You told them?!*"

"I told you they were going to ask me one day and I wasn't going to lie!" Bri reminds her. "I'm just surprised they hadn't asked sooner!"

Jack's voice is *thick* with loathing, "It was probably for the best because I don't even want to be in the same room with you! After everything you said about her that night, you're a *disgusting piece of*—." He stops himself. "Out of respect for Bri being in the room, I won't finish that. You never really were her friend, or you *never* would've even considered doing the evil and vile things you two did to her!" His face matches his disgust and revulsion towards her.

Katie says to Bri, "If I wasn't still your friend, then I wouldn't have come to warn you about—."

"My apologies, Jack." David cuts Katie off. "Nothing was so important it couldn't have waited until you both returned home."

"You have *nothing* to apologize for David!" Jack glares at Katie.

"Well, I hate she interrupted you two for *any* amount of time!"

Katie blurts, "Bri, the Worthington's are going to prostitute you—."

"*That's ridiculous!*" Bri interrupts her.

"I overheard Carlotta talking to someone in the background when I was talking to James on the phone!" Katie tells her.

"Seriously, Katie?!" Bri frowns. "Jack and I are married!"

Katie looks at Jack's wedding band and laughs at the ridiculousness of it. "You're actually playing it off that way and expect people to respect it?! All it does is create an invitation that you, Jack, and David are *not* monogamous!"

"*To you!*" Bri snaps. She gets up and carefully puts Jack's shirt on; James turns his back to her for privacy.

"It's legally binding, Katie," David interjects, "and technically, if Jack were to break it, *legally* I could have him put to death."

Bri stops her mouth from dropping. She knows there is nothing to worry about, but she never knew there were any serious consequences like that! Then again, going back over the centuries, it would make sense.

Before Katie can say anything, David asks, "James?"

James knows what David is going to say and replies, "*We're leaving!*"

"Wait!" Katie protests.

"*No, Katie,*" David speaking sternly again, "you're done here! Bri can decide later what she wants to do between the two of you. And you, of all people, should know she fiercely protects those she loves and cares about!" David lets that sink in. "Now, I'll see you all when you get back to Newhaven." They all say goodbye and David hangs up.

The images from memories Bri had buried threaten to break free, and she tries to keep them at bay. She hears Katie's cold voice as Bri walks into view.

"*Don't you think you owe me an explanation!*" Katie snaps.

"*Excuse me?!*" Bri shoots back, folding her arms.

"You knew I was trying to land Jack! You had David and you *seemed* so in-love, but what? David wasn't enough so now you have to be greedy and take Jack, too?! You sl—."

"*That's enough!*" Bri is angry and has an expression to match. "I don't *owe you* an explanation! *In fact, I don't owe you a damn thing!* Don't pretend to tell me it was Jack you wanted when you were with James right before that! James was the best catch you've ever had, or ever will have, and you tossed him aside like you just finished flipping through some magazine! Then you're busy having quickies with half the staff, and who knows how many guests at the wedding?! A wedding that Jack became 'The Noble Consort' of *his own choosing! No one forced him!*"

"So what? Wait a second! If 'Noble Consort' is another husband, then what's a 'Royal Consort' then?"

"The same thing as a 'noble consort' for a duke or duchess," James tells her, "only 'royal consort' for a king or queen."

Katie turns to Bri. "Then you should know——."

"*Get.Out!*" Bri enunciates and is livid. It's rare to see Bri like this, even for Katie. Bri gestures Jack and herself, "Like it or not, we *are* on *our honeymoon*, Katie, and *you* need to leave." She glares at Katie. "*Now!*"

Katie folds her arms and gives Bri a look as if to say, 'make me,' and Bri angrily steps forward, but Jack steps in and puts his arm around Bri's waist.

"Bri told you to leave, now leave or *I'll* make you!" Jack tells her. James grabs Katie's upper arm and forces her out the door. McMasters is right there and takes over in the hallway. James turns back to apologize, but Jack says, "We're good brother!"

The three of them hugged goodbye for now. James whispers an apology into Bri's ear, and that Amy filled him in on what she knew about what Katie did to her. Bri tells him he wasn't Katie's keeper.

"*Well*, you may be her babysitter for the rest of our time in Rome." Bri replies and they guys lightly laugh. Bri and Jack wave to James as they shut the door; James jogs to catch up with Katie and McMasters at the elevator. Bri asks Jack, "Do you think we could have a security guard at the elevator or something? I want McMasters to get his sleep since he chases after us throughout the day...I don't want anyone on this floor unless *we* specifically say that someone's okay to come up."

Jack hugs her and says, "I'll see what I can do."

Bri puts her hand on his arm. "What if I came with you and then we can go out for a little while, maybe see more of Rome at night?"

"I like the way you think, Amore Mia!" He says and kisses her tenderly.

They freshen up and she grabs her things. He holds her hand as they leave their room and take the elevator to the lobby. He approaches the reservation desk and they address him as Lord Carlisle, which he normally doesn't do; however, at David's request, he wants Jack to use his title, even hers when they're together, to keep her safe. McMasters agrees because hotels, car services, and other businesses are on an alert status when 'important people' are around. You'd think this would make them more of a target, but they're always a target; this way, it makes more people aware of their surroundings and other people. This will deter some criminals, but a few won't be and never will be, no matter what.

Jack greets the employee with McMasters by his side and asks, "I have a special request and I would like to speak to the manager if they're available."

"One moment, Lord Carlisle." The employee goes through the door behind him for a few minutes and comes back with the manager.

Jack, McMasters, and the manager step aside while Bri stays somewhat removed and looks at her phone. McMasters keeps a watchful eye on her and their surroundings as he listens to Jack and the manager talk, adding to the conversation here and there. Bri sees that Katie has blasted her phone with texts; she skims through them. It doesn't take long for Jack to make arrangements and the men shake hands before he and McMasters walk back over to her.

There is a look of anger, mixed with hurt and frustration, on Bri's face that Jack has never seen before. Then he remembers David reminding Katie of the fact that Bri fiercely protects those she loves. Bri is so angry; she is slightly shaking as she fights back the tears.

Jack takes her hand and leads her back upstairs to their room. He sits her on the couch, and he sits on the coffee table across from her.

"Amore Mia, let me see your phone." He softly says to her. She jerks her hand back, shaking her head. "Please. I'll send screenshots to David, then after he has read through them, the three of us can talk."

"*No, Jack!*" She shakes her head. "These are rancid and vile! I'm trying to reconcile them with this 'Katie,' against the Katie I thought I knew..."

He holds her cheek for her to look at him. "Amore Mia, *nothing* will top the shock, anger, and disgust of what she already did to you!" He takes her hand. "Bri, you *can't* reconcile with someone who *never existed!*"

He holds out his other hand for her phone. She doesn't hand her phone to him, but she doesn't resist him taking it this time either. He texts David about the screenshots before texting them to him. It takes time for both of them to read through all the texts; they read them more closely than she did. He video calls David who is obviously livid, and they talk about Katie's texts.

Jack says, "These are..." then says some phrases she thinks are Gaelic, which she can't translate; however, the sound of the anger in his voice is universal!

Jack and David see that the texts were an irate Katie who is angry at David and Jack, and jealous of Bri. Katie accuses both of them of changing Bri; turning Bri into someone Katie doesn't recognize anymore. How she's sorry to hit Bri with 'the truth,' how marriage can agree with some people, but not Bri...*she* is unrecognizable! These are the tame parts; the rest is increasingly vulgar and more viscous to the extreme viciousness women can be...even telling Bri that she wanted and asked for everything that was done to her that night; the night Bri refers to as 'once upon a nightmare.' Katie goes on to tell Bri that if people knew everything she wanted and asked for that night, "your precious reputation would be ruined and you would be seen for the whore you really are!"

"What are we going to do, David?" Jack asks. "I can't face Katie again, or it could be the first time I ever hit a woman. A scandal *none* of us need!" Implying Herst, too.

"Jack, you say that but we both know you'll avoid a scandal whenever you can. Personally, I'd like to cut all ties with this woman and shield Bri from her forever! Unfortunately, we can't make that decision for her."

"Agreed." Jack says. "This *has to be* her decision and we need to support whatever she decides to do..."

David reluctantly adds, "Even if it means Bri wants to help Katie."

Bri is barely audible when she looks over to Jack and down at David on the screen. "Our 'friendship,' if that's what we call it...*Ugh!* I'm done pretending and lying to her, *and to myself!*"

Bri is so frustrated she can't find the words, so she gets up and walks into the bedroom. Jack picks up the phone and finishes the conversation with David.

"We know that tone." David tells Jack, who faintly smiles. "I'm going to see to some things on my end. Take care of our girl and I'll see you both in a couple days."

"Will do!" And they say goodnight before they hang up.

Their room has a private hot tub that Bri had decided to use and tries to relax. After about five minutes of soaking, Jack joins her. He slips down next to her and he goes to wrap an arm around her, but she moves to straddle him and just hugs him tight. It takes a solid minute before he realizes what he hears; he can barely make it out she is crying over the loud jets of water.

He hugs her firmer, calmly saying, "Let it out, Amore Mia..." They sit like this for a few minutes.

When she sits back, she wipes her face with her wet hands saying, "Sorry."

He holds her face, "*Don't* be. I'm *always* here for you; so is David!"

She leans down to kiss him, then resting her forehead to his, she says, "Jack, right now I just need..." she takes a deep breath, "I just..." the lump makes it hard to speak, "*can't...*"

He stands with her, then he gently slides her down so she can stand. He leads her out and they dry off, but Jack does most of the work. Bri just stares into space. He leads her to the bedroom and helps her out of her bathing suit. He finishes drying her off, then picks her up and lays her in bed.

He says to her, "Lay on your front and let me massage your back."

She complies and he lays the sheet over her from the waist down. He finds some lotion and starts massaging. It takes some work, but his persistence for her to relax finally pays off. A few minutes pass before she breaks silence.

She inhales deeply and asks, "Did you read *all* her texts?"

He pauses for just a moment at the question, but then continues his massaging and replies, "Yes. And in all honesty, so did David."

Bri is working hard to talk and not cry again, only making fragmented sentences. "*How could...*I *never* would've...*I just...*I don't...*Ugh!*" There are enough pieces there for Jack to get the gist of what is going through her mind and what she is referring to.

Katie said Bri got everything she asked for that night; she wanted what Katie and her boyfriend did to her. Most of which Bri doesn't have actual memories of; she only knows of the disgusting and revolting things that were described in court and the couple of pictures she saw out of all that were taken that night, she didn't need, nor want, to see all of them. Now, Katie is taunting Bri that she has pictures that might 'accidentally' leak out into the media.

She starts to cry, "*Seriously*, leaking those pictures?!" It breaks his heart. "If those pictures are leaked, the court documents would need to be unsealed to offset her lies, then *everyone* would know *all* the appalling details of everything they ever did!"

"She hasn't considered that, or she is banking on you never releasing those records." He comments.

Her phone rings and by the ringtone Jack knows it's David. Jack gets up and answers it for her in the other room.

> "Oh good." David sounds relieved. "I was just thinking I should've called your phone when this one was already ringing. I can't relax enough to sleep. How is she?" David asks.

> "She's heartbroken." The anger surfaces in Jack's voice, "That woman is threatening to expose pictures of Bri, *of that assault*, which has me thinking bad thoughts!"

> "Me, too!" David replies, trying to think of a way to help Bri that stifles any actions Katie might take in retaliation.

> "I think it'll be good for her to see you at the airport when we all get back." Jack says.

> "Are you sure? I was planning on seeing you both at The Manor."

> "David, I'm good enough to get her through the next couple days, but she will need *you* to get her all the way through this."

> David tells him, "I'd *never* leave her with 'good enough,' Jack! You're the best! AND she'll need *us* to get her through this!"

"You're right," Jack agrees, "she does need both of us. We'll talk in the morning."

"Sounds good. Give her my love with a hug." David requests.

"Will do!"

Jack goes back into the bedroom. He finds Bri has cried herself to sleep and he covers her up better. He goes and gets ready for bed then slides in next to her, careful not to wake her; he hears her exhale a relaxing breath. He kisses her bare shoulder before settling in and going to sleep.

CHAPTER 43

Imperfectly Perfect Vineyard Tour

Jack wakes to Bri snuggling into him. He raises his arm so she can get closer and he watches her sleep for a while. He thinks about how wonderful her heart is and how psychotic a person must be to set her up like Katie did, then to say Bri deserved it?! *Katie is a revolting piece of filth!* He thinks to himself. He wishes he could've protected her from all of it then, but he and David will protect her from Katie now!

Jack lightly runs his fingers up and down her arm. He doesn't know she is awake until he feels her move and kisses the front part of his shoulder.

He hears her groggy voice say, *"I'm sorry I fell asleep on you last night..."*

"No apology needed, Amore Mia. How are you feeling?"

She rolls out of bed, grabbing his shirt and slipping it on as she goes to the restroom. She brushes her teeth before going back to bed and Jack slips into the bathroom next.

He crawls back into bed with her. "You never did answer my question. How—."

She kisses him, cutting him off. "No talking, Carlisle! More kissing!" She leans in but he pulls back.

"Are you trying to use sex to avoid answering?" He smirks.

"*Yes.*" She answers honestly. He smiles against her lips, then helps her by kissing her senseless. That is, until Bri breaks the kissing and sits up asking, "Ugh! *Why*?! *Whyyy* can't I get her out of my head?! *WHY* can't I focus on the hot sexy guy in front of me?!" She runs her hands into her hair, grasping her hair tight and she shuts her eyes.

"Shhh..." He pulls her back into bed and hugs her close. "Her insults against David are childish; her insults against me are obviously part of her jealousy. Setting up her best friend to be assaulted *and helping with it*, then to say you asked for it?! Well, all that is pretty telling of her true, *spiteful and heartless*, nature. Above all, I think it shows what a good person you are and how much you care about people. *But most importantly*, it shows how much better someone is with you *in* their life."

She rolls her eyes and scoffs. "*Trust me*, I'm pushing out vicious thoughts of revenge! Don't make me out to be better than I am! That's too much pressure for anyone!"

"*Bri*!" He moves to see her face. "Look at what happened when you two haven't seen much of each other over the last few months; at how much she has already changed!" He kisses her softly. "Remember, Amore Mia, this all started because of her jealousy, and compounded when I wouldn't shag, er, sleep with her. However, the jealousy began long ago because she convinced herself she couldn't measure up to you! There's not a strong enough word for setting up the nightmare and was *very much* a part of!" He feels her shudder.

"If you had taken her to The Black-Tic Party originally, maybe things would've been different?" She considers.

"No, it wouldn't!" He says with determination. "Bri, I was hooked the first day I watched you have a row with David in the stables! After that, she was *never* going to be in the cards!"

She lightly laughs. "Well, if you two *had* slept together, she would be bragging to me about 'having you first.'"

He rolls his eyes. "I had made a similar comment to her the night of the wedding when Katie said no one would know." He kisses the rings on her finger and she smiles lovingly at him. He says, "I was, I am, and will forever be, in-love with *you*! No relationship ever worked out because my heart was made *only for you*!" Jack continues. "I'm grateful for you and your love, for my friendship and brotherhood with David, and," he tangles his fingers in her hair, "I'm so indebted to him because of *his gift of you* in *my life*!" He pulls her lips to his and kisses her firmly and fiercely. Her bond with Jack solidified when they jumped off the waterfall together and she feels it growing stronger.

She taps a kiss to his lips and they rest their foreheads together. "I want to be in this moment with you, Jack."

He lifts his head. "Well, I'll give it my best shot!" His smoldering look is *loud and clear*...

493

Bri and Jack are finished getting ready for the day. Jack asks, "I'm sorry to bring her up again, but I just feel the need to ask...do you think Katie could just be returning back to who she really is?"

This surprises her. "Like our friendship was never real?!"

"More like 'not genuine' because *she* wasn't genuine, Amore Mia. You said something not too long ago that you felt a change or that something was off with her...It was brewing leading up to that ghastly night and actually changed that horrific night. You both have been trying to pretend it never happened, rather than deal with the fact that it did!" She is thinking about what he is saying. He also points out, "She knew you weren't going to be in DC that much longer and she is *desperately* trying to find a way *to stay* a significant person in your life! She focused on me to try to do that, but when that wasn't a possibility, her frustration mixed with jealousy took over."

"That sounds pretty desperate." She says lacking emotion, then realizes how that sounded and is mortified. "Oh Jack! I'm so sorry for the way that sounded! I didn't mean a relationship with you—."

He puts his fingers on her lips. "I understand, Amore Mia. You are talking about the subject of the conversation, *her*. It's fine, I promise! Besides, I'm *pretty* sure of how you feel about me!" He teases.

She giggles. "*Pretty* sure?! I guess I have some work to do!" She kisses him, walking him backwards to the bed and when he falls back onto it, she straddles him and leans down to kiss him.

They get ready for the day again. When Bri comes out of the bathroom, she sees Jack staring off into the mirror at nothing important. She hugs him to break his stare.

"Are you okay, Amore Mio?"

"Just thinking about how spending my life with you and *our* family is *all* I want!" He tells her. "After learning what Katie did to you, I'm more relieved than ever that I never dated her, nor slept with her! Katie tried to get me to sleep with her all night at the wedding, but at the end of the evening I tricked her into thinking I was going to join her, then I asked Stephen to get her safely to her room and keep her there. You can ask him—."

"*I trust you*," she interrupts, "so I don't need to ask anyone, Jack. I *never* want you to regret being honest with me; now lying to me would be a different story. Katie mentioned she was getting frustrated trying to get you interested in her. She loves getting a guy to *chase her* into bed, but if she does the chasing, well, she *usually* loses interest."

"What does that mean?" He asks, watching her tense up. "*Honesty* goes both ways, Amore Mia."

"There's *honesty*, then there's *not wanting to hurt your feelings unnecessarily*."

"Not if I want you to tell me." He tells her and she gives him a 'yeah, right' look. "Bri, I more than *loathe* that woman! *I really don't care what she thinks!*"

"Feelings can still be hurt, Jack!" She replies and sees his face's 'come on now' look. "*Fine.*" She takes a deep breath. "It wasn't going to end well for," using air quotes, "'playboy Jack,' no matter how good he was," she playfully smiles, "*or is...*" She bites her lower lip.

He chuckles. "*Explain that!*"

She giggles. "She heard the rumors around 'The Black-Tie Party' that you and David were playboys and had 'revolving doors.' She wanted to be the one who tamed you, the self-proclaimed 'life-bachelor,' only she never got you to chase her. Somewhere along the way, you became an *obsessive challenge* she just *had to conquer*. She has always felt she can get any man she wants."

"*Even yours.*" He slips in there.

She shrugs. "That is a powerful feeling over someone isn't it? Even now, if she could sleep with you and rub my face in it, then my life isn't as 'picture perfect' as her jealousy has her believing. *And conveniently forgetting* the battles I've went through in my life already, *including the nightmare she was very much a part of!*"

"True." Jack simply replies.

She rolls her eyes. "Only Katie doesn't see how she is coming off as desperate and pathetic. *Who wants a desperate person!*"

"Someone else who's already desperate." Jack throws out there.

"Right. And 'Playboy Jack' is *anything*, but desperate!" She grins. "Now, that guy, Richard McCleary, comes to mind!"

"*There's* two people who *should* be together!" He notes and Bri agrees.

They hear the knock of someone from room service with their breakfast. Jack finishes tucking in his shirt as he goes to answer the door. David sends Bri a 'good morning' text and she responds back. Jack comes in with a tray of breakfast food and they sit on the bed and eat.

"Either this is the best *French toast* I've ever had, or I'm extra hungry!"

Jack smiles. "We never ate last night." She looks so lovingly into his eyes, his heart squeezes. He tells her, "As you know David and I are a lot alike, even with the women we've dated..." he smirks, "and fall in-love with."

She laughs. "*And marry!*"

He playfully smiles. "*We've also been told* our *revolving doors* had the same type of women, underneath it all. Until you, until our first time together, I thought sex was just part of having a good time. I didn't know how good it could really be; how there really is a difference between making love and just having sex. Many times, sex was 'we had sex' and a few of those were better; but *none of them* have ever come close to this, *to us...*" he lovingly touches her cheek with the side of his forefinger, "*to you.* Even a quickie with you has a layer of making love that still makes it more meaningful." She has a little bit of tears in her eyes and a huge lump in her throat. "I love *you* so much, BriaLynn!" He sweetly kisses her. "It may sound weird, but I feel like David and I are partners in taking care of you—."

"*Of loving me!*" She has a huge grin.

He chuckles. "That's easy!"

"But taking care of me *isn't* easy?!" She teases and tickles him, finding out he is really ticklish. But she doesn't get to tickle him much before he grabs her hands to immobilize her.

"*Careful,* or I'll have to reciprocate." He smiles, pushing her back to lay on the bed. He kisses her, running his hand along her hourglass curve, before he abruptly stops and gets up, grabbing the breakfast tray.

She playfully gasps sitting up saying, "*You tease!* You know what they say about paybacks." When he looks back, she gives him a playful grin.

He laughs and stops at the door. "Oh, I'm counting on it, Amore Mia!" She giggles and he is happy she is feeling a little better.

Bri sees the juice glass on the dresser and something clicks: 'Tuscan Vineyards.' She remembers she wanted to visit this place and now she is afraid it may be too late.

Jack comes back and she asks, "Have you ever heard of 'Tuscan Vineyards?'"

He teases, "*Only* that they're famous for their 'love affair with grapes.'"

She rolls her eyes with a smile. "Do they do tours, *Smarty?*"

"I'm sure they would for *Lady Newhaven.*" He smirks. "Are you wanting to go?" He sees her hesitation with her title. "Amore Mia, we won't put them out more than just a leisurely tour, I promise. Can I make that appointment?"

"*Yes!* It's only the best tasting nonalcoholic wine and champagne I've ever had!" She tells him.

"You sound as if you've compared alcoholic wine and champagne to the nonalcoholic ones before. I thought you've never drank?"

"Oh, I did when I was younger, but I always hated the aftertaste of alcohol. I liked daiquiris and margaritas 'virgin' because I could taste the fruit with none of the alcohol aftertaste. Then, with my job, I'm around some people at events who end up having too much, or are completely drunk, and I sometimes have to navigate being groped and *need* to be sober! This is my choice and I'd *never* force my decision on anyone. David made it a point to serve mainly nonalcoholic wine and champagne at our engagement party and wedding out of love for me. However, on the same token, he respected that I didn't want to take that choice away from others either. So, if they wanted alcoholic anything, they could go to the bar for it...and we know Katie must've made countless trips..."

He squeezes her hand. "Had I known about 'Tuscan Vineyards' we could've set this up last week and had a steady supply shipping to Newhaven."

She laughs. "First, David did suggest that I ask you to take me, but honestly I had forgotten about it until now." She runs her finger down the middle of his chest. "I was a bit *preoccupied...*" she bites her lower lip with a flirty smile.

He takes her hand and says, "I'll give you that." He kisses her fingertip.

"Second, I don't think we need a 'steady supply,' but sending some different flavors home would be fantastic!"

Jack had the phone up to his ear as she finished her last statement and makes the arrangements. He sets up the appointment for as soon as they make it out there, and Jack texts McMasters.

"How do you do that? Just know the right number to call and 'poof,' it's all scheduled?!" She asks.

He laughs a little, "Gabriel." He sees her eyebrows shoot up. "Since you hired Gabriel to be your assistant, he wants to know what's going on with your schedule at all times. He prefers it this way, just like Mary, because he will always be in the loop to keep you organized for you duties and on time to your various appointments."

"*Good to know...*" She thinks out loud.

True to his routine, McMasters is waiting for them by their door at the time he said he would meet them there. They all walk to the elevator and then to the car waiting out front for them. They ride along for a while, and after driving through a charming little town, they turn onto a long driveway and at the end of it, they pull up to an incredible villa with the vineyards behind and around it, even along both sides of the driveway.

The manager of 'The Cidery and Vineyard' walks up to them, but Jack speaks first. "Signore Danesi, thank you *so much* for doing this on such short notice!" Jack says, shaking his hand.

Signore Danesi happily laughs. "My pleasure, Lord Carlisle."

Jack introduces Bri and then Signore Danesi shows them around. At the end of their tour, Signore Danesi takes them inside The Villa, to the cellar. As they walked through the large house, Jack notices how Bri is looking closely at everything inside, making him curious.

"Do you like the house, Amore Mia?"

"This place is *smashing*!" She teases with his accent. "Seriously though, there's simplicity, but exquisite attention to detail. It's Fascinating!" She continues to curiously look around.

"Sounds like you!" Jack says, placing his hand on the small of her back as he has her go through the cellar door and down the stairs after Signore Danesi, who is leading the way.

Jack has been looking for a villa to buy for years, but nothing ever looked right. Now he wants to find a place Bri would enjoy as well. If this is the style she likes, he will use this villa as an example to compare it with other estates.

"I've been instructed by the owners, all four of them in separate phone calls," he chuckles, "to personally bring you down here and let you pick a few bottles to take with you, Lady Newhaven." He says.

"All four?!" Bri asks, surprised.

"They are siblings. Their mother died a few months back and their father died years before her. They have their own lives and can't move back. They haven't sold the place, because they don't want to sell to some big company to be absorbed into their corporation." He explains.

She affectionately runs her hand down a wall of The Villa's cellar, "I hope they find some people to buy this place that will give it the love and respect it deserves, *and the business!*" Bri gestures the bottles. "The wines and champagnes *are amazing* and need to stay amazing!"

Signore Danesi chuckles. "*We* all *want that*!"

They pick out a couple bottles, but Bri picks out a third for her and David. Jack knows that's what she's doing and smiles lovingly at her. Jack places an order to be shipped to Newhaven, along with the bottles they just picked out.

Bri hugs him. "You're amazing, you know that, right?"

"Pretty sure that's only because of this gorgeous woman in my arms!" He taps a kiss into her lips.

Signore Danesi laughs. "It's *wonderful* when love is in the air!"

Jack asks Signore Danesi if he can show them around the rest of the place. He hesitates until Jack whispers in his ear so Bri won't hear, *"If she loves the rest of this place, I'm interested in buying the whole property, including the vineyard, and making it as seamless as possible for all who work here."*

Signore Danesi whispers with hope. *"No one will lose their job?"*

Jack shakes his head. *"Not unless you feel they need to go and we can talk about that."*

Signore Danesi laughs. *"Good!"*

Bri tells him, "Using your charm again for a tour of the house?"

Jack laughs and looks at Signore Danesi. "Luckily, Signore Danesi took pity!" He winks and Signore Danesi chuckles. "And he's going to show us the rest of this wonderful place!"

Bri smiles. *"Only if he doesn't get into trouble."*

"Oh, no! It will be fine!" Signore Danesi happily laughs.

He knows the owners would encourage the tour with Jack being interested in privately buying the house and vineyard. They talk as they walk around the house. Inside the 'Owner's Suite,' Bri sees a loft and she climbs up the stairs that is almost a ladder; Jack follows her. She looks around at, and through, all the windows around them, even tipping her head back to see the windows above them.

"Can you imagine having a telescope up here, all the *amazing* things one could see up in the sky at night?!" Jack looks up where she is looking and smiles, wrapping an arm around her. She asks, "I wonder if there's a room like this, or close to it, at The Manor that would have a view like this?"

"I'm not sure. I haven't been in every room in The Manor." He kisses her temple thinking he's going to have to remember to put a telescope up here if he's able to buy this place...

When they finish, Jack and Bri thank Signore Danesi for all his time. Signore Danesi secretly hands Jack the phone number of the son who is tasked with selling the property. Jack gives Signore Danesi his business card should anything come up. They shake hands and Jack gets in the car with Bri and they go back to the hotel.

CHAPTER 44

Imperfectly Perfect Company Banquet

That evening, Jack and Bri are getting ready for Jack's company party. In the closet is her red dress Jack bought for her, and she puts it on. Jack comes over with his tuxedo on, velvet box in hand, and zips her up. She turns to face him and he smiles.

 "Some finishing touches to highlight your beauty." He smiles adoringly at her. He opens the box with The Newhaven Necklace Set. He puts the necklace on, while she puts on the earrings.

"Jack, it just feels dangerous having this much money on display." She says, laying her hand on the necklace.

He gives her an understanding look. "McMasters will be coming with," he adds with a hint of a grin, "and he knows about the priceless jewelry."

"'Priceless.' *Not helping!*" She states. He opens the box with the tiara and she asks, "The tiara, too?!" Bri takes a deep breath, controlling her exhale through her mouth, trying not to freak out. "Jack, is the tiara necessary? There are more subtle ones."

"Amore Mia, this is one of those times where you're going to have to trust David and me. It's necessary because, for the first time, I'll be there as Lord Carlisle, who is escorting his wife, Lady Newhaven, The Marchioness of Newhaven, at this event. She is to become the next Duchess of Newhaven, so a 'subtle tiara' wouldn't be appropriate here. *I swear!*" He holds up his right hand. "Mother made sure to send these with me for this party!"

"Okay, but if I die because someone wants this stuff," she points to his chest, "I'll haunt you until the day you die!"

He snorts a laugh. "Well, then you won't have to haunt me for long!"

She furrows her eyebrows. "What do you mean?!"

"If anything happens to you on my watch, David will kill me, so I'll be along to join you soon enough!" He replies and she giggles, shaking her head.

She takes a deep breath and goes to put on the tiara. Jack watches as she pins it in her hair.

"Well, I *suppose* I better make a show of it for taking you off the market!" She smiles behind her pursed lips.

"That's my girl!" He winks.

They walk to the main door of their suite, and she grins saying, "We wouldn't want people to question your choice!"

He pauses and turns to her. "I'm being introduced with my title so no one will question *your* choice!" Her eyebrow goes up. "Most of the people coming here tonight have *no idea* I have a title *and I've dated some of the ladies in attendance!*" He gives her a slight smoldering look. "One look at you and they won't have any questions on my choice." He kisses the back of her hand.

She is about to argue, but he opens the door instead and they see McMasters waiting. He shakes Jack's hand and slightly bows to Bri and kisses her cheek.

McMasters smiles as he tells her, "You're looking very lovely this evening, *Lady Newhaven!*"

"Thank you." She replies. "*Hopefully,* things will go smoothly and you won't have a different thought later!"

"I'm sure it'll be fine." He tells her. "Security has been increased and the hotel has hired additional ones for the evening, but there's more provided by Watch Tower knowing you'll be attending." He looks at Jack. "I also asked for the long-time security employees, as we discussed."

"*Fantastic!* Thank you!" Jack responds.

McMasters asks them, "Are you two ready?"

"As ready as I can be!" She nervously lays her hand on the necklace.

"*Stop your fidgeting and relax!* You look *gorgeous,* Amore Mia! I need you to walk out of here with confidence, *and keep that confidence, for the* rest *of the night!*" She gives him a little nod. She quietly takes one more deep breath, inhaling and exhaling through her nose, as they walk down the hall to the elevators.

When Bri and Jack walk through the lobby, Bri has temporarily forgotten about Katie for the night; although Katie is in the lobby, hiding in a group of onlookers. She watches as they walk by, and she continues to watch them as they make their way to the hotel's Grand Ballroom. Jack had caught a glimpse of Katie, only he refuses to acknowledge her in *any* way. He wants to enjoy the evening with the woman he loves and adores.

Katie is continuing to fan the flames of anger and jealousy. She keeps texting Bri, wanting to ruin her evening with Jack. Unfortunately for Katie, Bri has turned the ringer off on her phone. The phone does default to a vibration mode for actual phone calls, with a short little 'dot' of a vibration for texts. None of that matters because she wouldn't hear or feel the slew of texts Katie sends to her phone that is in her wristlet, hanging from her wrist. The vibration setting is in case she forgets to turn the ringer back on later, or she can't find her phone.

As Bri and Jack enter the ballroom, they are introduced to the room by the M.C. and all eyes on them. They are taken to a table with company executives for Watchtower Investments and Bri can *feel* the whisperings around them.

"Lady Newhaven! So good to finally meet the woman who landed Jack! I'm Gerald Crestridge, CEO of Watchtower." He slightly bows his upper body and kisses the back of Bri's hand, then he happily shakes Jack's hand. "Good to see you, My Boy!"

"It's wonderful to meet you, Mr. and Mrs. Crestridge." Bri smiles and acknowledges the woman standing next to Mr. Crestridge. She shakes his wife's hand with a genuine smile.

"The pleasure is ours." Mrs. Crestridge happily replies. "I've been dying to meet The American Marchioness!"

"Congratulations, Jack!" Mr. Crestridge says. "It's about time you settled down!" He turns to Bri. "You're even lovelier than I imagined, and this guy here has dated some stunning ladies!"

"I told you she was the most gorgeous woman I've ever met!" Jack looks at her adoringly and Bri smiles sweetly at him. Another man approaches and Jack says to her, "Bri, this rascal here is Skeet Hutchins, the CFO and my mentor at the firm."

"*Ooo*! So, this is the man I need to talk to about some of your secrets!" Bri says, charming Skeet.

Skeet chuckles. "Save me a dance, Darlin,' and the stories I will tell you!"

"That's assuming I'll give up a dance!" Jack adds with a smoldering look, firmly wrapping his arm around Bri.

"Ignore him, Mister Hutchins!" She playfully glares at Jack. "If you'll give me the stories, I'll be happy to give you the *dances*!" She grins and they all laugh; Skeet laughing a bit more enthusiastically from his thicker waist.

They take their seats with the men pulling out the chairs for the ladies. Their meal courses were phenomenal and to Bri's pleasant surprise, conversations are easy to keep going. After Jack has finished eating, he drapes his arm on the back of Bri's chair. When Bri is finished eating, he holds her hand on his thigh. They continue to talk with the others at their table until everyone is finished eating.

The awards are next; however, there is first a presentation. Mr. Crestridge has Mr. Hutchins go up on stage to start things off.

"Good evening, Ladies and Gentlemen! All of you are here because you're the best of Watchtower!" There are cheers and applause. "Our reigning top producer, Jack Carlisle," Bri looks at him with a smile and he winks at her, "along with his team, are going to give us our presentation tonight rather than me. Jack, come on up!" Jack stands and sweetly kisses Bri's cheek, then heads up to the stage. There is louder applause with cheers and whistles when he walks to center stage. "Alright, Ladies, I know Jack is *way* better looking than me, but I feel I should break it to you that our Jack, here," he gestures Jack as he stands next to Mr. Hutchins, "has gotten himself married about a month ago." There are a few audible disappointed 'aws,' but lots of congratulatory applause. "My deepest and most heartfelt congratulations to you both, *Lord Carlisle*!" He chuckles. "Lady Newhaven definitely brings out your good side!"

Jack happily agrees and turns towards Bri, putting his hand on his heart. "That's because she *is* my *best* side!" He winks at her with aws and laughter. Jack addresses the audience, "Could I have my *spectacular* team join me up here?" Jack introduces each one as they join him on stage.

They all present an impressive presentation, followed by answering questions from the audience. It's easy to see Jack's brilliance in finance and investments, as well as his charisma with people. She can also see his team is completely loyal to him, and to each other!

When their presentation is finished, the awards are given out; Jack and his team winning a handful of them. Bri sees how Jack really is a *superstar* in his field! It makes so much more sense to her now; why he isn't worried he might be forgotten, because he is a *rock star* in his own right! She also understands more about how he made so much money, and David, believing in his best friend, has also made a ton of money, right along with the rest of the family and the corporation!

When the dancing started, Jack stands and asks Bri, "Will you do me the honor, Amore Mia?" He holds his hand out; she takes it with a smile.

Out on the dance floor, Bri recognizes the waltz, but Jack comments first. "Our very first dance was this waltz." He smiles and they take their positions.

"I remember!" Her eyes sparkle with love as she thinks back to that first party at 'The Worthington Estate.'

Not many are waltzing, so it's easy for people to watch and see how smooth their steps are together. The waltz ends and Jack nods to the DJ and looks at Bri who is giving him a curious look.

"I wanted to find a song for us." He gives her a sweet kiss and the song starts. Jack holds the woman he loves close and the world falls away for a little while.

She smiles, recognizing the song within the first few notes. "A timeless classic!" She lovingly kisses him as they dance to Etta James singing, 'At Last.'

He says next to her ear. "'At Last,' I found the love of my life and I get to love her forever!" She smiles with her eyes closed. He kisses her hand before tucking it against his chest. He whispers, "*I love you, Amore Mia!*"

"And I love you, Amore Mio!" She taps a kiss to his neck.

A few ladies have overheard this as they dance with their partners, wishing Jack would've said those very same words to them. They know he is a great guy and they really are happy he has found someone!

Jack and Bri mingle and he loves having her beside him. She is good at engaging people and keeping conversations flowing; her years in DC have come in handy. She dances with Jack's bosses, Mr. Crestridge and Mr. Hutchins, while Jack dances with their wives.

Mr. Hutchins tells her some hilarious stories, but it is plain to see that he means it when he says, "I'm proud of Jack and how far he's come! Most importantly, I'm excited for him to finally settle down and have a family of his own!"

Bri smiles kindly at him, then turns her head and looks at Jack. She feels so much love for him, her heart squeezes. Jack is dancing with Mrs. Hutchins and he looks over at Bri. He sees Bri's loving expression and he can't help giving her the same look back.

She says to Mr. Hutchins, "He'll be a *great* daddy."

"He most certainly will be!" He laughs a bit as the song ends.

Mr. Hutchins walks with Bri over to Jack and Mrs. Hutchins. Jack takes Bri's hand and leans into whisper, *"Would you hang in there for just a little longer? I'd like to show you off a bit more. I'll make it up to you later tonight."*

"I think I can manage." She answers with a playful smile. "But you don't have to make it up to me; I'm having a lot of fun!"

He gives her a look. *"Seriously?"*

"Are you kidding?!" She smiles, proud of him. *"I love seeing you in your element!"*

He chuckles. "Thank you for sharing this night with me, Amore Mia!" He holds her face and kisses her, then leads her around to a few more groups.

The last dance of the evening is a more recent love ballad. Jack holds Bri close, his arm wrapped around her low waist, just above her bum. He holds her hand over his heart, his cheek resting against hers, and his mouth next to her ear whispering, *"I love you"* and *"You're so incredibly beautiful, Amore Mia."* He pulls back towards the end of the song, so he can kiss her tenderly, all the way through the last note.

They say their goodbyes to certain people before they leave. Jack holds Bri's hand as they walk through the hotel lobby together. Up at the door of their hotel suite, they say goodnight to McMasters before they go inside, locking the door for the night.

Jack walks over to Bri and scoops her up in his arms, taking her to their bedroom. He helps take off her jewelry and tiara, then unzips her dress and helps her step out of it. He has her lie down on the bed as he sits at her feet. He starts with a foot massage that works up her legs, and into a full body massage...

CHAPTER 45

Imperfectly Imperfect Crossroads

The next morning, Bri's laying on her front, but facing Jack. He is lightly tracing his fingers around her back and he sees the side of her mouth curve slightly into a smile.

He kisses her shoulder. "Good morning, Gorgeous!"

"Good morning, *My Sexy Jack*!" Bri says as she wakes up.

He kisses her arm. "I have room service coming, but if you'd like to shower first, you could squeeze it in, if you hurry." She nods, sitting up; then goes into the bathroom.

When Jack is finished setting up breakfast up at the table, she comes out and she tells him, "I was just texting David quick after seeing a slew of *other* texts."

"Katie." He says flatly. "Eat as you talk to me about them." He pulls out her chair for her. "I'm assuming she texted you after she saw us in the lobby last night." She sits down.

"You saw her?" She asks.

He lays his napkin in his lap. "Yes, but I don't think she knew I had seen her, and I *certainly* wasn't going to act as if I did and ruin *our* evening. She has taken enough from you and, well, all of us."

Bri has tears from the sweetness of that statement and gives him an understanding smile. "I'll give you that."

She tells him about the slew of new texts from Katie about how David is treating her like, she uses air quotes, 'an American whore' to men of '*his* choosing' and refers to him as a 'noble pimp.' Reading that made her realize Katie's jealousy isn't just toxic, it is poisoning any part of the Katie she liked in her as a friend, *as a person*.

"I'm trying *not* to hate Katie. I want to be better than doing the easy thing, but she's making it difficult. I'd change phone numbers, but I still care too much not to be there if there really is an emergency, because she has *no one...*" She takes a deep breath. "Only now, I feel sorry for her."

"I just fell more in-love with you." Jack smiles sweetly at her. "After all that she has done, continues to do and say to you, you still care about her well-being! *You already are the better person, Amore Mia!*"

Bri tells Jack about the return text from Henry and Maggie; she had wondered what they knew and what their thoughts were. Unfortunately, what they knew wasn't good.

"Henry says her jealousy is like a plane in a deep nosedive and no one can pull her out of it." Bri tells Jack she has also texted Joe, who is angry about what happened and wants to see all the texts Katie sent. She sent them to him. "Now, we wait while he reads them."

"Off subject for a second," he says, "we need to finish our last little bit of packing, but is there anywhere you still want to go?" Jack had already started packing this morning after his workout and shower.

"I don't know. We've hit all the touristy things..." she thinks as she chews. "Pompeii! We haven't been there yet, but how far away is it?"

Jack had just taken a drink of orange juice and he puts the glass down slowly as he thinks. "By car, too long, but a flight to Naples, *maybe*; but a helicopter would be quickest."

"Are you sure?" Bri asks.

"I'd go anywhere with you, Gorgeous! And by the sound of it, even into a volcano!" He teases.

"Pompeii is at the *base* of Mount Vesuvius, so technically I'm not asking you to *jump* into a volcano." She teases back.

"And yet, I'd still jump!" He smiles his signature smile and Bri giggles as she shakes her head.

Jack reads through the texts on Bri's phone, skimming and skipping some that are too vulgar. There are some texts that don't make sense. After Joe read everything, he sends a text.

Joe responds simply: "No words."

Bri: "Yep. My thoughts, too!"

Joe: "I think you should proceed with caution when it comes to Katie. We know what she has done at her worst, and she did it *to you* while calling you her best friend! There could be no limit to what she is capable of, especially to you personally!"

B: "Good point."

Bri had moved to the couch and Jack comes over and sits by her, waiting patiently for her to finish her text to Joe. When she finishes, she turns to him but decides to straddle him again and hug him tight. He hugs her back just as tight, maybe a little tighter. He doesn't say anything, just holds her for as long as she needs.

When she is ready, she sits back on his lap and tells him more about Henry's and Maggie's responses. "They said she's been lost for a while. They've tried to have her over for dinner at their house, to help her get back on track, but she always has excuses, or cancels at the last minute. Now Katie is not taking their calls and barely returns texts." She rubs her hands over her face and breathes deeply. Jack rubs her thigh and waits for her to continue. "Joe feels she has a desperation about her, too; he says it's like she can't get enough drugs, alcohol, and sex..." She takes a deep breath, then holds his jaw, looking at his handsome face. She runs her hands down to his chest saying, "Let's change the subject." Her hands start to go downward.

Jack takes a deep breath, grabbing her hands before they get to his pants. "I can't believe I'm saying this, Amore Mia, but *no*. I know what you're trying to do, but you can't keep pushing this down and hope it will just go away."

"I can if I don't want to talk about it! I don't want to remember anything but *you* right now!"

He holds both her hands with one of his, then tangles the other in her hair to pull her in for a kiss. "I love you so much, Amore Mia! So, it *pains* me more than you know to say this, *but we can't*. One reason being there wouldn't be enough time; second, we need to clear your head." She reluctantly agrees. "Let's just get ready and leave for the airport a little early." Jack suggests.

She hugs him before she gets up to go get ready. Bri finds her turquoise dress, new shoes, and jewelry. She fixes her hair and puts on a little make up.

She sees Jack in a polo shirt, shorts, and sandals. "I'm thinking if I'm overly dressed for this trip..."

"*You're perfect!*" He kisses her deeply.

She hugs him tighter. "I'd have to argue that *you're* a specimen of perfection!"

He chuckles. "We can argue about it later." They both softly laugh as they gather their things to leave.

That afternoon, they are back in their hotel room and finish up their packing. They call the concierge to have their bags brought down to their car. A few minutes later, there is a knock on the door and it's not only the gentleman from concierge to collect their luggage, but McMasters is right there, too. Their luggage is put on the cart, while Jack and Bri grab their phones and things to take on the plane.

Walking through the lobby, Jack holds Bri's hand firmly to show her he's got her. About five minutes later they are checked out and outside in front of the hotel next to the waiting cars. Their luggage is being loaded in the trunk of their care when Katie walks out with James.

"Amy wasn't able to make it?" Bri asks James a little disappointed.

"Oh, she came for a couple of days and went back yesterday. She told me to give you this..." He hugs her for Amy.

Katie scoffs and gets into the car for her and James. Bri turns to James. "Why did Katie stay in Rome these last few days?"

James tells her, "She really did have various business meetings; Amy and I made sure to verify that!"

"That makes sense to some degree, I guess." Bri says and looks at the car Katie got into.

She and Jack watch James join her. Bri offhandedly says to Jack, "It's weird to think I once thought we were on our way to sisterhood..."

512

He hugs her. "I'm sorry, Bri! I never want anyone to play with your emotions like that, let alone do what she did to you! *I love you; David loves you; and our family loves you!*" He kisses her head.

She gives him a faint smile as she wipes a tear from her eye. "I love you both, more than I can put into words."

"Trust me, we feel it from you *and for you!*" He smiles sweetly.

She taps a kiss to his lips. "Jack, I can honestly say I've always thought yours and David's intentions were genuine."

"Good." He firmly kisses her before they get into their car.

On the plane, Jack is reclined back while Bri lays on his shoulder with a pillow and has a blanket draped across both of them; they sleep most of the flight. Katie and James were talking for a bit across from them before they napped. Katie took the couch, still pouting seeing Bri and Jack snuggled up together. She eventually falls asleep.

They all woke up when the plane was beginning its descent into Newhaven. Bri sat up next to Jack and he kisses her temple; Katie scoffs. A small part of Bri felt bad for Katie and thought maybe she shouldn't be so 'lovey-dovey' with Jack in front of her, but this was their honeymoon! It's Katie who crashed it! Bri loves Jack too much to take away from enjoying each other's love and company.

Jack remembers David is meeting them at the airport and he tells Bri. "I asked David a few days ago to be there when we land. I know you worry about me, but I know how happy you are with him, too! I love seeing you happy and as oddly as it might sound to you, I do enjoy watching you being happy with David, as David enjoys seeing you happy with me." Katie gets more annoyed with that and plunges her earbuds as deep as she can into her ears so she can't listen to anymore.

Jack shifts towards Bri and even though Katie had earbuds in, he still lowers his voice. "David was going to wait at The Manor for us, but with everything that has happened, well, I was there for you and I always will be, but I think you need him and us. I love you, Amore Mia!" He kisses her tenderly.

"*Jack*," she whispers, "*you'll* always *be what I need*!" She kisses him firmly and he deepens it. "I love you, Amore Mio." She hugs him for a long minute.

The flight attendant comes back one last time. "Is there anything else I can get for you, Lady Newhaven?"

Bri looks to Jack, James, and Katie replying, "No, I think we're all fine, Linda." Linda is pleasantly surprised Bri knew her name and slightly curtsies before turning and going to the front of the plane.

James smiles. "Jack and David are right about this!" Bri looks at Jack who winks at her. James says, "Not just anyone can live in this type of scenario, but you'll see how seamless this will become because of the brotherly bond of a deep love and friendship between them." She thinks about The King's interest in her being 'The Royal Consort."

"*Are you kidding me*?!" Katie blurts out.

"What's the problem Katie?" Jack asks in a monotone voice.

"*This*! How *delusional* you all are! This *won't* work! It'll *never* work because of basic human nature! *Of male testosterone and egos*!"

James frowns and tells her, "You sound jealous, Katie. I would've thought you would want Bri to be happy?"

"I wanted her to be happy *with David*! Not screwing around with Jack on the side! You'll eventually become territorial because you're men, and men have gigantic egos!" Her hands gesturing gigantic.

The plane is seconds from touching the runway. "Shut it, Katie!" Jack says in a firm voice. The plane touches down and everyone feels it when it does, holding onto something to steady themselves as the pilots brake. "I was *never* an option for you!"

"I guess we'll never know, will we?" She replies.

"*I KNOW, DAMNIT*!" Jack's anger boils over. "If Bri wasn't a Direct Bloodline and being *HER* Noble Consort wasn't possible, I NEVER would've married at all! I would've loved her from afar *for the rest of my life*!" He looks at Katie as he seethes with anger. "What bothers you most, Katie, is that you convinced yourself you could have any man you wanted, *including*

514

any man who was interested in Bri, or she was interested in!" Jack, James, and Bri see he is right by the smug look on her face. He stands and gets right up in her face to say, "Your jealous of the life she has–."

She scoffs, "I'm not jealous of a wh–."

Jack has a hand on her throat. He angrily tells her through gritted teeth, "I should squeeze the life right out of you," he gives Katie a look of disgust, then lets go, "but you're not worth it!"

When the plane comes to a stop, the flight attendant works at opening the door. Katie has collected her things and waits; she wants to be the first one off the plane.

"You will fail, Bri! Only this time, the entire world will see it!" Katie bites.

Jack grabs Katie's upper arm and firmly pulls her up and gets them closer to the door. "Linda, when you get the door open, would you kindly step aside right away?" Jack asks.

Linda looks over at them and sees Jack's angry face, which isn't normal for him. She nods and quickly does what she is asked to do.

Katie is angry. "I can't *believe* you!" She yells at Bri, fighting against Jack trying to get her off the plane. "You, *of all people*, are going to allow yourself to be used as a baby mill?!" Bri can feel a shift and finds herself feeling more disappointed in Katie. "Maybe you like being an aristocratic prostitute and being able to hide behind traditions––." She fights against leaving the plane, but Jack is too strong; he forces her out the door and down the stairs.

Bri gathers her things and finds herself thinking 'narcissism' and about the traits associated with it. James motions for her to go ahead of him and she smiles as she starts to pass him, then pauses.

"Thank you, James." She tells him.

He is confused. "For what?"

"For your support." She smiles and hugs him.

"Always!" He smiles and returns her hug, then he follows her off the plane.

Katie is watching for Bri to get off the plane. When she sees her coming down the stairs, she yells, "*You'll be seen for the whore you really are!*"

Jack is defensive of Bri. He pushes Katie's whole backside against the car with a bit of force. He sneers with disgust, "*The only whore is you!*"

She smirks. "You like to think that because you want to know I'll take care of any of your *needs*."

"Desperation doesn't look good on *any* woman!" He says. She glares and she goes to slap him across the face, but he catches her wrist. He tells her as she struggles to free her wrist. "I've never struck a lady before, *but you're pushing it*. Then again, you're not really a lady, are you?" She glares harder and he lets go of her wrist before he turns to walk over to Bri.

David coldly says to Katie, "*Wait here!*" His voice is authoritative, but security is right there, along with McMasters, so she has no choice but to comply.

David walks over to Bri and Jack. Jack is hugging Bri and telling her, "She's just trying to get under your skin because you're under hers."

They see David walking up as Katie makes another attempt. "Still think you're not a glorified prostitute?! Ask David about The King wanting *you* for *his* 'Royal Consort' and have *his* baby!" Katie glares at them with a smug look when she sees David is fuming. David has his hand on Jack's chest to stop him from charging at Katie.

Bri responds emotionless, "I know."

www.ingramcontent.com/pod-product-compliance
Lightning Source LLC
Chambersburg PA
CBHW071337020726
47502CB00001B/124